The Cambridge Edition
of The Works of
D. H. Lawrence

The texts of the Cambridge Edition of the Works of D. H. Lawrence have been established after careful study and comparison of all the surviving manuscripts, typescripts, proofs, and early printed editions. The words, sentences, even whole pages frequently omitted or altered by Lawrence's typists, editors, and printers are restored to their original form. The house-styling imposed on Lawrence by his printers is removed as far as possible, and the passages censored by his contemporary publishers are reinstated.

The Cambridge Edition, under its general editors, Professor James T. Boulton of the University of Birmingham and Professor Warren Roberts of the University of Texas at Austin, provides texts which are as close as can be determined to those which Lawrence himself would have wished to see printed.

D H LAWRENCE

WOMEN IN LOVE

Edited by
DAVID FARMER
LINDETH VASEY
and
JOHN WORTHEN

Introduction by
MELVYN BRAGG

GRAFTON BOOKS
A Division of the Collins Publishing Group

LONDON GLASGOW
TORONTO SYDNEY AUCKLAND

Published in paperback by
Grafton Books 1989

ISBN 0-586-05243-7

This edition first published in
Great Britain by Grafton Books 1988

This, the Cambridge Edition of the text of *Women in Love* now correctly established
from the original sources and first published in 1987, © the Estate of Frieda
Lawrence Ravagli 1987. Permission to reproduce this text entire or in part, or to
quote from it, can be granted only by the Literary Executor of the Estate, Laurence
Pollinger Ltd, 18 Maddox Street, Mayfair, London WIR OEU. Acknowledgement
is made to William Heinemann Ltd in the UK and the Viking Press in the USA,
who hold the exclusive book publication rights for the work as published (copyright
1920, 1921, 1922, 1936, 1948, 1950) in their respective territories, for the
authorisation granted to Cambridge University Press through the Frieda Lawrence
Ravagli Estate for use of the work as published in preparing the new scholarly text.

Introduction copyright © Melvyn Bragg 1988

Grafton Books
A Division of the Collins Publishing Group
8 Grafton Street, London WIX 3LA

Printed and bound in Great Britain by
Collins, Glasgow
Set in Times

CONTENTS

INTRODUCTION
BY MELVYN BRAGG

Women in Love is one of the finest novels of the twentieth century. It has gone in and out of fashion and will again slide evasively through that fool's gold of merely fashionable opinion. It is a novel of abstractions, of ideas and yet, unlike later and ultimately arid developments in that rarefied category, it maintains a vivid connection with naturalism, with character, location, the external world and with dramatic plot. It is undeniably excessive at times and now and then repetitive: blemishes which serve only to highlight the powerful strides of triumphant prose. Some will find it too rich but then they might question whether their palates are too thin: good books, as has been said, read you. The flaw – as in all novels of ideas – is that the conversations are not sufficiently distinguished between the characters: at times, any one of the four principals could be talking. That "flaw", though, can be seen as an advantage: the book can be read as a seamless discussion with the four principal characters exchanging and interchanging views as rapidly as those in a square dance exchange partners. And such views, such ideas! Again, over-rich for some tastes and quite out of tune with the current mix of smartness and snideness but for anyone drawn into the great British tradition of questing literature and non-conformist opinion, for anyone interested in thinking about how you live life wholly and seriously at this time, then *Women in Love* is not only a great novel but a remarkable testament.

Lawrence began to write it in 1913. It was not published until seven years later. For many of its several drafts (at least seven) it was known as "The Sisters" and part of a larger book which eventually became two: *The Rainbow* and *Women in Love*.

Those seven years – 1913–20 – were turbulent. The First World War drew into a deadly maelstrom not only the young men of Europe but also the ideas the society had lived by. Lawrence had eloped with Frieda Weekley in 1912 and, as she was German, his patriotism was tempered; indeed he was suspected of being a subversive and ordered to leave Cornwall by the military authorities in 1917. He had been there for 21 months. With Frieda he had begun what would become a ceaseless treadmill of travel – at its best a pilgrimage to new springs of light and inspiration, at its worst a bitter flight in poverty from one uneasy haven to another. His reputation was beginning to grow – especially with *Sons and Lovers* in 1913 and *The Prussian Officer and other stories* in 1914 but when *The Rainbow* came out a year later it was suppressed by court order and the first of an ever-growing number of comments and threats about obscenity began to be heard. He knew real poverty and the bitterness of seeing lesser talents applauded while he was starved of sales and praise. The English establishment took him up gleefully, this live, bright new element and then dropped him like a hot coal when he refused to be petted by them. He was not a well man even at that stage and the rift with his past had been brutal.

All in all the miracle of *Women in Love* is that it got written at all. That it was written so wonderfully well is proof of Lawrence's genius. "I consider this the best of my books," he wrote. Yet there was the despair: 1917 – "I have done a novel, which nobody will print, after the *Rainbow* experience. It has been the round of publishers by now, and rejected by all. I don't care. One might as well make roses bloom in January, as bring out living work into this present world of man." He became disillusioned with publishing, with England and with people. "I find people ultimately boring." The anger and anguish over the rejection of what he had toiled over so painstakingly and furiously distressed him deeply – "I *know* it is a good book."

Eventually, after many attempts, after cuts in the "sexual" passages and tuts over the "anti-England" passages, the book was published – 1920 in the USA and 1921 in the UK. The reviews were few and mostly opposed to the book although Rebecca West in the *New Statesman* declared it to be a "work of genius". Lawsuits were threatened – and one settled privately – by those he was supposed to have libelled in the bohemian London passages, and his portrait of Hermione cut him off forever from the influential social and literary court of Lady Ottoline Morrell. In those peculiar little hierarchies of snobbery and chummery which characterise London social-literary life this was to do Lawrence no good. On the other hand the book enjoyed real success in America – with five reprints by August 1923 – and it boosted his fortunes at a crucial time.

The story concerns the two Brangwen sisters, Ursula and Gudrun, and two men, Rupert Birkin and Gerald Crich. The women are schoolteachers in Lawrence's Nottinghamshire; Gudrun is also an artist and has returned from a quite successful start in London. Birkin is a school inspector. Gerald Crich is the rich local mineowner. The quartet becomes Birkin and Ursula, Gudrun and Gerald. Other characters of importance are Hermione with whom Birkin has had a long relationship before Ursula; the Crich family, especially the father; certain Metropolitan artists types and, towards the end, Loerke, a sculptor. The narrative conducts the four principals through courtship to marriage in one case and to a death in another.

The prose is heightened throughout. Some reviews described it as "poetic" prose but I think of it more as religious. It is more like a sermon than a poem although the lyrical pulse of the writing could well enable passages to be chanted aloud.

There is a terrible fury for purity at the heart of it. The engine of the novel is the character of Birkin, based on Lawrence himself. He is at once intolerable and splendid – a ridiculous and a magnificent figure. Out there is a wonderful world, says Birkin, like a Don Quixote of the text books – if only we could reach through to it. To get there, though, we have to destroy. To destroy the mechanical world of dead mechanical work; to destroy the equally mechanical ideas of marriage and domesticity; to destroy all forms of dependence and all the possession-culture which hems us in and makes us less free. Birkin is forever asking for that, like a diamond-tipped drill and yet he is also capable of unnerving switches, of lapses, of over-inflected pomposity, careless cruelty and what cannot be disguised as anything other than snobbery for "the common people" of the coalfields of Notting-hamshire. Yet we feel that, like an Old Testament prophet in the wilderness, it is for "the people's" greater life and joy that he is struggling: he will not soften it by sentimentality.

Gerald is drawn into a fascination with this man and with Gudrun who, in her own way, is fleeing the world as it has been given her and looking to find something bold and independent that she can take on her own terms. Between the two he pushes himself and is pushed beyond his limit. Ursula, in a sense the "norm" of the quartet, marries Birkin both because of and despite herself but in the process renounces all the achieved life she had worked for.

The novel is full of attempts to explain the state of emotions at times of considerable stress. Lawrence sees life between those who are drawn to each other as a battle, a flux, a never stable balance of power in which hate and love can follow as swiftly as love and sex. He is trying to grasp the essence, the "being" of his characters, hence the repetition, the motif, like a composer, like a bardic storyteller, keeping up the themes, never letting go of the beat of that particular life. It is exhilarating and for some it can be exhausting but it pierces the inner state of life with a success few other novelists have ever managed.

There is so much more to the novel. He is in full spate here in his torrential annihilation of the crippling desensitising and reductive effect of industry, of mechanism, of ugliness. Ideas bold and new then continue to ring true. His apprehensions about the future often have a weirdly prophetic ring as when he talks of men inventing a weapon which will destroy all mankind. There are discussions on education which were taken up generally fifty years later and a sexual credo still working its way through the bewildered layers of a once-superficially but also traditionally monogamous Christian society. Nor is he without the nerve to challenge his own deepest ideas: Birkin is forever checked by Ursula or by Gerald and in one scene a letter he has written to one of London's upper class bohemians is read aloud to howls of derision.

Yet for many readers, the sinews of the book will lie in the unsurpassed descriptions of action or of nature. Few scenes in the literature of action can compare with Gerald's attempt to control his Arab mare at a level crossing against the clanking of a train: or the rabbit which will not be held: or the catkins, the descriptions of snow, the lanterned boats on the night lake before the tragedy.

Women in Love has attracted and will continue to attract scholars and critics who wish to celebrate it further by pointing out the background tapestry, or by analysing the cluster of ideas and images which reinforce and echo each other. For the general reader it still remains, almost 70 years on, a thrilling ride through the mind and spirit of a man who believed that the novel could be everything and change everything.

WOMEN IN LOVE

Contents

Chapter I

Sisters

Ursula and Gudrun Brangwen sat one morning in the window-bay of their father's house in Beldover, working and talking. Ursula was stitching a piece of brightly-coloured embroidery, and Gudrun was drawing upon a board which she held on her knee. They were mostly silent, talking as their thoughts strayed through their minds.

"Ursula," said Gudrun, "don't you *really want* to get married?"

Ursula laid her embroidery in her lap and looked up. Her face was calm and considerate.

"I don't know," she replied. "It depends how you mean."

Gudrun was slightly taken aback. She watched her sister for some moments.

"Well," she said, ironically, "it usually means one thing!—But don't you think, anyhow, you'd be—" she darkened slightly—"in a better position than you are in now?"

A shadow came over Ursula's face.

"I might," she said. "But I'm not sure."

Again Gudrun paused, slightly irritated. She wanted to be quite definite.

"You don't think one needs the *experience* of having been married?" she asked.

"Do you think it need *be* an experience?" replied Ursula.

"Bound to be, in some way or other," said Gudrun, coolly. "Possibly undesirable, but bound to be an experience of some sort."

"Not really," said Ursula. "More likely to be the end of experience."

Gudrun sat very still, to attend to this.

"Of course," she said, "there's *that* to consider."

This brought the conversation to a close. Gudrun, almost angrily, took up her rubber and began to rub out part of her drawing. Ursula stitched absorbedly.

"You wouldn't consider a good offer?" asked Gudrun.

"I think I've rejected several," said Ursula.

"*Really*!" Gudrun flushed dark.—"But anything really worth while? Have you *really*?"

"A thousand a year, and an awfully nice man. I liked him awfully," said Ursula.

"Really! But weren't you fearfully tempted?"

"In the abstract—but not in the concrete," said Ursula. "When it comes to the point, one isn't even tempted.—Oh, if I were tempted, I'd marry like a shot.—I'm only tempted *not* to." The faces of both sisters suddenly lit up with amusement.

"Isn't it an amazing thing," cried Gudrun, "how strong the temptation is, not to!"

They both laughed, looking at each other. In their hearts they were frightened.

There was a long pause, whilst Ursula stitched and Gudrun went on with her sketch. The sisters were women, Ursula twenty-six and Gudrun twenty-five. But both had the remote, virgin look of modern girls, sisters of Artemis rather than of Hebe. Gudrun was very beautiful, passive, soft-skinned, soft-limbed. She wore a dress of dark-blue silky stuff, with ruches of blue and green linen lace in the neck and sleeves; and she had emerald-green stockings. Her look of confidence and diffidence contrasted with Ursula's sensitive expectancy. The provincial people, intimidated by Gudrun's perfect sang froid and exclusive bareness of manner, said of her: "She is a smart woman." She had just come back from London, where she had spent several years, working at an art-school, as a student, and living a studio life.

"I was hoping now for a man to come along," Gudrun said, suddenly catching her underlip between her teeth, and making a strange grimace, half sly smiling, half anguish.

Ursula was afraid.

"So you have come home, expecting him here?" she laughed.

"Oh my dear," cried Gudrun, strident, "I wouldn't go out of my way to look for him. But if there did happen to come along a highly attractive individual of sufficient means—well——" she tailed off ironically. Then she looked searchingly at Ursula, as if to probe her. "Don't you find yourself getting bored?" she asked of her sister. "Don't you find, that things fail to materialise? *Nothing materialises*! Everything withers in the bud."

"What withers in the bud?" asked Ursula.

"Oh, everything—oneself—things in general."

There was a pause, whilst each sister vaguely considered her fate.

"It does frighten one," said Ursula, and again there was a pause. "But do you hope to get anywhere by just marrying?"

"It seems to be the inevitable next step," said Gudrun.

Ursula pondered this, with a little bitterness. She was a class mistress herself, in Willey Green Grammar School, as she had been for some years.

"I know," she said, "it seems like that when one thinks in the abstract. But really imagine it: imagine any man one knows, imagine him coming home to one every evening, and saying 'Hello,' and giving one a kiss—"

There was a blank pause.

"Yes," said Gudrun, in a narrowed voice. "It's just impossible. The man makes it impossible."

"Of course there's children—" said Ursula, doubtfully.

Gudrun's face hardened.

"Do *really* want children, Ursula?" she asked coldly.

A dazzled, baffled look came on Ursula's face.

"One feels it is still beyond one," she said.

"*Do* you feel like that?" asked Gudrun. "I get no feeling whatever from the thought of bearing children."

Gudrun looked at Ursula with a mask-like, expressionless face. Ursula knitted her brows.

"Perhaps it isn't genuine," she faltered. "Perhaps one doesn't really want them, in one's soul—only superficially."

A hardness came over Gudrun's face. She did not want to be too definite.

"When one thinks of other people's children—" said Ursula.

Again Gudrun looked at her sister, almost hostile.

"Exactly," she said, to close the conversation.

The two sisters worked on in silence, Ursula having always that strange brightness of an essential flame that is caught, meshed, contravened. She lived a good deal by herself, to herself, working, passing on from day to day, and always thinking, trying to lay hold on life, to grasp it in her own understanding. Her active living was suspended, but underneath, in the darkness, something was coming to pass. If only she could break through the last integuments! She seemed to try to put her hands out, like an infant in the womb, and she could not, not yet. Still she had a strange prescience, an intimation of something yet to come.

She laid down her work and looked at her sister. She thought Gudrun so *charming*, so infinitely charming, in her softness and her fine, exquisite richness of texture and delicacy of line. There was a certain playfulness about her too, such a piquancy of ironic suggestion, such an untouched reserve. Ursula admired her with all her soul.

"Why did you come home, Prune?" she asked.

Gudrun knew she was being admired. She sat back from her drawing and looked at Ursula, from under her finely-curved lashes.

"Why did I come back, Ursula?" she repeated. "I have asked myself, a thousand times."

"And don't you know?"

"Yes, I think I do. I think my coming back home was just *reculer pour mieux sauter*."

And she looked with a long, slow look of knowledge at Ursula.

"I know!" cried Ursula, looking slightly dazzled and falsified, and as if she did *not* know. "But where can one jump *to*?"

"Oh, it doesn't matter," said Gudrun, somewhat superbly. "If one jumps over the edge, one is bound to land somewhere."

"But isn't it very risky?" asked Ursula.

A slow, mocking smile dawned on Gudrun's face.

"Ah!" she said, laughing. "What is it all but words!"

And so again she closed the conversation. But Ursula was still brooding.

"And how do you find home, now you have come back to it?" she asked.

Gudrun paused for some moments, coldly, before answering. Then, in a cold, truthful voice, she said:

"I find myself completely out of it."

"And father?"

Gudrun looked at Ursula, almost with resentment, as if brought to bay.

"I haven't thought about him: I've refrained," she said coldly.

"Yes," wavered Ursula; and the conversation was really at an end. The sisters found themselves confronted by a void, a terrifying chasm, as if they had looked over the edge.

They worked on in silence for some time. Gudrun's cheek was flushed with repressed emotion. She resented its having been called into being.

"Shall we go out and look at that wedding?" she asked at length, in a voice that was too casual.

"Yes!" cried Ursula, too eagerly, throwing aside her sewing and leaping up, as if to escape something, thus betraying the tension of the situation, and causing a friction of dislike to go over Gudrun's nerves.

As she went upstairs, Ursula was aware of the house, of her home round about her. And she loathed it, the sordid, too-familiar place! She was afraid at the depth of her feeling against the home, the milieu, the whole atmosphere and condition of this obsolete life. Her feeling frightened her.

The two girls were soon walking swiftly down the main road of Beldover, a wide street, part shops, part dwelling houses, utterly formless and sordid, without poverty. Gudrun, new from her life in Chelsea and

Sussex, shrank cruelly from this amorphous ugliness of a small colliery town in the midlands. Yet forward she went, through the whole sordid gamut of pettiness, the long, amorphous, gritty street. She was exposed to every stare, she passed on through a stretch of torment. It was strange that she should have chosen to come back and test the full effect of this shapeless, barren ugliness upon herself. Why had she wanted to submit herself to it, did she still want to submit herself to it, the insufferable torture of these ugly, meaningless people, this defaced countryside? She felt like a beetle toiling in the dust. She was filled with repulsion.

They turned off the main road, past a black patch of common-garden, where sooty cabbage stumps stood shameless. No one thought to be ashamed. No one was ashamed of it all.

"It is like a country in an underworld," said Gudrun. "The colliers bring it above-ground with them, shovel it up. Ursula, it's marvellous, it's really marvellous—it's really wonderful, another world. The people are all ghouls, and everything is ghostly. Everything is a ghoulish replica of the real world, a replica, a ghoul, all soiled, everything sordid. It's like being mad, Ursula."

The sisters were crossing a black path through a dark, soiled field. On the left was a large landscape, a valley with collieries, and opposite hills with cornfields and woods, all blackened with distance, as if seen through a veil of crape. White and black smoke rose up in steady columns, magic within the dark air. Near at hand came the long rows of dwellings, approaching curved up the hill-slope, in straight lines along the brow of the hill. They were of darkened red brick, brittle, with dark slate roofs.

The path on which the sisters walked was black, trodden-in by the feet of the recurrent colliers, and bounded from the field by iron fences; the stile that led again into the road was rubbed shiny by the moleskins of the passing miners. Now the two girls were going between some rows of dwellings, of the poorer sort. Women, their arms folded over their coarse aprons, standing gossiping at the end of their block, stared after the Brangwen sisters with that long, unwearying stare of aborigines; children called out names.

Gudrun went on her way half dazed. If this were human life, if these were human beings, living in a complete world, then what was her own world, outside? She was aware of her grass-green stockings, her large, grass-green velour hat, her full, soft coat, of a strong blue colour. And she felt as if she were treading in the air, quite unstable, her heart was contracted, as if at any minute she might be precipitated to the ground. She was afraid.

She clung to Ursula, who, through long usage was inured to this violation of a dark, uncreated, hostile world. But all the time her heart was crying, as if in the midst of some ordeal: "I want to go back, I want to go away, I want not to know it, not to know that this exists." Yet she must go forward.

Ursula could feel her suffering.

"You hate this, don't you?" she asked.

"It bewilders me," stammered Gudrun.

"You won't stay long," replied Ursula.

And Gudrun went along, grasping at release.

They drew away from the colliery region, over the curve of the hill, into the purer country of the other side, towards Willey Green. Still the faint glamour of blackness persisted over the fields and the wooded hills, and seemed darkly to gleam in the air. It was a spring day, chill, with snatches of sunshine. Yellow celandines showed out from the hedge-bottoms, and in the cottage gardens of Willey Green, currant-bushes were breaking into leaf, and little flowers were coming white on the grey alyssum that hung over the stone walls.

Turning, they passed down the high-road, that went between high banks, towards the church. There, in the lowest bend of the road, low under the trees and the wall of the churchyard, which was above their heads, stood a little group of expectant people, waiting to see the wedding. The daughter of the chief mine-owner of the district, Thomas Crich, was getting married to a naval officer.

"Let us go back," said Gudrun, swerving away. "There are all those people."

And she hung wavering in the road.

"Never mind them," said Ursula, "they're all right. They all know me, they don't matter."

"But must we go through them?" asked Gudrun.

"They're quite all right, really," said Ursula, going forward.

And together the two sisters approached the group of uneasy, watchful common people. They were chiefly women, colliers' wives of the more shiftless sort. They had watchful, underworld faces.

The two sisters held themselves tense, and went straight towards the gate. The women made way for them, but barely sufficient, as if grudging to yield ground. The sisters passed in silence through the stone gateway and up the steps, on the red carpet, a policeman estimating their progress.

"What price the stockings!" said a voice at the back of Gudrun. A sudden fierce anger swept over the girl, violent and murderous. She would have liked them all to be annihilated, cleared away, so that the world was left clear for her. How she hated walking up the churchyard path, along the red carpet, continuing in motion, in their sight.

"I won't go into the church," she said suddenly, with such final decision that Ursula immediately halted, turned round, and branched off up a small side path which led to the little private gate of the Grammar School, whose grounds adjoined those of the church.

Just inside the gate of the school shrubbery, outside the churchyard, Ursula sat down for a moment on the low stone wall under the laurel bushes, to rest. Behind her, the large red building of the school rose up peacefully, the windows all open for the holiday. Over the shrubs, before her, were the pale roofs and tower of the old church. The sisters were hidden by the foliage.

Gudrun sat down in silence. Her mouth was shut close, her face averted. She was regretting bitterly that she had ever come back. Ursula looked at her, and thought how amazingly beautiful she was, flushed with discomfiture. But she caused a constraint over Ursula's nature, a certain weariness. Ursula wished to be alone, freed from the tightness, the enclosure of Gudrun's presence.

"Are we going to stay here?" asked Gudrun.

"I was only resting a minute," said Ursula, getting up as if rebuked. "We will stand in the corner by the fives-court, we shall see everything from there."

For the moment, the sunshine fell brightly into the churchyard, there was a vague scent of sap and of spring, perhaps of violets from off the graves. Some white daisies were out, bright as angels. In the air, the unfolding leaves of a copper-beech were blood-red.

Punctually at eleven o'clock, the carriages began to arrive. There was a stir in the crowd at the gate, a concentration as a carriage drove up, wedding guests were mounting up the steps and passing along the red carpet to the church. They were all gay and excited because the sun was shining.

Gudrun watched them closely, with objective curiosity. She saw each one as a complete figure, like a character in a book, or a subject in a picture, or a marionette in a theatre, a finished creation. She loved to recognise their various characteristics, to place them in their true light, give them their own surroundings, settle them for ever as they passed before her along the path to the church. She knew them, they were finished, sealed and stamped and finished with, for her. There were none that had anything unknown, unresolved, until the Criches themselves began to appear. Then her interest was piqued. Here was something not quite so preconcluded.

There came the mother, Mrs Crich, with her eldest son Gerald. She was a queer unkempt figure, in spite of the attempts that had obviously been made to bring her into line for the day. Her face was pale, yellowish, with a clear, transparent skin, she leaned forward rather, her features were strongly marked, handsome, with a tense, unseeing, predative look. Her colourless hair was untidy, wisps floating down on to her sac coat of dark blue silk, from under her blue silk hat. She looked like a woman with a monomania, furtive almost, but heavily proud.

Her son was of a fair, sun-tanned type, rather above middle height, well-made, and almost exaggeratedly well-dressed. But about him also was the strange, guarded look, the unconscious glisten, as if he did not belong to the same creation as the people about him.

Gudrun lighted on him at once. There was something northern about him that magnetised her. In his clear northern flesh and his fair hair was a glisten like cold sunshine refracted through crystals of ice. And he looked so new, unbroached, pure as an arctic thing. Perhaps he was thirty years old, perhaps more. His gleaming beauty, maleness, like a young, good-humoured, smiling wolf did not blind her to the significant, sinister stillness in his bearing, the lurking danger of his unsubdued temper. "His totem is the wolf," she repeated to herself. "His mother is an old, unbroken wolf." And then she experienced a keen paroxysm, a transport, as if she had made some incredible discovery, known to nobody else on earth. A strange transport took possession of her, all her veins were in a paroxysm of violent sensation. "Good God!" she exclaimed to herself, "what is this?" And then, a moment after, she was saying assuredly, "I shall know more of that man." She was tortured with desire to see him again, a nostalgia, a necessity to see him again, to make sure it was not all a mistake, that she was not deluding herself, that she really felt this strange and overwhelming sensation on his account, this knowledge of him in her essence, this powerful apprehension of him. "Am I *really* singled out for him in some way, is there really some pale gold, arctic light that envelopes only us two?" she asked herself. And she could not believe it, she remained in a muse, scarcely conscious of what was going on around.

The bridesmaids were here, and yet the bridegroom had not come. Ursula wondered if something was amiss, and if the wedding would yet all go wrong. She felt troubled, as if it rested upon her. The chief bridesmaids had arrived. Ursula watched them come up the steps. One of them she knew, a tall, slow, reluctant woman with a weight of fair hair and a pale, long face. This was Hermione Roddice, a friend of the Criches. Now she came along, with her head held up, balancing an enormous flat hat of pale yellow velvet, on which were streaks of ostrich feathers, natural and grey. She drifted forward as if scarcely conscious, her long, blenched face lifted up, not to see the world. She was rich. She wore a dress of silky, frail velvet, of pale yellow colour, and she carried a lot of small rose-coloured cyclamens. Her shoes and stockings were of brownish grey, like the feathers on her hat, her hair was heavy, she drifted along with a peculiar fixity of the hips, a strange unwilling motion. She was impressive, in her lovely pale-yellow and brownish-rose, yet macabre, something repulsive. People were silent when she passed, impressed, roused, wanting to jeer, yet for some reason silenced. Her long, pale face, that she carried lifted up, somewhat in the Rossetti fashion, seemed almost drugged, as if a strange mass of thoughts coiled in the darkness within her, and she was never allowed to escape.

Ursula watched her with fascination. She knew her a little. She was the most remarkable woman in the midlands. Her father was a Derbyshire Baronet of the old school, she was a woman of the new school, full of intellectuality, and heavy, nerve-worn with consciousness. She was passionately interested in reform, her soul was given up to the public cause. But she was a man's woman, it was the manly world that held her.

She had various intimacies of mind and soul, with various men of capacity. Ursula knew, among these men, only Rupert Birkin, who was one of the school-inspectors for the county. But Gudrun had met others, in London. Moving with her artist friends in different kinds of society, Gudrun had already come to know a good many people of repute and standing. She had met Hermione twice, but they did not take to each other. It would be queer to meet again down here in the midlands, where their social standing was so diverse, after they had known each other on terms of equality in the houses of sundry acquaintances in town. For Gudrun had been a social success, and had her friends among the slack aristocracy that keeps touch with the arts.

Hermione knew herself to be well-dressed; she knew herself to be the social equal, if not far the superior, of anyone she was likely to meet in Willey Green. She knew she was accepted in the world of culture and of intellect. She was a *Kulturträger*, a medium for the culture of ideas. With all that was highest, whether in society or in thought or in public action, or even in art, she was at one, she moved among the foremost, at home with them. No one could put her down, no one could make mock of her, because she stood among the first, and those that were against her were below her, either in rank, or in wealth, or in high association of thought and progress and understanding. So, she was invulnerable. All her life, she had sought to make herself invulnerable, unassailable, beyond reach of the world's judgment.

And yet her soul was tortured, exposed. Even walking up the path to the church, confident as she was that in every respect she stood beyond all vulgar judgment, knowing perfectly that her appearance was complete and perfect, according to the first standards, yet she suffered a torture, under her confidence and her pride, feeling herself exposed to wounds and to mockery and to despite. She always felt vulnerable, vulnerable, there was always a secret chink in her armour. She did not know herself what it was. It was a lack of robust self, she had no natural sufficiency, there was a terrible void, a lack, a deficiency of being within her.

And she wanted someone to close up this deficiency, to close it up for ever. She craved for Rupert Birkin. When he was there, she felt complete, she was sufficient, whole. For the rest of time she was established on the sand, built over a chasm, and, in spite of all her vanity and securities, any common maid-servant of positive, robust temper could fling her down this bottomless pit of insufficiency, by the slightest movement of jeering or contempt. And all the while the pensive, tortured woman piled up her own defences of aesthetic knowledge, and culture, and world-visions, and disinterestedness. Yet she could never stop up the terrible gap of insufficiency.

If only Birkin would form a close and abiding connection with her, she would be safe during this fretful voyage of life. He could make her sound and triumphant, triumphant over the very angels of heaven. If only he would do it! But she was tortured with fear, with misgiving. She made herself beautiful, she strove so hard to come to that degree of beauty and advantage, when he should be convinced. But always there was a deficiency.

He was perverse too. He fought her off, he always fought her off. The more she strove to bring him to her, the more he battled her back. And they had been lovers now, for years. Oh, it was so wearying, so aching; she was so tired. But still she believed in herself. She knew he was trying to leave her. She knew he was trying to break away from her finally, to be free. But still she believed in her strength to keep him, she believed in her own higher knowledge. Her own knowledge was higher, she was the first touchstone of truth. She only needed his conjunction with her.

And this, this conjunction with her, which was his highest fulfilment also, with the perverseness of a wilful child he wanted to deny. With the wilfulness of an obstinate child, he wanted to break the holy connection that was between them.

He would be at this wedding; he was to be groom's man. He would be in the church, waiting. He would know when she came. She shuddered with nervous apprehension and desire as she went through the church door. He would be there, surely he would see how beautiful her dress was, surely he would see how she had made herself beautiful for him. He would understand, surely he would understand, he would be able to see how she was made for him, the first, how she was, for him, the highest. Surely at last he would be able to accept his highest fate, he would not deny her.

In a little convulsion of too-tired yearning, she entered the church and looked slowly along her cheeks for him, her slender body convulsed with agitation. As best man, he would be standing beside the altar. She looked slowly, deferring in her certainty.

And then, he was not there. A terrible storm came over her, as if she were drowning. She was possessed by a devastating hopelessness. And she approached mechanically to the altar. Never had she known such a pang of utter and final hopelessness. It was beyond death, so utterly null, desert.

The bridegroom and the groom's man had not yet come. There was a growing consternation outside. Ursula felt almost responsible. She could not bear it that the bride should arrive, and no groom. The wedding must not be a fiasco, it must not.

But here was the bride's carriage, adorned with ribbons and cockades. Gaily the grey horses curvetted to their destination at the church-gate, a laughter in the whole movement. Here was the quick of all laughter and pleasure. The door of the carriage was thrown open, to let out the very blossom of the day. The people on the roadway murmured faintly with the discontented murmuring of a crowd.

The father stepped out first into the air of the morning, like a shadow. He was a tall, thin, careworn man, with a thin black beard that was touched with grey. He waited at the door of the carriage patiently, self-obliterated.

In the opening of the doorway was a shower of fine foliage and flowers, a whiteness of satin and lace, and a sound of a gay voice saying:

"How do I get out?"

A ripple of satisfaction ran through the expectant people. They pressed near to receive her, looking with zest at the stooping blond head with its flower buds, and at the delicate, white, tentative foot that was reaching down to the step of the carriage. There was a sudden foaming rush, and the bride like a sudden surf-rush, floating all white beside her father in the morning shadow of trees, her veil flowing with laughter.

"That's done it!" she said.

She put her hand on the arm of her careworn, sallow father, and frothing her light draperies, proceeded over the eternal red carpet. Her father, mute and yellowish, his black beard making him look more careworn, mounted the steps stiffly, as if his spirit were absent; but the laughing mist of the bride went along with him undiminished.

And no bridegroom had arrived! It was intolerable for her. Ursula, her heart strained with anxiety, was watching the hill beyond; the white, descending road, that should give sight of him. There was a carriage. It was running. It had just come into sight. Yes, it was he. Ursula turned towards the bride and the people, and, from her place of vantage, gave an inarticulate cry. She wanted to warn them that he was coming. But her cry was inarticulate and inaudible, and she flushed deeply, between her desire and her wincing confusion.

The carriage rattled down the hill, and drew near. There was a shout from the people. The bride, who had just reached the top of the steps, turned round gaily to see what was the commotion. She saw a confusion among the people, a cab pulling up, and her lover dropping out of the carriage, and dodging among the horses and into the crowd.

"Tibs! Tibs!" she cried in her sudden, mocking excitement, standing high on the path in the sunlight and waving her bouquet. He, dodging with his hat in his hand, had not heard.

"Tibs!" she cried again, looking down to him.

He glanced up, unaware, and saw the bride and her father standing on the path above him. A queer, startled look went over his face. He hesitated for a moment. Then he gathered himself together for the leap, to overtake her.

"Ah-h-h!" came her strange, intaken cry, as, on the reflex, she started, turned, and fled, scudding with an unthinkable swift beating of her white feet and a fraying of her white garments, towards the church. Like a hound the young man was after her, leaping the steps and swinging past her father, his supple haunches working like those of a hound that bears down on the quarry.

"Ay, after her!", cried the vulgar women below, carried suddenly into the sport.

She, her flowers shaken from her like froth, was steadying herself to turn the angle of the church. She glanced behind, and with a wild cry of laughter and challenge, veered, poised, and was gone beyond the grey stone buttress. In another instant the bridegroom, bent forward as he ran, had caught the angle of the silent stone with his hand, and had swung himself out of sight, his supple, strong loins vanishing in pursuit.

Instantly cries and exclamations of excitement burst from the crowd at the gate. And then Ursula noticed again the dark, rather stooping figure of Mr Crich, waiting suspended on the path, watching with expressionless face the flight to the church. It was over, and he turned round to look behind him, at the figure of Rupert Birkin, who at once came forward and joined him.

"We'll bring up the rear," said Birkin, a faint smile on his face.

"Ay!" replied the father laconically.

And the two men turned together up the path.

Birkin was as thin as Mr Crich, pale and ill-looking. His figure was narrow but nicely made. He went with a slight trail of one foot, which came only from self-consciousness. Although he was dressed correctly for his part, yet there was an innate incongruity which caused a slight ridiculousness in his appearance. His nature was clever and separate, he did not fit at all in the conventional occasion. Yet he subordinated himself to the common idea, travestied himself.

He affected to be quite ordinary, perfectly and marvellously commonplace. And he did it so well, taking the tone of his surroundings, adjusting himself quickly to his interlocutor and his circumstance, that he achieved a verisimilitude of ordinary commonplaceness that usually propitiated his onlookers for the moment, disarmed them from attacking his singleness.

Now he spoke quite easily and pleasantly to Mr Crich, as they walked along the path; he played with situations like a man on a tight-rope: but always on a tight-rope, pretending nothing but ease.

"I'm sorry we are so late," he was saying. "We couldn't find a button-hook, so it took us a long time to button our boots. But you were to the moment."

"We are usually to time," said Mr Crich.

"And I'm always late," said Birkin. "But today I was *really* punctual, only accidentally not so. I'm sorry."

The two men were gone, there was nothing more to see, for the time. Ursula was left thinking about Birkin. He piqued her, attracted her, and annoyed her.

She wanted to know him more. She had spoken with him once or twice, but only in his official capacity as inspector. She thought he seemed to acknowledge some kinship between her and him, a natural, tacit understanding, a using of the same language. But there had been no time for the understanding to develop. And something kept her from him, as well as attracted her to him. There was a certain hostility, a hidden ultimate reserve in him, cold and inaccessible.

Yet she wanted to know him.

"What do you think of Rupert Birkin?" she asked, a little reluctantly, of Gudrun. She did not want to discuss him.

"What do I think of Rupert Birkin?" repeated Gudrun. "I think he's attractive—decidedly attractive.—What I can't stand about him is his way with other people—his way of treating any little fool as if she were his greatest consideration.—One feels so awfully sold, oneself."

"Why does he do it?" said Ursula.

"Because he has no real critical faculty—of people, at all events," said Gudrun. "I tell you, he treats any little fool as he treats me or you—and it's such an insult."

"Oh, it is," said Ursula. "One must discriminate."

"One *must* discriminate," repeated Gudrun.—"But he's a wonderful chap, in other respects—a marvellous personality. But you can't trust him."

"Yes," said Ursula vaguely. She was always forced to assent to Gudrun's pronouncements, even when she was not in accord altogether.

The sisters sat silent, waiting for the wedding-party to come out. Gudrun was impatient of talk. She wanted to think about Gerald Crich. She wanted to see if the strong feeling she had got from him was real. She wanted to have herself ready.

Inside the church, the wedding was going on. Hermione Roddice was thinking only of Birkin. He stood near her. She seemed to gravitate physically towards him. She wanted to stand touching him. She could hardly be sure he was near her, if she did not touch him. Yet she stood subjected through the wedding service.

She had suffered so bitterly when he did not come, that still she was dazed. Still she was gnawed as by a neuralgia, tormented by his potential absence from her. She had awaited him in a faint delirium of nervous torture. As she stood bearing herself pensively, the rapt look on her face, that seemed spiritual, like the angels, but which came from torture, gave her a certain poignancy that tore his heart with pity. He saw her bowed head, her rapt face, the face of an almost demoniacal ecstatic. Feeling him looking, she lifted her face and sought his eyes, her own beautiful grey eyes flaring him a great signal. But he avoided her look, she sank her head in torment and shame, the gnawing at her heart going on. And he too was tortured with shame, and ultimate dislike, and with acute pity for her, because he did not want to meet her eyes, he did not want to receive her flare of recognition.

The bride and bridegroom were married, the party went into the vestry. Hermione crowded involuntarily up against Birkin, to touch him. And he endured it.

Outside, Gudrun and Ursula listened for their father's playing on the organ. He would enjoy playing a wedding march.—Now the married pair were coming! The bells were ringing, making the air shake. Ursula wondered if the trees and the flowers could feel the vibration, and what they thought of it, this strange motion in the air. The bride was quite demure on the arm of the bridegroom, who stared up into the sky before him, shutting and opening his eyes unconsciously, as if he were neither here nor there. He looked rather comical, blinking and trying to be in the scene, when emotionally he was violated by his exposure to a crowd. He looked a typical naval officer, manly, and up to his duty.

Birkin came with Hermione. She had a rapt, triumphant look, like the fallen angels restored, yet still subtly demoniacal, now she held Birkin by the arm. And he was expressionless, neutralised, possessed by her as if it were his fate, without question.

Gerald Crich came, fair, good-looking, healthy, with a great reserve of energy. He was erect and complete, there was a strange stealth glistening through his amiable, almost happy appearance. Gudrun rose sharply and went away. She could not bear it. She wanted to be alone, to know this strange, sharp inoculation that had changed the whole temper of her blood.

Chapter II

Shortlands

The Brangwens went home to Beldover, the wedding-party gathered at Shortlands, the Criches' home. It was a long, low old house, a sort of manor farm, that spread along the top of a slope just beyond the narrow little lake of Willey Water. Shortlands looked across a sloping meadow that might be a park, because of the large, solitary trees that stood here and there, across the water of the narrow lake, at the wooded hill that successfully hid the colliery valley beyond, but did not quite hide the rising smoke. Nevertheless, the scene was rural and picturesque, very peaceful, and the house had a charm of its own.

It was crowded now with the family and the wedding guests. The father, who was not well, withdrew to rest. Gerald was host. He stood in the homely entrance hall, friendly and easy, attending to the men. He seemed to take pleasure in his social functions, he smiled, and was abundant in hospitality.

The women wandered about in a little confusion, chased hither and thither by the three married daughters of the house. All the while there could be heard the characteristic, imperious voice of one Crich woman or another calling, "Helen, come here a minute," "Marjory, I want you—here!" "Oh I say, Mrs Witham—." There was a great rustling of skirts, swift glimpses of smartly-dressed women, a child danced through the hall and back again, a maid-servant came and went hurriedly.

Meanwhile the men stood in calm little groups, chatting, smoking, pretending to pay no heed to the rustling animation of the women's world. But they could not really talk, because of the glassy ravel of women's excited, cold laughter and running voices. They waited, uneasy, suspended, rather bored. But Gerald remained as if genial and happy, unaware that he was waiting or unoccupied, knowing himself the very pivot of the occasion.

Suddenly Mrs Crich came noiselessly into the room, peering about with her strong, clear face. She was still wearing her hat, and her sac coat of blue silk.

"What is it, mother?" said Gerald.

"Nothing, nothing!" she answered vaguely.

And she went straight towards Birkin, who was talking to a Crich brother-in-law.

"How do you do, Mr Birkin," she said, in her low voice, that seemed to take no count of her guests. She held out her hand to him.

"Oh Mrs Crich," replied Birkin, in his readily-changing voice, "I couldn't come to you before."

"I don't know half the people here," she said, in her low voice. Her son-in-law moved uneasily away.

"And you don't like strangers?" laughed Birkin. "I myself can never see why one should take account of people, just because they happen to be in the room with one. Why *should* I know they are there?"

"Why indeed, why indeed!" said Mrs Crich, in her low, tense voice. "Except that they *are* there.—*I* don't know people whom I find in the house. The children introduce them to me—'Mother, this is Mr So-and-so.' I am no further. What has Mr So-and-so to do with his own name?—and what have I to do with either him or his name?"

She looked up at Birkin. She startled him. He was flattered too that she came to talk to him, for she took hardly any notice of anybody. He looked down at her tense clear face, with its heavy features, but he was afraid to look into her heavy-seeing blue eyes. He noticed instead how her hair looped in slack, slovenly strands over her rather beautiful ears, which were not quite clean. Neither was her neck perfectly clean. Even in that he seemed to belong to her, rather than to the rest of the company; though, he thought to himself, he was always well washed, at any rate at the neck and ears.

He smiled faintly, thinking these things. Yet he was tense, feeling that he and the elderly, estranged woman were conferring together like traitors, like enemies within the camp of the other people. He resembled a deer, that throws one ear back upon the trail behind, and one ear forward, to know what is ahead.

"People don't really matter," he said, rather unwilling to continue.

The mother looked up at him with sudden, dark interrogation, as if doubting his sincerity.

"How do you mean, *matter*?" she asked sharply.

"Not many people are anything at all," he answered, forced to go deeper than he wanted to. "They jingle and giggle. It would be much better if they were just wiped out. Essentially, they don't exist, they aren't there."

She watched him steadily while he spoke.

"But we don't imagine them," she said sharply.

"There's nothing to imagine, that's why they don't exist."

"Well," she said, "I would hardly go as far as that. There they are, whether they exist or no. It doesn't rest with me to decide on their existence. I only know that I can't be expected to take count of them all. You can't expect me to know them, just because they happen to be there. As far as *I* go they might as well not be there."

"Exactly," he replied.

"Mightn't they?" she asked again.

"Just as well," he repeated.

And there was a little pause.

"Except that they *are* there, and that's a nuisance," she said.

"There are my sons-in-law," she went on, in a sort of monologue. "Now Laura's got married, there's another. And I really don't know John from James yet. They come up to me, and call me mother. I know what they will say—'How are you, mother?' I ought to say, 'I am not your mother, in any sense.' But what is the use? There they are. I have had children of my own. I suppose I know them from another woman's children."

"One would suppose so," he said.

She looked at him, somewhat surprised, forgetting perhaps that she was talking to him. And she lost her thread.

She looked round the room, vaguely. Birkin could not guess what she was looking for, nor what she was thinking. Evidently she noticed her sons.

"Are my children all there?" she asked him, abruptly.

He laughed, startled, afraid perhaps.

"I scarcely know them, except Gerald," he replied.

"Gerald!" she exclaimed. "He's the most wanting of them all. You'd never think it, to look at him now, would you?"

"No," said Birkin.

The mother looked across at her eldest son, stared at him heavily for some time.

"Ay," she said, in an incomprehensible monosyllable, that sounded profoundly cynical. Birkin felt afraid, as if he dared not realise. And Mrs Crich moved away, forgetting him. But she returned on her traces.

"I should like him to have a friend," she said. "He has never had a friend."

Birkin looked down into her eyes, which were blue, and watching heavily. He could not understand them. "Am I my brother's keeper?" he said to himself, almost flippantly.

Then he remembered, with a slight shock, that that was Cain's cry. And Gerald was Cain, if anybody. Not that he was Cain, either, although he had slain his brother. There was such a thing as pure accident, and the consequences did not attach to one, even though one had killed one's brother in such wise. Gerald as a boy had accidentally killed his brother. What then? Why seek to draw a brand and a curse across the life that had caused the accident? A man can live by accident, and die by accident. Or can he not? Is every man's life subject to pure accident, is it only the race, the genus, the species, that has a universal reference? Or is this not true, is there no such thing as pure accident? Has *everything* that happens a universal significance? Has it? Birkin, pondering as he stood there, had forgotten Mrs Crich, as she had forgotten him.

He did not believe that there was any such thing as accident. It all hung together, in the deepest sense.

Just as he had decided this, one of the Crich daughters came up, saying:

"Won't you come and take your hat off, mother dear? We shall be sitting down to eat in a minute, and it's a formal occasion, darling, isn't it?"—She drew her arm through her mother's, and they went away. Birkin immediately went to talk with the nearest man.

The gong sounded for the luncheon. The men looked up, but no move was made to the dining-room. The women of the house seemed not to feel that the sound had meaning for them. Five minutes passed by. The elderly man-servant, Crowther, appeared in the doorway exasperatedly. He looked with appeal at Gerald. The latter took up a large, curved conch shell, that lay on a shelf, and without reference to anybody, blew a shattering blast. It was a strange, rousing noise, that made the heart beat. The summons was almost magical. Everybody came running, as if at a signal. And then the crowd in one impulse moved to the dining-room.

Gerald waited a moment, for his sister to play hostess. He knew his mother would pay no attention to her duties. But his sister merely crowded to her seat. Therefore the young man, slightly too dictatorial, directed the guests to their places.

There was a moment's lull, as everybody looked at the *hors d'oeuvres* that were being handed round. And out of this lull, a girl of thirteen or fourteen, with her long hair down her back, said in a calm, self-possessed voice:

"Gerald, you forget father, when you make that unearthly noise."

"Do I?" he answered. And then, to the company, "Father is lying down, he is not quite well."

"How is he, really?" called one of the married daughters, peeping round the immense wedding cake that towered up in the middle of the table shedding its artificial flowers.

"He has no pain, but he feels tired," replied Winifred, the girl with the hair down her back.

The wine was filled, and everybody was talking boisterously. At the far end of the table sat the mother, with her loosely-looped hair. She had Birkin for a neighbour. Sometimes she glanced fiercely down the rows of faces, bending forwards, and staring unceremoniously. And she would say, in a low voice, to Birkin:

"Who is that young man?"

"I don't know," Birkin answered discreetly.

"Have I seen him before?" she asked.

"I don't think so. *I* haven't," he replied.

And she was satisfied. Her eyes closed wearily, a peace came over her face, she looked like a queen in repose. Then she started, a little, social smile came on her face, for a moment she looked the pleasant hostess. For a moment she bent graciously, as if everyone were welcome and delightful. And then immediately the shadow came back, a sullen, eagle look was on her face, she glanced from under her brows like a sinister creature at bay, hating them all.

"Mother," called Diana, a handsome girl a little older than Winifred, "I may have wine, mayn't I?"

"Yes, you may have wine," replied the mother automatically, for she was perfectly indifferent to the question.

And Diana beckoned to the footman to fill her glass.

"Gerald shouldn't forbid me," she said calmly, to the company at large.

"All right Di," said her brother amiably.

And she glanced challenge at him as she drank from her glass.

There was a strange freedom, that almost amounted to anarchy, in the house. It was rather a resistance to authority, than liberty. Gerald had some command, by mere force of personality, not because of any granted position. There was a quality in his voice, amiable but dominant, that cowed the others, who were all younger than he.

Hermione was having a discussion with the bridegroom about nationality.

"No," she said, "I think that the appeal to patriotism is a mistake. It is like one house of business rivalling another house of business."

"Well you can hardly say that, can you?" exlaimed Gerald, who had a real *passion* for discussion. "You couldn't call a race a business concern, could you?—and nationality roughly corresponds to race, I think.—I think it is *meant* to."

There was a moment's pause. Gerald and Hermione were always strangely but politely and evenly inimical.

"*Do* you think race corresponds with nationality?" she asked musingly, with expressionless indecision.

Birkin knew she was waiting for him to participate. And dutifully he spoke up.

"I think Gerald is right—race is the essential element in nationality, in Europe at least," he said.

Again Hermione paused, as if to allow this statement to cool. Then she said, with strange assumption of authority:

"Yes, but even so, is the patriotic appeal an appeal to the racial instinct? Is it not rather an appeal to the proprietory instinct, the *commercial* instinct? And isn't this what we mean by nationality?"

"Probably," said Birkin, who felt that such a discussion was out of place and out of time.

But Gerald was now on the scent of argument.

"A race may have its commercial aspect," he said. "In fact it must. It is like a family. You *must* make provision. And to make provision you have got to strive against other families, other nations. I don't see why you shouldn't."

Again Hermione made a pause, domineering and cold, before she replied: "Yes, I think it is always wrong to provoke a spirit of rivalry. It makes bad blood. And bad blood accumulates."

"But you can't do away with the spirit of emulation altogether," said Gerald. "It is one of the necessary incentives to production and improvement."

"Yes," came Hermione's sauntering response. "I think you can do away with it."

"I must say," said Birkin, "I detest the spirit of emulation."

Hermione was biting a piece of bread, pulling it from between her teeth with her fingers, in a slow, slightly derisive movement. She turned to Birkin.

"You do hate it, yes," she said, intimate and gratified.

"Detest it," he repeated.

"Yes," she murmured, assured and satisfied.

"But," Gerald insisted, "you don't allow one man to take away his neighbour's living, so why should you allow one nation to take away the living from another nation?"

There was a long slow murmur from Hermione before she broke into speech, saying with a laconic indifference:

"It is not always a question of possessions, is it? It is not all a question of goods?"

Gerald was nettled by this implication of vulgar materialism.

"Yes, more or less," he retorted. "If I go and take a man's hat from off his head, that hat becomes a symbol of that man's liberty. When he fights me for his hat, he is fighting me for his liberty."

Hermione was nonplussed.

"Yes," she said, irritated. "But that way of arguing by imaginary instances is not supposed to be genuine, is it? A man does *not* come and take my hat from off my head, does he?"

"Only because the law prevents him," said Gerald.

"Not only," said Birkin. "Ninety-nine men out of a hundred don't want my hat."

"That's a matter of opinion," said Gerald.

"Or the hat," laughed the bridegroom.

"And if he does want my hat, such as it is," said Birkin, "why, surely it is open to me to decide, which is a greater loss to me, my hat, or my liberty as a free and indifferent man. If I am compelled to offer fight, I lose the latter. It is a question which is worth more to me, my pleasant liberty of conduct, or my hat."

"Yes," said Hermione, watching Birkin strangely. "Yes."

"But would you let somebody come and snatch your hat off your head?" the bride asked of Hermione.

The face of the tall straight woman turned slowly and as if drugged to this new speaker.

"No," she replied, in a low inhuman tone, that seemed to contain a chuckle. "No, I shouldn't let anybody take my hat off my head."

"How would you prevent it?" asked Gerald.

"I don't know," replied Hermione slowly. "Probably I should kill him."

There was a strange chuckle in her tone, a dangerous and convincing humour in her bearing.

"Of course," said Gerald, "I can see Rupert's point. It is a question to him whether his hat or his peace of mind is more important."

"Peace of body," said Birkin.

"Well, as you like there," replied Gerald. "But how are you going to decide this for a nation?"

"Heaven preserve me," laughed Birkin.

"Yes, but suppose you have to?" Gerald persisted.

"Then it is the same. If the national crown-piece is an old hat, then the thieving gent may have it."

"But *can* the national or racial hat be an old hat?" insisted Gerald.

"Pretty well bound to be, I believe," said Birkin.

"I'm not so sure," said Gerald.

"I don't agree, Rupert," said Hermione.

"All right," said Birkin.

"I'm all for the old national hat," laughed Gerald.

"And a fool you look in it," cried Diana, his pert sister who was just in her teens.

"Oh, we're quite out of our depths with these old hats," cried Laura Crich. "Dry up now, Gerald. We're going to drink toasts. Let us drink toasts. Toasts—glasses, glasses,—now then, toasts! Speech! Speech!"

Birkin, thinking about race or national death, watched his glass being filled with champagne. The bubbles broke at the rim, the man withdrew, and feeling a sudden thirst at the sight of the fresh wine, Birkin drank up his glass. A queer little tension in the room roused him. He felt a sharp constraint.

"Did I do it by accident, or on purpose?" he asked himself. And he decided that, according to the vulgar phrase, he had done it "accidentally on purpose." He looked round at the hired footman. And the hired footman came, with a silent step of cold servantlike disapprobation. Birkin decided that he detested toasts, and footmen, and assemblies, and mankind altogether, in most of its aspects. Then he rose to make a speech. But he was somehow disgusted.

At length it was over, the meal. Several men strolled out into the garden. There was a lawn, and flower-beds, and at the boundary an iron fence shutting off the little field or park. The view was pleasant: a high-road curving round the edge of a low lake, under the trees. In the spring air, the water gleamed and the opposite woods were purplish with new life. Charming Jersey cattle came to the fence, breathing hoarsely from their velvet muzzles at the human beings, expecting perhaps a crust.

Birkin leaned on the fence. A cow was breathing wet hotness on his hand.

"Pretty cattle, very pretty," said Marshall, one of the brothers-in-law. "They give the best milk you can have."

"Yes," said Birkin.

"Eh, my little beauty, eh, my beauty!" said Marshall, in a queer high falsetto voice, that caused the other man to have convulsions of laughter in his stomach.

"Who won the race, Lupton?" he called to the bridegroom, to hide the fact that he was laughing.

The bridegroom took his cigar from his mouth.

"The race?" he exclaimed. Then a rather thin smile came over his face. He did not want to say anything about the flight to the church door. "We got there together. At least she touched first, but I had my hand on her shoulder."

"What's this?" asked Gerald.

Birkin told him about the race of the bride and the bridegroom.

"Hm!" said Gerald, in disapproval. "What made you late then?"

"Lupton would talk about the immortality of the soul," said Birkin, "and then we hadn't got a button-hook."

"Oh God!" cried Marshall. "The immortality of the soul on your wedding day! Hadn't you got anything better to occupy your mind?"

"What's wrong with it?" asked the bridegroom, a clean-shaven naval man, flushing sensitively.

"Sounds as if you were going to be executed instead of married. The *immortality of the soul!*" repeated the brother-in-law, with most killing emphasis.

But he fell quite flat.

"And what did you decide?" asked Gerald, at once pricking up his ears at the thought of a metaphysical discussion.

"You don't want a soul, today, my boy," said Marshall. "It'd be in your road."

"Christ!, Marshall, go and talk to somebody else," cried Gerald, with sudden impatience.

"By God, I'm willing," said Marshall, in a temper. "Too much bloody soul, and talk altogether—"

He withdrew in a dudgeon, Gerald staring after him with angry eyes, that grew gradually calm and amiable as the stoutly-built form of the other man passed into the distance.

"There's one thing, Lupton," said Gerald, turning suddenly to the bridegroom. "Laura won't have brought such a fool into the family as Lottie did."

"Comfort yourself with that," laughed Birkin.

"I take no notice of them," laughed the bridegroom.

"What about this race then—who began it?" Gerald asked.

"We were late. Laura was at the top of the churchyard steps when our cab came up. She saw Lupton bolting towards her. And she fled.—But why do you look so cross? Does it hurt your sense of the family dignity?"

"It does rather," said Gerald. "If you're doing a thing, do it properly, and if you're not going to do it properly, leave it alone."

"Very nice aphorism," said Birkin.

"Don't you agree?" asked Gerald.

"Quite," said Birkin. "Only it bores me rather, when you become aphoristic."

"Damn you, Rupert, you want all the aphorisms your own way," said Gerald.

"No, I want them out of the way, and you're always shoving them in it."

Gerald smiled grimly at this humorism. Then he made a little gesture of dismissal, with his eyebrows.

"You don't believe in having any standard of behaviour at all, do you?" he challenged Birkin, censoriously.

"Standard—no. I hate standards. But they're necessary for the common ruck.—Anybody who is anything can just be himself and do as he likes."

"But what do you mean by being himself?" said Gerald. "Is that an aphorism or a cliché?"

"I mean just doing what you want to do. I think it was perfect good form in Laura to bolt from Lupton to the church door. It was almost a masterpiece in good form. It's the hardest thing in the world to act spontaneously on one's impulses—and it's the only really gentlemanly thing to do—provided you're fit to do it."

"You don't expect me to take you seriously, do you?" asked Gerald.

"Yes Gerald, you're one of the very few people I do expect that of."

"Then I'm afraid I can't come up to your expectations here, at any rate.—You think people should just do as they like?"

"I think they always do. But I should like them to like the purely individual thing in themselves, which makes them act in singleness. And they only like to do the collective thing."

"And I," said Gerald grimly, "shouldn't like to be in a world of people who acted individually and spontaneously, as you call it.—We should have everybody cutting everybody else's throat in five minutes."

"That means *you* would like to be cutting everybody's throat," said Birkin.

"How does that follow?" asked Gerald crossly.

"No man," said Birkin, "cuts another man's throat unless he wants to cut it, and unless the other man wants it cutting. This is a complete truth. It takes two people to make a murder: a murderer and a murderee. And a murderee is a man who is murderable. And a man who is murderable is a man who in a profound if hidden lust desires to be murdered."

"Sometimes you talk pure nonsense," said Gerald to Birkin. "As a matter of fact, none of us wants our throat cut, and most other people would like to cut it for us—some time or other—"

"It's a nasty view of things, Gerald," said Birkin, "and no wonder you are afraid of yourself and your own unhappiness."

"How am I afraid of myself?" said Gerald; "and I don't think I am unhappy."

"You seem to have a lurking desire to have your gizzard slit, and imagine every man has his knife up his sleeve for you," Birkin said.

"How do you make that out?" said Gerald.

"From you," said Birkin.

There was a pause of strange enmity between the two men, that was very near to love. It was always the same between them; always their talk brought them into a deadly nearness of contact, a strange, perilous intimacy which was either hate or love, or both. They parted with apparent inconcern, as if their going apart were a trivial occurrence. And they really kept it to the level of trivial occurrence. Yet the heart of each burned from the other. They burned with each other, inwardly. This they would never admit. They intended to keep their relationship a casual free-and-easy friendship, they were not going to be so unmanly and unnatural as to allow any heart-burning between them. They had not the faintest belief in deep relationship between man and man, and their disbelief prevented any development of their powerful but suppressed friendliness.

Chapter III

Class-room

A school-day was drawing to a close. In the class-room the last lesson was in progress, peaceful and still. It was elementary botany. The desks were littered with catkins, hazel˙ and willow, which the children had been sketching. But the sky had come over dark, as the end of the afternoon approached, there was scarcely light to draw any more. Ursula stood in front of the class, leading the children by questions to understand the structure and the meaning of the catkins.

A heavy, copper-coloured beam of light came in at the west window, gilding the outlines of the children's heads with red gold, and falling on the wall opposite in a rich, ruddy illumination. Ursula, however, was scarcely conscious of it. She was busy, the end of the day was here, the work went on as a peaceful tide that is at flood, hushed to retire.

This day had gone by like so many more, in an activity that was like a trance. At the end there was a little haste, to finish what was in hand. She was pressing the children with questions, so that they should know all they were to know, by the time the gong went. She stood in shadow in front of the class, with catkins in her hand, and she leaned towards the children, absorbed in the passion of instruction.

She heard, but did not notice the click of the door. Suddenly she started. She saw, in the shaft of ruddy, copper-coloured light near her, the face of a man. It was gleaming like fire, watching her, waiting for her to be aware. It startled her terribly. She thought she was going to faint. All her suppressed, subconscious fear sprang into being, with anguish.

"Did I startle you?" said Birkin, shaking hands with her. "I thought you had heard me come in."

"No," she faltered, scarcely able to speak.

He laughed, saying he was sorry. She wondered why it amused him.

"It is so dark," he said. "Shall we have the light?"

And moving aside, he switched on the strong electric lights. The class-room was distinct and hard, a strange place after the soft dim magic that filled it before he came. Birkin turned curiously to look at Ursula. Her eyes were round and wondering, bewildered, her mouth quivered slightly. She looked like one who is suddenly wakened. There was a living, tender beauty, like a tender light of dawn shining from her face. He looked at her with a new pleasure, feeling gay in his heart, irresponsible.

"You are doing catkins?" he asked, picking up a piece of hazel from a scholar's desk in front of him. "Are they as far out as this? I hadn't noticed them this year."

He looked absorbedly at the tassel of hazel in his hand.

"The red ones too!" he said, looking at the flickers of crimson that came from the female bud.

Then he went in among the desks, to see the scholars' books. Ursula watched his intent progress. There was a stillness in his motion that hushed the activities of her heart. She seemed to be standing aside in arrested silence, watching him move in another, concentrated world. His presence was so quiet, almost like a vacancy in the corporate air.

Suddenly he lifted his face to her, and her heart quickened at the flicker of his voice.

"Give them some crayons, won't you?" he said, "so that they can make the gynaecious flowers red, and the androgynous yellow. I'd chalk them in plain, chalk in nothing else, merely the red and the yellow. Outline scarcely matters in this case. There is just the one fact to emphasise."

"I haven't any crayons," said Ursula.

"There will be some somewhere—red and yellow, that's all you want."

Ursula sent out a boy on a quest.

"It will make the books untidy," she said to Birkin, flushing deeply.

"Not very," he said. "You must mark in these things obviously. It's the fact you want to emphasise, not a subjective impression to record. What's the fact?—red little spiky stigmas of the female flower, dangling yellow male catkin, yellow pollen flying from one to the other. Make a pictorial record of the fact, as a child does when drawing a face—two eyes, one nose, mouth with teeth—so ." And he drew a figure on the blackboard.

At that moment another vision was seen through the glass panels of the door. It was Hermione Roddice. Birkin went and opened to her.

"I saw your car," she said to him. "Do you mind my coming to find you? I wanted to see you when you were on duty."

She looked at him for a long time, intimate and playful, then she gave a short little laugh. And then only she turned to Ursula, who, with all the class, had been watching the little scene between the lovers.

"How do you do, Miss Brangwen," sang Hermione, in her slow, odd, singing fashion, that sounded almost as if she were poking fun. "Do you mind my coming in?"

Her grey, almost sardonic eyes rested all the while on Ursula, as if summing her up.

"Oh no," said Ursula.

"Are you *sure*?" repeated Hermione, with complete sang froid, and an odd, half-bullying effrontery.

"Oh no, I like it awfully," laughed Ursula, a little bit excited and bewildered, because Hermione seemed to be compelling her, coming very close to her, as if intimate with her; and yet, how could she be intimate?

This was the answer Hermione wanted. She turned satisfied to Birkin.

"What are you doing?" she sang, in her casual, inquisitive fashion.

"Catkins," he replied.

"Really!" she said. "And what do they learn about them?"

She spoke all the while in a mocking, half teasing fashion, as if making game of the whole business. She picked up a twig of the catkin, piqued by Birkin's attention to it.

She was a strange figure in the class-room, wearing a large, old cloak of greenish cloth, on which was a raised pattern of dull gold. The high collar, and the inside of the cloak, was lined with dark fur. Beneath she had a dress of fine lavender-coloured cloth, trimmed with fur, and her hat was close-fitting, made of fur and of the dull, green-and-gold figured stuff. She was tall and strange, she looked as if she had come out of some new, bizarre picture.

"Do you know the little red ovary flowers, that produce the nuts? Have you ever noticed them?" he asked her. And he came close and pointed them out to her, on the sprig she held.

"No," she replied. "What are they?"

"Those are the little seed-producing flowers, and the long catkins, they only produce pollen, to fertilise them."

"Do they, do they!" repeated Hermione, looking closely.

"From those little red bits, the nuts come; if they receive pollen from the long danglers."

"Little red flames, little red flames," murmured Hermione to herself. And she remained for some moments looking only at the small buds out of which the red flickers of the stigma issued.

"Aren't they beautiful? I think they're so beautiful," she said, moving close to Birkin, and pointing to the red filaments with her long, white finger.

"Had you never noticed them before?" he asked.

"No, never before," she replied.

"And now you will always see them," he said.

"Now I shall always see them," she repeated. "Thank you so much for showing me. I think they're so beautiful—little red flames—"

Her absorption was strange, almost rhapsodic. Both Birkin and Ursula were suspended. The little red pistillate flowers had some strange, almost mystic-passionate attraction for her.

The lesson was finished, the books were put away, at last the class was dismissed. And still Hermione sat at the table, with her chin in her hand, her elbow on the table, her long white face pushed up, not attending to anything. Birkin had gone to the window, and was looking from the brilliantly-lighted room on to the grey, colourless outside, where rain was noiselessly falling. Ursula put away her things in the cupboard.

At length Hermione rose and came near to her.

"Your sister has come home?" she said.

"Yes," said Ursula.

"And does she like being back in Beldover?"

"No," said Ursula.

"No. I wonder she can bear it. It takes all my strength, to bear the ugliness of this district, when I stay here.—Won't you come and see me? Won't you come with your sister to stay at Breadalby for a few days?—do—"

"Thank you very much," said Ursula.

"Then I will write to you," said Hermione. "You think your sister will come? I should be so glad. I think she is wonderful. I think some of her work is really wonderful. I have two water-wagtails, carved in wood, and painted—perhaps you have seen it?"

"No," said Ursula.

"I think it is perfectly wonderful—like a flash of instinct—"

"Her little carvings *are* strange," said Ursula.

"Perfectly beautiful—full of primitive passion—"

"Isn't it queer that she always likes little things?—she must always work small things, that one can put between one's hands, birds, and tiny animals. She likes to look through the wrong end of the opera glasses, and see the world that way.—Why is it, do you think?"

Hermione looked down at Ursula with that long, detached, scrutinising gaze that excited the younger woman.

"Yes," said Hermione at length. "It is curious. The little things seem to be more subtle to her—"

"But they aren't, are they? A mouse isn't any more subtle than a lion, is it?"

Again Hermione looked down at Ursula with that long scrutiny, as if she were following some train of thought of her own, and barely attending to the other's speech.

"I don't know," she replied.

"Rupert, Rupert," she sang mildly, calling him to her.

He approached in silence.

"Are little things more subtle than big things?" she asked, with the odd grunt of laughter in her voice, as if she were making game of him in the question.

"Dunno," he said.

"I hate subtleties," said Ursula.

Hermione looked at her slowly.

"Do you," she said.

"I always think they are a sign of weakness," said Ursula, up in arms, as if her prestige were threatened.

Hermione took no notice. Suddenly her face puckered, her brow was knit with thought, she seemed twisted in troublesome effort for utterance.

"Do you really think, Rupert," she asked, as if Ursula were not present, "do you really think it is worth while? Do you really think the children are better for being roused to consciousness?"

A dark flash went over his face, a silent fury. He was hollow-cheeked and pale, almost unearthly. And the woman, with her serious, conscience-harrowing question tortured him on the quick.

"They are not roused to consciousness," he said. "Consciousness comes to them, willy-nilly."

"But do you think they are better for having it quickened, stimulated? Isn't it better that they should remain unconscious of the hazel, isn't it better that they should see as a whole, without all this pulling to pieces, all this knowledge?"

"Would you rather, for yourself, know or not know, that the little red flowers are there, putting out for the pollen?" he asked harshly. His voice was brutal, scornful, cruel.

Hermione remained with her face lifted up, abstracted. He hung silent in irritation.

"I don't know," she replied, balancing mildly. "I don't know."

"But knowing is everything to you, it is all your life," he broke out. She slowly looked at him.

"Is it," she said.

"To know, that is your all, that is your life—you have only this, this knowledge," he cried. "There is only one tree, there is only one fruit, in your mouth."

Again she was some time silent.

"Is there," she said at last, with the same untouched calm. And then in a tone of whimsical inquisitiveness: "What fruit, Rupert?"

"The eternal apple," he replied in exasperation, hating his own metaphors.

"Yes," she said. There was a look of exhaustion about her. For some moments there was silence. Then, pulling herself together with a convulsed movement, Hermione resumed, in a sing-song, casual voice:

"But leaving me apart, Rupert; *do* you think the children are better, richer, happier, for all this knowledge, do you really think they are? Or is it better to leave them untouched, spontaneous. Hadn't they better be *animals*, simple animals, crude, violent, *anything*, rather than this self-consciousness, this incapacity to be spontaneous."

They thought she had finished. But with a queer rumbling in her throat she resumed, "Hadn't they better be anything than grow up crippled, crippled in their souls, crippled in their feelings—so thrown back—so turned back on themselves——incapable—" Hermione clenched her fist like one in a trance—"of any spontaneous action, always deliberate, always burdened with choice, never carried away."

Again they thought she had finished. But just as he was going to reply, she resumed her queer rhapsody—"never carried away, out of themselves, always conscious, always self-conscious, always aware of themselves.—— Isn't *anything* better than this? Better be animals, mere animals with no mind at all, than this, this *nothingness*—."

"But do you think it is knowledge that makes us unliving and self-conscious?" he asked irritably.

She opened her eyes and looked at him slowly.

"Yes," she said. She paused, watching him all the while, her eyes vague. Then she wiped her fingers across her brow, with a vague weariness. It irritated him bitterly. "It is the mind," she said, "and that is death." She raised her eyes slowly to him: "Isn't the mind—" she said, with the convulsed movement of her body, "isn't it our death? Doesn't it destroy all our spontaneity, all our instincts? Are not the young people growing up today, really dead before they have a chance to live?"

"Not because they have too much mind, but too little," he said brutally.

"Are you *sure*?" she cried. "It seems to me the reverse. They are over-conscious, burdened to death with consciousness."

"Imprisoned within a limited, false set of concepts," he cried.

But she took no notice of this, only went on with her own rhapsodic interrogation.

"When we have knowledge, don't we lose everything but knowledge?" she asked pathetically. "If I know about the flower, don't I lose the flower and have only the knowledge? Aren't we exchanging the substance for the shadow, aren't we forfeiting life for this dead quantity of knowledge? And what does it mean to me, after all? What does all this knowing mean to me? It means nothing."

"You are merely making words," he said; "knowledge means everything to you. Even your animalism, you want it in your head. You don't want to *be* an animal, you want to observe your own animal functions, to get a mental thrill out of them. It is all purely secondary—and more decadent than the most hide-bound intellectualism. What is it but the worst and last form of intellectualism, this love of yours for passion and the animal instincts? Passion and the instincts—you want them hard enough, but through your head, in your consciousness. It all takes place in your head, under that skull of yours.—Only you won't be conscious of what *actually* is: you want the lie that will match the rest of your furniture."

Hermione set hard and poisonous against this attack. Ursula stood covered with wonder and shame. It frightened her, to see how they hated each other.

"It's all that Lady of Shalott business," he said, in his strong, abstract voice. He seemed to be charging her before the unseeing air. "You've got that mirror, your own fixed will, your immortal understanding, your own tight conscious world, and there is nothing beyond it. There, in the mirror, you must have everything. But now you have come to all your conclusions, you want to go back and be like a savage, without knowledge. You want a life of pure sensation and 'passion.'"

He quoted the last word satirically against her. She sat convulsed with fury and violation, speechless, like a stricken pythoness of the Greek oracle.

"But your passion is a lie," he went on violently. "It isn't passion at all, it is your *will*. It's your bullying will. You want to clutch things and have them in your power. You want to have things in your power. And why? Because you haven't got any real body, any dark sensual body of life. You have no sensuality. You have only your will and your conceit of consciousness, and your lust for power, to *know*."

He looked at her in mingled hate and contempt, also in pain because she suffered, and in shame because he knew he tortured her. He had an impulse to kneel and plead for forgiveness. But a bitterer red anger burned up to fury in him. He became unconscious of her, he was only a passionate voice speaking.

"Spontaneous!" he cried. "You and spontaneity! You, the most deliberate thing that ever walked or crawled! You'd be verily deliberately spontaneous—that's you.—Because you want to have everything in your own volition, your deliberate voluntary consciousness.—You want it all in that loathsome little skull of yours, that ought to be cracked like a nut. For you'll be the same till it *is* cracked, like an insect in its skin.—If one cracked your skull perhaps one might get a spontaneous, passionate woman out of you, with real sensuality.—As it is, what you want is pornography—looking at yourself in mirrors, watching your naked animal actions in mirrors, so that you can have it all in your consciousness, make it all mental."

There was a sense of violation in the air, as if too much was said, the unforgivable. Yet Ursula was concerned now only with solving her own problems, in the light of his words. She was pale and abstracted.

"But do you really *want* sensuality?" she asked, puzzled.

Birkin looked at her, and became intent in his explanation.

"Yes," he said, "that, and nothing else, at this point. It is a fulfilment—the great dark knowledge you can't have in your head—the dark involuntary being. It is death to one self—but it is the coming into being of another."

"But how? How can you have knowledge not in your head?" she asked, quite unable to interpret his phrases.

"In the blood," he answered; "when the mind and the known world is drowned in darkness.—Everything must go—there must be the deluge. Then you find yourself a palpable body of darkness, a demon—"

"But why should I be a demon—?" she asked.

"*Woman wailing for her demon lover—*" he quoted—"Why, I don't know."

Hermione roused herself as from a death-annihilation.

"He is such a *dreadful* satanist, isn't he?" she drawled to Ursula, in a queer resonant voice, that ended in a shrill little laugh of pure ridicule. The two women were jeering at him, jeering him into nothingness. The laugh of the shrill, triumphant female sounded from Hermione, jeering him as if he were a neuter.

"No," he said. "You are the real devil who won't let life exist."

She looked at him with a long, slow look, malevolent, supercilious.

"You know all about it, don't you?" she said, with slow, cold, cunning mockery.

"Enough," he replied, his face fixing fine and clear like steel.

A horrible despair, and at the same time a sense of release, liberation, came over Hermione. She turned with a pleasant intimacy to Ursula.

NATIONAL HEALTH SERVICE—SCOTLAND

Dental Acceptance Card

Mr
Mrs } ....
Miss

Address ....

....

I accept you as a patient under the National Health Service for the dental treatment decided on when you consulted me on

....

Signature }
of Dentist } ....

THREE RULES FOR DENTAL HEALTH

1. Avoid sugary snacks and sugary drinks between meals.
2. Clean your teeth and gums thoroughly twice a day with a fluoride toothpaste and especially last thing at night.
3. Visit your dentist regularly to obtain advice and receive any necessary treatment.

Particulars of Appointments

Date	Time
~~SAT~~ TUES 5TH JUNE	4.45pm.
SAT 28TH JULY	9.30am.

Place of Treatment (Rubber Stamp)

S. E. SCOTT B.D.S.

49A HIGH STREET,

LINLITHGOW.

8431-7

Tel. 847923.

Note: Patients should give their dentist as much notice as possible if for any reason they are likely to be unable to keep an appointment. Failure to do so may result in treatment being delayed and the patient having to pay the dentist for the broken appointment.

It is a condition of receiving dental treatment under the National Health Service that a patient should, if required to do so attend for examination by a dental officer appointed by the Secretary of State.

Use of Dental Records: For the purpose of dental care details of treatment will be recorded and used mainly for accounting purposes. Some use may also be made of this information for statistical and research purposes to indicate the kind of dental services which patients require. A computer may be used for processing this information. Great care is taken however to ensure that high standards of confidentiality are maintained in respect of all information held for such purposes.

Ed Rep 2000m 12/89 (026286)

"You are sure you will come to Breadalby?" she said, urging.

"Yes, I should like to very much," replied Ursula.

Hermione looked down at her, gratified, reflecting, and strangely absent, as if possessed, as if not quite there.

"I'm so glad," she said, pulling herself together.—"Some time in about a fortnight? Yes?—I will write to you here, at the school, shall I?—Yes.—And you'll be sure to come?—Yes.—I shall be so glad. Goodbye!—Goo-oodbye—."

Hermione held out her hand and looked into the eyes of the other woman. She knew Ursula as an immediate rival, and the knowledge strangely exhilarated her. Also she was taking leave. It always gave her a sense of strength, advantage, to be departing and leaving the other behind. Moreover she was taking the man with her, if only in hate.

Birkin stood aside, fixed and unreal. But now, when it was his turn to bid goodbye, he began to speak again.

"There's the whole difference in the world," he said, "between the actual sensual being, and the vicious mental-deliberate profligacy our lot goes in for. In our night-time, there's always the electricity switched on, we watch ourselves, we get it all in the head, really.—You've got to lapse out before you can know what sensual reality is, lapse into unknowingness, and give up your volition. You've got to do it. You've got to learn not-to-be, before you can come into being.

"But we have got such a conceit of ourselves—that's where it is. We are so conceited, and so unproud. We've got no pride, we're all conceit, so conceited in our own papier-maché realised selves. We'd rather die than give up our little self-righteous self-opinionated self-will."

There was silence in the room. Both women were hostile and resentful. He sounded as if he were addressing a meeting. Hermione merely paid no attention, stood with her shoulders tight in a shrug of dislike.

Ursula was watching him as if furtively, not really aware of what she was seeing. There was a great physical attractiveness in him—a curious hidden richness, that came through his thinness and his pallor like another voice, conveying another knowledge of him. It was in the curves of his brows and his chin, rich, fine, exquisite curves, the powerful beauty of life itself. She could not say what it was. But there was a sense of richness and of liberty.

"But we are sensual enough, without making ourselves so, aren't we?" she asked, turning to him with a certain golden laughter flickering under her greenish eyes, like a challenge. And immediately the queer, careless, terribly attractive smile came over his eyes and brows, though his mouth did not relax.

"No," he said, "we aren't. We're too full of ourselves."

"Surely it isn't a matter of conceit," she cried.

"That and nothing else."

She was frankly puzzled.

"Don't you think that people are most conceited of all about their sensual powers?" she asked.

"That's why they aren't sensual—only sensuous—which is another matter. They're *always* aware of themselves—and they're so conceited, that rather than release themselves, and live in another world, from another centre, they'd—."

"You want your tea, don't you," said Hermione, turning to Ursula with a gracious kindliness. "You've worked all day—"

Birkin stopped short. A spasm of anger and chagrin went over Ursula. His face set. And he bade goodbye, as if he had ceased to notice her.

They were gone. Ursula stood looking at the door for some moments. Then she put out the lights. And having done so, she sat down again in her chair, absorbed and lost. And then she began to cry, bitterly, bitterly weeping: but whether for misery or joy, she never knew.

Chapter IV

Diver

The week passed away. On the Saturday it rained, a soft, drizzling rain that held off at times. In one of the intervals Gudrun and Ursula set out for a walk, going towards Willey Water. The atmosphere was grey and translucent, the birds sang sharply on the young twigs, the earth would be quickening and hastening in growth. The two girls walked swiftly, gladly, because of the soft, subtle rush of morning that filled the wet haze. By the road the blackthorn was in blossom, white and wet, its tiny amber grains burning faintly in the white smoke of blossom. Purple twigs were darkly luminous in the grey air, high hedges glowed like living shadows, hovering nearer, coming into creation. The morning was full of a new creation.

When the sisters came to Willey Water, the lake lay all grey and visionary, stretching into the moist, translucent vista of trees and meadow. Fine electric activity in sound came from the dumbles below the road, the birds piping one against the other, and water mysteriously plashing, issuing from the lake.

The two girls drifted swiftly along. In front of them, at the corner of the lake, near the road, was a mossy boat-house under a walnut tree, and a little landing-stage where a boat was moored, wavering like a shadow on the still grey water, below the green, decayed poles. All was shadowy with coming summer.

Suddenly, from the boat-house, a white figure ran out, frightening in its swift sharp transit, across the old landing-stage. It launched in a white arc through the air, there was a bursting of the water, and among the smooth ripples a swimmer was making out to space, in a centre of faintly heaving motion. The whole otherworld, wet and remote, he had to himself. He could move into the pure translucency of the grey, uncreated water.

Gudrun stood by the stone wall, watching.

"How I envy him," she said, in low, desirous tones.

"Ugh!" shivered Ursula. "So cold!"

"Yes, but how good, how really fine, to swim out there!"

The sisters stood watching the swimmer move further into the grey, moist, full space of the water, pulsing with his own small, invading motion, and arched over with mist and dim woods.

"Don't you wish it were you?" asked Gudrun, looking at Ursula.

"I do," said Ursula. "—But I'm not sure—it's *so* wet."

"No," said Gudrun, reluctantly.

She stood watching the motion on the bosom of the water, as if fascinated. He, having swum a certain distance, turned round and was swimming on his back, looking along the water at the two girls by the wall. In the faint wash of motion, they could see his ruddy face, and could feel him watching them.

"It is Gerald Crich," said Ursula.

"I know," replied Gudrun.

And she stood motionless gazing over the water at the face which washed up and down on the flood, as he swam steadily. From his separate element he saw them, and he exulted to himself because of his own advantage, his possession of a world to himself. He was immune and perfect. He loved his own vigorous, thrusting motion, and the violent impulse of the very cold water against his limbs, buoying him up. He could see the girls watching him a way off, outside, and that pleased him. He lifted his arm from the water, in a sign to them.

"He is waving," said Ursula.

"Yes," replied Gudrun.

They watched him. He waved again, with a strange movement of recognition across the difference.

"Like a Nibelung," laughed Ursula.

Gudrun said nothing, only stood still looking over the water.

Gerald suddenly turned, and was swimming away swiftly, with a side stroke. He was alone now, alone and immune in the middle of the waters, which he had all to himself. He exulted in his isolation in the new element, unquestioned and unconditioned. He was happy, thrusting with his legs and all his body, without bond or connection anywhere, just himself in the watery world.

Gudrun envied him almost painfully. Even this momentary possession of pure isolation and fluidity seemed to her so terribly desirable, that she felt herself as if damned, out there on the high-road.

"God, what it is to be a man!" she cried.

"What?" exclaimed Ursula, in surprise.

"The freedom, the liberty, the mobility!" cried Gudrun, strangely flushed and brilliant. "You're a man, you want to do a thing, you do it. You haven't the *thousand* obstacles a woman has in front of her."

Ursula wondered what was in Gudrun's mind, to occasion this outburst. She could not understand.

"What do you want to do?" she asked.

"Nothing," cried Gudrun, in swift refutation. "But supposing I did. Supposing I want to swim up that water. It is impossible, it is one of the impossibilities of life, for me to take my clothes off now and jump in. But isn't it *ridiculous*, doesn't it simply prevent our living!"

She was so hot, so flushed, so furious, that Ursula was puzzled.

The two sisters went on, up the road. They were passing between the trees just below Shortlands. They looked up at the long, low house, dim and glamorous in the wet morning, its cedar tree slanting before the windows. Gudrun seemed to be studying it closely.

"Don't you think it's attractive, Ursula?" asked Gudrun.

"Very," said Ursula. "Very peaceful and charming."

"It has form, too—it has a period."

"What period?"

"Oh, eighteenth century, for certain; Dorothy Wordsworth, and Jane Austen, don't you think?"

Ursula laughed.

"Don't you think so?" repeated Gudrun.

"Perhaps. But I don't think the Criches fit the period. I know Gerald is putting in a private electric plant, for lighting the house, and is making all kinds of latest improvements."

Gudrun shrugged her shoulders swiftly.

"Of course," she said, "that's quite inevitable."

"Quite," laughed Ursula. "He is several generations of youngness at one go. They hate him for it. He takes them all by the scruff of the neck, and fairly flings them along. He'll have to die soon, when he's made every possible improvement, and there will be nothing more to improve.—He's got *go*, anyhow."

"Certainly he's got go," said Gudrun. "In fact I've never seen a man that showed signs of so much. The unfortunate thing is, where does his *go* go to, what becomes of it?"

"Oh I know," said Ursula. "It goes in applying the latest appliances."

"Exactly," said Gudrun.

"You know he shot his brother?" said Ursula.

"Shot his brother!" cried Gudrun, frowning as if in disapprobation.

"Didn't you know? Oh yes!—I thought you knew. He and his brother were playing together with a gun. He told his brother to look down the gun, and it was loaded, and blew the top of his head off.—Isn't it a horrible story?"

"How fearful!" cried Gudrun. "But it is long ago?"

"Oh yes, they were quite boys," said Ursula. "I think it is one of the most horrible stories I know."

"And he of course did not know that the gun was loaded?"

"Yes. You see it was an old thing that had been lying in the stable for years. Nobody dreamed it would ever go off, and of course, no-one imagined it was loaded. But isn't it dreadful, that it should happen?"

"Frightful!" cried Gudrun. "And isn't it horrible too to think of such a thing happening to one, when one was a child, and having to carry the responsibility of it all through one's life. Imagine it, two boys playing together—then this comes upon them, for no reason whatever—out of the air. Ursula, it's very frightening! Oh, it's one of the things I can't bear. Murder, that is thinkable, because there's a will behind it. But a thing like that to *happen* to one—"

"Perhaps there *was* an unconscious will behind it," said Ursula. "This playing at killing has some primitive *desire* for killing in it, don't you think?"

"Desire!" said Gudrun, coldly, stiffening a little. "I can't see that they were even playing at killing. I suppose one boy said to the other, 'You look down the barrel while I pull the trigger, and see what happens.' It seems to me the purest form of accident."

"No," said Ursula. "I couldn't pull the trigger of the emptiest gun in the world, not if someone were looking down the barrel. One instinctively doesn't do it—one can't."

Gudrun was silent for some moments, in sharp disagreement.

"Of course," she said coldly, "if one is a woman, and grown up, one's instinct prevents one. But I cannot see how that applies to a couple of boys playing together."

Her voice was cold and angry.

"Yes," persisted Ursula.

At that moment they heard a woman's voice a few yards off say loudly: "Oh damn the thing!"

They went forward and saw Laura Crich and Hermione Roddice in the field on the other side of the hedge, and Laura Crich struggling with the gate, to get out. Ursula at once hurried up and helped to lift the gate.

"Thanks so much," said Laura, looking up flushed and amazon-like, yet rather confused. "It isn't right on the hinges."

"No," said Ursula. "And they're so heavy."

"Surprising!" cried Laura.

"How do you do," sang Hermione, from out of the field, the moment she could make her voice heard. "It's nice now. Are you going for a walk? Yes. Isn't the young green beautiful? So beautiful—quite burning. Good morning—good morning—you'll come and see me?—thank you so much—next week—yes—goodbye, go-o-o-dby-y-e."

Gudrun and Ursula stood and watched her slowly waving her head up and down, and waving her hand slowly in dismissal, smiling a strange affected smile, making a tall, queer, frightening figure, with her heavy fair hair slipping to her eyes. Then they moved off, as if they had been dismissed like inferiors. The four women parted.

As soon as they had gone far enough, Ursula said, her cheeks burning, "I do think she's impudent."

"Who, Hermione Roddice?" asked Gudrun. "Why?"

"The way she treats one—impudence!"

"Why Ursula, what did you notice that was so impudent?" asked Gudrun, rather coldly.

"Her whole manner—Oh, it's impossible, the way she tries to bully one. Pure bullying. She's an impudent woman. 'You'll come and see me,' as if we should be falling over ourselves for the privilege."

"I can't understand, Ursula, what you are so much put out about," said Gudrun, in some exasperation. "One knows those women are impudent—these free women who have emancipated themselves from the aristocracy."

"But it is so *unnecessary*—so vulgar," cried Ursula.

"No, I don't see it.—And if I did—pour moi, elle n'existe pas. I don't grant her the power to be impudent to me."

"Do you think she likes you?" asked Ursula.

"Well, no, I shouldn't think she did."

"Then why does she ask you to go to Breadalby and stay with her?"

Gudrun lifted her shoulders in a slow shrug.

"After all, she's got the sense to know we're not just the ordinary run," said Gudrun. "Whatever she is, she's not a fool. And I'd rather have somebody I detested, than the ordinary woman who keeps to her own set. Hermione Roddice does risk herself in some respects."

Ursula pondered this for a time.

"I doubt it," she replied. "Really, she risks nothing.—I suppose we ought to admire her for knowing she *can* invite us—school-teachers—and risk nothing."

"Precisely!" said Gudrun. "Think of the myriads of women that daren't do it. She makes the most of her privileges—that's something. I suppose, really, we should do the same, in her place."

"No," said Ursula, "no. It would bore me. I couldn't spend my time playing her games. It's infra dig."

The two sisters were like a pair of scissors, snipping off everything that came athwart them; or like a knife and a whetstone, the one sharpened against the other.

"Of course," cried Ursula suddenly, "she ought to thank her stars if we will go and see her. You are perfectly beautiful, a thousand times more beautiful than ever she is or was, and to my thinking, a thousand times more beautifully dressed, for she never looks fresh and natural, like a flower, always old, thought-out; and we *are* more intelligent than most people."

"Undoubtedly!" said Gudrun.

"And it ought to be admitted, simply," said Ursula.

"Certainly it ought," said Gudrun. "But you'll find that the really chic thing is to be so absolutely ordinary, so perfectly commonplace and like the person in the street, that you really are a masterpiece of humanity, not the person in the street actually, but the artistic creation of her—"

"How awful!" cried Ursula.

"Yes Ursula, it *is* awful, in most respects. You daren't be anything that isn't amazingly *à terre*, so much *à terre* that it is the artistic creation of ordinariness."

"It's very dull to create oneself into nothing better," laughed Ursula.

"Very dull!" retorted Gudrun. "Really Ursula, it *is* dull, that's just the word. One longs to be high-flown, and make speeches like Corneille, after it."

Gudrun was becoming flushed and excited over her own cleverness.

"Strut," said Ursula, "one wants to strut, to be a swan among geese."

"Exactly," cried Gudrun, "a swan among geese."

"They are all so busy playing the ugly duckling," cried Ursula, with mocking laughter. "And I don't feel a bit like a humble and pathetic ugly duckling. I do feel like a swan among geese—I can't help it. They make one feel so. And I don't care what *they* think of me.—*Je m'en fiche.*"

Gudrun looked up at Ursula with a queer, uncertain envy and dislike.

"Of course, the only thing to do is to despise them all—just all," she said.

The sisters went home again, to read and talk and work, and wait for Monday, for school. Ursula often wondered what else she waited for, besides the beginning and end of the school-week, and the beginning and end of the holidays. This was a whole life! Sometimes she had periods of tight horror, when it seemed to her that her life would pass away, and be gone, without having been more than this. But she never really accepted it. Her spirit was active, her life was like a shoot that is growing steadily, but which has not yet come above ground.

Chapter V

In the Train

One day at this time Birkin was called to London. He was not very fixed in his abode. He had rooms in Nottingham, because his work lay chiefly in that town. But often he was in London, or in Oxford. He moved about a great deal, his life seemed uncertain, without any definite rhythm, any organic meaning.

On the platform of the railway station he saw Gerald Crich, reading a newspaper, and evidently waiting for the train. Birkin stood some distance off, among the people. It was against his instinct to approach anybody.

From time to time, in a manner characteristic of him, Gerald lifted his head and looked round. Even though he was reading the newspaper closely, he must keep a watchful eye on his external surroundings. There seemed to be a dual consciousness running in him. He was thinking vigorously of something he read in the newspaper, and at the same time his eye ran over the surface of the life round him, and he missed nothing. Birkin, who was watching him, was irritated by this duality. He noticed, too, that Gerald seemed always to be at bay against everybody, in spite of his queer, genial, social manner when roused.

Now Birkin started violently at seeing this genial look flash on to Gerald's face, at seeing Gerald approaching with hand outstretched.

"Hallo Rupert, where are you going?"

"London. So are you I suppose."

"Yes—"

Gerald's eyes went over Birkin's face in curiosity.

"We'll travel together if you like," he said.

"Don't you usually go first?" asked Birkin.

"I can't stand the crowd," replied Gerald. "But third'll be all right. There's a restaurant car, we can have some tea."

The two men looked at the station clock, having nothing further to say.

"What were you reading in the paper?" Birkin asked.

Gerald looked at him quickly.

"Isn't it funny, what they *do* put in newspapers," he said. "Here are two leaders—" he held out his *Daily Telegraph*, "full of the ordinary newspaper cant—" he scanned the columns down—"and then there's this little—I dunno what you'd call it, essay, almost—appearing with the leaders, and saying there must arise a man who will give new values to things, give us new truths, a new attitude to life, or else we shall be a crumbling nothingness in a few years, a country in ruin—"

"I suppose that's a bit of newspaper cant, as well," said Birkin.

"It sounds as if the man meant it, and quite genuinely," said Gerald.

"Give it me," said Birkin, holding out his hand for the paper.

The train came, and they went on board, sitting on either side a little table, by the window, in the restaurant car. Birkin glanced over his paper, then looked up at Gerald, who was waiting for him.

"I believe the man means it," he said, "as far as he means anything."

"And do you think it's true? Do you think we really want a new gospel?" asked Gerald.

Birkin shrugged his shoulders.

"I think the people who say they want a new religion are the last to accept anything new. They want novelty right enough. But to stare straight at this life that we've brought upon ourselves, and reject it, absolutely smash up the old idols of ourselves, that we s'll never do. You've got very badly to want to get rid of the old, before anything new will appear—even in the self."

Gerald watched him closely.

"You think we ought to break up this life, just start and let fly?" he asked.

"This life—yes I do. We've got to bust it completely, or shrivel inside it, as in a tight skin. For it won't expand any more."

There was a queer little smile in Gerald's eyes, a look of amusement, calm and curious.

"And how do you propose to begin? I suppose you mean, reform the whole order of society?" he asked.

Birkin had a slight, tense frown between the brows. He too was impatient of the conversation.

"I don't propose at all," he replied. "When we really want to go for something better, we shall smash the old. Until then, any sort of proposal, or making proposals, is no more than a tiresome game for self-important people."

The little smile began to die out of Gerald's eyes, and he said, looking with a cool stare at Birkin:

"So you really think things are very bad?"

"Completely bad."

The smile appeared again.

"In what way?"

"Every way," said Birkin. "We are such dreary liars. Our one idea is to lie to ourselves. We have an ideal of a perfect world, clean and straight and sufficient. So we cover the earth with foulness, life is a blotch of labour, like insects scurrying in filth, so that your collier can have a pianoforte in his parlour, and you can have a butler and a motor-car in your up-to-date house, and as a nation we can sport the Ritz, or the Empire, Gaby Deslys and the Sunday newspapers. It is very dreary."

Gerald took a little time to readjust himself after this tirade.

"Would you have us live without houses—return to nature?" he asked.

"I would have nothing at all. People only do what they want to do—and what they are capable of doing. If they were capable of anything else, there would be something else."

Again Gerald pondered. He was not going to take offence at Birkin.

"Don't you think the collier's *pianoforte*, as you call it, is a symbol for something very real, a real desire for something higher, in the collier's life?"

"Higher!" cried Birkin. "Yes. Amazing heights of upright grandeur. It makes him so much higher in his neighbouring colliers' eyes. He sees himself reflected in the neighbouring opinion, like in a Brocken mist, several feet taller on the strength of the pianoforte, and he is satisfied. He lives for the sake of that Brocken spectre, the reflection of himself in the human opinion.—You do the same. If you are of high importance to humanity you are of high importance to yourself. That is why you work so hard at the mines. If you can produce coal to cook five thousand dinners a day, you are five thousand times more important than if you cooked only your own dinner."

"I suppose I am," laughed Gerald.

"Can't you see," said Birkin, "that to help my neighbour to eat is no more than eating myself. 'I eat, thou eatest, he eats, we eat, you eat, they eat'—and what then? Why should every man decline the whole verb. First person singular is enough for me."

"You've got to start with material things," said Gerald.

Which statement Birkin ignored.

"And we've got to live for *something*, we're not just cattle that can graze and have done with it," said Gerald.

"Tell me," said Birkin. "What do you live for?"

Gerald's face went baffled.

"What do I live for?" he repeated. "I suppose I live to work, to produce something, in so far as I am a purposive being. Apart from that, I live because I am living."

"And what's your work? Getting so many *more* thousands of tons of coal out of the earth every day. And when we've got all the coal we want, and all the plush furniture, and pianofortes, and the rabbits are all stewed and eaten, and we're all warm and our bellies are filled and we're listening to the young lady performing on the pianoforte—what then? What then, when you've made a real fair start with your material things?"

Gerald sat laughing at the words and the mocking humour of the other man. But he was cogitating too.

"We haven't got there yet," he replied. "A good many people are still waiting for the rabbit and the fire to cook it."

"So while you get the coal I must chase the rabbit?" said Birkin, mocking at Gerald.

"Something like that," said Gerald.

Birkin watched him narrowly. He saw the perfect good-humoured callousness, even strange, glistening malice, in Gerald, glistening through the plausible ethics of productivity.

"Gerald," he said, "I rather hate you."

"I know you do," said Gerald. "Why do you?"

Birkin mused inscrutably for some minutes.

"I should like to know if you are conscious of hating me," he said at last. "Do you ever consciously detest me—hate me with mystic hate?—There are odd moments when I hate you starrily."

Gerald was rather taken aback, even a little disconcerted. He did not quite know what to say.

"I may, of course, hate you sometimes," he said. "But I'm not aware of it—never acutely aware of it, that is."

"So much the worse," said Birkin.

Gerald watched him with curious eyes. He could not quite make him out.

"So much the worse, is it?" he repeated.

There was a silence between the two men for some time, as the train ran on. In Birkin's face was a little irritable tension, a sharp knitting of the brows, keen and difficult. Gerald watched him warily, carefully, rather calculatingly, for he could not decide what he was after.

Suddenly Birkin's eyes looked straight and overpowering into those of the other man.

"What do you think is the aim and object of your life, Gerald?" he asked.

Again Gerald was taken aback. He could not think what his friend was getting at. Was he poking fun, or not?

"At this moment, I couldn't say off-hand," he replied, with faintly ironic humour.

"Do you think love is the be-all and the end-all of life?" Birkin asked, with direct, attentive seriousness.

"Of my own life?" said Gerald.

"Yes."

There was a really puzzled pause.

"I can't say," said Gerald. "It hasn't been, so far."

"What has your life been, so far?"

"Oh—finding out things for myself—and getting experiences—and making things *go*."

Birkin knitted his brows like sharply moulded steel.

"I find," he said, "that one needs some one *really* pure single activity—I should call love a single pure activity. But I *don't* really love anybody—not now."

"Have you ever really loved anybody?" asked Gerald.

"Yes and no," replied Birkin.

"Not finally?" said Gerald.

"Finally—finally—no," said Birkin.

"Nor I," said Gerald.

"And do you want to?" said Birkin.

Gerald looked with a long, twinkling, almost sardonic look into the eyes of the other man.

"I don't know," he said.

"I do—I want to love," said Birkin.

"You do?"

"Yes. I want the finality of love."

"The finality of love," repeated Gerald. And he waited for a moment.

"Just one woman?" he added. The evening light, flooding yellow along the fields, lit up Birkin's face with a tense, abstract steadfastness. Gerald still could not make it out.

"Yes, one woman," said Birkin.

But to Gerald it sounded as if he were insistent rather than confident.

"I don't believe a woman, and nothing but a woman, will ever make my life," said Gerald.

"Not the centre and core of it—the love between you and a woman?" asked Birkin.

Gerald's eyes narrowed with a queer dangerous smile as he watched the other man.

"I never quite feel it that way," he said.

"You don't? Then wherein does life centre, for you?"

"I don't know—that's what I want somebody to tell me.—As far as I can make out, it doesn't centre at all. It is artificially held together by the social mechanism."

Birkin pondered as if he would crack something.

"I know," he said, "it just doesn't centre. The old ideals are dead as nails—nothing there. It seems to me there remains only this perfect union with a woman—sort of ultimate marriage—and there isn't anything else."

"And you mean if there isn't the woman, there's nothing?" said Gerald.

"Pretty well that—seeing there's no God."

"Then we're hard put to it," said Gerald. And he turned to look out of the window at the flying, golden landscape.

Birkin could not help seeing how beautiful and soldierly his face was, with a certain courage to be indifferent.

"You think it's heavy odds against us?" said Birkin.

"If we've got to make our life up out of a woman, one woman, woman only, yes, I do," said Gerald. "I don't believe I shall ever make up *my* life, at that rate."

Birkin watched him almost angrily.

"You are a born unbeliever," he said.

"I only feel what I feel," said Gerald. And he looked again at Birkin almost sardonically, with his blue, manly, sharp-lighted eyes. Birkin's eyes were at the moment full of anger. But swiftly they became troubled, doubtful, then full of a warm, rich affectionateness and laughter.

"It troubles me very much, Gerald," he said, wrinkling his brows.

"I can see it does," said Gerald, uncovering his mouth in a manly, quick, soldierly laugh.

Gerald was held unconsciously by the other man. He wanted to be near him, he wanted to be within his sphere of influence. There was something very congenial to him in Birkin. But yet, beyond this, he did not take much notice. He felt that he, himself, Gerald, had harder and more durable truths than any the other man knew. He felt himself older, more knowing. It was the quick-changing warmth and versatility and brilliant warm utterance he loved in his friend. It was the rich play of words and quick interchange of feelings he enjoyed. The real content of the words he never really considered: he himself knew better.

Birkin knew this. He knew that Gerald wanted to be *fond* of him without taking him seriously. And this made him go hard and cold. As the train ran on, he sat looking at the land, and Gerald fell away, became as nothing to him.

Birkin looked at the land, at the evening, and was thinking: "Well, if mankind is destroyed, if our race is destroyed like Sodom, and there is this beautiful evening with the luminous land and trees, I am satisfied. That which informs it all is there, and can never be lost. After all, what is mankind but just one expression of the incomprehensible. And if mankind passes away, it will only mean that this particular expression is completed and done. That which is expressed, and that which is to be expressed, cannot be diminished. There it is, in the shining evening. Let mankind pass away—time it did. The creative utterances will not cease, they will only be there. Humanity doesn't embody the utterance of the incomprehensible any more. Humanity is a dead letter. There will be a new embodiment, in a new way. Let humanity disappear as quick as possible."

Gerald interrupted him by asking,

"Where are you staying in London?"

Birkin looked up.

"With a man in Soho. I pay part of the rent of a flat, and stop there when I like."

"Good idea—have a place more or less your own," said Gerald.

"Yes. But I don't care for it much. I'm tired of the people I am bound to find there."

"What kind of people?"

"Art—music—London Bohemia—the most pettifogging calculating Bohemia that ever reckoned its pennies.—But there are a few decent people, decent in some respects. They are really very thorough rejecters of the world—perhaps they live only in the gesture of rejection and negation—but negatively something, at any rate."

"What are they?—painters, musicians?"

"Painters, musicians, writers—hangers-on, models, advanced young people, anybody who is openly at outs with the conventions, and belongs to nowhere particularly. They are often young fellows down from the University, and girls who are living their own lives, as they say."

"All loose?" said Gerald.

Birkin could see his curiosity was roused.

"In one way. Most bound, in another. For all their shockingness, all on one note."

He looked at Gerald, and saw how his blue eyes were lit up with a little flame of curious desire. He saw too how good-looking he was. Gerald was attractive, his blood seemed fluid and electric. His blue eyes burned with a keen, yet cold light, there was a certain beauty, a beautiful passivity in all his body, his moulding.

"We might see something of each other—I am in London for two or three days," said Gerald.

"Yes," said Birkin. "I don't want to go to the theatre, or the music hall—you'd better come round to the flat, and see what you make of Halliday and his crowd."

"Thanks—I should like to," laughed Gerald. "What are you doing tonight?"

"I promised to meet Halliday at the Pompadour. It's a bad place, but there is nowhere else."

"Where is it?" asked Gerald.

"Piccadilly Circus."

"Oh yes—well, shall I come round there?"

"By all means, it might amuse you."

The evening was falling. They had passed Bedford. Birkin watched the country, and was filled with a sort of hopelessness. He always felt this, on approaching London. His dislike of mankind, of the mass of mankind, amounted almost to an illness.

"'Where the quiet coloured end of evening smiles
                    Miles and miles—'"

he was murmuring to himself, like a man condemned to death. Gerald, who was very subtly alert, wary in all his senses, leaned forward and asked, smilingly:

"What were you saying?"

Birkin glanced at him, laughed, and repeated:

"'Where the quiet coloured end of evening smiles,
                    Miles and miles,
           Over pastures where the something something sheep
                    Half asleep—'"

Gerald also looked now at the country. And Birkin, who, for some reason was now tired and dispirited, said to him:

"I always feel doomed when the train is running into London. I feel such a despair, so hopeless, as if it were the end of the world."

"Really!" said Gerald. "And does the end of the world frighten you?"

Birkin lifted his shoulders in a slow shrug.

"I don't know," he said. "It does while it hangs imminent and doesn't fall.—But people give me a bad feeling—very bad."

There was a roused glad smile in Gerald's eyes.

"Do they?" he said. And he watched the other man critically.

In a few minutes the train was running through the disgrace of outspread London. Everybody in the carriage was on the alert, waiting to escape. At last they were under the huge arch of the station, in the tremendous shadow of the town. Birkin shut himself together—he was in now.

The two men went together in a taxi-cab.

"Don't you feel like one of the damned?" asked Birkin, as they sat in the little, swiftly-running enclosure, and watched the hideous great street.

"No," laughed Gerald.

"It is real death," said Birkin.

Chapter VI

Crême de Menthe

They met again in the café several hours later. Gerald went through the push doors into the large, lofty room where the faces and heads of the drinkers showed dimly through the haze of smoke, reflected more dimly, and repeated ad infinitum in the great mirrors on the walls, so that one seemed to enter a vague, dim world of shadowy drinkers humming within an atmosphere of blue tobacco smoke. There was, however, the red plush of the seats to give substance within the bubble of pleasure.

Gerald moved in his slow, observant, glistening-attentive motion down between the tables and the people whose shadowy faces looked up as he passed. He seemed to be entering in some strange element, passing into an illuminated new region, among a host of licentious souls. He was pleased, and entertained. He looked over all the dim, evanescent, strangely illuminated faces that bent across the tables. Then he saw Birkin rise and signal to him.

At Birkin's table was a girl with dark, soft, fluffy hair cut short in the artist fashion, hanging level and full almost like the Egyptian princes's. She was small and delicately made, with warm colouring and large, dark, hostile eyes. There was a delicacy, almost a beauty in all her form, and at the same time a certain attractive grossness of spirit, that made a little spark leap instantly alight in Gerald's eyes.

Birkin, who looked muted, unreal, his presence left out, introduced her as Miss Darrington. She gave her hand with a sudden, unwilling movement, looking all the while at Gerald with a dark, exposed stare. A glow came over him as he sat down.

The waiter appeared. Gerald glanced at the glasses of the other two. Birkin was drinking something green, Miss Darrington had a small liqueur glass that was empty save for a tiny drop.

"Won't you have some more—?"

"Brandy," she said, sipping her last drop and putting down the glass. The waiter disappeared.

"No," she said to Birkin. "He doesn't know I'm back. He'll be terwified when he sees me here."

She spoke her r's like w's, lisping with a slightly babyish pronunciation which was at once affected and true to her character. Her voice was dull and toneless.

"Where is he then?" asked Birkin.

"He's doing a private show at Lady Snellgrove's," said the girl. "Warens is there too."

There was a pause.

"Well then," said Birkin, in a dispassionate protective manner, "what do you intend to do?"

The girl paused sullenly. She hated the question.

"I don't intend to do anything," she replied. "I shall look for some sittings tomorrow."

"Who shall you go to?" asked Birkin.

"I shall go to Bentley's first. But I believe he's angwy with me for running away."

"That is from the Madonna?"

"Yes. And then if he doesn't want me, I know I can get work with Carmarthen."

"Carmarthen—?"

"Lord Carmarthen—he does photographs."

"Chiffon and shoulders—"

"Yes. But he's awfully decent."

There was a pause.

"And what are you going to do about Julius?" he asked.

"Nothing," she said. "I shall just ignore him."

"You've done with him altogether?"

But she turned aside her face sullenly, and did not answer the question.

Another young man came hurrying up to the table.

"Hallo Birkin! *Hallo Pussum*, when did you come back?" he said eagerly.

"Today."

"Does Halliday know?"

"I don't know. I don't care either."

"Ha-ha! The wind still sits in that quarter, does it? Do you mind if I come over to this table?"

"I'm talking to Wupert, do you mind?" she replied, coolly and yet appealingly, like a child.

"Open confession—good for the soul, eh?" said the young man. "Well, so long."

And giving a sharp look at Birkin and at Gerald, the young man moved off, with a swing of his coat skirts.

All this time Gerald had been completely ignored. And yet he felt that the girl was physically aware of his proximity. He waited, listened, and tried to piece together the conversation.

"Are you staying at the flat?" the girl asked, of Birkin.

"For three days," replied Birkin. "And you?"

"I don't know yet. I can always go to Bertha's."

There was a silence.

Suddenly the girl turned to Gerald, and said, in a rather formal, polite voice, with the distant manner of a woman who accepts her position as a social inferior, yet assumes an intimate *camaraderie* with the male she addresses:

"Do you know London well?"

"I can hardly say," he laughed. "I've been up a good many times, but I was never in this place before."

"You're not an artist, then?" she said, in a tone that placed him an outsider.

"No," he replied.

"He's a soldier, and an explorer, and a Napoleon of industry," said Birkin, giving Gerald his credentials for Bohemia.

"Are you a soldier?" asked the girl, with a cold, yet lively curiosity.

"No, I resigned my commission," said Gerald, "some years ago."

"He was in the last war," said Birkin.

"Were you really?" said the girl.

"And then he explored the Amazon," said Birkin, "and now he is ruling over coal-mines."

The girl looked at Gerald with steady, calm curiosity. He laughed, hearing himself described. He felt proud too, full of male strength. His blue, keen eyes were lit up with laughter, his ruddy face with its sharp fair hair was full of satisfaction, and glowing with life. He piqued her.

"How long are you staying?" she asked him.

"A day or two," he replied. "But there is no particular hurry."

Still she stared into his face with that slow, full gaze which was so curious and so exciting to him. He was acutely and delightfully conscious of himself, of his own attractiveness. He felt full of strength, able to give off a sort of electric power. And he was aware of her dark, hot-looking eyes upon him. She had beautiful eyes, dark, fully-opened, hot, naked in their looking at him. And on them there seemed to float a film of disintegration, a sort of misery and sullenness, like oil on water. She wore no hat, in the heated café, her loose, simple jumper was strung on a string round her neck. But it was made of rich peach-coloured crêpe-de-chine, that hung heavily and softly from her young throat and her slender wrists. Her appearance was simple and complete, really beautiful, because of her regularity and form, her soft dark hair falling full and level on either side of her head, her straight, small, softened features, Egyptian in the slight fulness of their curves, her slender neck, and the simple, rich-coloured smock hanging on her slender shoulders. She was very still, almost null, in her manner, apart and watchful.

She appealed to Gerald strongly. He felt an awful, enjoyable power over her, an instinctive cherishing very near to cruelty. For she was a victim. He felt that she was in his power, and he was generous. The electricity was turgid and voluptuously rich, in his limbs. He would be able to destroy her utterly in the strength of the discharge. But she was waiting in her separation, given.

They talked banalities for some time. Suddenly Birkin said:

"There's Julius!" and he half rose to his feet, motioning to the new-comer. The girl, with a curious, almost evil motion, looked round over her shoulder without moving her body. Gerald watched her dark, soft hair swing over her ears. He felt her watching intensely the man who was approaching, so he looked too. He saw a pale, full-built young man with rather long, solid fair hair hanging from under his black hat, moving cumbrously down the room, his face lit up with a smile at once naive and warm, and vapid. He approached straight towards Birkin, with a haste of welcome.

It was not till he was quite close that he perceived the girl. He recoiled, went pale, and said, in a high, squealing voice:

"Pussum, what are *you* doing here?"

The café looked up like animals when they hear a cry. Halliday hung motionless, an almost imbecile smile flickering palely on his face. The girl only stared at him with a black look in which flared an unfathomable hell of knowledge, and a certain impotence. She was limited by him.

"Why have you come back?" repeated Halliday, in the same high, hysterical voice. "I told you not to come back."

The girl did not answer, only stared in the same viscous, heavy fashion, straight at him, as he stood recoiled, as if for safety, against the next table.

"You know you wanted her to come back—come and sit down," said Birkin to him.

"No I didn't want her to come back, and I told her not to come back.—What have you come for, Pussum?"

"For nothing from *you*," she said in a heavy voice of resentment.

"Then why have you come back at *all*?" cried Halliday, his voice rising to a kind of squeal.

"She comes as she likes," said Birkin. "Are you going to sit down, or are you not?"

"No I won't sit down with Pussum," cried Halliday.

"I won't hurt you, you needn't be afwaid," she said to him, very curtly, and yet with a sort of protectiveness towards him, in her voice.

Halliday came and sat at the table, putting his hand on his heart, and crying:

"Oh, it's given me such a turn! Pussum, I wish you wouldn't do these things. Why did you come back?"

"Not for anything from you," she repeated.

"You've said that before," he cried in a high voice.

She turned completely away from him, to Gerald Crich, whose eyes were shining with a subtle amusement.

"Were you ever vewy much afwaid of the savages?" she asked in her calm, dull, childish voice.

"No—never very much afraid. On the whole they're harmless—they're not born yet, you can't feel really afraid of them. You know you can manage them."

"Do you weally? Aren't they very fierce?"

"Not very. There aren't many fierce things, as a matter of fact. There aren't many things, neither people nor animals, that have it in them to be really dangerous."

"Except in herds," interrupted Birkin.

"Aren't there really?" she said. "Oh, I thought savages were all so dangerous, they'd have your life before you could look round."

"Did you?" he laughed. "They are over-rated, savages. They're too much like other people, not exciting, after the first acquaintance."

"Oh, it's not so very wonderfully brave then, to be an explorer?"

"No. It's more a question of hardships than of terrors."

"Oh! And weren't you *ever* afraid?"

"In my life? I don't know. Yes, I'm afraid of some things—of being shut up, locked up anywhere—or being fastened. I'm afraid of being bound hand and foot."

She looked at him steadily with her dark eyes, that rested on him and roused him so deeply, that it left his upper self quite calm. It was rather delicious, to feel her drawing his self-revelations from him, as from the very innermost dark marrow of his body. She wanted to know. And her dark eyes seemed to be looking through into his naked organism. He felt, she was compelled to him, she was fated to come into contact with him, must have the seeing him and knowing him. And this roused a curious exultance. Also he felt, she must relinquish herself into his hands, and be subject to him. She was so profane, slave-like, watching him, absorbed by him. It was not that she was interested in what he said; she was absorbed by his self-revelation, by *him*, she wanted the secret of him, the experience of his male being.

Gerald's face was lit up with an uncanny smile, full of light and rousedness, yet unconscious. He sat with his arms on the table, his sun-browned, rather sinister hands, that were animal and yet very shapely and attractive, pushed forward towards her. And they fascinated her. And she knew, she watched her own fascination.

Other men had come to the table, to talk with Birkin and Halliday. Gerald said in a low voice, apart, to Pussum:

"Where have you come back from?"

"From the country," replied Pussum, in a very low, yet fully resonant voice. Her face closed hard. Continually she glanced at Halliday, and then a black flare came over her eyes. The heavy, fair young man ignored her completely; he was really afraid of her. For some moments she would be unaware of Gerald. He had not conquered her yet.

"And what has Halliday to do with it?" he asked, his voice still muted.

She would not answer for some seconds. Then she said, unwillingly:

"He made me go and live with him, and now he wants to throw me over. And yet he won't let me go to anybody else. He wants me to live hidden in the country. And then he says I persecute him, that he can't get rid of me."

"Doesn't know his own mind," said Gerald.

"He hasn't any mind, so he can't know it," she said. "He waits for what somebody tells him to do. He never does anything he wants to do himself—because he doesn't know what he wants. He's a perfect baby."

Gerald looked at Halliday for some moments, watching the soft, rather degenerate face of the young man. Its very softness was an attraction; it was a soft, warm, corrupt nature, into which one might plunge with gratification.

"But he has no hold over you, has he?" Gerald asked.

"You see he *made* me go and live with him, when I didn't want to," she replied. "He came and cried to me, tears, you never saw so many, saying *he couldn't* bear it unless I went back to him. And he wouldn't go away, he would have stayed for ever. He made me go back. Then every time he behaves in this fashion.—And now I'm going to have a baby, he wants to give me a hundred pounds and send me into the country, so that he would never see me nor hear of me again. But I'm not going to do it, after—"

A queer look came over Gerald's face.

"Are you going to have a child?" he asked incredulous. It seemed, to look at her, impossible, she was so young and so far in spirit from any childbearing.

She looked full into his face, and her dark, inchoate eyes had now a furtive look, and a look of a knowledge of evil, dark and indomitable. A flame ran secretly to his heart.

"Yes," she said. "Isn't it beastly?"

"Don't you want it?" he asked.

"I don't," she replied, emphatically.

"But—" he said, "how long have you known?"

"Ten weeks," she said.

All the time she kept her dark, inchoate eyes full upon him. He remained silent, thinking. Then, switching off and becoming cold, he asked, in a voice full of considerate kindness:

"Is there anything we can eat here? Is there anything you would like?"

"Yes," she said. "I should adore some oysters."

"All right," he said. "We'll have oysters."

And he beckoned to the waiter.

Halliday took no notice, until the little plate was set before her. Then suddenly he cried:

"Pussum, you can't eat oysters when you're drinking brandy."

"What has it got to do with you?" she asked.

"Nothing, nothing," he cried. "But you can't eat oysters when you're drinking brandy."

"I'm not drinking brandy," she replied, and she sprinkled the last drops of her liqueur over his face. He gave an odd squeal. She sat looking at him, as if indifferent.

"Pussum, why do you do that?" he cried in panic. He gave Gerald the impression that he was terrified of her, and that he loved his terror. He seemed to relish his own horror and hatred of her, turn it over and extract every flavour from it, in real panic. Gerald thought him a strange fool, and yet piquant.

"But Pussum," said another man, in a very small, quick, Eton voice, "you promised not to hurt him."

"I haven't hurt him," she answered.

"What will you drink?" the young man asked. He was dark, and smooth-skinned, and full of a stealthy vigour.

"I don't like porter, Maxim," she replied.

"You must ask for champagne," came the whispering, gentlemanly voice of the other.

Gerald suddenly realised that this was a hint to him.

"Shall we have champagne?" he asked, laughing.

"Yes please, dwy," she lisped, childishly.

Gerald watched her eating the oysters. She was delicate and finicking in her eating, her fingers were fine and seemed very sensitive in the tips, so she put her food apart with fine, small motions, she ate carefully, delicately. It pleased him very much to see her, and it irritated Birkin. They were all drinking champagne. Maxim, the prim young Russian with the smooth, warm-coloured face and black, oiled hair, was the only one who seemed to be perfectly calm and sober. Birkin was white and abstract, unnatural, Gerald was smiling with a constant bright, amused, cold light in his eyes, leaning a little protectively towards the Pussum, who was very handsome and soft, unfolded like some red lotus in dreadful flowering nakedness, vainglorious now, flushed with wine and with the excitement of men. Halliday looked foolish. One glass of wine was enough to make him drunk and giggling. Yet there was always a pleasant, warm naïveté about him, that made him attractive.

"I'm not afwaid of anything essept black-beetles," said the Pussum, looking up suddenly and staring with her black eyes, on which there seemed an unseeing film of flame, fully upon Gerald. He laughed dangerously, from the blood. Her childish speech caressed his nerves, and her burning, filmed eyes, turned now full upon him, oblivious of all her antecedents, gave him a sort of licence.

"I'm not," she protested. "I'm not afraid of other things. But black-beetles—ugh!—" she shuddered convulsively, as if the very thought were too much to bear.

"Do you mean," said Gerald, with the punctiliousness of a man who has been drinking, "that you are afraid of the sight of a black-beetle, or you are afraid of a black-beetle biting you, or doing you some harm?"

"Do they bite?" cried the girl.

"How perfectly loathsome!" exclaimed Halliday.

"I don't know," replied Gerald, looking round the table. "Do black-beetles bite?—But that isn't the point. Are you afraid of their biting, or is it a metaphysical antipathy?"

The girl was looking full upon him all the time with inchoate eyes.

"Oh, I think they're beastly, they're horrid," she cried. "If I see one, it gives me the creeps all over. If one were to crawl on me, I'm *sure* I should die—I'm sure I should."

"I hope not," whispered the young Russian.

"I'm sure I should, Maxim," she asseverated.

"Then one won't crawl on you," said Gerald, smiling and knowing. In some strange way, he understood her.

"It's metaphysical, as Gerald says," Birkin stated.

There was a little pause of uneasiness.

"And are you afraid of nothing else, Pussum?" asked the young Russian, in his quick, hushed, elegant manner.

"Not weally," she said. "I am afwaid of some things, but not weally the same. I'm not afwaid of *blood*."

"Not afwaid of blood!" exclaimed a young man with a thick, pale, jeering face, who had just come to the table and was drinking whisky.

The Pussum turned on him a sulky look of dislike, low and ugly.

"Aren't you really afraid of blud?" the other persisted, a sneer all over his face.

"No, I'm not," she retorted.

"Why, have you ever seen blood, except in a dentist's spittoon?" jeered the young man.

"I wasn't speaking to you," she replied rather superbly.

"You can answer me, can't you?" he said.

For reply, she suddenly jabbed a knife across his thick, pale hand. He started up with a vulgar curse.

"Show's what you are," said the Pussum in contempt.

"Curse you," said the young man, standing by the table and looking down at her with acrid malevolence.

"Stop that," said Gerald, in quick, instinctive command.

The young man stood looking down at her with sardonic contempt, a cowed, self-conscious look on his thick, pale face. The blood began to flow from his hand.

"Oh, how horrible, take it away!" squealed Halliday, turning green and averting his face.

"D'you feel ill?" asked the sardonic young man, in some concern. "Do you feel ill, Julius? Garn, it's nothing man, don't give her the pleasure of letting her think she's performed a feat—don't give her the satisfaction, man,—it's just what she wants."

"Oh!" squealed Halliday.

"He's going to cat, Maxim," said the Pussum warningly.

The suave young Russian rose and took Halliday by the arm, leading him away. Birkin, white and diminished, looked on as if he were displeased. The wounded, sardonic young man moved away, ignoring his bleeding hand in the most conspicuous fashion.

"He's an awful coward, really," said the Pussum to Gerald. "He's got such an influence over Julius."

"Who is he?" asked Gerald.

"He's a Jew, really. I can't bear him."

"Well, he's quite unimportant. But what's wrong with Halliday?"

"Julius's the most awful coward you've ever seen," she cried. "He always faints if I lift a knife—he's *tewwified* of me."

"Hm!" said Gerald.

"They're all afwaid of me," she said. "Only the Jew thinks he's going to show his courage. But he's the biggest coward of them all, really, because he's afwaid what people will think about him—and Julius doesn't care about that."

"They've a lot of valour between them," said Gerald good-humouredly.

The Pussum looked at him with a slow, slow smile. She was very handsome, flushed, and confident in dreadful knowledge. Two little points of light glinted on Gerald's eyes.

"Why do they call you Pussum, because you're like a cat?" he asked her.

"I expect so," she said.

The smile grew more intense on his face.

"You are, rather;—or a young, female panther."

"Oh god, Gerald!" said Birkin, in some disgust.

They both looked uneasily at Birkin.

"You're silent tonight, Wupert," she said to him, with a slight insolence, being safe with the other man.

Halliday was coming back, looking forlorn and sick.

"Pussum," he said, "I wish you wouldn't do these things—Oh!" he sank in his chair with a groan.

"You'd better go home," she said to him.

"I *will* go home," he said. "But won't you all come along. Won't you come round to the flat?" he said to Gerald. "I should be so glad if you would. Do—that'll be splendid.—I say?" He looked round for a waiter. "Get me a taxi." Then he groaned again. "Oh I do feel—perfectly ghastly! Pussum, you see what you do to me."

"Then why are you such an idiot," she said with sullen calm.

"But I'm *not* an idiot! Oh, how awful! Do come, everybody, it will be *so* splendid. Pussum, you are coming.—What?—Oh but you *must* come, yes, you must. What?—Oh, my dear girl, don't make a fuss now, I feel perfectly—Oh, it's so ghastly—Hc!-er!—Oh!"

"You know you can't drink," she said to him, coldly.

"I tell you it isn't drink—it's your disgusting behaviour, Pussum, it's nothing else.—Oh, how awful! Libidnikov, *do* let us go."

"He's only drunk one glass—only one glass," came the rapid, hushed voice of the young Russian.

They all moved off to the door. The girl kept near to Gerald, and seemed to be at one in her motion with him. He was aware of this, and filled with demon-satisfaction that his motion held good for two. He held her in the hollow of his will, and she was soft, secret, invisible in her stirring there.

They crowded five of them into the taxi-cab. Halliday lurched in first, and dropped into his seat against the other window. Then the Pussum took her place, and Gerald sat next to her. They heard the young Russian giving orders to the driver, then they were all seated in the dark, crowded close together, Halliday groaning and leaning out of the window. They felt the swift, muffled motion of the car.

The Pussum sat near to Gerald, and she seemed to become soft, subtly to infuse herself into his bones, as if she were passing into him in a black, electric flow. Her being suffused into his veins like a magnetic darkness, and concentrated at the base of his spine like a fearful source of power. Meanwhile her voice sounded out reedy and nonchalant, as she talked indifferently with Birkin and with Maxim. Between her and Gerald was this silence and this black, electric comprehension in the darkness. Then she found his hand, and grasped it in her own firm, small clasp. It was so utterly dark, and yet such a naked statement, that rapid vibrations ran through his blood and over his brain, he was no longer responsible. Still her voice rang on like a bell, tinged with a tone of mockery. And as she swung her head, her fine mane of hair just swept his face, and all his nerves were on fire, as with a subtle friction of electricity. But the great centre of his force held steady, a magnificent pride to him, at the base of his spine.

They arrived at a large block of buildings, went up in a lift, and presently a door was being opened for them by a Hindu. Gerald looked in surprise, wondering if he were a gentleman, one of the Hindus down from Oxford, perhaps. But no, he was the man-servant.

"Make tea, Hasan," said Halliday.

"There is a room for me?" said Birkin.

To both of which questions the man grinned, and murmured.

He made Gerald uncertain, because, being tall and slender and reticent, he looked like a gentleman.

"Who is your servant?" he asked of Halliday. "He looks a swell."

"Oh yes—that's because he's dressed in another man's clothes. He's anything but a swell, really. We found him in the road, starving. So I took him here, and another man gave him clothes. He's anything but what he seems to be—his only advantage is that he can't speak English and can't understand it, so he's perfectly safe."

"He's very dirty," said the young Russian swiftly and silently.

Directly, the man appeared in the doorway.

"What is it?" said Halliday.

The Hindu grinned, and murmured shyly:

"Want to speak to master."

Gerald watched curiously. The fellow in the doorway was good-looking and clean-limbed, his bearing was calm, he looked elegant, aristocratic. Yet he was half a savage, grinning foolishly. Halliday went out into the corridor to speak with him.

"What?" they heard his voice. "What? What do you say? Tell me again. What? Want money? Want *more* money? But what do you want money for?" There was the confused sound of the Hindu's talking, then Halliday appeared in the room, smiling also foolishly, and saying:

"He says he wants money to buy underclothing. Can anybody lend me a shilling? Oh thanks, a shilling will do to buy all the underclothes he wants." He took the money from Gerald and went out into the passage again, where they heard him saying, "You can't want more money, you had three and six yesterday. You mustn't ask for any more. Bring the tea in quickly."

Gerald looked round the room. It was an ordinary London sitting-room in a flat, evidently taken furnished, rather common and ugly. But there were several negro statues, wood-carvings from West Africa, strange and disturbing, the carved negroes looked almost like the foetus of a human being. One was of a woman sitting naked in a strange posture, and looking tortured, her abdomen stuck out. The young Russian explained that she was sitting in childbirth, clutching the ends of the band that hung from her neck, one in each hand, so that she could bear down, and help labour. The strange, transfixed, rudimentary face of the woman again reminded Gerald of a foetus, it was also rather wonderful, conveying the suggestion of the extreme of physical sensation, beyond the limits of mental consciousness.

"Aren't they rather obscene?" he asked, disapproving.

"I don't know," murmured the other rapidly. "I have never defined the obscene. I think they are very good."

Gerald turned away. There were one or two new pictures in the room, in the Futurist manner; there was a large piano. And these, with some ordinary London lodging-house furniture of the better sort, completed the whole.

The Pussum had taken off her hat and coat, and was seated on the sofa. She was evidently quite at home in the house, but uncertain, suspended. She did not quite know her position. Her alliance for the time being was with Gerald, and she did not know how far this was admitted by any of the men. She was considering how she should carry off the situation. She was determined to have her experience. Now, at this eleventh hour, she was not to be balked. Her face was flushed as with battle, her eye was brooding but inevitable.

The man came in with tea and a bottle of Kümmel. He set the tray on a little table before the couch.

"Pussum," said Halliday, "pour out the tea."

She did not move.

"Won't you do it?" Halliday repeated, in a state of nervous apprehension.

"I've not come back here as it was before," she said. "I only came because the others wanted me to, not for your sake."

"My dear Pussum, you know you are your own mistress. I don't want you to do anything but use the flat for your own convenience—you know it, I've told you so many times."

She did not reply, but silently, reservedly reached for the tea-pot. They all sat round and drank tea. Gerald could feel the electric connection between him and her so strongly, as she sat there quiet and withheld, that another set of conditions altogether had come to pass. Her silence and her immutability perplexed him. *How* was he going to come to her? And yet he felt it quite inevitable. He trusted completely to the current that held them. His perplexity was only superficial, new conditions reigned, the old were surpassed; here one did as one was possessed to do, no matter what it was.

Birkin rose. It was nearly one o'clock.

"I'm going to bed," he said. "Gerald, I'll ring you up in the morning at your place—or you ring me up here."

"Right," said Gerald, and Birkin went out.

When he was well gone, Halliday said in a stimulated voice, to Gerald:
"I say, won't you stay here—oh do!"

"You can't put everybody up," said Gerald.

"Oh but I can, perfectly—there are three more beds besides mine—do stay, won't you. Everything is quite ready—there is always somebody here—I always put people up—I love having the house crowded."

"But there are only two rooms," said the Pussum, in a cold, hostile voice, "now Rupert's here."

"I know there are only two rooms," said Halliday, in his odd, high way of speaking. "But what does that matter?"

He was smiling rather foolishly, and he spoke eagerly, with an insinuating determination.

"Julius and I will share one room," said the Russian in his discreet, precise voice. Halliday and he were friends since Eton.

"It's very simple," said Gerald, rising and pressing back his arms, stretching himself. Then he went again to look at one of the pictures. Every one of his limbs was turgid with electric force, and his back was tense like a tiger's, with slumbering fire. He was very proud.

The Pussum rose. She gave a black look at Halliday, black and deadly, which brought the rather foolish, pleased smile to that young man's face. Then she went out of the room, with a cold Goodnight to them all generally.

There was a brief interval, they heard a door close, then Maxim said, in his refined voice:

"That's all right."

He looked significantly at Gerald, and said again, with a slight nod:

"That's all right—you're all right."

Gerald looked at the smooth, ruddy, comely face, and at the strange, significant eyes, and it seemed as if the voice of the young Russian, so small and perfect, sounded in the blood rather than in the air.

"*I'm* all right then," said Gerald.

"Yes! Yes! You're all right," said the Russian.

Halliday continued to smile, and to say nothing.

Suddenly the Pussum appeared again in the door, her small, childish face looking sullen and vindictive.

"I know you want to catch me out," came her cold, rather resonant voice. "But I don't care, I don't care how much you catch me out."

She turned and was gone again. She had been wearing a loose dressing-gown of purple silk, tied round her waist. She looked so small and childish and vulnerable, almost pitiful. And yet the black looks of her eyes made Gerald feel drowned in some potent darkness that almost frightened him.

The men lit another cigarette and talked casually.

Chapter VII

Fetish

In the morning Gerald woke late. He had slept heavily. Pussum was still asleep, sleeping childishly and pathetically. There was something small and curled up and defenceless about her, that roused an unsatisfied flame of passion in the young man's blood, a devouring, avid pity. He looked at her again. But it would be too cruel to wake her. He subdued himself, and went away.

Hearing voices coming from the sitting-room, Halliday talking to Libidnikov, he went to the door and glanced in, knowing he might go about in this bachelor establishment in his trousers and shirt.

To his surprise he saw the two young men by the fire, stark naked. Halliday looked up, rather pleased.

"Good-morning," he said. "Oh—did you want towels?"

And stark naked, he went out into the hall, striding a strange, white figure between the unliving furniture. He came back with the towels, and took his former position, crouching seated before the fire on the fender.

"Don't you love to feel the fire on your skin?" he said.

"It *is* rather pleasant," said Gerald.

"How perfectly splendid it must be to be in a climate where one could do without clothing altogether," said Halliday.

"Yes," said Gerald, "if there weren't so many things that sting and bite."

"That's a disadvantage," murmured Maxim.

Gerald looked at him, and with a slight revulsion saw the human animal, golden skinned and bare, somehow humiliating. Halliday was different. He had a rather heavy, slack, broken beauty, white and firm. He was like a Christ in a Pietà. The animal was not there at all, only the heavy, broken beauty. And Gerald realised how Halliday's eyes were beautiful too, so blue and warm and confused, broken also in their expression. The fireglow fell on his heavy, rather bowed shoulders, he sat slackly crouched on the fender, his face was uplifted, degenerate, perhaps slightly disintegrate, and yet with a moving beauty of its own.

"Of course," said Maxim, "you've been in hot countries where the people go about naked."

"Oh really!" exclaimed Halliday. "Where?"

"South America—Amazon," said Gerald.

"Oh but how perfectly splendid! It's one of the things I want most to do—to live from day to day without *ever* putting on any sort of clothing whatever. If I could do that, I should feel I had lived."

"But why?" said Gerald. "I can't see that it makes so much difference."

"Oh, I think it would be perfectly splendid. I'm sure life would be entirely another thing—entirely different, and perfectly wonderful."

"But why?" asked Gerald. "Why should it?"

"Oh—one would *feel* things instead of merely looking at them. I should feel the air move against me, and feel the things I touched, instead of having only to look at them. I'm sure life is all wrong because it has become much too visual—we can neither hear nor feel nor understand, we can only see. I'm sure that is entirely wrong."

"Yes, that is true, that is true," said the Russian.

Gerald glanced at him, and saw him, his suave, golden coloured body with the black hair growing fine and freely, like tendrils, and his limbs like smooth plant-stems. He was so healthy and well-made, why did he make one ashamed, why did one feel repelled. Why should Gerald even dislike it, why did it seem to him to detract from his own dignity. Was that all a human being amounted to? So uninspired! thought Gerald.

Birkin suddenly appeared in the doorway, also in a state of nudity, towel and sleeping suit over his arm. He was very narrow and white, and somehow apart.

"There's the bath-room now, if you want it," he said generally, and was going away again, when Gerald called:

"I say, Rupert!"

"What?" The single white figure appeared again, a presence in the room.

"What do you think of that figure there? I want to know," Gerald asked.

Birkin, white and strangely present, went over to the carved figure of the negro woman in labour. Her nude, protuberant body crouched in a strange, clutching posture, her hands gripping the ends of the band, above her breast.

"It is art," said Birkin.

"Very beautiful, it's very beautiful," said the Russian.

They all drew near to look. Gerald looked at the group of naked men, the Russian golden and like a water-plant, Halliday tall and heavily, brokenly beautiful, Birkin very white and immediate, not to be defined, as he looked closely at the carven woman. Strangely elated, Gerald also lifted his eyes to the face of the wooden figure. And his heart contracted.

He saw vividly, with his spirit, the grey, forward-stretching face of the negro woman, African and tense, abstracted in utter physical stress. It was a terrible face, void, peaked, abstracted almost into meaninglessness by the weight of sensation beneath. He saw the Pussum in it. As in a dream, he knew her.

"Why is it art?" Gerald asked, shocked, resentful.

"It conveys a complete truth," said Birkin. "It contains the whole truth of that state, whatever you feel about it."

"But you can't call it *high* art," said Gerald.

"High! There are centuries and hundreds of centuries of development in a straight line, behind that carving; it is an awful pitch of culture, of a definite sort."

"What culture?" Gerald asked, in opposition. He hated the sheer African thing.

"Pure culture in sensation, culture in the physical consciousness, really *ultimate* physical consciousness, mindless, utterly sensual. It is so sensual as to be final, supreme."

But Gerald resented it. He wanted to keep certain illusions, certain ideas like clothing.

"You like the wrong things, Rupert," he said, "things against yourself."

"Oh, I know, this isn't everything," Birkin replied, moving away.

When Gerald went back to his room from the bath, he also carried his clothes. It seemed bad form in this house, not to go about naked. And after all, it was rather nice, there *was* a real simplicity. Still, it was rather funny, everybody being so deliberately nude.

The Pussum lay in her bed, motionless, her round, dark eyes like black, unhappy pools. He could only see the black, bottomless pools of her eyes. Perhaps she suffered. The sensation of her inchoate suffering roused the old sharp flame in him, a mordant pity, a passion almost of cruelty.

"You are awake now," he said to her.

"What time is it?" came her muted voice.

She seemed to flow back, almost like liquid, from his approach, to sink helplessly away from him. Her inchoate look of a violated slave, whose fulfilment lies in her further and further violation, made his nerves quiver with acutely desirable sensation. After all, his was the only will, she was the passive substance of his will. He tingled with the subtle, biting sensation. And then he knew, he must go away from her, there must be pure separation between them.

It was a quiet and ordinary breakfast, the four men all looking very clean and bathed. Gerald and the Russian were both correct and *comme il faut* in appearance and manner, Birkin was gaunt and sick, and looked a failure in his attempt to be a properly dressed man, like Gerald and Maxim. Halliday wore tweeds and a green flannel shirt, and a rag of a tie, which was just right for him. The Hindu brought in a great deal of soft toast, and looked exactly the same as he had looked the night before, statically the same.

At the end of the breakfast the Pussum appeared, in a purple silk wrap with a shimmering sash. She had recovered herself somewhat, but was mute and lifeless still. It was a torment to her when anybody spoke to her. Her face was like a small, fine mask, sinister too, masked with unwilling suffering. It was almost midday. Gerald rose and went away to his business, glad to get out. But he had not finished. He was coming back again at evening, they were all dining together, and he had booked seats for the party, excepting Birkin, at a music-hall.

At night they came back to the flat very late again, again flushed with drink. Again the man-servant—who invariably disappeared between the hours of ten and twelve at night—came in silently and inscrutably with tea, bending in a slow, strange, leopard-like fashion to put the tray softly on the table. His face was immutable, aristocratic-looking, tinged slightly with grey under the skin; he was young and good-looking. But Birkin felt a slight sickness, looking at him, and feeling the slight greyness an ash of corruption, the aristocratic inscrutability of expression a nauseating, bestial stupidity.

Again they talked cordially and rousedly together. But already a certain friability was coming over the party, Birkin was mad with irritation, Halliday was turning in an insane hatred against Gerald, the Pussum was becoming hard and cold, like a flint knife, and Halliday was laying himself out to her. And her intention, ultimately, was to capture Halliday, to have complete power over him.

In the morning they all stalked and lounged about again. But Gerald could feel a strange hostility to himself, in the air. It roused his obstinacy, and he stood up against it. He hung on for two more days. The result was a nasty and insane scene with Halliday on the fourth evening. Halliday turned with absurd animosity upon Gerald, in the Café. There was a row. Gerald was on the point of knocking-in Halliday's face; when he was filled with sudden disgust and indifference, and he went away, leaving Halliday in a foolish state of gloating triumph, the Pussum hard and established, and Maxim standing clear. Birkin was absent, he had gone out of town again.

Gerald was piqued because he had left without giving the Pussum money. It was true, she did not care whether he gave her money or not, and he knew it. But she would have been glad of ten pounds, and he would have been *very* glad to give them to her. Now he felt in a false position. He went away chewing his lips to get at the ends of his short clipped moustache. He knew the Pussum was merely glad to be rid of him. She had got her Halliday, whom she wanted. She wanted him completely in her power. Then she would marry him. She wanted to marry him. She had set her will on marrying Halliday. She never wanted to hear of Gerald again; unless, perhaps, she were in difficulty. Because after all, Gerald was what she called a man, and these others, Halliday, Libidnikov, Birkin, the whole Bohemian set, they were only half men. But it was half men she could deal with. She felt sure of herself with them. The real men, like Gerald, put her in her place too much.

Still, she respected Gerald, she really respected him. She had managed to get his address, so that she could appeal to him in time of distress. She knew he wanted to give her money. She would perhaps write to him on that inevitable rainy day.

Chapter VIII

Breadalby

Breadalby was a Georgian house with Corinthian pillars, standing among the softer, greener hills of Derbyshire, not far from Cromford. In front, it looked over a lawn, over a few trees, down to a string of fish-ponds in the hollow of the silent park. At the back were trees, among which were to be found the stables, and the big kitchen garden, behind which was a wood.

It was a very quiet place, some miles from the high-road, back from the Derwent valley, outside the show scenery. Silent and forsaken, the golden stucco showed between the trees, the house-front looked down the park, unchanged and unchanging.

Of late, however, Hermione had lived a good deal at the house. She had turned away from London, away from Oxford, towards the silence of the country. Her father was mostly absent, abroad, she was either alone in the house, with her visitors, of whom there were always several, or she had with her her brother, a bachelor, and a Liberal member of Parliament. He always came down when the House was not sitting, seemed always to be present in Breadalby, although he was most conscientious in his attendance to duty.

The summer was just coming in when Ursula and Gudrun went to stay the second time with Hermione. Coming along in the car, after they had entered the park, they looked across the dip, where the fish-ponds lay in silence, at the pillared front of the house, sunny and small like an English drawing of the old school, on the brow of the green hill, against the trees. There were small figures on the green lawn, women in lavender and yellow moving to the shade of the enormous, beautifully balanced cedar tree.

"Isn't it complete!" said Gudrun. "It is as final as an old aquatint." She spoke with some resentment in her voice, as if she were captivated unwillingly, as if she must admire against her will.

"Do you love it?" asked Ursula.

"I don't *love* it, but in its way, I think it is quite complete."

The motor-car ran down the hill and up again in one breath, and they were curving to the side door. A parlour-maid appeared, and then Hermione, coming forward with her pale face lifted, and her hands outstretched, advancing straight to the new-comers, her voice singing:

"Here you are—I'm so glad to see you—" she kissed Gudrun—"—so glad to see you—" she kissed Ursula and remained with her arm round her. "Are you very tired?"

"Not at all tired," said Ursula.

"Are you tired, Gudrun?"

"Not at all, thanks," said Gudrun.

"No—" drawled Hermione. And she stood and looked at them. The two girls were embarrassed because she would not move into the house, but must have her little scene of welcome there on the path. The servants waited.

"Come in," said Hermione at last, having fully taken in the pair of them. Gudrun was the more beautiful and attractive, she had decided again, Ursula was more physical, more womanly. She admired Gudrun's dress more. It was of green poplin, with a loose coat above it, of broad, dark-green and dark-brown stripes. The hat was of a pale, greenish straw, the colour of new hay, and it had a plaited ribbon of black and orange, the stockings were dark green, the shoes black. It was a good get-up, at once fashionable and individual. Ursula, in dark blue, was more ordinary, though she also looked well.

Hermione herself wore a dress of prune-coloured silk, with coral beads and coral coloured stockings. But her dress was both shabby and soiled, even rather dirty.

"You would like to see your rooms now, wouldn't you! Yes. We will go up now, shall we?"

Ursula was glad when she could be left alone in her room. Hermione lingered so long, made such a stress on one. She stood so near to one, pressing herself near upon one, in a way that was most embarrassing and oppressive. She seemed to hinder one's workings.

Lunch was served on the lawn, under the great tree, whose thick, blackish boughs came down close to the grass. There were present a young Italian woman, slight and fashionable, a young, athletic-looking Miss Bradley, a learned, dry Baronet of fifty, who was always making witticisms and laughing at them heartily in a harsh, horse-laugh, there was Rupert Birkin, and then a woman secretary, a Fräulein März, young and slim and pretty.

The food was very good, that was one thing. Gudrun, critical of everything, gave it her full approval. Ursula loved the situation, the white table by the cedar tree, the scent of new sunshine, the little vision of the leafy park, with far-off deer feeding peacefully. There seemed a magic circle drawn about the place, shutting out the present, enclosing the delightful, precious past, trees and deer and silence, like a dream.

But in spirit she was unhappy. The talk went on like a rattle of small artillery, always slightly sententious, with a sententiousness that was only emphasised by the continual crackling of a witticism, the continual spatter of verbal jest, designed to give a tone of flippancy to a stream of conversation that was all critical and general, a canal of conversation rather than a stream.

The attitude was mental and very wearying. Only the elderly sociologist, whose mental fibre was so tough as to be insentient, seemed to be thoroughly happy. Birkin was down in the mouth. Hermione appeared, with amazing persistence, to wish to ridicule him and make him look ignominious in the eyes of everybody. And it was surprising how she seemed to succeed, how helpless he seemed against her. He looked completely insignificant. Ursula and Gudrun, both very unused, were mostly silent, listening to the slow, rhapsodic sing-song of Hermione, or the verbal sallies of Sir Joshua, or the prattle of Fräulein, or the responses of the other two women.

Luncheon was over, coffee was brought out on to the grass, the party left the table and sat about in lounge chairs, in the shade or in the sunshine as they wished. Fräulein departed into the house, Hermione took up her embroidery, the little contessa took a book, Miss Bradley was weaving a basket out of fine grass, and there they all were on the lawn, in the early summer afternoon, working leisurely and spattering with half-intellectual, deliberate talk.

Suddenly there was the sound of the brakes and the shutting off of a motor-car.

"There's Salsie!" sang Hermione, in her slow, amusing sing-song. And laying down her work, she rose slowly, and slowly passed over the lawn, round the bushes, out of sight.

"Who is it?" asked Gudrun.

"Mr Roddice—Miss Roddice's brother—at least, I suppose it's he," said Sir Joshua.

"Salsie, yes, it is her brother," said the little contessa, lifting her head for a moment from her book, and speaking as if to give information, in her slightly deepened, guttural English.

They all waited. And then, round the bushes came the tall form of Alexander Roddice, striding romantically like a Meredith hero who remembers Disraeli. He was cordial with everybody, he was at once a host, with an easy, off-hand hospitality that he had learned for Hermione's friends. He had just come down from London, from the House. At once the atmosphere of the House of Commons made itself felt over the lawn: the Home Secretary had said such and such a thing, and he, Roddice, on the other hand, thought such and such a thing, and had said so-and-so to the P. M.

Now Hermione came round the bushes with Gerald Crich. He had come along with Alexander. Gerald was presented to everybody, was kept by Hermione for a few moments in full view, then he was led away, still by Hermione. He was evidently her guest of the moment.

There had been a split in the Cabinet; the minister for Education had resigned owing to adverse criticism. This started a conversation on education.

"Of course," said Hermione, lifting her face like a rhapsodist, "there *can* be no reason, no *excuse* for education, except the joy and beauty of knowledge in itself." She seemed to rumble and ruminate with subterranean thoughts for a minute, then she proceeded: "Vocational education *isn't* education, it is the close of education."

Gerald, on the brink of a discussion, sniffed the air with delight and prepared for action.

"Not necessarily," he said. "But isn't education really like gymnastics, isn't the end of education the production of a well-trained, vigorous, energetic mind?"

"Just as athletics produce a healthy body, ready for anything," cried Miss Bradley, in hearty accord.

Gudrun looked at her in silent loathing.

"Well—" rumbled Hermione, "I don't know. To me the pleasure of knowing is *so* great, so *wonderful*—nothing has meant so much to me in all life, as certain knowledge—no, I am sure—nothing."

"What knowledge, for example, Hermione?" asked Alexander.

Hermione lifted her face and rumbled—

"m- m- m- I don't know.———But one thing was the stars, when I really understood something about the stars. One feels so *uplifted*, so *unbounded*———"

Birkin looked at her in a white fury.

"What do you want to feel unbounded for?" he said sarcastically. "You don't want to *be* unbounded."

Hermione recoiled in offence.

"Yes, but one does have that limitless feeling," said Gerald. "It's like getting on top of the mountain and seeing the Pacific."

"Silent upon a peak in Dariayn," murmured the Italian, lifting her face for a moment from her book.

"Not necessarily in Darien," said Gerald, while Ursula began to laugh.

Hermione waited for the dust to settle, and then she said, untouched:

"Yes, it is the greatest thing in life—*to know*. It is really to be happy, to be *free*."

"Knowledge is, of course, liberty," said Malleson.

"In compressed tabloids," said Birkin, looking at the dry, stiff little body of the Baronet. Immediately Gudrun saw the famous sociologist as a flat bottle, containing tabloids of compressed liberty. That pleased her. Sir Joshua was labelled and placed forever in her mind.

"What does that mean, Rupert?" sang Hermione, in a calm snub.

"You can only have knowledge, strictly," he replied, "of things concluded, in the past. It's like bottling the liberty of last summer in the bottled gooseberries."

"Can one have knowledge only of the past?" asked the baronet, pointedly. "Could we call our knowledge of the laws of gravitation, for instance, knowledge of the past?"

"Yes," said Birkin.

"There is a most beautiful thing in my book," suddenly piped the little Italian woman. "It says the man came to the door and threw his eyes down the street."

There was a general laugh in the company. Miss Bradley went and looked over the shoulder of the contessa.

"See!" said the contessa.

"Bazarov came to the door and threw his eyes hurriedly down the street," she read.

Again there was a loud laugh, the most startling of which was the Baronet's, which rattled out like a clatter of falling stones.

"What is the book?" asked Alexander, promptly.

"*Fathers and Sons*, by Turgenev," said the little foreigner, pronouncing every syllable distinctly. She looked at the cover, to verify herself.

"An old American edition," said Birkin.

"Ha! of course—translated from the French," said Alexander, with a fine declamatory voice. "Bazarov ouvra la porte et jeta les yeux dans la rue."

He looked brightly round the company.

"I wonder what the 'hurriedly' was," said Ursula.

They all began to guess.

And then, to the amazement of everybody, the maid came hurrying with a large tea-tray. The afternoon had passed so swiftly.

Women in Love

After tea, they were all gathered for a walk.

"Would you like to come for a walk?" said Hermione to each of them, one by one. And they all said yes, feeling somehow like prisoners marshalled for exercise. Birkin only refused.

"Will you come for a walk, Rupert?"

"No, Hermione."

"But are you *sure?*"

"Quite sure."

There was a second's hesitation.

"And why not?" sang Hermione's question. It made her blood run sharp, to be thwarted in even so trifling a matter. She intended them all to walk with her in the park.

"Because I don't like trooping off in a gang," he said.

Her voice rumbled in her throat for a moment. Then she said, with a curious stray calm:

"Then we'll leave a little boy behind, if he's sulky."

And she looked really gay, while she insulted him. But it merely made him stiff.

She trailed off to the rest of the company, only turning to wave her handkerchief to him, and to chuckle with laughter, singing out:

"Goodbye, goodbye little boy."

"Goodbye impudent hag," he said to himself.

They all went through the park. Hermione wanted to show them the wild daffodils on a little slope. "This way, this way," sang her leisurely voice at intervals. And they had all to come this way. The daffodils were pretty, but who could see them? Ursula was stiff all over with resentment by this time, resentment of the whole atmosphere. Gudrun, mocking and objective, watched and registered everything.

They looked at the shy deer, and Hermione talked to the stag, as if he too were a boy she wanted to wheedle and fondle. He was male, so she must exert some kind of power over him. They trailed home by the fish-ponds, and Hermione told them about the quarrel of two male swans, who had striven for the love of the one lady. She chuckled and laughed as she told how the ousted lover had sat with his head buried under his wing, on the gravel.

When they arrived back at the house, Hermione stood on the lawn and sang out, in a strange, small, high voice that carried very far:

"Rupert! Rupert!" The first syllable was high and slow, the second dropped down. "Roo-o-opert."

But there was no answer. A maid appeared.

"Where is Mr Birkin, Alice?" asked the mild, straying voice of Hermione. But under the straying voice, what a persistent, almost insane *will*!

"I think he's in his room, my lady."

"Is he."

Hermione went slowly up the stairs, along the corridor, singing out in her high, small call:

"Ru-oo-pert! Ru-oo-pert!"

She came to his door, and tapped, still crying: "Roo-pert."

"Yes," sounded his voice at last.

"What are you doing?"

The question was mild and curious.

There was no answer. Then he opened the door.

"We've come back," said Hermione. "The daffodils are *so* beautiful."

"Yes," he said, "I've seen them."

She looked at him with her long, slow, impassive look, along her cheeks.

"Have you," she echoed. And she remained looking at him. She was stimulated above all things by this conflict with him, when he was like a sulky boy, helpless, and she had him safe at Breadalby. But underneath she knew the split was coming, and her hatred of him was subconscious and intense.

"What were you doing?" she reiterated, in her mild, indifferent tone. He did not answer, and she made her way, almost unconsciously, into his room. He had taken a Chinese drawing of geese from the boudoir, and was copying it, with much skill and vividness.

"You are copying the drawing," she said, standing near the table and looking down at his work. "Yes—How beautifully you do it! You like it very much, don't you?"

"It's a marvellous drawing," he said.

"Is it? I'm so glad you like it, because I've always been fond of it.—The Chinese ambassador gave it me."

"I know," he said.

"But why do you copy it?" she asked, casual and sing-song. "Why not do something original?"

"I want to know it," he replied. "One gets more of China, copying this picture, than reading all the books."

"And what do you get?"

She was at once roused, she laid as it were violent hands on him, to extract his secrets from him. She *must* know. It was a dreadful tyranny, an obsession in her, to know all he knew. For some time he was silent, hating to answer her. Then, compelled, he began:

"I know what centres they live from—what they perceive and feel—the hot, stinging centrality of a goose in the flux of cold water and mud—the curious bitter stinging heat of a goose's blood, entering their own blood like an inoculation of corruptive fire—fire of the cold-burning mud—the lotus mystery."

Hermione looked at him along her narrow, pallid cheeks. Her eyes were strange and drugged, heavy under their heavy, dropping lids. Her thin bosom shrugged convulsively. He stared back at her, devilish and unchanging. With another strange, sick convulsion, she turned away, as if she were sick, could feel dissolution setting-in in her body. For with her mind she was unable to attend to his words, he caught her, as it were, beneath all her defences, and destroyed her with some insidious occult potency.

"Yes," she said, as if she did not know what she were saying. "Yes." and she swallowed, and tried to regain her mind. But she could not, she was witless, decentralised. Use all her will as she might, she could not recover. She suffered the ghastliness of dissolution, broken and gone in a horrible corruption. And he stood and looked at her unmoved. She strayed out, pallid and preyed-upon like a ghost, like one attacked by the tomb-influences which dog us. And she was gone like a corpse, that has no presence, no connection. He remained hard and vindictive.

Hermione came down to dinner strange and sepulchral, her eyes heavy and full of sepulchral darkness, strength. She had put on a dress of stiff old greenish brocade, that fitted tight and made her look tall and rather terrible, ghastly. In the gay light of the drawing-room she was uncanny and oppressive. But seated in the half-light of the dining-room, sitting stiffly before the shaded candles on the table, she seemed a power, a presence. She listened and attended with a drugged attention.

The party was gay and extravagant in appearance, everybody had put on evening dress except Birkin and Joshua Malleson. The little Italian contessa wore a dress of tissue of orange and gold and black velvet in soft wide stripes, Gudrun was emerald green with strange net-work of grey, Ursula was in yellow with dull silver veiling, Miss Bradley was crimson and jet, Fräulein März wore pale blue. It gave Hermione a sudden convulsive sensation of pleasure, to see these rich colours under the candle-light. She was aware of the talk going on, ceaselessly, Joshua's voice dominating; of the ceaseless pitter-patter of women's light laughter and responses; of the brilliant colours and the white table and the shadow above and below; and she seemed in a swoon of gratification, convulsed with pleasure, and yet sick, like a *revenant*. She took very little part in the conversation, yet she heard it all, it was all hers.

They all went together into the drawing-room, as if they were one family, easily, without any attention to ceremony. Fräulein handed the coffee, everybody smoked cigarettes, or else long warden pipes of white clay, of which a sheaf was provided.

"Wiill you smooke?—cigarettes or pipe?" asked Fräulein prettily.

There was a circle of people, Sir Joshua with his eighteenth-century appearance, Gerald the amused, handsome young Englishman, Alexander tall and the handsome politician, democratic and lucid, Hermione strange like a long Cassandra, and the women lurid with colour, all dutifully smoking their long white pipes, and sitting in a half-moon in the comfortable, soft-lighted drawing-room, round the logs that flickered on the marble hearth.

The talk was very often political or sociological, and interesting, curiously anarchistic. There was an accumulation of powerful force in the room, powerful and destructive. Everything seemed to be thrown into the melting pot, and it seemed to Ursula they were all witches, helping the pot to bubble. There was an elation and a satisfaction in it all, but it was cruelly exhausting for the new-comers, this ruthless mental pressure, this powerful, consuming, destructive mentality that emanated from Joshua and Hermione and Birkin, and dominated the rest.

But a sickness, a fearful nausea gathered possession of Hermione. There was a lull in the talk, as it was arrested by her unconscious but all-powerful will.

"Salsie, won't you play something?" said Hermione, breaking off completely. "Won't somebody dance? Gudrun, you will dance, won't you? I wish you would. Anche tu, Palestra, ballerai?—si, per piacere. You too, Ursula."

Hermione rose and slowly pulled the gold-embroidered band that hung by the mantel, clinging to it for a moment, then releasing it suddenly. Like a priestess she looked, unconscious, sunk in a heavy half-trance. A servant came, and soon reappeared with armfuls of silk robes and shawls and scarves, mostly oriental, things that Hermione, with her love for beautiful extravagant dress, had collected gradually.

"The three women will dance together," she said.

"What shall it be?" asked Alexander, rising briskly.

"Vergini Delle Rocchette," said the contessa at once.

"They are so languid," said Ursula.

"The three witches from Macbeth," suggested Fräulein usefully.

It was finally decided to do Naomi and Ruth and Orpah. Ursula was Naomi, Gudrun was Ruth, the contessa was Orpah. The idea was to make a little ballet, in the style of the Russian Ballet of Pavlova and Nijinsky.

The contessa was ready first. Alexander went to the piano, a space was cleared, Orpah, in beautiful oriental clothes, began slowly to dance the death of her husband. Then Ruth came, and they wept together, and lamented, then Naomi came to comfort them. It was all done in dumb show, the women danced their emotion in gesture and motion. The little drama went on for a quarter of an hour.

Ursula was beautiful as Naomi. All her men were dead, it remained to her only to stand alone in indomitable assertion, demanding nothing. Ruth, woman-loving, loved her. Orpah, a vivid, sensational, subtle widow, would go back to the former life, a repetition. The interplay between the women was real and rather frightening. It was strange to see how Gudrun clung with heavy, desperate passion to Ursula, yet smiled with subtle malevolence against her, how Ursula accepted silently, unable to provide any more either for herself or for the other, but dangerous and indomitable, refuting her grief.

Hermione loved to watch. She could see the contessa's rapid, stoat-like sensationalism, Gudrun's ultimate but treacherous cleaving to the woman in her sister, Ursula's dangerous helplessness, as if she were helplessly weighted, and unreleased.

"That was very beautiful," everybody cried with one accord. But Hermione writhed in her soul, knowing what she could not know. She cried out for more dancing, and it was her will that set the contessa and Birkin moving mockingly in Malbrouk.

Gerald was excited by the desperate cleaving of Gudrun to Naomi. The essence of that female, subterranean recklessness and mockery penetrated his blood. He could not forget Gudrun's lifted, offered, cleaving, reckless, yet withal mocking weight. And Birkin, watching like a hermit crab from its hole, had seen the brilliant frustration and helplessness of Ursula. She was rich, full of dangerous power. She was like a strange unconscious bud of powerful womanhood. He was unconsciously drawn to her. She was his future.

Alexander played some Hungarian music, and they all danced, seized by the spirit. Gerald was marvellously exhilarated at finding himself in motion, moving towards Gudrun, dancing with feet that could not yet escape from the waltz and the two-step, but feeling his force stir along his limbs and his body, out of captivity. He did not know yet how to dance their convulsive, rag-time sort of dancing, but he knew how to begin. Birkin, when he could get free from the weight of the people present, whom he disliked, danced rapidly and with a real gaiety. And how Hermione hated him for this irresponsible gaiety.

"Now I see," cried the contessa excitedly, watching his purely gay motion, which he had all to himself. "Mr Birkin, he is a changer."

Hermione looked at her slowly, and shuddered, knowing that only a foreigner could have seen and have said this.

"Cosa vuol dire, Palestra?" she asked, sing-song.

"Look," said the contessa, in Italian. "He is not a man, he is a chameleon, a creature of change."

"He is not a man, he is treacherous, not one of us," sang itself over in Hermione's consciousness. And her soul writhed in the black subjugation to him, because of his power to escape, to exist, other than she did, because he was not consistent, not a man, less than a man. She hated him in a despair that shattered her and broke her down, so that she suffered sheer dissolution, like a corpse, and was unconscious of everything save the horrible sickness of dissolution that was taking place within her, body and soul.

The house being full, Gerald was given the smaller room, really the dressing-room, communicating with Birkin's bedroom. When they all took their candles and mounted the stairs, where the lamps were burning subduedly, Hermione captured Ursula and brought her into her own bedroom, to talk to her. A sort of constraint came over Ursula, in the big, strange bedroom. Hermione seemed to be bearing down on her, awful and inchoate, making some appeal. They were looking at some Indian silk shirts, gorgeous and sensual in themselves, their shape, their almost corrupt gorgeousness. And Hermione came near, and her bosom writhed, and Ursula was for a moment blank with panic. And for a moment, Hermione's haggard eyes saw the fear on the face of the other, there was again a sort of crash, a crashing down. And Ursula picked up a shirt of rich red and blue silk, made for a young princess of fourteen, and was crying mechanically:

"Isn't it wonderful—who would dare to put those two strong colours together——"

Then Hermione's maid entered silently, and Ursula, overcome with dread, escaped, carried away by powerful impulse.

Birkin went straight to bed. He was feeling happy, and sleepy. Since he had danced he was happy. But Gerald would talk to him. Gerald, in evening dress, sat on Birkin's bed when the other lay down, and must talk.

"Who are those two Brangwens?" Gerald asked.

"They live in Beldover."

"In Beldover! Who are they, then?"

"Teachers in the Grammar School."

There was a pause.

"They are?" said Gerald at length. "I thought I had seen them before."

"It disappoints you?" said Birkin.

"Disappoints me? No.—But how is it Hermione has them here?"

"She knew Gudrun in London—that's the younger one, the one with the darker hair—she's an artist—does sculpture and modelling."

"She's not a teacher in the Grammar School, then—only the other?"

"Both—Gudrun art mistress, Ursula a class mistress."

"And what's the father?"

"Handicraft instructor in the schools."

"Really!"

"Class-barriers are breaking down!"

Gerald was always uneasy under the slightly jeering tone of the other.

"That their father is handicraft instructor in a school? What does it matter to me?"

Birkin laughed. Gerald looked at his face, as it lay there laughing and bitter and indifferent, on the pillow, and he could not go away.

"I don't suppose you will see very much more of Gudrun, at least. She is a restless bird, she'll be gone in a week or two," said Birkin.

"Where will she go?"

"London, Paris, Rome—heaven knows. I always expect her to sheer off to Damascus or San Francisco; she's a bird of paradise. God knows what she's got to do with Beldover. It goes by contraries, like dreams."

Gerald pondered for a few moments.

"How do you know her so well?" he asked.

"I knew her in London," he replied, "in the Algernon Strange set. She'll know about Pussum and Libidnikov and the rest—even if she doesn't know them personally.—She was never quite that set—more conventional, in a way. I've known her for two years, I suppose."

"And she makes money, apart from her teaching?" asked Gerald.

"Some—irregularly. She can sell her models. She has a certain réclame."

"How much for?"

"A guinea—ten guineas—."

"And are they good? What are they?"

"I think sometimes they are marvellously good. That is hers, those two wagtails in Hermione's boudoir—you've seen them—they are carved in wood and painted."

"I thought it was savage carving again."

"No, hers.—That's what they are—animals and birds, sometimes odd small people in everyday dress, really rather wonderful when they come off. They have a sort of funniness that is quite unconscious and subtle."

"She might be a well-known artist one day?" mused Gerald.

"She might. But I think she won't. She drops her art if anything else catches her. Her contrariness prevents her taking it seriously—she must never be too serious, she feels she gives herself away. And she won't give herself away—she's always on the defensive. That's what I can't stand about her type.—By the way, how did things go off with Pussum after I left you? I haven't heard anything."

"Oh, rather disgusting. Halliday turned objectionable, and I only just saved myself from jumping in his stomach, in a real old-fashioned row."

Birkin was silent.

"Of course," he said, "Julius is really mad. On the one hand he's a religious maniac, and on the other, he is fascinated by obscenity. Either he is a pure servant, washing the feet of Christ, or else he is making obscene drawings of Jesus—action and reaction—and between the two, nothing. He is really split mad. He wants a pure lily, another girl, with a baby face,—the good old chaste love—and at the same time he *must* have the Pussum, just to defile himself with her."

"That's what I can't make out," said Gerald. "Does he love her, the Pussum, or doesn't he?"

"He neither does nor doesn't. She is the harlot, the actual harlot of adultery to him. And he's got a craving to throw himself away with her. Then he gets up and turns towards the lily of purity, the baby-faced girl, and so gets another thrill. It's the old game—action and reaction, and nothing between."

"I don't know," said Gerald, after a pause, "that he does insult the Pussum so very much. She strikes me as being rather foul."

"But I thought you liked her!" exclaimed Birkin. "I always felt fond of her.—I never had anything to do with her, personally, that's true."

"I liked her all right, for a couple of days," said Gerald. "But a week of her would have turned me over. There's a certain smell about the skin of those women, that in the end is sickening beyond words—even if you like it at first."

"I know," said Birkin. Then he added, rather fretfully, "But go to bed, Gerald. God knows what time it is."

Gerald looked at his watch, and at length rose off the bed, and went to his room. But he returned in a few minutes, in his shirt.

"One thing," he said, seating himself on the bed again; "we finished up rather stormily, and I never had time to give her anything."

"Money?" said Birkin. "She'll get what she wants from Halliday or from one of her acquaintances."

"But then," said Gerald, "I'd rather give her her dues, and settle the account."

"She doesn't care."

"No, perhaps not.—But one feels the account is left open, and one would rather it were closed."

"Would you?" said Birkin. He was looking at the white legs of Gerald, as the latter sat on the side of the bed in his shirt. They were white-skinned, full, muscular legs, handsome and decided. Yet they moved Birkin with a sort of pathos, tenderness, as if they were childish.

"I think I'd rather close the account," said Gerald, repeating himself vaguely.

"It doesn't matter, one way or another," said Birkin.

"You always say it doesn't matter," said Gerald, a little puzzled, looking down at the face of the other man affectionately.

"Neither does it," said Birkin.

"But she was a decent sort, really."

"Render unto Caesarina the things that are Caesarina's," said Birkin, turning aside. It seemed to him Gerald was talking for the sake of talking.

"Go away, it wearies me—it's too late at night," he said.

"I wish you'd tell me something that *did* matter," said Gerald, looking down all the time at the face of the other man, waiting for something. But Birkin turned his face aside.

"All right then, go to sleep," said Gerald, and he laid his hand affectionately on the other man's shoulder, and went away.

In the morning, when Gerald awoke and heard Birkin move, he called out:

"I still think I ought to give the Pussum ten pounds."

"Oh God," said Birkin, "don't be so matter-of-fact. Close the account in your own soul, if you like. It is there you can't close it."

"How do you know I can't?"

"Knowing you."

Gerald meditated for some moments.

"It seems to me the right thing to do, you know, with the Pussums, is to pay them."

"And the right thing for mistresses: keep them. And the right thing for wives: live under the same roof with them. Integer vitae scelerisque purus—" said Birkin.

"There's no need to be nasty about it," said Gerald.

"It bores me. I'm not interested in your peccadilloes."

"And I don't care whether you are or not—I am."

The morning was again sunny. The maid had been in and brought the water, and had drawn the curtains. Birkin, sitting up in bed, looked lazily and pleasantly out on the park, that was so green and deserted, romantic, belonging to the past. He was thinking how lovely, how sure, how formed, how final all the things of the past were—the lovely accomplished past—this house, so still and golden, the park slumbering its centuries of peace. And then, what a snare and a delusion, this beauty of static things—what a horrible, dead prison Breadalby really was, what an intolerable confinement, the peace! Yet it was better than the sordid scrambling conflict of the present. If only one might create the future after one's own heart—for a little pure truth, a little unflinching application of simple truth to life, the heart cried out ceaselessly.

"I can't see what you will leave me at all, to be interested in," came Gerald's voice from the lower room. "Neither the Pussums, nor the mines, nor anything else."

"You be interested in what you can, Gerald. Only I'm not interested myself," said Birkin.

"What am I to do at all, then?" came Gerald's voice.

"What you like.—What am I to do myself?"

In the silence Birkin could feel Gerald musing this fact.

"I'm blest if I know," came the good-humoured answer.

"You see," said Birkin, "part of you wants the Pussum, and nothing but the Pussum, part of you wants the mines, the business, and nothing but the business—and there you are—all in bits—"

"And part of me wants something else," said Gerald, in a queer quiet, real voice.

"What?" said Birkin, rather surprised.

"That's what I hoped you could tell me," said Gerald.

There was a silence for some time.

"I can't tell you—I can't find my own way, let alone yours. You might marry," Birkin replied.

"Who—the Pussum?" asked Gerald.

"Perhaps," said Birkin. And he rose and went to the window.

"That is your panacea," said Gerald. "But you haven't even tried it on yourself yet, and you are sick enough."

"I am," said Birkin. "Still, I shall come right."

"Through marriage?"

"Yes," Birkin answered obstinately.

"And no," added Gerald. "No, no, no, my boy."

There was a silence between them, and a strange tension of hostility. They always kept a gap, a distance between them, they wanted always to be free each of the other. Yet there was a curious heart-straining towards each other.

"Salvator femininus," said Gerald, satirically.

"Why not?" said Birkin.

"No reason at all," said Gerald, "if it really works. But whom will you marry?"

"A woman," said Birkin.

"Good," said Gerald.

Birkin and Gerald were the last to come down to breakfast. Hermione liked everybody to be early. She suffered when she felt her day was diminished, she felt she had missed her life. She seemed to grip the hours by the throat, to force her life from them. She was rather pale and ghastly, as if left behind, in the morning. Yet she had her power, her will was strangely pervasive. With the entrance of the two young men a sudden tension was felt.

She lifted her face, and said, in her amused sing-song:

"Good morning! Did you sleep well?—I'm so glad."

And she turned away, ignoring them. Birkin, who knew her well, saw that she intended to discount his existence.

"Will you take what you want from the sideboard," said Alexander, in a voice slightly suggesting disapprobation. "I hope the things aren't cold. Oh no!—Do you mind putting out the flame under the chafing-dish, Rupert? Thank you."

Even Alexander was rather authoritative where Hermione was cool. He took his tone from her, inevitably. Birkin sat down and looked at the table. He was so used to this house, to this room, to this atmosphere, through years of intimacy, and now he felt in complete opposition to it all, it had nothing to do with him. How well he knew Hermione, as she sat there, erect and silent and somewhat bemused, and yet so potent, so powerful! He knew her statically, so finally, that it was almost like a madness. It was difficult to believe one was not mad, that one was not a figure in the hall of kings in some Egyptian tomb, where the dead all sat immemorial and tremendous. How utterly he knew Joshua Malleson, who was talking in his harsh, yet rather mincing voice, endlessly, endlessly, always with a strong mentality working, always interesting, and yet always known, everything he said known beforehand, however novel it was, and clever. Alexander the up-to-date host, so bloodlessly free-and-easy, Fräulein so prettily chiming in just as she should, the little Italian countess taking no notice of anybody, only playing her little game, objective and cold, like a weasel watching everything, and extracting her own amusement, never giving herself in the slightest; then Miss Bradley, heavy and rather subservient, treated with cool, almost amused contempt by Hermione, and therefore slighted by everybody—how known it all was, like a game with the figures set out, the same figures, the Queen of chess, the knights, the pawns, the same now as they were hundreds of years ago, the same figures moving round in one of the innumerable permutations that make up the game. But the game is known, its going on is like a madness, it is so exhausted.

There was Gerald, an amused look on his face; the game pleased him. There was Gudrun, watching with steady, large, hostile eyes; the game fascinated her, and she loathed it. There was Ursula, with a slightly startled look on her face, as if she were hurt, and the pain were just outside her consciousness.

Suddenly Birkin got up and went out.

"That's enough," he said to himself, involuntarily.

Hermione knew his motion, though not in her consciousness. She lifted her heavy eyes and saw him lapse suddenly away, on a sudden, unknown tide, and the waves broke over her. Only her indomitable will remained static and mechanical, she sat at table making her musing, stray remarks. But the darkness had covered her, she was like a ship that has gone down. It was finished for her too, she was wrecked in the darkness. Yet the unfailing mechanism of her will worked on, she had that activity.

"Shall we bathe this morning?" she said, suddenly looking at them all.

"Splendid," said Joshua. "It is a perfect morning."

"Oh it is beautiful," said the Fräulein.

"Yes, let us bathe," said the Italian woman.

"We have no bathing suits," said Gerald.

"Have mine," said Alexander. "I must go to church and read the lessons. They expect me."

"Are you a Christian?" asked the Italian countess, with sudden interest.

"No," said Alexander. "I'm not. But I believe in keeping up the old institutions."

"They are so beautiful," said the Fräulein daintily.

"Oh they are," cried Miss Bradley.

They all trailed out on to the lawn. It was a sunny, soft morning in early summer, when life ran in the world subtly, like a reminiscence. The church bells were ringing a little way off, not a cloud was in the sky, the swans were like lilies on the water below, the peacocks walked with long, prancing steps across the shadow and into the sunshine of the grass. One wanted to swoon into the by-gone perfection of it all.

"Goodbye," called Alexander, waving his gloves cheerily, and he disappeared behind the bushes, on his way to church.

"Now," said Hermione, "shall we all bathe?"

"I won't," said Ursula.

"You don't want to?" said Hermione, looking at her slowly.

"No, I don't want to," said Ursula.

"Nor I," said Gudrun.

"What about my suit?" asked Gerald.

"I don't know," laughed Hermione, with an odd, amused intonation. "Will a handkerchief do—a large handkerchief?"

"That will do," said Gerald.

"Come along then," sang Hermione.

The first to run across the lawn was the little Italian, small and like a cat, her white legs twinkling as she went, ducking slightly her head, that was tied in a gold silk kerchief. She tripped through the gate and down the grass, and stood, like a tiny figure of ivory and bronze, at the water's edge, having dropped off her towelling, watching the swans, which came up in surprise. Then out ran Miss Bradley, like a large, soft plum in her dark-blue suit. Then Gerald came, a scarlet silk kerchief round his loins, his towels over his arms. He seemed to flaunt himself a little in the sun, lingering and laughing, strolling easily, looking white but natural in his nakedness. Then came Sir Joshua, in an overcoat, and lastly Hermione, striding with stiff grace from out of a great mantle of purple silk, her head tied up in purple and gold. Handsome was her stiff, long body, her straight-stepping white legs, there was a static magnificence about her as she let the cloak float loosely away from her striding. She crossed the lawn like some strange memory, and passed slowly and statelily towards the water.

There were three ponds, in terraces descending the valley, large and smooth and beautiful, lying in the sun. The water ran over a little stone

wall, over small rocks, splashing down from one pond to the level below.
The swans had gone out on to the opposite bank, the reds smelled sweet, a
faint breeze touched the skin.

Gerald had dived in, after Sir Joshua, and had swum to the end of the
pond. There he climbed out and sat on the wall. There was a dive, and the
little countess was swimming like a rat, to join him. They both sat in the
sun, laughing and crossing their arms on their breasts. Sir Joshua swam up
to them, and stood near them, up to his arm-pits in the water. Then
Hermione and Miss Bradley swam over, and they sat in a row on the
embankment.

"Aren't they terrifying? Aren't they really terrifying?" said Gudrun.
"Don't they look saurian? They are just like great lizards. Did ever you see
anything like Sir Joshua? But really, Ursula, he belongs to the primeval
world, when great lizards crawled about."

Gudrun looked in dismay on Sir Joshua, who stood up to the breast in
the water, his long, greyish hair washed down into his eyes, his neck set
into thick, crude shoulders. He was talking to Miss Bradley, who, seated
on the bank above, plump and big and wet, looked as if she might roll
and slither in the water almost like one of the slithering sea-lions in the
Zoo.

Ursula watched in silence. Gerald was laughing happily, between
Hermione and the Italian. He reminded her of Dionysos, because his hair
was really yellow, his figure so full and laughing. Hermione, in her large,
stiff, sinister grace, leaned near him, frightening, as if she were not
responsible for what she might do. He knew a certain danger in her, a
convulsive madness. But he only laughed the more, turning often to the
little countess, who was flashing up her face at him.

They all dropped into the water, and were swimming together like a
shoal of seals. Hermione was powerful and unconscious in the water, large
and slow and powerful, Palestra was quick and silent as a water rat, Gerald
wavered and flickered, a white natural shadow. Then, one after the other,
they waded out, and went up to the house.

But Gerald lingered a moment to speak to Gudrun.

"You don't like the water?" he said.

She looked at him with a long, slow, inscrutable look, as he stood before
her negligently, the water standing in beads all over his skin.

"I like it very much," she replied.

He paused, expecting some sort of explanation.

"And you swim?"

"Yes, I swim."

Still he would not ask her why she would not go in, then. He could feel something ironic in her. He walked away, piqued for the first time.

"Why wouldn't you bathe?" he asked her again, later, when he was once more the properly-dressed, correct young Englishman.

She hesitated a moment before answering, opposing his persistence.

"Because I didn't like the crowd," she replied.

He laughed, her phrase seemed to re-echo in his consciousness. The flavour of her slang was piquant to him. Whether he would or not, she signified the real world to him. He wanted to come up to her standards, fulfil her expectations. He knew that her criterion was the only one that mattered. The others were all outsiders, instinctively, whatever they might be socially. And Gerald could not help it, he was bound to strive to come up to her criterion, fulfil her idea of a man and a human-being.

After lunch, when all the others had withdrawn, Hermione and Gerald and Birkin lingered, finishing their talk. There had been some discussion, on the whole quite intellectual and artificial, about a new state, a new world of man. Supposing this old social state *were* broken and destroyed, then, out of the chaos, what then?

The great social idea, said Sir Joshua, was the *social* equality of man. No, said Gerald, the idea was, that every man was fit for his own little bit of a task—let him do that, and then please himself. The unifying principle was the work in hand. Only work, the business of production, held men together. It was mechanical, but then society *was* a mechanism. Apart from work they were isolated, free to do as they liked.

"Oh!" cried Gudrun. "Then we shan't have names any more—we shall be like the Germans, nothing but Herr Obermeister and Herr Unter-meister. I can imagine it—'I am Mrs Colliery-Manager Crich—I am Mrs Member-of-Parliament Roddice, I am Miss Art-Teacher Brangwen.' Very pretty that."

"Things would work very much better, Miss Art-Teacher Brangwen," said Gerald.

"What things, Mr Colliery-Manager Crich? The relation between you and me, *par exemple*?"

"Yes, for example," cried the Italian. "That which is between men and women—!"

"That is non-social," said Birkin, sarcastically.

"Exactly," said Gerald. "Between me and a woman, the social question does not enter. It is my own affair."

"A ten-pound note on it," said Birkin.

"You don't admit that a woman is a social being?" asked Ursula of Gerald.

"She is both," said Gerald. "She is a social being, as far as society is concerned. But for her own private self, she is a free agent, it is her own affair, what she does."

"But won't it be rather difficult to arrange the two halves?" asked Ursula.

"Oh no," replied Gerald. "They arrange themselves naturally—we see it now, everywhere."

"Don't you laugh so pleasantly till you're out of the wood," said Birkin.

Gerald knitted his brows in momentary irritation.

"Was I laughing?" he said.

"*If*," said Hermione at last, "we could only realise, that in the *spirit* we are all one, all equal in the spirit, all brothers there—the rest wouldn't matter, there would be no more of this carping and envy and this struggle for power, which destroys, only destroys."

This speech was received in silence, and almost immediately the party rose from table. But when the others had gone, Birkin turned round in bitter declamation, saying:

"It is just the opposite, just the contrary, Hermione. We are all different and unequal in spirit—it is only the *social* differences that are based on accidental material conditions. We are all abstractly or mathematically equal, if you like. Every man has hunger and thirst, two eyes, one nose and two legs. We're all the same in point of number. But spiritually, there is pure difference and neither equality nor inequality counts. It is upon these two bits of knowledge that you must found a state. Your democracy is an absolute lie—your brotherhood of man is a pure falsity, if you apply it further than the mathematical abstraction. We all drank milk first, we all eat bread and meat, we all want to ride in motor-cars—therein lies the beginning and the end of the brotherhood of man. But no equality.

"But I, myself, who am myself, what have I to do with equality—with any other man or woman? In the spirit, I am as separate as one star is from another, as different in quality and quantity. Establish a state on *that*. One man isn't any better than another, not because they are equal, but because they are intrinsically *other*, that there is no term of comparison. The minute you begin to compare, one man is seen to be far better than another, all the inequality you can imagine, is there by nature.

"I want every man to have his share in the world's goods, so that I am rid of his importunity, so that I can tell him: 'Now you've got what you want—you've got your fair share of the world's gear. Now, you one-mouthed fool, mind yourself and don't obstruct me.'"

Hermione was looking at him with leering eyes, along her cheeks. He could feel violent waves of hatred and loathing of all he said, coming out of her. It was dynamic hatred and loathing, coming strong and black out of the unconsciousness. She heard his words in her unconscious self, *consciously* she was as if deafened, she paid no heed to them.

"It *sounds* like megalomania, Rupert," said Gerald, genially.

Hermione gave a queer, grunting sound. Birkin stood back.

"Yes, let it," he said suddenly, the whole tone gone out of his voice, that had been so insistent, bearing everybody down. And he went away.

But he felt, later, a little compunction. He had been violent, cruel with poor Hermione. He wanted to recompense her, to make it up. He had hurt her, he had been vindictive. He wanted to be on good terms with her again.

He went into her boudoir, a remote and very cushiony place. She was sitting at her table writing letters. She lifted her face abstractedly when he entered, watched him go to the sofa, and sit down. Then she looked down at her paper again.

He took a large volume, which he had been reading before, and became minutely attentive to his author. His back was towards Hermione. She could not go on with her writing. Her whole mind was a chaos, darkness breaking in upon it, and herself struggling to gain control with her will, as a swimmer struggles with the swirling water. But in spite of her efforts she was borne down, darkness seemed to break over her, she felt as if her heart was bursting. The terrible tension grew stronger and stronger, it was most fearful agony, like being walled up.

And then she realised that his presence was the wall, his presence was destroying her. Unless she could break out, she must die most fearfully, walled up in horror. And he was the wall. She must break down the wall—she must break him down before her, the awful obstruction of him who obstructed her life to the last. It must be done, or she must perish most horribly.

Terrible shocks ran over her body, like shocks of electricity, as if many volts of electricity suddenly struck her down. She was aware of him sitting silently there, an unthinkable evil obstruction. Only this blotted out her mind, pressed out her very breathing, his silent, stooping back, the back of his head.

A terrible voluptuous thrill ran down her arms—she was going to know her voluptuous consummation. Her arms quivered and were strong, immeasurably and irresistibly strong. What delight, what delight in

strength, what delirium of pleasure! She was going to have her consummation of voluptuous ecstasy at last. It was coming! In utmost terror and
agony, she knew it was upon her now, in extremity of bliss. Her hand
closed on a blue, beautiful ball of lapis lazuli that stood on her desk for a
paper-weight. She rolled it round in her hand as she rose silently. Her
heart was a pure flame in her breast, she was purely unconscious in ecstasy.
She moved towards him and stood behind him for a moment in ecstasy.
He, closed within the spell, remained motionless and unconscious.

Then swiftly, in a flame that drenched down her body like fluid
lightning, and gave her a perfect, unutterable consummation, unutterable
satisfaction, she brought down the ball of jewel stone with all her force,
crash on his head. But her fingers were in the way, and deadened the blow.
Nevertheless down went his head on the table on which his book lay, the
stone slid aside and over his ear, it was one convulsion of pure bliss for her,
lit up by the crushed pain of her fingers. But it was not somehow complete.
She lifted her arm high to aim once more, straight down on the head that
lay dazed on the table. She must smash it, it must be smashed before her
ecstasy was consummated, fulfilled for ever. A thousand lives, a thousand
deaths mattered nothing now, only the fulfilment of this perfect ecstasy.

She was not swift, she could only move slowly. A strong spirit in him
woke him and made him lift his face and twist to look at her. Her arm was
raised, the hand clasping the ball of lapis lazuli. It was her left hand, he
realised again with horror that she was left-handed. Hurriedly, with a
burrowing motion, he covered his head under the thick volume of
Thucydides, and the blow came down, almost breaking his neck, and
shattering his heart.

He was shattered, but he was not afraid. Twisting round to face her, he
pushed the table over and got away from her. He was like a flask that is
smashed to atoms, he seemed to himself that he was all fragments,
smashed to bits. Yet his movements were perfectly coherent and clear, his
soul was entire and unsurprised.

"No you don't, Hermione," he said in a low voice. "I don't let you."

He saw her standing tall and livid and attentive, the stone clenched tense
in her hand.

"Stand away and let me go," he said, drawing near to her.

As if pressed back by some hand, she stood away, watching him all the
time without changing, like a neutralised angel confronting him.

"It is no good," he said, when he had gone past her. "It isn't I who will
die. You hear?"

He kept his face to her as he went out, lest she should strike again. While he was on his guard, she dared not move. And he was on his guard, she was powerless. So he had gone, and left her standing.

She remained perfectly rigid, standing as she was for a long time. Then she staggered to the couch and lay down, and went heavily to sleep. When she awoke, she remembered what she had done, but it seemed to her, she had only hit him, as any woman might do, because he tortured her. She was perfectly right. She knew that, spiritually, she was right. In her own infallible purity, she had done what must be done. She was right, she was pure. A drugged, almost sinister religious expression became permanent on her face.

Birkin, barely conscious, and yet perfectly direct in his motion, went out of the house and straight across the park, to the open country, to the hills. The brilliant day had become overcast, spots of rain were falling. He wandered on to a wild valley-side, where were thickets of hazel, many flowers, tufts of heather, and little clumps of young fir-trees, budding with soft paws. It was rather wet everywhere, there was a stream running down at the bottom of the valley, which was gloomy, or seemed gloomy. He was aware that he could not regain his consciousness, that he was moving in a sort of darkness.

Yet he wanted something. He was happy in the wet hill-side, that was overgrown and obscure with bushes and flowers. He wanted to touch them all, to saturate himself with the touch of them all. He took off his clothes, and sat down naked among the primroses, moving his feet softly among the primroses, his legs, his knees, his arms right up to the arm-pits, then lying down and letting them touch his belly, his breasts. It was such a fine, cool, subtle touch all over him, he seemed to saturate himself with their contact.

But they were too soft. He went through the long grass to a clump of young fir-trees, that were no higher than a man. The soft sharp boughs beat upon him, as he moved in keen pangs against them, threw little cold showers of drops on his belly, and beat his loins with their clusters of soft-sharp needles. There was a thistle which pricked him vividly, but not too much, because all his movements were too discriminate and soft. To lie down and roll in the sticky, cool young hyacinths, to lie on one's belly and cover one's back with handfuls of fine wet grass, soft as a breath, soft and more delicate and more beautiful than the touch of any woman; and then to sting one's thigh against the living dark bristles of the fir-boughs; and then to feel the light whip of the hazel on one's shoulders, stinging, and then to clasp the silvery birch-trunk against one's breast, its smoothness, its hardness, its vital knots and ridges—this was good, this was all very good, very satisfying. Nothing else would do, nothing else would satisfy, except this coolness and subtlety of vegetation travelling into one's blood. How fortunate he was, that there was this lovely, subtle, responsive vegetation, waiting for him, as he waited for it; how fulfilled he was, how happy!

As he dried himself a little with his handkerchief, he thought about Hermione and the blow. He could feel a pain on the side of his head. But after all, what did it matter? What did Hermione matter, what did people matter altogether? There was this perfect cool loneliness, so lovely and fresh and unexplored. Really, what a mistake he had made, thinking he wanted people, thinking he wanted a woman. He did not want a woman— not in the least. The leaves and the primroses and the trees, they were really lovely and cool and desirable, they really came into the blood and were added on to him. He was enrichened now immeasurably, and so glad.

It was quite right of Hermione to want to kill him. What had he to do with her? Why should he pretend to have anything to do with human beings at all? Here was his world, he wanted nobody and nothing but the lovely, subtle, responsive vegetation, and himself, his own living self.

It was necessary to go back into the world. That was true. But that did not matter, so one knew where one belonged. He knew now where he belonged. He knew where to plant himself, his seed:—along with the trees, in the folds of the delicious fresh growing leaves. This was his place, his marriage place. The world was extraneous.

He climbed out of the valley, wondering if he were mad. But if so, he preferred his own madness, to the regular sanity. He rejoiced in his own madness, he was free. He did not want that old sanity of the world, which was become so repulsive. He rejoiced in the new-found world of his madness. It was so fresh and delicate and so satisfying.

As for the certain grief he felt at the same time, in his soul, that was only the remains of an old ethic, that bade a human-being adhere to humanity. But he was weary of the old ethic, of the human being, and of humanity. He loved now the soft, delicate vegetation, that was so cool and perfect. He would overlook the old grief, he would put away the old ethic, he would be free in his new state.

He was aware of the pain in his head becoming more and more difficult every minute. He was walking now along the road to the nearest station. It was raining and he had no hat. But then plenty of cranks went out nowadays without hats, in the rain.

He wondered again how much of his heaviness of heart, a certain depression, was due to fear, fear lest anybody should have seen him naked lying with the vegetation. What a dread he had of mankind, of other people! It amounted almost to horror, to a sort of dream terror—his horror

of being observed by some other people. If he were on an island, like
Alexander Selkirk, with only the creatures and the trees, he would be free
and glad, there would be none of this heaviness, this misgiving. He could
love the vegetation and be quite happy and unquestioned, by himself.

He had better send a note to Hermione: she might trouble about him,
and he did not want the onus of this. So at the station, he wrote saying:

"I will go on to town—I don't want to come back to Breadalby for the
present. But it is quite all right—I don't want you to mind having biffed me,
in the least. Tell the others it is just one of my moods. You were quite right,
to biff me—because I know you wanted to. So there's the end of it."

In the train, however, he felt ill. Every motion was insufferable pain, and
he was sick. He dragged himself from the station into a cab, feeling his way
step by step, like a blind man, and held up only by a dim will.

For a week or two he was ill, but he did not let Hermione know, and she
thought he was sulking, there was a complete estrangement between them.
She became rapt, abstracted in her conviction of exclusive righteousness.
She lived in and by her own self-esteem, conviction of her own rightness of
spirit.

Chapter IX

Coal-Dust

Going home from school in the afternoon, the Brangwen girls descended the hill between the picturesque cottages of Willey Green till they came to the railway crossing. There they found the gate shut, because the colliery train was rumbling nearer. They could hear the small locomotive panting hoarsely as it advanced with caution between the embankments. The one-legged man in the little signal-hut by the road stared out from his obscurity like a crab from a snail-shell.

Whilst the two girls waited, Gerald Crich trotted up on a red Arab mare. He rode well and softly, pleased with the delicate quivering of the creature between his knees. And he was very picturesque, at least in Gudrun's eyes, sitting soft and close on the slender red mare, whose long tail flowed on the air. He saluted the two girls, and drew up at the crossing to wait for the gate, looking down the railway for the approaching train. In spite of her ironic smile at his picturesqueness, Gudrun liked to look at him. He was well-set and easy, his face with its warm tan showed up his whitish, coarse moustache, and his blue eyes were full of sharp light, as he watched the distance.

The locomotive chuffed slowly between the banks, hidden. The mare did not like it. She began to wince away, as if hurt by the unknown noise. But Gerald pulled her back and held her head to the gate. The sharp blasts of the chuffing engine broke with more and more force on her. The repeated sharp blows of unknown, terrifying noise struck through her till she was rocking with terror. She recoiled like a spring let go. But a glistening, half-smiling look came into Gerald's face. He brought her back again, inevitably.

The noise was released, the little locomotive with her clanking steel connecting-rod emerged on the high-road, clanking sharply. The mare rebounded like a drop of water from hot iron. Ursula and Gudrun pressed back into the hedge, in fear. But Gerald was heavy on the mare, and forced her back. It seemed as if he sank into her magnetically, and could thrust her back, against herself.

"The fool," cried Ursula, loudly. "Why doesn't he ride away till it's gone by."

Gudrun was looking at him with black-dilated, spell-bound eyes. But he sat glistening and obstinate, forcing the wheeling mare, which spun and swerved like a wind, and yet could not get out of the grasp of his will, nor escape from the mad clamour of terror that resounded through her, as the trucks thumped slowly, heavily, horrifying, one after the other, one pursuing the other, over the rails of the crossing.

The locomotive, as if wanting to see what could be done, put on the brakes, and back came the trucks rebounding on the iron buffers, striking like horrible cymbals, clashing nearer and nearer in frightful strident concussions. The mare opened her mouth and rose slowly, as if lifted up on a wind of terror. Then suddenly her fore feet struck out, as she convulsed herself utterly away from the horror. Back she went, and the two girls clung to each other, feeling she must fall backwards on top of him. But he leaned forward, his face shining with fixed amusement, and at last he brought her down, sank her down, and was bearing her back to the mark. But as strong as the pressure of his compulsion was the repulsion of her utter terror, throwing her back away from the railway, so that she spun round and round, on two legs, as if she were in the centre of some whirlwind. It made Gudrun faint with poignant dizziness, which seemed to penetrate to her heart.

"No—! No—! Let her go! Let her go, you fool, you *fool*——!" cried Ursula at the top of her voice, completely outside herself. And Gudrun hated her bitterly for being outside herself. It was unendurable that Ursula's voice was so powerful and naked.

A sharpened look came on Gerald's face. He bit himself down on the mare like a keen edge biting home, and *forced* her round. She roared as she breathed, her nostrils were two wide, hot holes, her mouth was apart, her eyes frenzied. It was a repulsive sight. But he held on her unrelaxed, with an almost mechanical relentlessness, keen as a sword pressing in to her. Both man and horse were sweating with violence. Yet he seemed calm as a ray of cold sunshine.

Meanwhile the eternal trucks were rumbling on, very slowly, threading one after the other, one after the other, like a disgusting dream that has no end. The connecting chains were grinding and squeaking as the tension varied, the mare pawed and struck away mechanically now, her terror fulfilled in her, for now the man encompassed her; her paws were blind and pathetic as she beat the air, the man closed round her, and brought her down, almost as if she were part of his own physique.

"And she's bleeding!—She's bleeding!" cried Ursula, frantic with opposition and hatred of Gerald. She alone understood him perfectly, in pure opposition.

Gudrun looked and saw the trickles of blood on the sides of the mare, and she turned white. And then on the very wound the bright spurs came down, pressing relentlessly. The world reeled and passed into nothingness for Gudrun, she could not know any more.

When she recovered, her soul was calm and cold, without feeling. The trucks were still rumbling by, the man and the mare were still fighting. But she herself was cold and separate, she had no more feeling for them. She was quite hard and cold and indifferent.

They could see the top of the hooded guard's-van approaching, the sound of the trucks was diminishing, there was hope of relief from the intolerable noise. The heavy panting of the half-stunned mare sounded automatically, the man seemed to be relaxing confidently, his will bright and unstained.

The guard's-van came up, and passed slowly, the guard staring out in his transition on the spectacle in the road. And, through the man in the closed wagon Gudrun could see the whole scene spectacularly, isolated and momentary, like a vision isolated in eternity.

Lovely, grateful silence seemed to trail behind the receding train. How sweet the silence is! Ursula looked with hatred on the buffers of the diminishing wagon. The gate-keeper stood ready at the door of his hut, to proceed to open the gate. But Gudrun sprang suddenly forward, in front of the struggling horse, threw off the latch and flung the gates asunder, throwing one half to the keeper, and running with the other half, forwards. Gerald suddenly let go the horse and leaped forwards, almost on to Gudrun. She was not afraid. As he jerked aside the mare's head, Gudrun cried, in a strange, high voice, like a gull, or like a witch screaming out from the side of the road:

"I should think you're proud."

The words were distinct and formed. The man, twisting aside on his dancing horse, looked at her in some surprise, some wondering interest. Then the mare's hoofs had danced three times on the drum-like sleepers of the crossing, and man and horse were bounding springily, unequally up the road.

The two girls watched them go. The gate-keeper hobbled thudding over the logs of the crossing, with his wooden leg. He had fastened the gate. Then he also turned, and called to the girls:

"A masterful young jockey, that;—'ll have his own road, if ever anybody would."

"Yes," cried Ursula, in her hot, overbearing voice. "Why couldn't he take the horse away, till the trucks had gone by? He's a fool, and a bully.

Does he think it's manly, to torture a horse? It's a living thing, why should he bully it and torture it?"

There was a pause, then the gate-keeper shook his head, and replied:

"Yes, it's as nice a little mare as you could set eyes on—beautiful little thing, beautiful.—Now you wouldn't see his father treat any animal like that—not you. They're as different as they welly can be, Gerald Crich and his father—two different men, different made."

There was a pause.

"But why does he do it?" cried Ursula, "why does he? Does he think he's grand, when he's bullied a sensitive creature, ten times as sensitive as himself?"

Again there was the cautious pause. Then again the man shook his head, as if he would say nothing, but would think the more.

"I expect he's got to train the mare to stand to anything," he replied. "A pure-bred Harab—not the sort of breed as is used to round here—different sort from our sort altogether. They say as he got her from Constantinople."

"He would!" said Ursula. "He'd better have left her to the Turks, I'm sure they would have had more decency towards her."

The man went in to drink his can of tea, the girls went on down the lane, that was deep in soft black dust. Gudrun was as if numbed in her mind by the sense of indomitable soft weight of the man, bearing down into the living body of the horse: the strong, indomitable thighs of the blond man clenching the palpitating body of the mare into pure control; a sort of soft white magnetic domination from the loins and thighs and calves, enclosing and encompassing the mare heavily into unutterable subordination, soft blood-subordination, terrible.

On the left, as the girls walked silently, the coal-mine lifted its great mounds and its patterned head-stocks, the black railway with the trucks at rest looked like a harbour just below, a large bay of railroad with anchored wagons.

Near the second level-crossing, that went over many bright rails, was a farm belonging to the collieries, and a great round globe of iron, a disused boiler, huge and rusty and perfectly round, stood silently in a paddock by the road. The hens were pecking round it, some chickens were balanced on the drinking trough, wagtails flew away in among trucks, from the water.

On the other side of the wide crossing, by the road-side, was a heap of pale-grey stones for mending the roads, and a cart standing, and a middle-aged man with whiskers round his face was leaning on his shovel, talking to a young man in gaiters, who stood by the horse's head. Both men were facing the crossing.

They saw the two girls appear, small, brilliant figures in the near distance, in the strong light of the late afternoon. Both wore light, gay summer dresses, Ursula had an orange-coloured knitted coat, Gudrun a pale yellow, Ursula wore canary yellow stockings, Gudrun bright rose, the figures of the two women seemed to glitter in progress over the wide bay of the railway crossing, white and orange and yellow and rose glittering in motion across a hot world silted with coal-dust.

The two men stood quite still in the heat, watching. The elder was a short, hard-faced, energetic man of middle age, the younger a laborer of twenty-three or so. They stood in silence watching the advance of the sisters. They watched whilst the girls drew near, and whilst they passed, and whilst they receded down the dusty road, that had dwellings on one side, and dusty young corn on the other.

Then the elder man, with the whiskers round his face, said in a prurient manner to the young man:

"What price that, eh? She'll do, won't she?"

"Which?" asked the young man, eagerly, with a laugh.

"Her with the red stockings.—What d' you say?—I'd give my week's wages for five minutes;—what!—just for five minutes."

Again the younger man laughed.

"Your Missis 'ud have summat to say to you," he replied.

Gudrun had turned round and looked at the two men. They were to her sinister creatures, standing watching after her, by the heap of pale grey slag. She loathed the man with whiskers round his face.

"You're first class, you are," the man said to her, and to the distance.

"Do you think it would be worth a week's wages?" said the younger man, musing.

"Do I? I'd put 'em bloody-well down this second—"

The younger man looked after Gudrun and Ursula objectively, as if he wished to calculate what there might be, that was worth his week's wages. He shook his head with fatal misgiving.

"No," he said. "It's not worth that to me."

"Isn't?" said the old man. "By God, if it isn't to me!"

And he went on shovelling his stones.

The girls descended between the houses with slate roofs and blackish brick walls. The heavy gold glamour of approaching sunset lay over all the colliery district, and the ugliness overlaid with beauty was like a narcotic to the senses. On the roads silted with black dust, the rich light fell more warmly, more heavily; over all the amorphous squalor a kind of magic was cast, from the glowing close of day.

"It has a foul kind of beauty, this place," said Gudrun, evidently suffering from the fascination. "Can't you feel, in some way, a thick, hot attraction in it? *I* can. And it quite stupefies me."

They were passing between blocks of miners' dwellings. In the back yards of several dwellings, a miner could be seen washing himself in the open on this hot evening, naked down to the loins, his great trousers of moleskin slipping almost away. Miners already cleaned were sitting on their heels, with their backs near the walls, talking and silent in pure physical well-being, tired, and taking physical rest. Their voices sounded out with strong intonation, and the broad dialect was curiously caressing to the blood. It seemed to envelop Gudrun in a laborer's caress, there was in the whole atmosphere a resonance of physical men, a glamorous thickness of labour and maleness surcharged in the air. But it was universal in the district, and therefore unnoticed by the inhabitants.

To Gudrun, however, it was potent and half-repulsive. She could never tell why Beldover was so utterly different from London and the south, why one's whole feelings were different, why one seemed to live in another sphere. Now she realised that this was the world of powerful, underworld men who spent most of their time in the darkness. In their voices she could hear the voluptuous resonance of darkness, the strong, dangerous underworld, mindless, inhuman. They sounded also like strange machines, heavy, oiled. The voluptuousness was like that of machinery, cold and iron.

It was the same every evening when she came home, she seemed to move through a wave of disruptive force, that was given off from the presence of thousands of vigorous, underworld, half-automatised colliers, and which went to the brain and the heart, awaking a fatal desire, and a fatal callousness.

There came over her a nostalgia for the place. She hated it, she knew how utterly cut off it was, how hideous and how sickeningly mindless. Sometimes she beat her wings like a new Daphne, turning not into a tree but a machine. And yet, she was overcome by the nostalgia. She struggled to get more and more into accord with the atmosphere of the place, she craved to get her satisfaction of it.

She felt herself drawn out at evening into the main street of the town, that was uncreated and ugly, and yet surcharged with this same potent atmosphere of intense, dark callousness. There were always miners about. They moved with their strange, distorted dignity, a certain beauty, an unnatural stillness in their bearing, a look of abstraction and half-resignation in their pale, often gaunt faces. They belonged to another world, they had a strange glamour, their voices were full of an intolerable deep resonance, like a machine's burring, a music more maddening than the siren's long ago.

She found herself, with the rest of the common women, drawn out on Friday evenings to the little market. Friday was pay-day for the colliers, and Friday night was market night. Every woman was abroad, every man was out, shopping with his wife, or gathering with his pals. The pavements were dark for miles around with people coming in, the little market-place on the crown of the hill, and the main street of Beldover were black with thickly-crowded men and women.

It was dark, the market-place was hot with kerosene flares, which threw a ruddy light on the grave faces of the purchasing wives, and on the pale abstract faces of the men. The air was full of the sound of criers and of people talking, thick streams of people moved on the pavements towards the solid crowd of the market. The shops were blazing and packed with women, in the streets were men, mostly men, miners of all ages. Money was spent with almost lavish freedom.

The carts that came could not pass through. They had to wait, the driver calling and shouting, till the dense crowd would make way. Everywhere, young fellows from the outlying district were making conversation with the girls, standing in the road and at the corners. The doors of the public-houses were open and full of light, men passed in and out in a continual stream, everywhere men were calling out to one another, or crossing to meet one another, or standing in little gangs and circles, discussing, endlessly discussing. The sense of talk, buzzing, jarring, half-secret, the endless mining and political wrangling, vibrated in the air like discordant machinery. And it was these voices which affected Gudrun almost to swooning. They aroused a strange, nostalgic ache of desire, something almost demoniacal, never to be fulfilled.

Like any other common girl of the district, Gudrun strolled up and down, up and down the length of the brilliant two-hundred paces of the pavement nearest the market-place. She knew it was a vulgar thing to do; her father and mother could not bear it; but the nostalgia came over her, she must be among the people. Sometimes she sat among the louts in the cinema: rakish-looking, unattractive louts they were. Yet she must be among them.

And, like any other common lass, she found her 'boy'. It was an electrician, one of the electricians introduced according to Gerald's new scheme. He was an earnest, clever man, a scientist with a passion for sociology. He lived alone in a cottage, in lodgings, in Willey Green. He was a gentleman, and sufficiently well-to-do. His landlady spread the reports about him: he *would* have a large wooden tub in his bedroom, and every time he came in from work, he *would* have pails and pails of water brought up, to bath in, then he put on clean shirt and underclothing *every* day, and clean silk socks; fastidious and exacting he was in these respects, but in every other way, most ordinary and unassuming.

Gudrun knew all these things. The Brangwens' house was one to which the gossip came naturally and inevitably. Palmer was in the first place a friend of Ursula's. But in his pale, elegant, serious face there showed the same nostalgia that Gudrun felt. He too must walk up and down the street on Friday evening. So he walked with Gudrun, and a friendship was struck up between them. But he was not in love with Gudrun; he *really* wanted Ursula, but for some strange reason, nothing could happen between her and him. He liked to have Gudrun about, as a fellow mind—but that was all. And she had no real feeling for him. He was a scientist, he had to have a woman to back him. But he was really impersonal, he had the fineness of an elegant piece of machinery. He was too cold, too destructive to care really for women, too great an egoist. He was polarised by the men. Individually he detested and despised them. In the mass they fascinated him, as machinery fascinated him. They were a new sort of machinery to him—but incalculable, incalculable.

So Gudrun strolled the streets with Palmer, or went to the cinema with him. And his long, pale, rather elegant face flickered as he made his sarcastic remarks. There they were, the two of them: two elegants, in one sense: in the other sense, two units, absolutely adhering to the people, teeming with the distorted colliers. The same secret seemed to be working in the souls of all alike, Gudrun, Palmer, the rakish young bloods, the gaunt, middle-aged men. All had a secret sense of power, and of inexpressible destructiveness, and of fatal half-heartedness, a sort of rottenness in the will.

Sometimes Gudrun would start aside, see it all, see how she was sinking in. And then she was filled with a fury of contempt and anger. She felt she was sinking into one mass with the rest—all so close and intermingled and breathless. It was horrible. She stifled. She prepared for flight, feverishly she flew to her work. But soon she let go. She started off into the country—the darkish, glamorous country. The spell was beginning to work again.

Chapter X

Sketch-Book

One morning the sisters were sketching by the side of Willey Water, at the remote end of the lake. Gudrun had waded out to a gravelly shoal, and was seated like a Buddhist, staring fixedly at the water-plants that rose succulent from the mud of the low shores. What she could see was mud, soft, oozy, watery mud, and from its festering chill, water-plants rose up, thick and cool and fleshy, very straight and turgid, thrusting out their leaves at right angles, and having dark lurid colours, dark green and blotches of black-purple and bronze. But she could feel their turgid fleshy structure as in a sensuous vision, she *knew* how they rose out of the mud, she *knew* how they thrust out from themselves, how they stood stiff and succulent against the air.

Ursula was watching the butterflies, of which there were dozens near the water, little blue ones suddenly snapping out of nothingness into a jewel-life, a large black-and-red one standing upon a flower and breathing with his soft wings, intoxicatingly, breathing pure, ethereal sunshine; two white ones wrestling in the low air; there was a halo round them; ah, when they came tumbling nearer they were orange-tips, and it was the orange that had made the halo. Ursula rose and drifted away, unconscious like the butterflies.

Gudrun, absorbed in a stupor of apprehension of surging water-plants, sat crouched on the shoal, drawing, not looking up for a long time, and then staring unconsciously, absorbedly at the rigid, naked, succulent stems. Her feet were bare, her hat lay on the bank opposite.

She started out of her trance, hearing the knocking of oars. She looked round. There was a boat with a gaudy Japanese parasol, and a man in white, rowing. The woman was Hermione, and the man was Gerald. She knew it instantly. And instantly she perished in the keen *frisson* of anticipation, an electric vibration in her veins, intense, much more intense than that which was always humming low in the atmosphere of Beldover.

Gerald was her escape from the heavy slough of the pale, underworld, automatic colliers—he started out of the mud. He was master. She saw his back, the movement of his white loins. But not that—it was the whiteness he seemed to enclose as he bent forwards, rowing. He seemed to stoop to something. His glistening, whitish hair seemed like the electricity of the sky.

"There's Gudrun," came Hermione's voice floating distinct over the water. "We will go and speak to her. Do you mind?"

Gerald looked round and saw the girl standing by the water's edge, looking at him. He pulled the boat towards her, magnetically, without thinking of her. In his world, his conscious world, she was still nobody. He knew that Hermione had a curious pleasure in treading down all the social differences, at least apparently, and he left it to her.

"How do you do, Gudrun?" sang Hermione, using the Christian name in the fashionable manner. "What are you doing?"

"How do you do, Hermione? I *was* sketching."

"Were you." The boat drifted nearer, till the keel ground on the bank. "May we see? I should like to *so* much."

It was no use resisting Hermione's deliberate intention.

"Well—" said Gudrun reluctantly, for she always hated to have her unfinished work exposed—"there's nothing in the least interesting."

"Isn't there. But let me see, will you?"

Gudrun reached out the sketch-book, Gerald stretched from the boat to take it. And as he did so, he remembered Gudrun's last words to him, and her face lifted up to him as he sat on the swerving horse. An intensification of pride went over his nerves, because he felt, in some way she was compelled by him. The exchange of feeling between them was strong and apart from their consciousness.

And as if in a spell, Gudrun was aware of his body, stretching and surging like the marsh-fire, stretching towards her, his hand coming straight forward like a stem. Her voluptuous, acute apprehension of him made the blood faint in her veins, her mind went dim and unconscious. And he rocked on the water perfectly, like the rocking of phosphorescence. He looked round at the boat. It was drifting off a little. He lifted the oar to bring it back. And the exquisite pleasure of slowly arresting the boat, in the heavy-soft water, was complete as a swoon.

"*That's* what you have done," said Hermione, looking searchingly at the plants on the shore, and comparing with Gudrun's drawing. Gudrun looked round in the direction of Hermione's long, pointing finger. "That is it, isn't it?" repeated Hermione, needing confirmation.

"Yes," said Gudrun automatically, taking no real heed.

"Let me look," said Gerald, reaching forward for the book. But Hermione ignored him, he must not presume, before she had finished. But he, his will as unthwarted and as unflinching as hers, stretched forward till he touched the book. A little shock, a storm of revulsion against him, shook

Hermione unconsciously. She released the book when he had not properly got it, and it tumbled against the side of the boat and bounced into the water.

"There!" sang Hermione, with a strange ring of malevolent victory. "I'm so sorry, so awfully sorry. Can't you get it, Gerald?"

This last was said in a note of anxious sneering that made Gerald's veins tingle with fine hate for her. He leaned far out of the boat, reaching down into the water. He could feel his position was ridiculous, his loins exposed behind him.

"It is of no importance," came the strong, clanging voice of Gudrun. She seemed to touch him. But he reached further, the boat swayed violently. Hermione, however, remained unperturbed. He grasped the book, under the water, and brought it up, dripping.

"I'm so dreadfully sorry—so dreadfully sorry," repeated Hermione. "I'm afraid it was all my fault."

"It's of no importance—really, I assure you—it doesn't matter in the least," said Gudrun loudly, with emphasis, her face flushed scarlet. And she held out her hand impatiently for the wet book, to have done with the scene. Gerald gave it to her. He was not quite himself.

"I'm so dreadfully sorry," repeated Hermione, till both Gerald and Gudrun were exasperated. "Is there nothing that can be done?"

"In what way?" asked Gudrun, with cool irony.

"Can't we save the drawings?"

There was a moment's pause, wherein Gudrun made evident all her refutation of Hermione's persistence.

"I assure you," said Gudrun, with cutting distinctness, "the drawings are quite as good as ever they were, for my purpose. I want them only for reference."

"But can't I give you a new book? I wish you'd let me do that. I feel so truly sorry. I feel it was all my fault."

"As far as I saw," said Gudrun, "it wasn't your fault at all. If there was any *fault*, it was Mr Crich's. But the whole thing is *entirely* trivial, and it really is ridiculous to take any notice of it."

Gerald watched Gudrun closely, whilst she repulsed Hermione. There was a body of cold power in her. He watched her with an insight that amounted to clairvoyance. He saw her a dangerous, hostile spirit, that could stand undiminished and unabated. It was so finished, and of such perfect gesture, moreover.

"I'm awfully glad if it doesn't matter," he said; "if there's no real harm done."

She looked back at him, with her fine blue eyes, and signalled full into his spirit, as she said, her voice ringing with intimacy almost caressive now it was addressed to him:

"Of course it doesn't matter in the *least*."

The bond was established between them, in that look, in her tone. In her tone, she made the understanding clear—they were of the same kind, he and she, a sort of diabolic freemasonry subsisted between them. Henceforward, she knew, she had her power over him. Wherever they met, they would be secretly associated. And he would be helpless in the association with her. Her soul exulted.

"Goodbye! I'm so glad you forgive me. Gooood-byyye!" Hermione sang her farewell, and waved her hand. Gerald automatically took the oar and pushed off. But he was looking all the time, with a glimmering, subtly-smiling admiration in his eyes, at Gudrun, who stood on the shoal shaking the wet book in her hand. She turned away and ignored the receding boat. But Gerald looked back as he rowed, beholding her, forgetting what he was doing.

"Aren't we going too much to the left?" sang Hermione, as she sat ignored under her coloured parasol.

Gerald looked round without replying, the oars balanced and glancing in the sun.

"I think it's all right," he said good-humouredly, beginning to row again without thinking of what he was doing. And Hermione disliked him extremely for his good-humoured obliviousness, she was nullified, she could not regain ascendancy.

Chapter XI

An Island

Meanwhile Ursula had wandered on from Willey Water along the course of the bright little stream. The afternoon was full of larks' singing. On the bright hill-sides was a subdued smoulder of gorse. A few forget-me-nots flowered by the water. There was a rousedness and a glancing everywhere.

She strayed absorbedly on, over the brooks. She wanted to go to the mill-pond above. The big mill-house was deserted, save for a laborer and his wife, who lived in the kitchen. So she passed through the empty farm-yard and through the wilderness of a garden, and mounted the bank by the sluice. When she got to the top, to see the old, velvety surface of the pond before her, she noticed a man on the bank, tinkering with a punt. It was Birkin sawing and hammering away.

She stood at the head of the sluice, looking at him. He was unaware of anybody's presence. He looked very busy, like a wild animal active and intent. She felt she ought to go away, he would not want her. He seemed to be so much occupied. But she did not want to go away. Therefore she moved along the bank till he would look up.

Which he soon did. The moment he saw her, he dropped his tools and came forward, saying:

"How do you do! I'm making the punt water-tight. Tell me if you think it is right."

She went along with him.

"You are your father's daughter, so you can tell me if it will do," he said.

She bent to look at the patched punt.

"I am sure I am my father's daughter," she said, fearful of having to judge. "But I don't know anything about carpentry. It *looks* right, don't you think?"

"Yes, I think. I hope it won't let me to the bottom, that's all. Though even so, it isn't a great matter, I should come up again. Help me to get it into the water, will you?"

With combined efforts they turned over the heavy punt and set it afloat.

"Now," he said, "I'll try it, and you can watch what happens. Then if it carries I'll take you over to the island."

"Do," she cried, watching anxiously.

The pond was large, and had that perfect stillness and the dark lustre of very deep water. There were two small islands overgrown with bushes and a few trees, towards the middle. Birkin pushed himself off, and veered clumsily in the pond. Luckily the punt drifted so that he could catch hold of a willow bough, and pull in to the island.

"Rather overgrown," he said, looking into the interior, "but very nice. I'll come and fetch you. The boat leaks a little."

In a moment he was with her again, and she stepped into the wet punt.

"It'll float us all right," he said, and manoeuvred again to the island.

They landed under a willow tree. She shrank from the little jungle of rank plants before her, evil-smelling fig-wort and hemlock. But he explored into it.

"I shall mow this down," he said, "and then it will be romantic—like *Paul et Virginie*."

"Yes, one could have lovely Watteau picnics here," cried Ursula with enthusiasm.

His face darkened.

"I don't want Watteau picnics here," he said.

"Only your Virginie," she laughed.

"Virginie enough," he smiled wryly. "No, I don't want her either."

Ursula looked at him closely. She had not seen him since Breadalby. He was very thin and hollow, with a ghastly look in his face.

"You have been ill, haven't you?" she asked, rather repulsed.

"Yes." he replied coldly.

They had sat down under the willow tree, and were looking at the pond, from their retreat on the island.

"Has it made you frightened?" she asked.

"What of?" he asked, turning his eyes to look at her. Something in him, inhuman and unmitigated, disturbed her, and shook her out of her ordinary self.

"It *is* frightening to be very ill, isn't it?" she said.

"It isn't pleasant," he said. "Whether one is really afraid of death, or not, I have never decided. In one mood, not a bit, in another, very much."

"But doesn't it make you feel ashamed? I think it makes one so ashamed, to be ill—illness is so terribly humiliating, don't you think?"

He considered for some minutes.

"Maybe," he said. "Though one knows all the time one's life isn't really right, at the source. That's the humiliation. I don't see that the illness counts so much, after that. One is ill because one doesn't live properly—can't. It's the failure to live that makes one ill, and humiliates one."

"But do you fail to live?" she asked, almost jeering.

"Why yes—I don't make much of a success of my days. One seems always to be bumping one's nose against the blank wall ahead."

Ursula laughed. She was frightened, and when she was frightened she always laughed and pretended to be jaunty.

"Your poor nose!" she said, looking at that feature of his face.

"No wonder it's ugly," he replied.

She was silent for some minutes, struggling with her own self-deception. It was an instinct in her, to deceive herself.

"But *I'm* happy—I think life is *awfully* jolly," she said.

"Good," he answered, with a certain cold indifference.

She reached for a bit of paper which had wrapped a small piece of chocolate she had found in her pocket, and began making a boat. He watched her without heeding her. There was something strangely pathetic and tender in her moving, unconscious finger-tips, that were agitated and hurt, really.

"I *do* enjoy things—don't you?" she asked.

"Oh yes! But it infuriates me that I can't get right, at the really growing part of me. I feel all tangled and messed up, and I *can't* get straight anyhow. I don't know what really to *do*. One must do something somewhere."

"Why should you always be *doing*?" she retorted. "It is so plebeian. I think it is much better to be really patrician, and to do nothing but just be oneself, like a walking flower."

"I quite agree," he said, "if one has burst into blossom. But I can't get my flower into blossom anyhow. Either it is blighted in the bud, or has got the smother-fly, or it isn't nourished. Curse it, it isn't even a bud. It is a contravened knot."

Again she laughed. He was so very fretful and exasperated. But she was anxious and puzzled. How was one to get out, anyhow. There must be a way out somewhere.

There was a silence, wherein she wanted to cry. She reached for another bit of chocolate paper, and began to fold another boat.

"And why is it," she asked at length, "that there is no flowering, no dignity of human life now?"

"The whole idea is dead. Humanity itself is dry-rotten really. There are myriads of human beings hanging on the bush—and they look very nice and rosy, your healthy young men and women. But they are apples of Sodom, as a matter of fact, Dead Sea Fruit, gall-apples. It isn't true that they have any significance—their insides are full of bitter, corrupt ash."

"But there *are* good people," protested Ursula.

"Good enough for the life of today. But mankind is a dead tree, covered with fine brilliant galls of people."

Ursula could not help stiffening herself against this, it was too picturesque and final. But neither could she help making him go on.

"And if it is so, *why* is it?" she asked, hostile. They were rousing each other to a fine passion of opposition.

"Why? Why are people all balls of bitter dust? Because they won't fall off the tree when they're ripe. They hang on to their old positions when the position is overpast, till they become infested with little worms and dry-rot."

There was a long pause. His voice had become hot and very sarcastic. Ursula was troubled and bewildered, they were both oblivious of everything but their own immersion.

"But even if everybody is wrong—where are *you* right?" she cried. "Where are you any better?"

"I?—I'm not right," he cried back. "At least my only rightness lies in the fact that I know it. I detest what I am, outwardly. I loathe myself as a human being. Humanity is a huge aggregate lie, and a huge lie is less than a small truth. Humanity is less, far less than the individual, because the individual may sometimes be capable of truth, and humanity is a tree of lies.——And they say that love is the greatest thing; they persist in *saying* this, the foul liars, and just look at what they do! Look at all the millions of people who repeat every minute that love is the greatest, and charity is the greatest— and see what they are doing all the time. By their works ye shall know them, for dirty liars and cowards, who daren't stand by their own actions, much less by their own words."

"But," said Ursula sadly, "that doesn't alter the fact that love is the greatest, does it? What they *do* doesn't alter the truth of what they say, does it?"

"Completely. If what they say *were* true, then they couldn't help fulfilling it. But they maintain a lie, and so they run amok at last. It's a lie to say that love is the greatest. You might as well say that hate is the greatest, since the opposite of everything balances.—What people want is hate— hate and nothing but hate. And in the name of righteousness and love, they get it. They distil themselves into nitro-glycerine, all the lot of them, out of very love.—It's the lie that kills. If we want hate, let us have it—death, murder, torture, violent destruction—let us have it: but not in the name of love.—But I abhor humanity, I wish it was swept away. It could go, and there would be no *absolute* loss, if every human being perished tomorrow. The reality would be untouched. Nay, it would be better. The real tree of life would then be rid of the most ghastly heavy crop of Dead Sea Fruit, the intolerable burden of myriad simulacra of people, an infinite weight of mortal lies."

"So you'd like everybody in the world destroyed?" said Ursula.

"I should indeed."

"And the world empty of people."

"Yes truly. You yourself, don't you find it a beautiful clean thought, a world empty of people, just uninterrupted grass, and a hare sitting up?"

The pleasant sincerity of his voice made Ursula pause to consider her own proposition. And really it *was* attractive: a clean, lovely, humanless world. It was the *really* desirable.—Her heart hesitated, and exulted.—But still, she was dissatisfied with *him*.

"But," she objected, "you'd be dead yourself, so what good would it do you?"

"I would die like a shot, to know that the earth would really be cleaned of *all* the people. It is the most beautiful and freeing thought. Then there would *never* be another foul humanity created, for a universal defilement."

"No," said Ursula, "there would be nothing."

"What! Nothing? Just because humanity was wiped out? You flatter yourself. There'd be everything."

"But how, if there were no people?"

"Do you think that creation depends on *man*! It merely doesn't.—There are the trees and the grass and birds. I much prefer to think of the lark rising up in the morning upon a humanless world.—Man is a mistake, he must go.—There is the grass, and hares and adders, and the unseen hosts, actual angels that go about freely when a dirty humanity doesn't interrupt them—and good pure-tissued demons: very nice."

It pleased Ursula, what he said, pleased her very much, as a phantasy. Of course it was only a pleasant fancy. She herself knew too well the actuality of humanity, its hideous actuality. She knew it could not disappear so cleanly and conveniently. It had a long way to go yet, a long and hideous way. Her subtle, feminine, demoniacal soul knew it well.

"If only man was swept off the face of the earth, creation would go on so marvellously, with a new start, non-human. Man is one of the mistakes of creation—like the ichthyosauri.—If only he were gone again, think what lovely things would come out of the liberated days; things straight out of the fire."

"But man will never be gone," she said, with insidious, diabolical knowledge of the horrors of persistence. "The world will go with him."

"Ah no," he answered, "not so. I believe in the proud angels and the demons that are our fore-runners. They will destroy us, because we are not proud enough. The ichthyosauri were not proud: they crawled and floundered as we do.—And besides, look at elder-flowers and bluebells—they are a sign that pure creation takes place—even the butterfly. But humanity never gets beyond the caterpillar stage—it rots in the chrysalis, it never will have wings. It is anti-creation, like monkeys and baboons."

Ursula watched him as he talked. There seemed a certain impatient fury in him, all the while, and at the same time a great amusement in everything, and a final tolerance. And it was this tolerance she mistrusted, not the fury. She saw that, all the while, in spite of himself, he would have to be trying to save the world. And this knowledge, whilst it comforted her heart somewhere with a little self-satisfaction, stability, yet filled her with a certain sharp contempt and hate of him. She wanted him to herself, she hated the Salvator Mundi touch. It was something diffuse and generalised about him, which she could not stand.—He would behave in the same way, say the same things, give himself as completely to anybody who came along, anybody and everybody who liked to appeal to him. It was despicable, a very insidious form of prostitution.

"But," she said, "you believe in individual love, even if you don't believe in loving humanity—?"

"I don't believe in love at all—that is, any more than I believe in hate, or in grief. Love is one of the emotions like all the others—and so it is all right whilst you feel it. But I can't see how it becomes an absolute. It is just part of human relationships, no more. And it is only part of *any* human relationship. And why one should be required *always* to feel it, any more than one always feels sorrow or distinct joy, I cannot conceive. Love isn't a desideratum—it is an emotion you feel or you don't feel, according to circumstance."

"Then why do you care about people at all?" she asked, "if you don't believe in love? Why do you bother about humanity?"

"Why do I? Because I can't get away from it."

"Because you love it," she persisted.

It irritated him.

"If I do love it," he said, "it is my disease."

"But it is a disease you don't want to be cured of," she said, with some cold sneering.

He was silent now, feeling she wanted to insult him.

"And if you don't believe in love, what *do* you believe in?" she asked, mocking. "Simply in the end of the world, and grass?"

He was beginning to feel a fool.

"I believe in the unseen hosts," he said.

"And nothing else?—You believe in nothing visible, except grass and birds?—Your world is a poor show."

"Perhaps it is," he said, cool and superior now he was offended, assuming a certain insufferable aloof superiority, and withdrawing into his distance.

Ursula disliked him. But also she felt she had lost something. She looked at him as he sat crouched on the bank. There was a certain priggish Sunday-school stiffness over him, priggish and detestable. And yet, at the same time, the moulding of him was so quick and attractive, it gave such a great sense of freedom: the moulding of his brows, his chin, his whole physique, something so alive, somewhere, in spite of the look of sickness.

And it was this duality in feeling which he created in her, that made a fine hate of him quicken in her bowels. There was his wonderful, desirable life-rapidity, the rare quality of an utterly desirable man: and there was at the same time this ridiculous, mean effacement into a Salvator Mundi and a Sunday-school teacher, a prig of the stiffest type.

He looked up at her. He saw her face strangely enkindled, as if suffused from within by a powerful sweet fire. His soul was arrested in wonder. She was enkindled in her own living fire. Arrested in wonder and in pure, perfect attraction, he moved towards her. She sat like a strange queen, almost supernatural in her glowing smiling richness.

"The point about love," he said, his consciousness quickly adjusting itself, "is that we hate the word because we have vulgarised it. It ought to be proscribed, tabooed from utterance, for many years, till we get a new, better idea."

There was a beam of understanding between them.

"But it always means the same thing," she said.

"Ah God, no, let it not mean that any more," he cried. "Let the old meanings go."

"But still it is love," she persisted. A strange, wicked yellow light shone at him in her eyes.

He hesitated, baffled, withdrawing.

"No," he said, "it isn't. Spoken like that, never in the world. You've no business to utter the word."

"I must leave it to you, to take it out of the Ark of the Covenant at the right moment," she mocked.

Again they looked at each other. She suddenly sprang up, turned her back to him, and walked away. He too rose slowly and went to the water's edge, where, crouching he began to amuse himself unconsciously. Picking a daisy he dropped it on the pond, so that the stem was a keel, the flower floated like a little water lily, staring with its open face up to the sky. It turned slowly round, in a slow, slow dervish dance, as it veered away.

He watched it, then dropped another daisy into the water, and after that another, and sat watching them with bright, absolved eyes, crouching near on the bank. Ursula turned to look. A strange feeling possessed her, as if something were taking place. But it was all intangible. And some sort of control was being put on her. She could not know. She could only watch the brilliant little discs of the daisies veering slowly in travel on the dark, lustrous water. The little flotilla was drifting into the light, a company of white specks in the distance.

"Do let us go to the shore, to follow them," she said, afraid of being any longer imprisoned on the island. And they pushed off in the punt.

She was glad to be on the free land again. She went along the bank towards the sluice. The daisies were scattered broadcast on the pond, tiny radiant things, like an exaltation, points of exaltation here and there. Why did they move her so strongly and mystically?

"Look," he said, "your boat of purple paper is escorting them, and they are a convoy of rafts."

Some of the daisies came slowly towards her, hesitating, making a shy bright little cotillon on the dark clear water. Their gay bright candour moved her so much as they came near, that she was almost in tears.

"Why are they so lovely?" she cried. "Why do I think them so lovely?"

"They are nice flowers," he said, her emotional tones putting a constraint on him.

"You know that a daisy is a company of florets, a concourse, become individual. Don't the botanists put it highest in the line of development? I believe they do."

"The compositae, yes, I think so," said Ursula, who was never very sure of anything. Things she knew perfectly well, at one moment, seemed to become doubtful the next.

"Explain it so, then," he said. "The daisy is a perfect little democracy, so it's the highest of flowers, hence its charm."

"No," she cried, "no—never. It isn't democratic."

"No," he admitted. "It's the golden mob of the proletariat, surrounded by a showy white fence of the idle rich."

"How hateful—your hateful social orders!" she cried.

"Quite! It's a daisy—we'll leave it alone."

"Do. Let it be a dark horse for once," she said: "if anything can be a dark horse to you," she added satirically.

They stood aside, forgetful. As if a little stunned, they both were motionless, barely conscious. The little conflict into which they had fallen had torn their consciousness and left them like two impersonal forces, there in contact.

He became aware of the lapse. He wanted to say something, to get on to a new more ordinary footing.

"You know," he said, "that I am having rooms here at the mill? Don't you think we can have some good times?"

"Oh are you?" she said, ignoring all his implication of admitted intimacy.

He adjusted himself at once, became normally distant.

"If I find I can live sufficiently by myself," he continued, "I shall give up my work altogether. It has become dead to me. I don't believe in the humanity I pretend to be part of, I don't care a straw for the social ideals I live by, I hate the dying organic form of social mankind—so it can't be anything but trumpery, to work at education. I shall drop it as soon as I am clear enough—tomorrow perhaps—and be by myself."

"Have you enough to live on?" asked Ursula.

"Yes—I've about four hundred a year. That makes it easy for me."

There was a pause.

"And what about Hermione?" asked Ursula.

"That's over, finally—a pure failure, and never could have been anything else."

"But you still know each other?"

"We could hardly pretend to be strangers, could we?"

There was a stubborn pause.

"But isn't that a half-measure?" asked Ursula at length.

"I don't think so," he said. "You'll be able to tell me if it is."

Again there was a pause of some minutes duration. He was thinking.

"One must throw everything away, everything—let everything go, to get the one last thing one wants," he said.

"What thing?" she asked, in challenge.

"I don't know—freedom together," he said.

She had wanted him to say 'love.'

There was heard a loud barking of the dogs below. He seemed disturbed by it. She did not notice. Only she thought he seemed uneasy.

"As a matter of fact," he said, in rather a small voice, "I believe that is

Hermione come now, with Gerald Crich. She wanted to see the rooms before they are furnished."

"I know," said Ursula. "She will superintend the furnishing for you."

"Probably. Does it matter?"

"Oh no, I should think not," said Ursula. "Though personally, I can't bear her. I think she is a lie, if you like, you who are always talking about lies." Then she ruminated for a moment, when she broke out: "Yes, and I do mind if she furnishes your rooms—I do mind. I mind that you keep her hanging on at all."

He was silent now, frowning.

"Perhaps," he said. "I don't *want* her to furnish the rooms here—and I don't keep her hanging on. Only, I needn't be churlish to her, need I?——At any rate, I shall have to go down and see them now. You'll come, won't you?"

"I don't think so," she said coldly and irresolutely.

"Won't you? Yes do. Come and see the rooms as well. Do come."

Chapter XII

Carpeting

He set off down the bank, and she went unwillingly with him. Yet she would not have stayed away, either.

"We know each other well, you and I, already," he said. She did not answer.

In the large, darkish kitchen of the mill, the laborer's wife was talking shrilly to Hermione and Gerald, who stood, he in white and she in a glistening bluish foulard, strangely luminous in the dusk of the room; whilst from the cages on the walls, a dozen or more canaries sang at the top of their voices. The cages were all placed round a small square window at the back, where the sunshine came in, a beautiful beam, filtering through green leaves of a tree. The voice of Mrs Salmon shrilled against the noise of the birds, which rose ever more wild and triumphant, and the woman's voice went up and up against them, and the birds replied with wild animation.

"Here's Rupert!" shouted Gerald in the midst of the din. He was suffering badly, being very sensitive in the ear.

"O-o-h them birds, they won't let you speak—!" shrilled the laborer's wife in disgust. "I'll cover them up."

And she darted here and there, throwing a duster, an apron, a towel, a table-cloth over the cages of the birds.

"Now will you stop it, and let a body speak for your row," she said, still in a voice that was too high.

The party watched her. Soon the cages were covered, they had a strange funereal look. But from under the towels odd defiant trills and bubblings still shook out.

"Oh, they won't go on," said Mrs Salmon reassuringly. "They'll go to sleep now."

"Really," said Hermione, politely.

"They will," said Gerald. "They will go to sleep automatically, now the impression of evening is produced."

"Are they so easily deceived?" cried Ursula.

"Oh yes," replied Gerald. "Don't you know the story of Fabre, who, when he was a boy, put a hen's head under her wing, and she straight away went to sleep? It's quite true."

"And did that make him a naturalist?" asked Birkin.

"Probably," said Gerald.

Meanwhile Ursula was peeping under one of the cloths. There sat the canary in a corner, bunched and fluffed up for sleep.

"How ridiculous!" she cried. "It really thinks the night has come! How absurd! Really, how can one have any respect for a creature that is so easily taken in!"

"Yes," sang Hermione, coming also to look. She put her hand on Ursula's arm and chuckled a low laugh. "Yes, doesn't he look comical?" she chuckled. "Like a stupid husband."

Then, with her hand still on Ursula's arm, she drew her away, saying, in her mild sing-song:

"How did you come here? We saw Gudrun too."

"I came to look at the pond," said Ursula, "and I found Mr Birkin there."

"Did you.——This is quite a Brangwen land, isn't it!"

"I'm afraid I hoped so," said Ursula. "I ran here for refuge, when I saw you down the lake just putting off."

"Did you!—And now we've run you to earth!"

Hermione's eyelids lifted with an uncanny movement, amused but overwrought. She had always her strange, rapt look, unnatural and irresponsible.

"I was going on," said Ursula. "Mr Birkin wanted me to see the rooms. Isn't it delightful to live here? It is perfect."

"Yes," said Hermione, abstractedly. Then she turned right away from Ursula, ceased to know her existence.

"How do you feel, Rupert?" she sang in a new, affectionate tone, to Birkin.

"Very well," he replied.

"Were you quite comfortable?" The curious, sinister, rapt look was on Hermione's face, she shrugged her bosom in a convulsed movement, and seemed like one half in a trance.

"Quite comfortable," he replied.

There was a long pause, whilst Hermione looked at him for a long time, from under her heavy, drugged eyelids.

"And you think you'll be happy here?" she said at last.

"I'm sure I shall."

"I'm sure I shall do anything for him as I can," said the laborer's wife.

"And I'm sure our mester will; so I *hope* as he'll find himself comfortable."

Hermione turned and looked at her slowly.

"Thank you so much," she said, and then she turned completely away again. She recovered her position, and lifting her face towards him, and addressing him exclusively, she said:

"Have you measured the rooms?"

"No," he said, "I've been mending the punt."

"Shall we do it now?" she said slowly, balanced and dispassionate.

"Have you got a tape measure, Mrs Salmon?" he said, turning to the woman.

"Yes sir, I think I can find you one," replied the woman, bustling immediately to a basket. "This is the only one I've got, if it will do."

Hermione took it, though it was offered to him.

"Thank you so much," she said. "It will do very nicely. Thank you so much." Then she turned to Birkin, saying with a little gay movement: "Shall we do it now, Rupert?"

"What about the others, they'll be bored," he said reluctantly.

"Do you mind?" said Hermione, turning to Ursula and Gerald vaguely.

"Not in the least," they replied.

"Which room shall we do first?" she said, turning again to Birkin, with the same gaiety, now she was going to *do* something with him.

"We'll take them as they come," he said.

"Should I be getting your teas ready, while you do that?" said the laborer's wife, also gay because *she* had something to do.

"Would you?" said Hermione, turning to her with the curious motion of intimacy that seemed to envelop the woman, draw her almost to Hermione's breast, and which left the others standing apart. "I should be so glad. Where shall we have it?"

"Where you would like it, my lady! Shall it be in here, or out on the grass?"

"Where shall we have tea?" sang Hermione to the company at large.

"On the bank by the pond. And *we'll* carry the things up, if you'll just get them ready, Mrs Salmon," said Birkin.

"All right," said the pleased woman.

The party moved down the passage into the front room. It was empty, but clean and sunny. There was a window looking on to the tangled front garden.

"This is the dining room," said Hermione. "We'll measure it this way, Rupert—you go down there—"

"Can't I do it for you," said Gerald, coming to take the end of the tape.

"No thank you," cried Hermione, stooping to the ground in her bluish, brilliant foulard. It was a great joy to her to *do* things, and to have the ordering of the job, with Birkin. He obeyed her subduedly. Ursula and Gerald looked on. It was a peculiarity of Hermione's, that at every moment, she had one intimate, and turned all the rest of those present into onlookers. This raised her into a state of triumph.

They measured and discussed in the dining-room, and Hermione decided what the floor coverings must be. It sent her into a strange, convulsed anger, to be thwarted. Birkin always let her have her way, for the moment.

Then they moved across, through the hall, to the other front room, that was a little smaller than the first.

"This is the study," said Hermione. "Rupert, I have a rug that I want you to have for here. Will you let me give it you? Do—I want to give it you."

"What is it like?" he asked ungraciously.

"You haven't seen it. It is chiefly rose red, then blue, a metallic, mid-blue, and a very soft dark blue. I think you would like it. Do you think you would?"

"It sounds very nice," he replied. "What is it? Oriental? With a pile?"

"Yes. Persian! It is made of camel's hair, silky. I think it is called Bergamos:—twelve feet by seven—. Do you think it would do?"

"It would *do*," he said. "But why should you give me an expensive rug? I can manage perfectly well with my old Oxford Turkish."

"But may I give it you? Do let me."

"How much did it cost?"

She looked at him, and said:

"I don't remember. It was quite cheap."

He looked at her, his face set.

"I don't want to take it, Hermione," he said.

"Do let me give it to the rooms," she said, going up to him and putting her hand on his arm lightly, pleadingly. "I shall be so disappointed."

"You know I don't want you to give me things," he repeated helplessly.

"I don't want to give you *things*," she said teasingly. "But will you have this?"

"All right," he said, defeated, and she triumphed.

They went upstairs. There were two bedrooms to correspond with the rooms downstairs. One of them was half furnished, and Birkin had evidently slept there. Hermione went round the room carefully, taking in every detail, as if absorbing the evidence of his presence, in all the inanimate things. She felt the bed and examined the coverings.

"Are you *sure* you were quite comfortable?" she said, pressing the pillow.

"Perfectly," he replied coldly.

"And you were warm? There is no down quilt. I am sure you need one. You mustn't have a great pressure of clothes."

"I've got one," he said. "It is coming down."

They measured the rooms, and lingered over every consideration. Ursula stood at the window and watched the woman carrying the tea up the bank to the pond. She hated the palaver Hermione made, she wanted to drink tea, she wanted anything but this fuss and business.

At last they all mounted the grassy bank, to the picnic. Hermione poured out tea. She ignored now Ursula's presence. And Ursula, recovering from her ill-humour, turned to Gerald saying:

"Oh, I hated you so much the other day, Mr Crich."

"What for?" said Gerald, wincing slightly away.

"For treating your horse so badly. Oh, I hated you so much!"

"What did he do?" sang Hermione.

"He made his lovely sensitive Arab horse stand with him at the railway crossing whilst a horrible lot of trucks went by; and the poor thing, she was in a perfect frenzy, a perfect agony. It was the most horrible sight you can imagine."

"Why did you do it, Gerald?" asked Hermione, calm and interrogative.

"She must learn to stand—what use is she to me, in this country, if she shies and goes off every time an engine whistles."

"But why inflict unnecessary torture?" said Ursula. "Why make her stand all that time at the crossing? You might just as well have ridden back up the road, and saved all that horror. Her sides were bleeding where you had spurred her. It was too horrible—!"

Gerald stiffened.

"I have to use her," he replied. "And if I'm going to be sure of her at *all*, she'll have to learn to stand noises."

"Why should she?" cried Ursula in a passion. "She is a living creature, why should she stand anything, just because you choose to make her? She has as much right to her own being, as you have to yours."

"There I disagree," said Gerald. "I consider that mare is there for my use. Not because I bought her, but because that is the natural order. It is more natural for a man to take a horse and use it as he likes, than for him to go down on his knees to it, begging it to do as it wishes, and to fulfil its own marvellous nature."

Ursula was just breaking out, when Hermione lifted her face and began, in her musing sing-song:

"I do think—I do really think we must have the *courage* to use the lower animal life for our needs. I do think there is something wrong, when we look on every living creature as if it were ourself. I do feel, that it is false to project our own feelings on every animate creature. It is a lack of discrimination, a lack of criticism."

"Quite," said Birkin sharply. "Nothing is so detestable as the maudlin attributing of human feelings and consciousness to animals."

"Yes," said Hermione, wearily, "we must really take a position. Either we are going to use the animals, or they will use us."

"That's a fact," said Gerald. "A horse has got a will like a man, though it has no *mind*, strictly. And if your will isn't master, then the horse is master of you. And this is a thing I can't help. I can't help being master of the horse."

"If only we could learn how to use our will," said Hermione, "we could do anything. The will can cure anything, and put anything right. That I am convinced of—if only we use the will properly, intelligently."

"What do you mean by using the will properly?" said Birkin.

"A very great doctor taught me," she said, addressing Ursula and Gerald vaguely. "He told me, for instance, that to cure oneself of a bad habit, one should *force* oneself to do it, when one would not do it;—make oneself do it—and then the habit would disappear."

"How do you mean?" said Gerald.

"If you bite your nails, for example. Then, when you don't want to bite your nails, bite them—make yourself bite them. And you would find the habit was broken."

"Is that so?" said Gerald.

"Yes. And in so many things, I have *made* myself well. I was a very queer and nervous girl. And by learning to use my will, simply by using my will, I *made* myself right."

Ursula looked all the while at Hermione, as she spoke in her slow, dispassionate, and yet strangely tense voice. A curious thrill went over the younger woman. Some strange, dark, convulsive power was in Hermione, fascinating and repelling.

"It is fatal to use the will like that," cried Birkin harshly, "disgusting. Such a will is an obscenity."

Hermione looked at him for a long time, with her shadowed, heavy eyes.

Her face was soft and pale and thin, almost phosphorescent, her jaw was lean.

"I'm sure it isn't," she said at length. There always seemed an interval, a strange split between what she seemed to feel and experience, and what she actually said and thought. She seemed to catch her thoughts at length from off the surface of a maelström of chaotic black emotions and reactions, and Birkin was always filled with repulsion, she caught so infallibly, her will never failed her. Her voice was always dispassionate and tense, and perfectly confident. Yet she shuddered with a sense of nausea, a sort of sea-sickness that always threatened to overwhelm her mind. But her mind remained unbroken, her will was still perfect. It almost sent Birkin mad. But he would never, never dare to break her will, and let loose the maelström of her subconsciousness, and see her in her ultimate madness. Yet he was always striking at her.

"And of course," he said to Gerald, "horses *haven't* got a complete will, like human beings. A horse has no *one* will. Every horse, strictly, has two wills. With one will, it wants to put itself in the human power completely,—and with the other, it wants to be free, wild. The two wills sometimes lock—you know that, if ever you've felt a horse bolt, while you've been driving it."

"I have felt a horse bolt while I was driving it," said Gerald, "but it didn't make me know it had two wills. I only knew it was frightened."

Hermione had ceased to listen. She simply became oblivious when these subjects were started.

"Why should a horse want to put itself in the human power?" asked Ursula. "That is quite incomprehensible to me. I don't believe it ever wanted it."

"Yes it did. It's the last, perhaps highest, love-impulse: resign your will to the higher being," said Birkin.

"What curious notions you have of love," jeered Ursula.

"And woman is the same as horses: two wills act in opposition inside her. With one will, she wants to subject herself utterly. With the other she wants to bolt, and pitch her rider to perdition."

"Then I'm a bolter," said Ursula, with a burst of laughter.

"It's a dangerous thing to domesticate even horses, let alone women," said Birkin. "The dominant principle has some rare antagonists."

"Good thing too," said Ursula.

"Quite," said Gerald, with a faint smile. "There's more fun."

Hermione could bear no more. She rose, saying in her easy sing-song:

"Isn't the evening beautiful! I get filled sometimes with such a great sense of beauty, that I feel I can hardly bear it."

Ursula, to whom she had appealed, rose with her, moved to the last impersonal depths. And Birkin seemed to her almost a monster of hateful arrogance. She went with Hermione along the bank of the pond, talking of beautiful, soothing things, picking the gentle cowslips.

"Wouldn't you like a dress," said Ursula to Hermione, "of this yellow spotted with orange—a cotton dress?"

"Yes," said Hermione, stopping and looking at the flower, letting the thought come home to her and soothe her. "Wouldn't it be pretty? I should *love* it."

And she turned smiling to Ursula, in a feeling of real affection.

But Gerald remained with Birkin, wanting to probe him to the bottom, to know what he meant by the dual will in horses. A flicker of excitement danced on Gerald's face.

Hermione and Ursula strayed on together, united in a sudden bond of deep affection and closeness.

"I really do *not* want to be forced into all this criticism and analysis of life. I really *do* want to see things in their entirety, with their beauty left to them, and their wholeness, their natural holiness.—Don't you feel it, don't you feel you *can't* be tortured into any more knowledge?" said Hermione, stopping in front of Ursula, and turning to her with clenched fists thrust downwards.

"Yes," said Ursula. "I do. I am sick of all this poking and prying."

"I'm so glad you are. Sometimes," said Hermione, again stopping arrested in her progress and turning to Ursula, "sometimes I wonder if I *ought* to submit to all this realisation, if I am not being weak in rejecting it.—But I feel I *can't*—I *can't*. It seems to destroy *everything*. All the beauty and the,—and the true holiness is destroyed,—and I feel I can't live without them."

"And it would be simply wrong to live without them," cried Ursula. "No, it is so *irreverent* to think that everything must be realised in the head. Really, something must be left to the Lord, there always is and always will be."

"Yes," said Hermione, reassured like a child, "it should, shouldn't it? And Rupert—" she lifted her face to the sky, in a muse—"he *can* only tear things to pieces. He really *is* like a boy who must pull everything to pieces to see how it is made. And I can't think it is right—it does seem so irreverent, as you say."

"Like tearing open a bud to see what the flower will be like," said Ursula.

"Yes. And that kills everything, doesn't it? It doesn't allow any possibility of flowering."

"Of course not," said Ursula. "It is purely destructive."

"It is, isn't it!"

Hermione looked long and slow at Ursula, seeming to accept confirmation from her. Then the two women were silent. As soon as they were in accord, they began mutually to mistrust each other. In spite of herself, Ursula felt herself recoiling from Hermione. It was all she could do to restrain her revulsion.

They returned to the men, like two conspirators who have withdrawn to come to an agreement. Birkin looked up at them. Ursula hated him for his cold watchfulness. But he said nothing.

"Shall we be going?" said Hermione. "Rupert, you are coming to Shortlands to dinner? Will you come at once, will you come now, with us?"

"I'm not dressed," replied Birkin. "And you know Gerald stickles for the convention."

"I don't stickle for it," said Gerald. "But if you'd got as sick as I have of rowdy go-as-you-please in the house, you'd prefer it if people were peaceful and conventional, at least at meals."

"All right," said Birkin.

"But can't we wait for you while you dress?" persisted Hermione.

"If you like."

He rose to go indoors. Ursula said she would take her leave.

"Only," she said, turning to Gerald, "I must say that, however man is lord of the beast and the fowl, I still don't think he has any right to violate the feelings of the inferior creation. I still think it would have been much more sensible and nice of you if you'd trotted back up the road while the train went by, and been considerate."

"I see," said Gerald, smiling, but somewhat annoyed. "I must remember another time."

"They all think I'm an interfering female," thought Ursula to herself, as she went away. But she was in arms against them.

She ran home plunged in thought. She had been very much moved by Hermione, she had really come into contact with her, so that there was a sort of league between the two women. And yet she could not bear her. But she put the thought away. "She's really good," she said to herself. "She really wants what is right." And she tried to feel at one with Hermione, and to shut off from Birkin. She was strictly hostile to him. But she was held to him by some bond, some deep principle. This at once irritated her and saved her.

Only now and again, violent little shudders would come over her, out of her subconsciousness, and she knew it was the fact that she had stated her challenge to Birkin, and he had, consciously or unconsciously, accepted. It was a fight to the death between them—or to new life: though in what the conflict lay, no one could say.

Chapter XIII

Mino

The days went by, and she received no sign. Was he going to ignore her, was he going to take no further notice of her secret? A dreary weight of anxiety and acrid bitterness settled on her. And yet Ursula knew she was only deceiving herself, that he *would* proceed. She said no word to anybody.

Then, sure enough, there came a note from him, asking if she would come to tea, with Gudrun, to his rooms in town.

"Why does he ask Gudrun as well?" she asked herself at once. "Does he want to protect himself, or does he think I would not go alone?"

She was tormented by the thought that he wanted to protect himself. But at the end of all, she only said to herself:

"I don't *want* Gudrun to be there, because I want him to say something more to me. So I shan't tell Gudrun anything about it, and I shall go alone. Then I shall know."

She found herself sitting on the tram-car, mounting up the hill going out of the town, to the place where he had his lodging. She seemed to have passed into a kind of dream world, absolved from the conditions of actuality. She watched the sordid streets of the town go by beneath her, as if she were a spirit disconnected from the material universe. What had it all to do with her? She was palpitating and formless within the flux of the ghost life. She could not consider any more, what anybody would say of her or think about her. People had passed out of her range, she was absolved. She had fallen strange and dim, out of the sheath of the material life, like a berry falls from the only world it has ever known, down out of the sheath on to the real unknown.

Birkin was standing in the middle of the room, when she was shown in by the landlady. He too was moved outside himself. She saw him agitated and shaken, a frail, unsubstantial body silent like the node of some violent force, that came out from him and shook her almost into a swoon.

"You are alone?" he said.

"Yes—Gudrun couldn't come."

He instantly guessed why.

And they were both seated in silence, in the terrible tension of the room.

She was aware that it was a pleasant room full of light and very restful in its form—aware also of a fuchsia tree, with dangling scarlet and purple flowers.

"How nice the fuchsias are!" she said, to break the silence.

"Aren't they!—Did you think I had forgotten what I said?"

A swoon went over Ursula's mind.

"I don't want you to remember it—if you don't want to," she struggled to say, through the dark mist that covered her.

There was silence for some moments.

"No," he said. "It isn't that. Only—if we are going to know each other, we must pledge ourselves for ever. If we are going to make a relationship, even of friendship, there must be something final and infallible about it."

There was a clang of mistrust and almost anger in his voice. She did not answer. Her heart was too much contracted. She could not have spoken.

Seeing she was not going to reply, he continued, almost bitterly, giving himself away:

"I can't say it is love I have to offer—and it isn't love I want. It is something much more impersonal and harder,—and rarer."

There was a silence, out of which she said:

"You mean you don't love me?"

She suffered furiously, saying that.

"Yes, if you like to put it like that.—Though perhaps that isn't true. I don't know. At any rate, I don't feel the emotion of love for you—no, and I don't want to. Because it gives out in the last issues."

"Love gives out in the last issues?" she asked, feeling numb to the lips.

"Yes, it does. At the very last, one is alone, beyond the influence of love. There is a real impersonal me, that is beyond love, beyond any emotional relationship. So it is with you. But we want to delude ourselves that love is the root. It isn't. It is only the branches. The root is beyond love, a naked kind of isolation, an isolated me, that does *not* meet and mingle, and never can."

She watched him with wide, troubled eyes. His face was incandescent in its abstract earnestness.

"And you mean you can't love?" she asked, in trepidation.

"Yes, if you like.—I have loved. But there is a beyond, where there is no love."

She could not submit to this. She felt it swooning over her. But she could not submit.

"But how do you know—if you have never *really* loved?" she asked.

"It is true, what I say: there is a beyond, in you, in me, which is further than love, beyond the scope, as stars are beyond the scope of vision, some of them."

"Then there *is* no love," cried Ursula.

"Ultimately, no, there is something else. But ultimately, there *is* no love."

Ursula was given over to this statement for some moments. Then she half rose from her chair, saying, in a final, repellant voice:

"Then let me go home—what am I doing here!"

"There is the door," he said. "You are a free agent."

He was suspended finely and perfectly in this extremity. She hung motionless for some seconds, then she sat down again.

"If there is no love, what is there?" she cried, almost jeering.

"Something," he said, looking at her, battling with his soul, with all his might.

"What?"

He was silent for a long time, unable to be in communication with her whilst she was in this state of opposition.

"There is," he said, in a voice of pure abstraction, "a final me which is stark and impersonal and beyond responsibility. So there is a final you. And it is there I would want to meet you—not in the emotional, loving plane—but there beyond, where there is no speech and no terms of agreement. There we are two stark, unknown beings, two utterly strange creatures, I would want to approach you, and you me.—And there could be no obligation, because there is no standard for action there, because no understanding has been reaped from that plane. It is quite inhuman,—so there can be no calling to book, in any form whatsoever—because one is outside the pale of all that is accepted, and nothing known applies. One can only follow the impulse, taking that which lies in front, and responsible for nothing, asked for nothing, giving nothing, only each taking according to the primal desire."

Ursula listened to this speech, her mind dumb and almost senseless, that he said was so unexpected and so untoward.

"It is just purely selfish," she said.

"If it is pure, yes. But it isn't selfish at all. Because I don't *know* what I want of you. I deliver *myself* over to the unknown, in coming to you, I am without reserves or defences, stripped entirely into the unknown. Only there needs the pledge between us, that we will both cast off everything, cast off ourselves even, and cease to be, so that that which is perfectly ourselves can take place in us."

She pondered along her own line of thought.

"But it is because you love me, that you want me?" she persisted.

"No it isn't. It is because I believe in you—if I *do* believe in you."

"Aren't you sure?" she laughed, suddenly hurt.

He was looking at her steadfastly, scarcely heeding what she said.

"Yes, I must believe in you, or else I shouldn't be here saying this," he replied. "But that is all the proof I have. I don't feel any very strong belief at this particular moment."

She disliked him for his sudden relapse into weariness and faithlessness.

"But don't you think me good-looking?" she persisted, in a mocking voice.

He looked at her, to see if he felt that she was good-looking.

"I don't *feel* that you're good-looking," he said.

"Not even attractive?" she mocked, bitingly.

He knitted his brows in sudden exasperation.

"Don't you see that it's not a question of visual appreciation in the least," he cried. "I don't *want* to see you. I've seen plenty of women, I'm sick and weary of seeing them. I want a woman I don't see."

"I'm sorry I can't oblige you by being invisible," she laughed.

"Yes," he said, "you are invisible to me, if you don't force me to be visually aware of you. But I don't want to see you or hear you."

"What did you ask me to tea for, then?" she mocked.

But he would take no notice of her. He was talking to himself.

"I want to find you, where you don't know your own existence, the you that your common self denies utterly. But I don't want your good looks, and I don't want your womanly feelings, and I don't want your thoughts nor opinions nor your ideas—they are all bagatelles to me."

"You are very conceited, Monsieur," she mocked. "How do you know what my womanly feelings are, or my thoughts or my ideas? You don't even know what I think of you now."

"Nor do I care in the slightest."

"I think you are very silly. I think you want to tell me you love me, and you go all this way round to do it."

"All right," he said, looking up with sudden exasperation. "Now go away then, and leave me alone. I don't want any more of your meretricious persiflage."

"Is it really persiflage?" she mocked, her face really relaxing into laughter. She interpreted it, that he had made a deep confession of love to her. But he was so absurd in his words, also.

They were silent for many minutes, she was pleased and elated like a child. His concentration broke, he began to look at her simply and naturally.

"What I want is a strange conjunction with you—" he said quietly: "—not meeting and mingling;—you are quite right:—but an equilibrium, a pure balance of two single beings:—as the stars balance each other."

She looked at him. He was very earnest, and earnestness was always rather ridiculous, commonplace, to her. It made her feel unfree and uncomfortable. Yet she liked him so much. But why drag in the stars!

"Isn't this rather sudden?" she mocked.

He began to laugh.

"Best to read the terms of the contract, before we sign," he said.

A young grey cat that had been sleeping on the sofa jumped down and stretched, rising on its long legs, and arching its slim back. Then it sat considering for a moment, erect and kingly. And then, like a dart, it had shot out of the room, through the open window-doors, and into the garden.

"What's he after?" said Birkin, rising.

The young cat trotted lordly down the path, waving his tail. He was an ordinary tabby with white paws, a slender young gentleman. A crouching, fluffy, brownish-grey cat was stealing up the side of the fence. The Mino walked statelily up to her, with manly nonchalance. She crouched before him and pressed herself on the ground in humility, a fluffy soft outcast, looking up at him with wild eyes that were green and lovely as great jewels. He looked casually down on her. So she crept a few inches further, proceeding on her way to the back door, crouching in a wonderful soft, self-obliterating manner, and moving like a shadow.

He, going statelily on his slim legs, walked after her, then suddenly, for pure excess, he gave her a light cuff with his paw on the side of her face. She ran off a few steps, like a blown leaf along the ground, then crouched unobtrusively, in submissive, wild patience. The Mino pretended to take no notice of her. He blinked his eyes superbly at the landscape. In a minute she drew herself together and moved softly, a fleecy brown-grey shadow, a few paces forward. She began to quicken her pace, in a moment she would be gone like a dream, when the young grey lord sprang before her, and gave her a light handsome cuff. She subsided at once, submissively.

"She is a wild cat," said Birkin. "She has come in from the woods."

The eyes of the stray cat flared round for a moment, like great green fires staring at Birkin. Then she had rushed in a soft swift rush, half way down the garden. There she paused to look round. The Mino turned his face in pure superiority to his master, and slowly closed his eyes, standing in statuesque young perfection. The wild cat's round, green, wondering eyes were staring all the while like uncanny fires. Then again, like a shadow, she slid towards the kitchen.

In a lovely springing leap, like a wind, the Mino was upon her, and had boxed her twice, very definitely, with a white, delicate fist. She sank and slid back, unquestioning. He walked after her, and cuffed her once or twice, leisurely, with sudden little blows of his magic white paws.

"Now why does he do that?" cried Ursula in indignation.

"They are on intimate terms," said Birkin.

"And is that why he hits her!" cried Ursula.

"Yes," laughed Birkin, "I think he wants to make it quite obvious to her."

"Isn't it horrid of him!" she cried; and going out into the garden she called to the Mino:

"Stop it, don't bully. Stop hitting her."

The stray cat vanished like a swift, invisible shadow. The Mino glanced at Ursula, then looked from her disdainfully to his master.

"Are you a bully, Mino?" Birkin asked.

The young slim cat looked at him, and slowly narrowed its eyes. Then it glanced away at the landscape, looking into the distance as if completely oblivious of the two human beings.

"Mino," said Ursula, "I don't like you. You are a bully like all the males."

"No," said Birkin, "he is justified. He is not a bully. He is only insisting to the poor stray that she shall acknowledge him as a sort of fate, her own fate: because you can see she is fluffy and promiscuous as the wind. I am with him entirely. He wants superfine stability."

"Yes, I know!" cried Ursula. "He wants his own way—I know what your fine words work down to—bossiness, I call it, bossiness."

The young cat again glanced at Birkin in disdain of the noisy woman.

"I quite agree with you, Miciotto," said Birkin to the cat. "Keep your male dignity, and your higher understanding."

Again the Mino narrowed his eyes as if he were looking at the sun. Then, suddenly affecting to have no connection at all with the two people, he went trotting off, with assumed spontaneity and gaiety, his tail erect, his white feet blithe.

"Now he will find the belle sauvage once more, and entertain her with his superior wisdom," laughed Birkin.

Ursula looked at the man who stood in the garden with his hair blowing and his eyes smiling ironically, and she cried:

"Oh it makes me so cross, this assumption of male superiority! And it is such a lie! One wouldn't mind if there were any justification for it."

"The wild cat," said Birkin, "doesn't mind. She perceives that it is justified."

"Does she!" cried Ursula. "And tell it to the Horse Marines."

"To them also."

"It is just like Gerald Crich with his horse—a lust for bullying—a real Wille zur Macht—so base, so petty."

"I agree that the Wille zur Macht is a base and petty thing. But with the Mino, it is the desire to bring this female cat into a pure stable equilibrium, a transcendent and abiding *rapport* with the single male.—Whereas without him, as you see, she is a mere stray, a fluffy sporadic bit of chaos. It is a volonté de pouvoir, if you like, a will to ability, taking pouvoir as a verb."

"Ah—! Sophistries! It's the old Adam."

"Oh yes. Adam kept Eve in the indestructible paradise, when he kept her single with himself, like a star in its orbit."

"Yes—yes—" cried Ursula, pointing her finger at him. "There you are—a star in its orbit! A satellite!—a satellite of Mars—that's what she is to be! There—there—you've given yourself away! You want a satellite, Mars and his satellite! You've said it—you've said it—you've dished yourself!"

He stood smiling in frustration and amusement and irritation and admiration and love. She was so quick, and so lambent, like discernible fire, and so vindictive, and so rich in her dangerous flamy sensitiveness.

"I've not said it at all," he replied, "if you will give me a chance to speak."

"No, no!" she cried. "I won't let you speak. You've said it, 'a satellite,' you're not going to wriggle out of it. You've said it."

"You'll never believe now that *I haven't* said it," he answered. "I neither implied nor indicated nor mentioned a satellite, nor intended a satellite, never."

"*You prevaricator!*" she cried, in real indignation.

"Tea is ready, sir," said the landlady from the doorway.

They both looked at her, very much as the cats had looked at them, a little while before.

"Thank you, Mrs Daykin."

An interrupted silence fell over the two of them, a moment of breach.

"Come and have tea," he said.

"Yes, I should love it," she replied, gathering herself together.

They sat facing each other across the tea-table.

"I did not say, nor imply, a satellite. I meant two single equal stars balanced in conjunction—"

"You gave yourself away, you gave away your little game completely," she cried, beginning at once to eat. He saw that she would take no further heed of his expostulations, so he began to pour the tea.

"What *good* things to eat!" she cried.

"Take your own sugar," he said.

He handed her her cup. He had everything so nice, such pretty cups and plates, painted with mauve-lustre and green, also shapely bowls and glass plates, and old spoons, on a woven cloth of pale grey and black and purple. It was very rich and fine. But Ursula could see Hermione's influence.

"Your things are so lovely!" she said, almost angrily.

"*I* like them. It gives me real pleasure to use things that are attractive in themselves—pleasant things. And Mrs Daykin is good. She thinks everything is wonderful, for my sake."

"Really," said Ursula, "landladies are better than wives, nowadays. They certainly *care* a great deal more. It is much more beautiful and complete here now, than if you were married."

"But think of the emptiness within," he laughed.

"No," she said. "I am jealous that men have such perfect landladies and such beautiful lodgings. There is nothing left them to desire."

"In the house-keeping way, we'll hope not. It is disgusting, people marrying for a home."

"Still," said Ursula, "a man has very little need for a woman now, has he?"

"In outer things, maybe—except to share his bed and bear his children. But essentially, there is just the same need as ever there was. Only nobody takes the trouble to be essential."

"How essential?" she asked.

"I do think," he said, "that the world is only held together by the mystic conjunction, the ultimate unison between people—a bond. And the immediate bond is between man and woman."

"But it's such old hat," said Ursula. "Why should love be a bond?—No, I'm not having any."

"If you are walking westward," he said, "you forfeit the northern and eastward and southern direction.—If you admit a unison, you forfeit all the possibilities of chaos."

"But love is freedom," she declared.

"Don't cant to me," he replied. "Love is a direction which excludes all other directions. It's a freedom *together*, if you like."

"No," she said, "love includes everything."

"Sentimental cant," he replied. "You want the state of chaos, that's all. It is ultimate nihilism, this freedom-in-love business, this freedom which is love and love which is freedom.—As a matter of fact, if you enter into a pure unison, it is irrevocable, and it is never pure till it is irrevocable. And when it is irrevocable, it is one way, like the path of a star."

"Ha!" she cried bitterly. "It is the old dead morality."

"No," he said, "it is the law of creation. One is committed. One must commit oneself to a conjunction with the other—forever. But it is not selfless—it is a maintaining of the self in mystic balance and integrity—like a star balanced with another star."

"I don't trust you when you drag in the stars," she said. "If you were quite true, it wouldn't be necessary to be so far-fetched."

"Don't trust me then," he said, angry. "It is enough that I trust myself."

"And that is where you make another mistake," she replied. "You *don't* trust yourself. You don't fully believe yourself what you are saying. You don't really want this conjunction, otherwise you wouldn't talk so much about it, you'd get it."

He was suspended for a moment, arrested.

"How?" he said.

"By just loving," she retorted in defiance.

He was still a moment, in anger. Then he said:

"I tell you, I don't believe in love like that. I tell you, you want love to administer to your egotism, to subserve you. Love is a process of subservience with you—and with everybody. I hate it."

"No," she cried, pressing back her head like a cobra, her eyes flashing. "It is a process of pride—I want to be proud—"

"Proud and subservient, proud and subservient, I know you," he retorted dryly. "Proud and subserved, then subservient to the proud—I know you and your love. It is a tick-tack, tick-tack, a dance of opposites."

"Are you so sure?" she mocked wickedly, "what my love is?"

"Yes, I am," he retorted.

"So cocksure!" she said. "How can anybody ever be right, who is so cocksure? It shows you are wrong."

He was silent in chagrin.

They had talked and struggled till they were both wearied out.

"Tell me about yourself and your people," he said.

And she told him about the Brangwens, and about her mother, and about Skrebensky, her first love, and about her later experiences. He sat very still, watching her as she talked. And he seemed to listen with reverence. Her face was beautiful and full of baffled light as she told him all the things that had hurt her or perplexed her so deeply. He seemed to warm and comfort his soul at the beautiful light of her nature.

"If she *really* could pledge herself," he thought to himself, with passionate insistence but hardly any hope. Yet a curious little irresponsible laughter appeared in his heart.

"We have all suffered so much," he mocked, ironically.

She looked up at him, and a flash of wild gaiety went over her face, a strange flash of yellow light coming from her eyes.

"Haven't we!" she cried, in a high, reckless cry. "It is almost absurd, isn't it?"

"Quite absurd," he said. "Suffering bores me, any more."

"So it does me."

He was almost afraid of the mocking recklessness of her splendid face. Here was one who would go the whole lengths of heaven or hell, whichever she had to go. And he mistrusted her, he was afraid of a woman capable of such abandon, such dangerous thoroughness of destructivity. Yet he chuckled within himself also.

She came over to him and put her hand on his shoulder, looking down at him with strange golden-lighted eyes, very tender, but with a curious devilish look lurking underneath.

"Say you love me, say 'my love' to me," she pleaded.

He looked back into her eyes, and saw. His face flickered with sardonic comprehension.

"I love you right enough," he said, grimly. "But I want it to be something else."

"But why? But why?" she insisted, bending her wonderful luminous face to him. "Why isn't it enough?"

"Because we can go one better," he said, putting his arms round her.

"No, we can't," she said, in a strong, voluptuous voice of yielding. "We can only love each other. Say 'my love' to me, say it, say it."

She put her arms round his neck. He enfolded her, and kissed her subtly, murmuring in a subtle voice of love, and irony, and submission:

"Yes,—my love, yes,—my love. Let love be enough then.—I love you then—I love you. I'm bored by the rest."

"Yes," she murmured, nestling very sweet and close to him.

Chapter XIV

Water-Party

Every year Mr Crich gave a more-or-less public water-party on the lake. There was a little pleasure-launch on Willey Water, and several rowing boats, and guests could take tea either in the marquee that was set up in the grounds of the house, or they could picnic in the shade of the great walnut tree at the boat-house by the lake. This year the staff of the Grammar School was invited, along with the chief officials of the firm. Gerald and the younger Criches did not care for this party, but it had become customary now, and it pleased the father, as being the only occasion when he could gather some people of the district together in festivity with him. For he loved to give pleasures to his dependents and to those poorer than himself. But his children preferred the company of their own equals in wealth. They hated their inferiors' humility or gratitude or awkwardness. Nevertheless they were willing to attend at this festival, as they had done almost since they were children, the more so, as they all felt a little guilty now, and unwilling to thwart their father any more, since he was so ill in health. Therefore, quite cheerfully Laura prepared to take her mother's place as hostess, and Gerald assumed responsibility for the amusements on the water.

Birkin had written to Ursula saying he expected to see her at the party, and Gudrun, although she scorned the patronage of the Criches, would nevertheless accompany her mother and father if the weather were fine.

The day came blue and full of sunshine, with little wafts of wind. The sisters both wore dresses of white cotton crape, and hats of soft grass. But Gudrun had a sash of brilliant black and pink and yellow colour wound broadly round her waist, and she had pink silk stockings, and black and pink and yellow decoration on the brim of her hat, weighing it down a little. She carried also a yellow silk coat over her arm, so that she looked remarkable, like a painting from the Salon. Her appearance was a sore trial to her father, who said angrily:

"Don't you think you might as well get yourself up for a Christmas cracker, an' ha' done with it?"

But Gudrun looked handsome and brilliant, and she wore her clothes in pure defiance. When people stared at her, and giggled after her, she made a point of saying loudly, to Ursula:

"Regarde, regarde ces gens-là! Ne sont-ils pas des hiboux incroyables?" And with the words of French in her mouth, she would look over her shoulder at the giggling party.

"No, really, it's impossible!" Ursula would reply distinctly.

And so the two girls took it out of their universal enemy. But their father became more and more enraged.

Ursula was all snowy white, save that her hat was pink, and entirely without trimming, and her shoes were dark red, and she carried an orange-coloured coat. And in this guise they were walking all the way to Shortlands, their father and mother going in front.

They were laughing at their mother, who, dressed in a summer material of black and purple stripes, and wearing a hat of purple straw, was setting forth with much more of the shyness and trepidation of a young girl than her daughters ever felt, walking demurely beside her husband, who, as usual, looked rather crumpled in his best suit, as if he were the father of a young family and had been holding the baby whilst his wife got dressed.

"Look at the young couple in front," said Gudrun calmly. Ursula looked at her mother and father, and was suddenly seized with uncontrollable laughter. The two girls stood in the road and laughed till the tears ran down their faces, as they caught sight again of the shy, unworldly couple of their parents going on ahead.

"We are roaring at you, mother," called Ursula, helplessly following after her parents.

Mrs Brangwen turned round with a slightly puzzled, exasperated look.

"Oh indeed!" she said. "What is there so very funny about *me*, I should like to know?"

She could not understand that there could be anything amiss with her appearance. She had a perfect calm sufficiency, an easy indifference to any criticism whatsoever, as if she were beyond it. Her clothes were always rather odd, and as a rule slip-shod, yet she wore them with a perfect ease and satisfaction. Whatever she had on, so long as she was barely tidy, she was right, beyond remark; such an aristocrat she was by instinct.

"You look so stately, like a country Baroness," said Ursula, laughing with a little tenderness at her mother's naive puzzled air.

"*Just* like a country Baroness!" chimed in Gudrun.

Now the mother's natural hauteur became self-conscious, and the girls shrieked again.

"Go home, you pair of idiots, great giggling idiots!" cried the father inflamed with irritation.

"Mm-m-er!" booed Ursula, pulling a face at his crossness.

The yellow lights danced in his eyes, he leaned forward in real rage.

"Don't be so silly as to take any notice of the great gabies," said Mrs Brangwen, turning on her way.

"I'll see if I'm going to be followed by a pair of giggling yelling jackanapes—" he cried vengefully.

The girls stood still, laughing helplessly at his fury, upon the path beside the hedge.

"Why you're as silly as they are, to take any notice," said Mrs Brangwen also becoming angry now he was really enraged.

"There are some people coming, father," cried Ursula, with mocking warning. He glanced round quickly, and went on to join his wife, walking stiff with rage. And the girls followed, weak with laughter.

When the people had passed by, Brangwen cried in a loud, stupid voice:

"I'm going back home if there's any more of this. I'm damned if I'm going to be made a fool of in this fashion, in the public road."

He was really out of temper. At the sound of his blind, vindictive voice, the laughter suddenly left the girls, and their hearts contracted with contempt. They hated his words "in the public road." What did they care for the public road?—But Gudrun was conciliatory.

"But we weren't laughing to *hurt* you," she cried, with an uncouth gentleness which made her parents uncomfortable. "We were laughing because we're fond of you."

"We'll walk on in front, if they are *so* touchy," said Ursula, angry.

And in this wise they arrived at Willey Water. The lake was blue and fair, the meadows sloped down in sunshine on one side, the thick dark woods dropped steeply on the other. The little pleasure-launch was fussing out from the shore, twanging its music, crowded with people, flapping its paddles. Near the boat-house was a throng of gaily-dressed persons, small in the distance. And on the high-road, some of the common people were standing along the hedge, looking at the festivity beyond, enviously, like souls not admitted to paradise.

"My eye!" said Gudrun, sotto voce, looking at the motley of guests, "there's a pretty crowd if you like! Imagine yourself in the midst of that, my dear."

Gudrun's apprehensive horror of people in the mass unnerved Ursula.

"It looks rather awful," she said anxiously.

"And imagine what they'll be like—*imagine*!" said Gudrun, still in that unnerving, subdued voice. Yet she advanced determinedly.

"I suppose we can get away from them," said Ursula anxiously.

"We're in a pretty fix if we can't," said Gudrun. Her extreme ironic loathing and apprehension was very trying to Ursula.

"We needn't stay," she said.

"I certainly shan't stay five minutes among that little lot," said Gudrun.

They advanced nearer, till they saw the policemen at the gates.

"Policemen to keep you in, too!" said Gudrun. "My word, this is a beautiful affair."

"We'd better look after father and mother," said Ursula anxiously.

"Mother's *perfectly* capable of getting through this little celebration," said Gudrun with some contempt.

But Ursula knew that her father felt uncouth and angry and unhappy, so she was far from her ease. They waited outside the gate till their parents came up. The tall, thin man in his crumpled clothes was unnerved and irritable as a boy, finding himself on the brink of this social function. He did not feel a gentleman, he did not feel anything except pure exasperation.

Ursula took her place at his side, they gave their tickets to the policemen, and passed in on to the grass, four abreast: the tall, hot, ruddy-dark man with his narrow boyish brow drawn with irritation, the fresh-faced, easy woman, perfectly collected though her hair was slipping on one side, then Gudrun, her eyes round and dark and staring, her full soft face impassive, almost sulky, so that she seemed to be backing away in antagonism even whilst she was advancing; and then Ursula, with the odd, brilliant, dazzled look on her face, that always came when she was in some false situation.

Birkin was the good angel. He came smiling to them with his affected social grace, that somehow was never *quite* right. But he took off his hat and smiled at them with a real smile in his eyes, so that Brangwen cried out heartily in relief:

"How do you do? You're better, are you?"

"Yes, I'm better. How do you do, Mrs Brangwen? I know Gudrun and Ursula very well."

His eyes smiled full of natural warmth. He had a soft, flattering manner with women, particularly with women who were not young.

"Yes," said Mrs Brangwen, cool but yet gratified. "I have heard speak of you often enough."

He laughed. Gudrun looked aside, feeling she was being belittled. People were standing about in groups, some women were sitting in the shade of the walnut tree, with cups of tea in their hands, a waiter in evening dress was hurrying round, some girls were simpering with parasols, some young men, who had just come in from rowing, were sitting cross-legged on the grass, coatless, their shirt-sleeves rolled up in manly fashion, their hands resting on their white flannel trousers, their gaudy ties floating about, as they laughed and tried to be witty with the young damsels.

"Why," thought Gudrun churlishly, "don't they have the manners to put their coats on, and not to assume such intimacy in their appearance."

She abhorred the ordinary young man, with his hair plastered back, and his easy-going chumminess.

Hermione Roddice came up, in a handsome gown of white lace, trailing an enormous silk shawl blotched with great embroidered flowers, and balancing an enormous plain hat on her head. She looked striking, astonishing, almost macabre, so tall, with the fringe of her great cream-coloured vividly-blotched shawl trailing on the ground after her, her thick hair coming low over her eyes, her face strange and long and pale, and the blotches of brilliant colour drawn round her.

"Doesn't she look *weird*!" Gudrun heard some girls titter behind her. And she could have killed them.

"How do you do!" sang Hermione, coming up very kindly, and glancing slowly over Gudrun's father and mother. It was a trying moment, exasperating for Gudrun. Hermione was really so strongly entrenched in her class superiority, she could come up and know people out of simple curiosity, as if they were creatures on exhibition. Gudrun would do the same herself. But she resented being in the position when somebody might do it to her.

Hermione, very remarkable, and distinguishing the Brangwens very much, led them along to where Laura Crich stood receiving the guests.

"This is Mrs Brangwen," sang Hermione, and Laura, who wore a stiff embroidered linen dress, shook hands and said she was glad to see her. Then Gerald came up, dressed in white, with a black-and-brown blazer, and looking handsome. He too was introduced to the Brangwen parents, and immediately he spoke to Mrs Brangwen as if she were a lady, and to Brangwen as if he were *not* a gentleman. Gerald was so obvious in his demeanour. He had to shake hands with his left hand, because he had hurt his right, and carried it, bandaged up, in the pocket of his jacket. Gudrun was *very* thankful that none of her party asked him what was the matter with the hand.

The steam launch was fussing in, all its music jingling, people calling excitedly from on board. Gerald went to see to the debarkation, Birkin was getting tea for Mrs Brangwen, Brangwen had joined a Grammar-School group, Hermione was sitting down by their mother, the girls went to the landing-stage to watch the launch come in.

She hooted and tooted gaily, then her paddles were silent, the ropes were thrown ashore, she drifted in with a little bump. Immediately the passengers crowded excitedly to come ashore.

"Wait a minute, wait a minute," shouted Gerald in sharp command.

They must wait till the boat was tight on the ropes, till the small gangway was put out. Then they streamed ashore, clamouring as if they had come from America.

"Oh it's *so* nice!" the young girls were crying. "It's quite lovely."

The waiters from on board ran out to the boat-house with baskets, the captain lounged on the little bridge. Seeing all safe, Gerald came to Gudrun and Ursula.

"You wouldn't care to go on board for the next trip, and have tea there?" he asked.

"No thanks," said Gudrun coldly.

"You don't care for the water?"

"For the water? Yes, I like it very much."

He looked at her, his eyes searching.

"You don't care for going on a launch, then?"

She was slow in answering, and then she spoke slowly.

"No," she said. "I can't say that I do."

Her colour was high, she seemed angry about something.

"Un peu trop de monde," said Ursula, explaining.

"Eh? *Trop de monde*!" He laughed shortly. "Yes, there's a fair number of 'em."

Gudrun turned on him brilliantly.

"Have you ever been from Westminster Bridge to Richmond on one of the Thames steamers?" she cried.

"No," he said, "I can't say I have."

"Well, it's one of the most *vile* experiences I've ever had." She spoke rapidly and excitedly, the colour high in her cheeks. "There was absolutely nowhere to sit down, nowhere, a man just above sang 'Rocked in the Cradle of the Deep' the *whole* way; he was blind and he had a small organ, one of those portable organs, and he expected money; so you can imagine what *that* was like; there came a constant smell of luncheon from below, and puffs of hot oily machinery; the journey took hours and hours and hours; and for miles, literally for miles, dreadful boys ran with us on the shore, in that *awful* Thames mud, going in *up to the waist*—they had their trousers turned back, and they went up to their hips in that indescribable

Thames mud, their faces always turned to us, and screaming, exactly like carrion creatures, screaming ''Ere y'are sir, 'ere y'are sir, 'ere y'are sir,' exactly like some foul carrion objects, perfectly obscene; and paterfamilias on board, laughing when the boys went right down in that awful mud, occasionally throwing them a ha'penny. And if you'd seen the intent look on the faces of those boys, and the way they darted in the filth when a coin was flung—really, no vulture or jackal could dream of approaching them, for foulness. I *never* would go on a pleasure boat again—never.''

Gerald watched her all the time she spoke, his eyes glittering with faint rousedness. It was not so much what she said: it was she herself who roused him, roused him with a small, vivid pricking.

"Of course," he said, "every civilised body is bound to have its vermin."

"Why?" cried Ursula. "*I* don't have vermin."

"And it's not that—it's the *quality* of the whole thing—paterfamilias laughing and thinking it sport, and throwing the ha'pennies, and materfamilias spreading her fat little knees and eating, continually eating—" replied Gudrun.

"Yes," said Ursula. "It isn't the boys so much who are vermin; it's the people themselves, the whole body politic, as you call it."

Gerald laughed.

"Never mind," he said. "You shan't go on the launch."

Gudrun flushed quickly at his rebuke. There were a few moments of silence. Gerald, like a sentinel, was watching the people who were going on to the boat. He was very good-looking and self-contained, but his air of soldierly alertness was rather irritating.

"Will you have tea here then, or go across to the house, where there's a tent on the lawn?" he asked.

"Can't we have a rowing boat, and get out?" asked Ursula, who was always rushing in too fast.

"To get out?" smiled Gerald.

"You see," cried Gudrun, flushing at Ursula's outspoken rudeness, "we don't know the people, we are almost *complete* strangers here."

"Oh, I can soon set you up with a few acquaintances," he said easily.

Gudrun looked at him, to see if it were ill-meant. Then she smiled at him.

"Ah," she said, "you know what we mean. Can't we go up there, and explore that coast?" She pointed to a grove on a hillock of the meadow-side, near the shore, half way down the lake. "That looks perfectly lovely. We might even bathe. Isn't it beautiful in this light!—Really, it's like one of the reaches of the Nile—as one imagines the Nile."

Gerald smiled at her factitious enthusiasm for the distant spot.

"You're sure it's far enough off?" he asked ironically, adding at once: "Yes, you might go there, if we could get a boat. They seem to be all out." He looked round the lake and counted the rowing boats on its surface.

"How lovely it would be!" cried Ursula wistfully.

"And don't you want tea?" he said.

"Oh," said Gudrun, "we could just drink a cup, and be off."

He looked from one to the other, smiling. He was somewhat offended—yet sporting.

"Can you manage a boat pretty well?" he asked.

"Yes," replied Gudrun, coldly, "pretty well."

"Oh yes," cried Ursula. "We can both of us row like water-spiders."

"You can?—There's a light little canoe of mine, that I didn't take out for fear somebody should drown themselves. Do you think you'd be safe in that?"

"Oh perfectly," said Gudrun.

"What an angel!" cried Ursula.

"Don't, for *my* sake, have an accident—because I'm responsible for the water."

"Sure," pledged Gudrun.

"Besides, we can both swim quite well," said Ursula.

"Well—then I'll get them to put you up a tea-basket, and you can picnic all to yourselves,—that's the idea, isn't it?"

"How fearfully good! How frightfully nice if you could!" cried Gudrun warmly, her colour flushing up again. It made the blood stir in his veins, the subtle way she turned to him and infused her gratitude into his body.

"Where's Birkin?" he said, his eyes twinkling. "He might help me to get it down."

"But what about your hand? Isn't it hurt?" asked Gudrun, rather muted, as if avoiding the intimacy. This was the first time the hurt had been mentioned. The curious way she skirted round the subject sent a new, subtle caress through his veins. He took his hand out of his pocket. It was bandaged. He looked at it, then put it in his pocket again. Gudrun quivered at the sight of the wrapped up paw.

"Oh, I can manage with one hand. The canoe is as light as a feather," he said. "There's Rupert!—Rupert!"

Birkin turned from his social duties and came towards them.

"What have you done to it?" asked Ursula, who had been aching to put the question for the last half hour.

"To my hand?" said Gerald. "I trapped it in some machinery."

"Ugh!" said Ursula. "And did it hurt it much?"

"Yes," he said. "It did at the time. It's getting better now. It crushed the fingers."

"Oh," cried Ursula, as if in pain, "I hate people who hurt themselves. I can *feel* it." And she shook her hand.

"What do you want?" said Birkin.

The two men carried down the slim brown boat, and set it on the water.

"You're quite sure you'll be safe in it?" Gerald asked.

"Quite sure," said Gudrun. "I wouldn't be so mean as to take it, if there was the slightest doubt. But I've had a canoe at Arundel, and I assure you I'm perfectly safe."

So saying, having given her word like a man, she and Ursula entered the frail craft, and pushed gently off. The two men stood watching them. Gudrun was paddling. She knew the men were watching her, and it made her slow and rather clumsy. The colour flew in her face like a flag.

"Thanks awfully," she called back to him, from the water, as the boat slid away. "It's lovely—like sitting in a leaf."

He laughed at the fancy. Her voice was shrill and strange, calling from the distance. He watched her as she paddled away. There was something child-like about her, trustful and deferential, like a child. He watched her all the while, as she rowed. And to Gudrun it was a real delight, in make-believe, to be the child-like, clinging woman to the man who stood there on the quay, so good-looking and efficient in his white clothes, and moreover the most important man she knew at the moment. She did not take any notice of the wavering, indistinct, lambent Birkin, who stood at his side. One figure at a time occupied the field of her attention.

The boat rustled lightly along the water. They passed the bathers whose striped tents stood between the willows of the meadow's edge, and drew along the open shore, past the meadows that sloped golden in the light of the already late afternoon. Other boats were stealing under the wooded shore opposite, they could hear people's laughter and voices. But Gudrun rowed on towards the clump of trees that balanced perfect in the distance, in the golden light.

The sisters found a little place where a tiny stream flowed into the lake, with reeds and flowery marsh of pink willow herb, and a gravelly bank to the side. Here they ran delicately ashore, with their frail boat, the two girls took off their shoes and stockings and went through the water's edge to the grass. The tiny ripples of the lake were warm and clear, they lifted their boat on to the bank, and looked round with joy. They were quite alone in a forsaken little stream-mouth, and on a knoll just behind was the clump of trees.

"We will bathe just for a moment," said Ursula, "and then we'll have tea."

They looked round. Nobody could notice them, or could come up in time to see them. In less than a minute Ursula had thrown off her clothes and had slipped naked into the water, and was swimming out. Quickly, Gudrun joined her. They swam silently and blissfully for a few minutes, circling round their little stream-mouth. Then they slipped ashore and ran into the grove again, like nymphs.

"How lovely it is to be free," said Ursula, running swiftly here and there between the tree trunks, quite naked, her hair blowing loose. The grove was of beech-trees, big and splendid, a steel-grey scaffolding of trunks and boughs, with level sprays of strong green here and there, whilst through the northern side the distance glimmered open as through a window.

When they had run and danced themselves dry, the girls quickly dressed and sat down to the fragrant tea. They sat on the northern side of the grove, in the yellow sunshine facing the slope of the grassy hill, alone in a little wild world of their own. The tea was hot and aromatic, there were delicious little sandwiches of cucumber and of caviare, and winy cakes.

"Are you happy, Prune?" cried Ursula in delight, looking at her sister.

"Ursula, I'm perfectly happy," replied Gudrun gravely, looking at the westering sun.

"So am I."

When they were together, doing the things they enjoyed, the two sisters were quite complete in a perfect world of their own. And this was one of the perfect moments of freedom and delight, such as children alone know, when all seems a perfect and blissful adventure.

When they had finished tea, the two girls sat on, silent and serene. Then Ursula, who had a beautiful strong voice, began to sing to herself, softly: "Ännchen von Tharau." Gudrun listened, as she sat beneath the trees, and the yearning came into her heart. Ursula seemed so peaceful and sufficient unto herself, sitting there unconsciously crooning her song, strong and unquestioned at the centre of her own universe. And Gudrun felt herself outside. Always this desolating, agonised feeling, that she was outside of life, an onlooker, whilst Ursula was a partaker, caused Gudrun to suffer from a sense of her own negation, and made her, that she must always demand the other to be aware of her, to be in connection with her.

"Do you mind if I do Dalcroze to that tune, Hurtler?" she asked in a curious muted tone, scarce moving her lips.

"What did you say?" asked Ursula, looking up in peaceful surprise.

"Will you sing while I do Dalcroze?" said Gudrun, suffering at having to repeat herself.

Ursula thought a moment, gathering her straying wits together.

"While you do——?" she asked vaguely.

"Dalcroze movements," said Gudrun, suffering tortures of self-consciousness, even because of her sister.

"Oh Dalcroze! I couldn't catch the name. *Do*—I should love to see you," cried Ursula, with childish surprised brightness. "What shall I sing?"

"Sing anything you like, and I'll take the rhythm from it."

But Ursula could not for her life think of anything to sing. However, she suddenly began, in a laughing, teasing voice:

"My love——is a high-born lady—"

Gudrun, looking as if some invisible chain weighed on her hands and feet, began slowly to dance in the eurythmic manner, pulsing and fluttering rhythmically with her feet, making slower, regular gestures with her hands and arms, now spreading her arms wide, now raising them above her head, now flinging them softly apart, and lifting her face, her feet all the time beating and running to the measure of the song, as if it were some strange incantation, her white, rapt form drifting here and there in a strange impulsive rhapsody, seeming to be lifted on a breeze of incantation, shuddering with strange little runs. Ursula sat on the grass, her mouth open in her singing, her eyes laughing as if she thought it was a great joke, but a yellow light flashing up in them, as she caught some of the unconscious ritualistic suggestion of the complex shuddering and waving and drifting of her sister's white form, that was clutched in pure, mindless, tossing rhythm, and a will set powerful in a kind of hypnotic influence.

"My love is a high-born lady—She is-s-s—rather dark than shady—" rang out Ursula's laughing, satiric song, and quicker, fiercer went Gudrun in the dance, stamping as if she were trying to throw off some bond, flinging her hands suddenly and stamping again, then rushing with face uplifted and throat full and beautiful, and eyes half closed, sightless. The sun was low and yellow, sinking down, and in the sky floated a thin, ineffectual moon.

Ursula was quite absorbed in her song, when suddenly Gudrun stopped and said mildly, ironically:

"Ursula!"

"Yes?" said Ursula, opening her eyes out of the trance.

Gudrun was standing still and pointing, a mocking smile on her face, towards the side.

"Ugh!" cried Ursula in sudden panic, starting to her feet.

"They're quite all right," rang out Gudrun's sardonic voice.

On the left stood a little cluster of Highland cattle, vividly coloured and fleecy in the evening light, their horns branching into the sky, pushing forward their muzzles inquisitively, to know what it was all about. Their eyes glittered through their tangle of hair, their naked nostrils were full of shadow.

"Won't they do anything?" cried Ursula in fear.

Gudrun, who was usually frightened of cattle, now shook her head in a queer, half-doubtful, half-sardonic motion, a faint smile round her mouth.

"Don't they look charming, Ursula?" cried Gudrun, in a high, strident voice, something like the scream of a sea-gull.

"Charming," cried Ursula in trepidation. "But won't they do anything to us?"

Again Gudrun looked back at her sister with an enigmatic smile, and shook her head.

"I'm sure they won't," she said, as if she had to convince herself also, and yet, as if she were confident of some secret power in herself, and had to put it to the test. "Sit down and sing again," she called in her high, strident voice.

"I'm frightened," cried Ursula, in a pathetic voice, watching the group of sturdy short cattle, that stood with their knees planted, and watched with their dark, wicked eyes, through the matted fringe of their hair. Nevertheless, she sank down again, in her former posture.

"They are quite safe," came Gudrun's high call. "Sing something, you've only to sing something."

It was evident she had a strange passion to dance before the sturdy, handsome cattle.

Ursula began to sing, in a false, quavering voice:

"Way down in Tennessee———"

She sounded purely anxious. Nevertheless Gudrun, with her arms outspread and her face uplifted, went in a strange, palpitating dance towards the cattle, lifting her body towards them as if in a spell, her feet pulsing as if in some little frenzy of unconscious sensation, her arms, her wrists, her hands stretching and heaving and falling and reaching and reaching and falling, her breasts lifted and shaken towards the cattle, her throat exposed as in some voluptuous ecstasy towards them, whilst she drifted imperceptibly nearer, an uncanny white figure carried away in its own rapt trance, ebbing in strange fluctuations upon the cattle, that waited, and ducked their heads a little in sudden contraction from her, watching all the time as if hypnotised, their bare horns branching in the clear light, as the white figure of the woman ebbed upon them, in the slow, hypnotising convulsion of the dance. She could feel them just in front of her, it was as if she had the electric pulse from their breasts running into her hands. Soon she would touch them, actually touch them. A terrible shiver of fear and pleasure went through her. And all the while, Ursula spell-bound kept up her high-pitched thin, irrelevant song, which pierced the fading evening like an incantation.

Gudrun could hear the cattle breathing heavily with helpless fear and fascination. Oh, they were brave little beasts, these wild Scotch bullocks, wild and fleecy. Suddenly one of them snorted, ducked its head, and backed.

"Hue! Hi—eee!" came a sudden loud shout from the edge of the grove. The cattle broke and fell back quite spontaneously, went running up the hill, their fleece waving like fire to their motion. Gudrun stood suspended, out on the grass, Ursula rose to her feet.

It was Gerald and Birkin come to find them, and Gerald had cried out to frighten off the cattle.

"What do you think you're doing?" he now called, in a high, wondering, vexed tone.

"Why have you come—?" came back Gudrun's strident cry of anger.

"What do you think you were doing?" Gerald repeated, automatically.

"We were doing eurythmics," laughed Ursula, in a shaken voice.

Gudrun stood aloof looking at them with large dark eyes of resentment, suspended for a few moments. Then she walked away up the hill, after the cattle, which had gathered in a little, spell-bound cluster higher up.

"Where are you going?" Gerald called after her. And he followed her up the hill-side. The sun had gone behind the hill, and shadows were clinging to the earth, the sky above was full of travelling light.

"A poor song for a dance," said Birkin to Ursula, standing before her with a sardonic, flickering laugh on his face. And in another second, he was singing softly to himself, and dancing a grotesque step-dance in front of her, his limbs and body shaking loose, his face flickering palely, a constant thing, whilst his feet beat a rapid mocking tattoo, and his body seemed to hang all loose and quaking in between, like a shadow.

"I think we've all gone mad," she said, laughing rather frightened.

"Pity we aren't madder," he answered, as he kept up the incessant shaking dance. Then suddenly he leaned up to her and kissed her fingers lightly, putting his face to hers and looking into her eyes with a pale grin. She stepped back, affronted.

"Offended—?" he asked ironically, suddenly going quite still and reserved again. "I thought you liked the light fantastic."

"Not like that," she said, confused and bewildered, almost affronted. Yet somewhere inside her she was fascinated by the sight of his loose, vibrating body, perfectly abandoned to its own dropping and swinging, and by the pallid, sardonic-smiling face above. Yet automatically she stiffened herself away, and disapproved. It seemed almost an obscenity, in a man who talked as a rule so very seriously.

"Why not like that?" he mocked. And immediately he dropped again into the incredibly rapid, slack-waggling dance, watching her malevolently. And moving in the rapid, stationary dance, he came a little nearer, and reached forward with an incredibly mocking, satiric gleam on his face, and would have kissed her again, had she not started back.

"No, don't!" she cried, really afraid.

"Cordelia after all," he said satirically.

She was stung, as if this were an insult. She knew he intended it as such, and it bewildered her.

"And you," she cried in retort, "why do you always take your soul in your mouth, so frightfully full!"

"So that I can spit it out the more readily," he said, pleased by his own retort.

Gerald Crich, his face narrowing to an intent gleam, followed up the hill with quick strides, straight after Gudrun. The cattle stood with their noses together on the brow of a slope, watching the scene below, the men in white hovering about the white forms of the women, watching above all Gudrun, who was advancing slowly towards them. She stood a moment, glancing back at Gerald, and then at the cattle.

Then in a sudden motion, she lifted her arms and rushed sheer upon the long-horned bullocks, in shuddering irregular runs, pausing for a second and looking at them, then lifting her hands and running forward with a flash, till they ceased pawing the ground, and gave way, snorting with terror, lifting their heads from the ground and flinging themselves away, galloping off into the evening, becoming tiny in the distance, and still not stopping.

Gudrun remained staring after them, with a mask-like, defiant face.

"Why do you want to drive them mad?" asked Gerald, coming up with her.

She took no notice of him, only averted her face from him.

"It's not safe, you know," he persisted. "They're nasty, when they do turn."

"Turn where? Turn away?" she mocked loudly.

"No," he said, "turn against you."

"Turn against *me*?" she mocked.

He could make nothing of this.

"Any way, they gored one of the farmer's cows to death, the other day," he said.

"What do I care?" she said.

"*I* cared though," he replied, "seeing that they're my cattle."

"How are they yours! You haven't swallowed them. Give me one of them now," she said, holding out her hand.

"You know where they are," he said, pointing over the hill. "You can have one if you'd like it sent to you later on."

She looked at him inscrutably.

"You think I'm afraid of you and your cattle, don't you?" she asked.

His eyes narrowed dangerously. There was a faint domineering smile on his face.

"Why should I think that?" he said.

She was watching him all the time with her dark, dilated, inchoate eyes. She leaned forward and swung round her arm, catching him a light blow on the face with the back of her hand.

"That's why," she said, mocking.

And she felt in her soul an unconquerable desire for deep violence against him. She shut off the fear and dismay that filled her conscious mind. She wanted to do as she did, she was not going to be afraid.

He recoiled from the slight blow on his face. He became deadly pale, and a dangerous flame darkened his eyes. For some seconds he could not speak, his lungs were so suffused with blood, his heart stretched almost to bursting with a great gush of ungovernable emotion. It was as if some reservoir of black emotion had burst within him, and swamped him.

"You have struck the first blow," he said at last, forcing the words from his lungs, in a voice so soft and low, it sounded like a dream within her, not spoken in the outer air.

"And I shall strike the last," she retorted involuntarily, with confident assurance. He was silent, he did not contradict her.

She stood negligently, staring away from him, into the distance. On the edge of her consciousness the question was asking itself, automatically, "Why *are* you behaving in this *impossible* and ridiculous fashion?" But she was sullen, she half shoved the question out of herself. She could not get it clean away, so she felt self-conscious.

Gerald, very pale, was watching her closely. His eyes were lit up with intent lights, absorbed and gleaming. She turned suddenly on him.

"It's you who make me behave like this, you know," she said, almost suggestive.

"I? How?" he said.

But she turned away, and set off towards the lake. Below, on the water, lanterns were coming alight, faint ghosts of warm flame floating in the pallor of the first twilight. The earth was spread with darkness, like lacquer, overhead was a pale sky, all primrose, and the lake was pale as milk in one part. Away at the landing-stage, tiniest points of coloured rays were stringing themselves in the dusk. The launch was being illuminated. All round, shadow was gathering from the trees.

Gerald, white like a presence in his summer clothes, was following down the open grassy slope. Gudrun waited for him to come up. Then she softly put out her hand and touched him, saying softly:

"Don't be angry with me."

A flame flew over him, and he was unconscious. Yet he stammered:

"I'm not angry with you. I'm in love with you."

His mind was gone, he grasped for sufficient mechanical control, to save himself. She laughed a silvery little mockery, yet intolerably caressive.

"That's one way of putting it," she said.

The terrible swooning burden on his mind, the awful swooning, the loss of all his control, was too much for him. He grasped her arm in his one hand, as if his hand were iron.

"It's all right, then, is it?" he said, holding her arrested.

She looked at the face with the fixed eyes, set before her, and her blood ran cold.

"Yes, it's all right," she said softly, as if drugged, her voice crooning and witch-like.

He walked on beside her, a striding, mindless body. But he recovered a little as he went. He suffered badly. He had killed his brother when a boy, and was set apart, like Cain.

They found Birkin and Ursula sitting together by the boats, talking and laughing. Birkin had been teasing Ursula.

"Do you smell this little marsh?" he said, sniffing the air. He was very sensitive to scents, and quick in understanding them.

"It's rather nice," she said.

"No," he replied, "alarming."

"Why alarming?" she laughed.

"It seethes and seethes, a river of darkness," he said, "putting forth lilies and snakes, and the ignis fatuus, and rolling all the time onward. That's what we never take into count—that it rolls onwards."

"What does?"

"The other river, the black river. We always consider the silver river of life, rolling on and quickening all the world to a brightness, on and on to heaven, flowing into a bright eternal sea, a heaven of angels thronging.— But the other is our real reality—"

"But what other? I don't see any other," said Ursula.

"It is your reality, nevertheless," he said; "the dark river of dissolution.—You see it rolls in us just as the other rolls—the black river of corruption. And our flowers are of this—our sea-born Aphrodite, all our white phosphorescent flowers of sensuous perfection, all our reality, nowadays."

"You mean that Aphrodite is really deathly?" asked Ursula.

"I mean she is the flowering mystery of the death-process, yes," he replied. "When the stream of synthetic creation lapses, we find ourselves part of the inverse process, the flood of destructive creation. Aphrodite is born in the first spasm of universal dissolution—then the snakes and swans and lotus—marsh-flowers—and Gudrun and Gerald—born in the process of destructive creation."

"And you and me—?" she asked.

"Probably," he replied. "In part, certainly. Whether we are that, in toto, I don't yet know."

"You mean we are flowers of dissolution—fleurs du mal?—I don't feel as if I were," she protested.

He was silent for a time.

"I don't feel as if we were, *altogether*," he replied. "Some people are pure flowers of dark corruption—lilies. But there ought to be some roses, warm and flamy.—You know Herakleitos says 'a dry soul is best.' I know so well what that means. Do you?"

"I'm not sure," Ursula replied. "But what if people *are* all flowers of dissolution—when they're flowers at all—what difference does it make?"

"No difference—and all the difference. Dissolution rolls on, just as production does," he said. "It is a progressive process—and it ends in universal nothing—the end of the world, if you like.—But why isn't the end of the world as good as the beginning?"

"I suppose it isn't," said Ursula, rather angry.

"Oh yes, ultimately," he said. "It means a new cycle of creation after—but not for us. If it is the end, then we are of the end—fleurs du mal if you like. If we are fleurs du mal, we are not roses of happiness, and there you are."

"But I think I am," said Ursula. "I think I am a rose of happiness."

"Ready-made?" he asked ironically.

"No—real," she said, hurt.

"If we are the end, we are not the beginning," he said.

"Yes we are," she said. "The beginning comes out of the end."

"After it, not out of it. After us, not out of us."

"You are a devil, you know, really," she said. "You want to destroy our hope. You *want* us to be deathly."

"No," he said, "I only want us to *know* what we are."

"Ha!" she cried in anger. "You only want us to know death."

"You're quite right," said the soft voice of Gerald, out of the dusk behind.

Birkin rose. Gerald and Gudrun came up. They all began to smoke, in the moments of silence. One after another, Birkin lighted their cigarettes. The match flickered in the twilight, and they were all smoking peacefully by the water-side. The lake was dim, the light dying from off it, in the midst of the dark land. The air all round was intangible, neither here nor there, and there was an unreal noise of banjoes, or suchlike music.

As the golden swim of light overhead died out, the moon gained brightness, and seemed to begin to smile forth her ascendancy. The dark woods on the opposite shore melted into universal shadow. And amid this universal undershadow, there was a scattered intrusion of lights. Far down the lake were fantastic pale strings of colour, like beads of wan fire, green and red and yellow. The music came out in a little puff, as the launch, all illuminated, veered into the great shadow, stirring her outlines of half-living lights, puffing out her music in little drifts.

All were lighting up. Here and there, close against the faint water, and at the far end of the lake, where the water lay milky in the last whiteness of the sky, and there was no shadow, solitary, frail flames of lanterns floated from the unseen boats. There was a sound of oars, and a boat passed from the pallor into the darkness under the wood, where her lanterns seemed to kindle into fire, hanging in ruddy lovely globes. And again, in the lake, shadowy red gleams hovered in reflection about the boat. Everywhere were these noiseless ruddy creatures of fire drifting near the surface of the water, caught at by the rarest, scarce visible reflections.

Birkin brought the lanterns from the bigger boat, and the four shadowy white figures gathered round, to light them. Ursula held up the first, Birkin lowered the light from the rosy, glowing cup of his hands, into the depths of the lantern. It was kindled, and they all stood back to look at the great blue moon of light that hung from Ursula's hand, casting a strange gleam on her face. It flickered, and Birkin went bending over the well of light. His face shone out like an apparition, so unconscious, and again, something demoniacal. Ursula was dim and veiled, looming over him.

"That is all right," said his voice softly.

She held up the lantern. It had a flight of storks streaming through a turquoise sky of light, over a dark earth.

"This is beautiful," she said.

"Lovely," echoed Gudrun, who wanted to hold one also, and lift it up full of beauty.

"Light one for me," she said. Gerald stood by her, incapacitated. Birkin lit the lantern she held up. Her heart beat with anxiety, to see how beautiful it would be. It was primrose yellow, with tall straight flowers growing darkly from their dark leaves, lifting their heads into the primrose day, while butterflies hovered about them, in the pure clear light.

Gudrun gave a little cry of excitement, as if pierced with delight.

"Isn't it beautiful, oh, isn't it beautiful!"

Her soul was really pierced with beauty, she was translated beyond herself. Gerald leaned near to her, into her zone of light, as if to see. He came close to her, and stood touching her, looking with her at the primrose-shining globe. And she turned her face to his, that was faintly bright in the light of the lantern, and they stood together in one luminous union, close together and ringed round with light, all the rest excluded.

Birkin looked away, and went to light Ursula's second lantern. It had a pale ruddy sea-bottom, with black crabs and sea-weed moving sinuously under a transparent sea, that passed into flamy ruddiness above.

"You've got the heavens above, and the waters under the earth," said Birkin to her.

"Anything but the earth itself," she laughed, watching his live hands that hovered to attend to the light.

"I'm dying to see what my second one is," cried Gudrun, in a vibrating rather strident voice, that seemed to repel the others from her.

Birkin went and kindled it. It was of a lovely deep blue colour, with a red floor, and a great white cuttle-fish flowing in white soft streams all over it. The cuttle-fish had a face that stared straight from the heart of the light, very fixed and coldly intent.

"How truly terrifying!" exclaimed Gudrun, in a voice of horror. Gerald, at her side, gave a low laugh.

"But isn't it really fearful!" she cried in dismay.

Again he laughed, and said:

"Change it with Ursula, for the crabs."

Gudrun was silent for a moment.

"Ursula," she said, "could you bear to have this fearful thing?"

"I think the colouring is *lovely*," said Ursula.

"So do I," said Gudrun. "But could you *bear* to have it swinging to your boat? Don't you want to destroy it *at once*?"

"Oh no," said Ursula. "I don't want to destroy it."

"Well—do you mind having it instead of the crabs? Are you sure you don't mind?"

Gudrun came forward to exchange lanterns.

"No," said Ursula, yielding up the crabs and receiving the cuttle-fish.

Yet she could not help feeling rather resentful at the way in which Gudrun and Gerald should assume a right over her, a precedence.

"Come then," said Birkin. "I'll put them on the boats."

He and Ursula were moving away to the big boat.

"I suppose you'll row me back, Rupert," said Gerald, out of the pale shadow of the evening.

"Won't you go with Gudrun in the canoe?" said Birkin. "It'll be more interesting."

There was a moment's pause. Birkin and Ursula stood dimly, with their swinging lanterns, by the water's edge. The world was all illusive.

"Is that all right?" said Gudrun to him.

"It'll suit *me* very well," he said. "But what about you, and the rowing? I don't see why you should pull me."

"Why not?" she said. "I can pull you as well as I could pull Ursula." By her tone he could tell she wanted to have him in the boat to herself, and that she was subtly gratified that she should have power over them both. He gave himself, in a strange, electric submission.

She handed him the lanterns, whilst she went to fix the cane at the end of the canoe. He followed after her, and stood with the lanterns dangling against his white-flannelled thighs, emphasising the shadow around.

"Kiss me before we go," came his voice softly from out of the shadow above.

She stopped her work in real, momentary astonishment.

"But why?" she exclaimed, in pure surprise.

"Why?" he echoed, ironically.

And she looked at him fixedly for some moments. Then she leaned forward and kissed him, with a slow, luxurious kiss, lingering on the mouth. And then she took the lanterns from him, while he stood swooning with the perfect fire that burned in all his joints.

They lifted the canoe into the water, Gudrun took her place, and Gerald pushed off.

"Are you sure you don't hurt your hand, doing that?" she asked, solicitous. "Because I could have done it *perfectly*."

"I don't hurt myself," he said in a low, soft voice, that caressed her with inexpressible beauty.

And she watched him as he sat near her, very near to her, in the stern of the canoe, his legs coming towards hers, his feet touching hers. And she paddled softly, lingeringly, longing for him to say something meaningful to her. But he remained silent.

"You like this, do you?" she said, in a gentle, solicitous voice.

He laughed shortly.

"There is a space between us," he said, in the same low, unconscious voice, as if something were speaking out of him. And she was as if magically aware of their being balanced in separation, in the boat. She swooned with acute comprehension and pleasure.

"But I'm very near," she said caressively, gaily.

"Yet distant, distant," he said. Again she was silent with pleasure, before she answered, speaking with a reedy, thrilled voice:

"Yet we cannot very well change, whilst we are on the water."—She caressed him subtly and strangely, having him completely at her mercy.

A dozen or more boats on the lake swung their rosy and moon-like lanterns low on the water, that reflected as from a fire. In the distance, the steamer twanged and thrummed and washed with her faintly-splashing paddles, trailing her strings of coloured lights, and occasionally lighting up the whole scene luridly with an effusion of fireworks, Roman candles and sheafs of stars and other simple effects, illuminating the surface of the water, and showing the boats creeping round, low down. Then the lovely darkness fell again, the lanterns and the little threaded lights glimmered softly, there was a muffled knocking of oars and a waving of music.

Gudrun paddled almost imperceptibly. Gerald could see, not far ahead, the rich blue and the rose globes of Ursula's lanterns swaying softly cheek to cheek as Birkin rowed, and iridescent, evanescent gleams chasing in the wake. He was aware, too, of his own delicately coloured lights casting their softness behind him.

Gudrun rested her paddle and looked round. The canoe lifted with the lightest ebbing of the water. Gerald's white knees were very near to her.

"Isn't it beautiful!" she said softly, as if reverently.

She looked at him, as he leaned back against the faint crystal of the lantern-light. She could see his face, although it was a pure shadow. But it was a piece of twilight. And her breast was keen with passion for him, he was so beautiful in his male stillness and mystery. It was a certain pure effluence of maleness, like an aroma from his softly, firmly moulded contours, a certain rich perfection of his presence, that touched her with an ecstasy, a thrill of pure intoxication. She loved to look at him. For the present she did not want to touch him, to know the further, satisfying substance of his living body. He was purely intangible, yet so near. Her hands lay on the paddle like slumber, she only wanted to see him like a crystal shadow, to feel his essential presence.

"Yes," he said vaguely. "It is very beautiful."

He was listening to the faint near sounds, the dropping of water-drops from the oar-blades, the slight drumming of the lanterns behind him, as they rubbed against one another, the occasional rustling of Gudrun's full skirt, an alien land noise. His mind was almost submerged, he was almost transfused, lapsed out for the first time in his life, into the things about him. For he always kept such a keen attentiveness, concentrated and unyielding in himself. Now he had let go, imperceptibly he was melting into oneness with the whole. It was like pure, perfect sleep, his first great sleep of life. He had been so insistent, so guarded, all his life. But here was sleep, and peace, and perfect lapsing out.

"Shall I row to the landing-stage?" asked Gudrun wistfully.

"Anywhere," he answered. "Let it drift."

"Tell me then, if we are running into anything," she replied, in that very quiet, toneless voice of sheer intimacy.

"The lights will show," he said.

So they drifted almost motionless, in silence. He wanted silence, pure and whole. But she was uneasy yet for some word, for some assurance.

"Nobody will miss you?" she asked, anxious for some communication.

"Miss me?" he echoed. "No! Why?"

"I wondered if anybody would be looking for you."

"Why should they look for me?" And then he remembered his manners. "But perhaps you want to get back," he said, in a changed voice.

"No, I don't want to get back," she replied. "No, I assure you."

"You're quite sure it's all right for you?"

"Perfectly all right."

And again they were still. The launch twanged and hooted, somebody was singing. Then as if the night smashed, suddenly there was a great shout, a confusion of shouting warring on the water, then the horrid noise of paddles reversed and churned violently.

Gerald sat up, and Gudrun looked at him in fear.

"Somebody in the water," he said, angrily, and desperately, looking keenly across the dusk. "Can you row up?"

"Where, to the launch?" asked Gudrun, in nervous panic.

"Yes."

"You'll tell me if I don't steer straight," she said, in nervous apprehension.

"You keep pretty level," he said, and the canoe hastened forward. The shouting and the noise continued, sounding horrid through the dusk, over the surface of the water.

"Wasn't this *bound* to happen?" said Gudrun, with heavy, hateful irony.

But he hardly heard, and she glanced over her shoulder to see her way. The half-dark waters were sprinkled with lovely bubbles of swaying lights, the launch did not look far off. She was rocking her lights in the early night. Gudrun rowed as hard as she could. But now that it was a serious matter, she seemed uncertain and clumsy in her stroke, it was difficult to paddle swiftly. She glanced at his face. He was looking fixedly into the darkness, very keen and alert and single in himself, instrumental. Her heart sank, and she seemed to die a death. "Of course," she said to herself, "nobody will be drowned. Of course they won't. It would be too extravagant and sensational." But her heart was cold, because of his sharp, impersonal face. It was as if he belonged naturally to dread and catastrophe, as if he were himself again.

Then there came a child's voice, a girl's high, piercing shriek:

"*Di—Di—Di—Di—Oh Di—Oh Di—Oh Di*!"

The blood ran cold in Gudrun's veins.

"It's Diana, is it," muttered Gerald. "The young monkey, she'd have to be up to some of her tricks."

And he glanced again at the paddle, the boat was not going quickly enough for him. It made Gudrun almost helpless at the rowing, this nervous stress. She kept up with all her might. Still the voices were calling and answering. "Where, Where? There you are—that's it. Which? No—No-o-o. Damn it all, here, *here*—" Boats were hurrying from all directions to the scene, coloured lanterns could be seen waving close to the surface of the lake, reflections swaying after them in uneven haste. The steamer hooted again, for some unknown reason. Gudrun's boat was travelling quickly, the lanterns were swinging behind Gerald.

And then again came the child's high, screaming voice, with a note of weeping and impatience in it now:

"*Di—Oh Di—Oh Di—Di—*!"

It was a terrible sound, coming through the obscure air of the evening.

"You'd be better if you were in bed, Winnie," Gerald muttered to himself.

He was stooping unlacing his shoes, pushing them off with the foot. Then he threw his soft hat into the bottom of the boat.

"You can't go into the water with your hurt hand," said Gudrun, panting, in a low voice of horror.

"What?—It won't hurt."

He had struggled out of his jacket, and had dropped it between his feet. He sat bare-headed, all in white now. He felt the belt at his waist. They were nearing the launch, which stood still big above them, its myriad lamps making lovely darts, and sinuous running tongues of ugly red and green and yellow on the lustrous dark water, under the shadow.

"*Oh get her out! Oh Di, darling! Oh get her out! Oh Daddy, Oh Daddy!*" moaned the child's voice, in distraction. Somebody was in the water, with a life-belt. Two boats paddled near, their lanterns swinging ineffectually, the boats nosing round.

"Hi there—Rockley!—hi there!"

"Mr Gerald!" came the captain's terrified voice. "Miss Diana's in the water."

"Anybody gone in for her?" came Gerald's sharp voice.

"Young Doctor Brindell, sir."

"Where?"

"Can't see no signs of them, sir. Everybody's looking, but there's nothing so far."

There was a moment's ominous pause.

"Where did she go in?"

"I think—about where that boat is," came the uncertain answer, "that one with red and green lights."

"Row there," said Gerald quietly to Gudrun.

"*Get her out, Gerald, Oh get her out*," the child's voice was crying anxiously. He took no heed.

"Lean back that way," said Gerald to Gudrun, as he stood up in the frail boat. "She won't upset."

In another moment, he had dropped clean down, soft and plumb, into the water. Gudrun was swaying violently in her boat, the agitated water shook with transient lights, she realised that it was faintly moonlight, and that he was gone. So it was possible to be gone. A terrible sense of fatality robbed her of all feeling and thought. So he was gone out of the world, there was merely the same world, and absence, his absence. The night seemed large and vacuous. Lanterns swayed here and there, people were talking in an undertone on the launch and in the boats. She could hear Winifred moaning: "*Oh do find her Gerald, do find her,*" and someone trying to comfort the child. Gudrun paddled aimlessly here and there. The terrible, massive, cold, boundless surface of the water terrified her beyond words. Would he never come back? She felt she must jump into the water too, to know the horror also.

She started, hearing someone say: "There he is." She saw the movement of his swimming, like a water-rat. And she rowed involuntarily to him. But he was near another boat, a bigger one. Still she rowed towards him. She must be very near. She saw him—he looked like a seal. He looked like a seal as he took hold of the side of the boat. His fair hair was washed down on his round head, his face seemed to glisten suavely. She could hear him panting.

Then he clambered into the boat. Oh, and the beauty of the subjection of his loins, white and dimly luminous as he climbed over the side of the boat, made her want to die, to die. The beauty of his dim and luminous loins as he climbed into the boat, his back rounded and soft—ah, this was too much for her, too final a vision. She knew it, and it was fatal. The terrible hopelessness of fate, and of beauty, such beauty!

He was not like a man to her, he was an incarnation, a great phase of life. She saw him press the water out of his face, and look at the bandage on his hand. And she knew it was all no good, and that she would never go beyond him, he was the final approximation of life to her.

"Put the lights out, we shall see better," came his voice, sudden and mechanical and belonging to the world of man. She could scarcely believe it. She could scarcely believe there was a world of man. She leaned round and blew out her lanterns. They were difficult to blow out. Everywhere the lights were gone, save the coloured points on the sides of the launch. The bluey-grey, early night spread level around, the moon was overhead, there were shadows of boats here and there.

Again there was a splash, and he was gone under. Gudrun sat, sick at heart, frightened of the great, level surface of the water, so heavy and deadly. She was so alone, with the level, unliving field of the water stretching beneath her. It was not a good isolation, it was a terrible, cold separation of suspense. She was suspended upon the surface of the insidious reality until such time as she also should disappear beneath it.

Then she knew, by a stirring of voices, that he had climbed out again, into a boat. She sat wanting connection with him. Strenuously she claimed her connection with him, across the invisible space of the water! But round her heart was an isolation unbearable, through which nothing would penetrate.

"Take the launch in. It's no use keeping her there. Get lines for the dragging," came the decisive, instrumental voice, that was full of the sound of the world.

The launch began gradually to beat the waters.

"*Gerald! Gerald?*" came the wild crying voice of Winifred. He did not answer. Slowly the launch drifted round in a pathetic, clumsy circle, and slunk away to the land, retreating into the dimness. The wash of her paddles grew duller. Gudrun rocked in her light boat, and dipped the paddle automatically to steady herself.

"Gudrun?" called Ursula's voice.

"Ursula!"

The boats of the two sisters pulled together.

"Where is Gerald?" said Gudrun.

"He's dived again," said Ursula plaintively. "And I know he ought not, with his hurt hand and everything."

"I'll take him in home this time," said Birkin.

The boats swayed again from the wash of the steamer. Gudrun and Ursula kept a look-out for Gerald.

"There he is!" cried Ursula, who had the sharpest eyes. He had not been long under. Birkin pulled towards him, Gudrun following. He swam slowly, and caught hold of the boat with his wounded hand. It slipped, and he sank back.

"Why don't you help him?" cried Ursula sharply.

He came again, and Birkin leaned to help him in to the boat. Gudrun again watched Gerald climb out of the water, but this time slowly, heavily, with the blind clambering motions of an amphibious beast, clumsy. Again the moon shone with faint luminosity on his white, wet figure, on the stooping back and the rounded loins. But it looked defeated now, his body, it clambered and fell with slow clumsiness. He was breathing hoarsely too, like an animal that is suffering. He sat slack and motionless in the boat, his head blunt and blind like a seal's, his whole appearance inhuman, unknowing. Gudrun shuddered as she mechanically followed his boat. Birkin rowed without speaking to the landing-stage.

"Where are you going?" Gerald asked suddenly, as if just waking up.

"Home," said Birkin.

"Oh no!" said Gerald imperiously. "We can't go home while they're in the water. Turn back again, I'm going to find them." The women were frightened, his voice was so imperative and dangerous, almost mad, not to be opposed.

"No," said Birkin. "You can't." There was a strange fluid compulsion in his voice. Gerald was silent, in a battle of wills. It was as if he would kill the other man. But Birkin rowed evenly and unswerving, with an inhuman inevitability.

"Why should you interfere?" said Gerald, in hate.

Birkin did not answer. He rowed towards the land. And Gerald sat mute, like a dumb beast, panting, his teeth chattering, his arms inert, his head like a seal's head.

They came to the landing-stage. Wet and naked-looking, Gerald climbed up the few steps. There stood his father, in the night.

"Father!" he said.

"Yes my boy?—Go home and get those things off."

"We shan't save them, father," said Gerald.

"There's hope yet, my boy."

"I'm afraid not. There's no knowing where they are. You can't find them. And there's a current, as cold as hell."

"We'll let the water out," said the father. "Go home you and look to yourself. See that he's looked after, Rupert," he added in a neutral voice.

"Well father, I'm sorry. I'm sorry. I'm afraid it's my fault. But it can't be helped; I've done what I could for the moment. I could go on diving, of course—not much, though—and not much use—"

He moved away barefoot, on the planks of the platform. Then he trod on something sharp.

"Of course, you've got no shoes on," said Birkin.

"His shoes are here!" cried Gudrun from below. She was making fast her boat.

Gerald waited for them to be brought to him. Gudrun came with them. He pulled them on his feet.

"If you once die," he said, "then when it's over, it's finished. Why come to life again? There's room under that water there for thousands."

"Two is enough," she said, murmuring.

He dragged on his second shoe. He was shivering violently, and his jaw shook as he spoke.

"That's true," he said, "maybe. But it's curious how much room there seems, a whole universe under there; and as cold as hell, you're as helpless as if your head was cut off." He could scarcely speak, he shook so violently.

"There's one thing about our family, you know," he continued. "Once anything goes wrong, it can never be put right again—not with us. I've noticed it all my life—you can't put a thing right, once it has gone wrong."

They were walking across the high-road to the house.

"And do you know, when you are down there, it is so cold, actually, and so endless, so different really from what it is on top, so endless—you wonder how it is so many are alive, why we're all up here.—Are you going? I shall see you again, shan't I? Goodnight, and thank you. Thank you very much."

The two girls waited a while, to see if there were any hope. The moon shone clearly overhead, an almost impertinent brightness, the small dark boats clustered on the water, there were voices and subdued shouts. But it was all to no purpose. Gudrun went home when Birkin returned.

He was commissioned to open the sluice that let out the water from the lake, which was pierced at one end, near the high-road, thus serving as a reservoir to supply with water the distant mines, in case of necessity. "Come with me," he said to Ursula. "And then I will walk home with you, when I've done this."

He called at the water-keeper's cottage and took the key of the sluice. They went through a little gate from the high-road, to the head of the water, where was a great stone basin which received the overflow, and a flight of stone steps descended into the depths of the water itself. At the head of the steps was the lock of the sluice-gate.

The night was silver-grey and perfect, save for the scattered, restless sound of voices. The grey sheen of the moonlight caught the stretch of water, dark boats plashed and moved. But Ursula's mind ceased to be receptive, everything was unimportant and unreal.

Birkin fixed the iron handle of the sluice, and turned it with a wrench. The cogs began slowly to rise. He turned and turned, like a slave, his white figure become distinct. Ursula looked away. She could not bear to see him winding heavily and laboriously, bending and rising mechanically like a slave, turning the handle.

Then, a real shock to her, there came a loud splashing of water from out of the dark, tree-filled hollow beyond the road, a splashing that deepened rapidly to a harsh roar, and then became a heavy, booming noise of a great body of water falling solidly all the time. It occupied the whole of the night, this great steady booming of water, everything was drowned within it, drowned and lost. Ursula seemed to have to struggle for her life. She put her hands over her ears, and looked at the high, bland moon.

"Can't we go now?" she cried to Birkin, who was watching the water on the steps, to see if it would get any lower. It seemed to fascinate him. He looked up at her and nodded.

The little dark boats had moved nearer, people were crowding curiously along the hedge by the high-road, to see what was to be seen. Birkin and Ursula went to the cottage with the key, then turned their backs on the lake. She was in great haste. She could not bear the terrible crushing boom of the escaping water.

"Do you think they are dead?" she cried in a high voice, to make herself heard.

"Yes," he replied.

"Isn't it horrible!"

He paid no heed. They walked up the hill, further and further away from the noise.

"Do you mind very much?" she asked him.

"I don't mind about the dead," he said, "once they are dead. The worst of it is, they cling on to the living, and won't let go."

She pondered for a time.

"Yes," she said. "The *fact* of death doesn't really seem to matter much, does it?"

"No," he said. "What does it matter if Diana Crich is alive or dead?"

"Doesn't it!" she said, shocked.

"No, why should it? Better she were dead—she'll be much more real. She'll be positive in death. In life she was a fretting, negated thing."

"You are rather horrible," murmured Ursula.

"No! I'd rather Diana Crich were dead. Her living, somehow, was all wrong. As for the young man, poor devil—he'll find his way out quickly instead of slowly. Death is all right—nothing better."

"Yet *you* don't want to die," she challenged him.

He was silent for a time. Then he said, in a voice that was frightening to her in its change:

"I should like to be through with it—I should like to be through with the death-process."

"And aren't you?" asked Ursula nervously.

They walked on for some way in silence, under the trees. Then he said, slowly, as if afraid:

"There is life which belongs to death, and there is life which isn't death. One is tired of the life that belongs to death—our kind of life. But whether it is finished, God knows. I want love that is like sleep, like being born again, vulnerable as a baby that just comes into the world."

Ursula listened, half attentive, half avoiding what he said. She seemed to catch the drift of his statement, and then she drew away. She wanted to hear, but she did not want to be implicated. She was reluctant to yield there, where he wanted her, to yield, as it were, her very identity.

"Why should love be like sleep?" she asked sadly.

"I don't know. So that it is like death—I *do* want to die from this life—and yet it is more than life itself. One is delivered over like a naked infant from the womb, all the old defences and the old body gone, a new air around one, that has never been breathed before."

She listened, making out what he said. She knew, as well as he knew, that words themselves do not convey meaning, that they are but a gesture we make, a dumb show like any other. And she seemed to feel his gesture through her blood, and she drew back, even though her desire sent her forward.

"But," she said gravely, "didn't you say you wanted something that was *not* love—something beyond love?"

He turned in confusion. There was always confusion in speech. Yet it must be spoken. Whichever way one moved, if one were to move forwards, one must break a way through. And to know, to give utterance, was to break a way through the walls of the prison, as the infant in labour strives through the walls of the womb. There is no new movement now, without the breaking through of the old body, deliberately, in knowledge, in the struggle to get out.

"I don't want love," he said. "I don't want to know you. I want to be gone out of myself, and you to be lost to yourself, so we are found different.— One shouldn't talk when one is tired and wretched.—One Hamletises, and it seems a lie.—Only believe me when I show a bit of healthy pride and insouciance. I hate myself serious."

"Why shouldn't you be serious?" she said.

He thought for a minute, then he said, sulkily:

"I don't know."

Then they walked on in silence, at outs. He was vague and lost.

"Isn't it strange," she said, suddenly putting her hand on his arm, with a loving impulse, "how we always talk like this! I suppose we do love each other, in some way."

"Oh yes," he said; "too much."

She laughed almost gaily.

"You'd have to have it your own way, wouldn't you?" she teased. "You could never take it on trust."

He changed, laughed softly, and turned and took her in his arms, in the middle of the road.

"Yes," he said softly.

And he kissed her face and brow, slowly, gently, with a sort of delicate happiness which surprised her extremely, and to which she could not respond. They were soft, blind kisses, perfect in their stillness. Yet she held back from them. It was like strange moths, very soft and silent, settling on her from the darkness of her soul. She was uneasy. She drew away.

"Isn't somebody coming?" she said.

So they looked down the dark road, then set off again walking towards Beldover. Then suddenly, to show him she was no shallow prude, she stopped and held him tight, hard against her, and covered his face with hard, fierce kisses of passion. In spite of his otherness, the old blood beat up in him.

"Not this, not this," he whimpered to himself, as the first perfect mood of softness and sleep-loveliness ebbed back away from the rushing of passion that came up his limbs and over his face as she drew him. And soon he was a perfect hard flame of passionate desire for her. Yet in the small core of the flame was an unyielding anguish of another thing. But this also was lost; he only wanted her, with an extreme desire that seemed inevitable as death, beyond question.

Then, satisfied and shattered, fulfilled and destroyed, he went home away from her, drifting vaguely through the darkness, lapsed into the old fire of burning passion. Far away, far away, there seemed to be a small lament in the darkness. But what did it matter? What did it matter, what did anything matter save this ultimate and triumphant experience of physical passion, that had blazed up anew like a new spell of life. "I was becoming quite dead-alive, nothing but a word-bag," he said in triumph, scorning his other self. Yet somewhere far off and small, the other hovered.

The men were still dragging the lake when he got back. He stood on the bank and heard Gerald's voice. The water was still booming in the night, the moon was fair, the hills beyond were elusive. The lake was sinking. There came the raw smell of the banks, in the night air.

Up at Shortlands there were lights in the windows, as if nobody had gone to bed. On the landing-stage was the old doctor, the father of the young man who was lost. He stood quite silent, waiting. Birkin also stood and watched. Gerald came up in a boat.

"You still here, Rupert?" he said. "We can't get them. The bottom slopes, you know, very steep. The water lies between two very sharp slopes, with little branch valleys, and God knows where the drift will take you. It isn't as if it was a level bottom. You never know where you are, with the dragging."

"Is there any need for you to be working?" said Birkin. "Wouldn't it be much better if you went to bed?"

"To bed! Good God, do you think I should sleep? We'll find 'em, before I go away from here."

"But the men would find them just the same without you—why should you insist?"

Gerald looked up at him. Then he put his hand affectionately on Birkin's shoulder, saying:

"Don't you bother about me, Rupert. If there's anybody's health to think about, it's yours, not mine. How do you feel yourself?"

"Very well.—But you, you spoil your own chance of life—you waste your best self."

Gerald was silent for a moment. Then he said:

"Waste it? What else is there to do with it?"

"But leave this, won't you? You force yourself into horrors, and put a mill-stone of beastly memories round your neck! Come away now."

"A mill-stone of beastly memories!" Gerald repeated. Then he put his hand again affectionately on Birkin's shoulder. "God, you've got such a telling way of putting things, Rupert, you have."

Birkin's heart sank. He was irritated and weary of having a telling way of putting things.

"Won't you leave it? Come over to my place—?" he urged, as one urges a drunken man.

"No," said Gerald coaxingly, his arm across the other man's shoulder. "Thanks very much, Rupert—I shall be glad to come tomorrow, if that'll do. You understand, don't you? I want to see this job through. But I'll come tomorrow, right enough. Oh, I'd rather come and have a chat with you than—than do anything else, I verily believe. Yes, I would. You mean a lot to me, Rupert, more than you know."

"What do I mean, more than I know?" asked Birkin irritably. He was acutely aware of Gerald's hand on his shoulder. And he did not want this altercation. He wanted the other man to come out of the ugly misery.

"I'll tell you another time," said Gerald, coaxingly.

"Come along with me now—I want you to come," said Birkin.

There was a pause, intense and real. Birkin wondered why his own heart beat so heavily.—Then Gerald's fingers gripped hard and communicative into Birkin's shoulder, as he said:

"No, I'll see this job through, Rupert. Thank you—I know what you mean. We're all right, you know, you and me."

"I may be all right, but I'm sure you're not, mucking about here," said Birkin.

And he went away.

The bodies of the dead were not recovered till towards dawn. Diana had her arms tight round the neck of the young man, choking him.

"She killed him," said Gerald.

The moon sloped down the sky and sank at last, the lake was sunk to quarter size, it had horrible raw banks of clay, that smelled of raw rottenish water. Dawn roused faintly behind the eastern hill. The water still boomed through the sluice.

As the birds were whistling for the first morning, and the hills at the back of the desolate lake stood radiant with new mists, there was a straggling procession up to Shortlands, men bearing the bodies on a stretcher, Gerald going beside them, the two grey-bearded fathers following in silence. Indoors the family was all sitting up, waiting. Somebody must go to tell the mother, in her room. The doctor in secret struggled to bring back his son, till he himself was exhausted.

Over all the outlying district was a hush of dreadful excitement on that Sunday morning. The colliery people felt as if this catastrophe had happened directly to themselves, indeed they were more shocked and frightened than if their own men had been killed. Such a tragedy at Shortlands, the high home of the district! One of the young mistresses, persisting in dancing on the cabin roof of the launch, wilful young madam, drowned in the midst of the festival, with the young doctor! Everywhere, on the Sunday morning, the colliers wandered about, discussing the calamity. At all the Sunday dinners of the people, there seemed a strange presence. It was as if the angel of death were very near, there was a sense of the supernatural in the air. The men had excited, startled faces, the women looked solemn, some of them had been crying. The children enjoyed the excitement at first. There was an intensity in the air, almost magical. Did all enjoy it? Did all enjoy the thrill?

Gudrun had wild ideas of rushing to comfort Gerald. She was thinking all the time of the perfect comforting, reassuring thing to say to him. She was shocked and frightened, but she put that away, thinking of how she should deport herself with Gerald: act her part. That was the real thrill: how she should act her part.

Ursula was deeply and passionately in love with Birkin, and she was capable of nothing. She was perfectly callous about all the talk of the accident, but her estranged air looked like trouble. She merely sat by herself, whenever she could, and longed to see him again. She wanted him to come to the house—she would not have it otherwise, he must come at once. She was waiting for him. She stayed indoors all the day, waiting for him to knock at the door. Every minute, she glanced automatically at the window. He would be there.

Chapter XV

Sunday Evening

As the day wore on, the life-blood seemed to ebb away from Ursula, and within the emptiness a heavy despair gathered. Her passion seemed to bleed to death, and there was nothing. She sat suspended in a state of complete nullity, harder to bear than death.

"Unless something happens," she said to herself, in the perfect lucidity of final suffering, "I shall die. I am at the end of my line of life."

She sat crushed and obliterated in a darkness that was the border of death. She realised how all her life she had been drawing nearer and nearer to this brink, where there was no beyond, from which one had to leap like Sappho into the unknown. The knowledge of the imminence of death was like a drug. Darkly, without thinking at all, she knew that she was near to death. She had travelled all her life along the line of fulfilment, and it was nearly concluded. She knew all she had to know, she had experienced all she had to experience, she was fulfilled in a kind of bitter ripeness, there remained only to fall from the tree into death. And one must fulfil one's development to the end, must carry the adventure to its conclusion. And the next step was over the border into death. So it was then! There was a certain peace in the knowledge.

After all, when one was fulfilled, one was happiest in falling into death, as a bitter fruit plunges in its ripeness downwards. Death is a great consummation, a consummating experience. It is a development from life. That we know, while we are yet living. What then need we think for further? One can never see beyond the consummation. It is enough that death is a great and conclusive experience. Why should we ask what comes after the experience, when the experience is still unknown to us? Let us die, since the great experience is the one that follows now upon all the rest, death, which is the next great crisis in front of which we have arrived. If we wait, if we balk the issue, we do but hang about the gates in undignified uneasiness. There it is, in front of us, as in front of Sappho, the illimitable space. Thereinto goes the journey. Have we not the courage to go on with our journey, must we cry 'I daren't.'? On ahead we will go, into death, and whatever death may mean. If a man can see the next step to be taken, why

173

should he fear the next but one? Why ask about the next but one? Of the next step we are certain. It is the step into death.

"I shall die—I shall quickly die," said Ursula to herself, clear as if in a trance, clear, calm, and certain beyond human certainty. But somewhere behind, in the twilight, there was a bitter weeping and a hopelessness. That must not be attended to. One must go where the unfaltering spirit goes, there must be no balking the issue, because of fear. No balking the issue, no listening to the lesser voices. If the deepest desire be now, to go on into the unknown of death, shall one forfeit the deepest truth for one more shallow?

"Then let it end," she said to herself. It was a decision. It was not a question of taking one's life—she would *never* kill herself, that was repulsive and violent. It was a question of *knowing* the next step. And the next step led into the space of death. Did it?—or was there———?

Her thoughts drifted into unconsciousness, she sat as if asleep beside the fire. And then the thought came back. The space of death! Could she give herself to it? Ah yes—it was a sleep. She had had enough. So long she had held out and resisted. Now was the time to relinquish, not to resist any more.

In a kind of spiritual trance, she yielded, she gave way, and all was dark. She could feel, within the darkness, the terrible assertion of her body, the unutterable anguish of dissolution, the only anguish that is too much, the far-off, awful nausea of dissolution set in within the body.

"Does the body correspond so immediately with the spirit?" she asked herself. And she knew, with the clarity of ultimate knowledge, that the body is only one of the manifestations of the spirit, the transmutation of the integral spirit is the transmutation of the physical body as well.—Unless I set my will, unless I absolve myself from the rhythm of life, fix myself and remain static, cut off from living, absolved within my own will. But better die than live mechanically a life that is a repetition of repetitions. To die is to move on with the invisible. To die is also a joy, a joy of submitting to that which is greater than the known, namely, the pure unknown. That is a joy. But to live mechanised and cut off within the motion of the will, to live as an entity absolved from the unknown, that is shameful and ignominious. There is no ignominy in death. There is complete ignominy in an unreplenished, mechanised life. Life indeed may be ignominious, shameful to the soul. But death is never a shame. Death itself, like the illimitable space, is beyond our sullying.

Tomorrow was Monday. Monday, the beginning of another school-week! Another shameful, barren school-week, mere routine and mechanical activity. Was not the adventure of death infinitely preferable? Was not death infinitely more lovely and noble than such a life? A life of barren routine, without inner meaning, without any real significance. How sordid life was, how it was a terrible shame to the soul, to live now! How much cleaner and more dignified to be dead! One could not bear any more of this shame of sordid routine and mechanical nullity. One might come to fruit in death. She had had enough. For where was life to be found? No flowers grow upon busy machinery, there is no sky to a routine, there is no space to a rotary motion. And all life was a rotary motion, mechanised, cut off from reality. There was nothing to look for from life—it was the same in all countries and all peoples. The only window was death. One could look out on to the great dark sky of death with elation, as one had looked out of the class-room window as a child, and seen perfect freedom in the outside. Now one was not a child, and one knew that the soul was a prisoner within this sordid vast edifice of life, and there was no escape, save in death.

But what a joy! What a gladness to think that whatever humanity did, it could not seize hold of the kingdom of death, to nullify that. The sea they turned into a murderous alley and a soiled road of commerce, disputed like the dirty land of a city every inch of it. The air they claimed too, shared it up, parcelled it out to certain owners, they trespassed in the air to fight for it. Everything was gone, walled in, with spikes on top of the walls, and one must ignominiously creep between the spiky walls through a labyrinth of life.

But the great, dark, illimitable kingdom of death, there humanity was put to scorn. So much they could do upon earth, the multifarious little gods that they were. But the kingdom of death put them all to scorn, they dwindled into their true vulgar silliness in face of it.

How beautiful, how grand and perfect death was, how good to look forward to. There one would wash off all the lies and ignominy and dirt that had been put upon one here, a perfect bath of cleanness and glad refreshment, and go unknown, unquestioned, unabased. After all, one was rich, if only in the promise of perfect death. It was a gladness above all, that this remained to look forward to, the pure inhuman otherness of death. Whatever life might be, it could not take away death, the inhuman transcendent death. Oh, let us ask no question of it, what it is or is not. To know is human, and in death we do not know, we are not human. And the joy of this compensates for all the bitterness of knowledge and the sordidness of our humanity. In death we shall not be human, and we shall not know. The promise of this is our heritage, we look forward like heirs to their majority.

Ursula sat quite still and quite forgotten, alone by the fire in the drawing-room. The children were playing in the kitchen, all the others were gone to church. And she was gone into the ultimate darkness of her own soul.

She was startled by hearing the bell ring, away in the kitchen, the children came scudding along the passage in delicious alarm.

"Ursula, there's somebody."

"I know. Don't be silly," she replied. She too was startled, almost frightened. She dared hardly go to the door.

Birkin stood on the threshold, his rain-coat turned up to his ears. He had come now, now she was gone far away. She was aware of the rainy night behind him.

"Oh is it you?" she said.

"I am glad you are at home," he said in a low voice, entering the house.

"They are all gone to church."

He took off his coat and hung it up. The children were peeping at him round the corner.

"Go and get undressed now, Billy and Dora," said Ursula. "Mother will be back soon, and she'll be disappointed if you're not in bed."

The children, in a sudden angelic mood, retired without a word. Birkin and Ursula went into the drawing-room. The fire burned low. He looked at her, and wondered at the luminous delicacy of her beauty, and the wide shining of her eyes. He watched from a distance, with wonder in his heart, she seemed transfigured with light.

"What have you been doing all day?" he asked her.

"Only sitting about," she said.

He looked at her. There was a change in her. But she was separate from him. She remained apart, in a kind of brightness. They both sat silent in the soft light of the lamp. He felt he ought to go away again, he ought not to have come. Still he did not gather enough resolution to move. But he was *de trop*, her mood was absent and separate.

Then there came the voices of the two children calling shyly outside the door, softly, with self-excited timidity:

"Ursula! Ursula!"

She rose and opened the door. On the threshold stood the two children in their long nightgowns, with wide-eyed, angelic faces. They were being very good for the moment, playing the rôle perfectly of two obedient children.

"Shall you take us to bed!" said Billy, in a loud whisper.

"Why, you *are* angels tonight," she said softly. "Won't you come and say goodnight to Mr Birkin?"

The children merged shyly into the room, on bare feet. Billy's face was wide and grinning, but there was a great solemnity of being good in his round blue eyes. Dora, peeping from the floss of her fair hair, hung back like some tiny Dryad, that has no soul.

"Will you say goodnight to me?" asked Birkin, in a voice that was strangely soft and smooth. Dora drifted away at once, like a leaf lifted on a breath of wind. But Billy went softly forward, slow and willing, lifting his pinched-up mouth implicitly to be kissed. Ursula watched the full, gathered lips of the man gently touch those of the boy, so gently. Then Birkin lifted his fingers and touched the boy's round, confiding cheek, with a faint touch of love. Neither spoke. Billy seemed angelic like a cherub boy, or like an acolyte, Birkin was a tall, grave angel looking down to him.

"Are you going to be kissed?" Ursula broke in, speaking to the little girl. But Dora edged away like a tiny Dryad that will not be touched.

"Won't you say Goodnight to Mr Birkin? Go, he's waiting for you," said Ursula. But the girl-child only made a little motion away from him.

"Silly Dora, silly Dora!" said Ursula.

Birkin felt some mistrust and antagonism in the small child. He could not understand it.

"Come then," said Ursula. "Let us go before mother comes."

"Who'll hear us say our prayers?" asked Billy anxiously.

"Whom you like."

"Won't *you*?"

"Yes, I will."

"Ursula?"

"Well Billy?"

"Is it *whom* you like."

"That's it."

"Well what is *whom*?"

"It's the accusative of who."

There was a moment's contemplative silence, then the confiding:

"Is it?"

Birkin smiled to himself as he sat by the fire. When Ursula came down he sat motionless, with his arms on his knees. She saw him, how he was motionless and ageless, like some crouching idol, some image of a deathly religion. He looked round at her, and his face, very pale and unreal, seemed to gleam with a whiteness almost phosphorescent.

"Don't you feel well?" she asked, in indefinable repulsion.

"I hadn't thought about it."

"But don't you know without thinking about it?"

He looked at her, his eyes dark and swift, and he saw her revulsion. He did not answer her question.

"Don't you know whether you are unwell or not, without thinking about it?" she persisted.

"Not always," he said coldly.

"But don't you think that's very wicked?"

"Wicked?"

"Yes. I think it's *criminal* to have so little connection with your own body that you don't even know when you are ill."

He looked at her darkly.

"Yes," he said.

"Why don't you stay in bed when you are seedy? You look perfectly ghastly."

"Offensively so?" he asked ironically.

"Yes, quite offensive. Quite repelling."

"Ah!—Well that's unfortunate."

"And it's raining, and it's a horrible night. Really, you shouldn't be forgiven for treating your body like it—you *ought* to suffer, a man who takes as little notice of his body as that."

"—takes as little notice of his body as that," he echoed mechanically.

This cut her short, and there was silence.

The others came in from church, and the two had the girls to face, then the mother and Gudrun, and then the father and the boy.

"Good-evening," said Brangwen, faintly surprised. "Came to see me, did you?"

"No," said Birkin, "not about anything in particular, that is. The day was dismal, and I thought you wouldn't mind if I called in."

"It *has* been a depressing day," said Mrs Brangwen sympathetically. At that moment the voices of the children were heard calling from upstairs: "Mother! Mother!" She lifted her face and answered mildly into the distance: "I shall come up to you in a minute Doysie." Then to Birkin: "There is nothing fresh at Shortlands, I suppose?—Ah," she sighed, "no, poor things, I should think not."

"You've been over there today, I suppose?" asked the father.

"Gerald came round to tea with me, and I walked back with him. The house is overexcited and unwholesome, I thought."

"I should think they were people who hadn't much restraint," said Gudrun.

"Or too much," Birkin answered.

"Oh yes, I'm sure," said Gudrun, almost vindictively; "One or the other."

"They all feel they ought to behave in some unnatural fashion," said Birkin. "When people are in grief, they would do better to cover their faces and keep in retirement, as in the old days."

"Certainly!" cried Gudrun, flushed and inflammable. "What can be worse than this public grief—what is more horrible, more false! If *grief* is not private, and hidden, what is?"

"Exactly," he said. "I felt ashamed when I was there and they were all going about in a lugubrious false way, feeling they must not be natural or ordinary."

"Well—" said Mrs Brangwen, offended at this criticism, "it isn't so easy to bear a trouble like that."

And she went upstairs to the children.

He remained only a few minutes longer, then took his leave. When he was gone Ursula felt such a poignant hatred of him, that all her brain seemed turned into a sharp crystal of fine hatred. Her whole nature seemed sharpened and intensified into a pure dart of hate. She could not imagine what it was. It merely took hold of her, the most poignant and ultimate hatred, pure and clear and beyond thought. She could not think of it at all, she was translated beyond herself. It was like a possession. She felt she was possessed. And for several days she went about possessed by this exquisite force of hatred against him. It surpassed anything she had ever known before, it seemed to throw her out of the world into some terrible region where nothing of her old life held good. She was quite lost and dazed, really dead to her own life.

It was so completely incomprehensible and irrational. She did not know *why* she hated him, her hate was quite abstract. She had only realised with a shock that stunned her, that she was overcome by this pure trans-portation. He was the enemy, fine as a diamond, and as hard and jewel-like, the quintessence of all that was inimical.

She thought of his face, white and purely wrought, and of his eyes that had such a dark, constant will of assertion, and she touched her own forehead, to feel if she were mad, she was so transfigured in white flame of essential hate.

It was not temporal, her hatred, she did not hate him for this or for that;

she did not want to do anything to him, to have any connection with him. Her relation was ultimate and utterly beyond words, the hate was so pure and gem-like. It was as if he were a beam of essential enmity, a beam of light that did not only destroy her, but denied her altogether, revoked her whole world. She saw him as a clear stroke of uttermost contradiction, a strange gem-like being whose existence defined her own non-existence. When she heard he was ill again, her hatred only intensified itself a few degrees, if that were possible. It stunned her and annihilated her, but she could not escape it. She could not escape this transfiguration of hatred that had come upon her.

Chapter XVI

Man to Man

He lay sick and unmoved, in pure opposition to everything. He knew how near to breaking was the vessel that held his life. He knew also how strong and durable it was. And he did not care. Better a thousand times take one's chance with death, than accept a life one did not want. But best of all to persist and persist and persist for ever, till one were satisfied in life.

He knew that Ursula was referred back to him. He knew his life rested with her. But he would rather not live than accept the love she proffered. The old way of love seemed a dreadful bondage, a sort of conscription. What it was in him he did not know, but the thought of love, marriage, and children, and a life lived together, in the horrible privacy of domestic and connubial satisfaction, was repulsive. He wanted something clearer, more open, cooler, as it were. The hot narrow intimacy between man and wife was abhorrent. The way they shut their doors, these married people, and shut themselves in to their own exclusive alliance with each other, even in love, disgusted him. It was a whole community of mistrustful couples insulated in private houses or private rooms, always in couples, and no further life, no further immediate, no disinterested relationship admitted: a kaleidoscope of couples, disjoined, separatist, meaningless entities of married couples. True, he hated promiscuity even worse than marriage, and a liaison was only another kind of coupling, reactionary from the legal marriage. Reaction was a greater bore than action.

On the whole, he hated sex, it was such a limitation. It was sex that turned a man into a broken half of a couple, the woman into the other broken half. And he wanted to be single in himself, the woman single in her self. He wanted sex to revert to the level of the other appetites, to be regarded as a functional process, not as a fulfilment. He believed in sex marriage. But beyond this, he wanted a further conjunction, where man had being and woman had being, two pure beings, each constituting the freedom of the other, balancing each other like two poles of one force, like two angels, or two demons.

He wanted so much to be free, not under the compulsion of any need for unification, or tortured by unsatisfied desire. Desire and aspiration should find their object without all this torture, as now, in a world of plenty of water, simple thirst is inconsiderable, satisfied almost unconsciously. And he wanted to be with Ursula as free as with himself, single and clear and cool, yet balanced, polarised with her. The merging, the clutching, the mingling of love was become madly abhorrent to him.

But it seemed to him, woman was always so horrible and clutching, she had such a lust for possession, a greed of self-importance in love. She wanted to have, to own, to control, to be dominant. Everything must be referred back to her, to Woman, the Great Mother of everything, out of whom proceeded everything and to whom everything must finally be rendered up.

It filled him with almost insane fury, this calm assumption of the Magna Mater, that all was hers, because she had borne it. Man was hers, because she had borne him. A Mater Dolorosa, she had borne him, a Magna Mater, she now claimed him again, soul and body, sex, meaning, and all. He had a horror of the Magna Mater, she was detestable.

She was on a very high horse again, was woman, the Great Mother. Did he not know it in Hermione. Hermione, the humble, the subservient, what was she all the while but the Mater Dolorosa, in her subservience claiming, with horrible, insidious arrogance and female tyranny, her own again, claiming back the man she had borne in suffering. By her very suffering and humility she bound her son with chains, she held him her everlasting prisoner.

And Ursula, Ursula was the same—or the inverse. She too was the awful, arrogant queen of life, as if she were a queen bee on whom all the rest depended. He saw the yellow flare in her eyes, he knew the unthinkable overweening assumption of primacy in her. She was unconscious of it herself. She was only too ready to knock her head on the ground before a man. But this was only when she was so certain of her man, that she could worship him as a woman worships her own infant, with a worship of perfect possession.

It was intolerable, this possession at the hands of woman. Always a man must be considered as the broken-off fragment of a woman, and the sex was the still aching scar of the laceration. Man must be added on to a woman, before he had any real place or wholeness.

And why? Why should we consider ourselves, men and women, as broken fragments of one whole. It is not true. We are not broken fragments of one whole. Rather we are the singling away into purity and clear being, of things that were mixed. Rather the sex is that which remains in us of the mixed, the unresolved. And passion is the further separating of this mixture, that which is manly being taken into the being of the man, that which is womanly passing to the woman, till the two are clear and whole as angels, the admixture of sex in the highest sense surpassed, leaving two single beings, constellated together like two stars.

In the old age, before sex was, we were mixed, each one a mixture. The process of singling into individuality resulted in the great polarisation of sex. The womanly drew to one side, the manly to the other. But the separation was imperfect even then. And so our world-cycle passes. There is now to come the new day, where we are beings each of us, fulfilled in difference. The man is pure man, the woman pure woman, they are perfectly polarised. But there is no longer any of the horrible merging, mingling, self-abnegation of love. There is only the pure duality of polarisation, each one free from any contamination of the other. In each, the individual is primal, sex is subordinate, but perfectly polarised. Each has a single, separate being, with its own laws. The man has his pure freedom, the woman hers. Each acknowledges the perfection of the polarised sex-circuit. Each admits the different nature in the other.

So Birkin meditated whilst he was ill. He liked sometimes to be ill enough to take to his bed. For then he got better very quickly, and things came to him clear and sure.

Whilst he was laid up, Gerald came to see him. The two men had a deep, uneasy feeling for each other. Gerald's eyes were quick and restless, his whole manner tense and impatient, he seemed strung up to some activity. According to conventionality, he wore black clothes, he looked formal, handsome and *comme il faut*. His hair was fair almost to whiteness, sharp like splinters of light, his face was keen and ruddy, his body seemed full of northern energy.

Gerald really loved Birkin, though he never quite believed in him. Birkin was too unreal;—clever, whimsical, wonderful, but not practical enough. Gerald felt that his own understanding was much sounder and safer. Birkin was delightful, a wonderful spirit, but after all, not to be taken seriously, not quite to be counted as a man among men.

"Why are you laid up again?" he asked, kindly, taking the sick man's hand. It was always Gerald who was protective, offering the warm shelter of his physical strength.

"For my sins, I suppose," Birkin said, smiling a little ironically.

"For your sins? Yes, probably that is so.—You should sin less, and keep better in health."

"You'd better teach me," said Birkin.

He looked at Gerald with ironic eyes.

"How are things with you?" asked Birkin.

"With me?" Gerald looked at Birkin, saw he was serious, and a warm light came into his eyes. "I don't know that they're any different. I don't see how they could be. There's nothing to change."

"I suppose you are conducting the business as successfully as ever, and ignoring the demands of the soul."

"That's it," said Gerald; "at least as far as the business is concerned. I couldn't say about the soul, I'm sure."

"No."

"Surely you don't expect me to?" laughed Gerald.

"No.—How are the rest of your affairs progressing, apart from the business?"

"The rest of my affairs? What are those? I couldn't say; I don't know what you refer to."

"Yes you do," said Birkin. "Are you gloomy or cheerful?—And what about Gudrun Brangwen?"

"What about her?" A confused look came over Gerald. "Well," he added, "I don't know. I can only tell you, she gave me a hit over the face the last time I saw her."

"A hit over the face! What for?"

"That I couldn't tell you, either."

"Really!—But when?"

"The night of the party—when Diana was drowned. She was driving the cattle up the hill, and I went after her—you remember."

"Yes, I remember. But what made her do that? You didn't definitely ask her for it, I suppose?"

"I? No, not that I know of. I merely said to her, that it was dangerous to drive those Highland bullocks—as it *is*. She turned in such a way, and said—'I suppose you think I'm afraid of you and your cattle, don't you?'—So I asked her 'Why—?'—And for answer she flung me a back-hander across the face."

Birkin laughed quickly, as if it pleased him. Gerald looked at him, wondering, and began to laugh as well, saying:

"I didn't laugh at the time, I assure you. I was never so taken aback in my life."

"And weren't you furious?"

"Furious? I should think I was. I'd have murdered her for two pins."

"Hm!" ejaculated Birkin. "Poor Gudrun, wouldn't she suffer afterwards for having given herself away!" He was hugely delighted.

"Would she suffer?" asked Gerald, also amused now.

Both men smiled in malice and amusement.

"Badly, I'm sure; seeing how self-conscious she is."

"She is self-conscious is she? Then what made her do it? For I certainly think it was quite uncalled for, and quite unjustified."

"I suppose it was a sudden impulse."

"Yes, but how do you account for her having such an impulse? I'd done her no hurt."

Birkin shook his head.

"The Amazon suddenly came up in her I suppose," he said.

"Well," replied Gerald, "I'd rather it had been the Orinoco."

They both laughed at the poor joke. Gerald was thinking how Gudrun had said she would strike the last blow too. But some reserve made him keep this back from Birkin.

"And you resent it?" Birkin asked.

"I don't *resent* it. I don't care a tinker's curse about it." He was silent a moment, then he added, laughing, "No, I'll see it through, that's all. She seemed sorry afterwards."

"Did she? You've not met since that night?"

Gerald's face clouded.

"No," he said. "We've been—you can imagine how it's been, since the accident."

"Yes. Is it calming down?"

"I don't know. It's a shock, of course. But I don't believe mother minds. I really don't believe she takes any notice. And what's so funny, she used to be all for the children—nothing mattered, nothing whatever mattered but the children. And now, she doesn't take any more notice than if it was one of the servants."

"No? Did it upset *you* very much?"

"It's a shock. But I don't feel it very much, really. I don't feel any different. We've all got to die, and it doesn't seem to make any great difference, anyhow, whether you die or not. I can't feel any *grief*, you know. It leaves me cold. I can't quite account for it."

"You don't care if you die or not?" asked Birkin.

Gerald looked at him with eyes blue as the blue-fibred steel of a weapon. He felt awkward, but indifferent. As a matter of fact, he did care terribly, with a great fear.

"Oh," he said, "I don't want to die, why should I? But I never trouble. The question doesn't seem to be on the carpet for me at all. It doesn't interest me, you know."

"'Timor mortis conturbat me'," quoted Birkin, adding—"No, death doesn't really seem the point any more. It curiously doesn't concern one. It's like an ordinary tomorrow."

Gerald looked closely at his friend. The eyes of the two men met, and an unspoken understanding was exchanged.

Gerald narrowed his eyes, his face was cool and unscrupulous as he looked at Birkin, impersonally, with a vision that ended in a point in space, strangely keen-eyed and yet blind.

"If death isn't the point," he said, in a strangely abstract, cold, fine voice—"what is?" He sounded as if he had been found out.

"What is?" re-echoed Birkin. And there was a mocking silence.

"There's a long way to go, after the point of intrinsic death, before we disappear," said Birkin.

"There is," said Gerald. "But what sort of way?" He seemed to press the other man for knowledge which he himself knew far better than Birkin did.

"Right down the slopes of degeneration—mystic, universal degeneration.—There are many stages of pure degradation to go through: agelong. We live on long after our death, and progressively, aeons of progressive devolution."

Gerald listened with a faint, fine smile on his face, all the time, as if, somewhere, he knew so much better than Birkin, all about this: as if his own knowledge were direct and personal, whereas Birkin's was a matter of observation and inference, not quite hitting the nail on the head:—though aiming near enough at it.—But he was not going to give himself away. If Birkin could get at the secrets, let him. Gerald would never help him. Gerald would be a dark horse to the end.

"Of course," he said, with a startling change of conversation, "it is father who really feels it. It will finish him. For him the world collapses.—All his care now is for Winnie—he must save Winnie.—He says she ought to be sent away to school, but she won't hear of it, and he'll never do it.—Of course she *is* in rather a queer way. We're all of us curiously bad at living. We can do things—but we can't get on with life at all.—It's curious—a family failing."

"She oughtn't to be sent away to school," said Birkin, who was considering the new proposition.

"She oughtn't? Why?"

"She's a queer child—a special child, more special even than you. And in my opinion special children should never be sent away to school. Only moderately ordinary children should be sent to school,—so it seems to me."

"I'm inclined to think just the opposite. I think it would probably make her more normal if she went away and mixed with other children."

"She wouldn't mix, you see. *You* never really mixed, did you? And she wouldn't be willing even to pretend to. She's proud, and solitary, and naturally apart. If she has a single nature, why do you want to make her gregarious?"

"No, I don't want to make her anything. But I think school would be good for her."

"Was it good for *you?*"

Gerald's eyes narrowed uglily. School had been torture to him. Yet he had not questioned whether one should go through this torture. He seemed to believe in education through subjection and torment.

"I hated it at the time, but I can see it was necessary," he said. "It brought me into line a bit—and you can't live unless you do come into line somewhere."

"Well," said Birkin, "I begin to think that you can't live unless you keep entirely out of the line. It's no good trying to toe the line, when your one impulse is to smash up the line.—Winnie is a special nature, and for special natures you must give a special world."

"Yes, but where's your special world?" said Gerald.

"Make it.—Instead of chopping yourself down to fit the world, chop the world down to fit yourself.—As a matter of fact, two exceptional people make another world. You and I, we make another, separate world.—You don't *want* a world same as your brothers-in-law.—It's just the special quality you value. Do you *want* to be normal or ordinary?—It's a lie. You want to be free and extraordinary, in an extraordinary world of liberty."

Gerald looked at Birkin with subtle eyes of knowledge. But he would never openly admit what he felt. He knew more than Birkin, in one direction—much more. And this gave him his gentle love for the other man, as if Birkin were in some way young, innocent, child-like: so amazingly clever, but incurably innocent.

"Yet you are so banal as to consider me chiefly a freak," said Birkin pointedly.

"A freak!" exclaimed Gerald, startled. And his face opened suddenly, as if lighted with simplicity, as when a flower opens out of the cunning bud.

"No—I never consider you a freak." And he watched the other man with strange eyes, that Birkin could not understand. "I feel," Gerald continued, "that there is always an element of uncertainty about you—perhaps you are uncertain about yourself. But I'm never sure of you. You can go away and change as easily as if you had no soul."

He looked at Birkin with penetrating eyes. Birkin was amazed. He thought he had all the soul in the world. He stared in amazement. And Gerald, watching, saw the amazing attractive goodliness of his eyes, a young, spontaneous goodness that attracted the other man infinitely, yet filled him with bitter chagrin, because he mistrusted it so much. He knew Birkin could do without him—could forget, and not suffer. This was always present in Gerald's consciousness, filling him with bitter unbelief: this consciousness of the young, animal-like spontaneity of detachment. It seemed almost like hypocrisy and lying, sometimes, oh, often, on Birkin's part, to talk so deeply and importantly.

Quite other things were going through Birkin's mind. Suddenly he saw himself confronted with another problem—the problem of love and eternal conjunction between two men. Of course this was necessary—it had been a necessity inside himself all his life—to love a man purely and fully. Of course he had been loving Gerald all along, and all along denying it.

He lay in the bed and wondered, whilst his friend sat beside him, lost in brooding. Each man was gone in his own thoughts.

"You know how the old German knights used to swear a Blutbrüder-schaft," he said to Gerald, with quite a new happy activity in his eyes.

"Make a little wound in their arms, and rub each other's blood into the cut?" said Gerald.

"Yes—and swear to be true to each other, of one blood, all their lives.—That is what we ought to do. No wounds, that is obsolete.—But we ought to swear to love each other, you and I, implicitly and perfectly, finally, without any possibility of going back on it."

He looked at Gerald with clear, happy eyes of discovery. Gerald looked down at him, attracted, so deeply bondaged in fascinated attraction, that he was mistrustful, resenting the bondage, hating the attraction.

"We will swear to each other, one day, shall we?" pleaded Birkin. "We will swear to stand by each other—be true to each other—ultimately—infallibly—given to each other, organically—without possibility of taking back."

Birkin sought hard to express himself. But Gerald hardly listened. His face shone with a certain luminous pleasure. He was pleased. But he kept his reserve. He held himself back.

"Shall we swear to each other, one day?" said Birkin, putting out his hand towards Gerald.

Gerald just touched the extended fine, living hand, as if withheld and afraid.

"We'll leave it till I understand it better," he said, in a voice of excuse.

Birkin watched him. A little sharp disappointment, perhaps a touch of contempt came into his heart.

"Yes," he said. "You must tell me what you think, later. You know what I mean? not sloppy emotionalism. An impersonal union that leaves one free."

They lapsed both into silence. Birkin was looking at Gerald all the time. He seemed now to see, not the physical, animal man, which he usually saw in Gerald, and which he usually liked so much, but the man himself, complete, and as if fated, doomed, limited. This strange sense of fatality in Gerald, as if he were limited to one form of existence, one knowledge, one activity, a sort of fatal halfness, which to himself seemed wholeness, always overcame Birkin after their moments of passionate approach, and filled him with a sort of contempt, or boredom. It was the insistence on the limitation which so bored Birkin in Gerald. Gerald could never fly away from himself, in real indifferent gaiety. He had a clog, a sort of monomania.

There was silence for a time. Then Birkin said, in a lighter tone, letting the stress of the contact pass:

"Can't you get a good governess for Winifred?—somebody exceptional?"

"Hermione Roddice suggested we should ask Gudrun to teach her to draw and to model in clay. You know Winnie is astonishingly clever with that plasticine stuff. Hermione declares she is an artist." Gerald spoke in the usual animated, chatty manner, as if nothing unusual had passed. But Birkin's manner was full of reminder.

"Really! I didn't know that.—Oh well then, if Gudrun *would* teach her, it would be perfect—couldn't be anything better—if Winifred is an artist. Because Gudrun somewhere is one. And every true artist is the salvation of every other."

"I thought they got on so badly, as a rule."

"Perhaps. But only artists produce for each other the world that is fit to live in. If you can arrange *that* for Winifred, it is perfect."

"But you think she wouldn't come?"

"I don't know. Gudrun is rather self-opinionated. She won't go cheap, anywhere. Or if she does, she'll pretty soon take herself back. So whether she would condescend to do private teaching, particularly here, in

Beldover, I don't know. But it would be just the thing. Winifred has got a special nature. And if you can put into her way the means of being self-sufficient, that is the best thing possible.—She'll never get on with the ordinary life. You find it difficult enough yourself, and she is several skins thinner than you are. It is awful to think what her life will be like unless she does find a means of expression, some way of fulfilment. You can see what mere leaving it to fate brings. You can see how much marriage is to be trusted to—look at your own mother."

"Do you think mother is abnormal?"

"No! I think she only wanted something more, or other than the common run of life. And not getting it, she has gone wrong, perhaps."

"After producing a brood of wrong children," said Gerald gloomily.

"No more wrong than any of the rest of us," Birkin replied. "The most normal people have the worst subterranean selves, take them one by one."

"Sometimes I think it is a curse to be alive," said Gerald, with sudden impotent anger.

"Well," said Birkin, "why not! Let it be a curse sometimes to be alive—at other times it is anything but a curse. You've got plenty of zest in it really."

"Less than you'd think," said Gerald, revealing a strange poverty in his look at the other man.

There was silence, each thinking his own thoughts.

"She's a teacher already, isn't she?" said Gerald. "I don't see what she has to distinguish between teaching at the Grammar School, and coming to teach Win."

"The difference between a public servant and a private one. The only nobleman today, king and only aristocrat, is the public, the public. You are quite willing to serve the public—but to be a private tutor—"

"I don't want to serve either—"

"No! And Gudrun will probably feel the same."

Gerald thought for a few minutes. Then he said:

"At all events, father won't make her feel like a private servant. He will be fussy and grateful enough."

"So he ought—and so ought all of you.—Do you think you can hire a woman like Gudrun Brangwen with money?—She is your equal like anything—probably your superior."

"Is she!" said Gerald.

"Yes. And if you haven't the guts to know it, I hope she'll leave you to your own devices."

"Nevertheless," said Gerald, "if she is my equal, I wish she weren't a teacher, because I don't think teachers as a rule are my equal."

"Nor do I, damn them. But am I a teacher because I teach, or a parson because I preach?—It bores me—."

Gerald laughed. He was always uneasy on this score. He did not *want* to claim social superiority, yet he *would* not claim intrinsic personal superiority, because he would never base his standard of values on pure being. So he wobbled upon a tacit assumption of social standing. Now Birkin wanted him to accept the fact of intrinsic difference between human beings, which he did not intend to accept. It was against his social honor, his principle. He rose to go.

"I've been neglecting my business all this while," he said, smiling.

"I ought to have reminded you before," Birkin replied, laughing and mocking.

"I knew you'd say something like that," laughed Gerald, rather uneasily.

"Did you!"

"Yes, Rupert. It wouldn't do for us all to be like you are—we should soon be in the cart. When I am above the world, I shall ignore all businesses."

"Of course, we're not in the cart now," said Birkin, satirically.

"Not as much as you make out. At any rate, we have enough to eat and drink—"

"And be satisfied," added Birkin.

Gerald came near the bed, and stood looking down at Birkin whose throat was exposed, whose tossed hair fell attractively on the warm brow, above the eyes that were so unchallenged and still in the satirical face. Gerald, full-limbed and turgid with energy, stood unwilling to go, he was held by the presence of the other man. He had not the power to go away.

"So," said Birkin, "goodbye." And he reached out his hand from under the bed-clothes, smiling with a glimmering look.

"Goodbye," said Gerald, taking the warm hand of his friend in a firm grasp. "I shall come again. I miss you down at the mill."

"I'll be there in a few days," said Birkin.

The eyes of the two men met again. Gerald's, that were keen as a hawk's, were suffused now with warm light and with unadmitted love, Birkin looked back as out of the darkness, unsounded and unknown, yet with a kind of warmth, that seemed to flow over Gerald's brain like a fertile sleep.

"Goodbye then. There's nothing I can do for you?"

"Nothing, thanks."

Birkin watched the black-clothed form of the other man move out of the door, the bright head was gone, he turned over to sleep.

Chapter XVII

The Industrial Magnate

In Beldover, there was both for Ursula and for Gudrun an interval. It seemed to Ursula as if Birkin had gone out of her for the time, he had lost his significance, he scarcely mattered in her world. She had her own friends, her own activities, her own life. She turned back to the old ways with zest, away from him.

And Gudrun, after feeling every moment in all her veins conscious of Gerald Crich, connected even physically with him, was now almost indifferent to the thought of him. She was nursing new schemes for going away and trying a new form of life. All the time, there was something in her urging her to avoid the final establishing of a relationship with Gerald. She felt it would be wiser and better to have no more than a casual acquaintance with him.

She had a scheme for going to St. Petersburg, where she had a friend who was a sculptor like herself, and who lived with a wealthy Russian whose hobby was jewel-making. The emotional, rather rootless life of the Russians appealed to her. She did not want to go to Paris. Paris was dry, and essentially boring. She would like to go to Rome, Munich, Vienna, or to St. Petersburg or Moscow. She had a friend in St. Petersburg and a friend in Munich. To each of these she wrote, asking about rooms.

She had a certain amount of money. She had come home partly to save, and now she had sold several pieces of work, she had been praised in various shows. She knew she could become quite the "go," if she went to London. But she knew London, she wanted something else. She had seventy pounds, of which nobody knew anything. She would move soon, as soon as she heard from her friends. Her nature, in spite of her apparent placidity and calm, was profoundly restless.

The sisters happened to call in a cottage in Willey Green to buy honey. Mrs Kirk, a stout, pale, sharp-nosed woman, sly, honied, with something shrewish and cat-like beneath, asked the girls into her too-cosy, too tidy kitchen. There was a cat-like comfort and cleanliness everywhere.

"Yes, Miss Brangwen," she said, in her slightly whining, insinuating voice, "and how do you like being back in the old place then?"

Gudrun, whom she addressed, hated her at once.

"I don't care for it," she replied abruptly.

"You don't? Ay, well, I suppose you find a difference from London. You like life, and big, grand places. Some of us has to be content with Willey Green and Beldover.—And what do you think of our Grammar School, as there's so much talk about?"

"What do I think of it?" Gudrun looked round at her slowly. "Do you mean, do I think it's a good school?"

"Yes. What is your opinion of it?"

"I *do* think it's a good school."

Gudrun was very cold and repelling. She knew the common people hated the school.

"Ay, you do, then! I've heard so much, one way and the other. It's nice to know what those that's in it feel. But opinions vary, don't they? Mr Crich up at Shortlands is all for it. Ay, poor man, I'm afraid he's not long for this world. He's very poorly."

"Is he worse?" asked Ursula.

"Eh, yes—since they lost Miss Diana. He's gone off to a shadow. Poor man, he's had a world of trouble."

"Has he?" asked Gudrun, faintly ironic.

"He has, a world of trouble. And as nice and kind a gentleman as ever you could wish to meet.—His children don't take after him."

"I suppose they take after their mother?" said Ursula.

"In many ways." Mrs Kirk lowered her voice a little. "She was a proud, haughty lady when she came into these parts—my word, she was that! She mustn't be looked at, and it was worth your life to speak to her."

The woman made a dry, sly face.

"Did you know her when she was first married?"

"Yes, I knew her. I nursed three of her children. And proper little terrors they were, little fiends—that Gerald was a demon if ever there was one, a proper demon, ay, at six month's old."

A curious malicious, sly tone came into the woman's voice.

"Really!" said Gudrun.

"That wilful, masterful—he'd mastered one nurse at six months. Kick, and scream, and struggle like a demon! Many's the time I've pinched his little bottom for him, when he was a child in arms.—Ay, and he'd have been better if he'd had it pinched oftener. But she wouldn't have them corrected—no-o, wouldn't hear of it. I can remember the rows she had with Mr Crich, my word!—When he'd got worked up, properly worked up till he could stand no more, he'd lock the study door and whip them. But she paced up and down all the while like a tiger outside, like a tiger, with very murder in her face. She had a face that could *look* death. And when the door was opened, she'd go in with her hands lifted—'What have you been doing to *my* children, you coward.'—She was like one out of her mind. I believe he was frightened of her;—he had to be driven mad before he'd lift a finger. Didn't the servants have a life of it! And didn't we used to be thankful when one of them caught it. They were the torment of your life."

"Really!" said Gudrun.

"In every possible way. If you wouldn't let them smash their pots on the table, if you wouldn't let them drag the kitten about with a string round its neck, if you wouldn't give them whatever they asked for, every mortal thing—then there was a shine on, and their mother coming in asking—'What's the matter with him? What have you done to him? What is it, Darling?' And then she'd turn on you as if she'd trample you under her feet.—But she didn't trample on me. I was the only one that could do anything with her demons—for she wasn't going to be bothered with them herself. No, *she* took no trouble for them. But they must just have their way, they mustn't be spoken to. And master Gerald was the beauty. I left when he was a year and a half, I could stand no more. But I pinched his little bottom for him when he was in arms, I did, when there was no holding him—and I'm not sorry I did—."

Gudrun went away in fury and loathing. The phrase, 'I pinched his little bottom for him,' sent her into a white, stony fury. She could not bear it, she wanted to have the woman taken out at once and strangled. And yet there the phrase was lodged in her mind for ever, beyond escape. She felt, one day, she would *have* to tell him, to see how he took it. And she loathed herself for the thought.

But at Shortlands the life-long struggle was coming to a close. The father was ill and was going to die. He had bad internal pains, which took away all his attentive life, and left him with only a vestige of his consciousness. More and more a silence came over him, he was less and less acutely aware of his surroundings. The pain seemed to absorb his activity. He knew it was there, he knew it would come again. It was like something lurking in the darkness within him. And he had not the power, or the will, to seek it out and to know it. There it remained in the darkness, the great pain, tearing him at times, and then lying silent. And when it tore him he crouched in silent subjection under it, and when it left him alone again, he refused to know of it. It was within the darkness, let it remain unknown. So he never admitted it, except in a secret corner of himself, where all his never-revealed fears and secrets were accumulated. For the rest, he had a pain, it went away, it made no difference. It even stimulated him, excited him.

But it gradually absorbed his life. Gradually it drew away all his potentiality, it bled him into the dark, it weaned him of life and drew him away into the darkness. And in this twilight of his life, little remained visible to him. The business, his work, that was gone entirely. His public interests had disappeared as if they had never been. Even his family had become extraneous to him, he could only remember, in some slight, non-essential part of himself, that such and such were his children. It was superficial fact, not vital to him. He had to make an effort to know their relation to him. Even his wife barely existed. She indeed was like the darkness, like the pain within him. By some strange association, the darkness that contained the pain and the darkness that contained his wife were identical. All his thoughts and understandings became blurred and fused, and now his wife and the consuming pain were the same dark secret power against him, that he never faced. He never drove the dread out of its lair within him. He only knew that there was a dark place, and something inhabiting this darkness which issued from time to time and rent him. But he dared not penetrate and drive the beast into the open. He had rather ignore its existence. Only, in his vague way, the dread was his wife, the destroyer, and it was the pain, the destruction, a darkness which was one and both.

He very rarely saw his wife. She kept her room. Only occasionally she came forth, with her head stretched forward, and in her low, possessed voice, she asked him how he was. And he answered her, in the habit of more than thirty years: "Well, I don't think I'm any the worse, dear." But he was frightened of her, underneath this safeguard of habit, frightened almost to the verge of death.

But all his life, he had been so constant to his lights, he had never broken down. He would die even now without breaking down, without knowing what his feelings were, towards her. All his life, he had said: "Poor Christiana, she has such a strong temper." With unbroken will, he had stood by his position with regard to her, he had substituted pity for all his hostility, pity had been his shield and his safeguard, and his infallible weapon. And still, in his consciousness, he was sorry for her, her nature was so violent and so impatient.

But now his pity, with his life, was wearing thin, and the dread, almost amounting to horror, was rising into being. But before the armour of his pity really broke, he would die, as an insect when its shell is cracked. This was his final resource. Others would live on, and know the living death, the

ensuing process of hopeless chaos. He would not. He denied death its
victory.

He had been so constant to his lights, so constant to charity, and to his
love for his neighbour. Perhaps he had loved his neighbour even better
than himself—which is going one further than the commandment.
Always, this flame had burned in his heart, sustaining him through
everything, the welfare of the people. He was a large employer of labour,
he was a great mine-owner. And he had never lost this from his heart, that
in Christ he was one with his workmen. Nay, he had felt inferior to them,
as if they, through poverty and labour, were nearer to God than he. He
had always the unacknowledged belief, that it was his workmen, the
miners, who held in their hands the means of salvation. To move nearer to
God, he must move towards his miners, his life must gravitate towards
theirs. They were, unconsciously, his idol, his God made manifest. In
them he worshipped the highest, the great, sympathetic, mindless
Godhead of humanity.

And all the while, his wife had opposed him like one of the great demons
of hell. Strange, like a bird of prey, with the fascinating beauty and
abstraction of a hawk, she had beat against the bars of his philanthropy,
and like a hawk in a cage, she had sunk into silence. By force of circumstance, because all the world combined to make the cage unbreakable, he
had been too strong for her, he had kept her prisoner. And because she
was his prisoner, his passion for her had always remained keen as death.
He had always loved her, loved her with intensity. Within the cage, she was
denied nothing, she was given all licence.

But she had gone almost mad. Of wild and overweening temper, she
could not bear the humiliation of her husband's soft, half-appealing
kindness to everybody. He was not deceived by the poor. He knew they
came and sponged on him, and whined to him, the worse sort; the majority,
luckily for him, were much too proud to ask for anything, much too
independent to come knocking at his door. But in Beldover, as everywhere
else, there were the whining, parasitic, foul human beings who come
crawling after charity, and feeding on the living body of the public like lice.
A kind of fire would go over Christiana Crich's brain, as she saw two more
pale-faced, creeping women in objectionable black clothes, cringing
lugubriously up the drive to the door. She wanted to set the dogs on them,
"Hi Rip! Hi Ring! Ranger! At 'em boys, set 'em off." But Crowther, the
butler, with all the rest of the servants, was Mr Crich's man. Nevertheless,
when her husband was away, she would come down like a wolf on the
crawling supplicants; "What do you people want? There is nothing for you

here. You have no business on the drive at all. Crowther, drive them away, and let no more of them through the gate."

The servants had to obey her. And she would stand watching with an eye like the eagle's, whilst the groom in clumsy confusion drove the lugubrious persons down the drive, as if they were rusty fowls scuttling before him.

But they learned to know, from the lodge-keeper, when Mr Crich was away, and they timed their visits. How many times, in the first years, would Crowther knock softly at the door: "Person to see you, sir."

"What name?"

"Grocock, sir."

"What do they want?" The question was half impatient, half gratified. He liked hearing appeals to his charity.

"About a child, sir."

"Show them into the library, and tell them they shouldn't come after eleven o'clock in the morning."

"Why do you get up from dinner?—send them off," his wife would say abruptly.

"Oh, I can't do that. It's no trouble just to hear what they have to say."

"How many more have been here today? Why don't you establish open house for them? They would soon oust me and the children."

"You know dear, it doesn't hurt me to hear what they have to say. And if they really are in trouble—well, it is my duty to help them out of it."

"It's your duty to invite all the rats in the world to gnaw at your bones."

"Come, Christiana, it isn't like that. Don't be uncharitable."

But she suddenly swept out of the room, and out to the study. There sat the meagre charity-seekers, looking as if they were at the doctor's.

"Mr Crich can't see you. He can't see you at this hour. Do you think he is your property, that you can come whenever you like? You must go away, there is nothing for you here."

The poor people rose in confusion. But Mr Crich, pale and black-bearded and deprecating, came behind her, saying:

"Yes, I don't like you coming as late as this. I'll hear any of you in the morning part of the day, but I can't really do with you after.—What's amiss then, Gittins? How is your Missis?"

"Why, she's sunk very low, Mester Crich, she's a'most gone, she is—"

Sometimes, it seemed to Mrs Crich as if her husband were some subtle funeral bird, feeding on the miseries of the people. It seemed to her he was never satisfied unless there was some sordid tale being poured out to him, which he drank in with a sort of mournful, sympathetic satisfaction. He would have no *raison d'être* if there were no lugubrious miseries in the world, as an undertaker would have no meaning if there were no funerals.

Mrs Crich recoiled back upon herself, she recoiled away from this world of creeping democracy. A band of tight, baleful exclusion fastened round her heart, her isolation was fierce and hard, her antagonism was passive but terribly pure, like that of a hawk in a cage. As the years went on, she lost more and more count of the world, she seemed rapt in some glittering abstraction, almost purely unconscious. She would wander about the house and about the surrounding country, staring keenly and seeing nothing. She rarely spoke, she had no connection with the world. And she did not even think. She was consumed in a fierce tension of opposition, like the negative pole of a magnet.

And she bore many children. For, as time went on, she never opposed her husband in word or deed. She took no notice of him, externally. She submitted to him, let him take what he wanted and do as he wanted with her. She was like a hawk that sullenly submits to everything. The relation between her and her husband was wordless and unknown, but it was deep, awful, a relation of utter interdestruction. And he, who triumphed in the world, he became more and more hollow in his vitality, the vitality was bled from within him, as by some hemorrhage. She was hulked like a hawk in a cage, but her heart was fierce and undiminished within her, though her mind was destroyed.

So to the last he would go to her and hold her in his arms, sometimes, before his strength was all gone. The terrible white, destructive light that burned in her eyes only excited and roused him. Till he was bled to death, and then he dreaded her more than anything. But he always said to himself, how happy he had been, how he had loved her with a pure and consuming love ever since he had known her. And he thought of her as pure, chaste, the white flame which was known to him alone, the flame of her sex, was a white flower of snow to his mind. She was a wonderful white snow-flower, which he had desired infinitely. And now he was dying with all his ideas and interpretations intact. They would only collapse when the breath left his body. Till then they would be pure truths for him. Only death would show the perfect completeness of the lie. Till death, she was his white snow-flower. He had subdued her, and her subjugation was to him an infinite chastity in her, a virginity which he could never break, and which dominated him as by a spell.

She had let go the outer world, but within herself she was unbroken and unimpaired. She only sat in her room like a moping, dishevelled hawk, motionless, mindless. Her children, for whom she had been so fierce in her youth, now meant scarcely anything to her. She had lost all that, she was quite by herself. Only Gerald, the gleaming, had some existence for her. But of late years, since he had become head of the business, he too was forgotten.

Whereas the father, now he was dying, turned for compassion to Gerald. There had always been opposition between the two of them. Gerald had feared and despised his father, and to a great extent had avoided him all through boyhood and young manhood. And the father had felt very often a real dislike of his eldest son, which, never wanting to give way to, he had refused to acknowledge. He had ignored Gerald as much as possible, leaving him alone.

Since, however, Gerald had come home and assumed responsibility in the firm, and had proved such a wonderful director, the father, tired and weary of all outside concerns, had put all his trust of these things in his son, implicitly, leaving everything to him, and assuming a rather touching dependence on the young enemy. This immediately roused a poignant pity and allegiance in Gerald's heart, always shadowed by contempt and by the unadmitted enmity. For Gerald was in reaction against Charity, yet he was dominated by it; it assumed supremacy in the inner life, and he could not confute it. So he was partly subject to that which his father stood for, but he was in reaction against it. Now he could not save himself. A certain pity and grief and tenderness for his father overcame him, in spite of the deeper, more sullen hostility.

The father won shelter from Gerald through compassion. But for love he had Winifred. She was his youngest child, she was the only one of his children whom he had ever closely loved. And her he loved with all the great, overweening, sheltering love of a dying man. He wanted to shelter her infinitely, infinitely, to wrap her in warmth and love and shelter, perfectly. If he could save her she should never know one pain, one grief, one hurt. He had been so right all his life, so constant in his kindness and his goodness. And this was his last passionate righteousness, his love for the child Winifred. Some things troubled him yet. The world had passed away from him, as his strength ebbed. There were no more poor and injured and humble to protect and succour. These were all lost to him. There were no more sons and daughters to trouble him, and to weigh on him as an unnatural responsibility. These too had faded out of reality. All these things had fallen out of his hands, and left him free.

There remained the covert fear and horror of his wife, as she sat mindless and strange in her room, or as she came forth with slow, prowling step, her head bent forward. But this he put away. Even his life-long righteousness, however, would not quite deliver him from the inner horror. Still, he could keep it sufficiently at bay. It would never break forth openly. Death would come first.

Then there was Winifred! If only he could be sure about her, if only he could be sure. Since the death of Diana, and the development of his illness, his craving for surety with regard to Winifred amounted almost to obsession. It was as if, even dying, he must have some anxiety, some responsibility of love, of Charity, upon his heart.

She was an odd, sensitive, inflammable child, having her father's dark hair and quiet bearing, but being quite detached, momentaneous. She was like a changeling indeed, as if her feelings did not matter to her, really. She often seemed to be talking and playing like the gayest and most childish of children, she was full of the warmest, most delightful affection for a few things—for her father, and for her animals in particular. But if she heard that her beloved kitten Leo had been run over by the motor-car, she put her head on one side, and replied, with a faint contraction like resentment on her face: "Has he?" Then she took no more notice. She only disliked the servant who would force bad news on her, and wanted her to be sorry. She wished not to know, and that seemed her chief motive. She avoided her mother, and most of the members of her family. She *loved* her Daddy, because he wanted her always to be happy, and because he seemed to become young again, and irresponsible in her presence. She liked Gerald, because he was so self-contained. She loved people who would make life a game for her. She had an amazing instinctive critical faculty, and was a pure anarchist, a pure aristocrat at once. For she accepted her equals wherever she found them, and she ignored with blithe indifference her inferiors, whether they were her brothers and sisters, or whether they were wealthy guests of the house, or whether they were the common people or the servants. She was quite single and by herself, deriving from nobody. It was as if she were cut off from all purpose or continuity, and existed simply moment by moment.

The father, as by some strange final illusion, felt as if all his fate depended on his ensuring to Winifred her happiness. She who could never suffer, because she never formed vital connections, she who could lose the dearest things of her life and be just the same the next day, the whole memory dropped out, as if deliberately, she whose will was so strangely and easily free, anarchistic, almost nihilistic, who like a soulless bird flits on its own will, without attachment or responsibility beyond the moment, who in her every motion snapped the threads of serious relationship, with blithe, free hands, really nihilistic, because never troubled, she must be the object of her father's final passionate solicitude.

When Mr Crich heard that Gudrun Brangwen might come to help Winifred with her drawing and modelling he saw a road to salvation for his child. He believed that Winifred had talent, he had seen Gudrun, he knew that she was an exceptional person. He could give Winifred into her hands as into the hands of a right being. Here was a direction and a positive force to be lent to his child, he need not leave her directionless and defenceless. If he could but graft the girl on to some tree of utterance before he died, he would have fulfilled his responsibility. And here it could be done. He did not hesitate to appeal to Gudrun.

Meanwhile, as the father drifted more and more out of life, Gerald experienced more and more a sense of exposure. His father after all had stood for the living world to him. Whilst his father lived, Gerald was not responsible for the world. But now his father was passing away, Gerald found himself left exposed and unready before the storm of living, like the mutinous first mate of a ship that has lost its captain, and who sees only a terrible chaos in front of him. He did not inherit an established order and a living idea. The whole unifying idea of mankind seemed to be dying with his father, the centralising force that had held the whole together seemed to collapse with his father, the parts were ready to go asunder in terrible disintegration. Gerald was as if left on board of a ship that was going asunder beneath his feet, he was in charge of a vessel whose timbers were all coming apart.

He knew that all his life he had been wrenching at the frame of life to break it apart. And now, with something of the terror of a destructive child, he saw himself on the point of inheriting his own destruction. And during the last months, under the influence of death, and of Birkin's talk, and of Gudrun's penetrating being, he had lost entirely that mechanical certainty that had been his triumph. Sometimes spasms of hatred came over him, against Birkin and Gudrun and that whole set. He wanted to go back to the dullest conservatism, to the most stupid of conventional people. He wanted to revert to the strictest Toryism. But the desire did not last long enough to carry him into action.

During his childhood and his boyhood he had wanted a sort of savage freedom. The days of Homer were his ideal, when a man was chief of an army of heroes, or spent his years in wonderful Odyssey. He hated remorselessly the circumstances of his own life, so much so that he never really saw Beldover and the colliery valley. He turned his face entirely away from the blackened mining region that stretched away on the right hand of Shortlands, he turned entirely to the country and the woods beyond Willey Water. It was true that the panting and rattling of the coal-mines could always be heard at Shortlands. But from his earliest childhood, Gerald had paid no heed to this. He had ignored the whole of the industrial sea which surged in coal-blackened tides against the grounds of the house. The world was really a wilderness where one hunted and swam and rode. He rebelled against all authority. Life was a condition of savage freedom.

Then he had been sent away to school, which was so much death to him. He refused to go to Oxford, choosing a German university. He had spent a certain time at Bonn, at Berlin, and at Frankfurt. There, a curiosity had been aroused in his mind. He wanted to see and to know, in a curious objective fashion, as if it were an amusement to him. Then he must try war. Then he must travel into the savage regions that had so attracted him.

The result was, he found humanity very much alike everywhere, and to a mind like his, curious and cold, the savage was duller, less exciting than the European. So he took hold of all kinds of sociological ideas, and ideas of reform. But they never went more than skin-deep, they were never more than a mental amusement. Their interest lay chiefly in the reaction against the positive order, the destructive reaction.

He discovered at last a real adventure in the coal-mines. His father asked him to help in the firm. Gerald had been educated in the science of mining, and it had never interested him. Now, suddenly, with a sort of exultation, he laid hold of the world.

There was impressed photographically on his consciousness the great industry. Suddenly, it was real, he was part of it. Down the valley ran the colliery railway, linking mine with mine. Down the railway ran the trains, short trains of heavily-laden trucks, long trains of empty wagons, each one bearing in big white letters the initials:

"C. B. & Co."

These white letters on all the wagons he had seen since his first childhood, and it was as if he had never seen them, they were so familiar, and so ignored. Now at last he saw his own name written on the wall. Now he had a vision of power.

So many wagons, bearing his initial, running all over the country. He saw them as he entered London in the train, he saw them at Dover. So far his power ramified. He looked at Beldover, at Selby, at Whatmore, at Lethley Bank, the great colliery villages which depended entirely on his mines. They were hideous and sordid, during his childhood they had been sores in his consciousness. And now he saw them with pride. Four raw new towns, and many ugly industrial hamlets were crowded under his dependence. He saw the stream of miners flowing along the causeways from the mines at the end of the afternoon, thousands of blackened, slightly distorted human beings with red mouths, all moving subjugate to his will. He pushed slowly in his motor-car through the little market-top on Friday nights in Beldover, through a solid mass of human beings that were making their purchases and doing their weekly spending. They were all subordinate to him. They were ugly and uncouth, but they were his instruments. He was the God of the machine. They made way for his motor-car automatically, slowly.

He did not care whether they made way with alacrity, or grudgingly. He did not care what they thought of him. His vision had suddenly crystallised. Suddenly he had conceived the pure instrumentality of mankind. There had been so much humanitarianism, so much talk of sufferings and feelings. It was ridiculous. The sufferings and feelings of individuals did not matter in the least. They were mere conditions, like the weather. What mattered was the pure instrumentality of the individual. As a man as of a knife: does it cut well? Nothing else mattered.

Everything in the world has its function, and is good or not good in so far as it fulfils this function more or less perfectly. Was a miner a good miner? Then he was complete. Was a manager a good manager? That was enough. Gerald himself, who was responsible for all this industry, was he a good director? If he were, he had fulfilled his life. The rest was by-play.

The mines were there, they were old. They were giving out, it did not pay to work the seams. There was talk of closing down two of them. It was at this point that Gerald arrived on the scene.

He looked around. There lay the mines. They were old, obsolete. They were like old lions, no more good. He looked again. Pah! the mines were nothing but the clumsy efforts of impure minds. There they lay, abortions of a half-trained mind. Let the idea of them be swept away. He cleared his brain of them, and thought only of the coal in the under earth. How much was there?

There was plenty of coal. The old workings could not get at it, that was all. Then break the neck of the old workings. The coal lay there in its seams, even though the seams were thin. There it lay, inert matter, as it had always lain, since the beginning of time, subject to the will of man. The will of man was the determining factor. Man was the arch-god of earth. His mind was obedient to serve his will. Man's will was the absolute, the only absolute.

And it was his will to subjugate Matter to his own ends. The subjugation itself was the point, the fight was the be-all, the fruits of victory were mere results. It was not for the sake of money that Gerald took over the mines. He did not care about money, fundamentally. He was neither ostentatious nor luxurious, neither did he care about social position, not finally. What he wanted was the pure fulfilment of his own will in the struggle with the natural conditions. His will was now, to take the coal out of the earth, profitably. The profit was merely the condition of victory, but the victory itself lay in the feat achieved. He vibrated with zest before the challenge. Every day he was in the mines, examining, testing, he consulted experts, he gradually gathered the whole situation into his mind, as a general grasps the plan of his campaign.

Then there was need for a complete break. The mines were run on an old system, an obsolete idea. The initial idea had been, to obtain as much money from the earth as would make the owners comfortably rich, would allow the workmen sufficient wages and good conditions, and would increase the wealth of the country altogether. Gerald's father, following in the second generation, having a sufficient fortune, had thought only of the men. The mines, for him, were primarily great fields to produce bread and plenty for all the hundreds of human beings gathered about them. He had lived and striven with his fellow owners to benefit the men every time. And the men had been benefited in their fashion. There were few poor, and few needy. All was plenty, because the mines were good and easy to work. And the miners, in those days, finding themselves richer than they might have expected, felt glad and triumphant. They thought themselves well-off, they congratulated themselves on their good-fortune, they remembered how their fathers had starved and suffered, and they felt that better times had come. They were grateful to those others, the pioneers, the new owners, who had opened out the pits, and let forth this stream of plenty.

But man is never satisfied, and soon the miners, from gratitude to their owners, passed on to murmuring. Their sufficiency decreased with knowledge, they wanted more. Why should the masters be so out-of-all-proportion rich?

There was a crisis when Gerald was a boy, when the Masters' Federation closed down the mines because the men would not accept a reduction. This lock-out had forced home the new conditions to Thomas Crich. Belonging to the Federation, he had been compelled by his honor to close the pits against his men. He, the father, the patriarch, was forced to deny the means of life to his sons, his people. He, the rich man who would hardly enter heaven because of his possessions, must now turn upon the poor, upon those who were nearer Christ than himself, those who were humble and despised and closer to perfection, those who were manly and noble in their labours, and must say to them: "Ye shall neither labour nor eat bread."

It was this recognition of the state of war which really broke his heart. He wanted his industry to be run on love, Oh, he wanted love to be the directing power even of the mines. And now, from under the cloak of love, the sword was cynically drawn, the sword of mechanical necessity.

This really broke his heart. He must have the illusion—and now the illusion was destroyed.—The men were not against *him*, but they were against the masters. It was war, and willy nilly he found himself on the wrong side, in his own conscience. Seething masses of miners met daily, carried away by a new religious impulse. The idea flew through them: "All men are equal on earth," and they would carry the idea to its material fulfilment. After all, is it not the teaching of Christ? And what is an idea, if not the germ of action in the material world. "All men are equal in spirit, they are all sons of God. Whence then this obvious disquality?" It was a religious creed pushed to its material conclusion. Thomas Crich at least had no answer. He could but admit, according to his sincere tenets, that the disquality was wrong. But he could not give up his goods, which were the stuff of disquality. So the men would fight for their rights. The last impulses of the last religious passion left on earth, the passion for equality, inspired them.

Seething mobs of men marched about, their faces lighted up as for holy war, with a smoke of cupidity. How disentangle the passion for equality from the passion of cupidity, when begins the fight for equality of possessions? But the God was the machine. Each man claimed equality in the Godhead of the great productive machine. Every man equally was part of this Godhead.—But somehow, somewhere, Thomas Crich knew this was false. When the machine is the Godhead, and production or work is worship, then the most mechanical mind is purest and highest, the representative of God on earth—and the rest are subordinate, each according to his degree.

Riots broke out, Whatmore pit-head was in flames. This was the pit furthest in the country, near the woods. Soldiers came. From the windows of Shortlands, on that fatal day, could be seen the flare of fire in the sky not far off, and now the little colliery train, with the workmen's carriages which were used to convey the miners to the distant Whatmore, was crossing the valley full of soldiers, full of red-coats. Then there was the far-off sound of firing, then the later news that the mob was dispersed, one man was shot dead, the fire was put out.

Gerald, who was a boy, was filled with the wildest excitement and delight. He longed to go with the soldiers to shoot the men. But he was not allowed to go out of the lodge gates. At the gates were stationed sentries with guns. Gerald stood near them in delight, whilst gangs of derisive miners strolled up and down the lanes, calling and jeering:

"Now then, three ha'porth o' coppers, let's see thee shoot thy gun." Insults were chalked on the walls and the fences, the servants left.

And all this while Thomas Crich was breaking his heart, and giving away hundreds of pounds in charity. Everywhere there was free food, a surfeit of free food. Anybody could have bread for asking, and a loaf cost only three-ha'pence. Every day there was a free tea somewhere, the children had never had so many treats in their lives. On Friday afternoon great basketfuls of buns and cakes were taken into the schools, and great pitchers of milk, the school-children had what they wanted. They were sick with eating too much cake and milk.

And then it came to an end, and the men went back to work. But it was never the same as before. There was a new situation created, a new idea reigned. Even in the machine, there should be equality. No part should be subordinate to any other part: all should be equal. The instinct for chaos had entered. Mystic equality lies in abstraction, not in having or in doing, which are processes. In function and process, one man, one part, must of necessity be subordinate to another. It is a condition of being.—But the desire for chaos had risen, and the idea of mechanical equality was the weapon of disruption which should execute the will of man, the will for chaos.

Gerald was a boy at the time of the strike, but he longed to be a man, to fight the colliers.—The father however was trapped between two half-truths, and broken. He wanted to be a pure Christian, one and equal with all men. He even wanted to give away all he had, to the poor.—Yet he was a great promoter of industry, and he knew perfectly that he must keep his goods and keep his authority. This was as divine a necessity in him, as the need to give away all he possessed—more divine, even, since this was the necessity he acted upon. Yet because he did *not* act on the other ideal, it dominated him, he was dying of chagrin because he must forfeit it. He wanted to be a father of loving-kindness and sacrificial benevolence. The colliers shouted to him about his thousands a year. They would not be deceived.

When Gerald grew up in the ways of the world, he shifted the position. He did not care about the equality. The whole Christian attitude of love and self-sacrifice was old hat. He knew that position and authority were the right thing in the world, and it was useless to cant about it. They were the right thing, for the simple reason that they were functionally necessary. They were not the be-all and the end-all. It was like being part of a machine. He himself happened to be a controlling, central part, the masses of men were the parts variously controlled. This was merely as it happened. As well get excited because a central hub drives a hundred outer wheels—or because the whole universe wheels round the sun. After all, it would be mere silliness to say that the moon and the earth and Saturn and Jupiter and Venus have just as much right to be the centre of the universe, each of them separately, as the sun. Such an assertion is made merely in the desire of chaos.

Without bothering to *think* to a conclusion, Gerald jumped to a conclusion. He abandoned the whole democratic-equality problem as a problem of silliness. What mattered was the great social productive machine. Let that work perfectly, let it produce a sufficiency of everything, let every man be given a rational portion, greater or less according to his functional degree or magnitude, and then, provision made, let the devil supervene, let every man look after his own amusements and appetites, so long as he interfered with nobody.

So Gerald set himself to work, to put the great industry in order. In his travels, and in his accompanying readings, he had come to the conclusion that the essential secret of life was harmony. He did not define to himself at all clearly what harmony was. The word pleased him, he felt he had come to his own conclusions. And he proceeded to put his philosophy into practice by forcing order into the established world, translating the mystic word harmony into the practical word organisation.

Immediately he *saw* the firm, he realised what he could do. He had a fight to fight with Matter, with the earth and the coal it enclosed. This was the sole idea, to turn upon the inanimate matter of the underground, and reduce it to his will. And for this fight with matter, one must have perfect instruments in perfect organisation, a mechanism so subtle and harmonious in its workings that it represents the single mind of man, and by its relentless repetition of given movement, will accomplish a purpose irresistibly, inhumanly. It was this inhuman principle in the mechanism he wanted to construct that inspired Gerald with an almost religious exaltation. He, the man, could interpose a perfect, changeless, godlike medium between himself and the Matter he had to subjugate. There were two opposites, his will and the resistant Matter of the earth. And between these he could establish the very expression of his will, the incarnation of his power, a great and perfect machine, a system, an activity of pure order, pure mechanical repetition, repetition ad infinitum, hence eternal and infinite. He found his eternal and his infinite in the pure machine-principle of perfect co-ordination into one pure, complex, infinitely repeated motion, like the spinning of a wheel; but a productive spinning, as the revolving of the universe may be called a productive spinning, a productive repetition through eternity, to infinity. And this is the God-motion, this productive repetition ad infinitum. And Gerald was the God of the Machine, Deus ex Machina. And the whole productive will of man was the Godhead.

He had his life-work now, to extend over the earth a great and perfect system in which the will of man ran smooth and unthwarted, timeless, a Godhead in process. He had to begin with the mines. The terms were given: first the resistant Matter of the underground; then the instruments of its subjugation, instruments human and metallic; and finally his own pure will, his own mind. It would need a marvellous adjustment of myriad instruments, human, animal, metallic, kinetic, dynamic, a marvellous casting of myriad tiny wholes in to one great perfect entirety. And then, in this case there was perfection attained, the will of the highest was perfectly fulfilled, the will of mankind was perfectly enacted; for was not mankind mystically contradistinguished against inanimate Matter, was not the history of mankind just the history of the conquest of the one by the other?

The miners were overreached. While they were still in the toils of divine equality of man, Gerald had passed on, granted essentially their case, and proceeded in his quality of human being to fulfil the will of mankind as a whole. He merely represented the miners in a higher sense when he perceived that the only way to fulfil perfectly the will of man was to establish the perfect, inhuman machine. But he represented them very essentially, they were far behind, out of date, squabbling for their material equality. The desire had already transmuted into this new and greater desire, for a perfect intervening mechanism between man and Matter, the desire to translate the Godhead into pure mechanism.

As soon as Gerald entered the firm, the convulsion of death ran through the old system. He had all his life been tortured by a furious and destructive demon, which possessed him sometimes like an insanity. This temper now entered like a virus into the firm, and there were cruel eruptions. Terrible and inhuman were his examinations into every detail; there was no privacy he would spare, no old sentiment but he would turn it over. The old grey managers, the old grey clerks, the doddering old pensioners, he looked at them, and removed them as so much lumber. The whole concern seemed like a hospital of invalid employees. He had no emotional qualms. He arranged what pensions were necessary, he looked for efficient substitutes, and when these were found, he substituted them for the old hands.

"I've a pitiful letter here from Letherinton," his father would say, in a tone of deprecation and appeal. "Don't you think the poor fellow might keep on a little longer. I always fancied he did very well."

"I've got a man in his place now, father. He'll be happier out of it, believe me. You think his allowance is plenty, don't you?"

"It is not the allowance that he wants, poor man. He feels it very much, that he is superannuated. Says he thought he had twenty more years of work in him yet."

"Not of this kind of work I want. He doesn't understand."

The father sighed. He wanted not to know any more. He believed the pits would have to be overhauled if they were to go on working. And after all, it would be worst in the long run for everybody, if they must close down. So he could make no answer to the appeals of his old and trusty servants, he could only repeat "Gerald says."

So the father withdrew more and more out of the light. The whole frame of the real life was broken for him. He had been right according to his lights. And his lights had been those of the great religion. Yet they seemed to have become obsolete, to be superseded in the world. He could not understand. He only withdrew his lights into an inner room, into the silence. The beautiful candles of belief, that would not do to light the world any more, they would still burn sweetly and sufficiently in the inner room of his soul, and in the silence of his retirement.

Gerald rushed into the reform of the firm, beginning with the office. It was needful to economise severely, to make possible the great alterations he must introduce.

"What are these widows' coals?" he asked.

"We have always allowed all widows of men who worked for the firm a load of coals every three months."

"They must pay cost price henceforward. The firm is not a charity institution, as everybody seems to think."

Widows, these stock figures of sentimental humanitarianism, he felt a dislike at the thought of them. They were almost repulsive. Why were they not immolated on the pyre of the husband, like the sati in India? At any rate, let them pay the cost of their coals.

In a thousand ways he cut down the expenditure, in ways so fine as to be hardly noticeable to the men. The miners must pay for the cartage of their coals, heavy cartage too; they must pay for their tools, for the sharpening, for the care of lamps, for many trifling things that made the bill of charges against every man mount up to a shilling or so in the week. It was not grasped very definitely by the miners, though they were sore enough. But it saved hundreds of pounds every week for the firm.

Gradually Gerald got hold of everything. And then began the great reform. Expert engineers were introduced in every department. An enormous electric plant was installed, both for lighting and for haulage underground, and for power. The electricity was carried to every mine. New machinery was brought from America, such as the miners had never seen before, great iron men, as the cutting machines were called, and unusual appliances. The working of the pits was thoroughly changed, all the control was taken out of the hands of the miners, the butty system was abolished. Everything was run on the most accurate and delicate scientific method, educated and expert men were in control everywhere, the miners were reduced to mere mechanical instruments. They had to work hard, much harder than before, the work was terrible and heart-breaking in its mechanicalness.

But they submitted to it all. The joy went out of their lives, the hope seemed to perish as they became more and more mechanised. And yet they accepted the new conditions. They even got a further satisfaction out of them. At first they hated Gerald Crich, they swore to do something to him, to murder him. But as time went on, they accepted everything with some fatal satisfaction. Gerald was their high priest, he represented the religion they really felt. His father was forgotten already. There was a new world, a new order, strict, terrible, inhuman, but satisfying in its very destructiveness. The men were satisfied to belong to the great and wonderful machine, even whilst it destroyed them. It was what they wanted, it was the highest that man had produced, the most wonderful and superhuman. They were exalted by belonging to this great and superhuman system which was beyond feeling or reason, something really godlike. Their hearts died within them, but their souls were satisfied. It was what they wanted. Otherwise Gerald could never have done what he did. He was just ahead of them in giving them what they wanted, this participation in a great and perfect system that subjected life to pure mathematical principles. This was a sort of freedom, the sort they really wanted. It was the first great step in undoing, the first great phase of chaos, the substitution of the mechanical principle for the organic, the destruction of the organic purpose, the organic unity, and the subordination of every organic unit to the great mechanical purpose. It was pure organic disintegration and pure mechanical organisation. This is the first and finest state of chaos.

Gerald was satisfied. He knew the colliers said they hated him. But he had long ceased to hate them. When they streamed past him at evening, their heavy boots slurring on the pavement wearily, their shoulders slightly distorted, they took no notice of him, they gave him no greeting whatever, they passed in a grey-black stream of unemotional acceptance. They were not important to him, save as instruments, nor he to them, save as a supreme instrument of control. As miners they had their being, he had his being as director. He admired their qualities. But as men, personalities, they were just accidents, sporadic little unimportant phenomena.—And tacitly, the men agreed to this. For Gerald agreed to it in himself.

He had succeeded. He had converted the industry into a new and terrible purity. There was a greater output of coal than ever, the wonderful and delicate system ran almost perfectly. He had a set of really clever engineers, both mining and electrical, and they did not cost much. A highly educated man cost very little more than a workman. His managers, who were all rare men, were no more expensive than the old bungling fools of his father's day, who were merely colliers promoted. His chief manager, who had twelve hundred a year, saved the firm at least five thousand. The whole system was now so perfect that Gerald was hardly necessary any more.

It was so perfect, that sometimes, a strange fear came over him, and he did not know what to do. He went on for some years in a sort of trance of activity. What he was doing seemed supreme, he was almost like a divinity. He was a pure and exalted activity.

But now he had succeeded—he had finally succeeded. And once or twice lately, when he was alone in the evening and had nothing to do, he had suddenly stood up in terror, not knowing what he was. And he went to the mirror and looked long and closely at his own face, at his own eyes, seeking for something. He was afraid, in mortal dry fear, but he knew not what of. He looked at his own face. There it was, shapely and healthy and the same as ever, yet somehow, it was not real, it was a mask. He dared not touch it, for fear it should prove to be only a composition mask. His eyes were blue and keen as ever, and as firm in their sockets. Yet he was not sure that they were not blue false bubbles that would burst in a moment and leave clear annihilation. He could see the darkness in them, as if they were only bubbles of darkness. He was afraid that one day he would break down and be a purely meaningless babble lapping round a darkness.

But his will yet held good, he was able to go away and read, and think about things. He liked to read books about the primitive man, books of anthropology, and also works of speculative philosophy. His mind was very active. But it was like a bubble floating in the darkness. At any moment it might burst and leave him in chaos. He would not die. He knew that. He would go on living, but the meaning would have collapsed out of him, his divine reason would be gone. In a strangely indifferent, sterile way, he was frightened. But he could not react even to the fear. It was as if his centres of feeling were drying up. He remained calm, calculative and healthy, and quite freely deliberate, even whilst he felt, with faint, small, but final, sterile horror, that his mystic reason was breaking, giving way now, at this crisis.

And it was a strain. He knew there was no equilibrium. He would have to go in some direction, shortly, to find relief. Only Birkin kept the fear definitely off him, saved him his quick sufficiency in life, by the odd mobility and changeableness which seemed to contain the quintessence of faith. But then Gerald must always come away from Birkin, as from a church service, back to the outside real world of work and life. There it was, it did not alter, and words were futilities. He had to keep himself in reckoning with the world of work and material life. And it became more and more difficult, such a strange pressure was upon him, as if the very middle of him were a vacuum, and outside were an awful tension.

He had found his most satisfactory relief in women. After a debauch with some desperate woman, he went on quite easy and forgetful. The devil of it was, it was so hard to keep up his interest in women nowadays. He didn't care about them any more. A Pussum was all right in her way, but she was an exceptional case, and even she mattered extremely little. No, women, in that sense, were useless to him any more. He felt that his *mind* needed acute stimulation, before he could be physically roused.

Chapter XVIII

Rabbit

Gudrun knew that it was a critical thing for her to go to Shortlands. She knew it was equivalent to accepting Gerald Crich as a lover. And though she hung back, disliking the condition, yet she knew she would go on. She equivocated. She said to herself, in torment recalling the blow and the kiss, "After all, what is it? What is a kiss? What even is a blow? It is an instant, vanished at once. I can go to Shortlands just for a time, before I go away, if only to see what it is like." For she had an insatiable curiosity to see and to know everything.

She also wanted to know what Winifred was really like. Having heard the child calling from the steamer in the night, she felt some mysterious connection with her.

Gudrun talked with the father in the library. Then he sent for his daughter. She came accompanied by Mademoiselle.

"Winnie, this is Miss Brangwen, who will be so kind as to help you with your drawing and making models of your animals," said the father.

The child looked at Gudrun for a moment with interest, before she came forward and with face averted offered her hand. There was a complete sang froid and indifference under Winifred's childish reserve, a certain irresponsible callousness.

"How do you do?" said the child, not lifting her face.

"How do you do," said Gudrun.

Then Winifred stood aside, and Gudrun was introduced to Mademoiselle.

"You have a fine day for your walk," said Mademoiselle, in a bright manner.

"*Quite* fine," said Gudrun.

Winifred was watching from her distance. She was as if amused, but rather unsure as yet what this new person was like. She saw so many new persons, and so few who became real to her. Mademoiselle was of no count whatever, the child merely put up with her, calmly and easily, accepting her little authority with faint scorn, compliant out of childish arrogance of indifference.

"Well Winifred," said the father, "aren't you glad Miss Brangwen has come? She makes animals and birds in wood and in clay, that the people in London write about in the papers, praising them to the skies."

Winifred smiled slightly.

"Who told you, Daddy?" she asked.

"Who told me? Hermione told me, and Rupert Birkin."

"Do you know them?" Winifred asked, of Gudrun, turning to her with faint challenge.

"Yes," said Gudrun.

Winifred readjusted herself a little. She had been ready to accept Gudrun as a sort of servant. Now she saw it was on terms of friendship they were intended to meet. She was rather glad. She had so many half inferiors, whom she tolerated with perfect good-humour.

Gudrun was very calm. She also did not take these things very seriously. A new occasion was mostly spectacular to her. However, Winifred was a detached, ironic child, she would never attach herself. Gudrun liked her and was intrigued by her. The first meetings went off with a certain humiliating clumsiness. Neither Winifred nor her instructress had any social grace.

Soon however, they met in a kind of make-believe world. Winifred did not notice human beings, unless they were like herself, playful and slightly mocking. She would accept nothing but the world of amusement, and the serious people of her life were the animals she had for pets. On those she lavished, almost ironically, her affection and her companionship. To the rest of the human scheme she submitted with a faint bored indifference.

She had a pekinese dog called Looloo, which she loved.

"Let us draw Looloo," said Gudrun, "and see if we can get his Looliness, shall we?"

"Darling!" cried Winifred, rushing to the dog, that sat with contemplative sadness on the hearth, and kissing its bulging brow. "Darling one, will you be drawn? Shall its mummy draw its portrait?" Then she chuckled gleefully, and turning to Gudrun, said: "Oh let's!"

They proceeded to get pencils and paper, and were ready.

"Beautifullest," cried Winifred, hugging the dog, "sit still while its mummy draws its beautiful portrait." The dog looked up at her with grievous resignation in its large, prominent eyes. She kissed it fervently, and said: "I wonder what mine will be like. It's sure to be awful."

As she sketched she chuckled to herself, and cried out at times:

"Oh darling, you're so beautiful!"

And again chuckling, she rushed to embrace the dog, in penitence, as if she were doing him some subtle injury. He sat all the time with the resignation and fretfulness of ages on his dark velvety face. She drew slowly, with a wicked concentration in her eyes, her head on one side, an intense stillness over her. She was as if working the spell of some enchantment. Suddenly she had finished. She looked at the dog, and then at her drawing, and then cried, with real grief for the dog, and at the same time a wicked exultation:

"My beautiful, why did they?"

She took her paper to the dog, and held it under his nose. He turned his head aside as in chagrin and mortification, and she impulsively kissed his velvety bulging forehead.

"'s a Loolie, 's a little Loozie! Look at his portrait, darling, look at his portrait, that his mother has done of him." She looked at her paper and chuckled. Then, kissing the dog once more, she rose and came gravely to Gudrun, offering her the paper.

It was a grotesque little diagram of a grotesque little animal, so wicked and so comical, a slow smile came over Gudrun's face, unconsciously. And at her side Winifred chuckled with glee, and said:

"It isn't like him, is it? He's much lovelier than that. He's *so* beautiful— mmm, Looloo, my sweet darling." And she flew off to embrace the chagrined little dog. He looked up at her with reproachful, saturnine eyes, vanquished in his extreme agedness of being. Then she flew back to her drawing, and chuckled with satisfaction.

"It isn't like him, is it?" she said to Gudrun.

"Yes, it's very like him," Gudrun replied.

The child treasured her drawing, carried it about with her, and showed it, with a silent embarrassment, to everybody.

"Look," she said, thrusting the paper into her father's hand.

"Why that's Looloo!" he exclaimed. And he looked down in surprise, hearing the almost inhuman chuckle of the child at his side.

Gerald was away from home when Gudrun first came to Shortlands. But the first morning he came back he watched for her. It was a sunny, soft morning, and he lingered in the garden paths, looking at the flowers that had come out during his absence. He was clean and fit as ever, shaven, his fair hair scrupulously parted at the side, bright in the sunshine, his short, fair moustache closely clipped, his eyes with their humorous kind twinkle, which was so deceptive. He was dressed in black, his clothes sat well on his well-nourished body. Yet as he lingered before the flower-beds in the morning sunshine, there was a certain isolation, a fear about him, as of something wanting.

Gudrun came up quickly, unseen. She was dressed in blue, with woollen yellow stockings, like the Blue coat boys. He glanced up in surprise. Her stockings always disconcerted him, the pale-yellow stockings and the rather heavy black shoes. Winifred, who had been playing about the garden with Mademoiselle and the dogs, came flitting towards Gudrun. The child wore a dress of black-and-white stripes. Her hair was rather short, cut round and hanging level in her neck.

"We're going to do Bismarck, aren't we?" she said, linking her hand through Gudrun's arm.

"Yes, we're going to do Bismarck. Do you want to?"

"Oh yes—Oh I do! I want most awfully to do Bismarck. He looks *so* splendid this morning, so *fierce*. He's almost as big as a lion." And the child chuckled sardonically at her own hyperbole. "He's a real king, he really is."

"Bonjour mademoiselle," said the little French governess, wavering up with a slight bow, a bow of the sort that Gudrun loathed, insolent.

"Winifred veut tant faire le portrait de Bismarck—! Oh, mais toute la matinée c'est—'We will do Bismarck this morning!'—Bismarck, Bismarck, toujours Bismarck! C'est un lapin, n'est-ce pas, mademoiselle?"

"Oui, c'est un grand lapin blanc et noir. Vous ne l'avez pas vu?" said Gudrun in her good, but rather heavy French.

"Non, mademoiselle, Winifred n'a jamais voulu me le faire voir. Tant de fois je le lui ai demandé, 'Qu'est-ce donc que ce Bismarck, Winifred?' Mais elle n'a pas voulu me le dire. Son Bismarck, c'était un mystère."

"Oui, c'est un mystère, vraiment un mystère! Miss Brangwen, say that Bismarck is a mystery," cried Winifred.

"Bismarck is a mystery, Bismarck, c'est un mystère, der Bismarck, er ist ein Wunder," said Gudrun, in mocking incantation.

"Ja, er ist ein Wunder," repeated Winifred, with odd seriousness, under which lay a wicked chuckle.

"Ist er auch ein Wunder?" came the slightly insolent sneering of Mademoiselle.

"Doch!" said Winifred briefly, indifferent.

"Doch ist er nicht ein König. Beesmarck, he was not a king, Winifred, as you have said. He was only—il n'était que chancelier."

"Qu'est-ce qu'un chancelier?" said Winifred, with slightly contemptuous indifference.

"A chancelier is a chancellor, and a chancellor is I believe, a sort of judge," said Gerald coming up and shaking hands with Gudrun. "You'll have made a song of Bismarck soon," said he.

Mademoiselle waited, and discreetly made her inclination, and her greeting.

"So they wouldn't let you see Bismarck, Mademoiselle?" he said.

"Non monsieur."

"Ah, very mean of them. What are you going to do to him, Miss Brangwen? I want him sent to the kitchen and cooked."

"Oh no," cried Winifred.

"We're going to draw him," said Gudrun.

"Draw him and quarter him and dish him up," he said, being purposely fatuous.

"Oh *no*!" cried Winifred with emphasis, chuckling.

Gudrun detected the tang of mockery in him, and she looked up and smiled into his face. He felt his nerves caressed. Their eyes met in knowledge.

"How do you like Shortlands?" he asked.

"Oh, very much," she said, with nonchalance.

"Glad you do. Have you noticed these flowers?"

He led her along the path. She followed intently. Winifred came, and the governess lingered in the rear. They stopped before some veined salpiglossis flowers.

"Aren't they wonderful!" she cried, looking at them absorbedly. Strange how her reverential, almost ecstatic admiration of the flowers caressed his nerves. She stooped down, and touched the trumpets, with infinitely fine and delicate-touching finger-tips. It filled him with ease to see her. When she rose, her eyes, hot with the beauty of the flowers, looked into his.

"What are they?" she asked.

"Sort of petunia, I suppose," he answered. "I don't really know them."

"They are quite strangers to me," she said.

They stood together in a false intimacy, a nervous contact. And he was in love with her.

She was aware of Mademoiselle standing near, like a little French beetle, observant and calculative. She moved away with Winifred, saying they would go to find Bismarck.

Gerald watched them go, looking all the while at the soft, full, still body of Gudrun, in its silky cashmere. How silky and rich and soft her body must be. An access of worship came over his mind, she was the all-desirable, the all-beautiful. He wanted only to come to her, nothing more. He was only this, this being that should come to her, and be given to her.

At the same time he was finely and acutely aware of Mademoiselle's neat, brittle finality of form. She was like some elegant beetle with thin ankles, perched on her high heels, her glossy black dress perfectly correct, her dark hair done high and admirably. How repulsive her completeness and her finality was! He loathed her.

Yet he did admire her. She was perfectly correct. And it did rather annoy him, that Gudrun came dressed in startling colours, like a macaw, when the family was in mourning. Like a macaw she was! He watched the lingering way she took her feet from the ground. And her ankles were pale yellow, and her dress a deep blue. Yet it pleased him. It pleased him very much. He felt the challenge in her very attire—she challenged the whole world. And he smiled as to the note of a trumpet.

Gudrun and Winifred went through the house to the back, where were the stables and the out-buildings. Everywhere was still and deserted. Mr Crich had gone out for a short drive, the stable-man had just led round Gerald's horse. The two girls went to the hutch that stood in a corner, and looked at the great black-and-white rabbit.

"Isn't he beautiful! Oh, do look at him listening! Doesn't he look silly!" she laughed quickly, then added "Oh, do let's do him listening, do let us, he listens with so much of himself;—don't you darling Bismarck?"

"Can we take him out?" said Gudrun.

"He's very strong. He really is *extremely* strong." She looked at Gudrun, her head on one side, in odd calculating mistrust.

"But we'll try, shall we?"

"Yes, if you like. But he's a *fearful* kicker!"

They took the key to unlock the door. The rabbit exploded in a wild rush round the hutch.

"He scratches most awfully sometimes," cried Winifred in excitement. "Oh do look at him, isn't he wonderful!" The rabbit tore round the hutch in a flurry. "Bismarck!" cried the child, in rousing excitement. "How *dreadful* you are! You are beastly." Winifred looked up at Gudrun with some misgiving in her wild excitement. Gudrun smiled sardonically with her mouth. Winifred made a strange crooning noise of unaccountable excitement. "Now he's still!" she cried, seeing the rabbit settled down in a far corner of the hutch.—"Shall we take him now?" she whispered excitedly, mysteriously, looking up at Gudrun and edging very close. "Shall we get him now?"—She chuckled wickedly to herself.

They unlocked the door of the hutch. Gudrun thrust in her arm and seized the great, lusty rabbit as it crouched still, she grasped its long ears. It set its four feet flat, and thrust back. There was a long scraping sound as it was hauled forward, and in another instant it was in mid-air, lunging wildly, its body flying like a spring coiled and released, as it lashed out, suspended from the ears. Gudrun held the black-and-white tempest at arms' length, averting her face. But the rabbit was magically strong, it was all she could do to keep her grasp. She almost lost her presence of mind.

"Bismarck, Bismarck, you are behaving *terribly*," said Winifred in a rather frightened voice, "Oh do put him down, he's beastly."

Gudrun stood for a moment astounded by the thunder-storm that had sprung into being in her grip. Then her colour came up, a heavy rage came over her like a cloud. She stood shaken as a house in a storm, and utterly overcome. Her heart was arrested with fury at the mindlessness and the bestial stupidity of this struggle, her wrists were badly scored by the claws of the beast, a heavy cruelty welled up in her.

Gerald came round as she was trying to capture the flying rabbit under her arm. He saw, with subtle recognition, her sullen passion of cruelty.

"You should let one of the men do that for you," he said, hurrying up.

"Oh he's *so* horrid!" cried Winifred, almost frantic.

He held out his nervous, sinewy hand and took the rabbit by the ears, from Gudrun.

"It's most *fearfully* strong," she cried, in a high voice, like the crying of a seagull, strange and vindictive.

The rabbit made itself into a ball in the air, and lashed out, flinging itself into a bow. It really seemed demoniacal. Gudrun saw Gerald's body tighten, saw a sharp blindness come into his eyes.

"I know these beggars of old," he said.

The long, demon-like beast lashed out again, spread on the air as if it were flying, looking something like a dragon, then closing up again, inconceivably powerful and explosive. The man's body, strung to its efforts, vibrated strongly. Then a sudden sharp, white-edged wrath came up in him. Swift as lightning he drew back and brought his free hand down like a hawk on the neck of the rabbit. Simultaneously, there came the unearthly, abhorrent scream of a rabbit in the fear of death. It made one immense writhe, tore his wrists and his sleeves in a final convulsion, all its belly flashed white in a whirlwind of paws, and then he had slung it round and had it under his arm, fast. It cowered and skulked. His face was gleaming with a smile.

"You wouldn't think there was all that force in a rabbit," he said, looking at Gudrun. And he saw her eyes black as night in her pallid face, she looked almost unearthly. The scream of the rabbit, after the violent tussle, seemed to have torn the veil of her consciousness. He looked at her, and the whitish, electric gleam in his face intensified.

"I don't really like him," Winifred was crooning. "I don't care for him as I do for Loozie. He's hateful really—."

A smile twisted Gudrun's face, as she recovered. She knew she was revealed.

"Don't they make the most fearful noise when they scream?" she cried, the high note in her voice, like a seagull's cry.

"Abominable," he said.

"He shouldn't be so silly, when he has to be taken out," Winifred was saying, putting out her hand and touching the rabbit tentatively, as it skulked under his arm, motionless as if it were dead.

"He's not dead, is he Gerald?" she asked.

"No, he ought to be," he said.

"Yes, he ought!" cried the child with a sudden flash of amusement. And she touched the rabbit with more confidence. "His heart is beating *so* fast. Isn't he funny? He really is."

"Where do you want him?" asked Gerald.

"In the little green court," she said.

Gudrun looked at Gerald with strange, darkened eyes, strained with underworld knowledge, almost supplicating, like those of a creature which is at his mercy, yet which is his ultimate victor. He did not know what to say to her. He felt the mutual hellish recognition. And he felt he ought to say something, to cover it. He had the power of lightning in his nerves, she seemed like a soft recipient of his magical, hideous white fire. He was unconfident, he had qualms of fear.

"Did he hurt you?" he asked.

"No," she said.

"He's an insensible beast," he said, turning his face away.

They came to the little court, which was shut in by old red walls, in whose crevices wall-flowers were growing. The grass was soft and fine and old, a level floor carpeting the court, the sky was blue overhead. Gerald tossed the rabbit down. It crouched still and would not move. Gudrun watched it with faint horror.

"Why doesn't it move?" she cried.

"It's skulking," he said.

She looked up at him, and a slight sinister smile contracted her white face.

"Isn't it a *fool*!" she cried. "Isn't it a sickening *fool*?"

The vindictive mockery in her voice made his brain quiver. Glancing up at him, into his eyes, she revealed again the mocking, white-cruel recognition. There was a league between them, abhorrent to them both. They were implicated with each other in abhorrent mysteries.

"How many scratches have you?" he asked, showing his hard forearm, white and hard and torn in red gashes.

"How really vile!" she cried, flushing with a sinister vision. "Mine is nothing."

She lifted her arm and showed a deep red score down the silken white flesh.

"What a devil!" he exclaimed. But it was as if he had had knowledge of her in the long red rent of her forearm, so silken and soft. He did not want to touch her. He would have to make himself touch her, deliberately. The long, shallow red rip seemed torn across his own brain, tearing the surface of his ultimate consciousness, letting through the forever unconscious, unthinkable red ether of the beyond, the obscene beyond.

"It doesn't hurt you very much, does it?" he asked, solicitous.

"Not at all," she cried.

And suddenly the rabbit, which had been crouching as if it were a flower, so still and soft, suddenly burst into life. Round and round the court it went, as if shot from a gun, round and round like a furry meteorite, in a tense hard circle that seemed to bind their brains. They all stood in amazement, smiling uncannily, as if the rabbit were obeying some unknown incantation. Round and round it flew, on the grass under the old red walls, like a storm.

And then quite suddenly it settled down, hobbled among the grass, and sat considering, its nose twitching like a bit of fluff in the wind. After having considered for a few minutes, a soft bunch with a black, open eye, which perhaps was looking at them, perhaps was not, it hobbled calmly forward and began to nibble the grass with that mean motion of a rabbit's quick eating.

"It's mad," said Gudrun. "It is most decidedly mad."

He laughed.

"The question is," he said, "what is madness? I don't suppose it is rabbit-mad."

"Don't you think it is?" she asked.

"No. That's what it is to be a rabbit."

There was a queer, faint, obscene smile over his face. She looked at him and saw him, and knew that he was initiate as she was initiate. This thwarted her, and contravened her, for the moment.

"God be praised we aren't rabbits," she said, in a high, shrill voice.

The smile intensified a little, on his face.

"Not rabbits?" he said, looking at her fixedly.

Slowly her face relaxed into a smile of obscene recognition.

"Ah Gerald," she said, in a strong, slow, almost man-like way. "—All that, and more." Her eyes looked up at him with shocking nonchalance.

He felt again as if she had hit him across the face—or rather, as if she had torn him across the breast, dully, finally. He turned aside.

"Eat, eat my darling!" Winifred was softly conjuring the rabbit, and creeping forward to touch it. It hobbled away from her. "Let its mother stroke its fur then, darling, because it is so mysterious——"

Chapter XIX

Moony

After his illness Birkin went to the south of France for a time. He did not write, nobody heard anything of him. Ursula, left alone, felt as if everything were lapsing out. There seemed to be no hope in the world. One was a tiny little rock with the tide of nothingness rising higher and higher. She herself was real, and only herself—just like a rock in a wash of flood-water. The rest was all nothingness. She was hard and indifferent, isolated in herself.

There was nothing for it now, but contemptuous, resistant indifference. All the world was lapsing into a grey wish-wash of nothingness, she had no contact and no connection anywhere. She despised and detested the whole show. From the bottom of her heart, from the bottom of her soul, she despised and detested people, adult people. She loved only children and animals: children she loved passionately, but coldly. They made her want to hug them, to protect them, to give them life. But this very love, based on pity and despair, was only a bondage and a pain to her. She loved best of all the animals, that were single and unsocial as she herself was. She loved the horses and cows in the field. Each was single and to itself, magical. It was not referred away to some detestable social principle. It was incapable of soulfulness and tragedy, which she detested so profoundly.

She could be very pleasant and flattering, almost subservient, to people she met. But no one was taken in. Instinctively each felt her contemptuous mockery of the human being in himself, or herself. She had a profound grudge against the human being. That which the word "human" stood for was despicable and repugnant to her.

Mostly her heart was closed in this hidden, unconscious strain of contemptuous ridicule. She thought she loved, she thought she was full of love. This was her idea of herself. But the strange brightness of her presence, a marvellous radiance of intrinsic vitality, was a luminousness of supreme repudiation, repudiation, nothing but repudiation.

Yet, at moments, she yielded and softened, she wanted pure love, only pure love. This other, this state of constant unfailing repudiation, was a strain, a suffering also. A terrible desire for pure love overcame her again.

She went out one evening, numbed by this constant essential suffering. Those who are timed for destruction must die now. The knowledge of this reached a finality, a finishing in her. And the finality released her. If fate would carry off in death or downfall all those who were timed to go, why need she trouble, why repudiate any further. She was free of it all, she could seek a new union elsewhere.

Ursula set off to Willey Green, towards the mill. She came to Willey Water. It was almost full again, after its period of emptiness. Then she turned off through the woods. The night had fallen, it was dark. But she forgot to be afraid, she who had such great sources of fear. Among the trees, far from any human beings, there was a sort of magic peace. The more one could find a pure loneliness, with no taint of people, the better one felt. She was in reality terrified, horrified in her apprehension of people.

She started, noticing something on her right hand, between the tree trunks. It was like a great presence, watching her, dodging her. She started violently. It was only the moon, risen through the thin trees. But it seemed so mysterious, with its white and deathly smile. And there was no avoiding it. Night or day, one could not escape the sinister face, triumphant and radiant like this moon, with a high smile. She hurried on, cowering from the white planet. She would just see the pond at the mill before she went home.

Not wanting to go through the yard, because of the dogs, she turned off along the hill-side to descend on the pond from above. The moon was transcendent over the bare, open space, she suffered from being exposed to it. There was a glimmer of nightly rabbits across the ground. The night was as clear as crystal, and very still. She could hear a distant coughing of a sheep.

So she swerved down to the steep, tree-hidden bank above the pond, where the alders twisted their roots. She was glad to pass into the shade out of the moon. There she stood, at the top of the fallen-away bank, her hand on the rough trunk of a tree, looking at the water, that was perfect in its stillness, floating the moon upon it. But for some reason she disliked it. It did not give her anything. She listened for the hoarse rustle of the sluice. And she wished for something else out of the night, she wanted another night, not this moon-brilliant hardness. She could feel her soul crying out in her, lamenting desolately.

She saw a shadow moving by the water. It would be Birkin. He had come back then, unawares. She accepted it without remark, nothing mattered to her. She sat down among the roots of the alder tree, dim and veiled, hearing the sound of the sluice like dew distilling audibly into the night. The islands were dark and half revealed, the reeds were dark also, only some of them had a little frail fire of reflection. A fish leaped secretly, revealing the light in the pond. This fire of the chill night breaking constantly on to the pure darkness, repelled her. She wished it were perfectly dark, perfectly, and noiseless and without motion. Birkin, small and dark also, his hair tinged with moonlight, wandered nearer. He was quite near, and yet he did not exist in her. He did not know she was there. Supposing he did something he would not wish to be seen doing, thinking he was quite private? But there, what did it matter? What did the small privacies matter? How could it matter, what he did? How can there be any secrets, we are all the same organisms? How can there be any secrecy, when everything is known to all of us?

He was touching unconsciously the dead husks of flowers as he passed by, and talking disconnectedly to himself.

"You can't go away," he was saying. "There *is* no away. You only withdraw upon yourself."

He threw a dead flower-husk on to the water.

"An antiphony—they lie, and you sing back at them.—There wouldn't have to be any truth, if there weren't any lies—then one needn't assert anything—"

He stood still, looking at the water, and throwing upon it the husks of the flowers.

"Cybele—curse her! The accursed Syria Dea!—Does one begrudge it her?—What else is there—?"

Ursula wanted to laugh loudly and hysterically, hearing his isolated voice speaking out. It was so ridiculous.

He stood staring at the water. Then he stooped and picked up a stone, which he threw sharply at the pond. Ursula was aware of the bright moon leaping and swaying, all distorted, in her eyes. It seemed to shoot out arms of fire like a cuttle-fish, like a luminous polyp, palpitating strongly before her.

And his shadow on the border of the pond, was watching for a few moments, then he stooped and groped on the ground. Then again there was a burst of sound, and a burst of brilliant light, the moon had exploded on the water, and was flying asunder in flakes of white and dangerous fire. Rapidly, like white birds, the fires all broken rose across the pond, fleeing in clamorous confusion, battling with the flock of dark waves that were forcing their way in. The furthest waves of light, fleeing out, seemed to be clamouring against the shore for escape, the waves of darkness came in heavily, running under towards the centre. But at the centre, the heart of all, was still a vivid, incandescent quivering of a white moon not quite destroyed, a white body of fire writhing and striving and not even now broken open, not yet violated. It seemed to be drawing itself together with strange, violent pangs, in blind effort. It was getting stronger, it was re-asserting itself, the inviolable moon. And the rays were hastening in in thin lines of light, to return to the strengthened moon, that shook upon the water in triumphant reassumption.

Birkin stood and watched, motionless, till the pond was almost calm, the moon was almost serene. Then, satisfied of so much, he looked for more stones. She felt his invisible tenacity. And in a moment again, the broken lights scattered in explosion over her face, dazzling her; and then, almost immediately, came the second shot. The moon leapt up white and burst through the air. Darts of bright light shot asunder, darkness swept over the centre. There was no moon, only a battlefield of broken lights and shadows, running close together. Shadows, dark and heavy, struck again and again across the place where the heart of the moon had been, obliterating it altogether. The white fragments pulsed up and down, and could not find where to go, apart and brilliant on the water like the petals of a rose that a wind has blown far and wide.

Yet again, they were flickering their way to the centre, finding the path blindly, enviously. And again, all was still, as Birkin and Ursula watched. The waters were loud on the shore. He saw the moon regathering itself insidiously, saw the heart of the rose intertwining vigorously and blindly, calling back the scattered fragments, winning home the fragments, in a pulse and an effort of return.

And he was not satisfied. Like a madness, he must go on. He got large stones, and threw them, one after the other, at the white-burning centre of the moon, till there was nothing but a rocking of hollow noise, and a pond surged up, no moon any more, only a few broken flakes tangled and glittering broadcast in the darkness, without aim or meaning, a darkened confusion, like a black and white kaleidoscope tossed at random. The hollow night was rocking and crashing with noise, and from the sluice came sharp, regular flashes of sound. Flakes of light appeared here and there, glittering tormented among the shadows, far off, in strange places, among the dripping shadow of the willow on the island. Birkin stood and listened, and was satisfied.

Ursula was dazed, her mind was all gone. She felt she had fallen to the ground and was spilled out, like water on the earth. Motionless and spent, she remained in the gloom. Though even now she was aware, unseeing, that in the darkness was a little tumult of ebbing flakes of light, a cluster dancing secretly in a round, twining and coming stealthily together. They were gathering a heart again, they were coming once more into being. Gradually the fragments caught together, re-united, heaving, rocking, dancing, falling back as in panic, but working their way home again persistently, making semblance of fleeing away when they had advanced, but always flickering nearer, a little closer to the mark, the cluster growing mysteriously larger and brighter, as gleam after gleam fell in with the whole, until a ragged rose, a distorted, frayed moon was shaking upon the waters again, re-asserted, renewed, trying to recover from its convulsion, to get over the disfigurement and the agitation, to be whole and composed, at peace.

Birkin lingered vaguely by the water. Ursula was afraid that he would stone the moon again. She slipped from her seat and went down to him, saying:

"You won't throw stones at it any more, will you?"

"How long have you been there?" he asked.

"All the time. You won't throw any more stones, will you?"

"I wanted to see if I could make it be quite gone off the pond," he said.

"Yes, it was horrible, really. Why should you hate the moon? It hasn't done you any harm, has it?"

"Was it hate?" he said.

And they were silent for a few minutes.

"When did you come back?" she said.

"Today."

"Why did you never write?"

"I could find nothing to say."

"Why was there nothing to say?"

"I don't know. Why are there no daffodils now?"

"No."

Again there was a space of silence. Ursula looked at the moon. It had gathered itself together, and was quivering slightly.

"Was it good for you, to be alone?" she asked.

"Perhaps. Not that I know much. But I got over a good deal. Did you do anything important?"

"No. I looked at England, and thought I'd done with it."

"Why England?" he asked in surprise.

"I don't know, it came like that."

"It isn't a question of nations," he said. "France is far worse."

"Yes, I know. I felt I'd done with it all."

They went and sat down on the roots of the trees, in the shadow. And being silent, he remembered the beauty of her eyes, which were sometimes filled with light, like spring, suffused with wonderful promise. So he said to her, slowly, with difficulty:

"There is a golden light in you, which I wish you would give me." It was as if he had been thinking of this for some time.

She was startled, she seemed to leap clear of him. Yet also she was pleased.

"What kind of a light?" she asked.

But he was shy, and did not say any more. So the moment passed for this time. And gradually a feeling of sorrow came over her.

"My life is so unfulfilled," she said.

"Yes," he answered briefly, not wanting to hear this.

"And I feel as if nobody would ever really love me," she said.

But he did not answer.

"You think, don't you," she said slowly, "that I only want physical things? It isn't true. I want you to serve my spirit."

"I know you do. I know you don't want physical things by themselves.—But, I want you to give me—to give your spirit to me—that golden light which is you—which you don't know—give it me—"

After a moment's silence she replied:

"But how can I, you don't love me! You only want your own ends. You don't want to serve *me*, and yet you want me to serve you. It is so one-sided."

It was a great effort to him to maintain this conversation, and to press for the thing he wanted from her, the surrender of her spirit.

"It is different," he said. "The two kinds of service are so different. I serve you in another way—not through *yourself*,—somewhere else.—But I want us to be together without bothering about ourselves—to be really together because we *are* together, as if it were a phenomenon, not a thing we have to maintain by our own effort."

"No," she said, pondering. "You are just egocentric.—You never have any enthusiasm, you never come out with any spark, towards me. You want yourself, really, and your own affairs. And you want me just to be there, to serve you."

But this only made him shut off from her.

"Ah well," he said, "words make no matter, any way. The thing *is* between us, or it isn't."

"You don't even love me," she cried.

"I do," he said angrily. "But I want—" His mind saw again the lovely golden light of spring transfused through her eyes, as through some wonderful window. And he wanted her to be with him there, in this world of proud indifference. But what was the good of telling her he wanted this company in proud indifference. What was the good of talking, any way? It must happen beyond the sound of words. It was merely ruinous to try to work her by conviction. This was a paradisal bird that could never be netted, it must fly by itself to the heart.

"I always think I am going to be loved—and then I am let down. You *don't* love me, you know. You don't want to serve me. You only want yourself."

A shiver of rage went over his veins, at this repeated: "You don't want to serve me." All the paradisal disappeared from him.

"No," he said, irritated, "I don't want to serve you, because there is nothing there to serve. What you want me to serve, is nothing, mere nothing. It isn't even you, it is your mere female quality. And I wouldn't give a straw for your female ego—it's a rag doll."

"Ha!" she laughed in mockery. "That's all you think of me, is it? And then you have the impudence to say you love me!"

She rose in anger, to go home.

"You want the paradisal unknowing," she said, turning round on him as he still sat half-visible in the shadow. "I know what that means, thank you. You want me to be your thing, never to criticise you or to have anything to say for myself. You want me to be a mere *thing* for you! No thank you! *If* you want that, there are plenty of women who will give it you. There are plenty of women who will lie down for you to walk over them—*go* to them then, if that's what you want—go to them."

"No," he said, outspoken with anger. "I want you to drop your assertive *will*, your frightened apprehensive self-insistence, that is what I want.—I want you to trust yourself so implicitly, that you can let yourself go."

"Let myself go!" She re-echoed in mockery. "*I* can let myself go, easily enough. It is you who can't let yourself go, it is you who hang on to yourself as if it were your only treasure. *You*—*you* are the Sunday school teacher—*you*—you preacher."

The amount of truth that was in this made him stiff and unheeding of her.

"I don't mean let yourself go in the Dionysic ecstatic way," he said. "I know you can do that. But I hate ecstasy, Dionysic or any other. It's like going round in a squirrel cage.—I want you not to care about yourself, just to be there and not to care about yourself, not to insist—be glad and sure and indifferent."

"Who insists?" she mocked. "Who is it that keeps on insisting?—It isn't *me*!"

There was a weary, mocking bitterness in her voice. He was silent for some time.

"I know," he said. "While ever either of us insists to the other, we are all wrong.—But there we are, the accord doesn't come."

They sat in stillness under the shadow of the trees by the bank. The night was white around them, they were in the darkness, barely conscious.

Gradually, the stillness and peace came over them. She put her hand tentatively on his. Their hands clasped softly and silently, in peace.

"Do you really love me?" she said.

He laughed.

"I call that your war-cry," he replied, amused.

"Why!" she cried, amused and really wondering.

"Your insistence—your war-cry—'A Brangwen, A Brangwen,' an old battle-cry.—Yours is 'Do you love me?—Yield knave, or die.'"

"No," she said, pleading, "not like that. Not like that. But I must know that you love me, mustn't I?"

"Well then, know it and have done with it."

"But do you?"

"Yes, I do. I love you, and I know it's final. It is final, so why say any more about it."

She was silent for some moments, in delight and doubt.

"Are you sure?" she said, nestling happily near to him.

"Quite sure—so now have done—accept it and have done."

She was nestled quite close to him.

"Have done with what?" she murmured, happily.

"With bothering," he said.

She clung nearer to him. He held her close, and kissed her softly, gently. It was such peace and heavenly freedom, just to fold her and kiss her gently, and not to have any thoughts or any desires or any will, just to be still with her, to be perfectly still and together, in a peace that was not sleep, but content in bliss. To be content in bliss, without desire or insistence anywhere, this was heaven: to be together in happy stillness.

For a long time she nestled to him, and he kissed her softly, her hair, her face, her ears, gently, softly, like dew falling. But his warm breath on her ears disturbed her again, kindled the old destructive fires. She cleaved to him, and he could feel his blood changing like quicksilver.

"But we'll be still, shall we?" he said.

"Yes," she said, as if submissively.

And she continued to nestle against him.

But in a little while she drew away and looked at him.

"I must be going home," she said.

"Must you—how sad," he replied.

She leaned forward and put up her mouth to be kissed.

"Are you really sad?" she murmured, smiling.

"Yes," he said. "I wish we could stay as we were, always."

"Always! Do you?" she murmured, as he kissed her. And then, out of a full throat, she crooned "Kiss me! Kiss me!" And she cleaved close to him. He kissed her many times. But he too had his idea and his will. He wanted only gentle communion, no other, no passion now.—So that soon she drew away, put on her hat and went home.

The next day, however, he felt wistful and yearning. He thought he had been wrong, perhaps. Perhaps he had been wrong to go to her with an idea of what he wanted. Was it really only an idea, or was it the interpretation of a profound yearning?—If the latter, how was it he was always talking about sensual fulfilment. The two did not agree very well.

Suddenly he found himself face to face with a situation. It was as simple as this: fatally simple. On the one hand, he knew he did want a further sensual experience—something deeper, darker than ordinary life could give. He remembered the African fetishes he had seen at Halliday's so often. There came back to him one, a statuette about two feet high, a tall, slim, elegant figure from West Africa, in dark wood, glossy and suave. It was a woman, with hair dressed high, like a melon-shaped dome. He remembered her vividly: she was one of his soul's intimates. Her body was long and elegant, her face was crushed tiny like a beetle's, she had rows of round heavy collars, like a column of quoits, on her neck. He remembered her: her astonishing cultured elegance, her diminished, beetle face, the astounding long elegant body, on short, ugly legs, with such protuberant buttocks, so weighty and unexpected below her slim long loins. She knew what he himself did not know. She had thousands of years of purely sensual, purely unspiritual knowledge behind her. It must have been thousands of years since her race had died, mystically: that is, since the relation between the senses and the outspoken mind had broken, leaving the experience all in one sort, mystically sensual. Thousands of years ago, that which was imminent in himself must have taken place in these Africans: the goodness, the holiness, the desire for creation and productive happiness must have lapsed, leaving the single impulse for knowledge in one sort, mindless progressive knowledge through the senses, knowledge arrested and ending in the senses, mystic knowledge in disintegration and dissolution, knowledge such as the beetles have, which live purely within the world of corruption and cold dissolution. This was why her face looked like a beetle's: this was why the Egyptians worshipped the ball-rolling scarab: because of the principle of knowledge in dissolution and corruption.

There is a long way we can travel, after the death-break: after that point where the soul in intense suffering breaks, breaks away from its organic hold like a leaf that falls. We fall from the connection with life and hope, we lapse from pure integral being, from creation and liberty, and we fall into the long, long African process of purely sensual understanding, knowledge in the mystery of dissolution.

He realised now that this is a long process—thousands of years it takes, after the death of the creative spirit. He realised that there were great mysteries to be unsealed, sensual, mindless, dreadful mysteries, far beyond the phallic cult. How far, in their inverted culture, had these West Africans gone beyond phallic knowledge? Very, very far. Birkin recalled again the female figure: the elongated, long, long body, the curious, unexpected heavy buttocks, the long, imprisoned neck, the face with tiny features like a beetle's. This was far beyond any phallic knowledge, sensual subtle realities far beyond the scope of phallic investigation.

There remained this way, this awful African process, to be fulfilled. It would be done differently by the white races. The white races, having the arctic north behind them, the vast abstraction of ice and snow, would fulfil a mystery of ice-destructive knowledge, snow-abstract annihilation. Whereas the West Africans, controlled by the burning death-abstraction of the Sahara, had been fulfilled in sun-destruction, the putrescent mystery of sun-rays.

Was this then all that remained? Was there left now nothing but to break off from the happy creative being, was the time up? Is our day of creative life finished? Does there remain to us only the strange, awful afterwards of the knowledge in dissolution, the African knowledge, but different in us, who are blond and blue-eyed from the north?

Birkin thought of Gerald. He was one of these strange white wonderful demons from the north, fulfilled in the destructive frost-mystery. And was he fated to pass away in this knowledge, this one process of frost-knowledge, death by perfect cold? Was he a messenger, an omen of the universal dissolution into whiteness and snow?

Birkin was frightened. He was tired too, when he had reached this length of speculation. Suddenly his strange, strained attention gave way, he could not attend to these mysteries any more.—There was another way, the way of freedom. There was the Paradisal entry into pure, single being, the individual soul taking precedence over love and desire for union, stronger than any pangs of emotion, a lovely state of free proud singleness, which accepts the obligation of the permanent connection with others, and with the other, submits to the yoke and leash of love, but never forfeits its own proud individual singleness, even while it loves and yields.

This was the other way, the remaining way. And he must run to follow it. He thought of Ursula, how sensitive and delicate she really was, her skin so over-fine, as if one skin were wanting. She was really so marvellously gentle and sensitive. Why did he ever forget it? He must go to her at once. He must ask her to marry him. They must marry at once, and so make a definite pledge, enter into a definite communion. He must set out at once and ask her, this moment. There was no moment to spare.

He drifted on swiftly to Beldover, half-unconscious of his own movement. He saw the town on the slope of the hill, not straggling, but as if walled-in with the straight, final streets of miners-dwellings, making a great square, and it looked like Jerusalem to his fancy. The world was all strange and transcendent.

Rosalind opened the door to him. She started slightly, as a young girl will, and said:

"Oh, I'll tell father."

With which she disappeared, leaving Birkin in the hall, looking at some reproductions from Picasso, lately introduced by Gudrun. He was admiring the almost wizard, sensuous apprehension of the earth, when Will Brangwen appeared, rolling down his shirt-sleeves.

"Well," said Brangwen, "I'll get a coat." And he too disappeared for a moment. Then he returned, and opened the door of the drawing-room, saying:

"You must excuse me, I was just doing a bit of work in the shed. Come inside, will you."

Birkin entered and sat down. He looked at the bright, reddish face of the other man, at the narrow brow and the very bright eyes, and at the rather sensual lips that unrolled wide and expansive under the black cropped moustache. How curious it was that this was a human being! What Brangwen thought himself to be, how meaningless it was, confronted with the reality of him. Birkin could see only a strange, inexplicable, almost patternless collection of passions and desires and suppressions and traditions and mechanical ideas, all cast unfused and disunited into this slender, bright-faced man of nearly fifty, who was as unresolved now as he was at twenty, and as uncreated. How could he be the parent of Ursula, when he was not created himself? He was not a parent. A slip of living flesh had been transmitted through him, but the spirit had not come from him.

The spirit had not come from any ancestor, it had come out of the unknown. A child is the child of the mystery, or it is uncreated.

"The weather's not so bad as it has been," said Brangwen, after waiting a moment. There was no connection between the two men.

"No," said Birkin. "It was full moon two days ago."

"Oh! You believe in the moon then, affecting the weather?"

"No, I don't think I do. I don't really know enough about it."

"You know what they say?—The moon and the weather may change together, but the change of the moon won't change the weather."

"Is that it?" said Birkin. "I hadn't heard it."

There was a pause. Then Birkin said:

"Am I hindering you? I called to see Ursula, really. Is she at home?"

"I don't believe she is. I believe she's gone to the library. I'll just see."

Birkin could hear him enquiring in the dining-room.

"No," he said, coming back. "But she won't be long. You wanted to speak to her?"

Birkin looked across at the other man with curious calm, clear eyes.

"As a matter of fact," he said, "I wanted to ask her to marry me."

A point of light came on the golden-brown eyes of the elder man.

"O-oh?" he said, looking at Birkin, then dropping his eyes before the calm, steadily watching look of the other: "Was she expecting you then?"

"No," said Birkin.

"No?—I didn't know anything of—of this sort was on foot—." Brangwen smiled awkwardly.

Birkin looked back at him, and said to himself: "I wonder why it should be 'on foot'!" Aloud he said:

"No, it's perhaps rather sudden." At which, thinking of his relationship with Ursula, he added—"but I don't know—"

"Quite sudden, is it?—Oh!" said Brangwen, rather baffled and annoyed.

"In one way," replied Birkin, "—not in another."

There was a moment's pause, after which Brangwen said:

"Well, she pleases herself—"

"Oh yes!" said Birkin, calmly.

A vibration came into Brangwen's strong voice, as he replied:

"Though I shouldn't want her to be in too big a hurry, either. It's no good looking round afterwards, when it's too late."

"Oh, it need never be too late," said Birkin, "as far as that goes."

"How do you mean?" asked the father.

"If one repents being married, the marriage is at an end," said Birkin.

"You think so?"

"Certainly."

"Ay, well that may be your way of looking at it."

Birkin, in silence, thought to himself: "So it may. As for *your* way of looking at it, William Brangwen, it needs a little explaining."

"I suppose," said Brangwen, "you know what sort of people we are?—What sort of a bringing-up she's had?"

"'*She*'," thought Birkin to himself, remembering his childhood's corrections, "is the cat's mother."

"*Do* I know what sort of a bringing-up she's had?" he asked simply.

He seemed to annoy Brangwen intentionally.

"Well," he said, "she's had everything that's right for a girl to have—as far as was possible, as far as we could give it her."

"I'm sure she has," said Birkin.

Which caused a most perilous full-stop. The father was becoming exasperated. There was something naturally irritant to him in Birkin's mere presence.

"And I don't want to see her going back on it all," he said, in a clanging voice.

"Why?" said Birkin.

This monosyllable exploded in Brangwen's brain like a shot.

"Why!" he repeated. "Why don't I? Because I don't believe in your new-fangled ways and your new-fangled ideas—in and out like a frog in a gallipot. It would never do for me."

Birkin watched him with steady, emotionless eyes. The radical antagonism in the two men was rousing.

"Yes, but are my ways and ideas new-fangled?" asked Birkin.

"Are they?" Brangwen caught himself up. "I'm not speaking of you in particular," he said. "What I mean is that my children have been brought up to think and do according to the religion I was brought up in myself, and I don't want to see them going away from that."

There was a dangerous pause.

"And beyond this—?" asked Birkin.

The father hesitated. He was in a nasty position.

"Eh? What do you mean?—All I want to say, is that my daughter—" he tailed off into silence, overcome by futility. He knew that in some way he was off the track.

"Of course," said Birkin, "I don't want to hurt anybody or influence anybody. Ursula does exactly as she pleases."

There was a complete silence, because of the utter failure in mutual understanding. Birkin felt bored. Her father was not a coherent human being, he was a roomful of old echoes. The eyes of the younger man rested on the face of the elder. Brangwen looked up, and saw Birkin looking at him. His face was covered with inarticulate anger and humiliation and sense of inferiority in strength.

"And as for beliefs, that's one thing," he said. "But I'd rather see my daughters dead tomorrow than that they should be at the beck and call of the first man that likes to come and whistle after them."

A queer, painful light came into Birkin's eyes.

"As to that," he said, "I only know that it's much more likely that it's I who am at the beck and call of the woman, than she at mine."

Again there was a pause. The father was somewhat bewildered.

"I know," he said, "she'll please herself—she always has done. I've done my best for them—but that doesn't matter. They've got themselves to please, and if they can help it they'll please nobody *but* themselves. But she's a right to consider her mother, and me as well—"

Brangwen was thinking his own thoughts.

"And I tell you this much, I would rather bury them, than see them getting into a lot of loose ways such as you see everywhere nowadays.—I'd rather bury them—"

"Yes but, you see," said Birkin slowly, rather wearily, bored again by this new turn, "they won't give either you or me the chance to bury them, because they're not to be buried."

Brangwen looked at him in a sudden flare of impotent anger.

"Now, Mr Birkin," he said, "I don't know what you've come here for, and I don't know what you're asking for.—But my daughters are my daughters—and it's my business to look after them while I can."

Birkin's brows knitted suddenly, his eyes concentrated in mockery. But he remained perfectly stiff and still. There was a pause.

"I've nothing against you marrying Ursula," Brangwen began again at length. "It's got nothing to do wi' me. She'll do as she likes, me or no me."

Birkin turned away, looking out of the window and letting go his consciousness. After all, what good was this? It was hopeless to keep it up. He would sit on till Ursula came home, then speak to her, then go away. He would not accept trouble at the hands of her father. It was all unnecessary, and he himself need not have provoked it.

The two men sat in complete silence, Birkin almost unconscious of his own whereabouts. He had come to ask her to marry him—well then, he would wait on, and ask her. As for what she said, whether she accepted or not, he did not think about it. He would say what he had come to say, and that was all he was conscious of. He accepted the complete insignificance of this household, for him. But everything now was as if fated. He could see one thing ahead, and no more. From the rest, he was absolved entirely for the time being. It had to be left to fate and chance to resolve the issues.

At length they heard the gate. They saw her coming up the steps with a bundle of books under her arm. Her face was bright and abstracted as usual, with the abstraction, that look of being not quite *there*, not quite present to the facts of reality, that galled her father so much. She had a maddening faculty of assuming a light of her own, which excluded the reality, and within which she looked radiant as if in sunshine.

They heard her go into the dining-room, and drop her armful of books on the table.

"Did you bring me that 'Girl's Own'?" cried Rosalind.

"Yes, I brought it. But I forgot which one it was you wanted."

"You would," cried Rosalind angrily.—"It's right, for a wonder."

Then they heard her say something in a lowered tone.

"Where?" cried Ursula.

Again her sister's voice was muffled.

Brangwen opened the door, and called, in his strong, brazen voice: "Ursula."

She appeared in a moment, wearing her hat.

"Oh how do you do!" she cried, seeing Birkin, and all dazzled as if taken by surprise. He wondered at her, knowing she was aware of his presence. She had her queer, radiant, breathless manner, as if confused by the actual world, unreal to it, having a complete bright world of her self alone.

"Have I interrupted a conversation?" she asked.

"No, only a complete silence," said Birkin.

"Oh," said Ursula, vaguely, absent. Their presence was not vital to her, she was withheld, she did not take them in. It was a subtle insult that never failed to exasperate her father.

"Mr Birkin came to speak to *you*, not to me," said her father.

"Oh, did he!" she exclaimed vaguely, as if it did not concern her. Then, recollecting herself, she turned to him rather radiantly, but still quite superficially, and said: "Was it anything special?"

"I hope so," he said, ironically.

"—To propose to you, according to all accounts," said her father.

"Oh," said Ursula.

"Oh," mocked her father, imitating her. "Have you nothing more to say?"

She winced as if violated.

"Did you really come to propose to me?" she asked of Birkin, as if it were a joke.

"Yes," he said. "I suppose I came to 'propose.'" He seemed to fight shy of the last word.

"Did you!" she cried, with her vague radiance. He might have been saying anything whatsoever. She seemed pleased.

"Yes," he answered. "I wanted to—I wanted you to agree to marry me."

She looked at him. His eyes were flickering with mixed lights, wanting something of her, yet not wanting it. She shrank a little, as if she were exposed to his eyes, and as if it were a pain to her. She darkened, her soul clouded over, she turned aside. She had been driven out of her own radiant, single world. And she dreaded contact, it was almost unnatural to her at these times.

"Yes," she said vaguely, in a doubting, absent voice.

Birkin's heart contracted swiftly, in a sudden fire of bitterness. It all meant nothing to her. He had been mistaken again. She was in some self-satisfied world of her own. He and his hopes were accidentals, violations to her. It drove her father to a pitch of mad exasperation. He had had to put up with this all his life, from her.

"Well, what do you say?" he cried.

She winced. Then she glanced down at her father, half-frightened, and she said:

"I didn't speak, did I?" as if she were afraid she might have committed herself.

"No," said her father, exasperated. "But you needn't look like an idiot. You've got your wits, haven't you?"

She ebbed away in silent hostility.

"I've got my wits, what does that mean?" she repeated, in a sullen voice of antagonism.

"You heard what was asked you, didn't you?" cried her father in anger.

"Of course I heard."

"Well then, can't you answer?" thundered her father.

"Why should I?"

At the impertinence of this retort, he went stiff. But he said nothing.

"No," said Birkin, to help out the occasion, "there's no need to answer at once. You can say when you like."

Her eyes flashed with a powerful yellow light.

"Why should I say anything?" she cried. "You do this off your *own* bat, it has nothing to do with me. Why do you both want to bully me!"

"Bully you! Bully you!" cried her father, in bitter, rancorous anger.

"Bully you! Why, it's a pity you can't be bullied into some sense and decency. Bully you! *You'll* see to that, you self-willed bargust."

She stood suspended in the middle of the room, her face glimmering and dangerous. She was set in satisfied defiance. Birkin looked up at her. He too was angry.

"But no-one is bullying you," he said, in a very soft, dangerous voice also.

"Oh yes," she cried. "You both want to force me into something."

"That is an illusion of yours," he said ironically.

"Illusion!" cried her father. "A self-opinionated fool, that's what she is."

Birkin rose, saying:

"However, we'll leave it for the time being."

And without another word, he walked out of the house.

"You fool!—You fool!" her father cried to her, with extreme bitterness. She left the room, and went upstairs, singing to herself. But she was terribly fluttered, as after some dreadful fight. From her window, she could see Birkin going up the road. He went in such a blithe drift of rage, that her mind wondered over him. He was ridiculous, but she was afraid of him. She was as if escaped from some danger.

Her father sat below, powerless in humiliation and chagrin. It was as if he were possessed with all the devils, after one of these unaccountable conflicts with Ursula. He hated her as if his only reality were in hating her to the last degree. He had all hell in his heart. But he went away, to escape himself. He knew he must despair, yield, give in to despair, and have done.

Ursula's face closed, she completed herself against them all. Recoiling upon herself, she became hard and self-completed, like a jewel. She was bright and invulnerable, quite free and happy, perfectly liberated in her self-possession. Her father had to learn not to see her blithe obliviousness, or it would have sent him mad. She was so radiant with all things, in her possession of perfect hostility.

She would go on now for days like this, in this bright frank state of seemingly pure spontaneity, so essentially oblivious of the existence of anything but herself, but so ready and facile in her interest. Ah it was a bitter thing for a man to be near her, and her father cursed his fatherhood. But he must learn not to see her, not to know.

She was perfectly stable in resistance when she was in this state: so bright and radiant and attractive in her pure opposition, so very pure, and yet mistrusted by everybody, disliked on every hand. It was her voice, curiously clear and repellant, that gave her away. Only Gudrun was in

accord with her. It was at these times that the intimacy between the two
sisters was most complete, as if their intelligence were one. They felt a
strong, bright bond of understanding between them, surpassing everything
else. And during all these days of blind bright abstraction and intimacy of
his two daughters, the father seemed to breathe an air of death, as if he
were destroyed in his very being. He was irritable to madness, he could not
rest, his daughters seemed to be destroying him. But he was inarticulate
and helpless against them. He was forced to breathe the air of his own
death. He cursed them in his soul, and only wanted, that they should be
removed from him.

They continued radiant in their easy female transcendency, beautiful to
look at. They exchanged confidences, they were intimate in their revel-
ations to the last degree, giving each other at last every secret. They
withheld nothing, they told everything, till they were over the border of
evil. And they armed each other with knowledge, they extracted the
subtlest flavours from the apple of knowledge. It was curious how their
knowledge was complementary, that of each to that of the other.

Ursula saw her men as sons, pitied their yearning and admired their
courage, and wondered over them as a mother wonders over her child,
with a certain delight in their novelty. But to Gudrun, they were the
opposite camp. She feared them and despised them, and respected their
activities even overmuch.

"Of course," she said easily, "there is a quality of life in Birkin which is
quite remarkable. There is an extraordinary rich spring of life in him,
really amazing, the way he can give himself to things. But there are so many
things in life that he simply doesn't know. Either he is not aware of their
existence at all, or he dismisses them as merely negligible—things which
are vital to the other person. In a way, he is not clever enough, he is too
intense in spots."

"Yes," cried Ursula, "too much of a preacher. He is really a priest."

"Exactly! He can't hear what anybody else has to say—he simply cannot
hear. His own voice is so loud."

"Yes. He cries you down."

"He cries you down," repeated Gudrun. "And by mere force of
violence. And of course it is hopeless. Nobody is convinced by violence. It
makes talking to him impossible—and living with him I should think would
be more than impossible."

"You don't think one could live with him?" asked Ursula.

"I think it would be too wearing, too exhausting. One would be shouted
down every time, and rushed into his way without any choice. He would

want to control you entirely. He cannot allow that there is any other mind than his own. And then the real clumsiness of his mind is its lack of self-criticism—. No, I think it would be perfectly intolerable."

"Yes," assented Ursula vaguely. She only half agreed with Gudrun. "The nuisance is," she said, "that one would find almost any man intolerable after a fortnight."

"It's perfectly dreadful," said Gudrun. "But Birkin—he is too positive. He couldn't bear it if you called your soul your own. Of him that is strictly true."

"Yes," said Ursula. "You must have *his* soul."

"Exactly! And what can you conceive more deadly?"

This was all so true, that Ursula felt jarred to the bottom of her soul, with ugly distaste. She went on, with the discord jarring and jolting through her, in the most barren of misery.

Then there started a revulsion from Gudrun. She finished life off so thoroughly, she made things so ugly and so final. As a matter of fact, even if it were as Gudrun said, about Birkin, other things were true as well. But Gudrun would draw two lines under him and cross him out like an account that is settled. There he was, summed up, paid for, settled, done with. And it was such a lie. This finality of Gudrun's, this dispatching of people and things in a sentence, it was all such a lie. Ursula began to revolt from her sister.

One day as they were walking along the lane, they saw a robin sitting on the top twig of a bush, singing shrilly. The sisters stood to look at him. An ironical smile flickered on Gudrun's face.

"Doesn't he feel important?" smiled Gudrun.

"Doesn't he!" exclaimed Ursula, with a little ironical grimace. "Isn't he a little Lloyd George of the air!"

"Isn't he! Little Lloyd Georges of the air! That's just what they are," cried Gudrun in delight. Then for days, Ursula saw the persistent, obtrusive birds as stout, short politicians lifting up their voices from the platform, little men who must make themselves heard at any cost.

But even from this there came the revulsion. Some yellow-ammers suddenly shot along the road in front of her. And they looked to her so uncanny and inhuman, like flaring yellow barbs shooting through the air on some weird, living errand, that she said to herself: "After all, it is impudence to call them little Lloyd Georges. They are really unknown to us, they are the unknown forces. It is impudence to look at them as if they were the same as human beings. They are of another world. How stupid anthropomorphism is! Gudrun is really impudent, insolent, making herself the measure of everything, making everything come down to human standards. Rupert is quite right, human beings are boring, painting the universe with their own image. The universe is non-human, thank God." It seemed to her irreverence, destructive of all true life, to make little Lloyd Georges of the birds. It was such a lie towards the robins, and such a defamation. Yet she had done it herself. But under Gudrun's influence: so she exonerated herself.

So she withdrew away from Gudrun and from that which she stood for, she turned in spirit towards Birkin again. She had not seen him since the fiasco of his proposal. She did not want to, because she did not want the question of her acceptance thrust upon her. She knew what Birkin meant when he asked her to marry him; vaguely, without putting it into speech, she knew. She knew what kind of love, what kind of surrender he wanted. And she was not at all sure that this was the kind of love that she herself wanted. She was not at all sure that it was this mutual unison in separateness that she wanted. She wanted unspeakable intimacies. She wanted to have him, utterly, finally to have him as her own, oh, so unspeakably, in intimacy. To drink him down—ah, like a life-draught. She made great professions, to herself, of her willingness to warm his foot-soles between her breasts, after the fashion of the nauseous Meredith poem. But only on condition that he, her lover, loved her absolutely, with complete self-abandon. And subtly enough, she knew he would never abandon himself *finally* to her. He did not believe in final self-abandonment. He said it openly. It was his challenge. She was prepared to fight him for it. For she believed in an absolute surrender to love. She believed that love by far surpassed the individual. He said the individual was *more* than love, or than any relationship. For him, the bright, single soul accepted love as one of its conditions, a condition of its own equilibrium. She believed that love was *everything*. Man must render himself up to her: he must be quaffed to the dregs by her. Let him be *her man* utterly, and she in return would be his humble slave—whether he wanted it or not.

Chapter XX

Gladiatorial

After the fiasco of the proposal, Birkin had hurried blindly away from Beldover, in a whirl of fury. He felt he had been a complete fool, that the whole scene had been a farce of the first water. But that did not trouble him at all. He was deeply, mockingly angry that Ursula persisted always in this old cry: "Why do you want to bully me?", and in her bright, insolent abstraction.

He went straight to Shortlands. There he found Gerald standing with his back to the fire, in the library, as motionless as a man is, who is completely and emptily restless, utterly hollow. He had done all the work he wanted to do—and now there was nothing. He could go out in the car, he could run to town. But he did not want to go out in the car, he did not want to run to town, he did not want to call on the Thirlbys. He was suspended motionless, in an agony of inertia, like a machine that is without power.

This was very bitter to Gerald, who had never known what boredom was, who had gone from activity to activity, never at a loss. Now, gradually, everything seemed to be stopping in him. He did not want any more to do the things that offered. Something dead within him just refused to respond to any suggestion. He cast over in his mind, what it would be possible to do, to save himself from this misery of nothingness, relieve the stress of this hollowness. And there were only three things left, that would rouse him, make him live. One was to drink or smoke hashish, the other was to be soothed by Birkin, and the third was woman. And there was no one for the moment to drink with. Nor was there a woman. And he knew Birkin was out. So there was nothing to do but to bear the stress of his own emptiness.

When he saw Birkin his face lit up in a sudden, wonderful smile:

"By God, Rupert," he said, "I'd just come to the conclusion that nothing in the world mattered except somebody to take the edge off one's being alone: the right somebody."

The smile in his eyes was very astonishing, as he looked at the other man. It was the pure gleam of relief. His face was pallid and even haggard.

"The right woman, I suppose you mean," said Birkin spitefully.

"Of course, for choice. Failing that, an amusing man."

He laughed as he said it. Birkin sat down near the fire.

"What were you doing?" he asked.

"I? Nothing. I'm in a bad way just now, everything's on edge, and I can neither work nor play. I don't know whether it's a sign of old age, I'm sure."

"You mean you're bored?"

"Bored! I don't know.—I can't apply myself. And I feel the devil is either very present inside me, or dead."

Birkin glanced up and looked in his eyes.

"You should try hitting something," he said.

Gerald smiled.

"Perhaps," he said. "So long as it was something worth hitting."

"Quite!" said Birkin, in his soft voice.

There was a long pause, during which each man could feel the presence of the other.

"One has to wait," said Birkin.

"Ah God! Waiting! What are we waiting for?"

"Some old Johnny says there are three cures for *ennui*: sleep, drink, and travel," said Birkin.

"All cold eggs," said Gerald. "In sleep, you dream, in drink you curse, and in travel you yell at a porter.—No, work and love are the two. When you're not at work you should be in love."

"Be it then," said Birkin.

"Give me the object," said Gerald. "The possibilities of love exhaust themselves."

"Do they? And then what?"

"Then you die," said Gerald.

"So you ought," said Birkin.

"I don't see it," replied Gerald. He took his hands out of his trousers pockets, and reached for a cigarette. He was tense and nervous. He lit the cigarette over a lamp, reaching forward and drawing steadily. He was dressed for dinner, as usual in the evening, although he was alone.

"There's a third one even to your two," said Birkin. "Work, love, and fighting. You forget the fight."

"I suppose I do," said Gerald. "Did you ever do any boxing—?"

"No, I don't think I did," said Birkin.

"Ay—" Gerald lifted his head and blew the smoke slowly into the air.

"Why?" said Birkin.

"Nothing.—I thought we might have a round. It is perhaps true, that I want something to hit. It's a suggestion."

"So you think you might as well hit me?" said Birkin.

"You? Well—! Perhaps—! In a friendly kind of way, of course."

"Quite!" said Birkin, bitingly.

Gerald stood leaning back against the mantel-piece. He looked down at Birkin, and his eyes flashed with a sort of terror, like the eyes of a stallion, that are bloodshot and overwrought, turned glancing backwards in a stiff terror.

"I feel that if I don't watch myself, I shall find myself doing something silly," he said.

"Why not do it?" said Birkin coldly.

Gerald listened with quick impatience. He kept glancing down at Birkin, as if looking for something from the other man.

"I used to do some Japanese wrestling," said Birkin. "A Jap lived in the same house with me in Heidelberg, and he taught me a little. But I was never much good at it."

"You did!" exclaimed Gerald. "That's one of the things I've never even seen done. You mean jiu-jitsu, I suppose?"

"Yes. But I am no good at those things—they don't interest me."

"They don't? They do me.—What's the start?"

"I'll show you what I can, if you like," said Birkin.

"You will?" A queer, smiling look tightened Gerald's face for a moment, as he said, "Well, I'd like it very much."

"Then we'll try jiu-jitsu. Only you can't do much in a starched shirt."

"Then let us strip, and do it properly.—Half a minute—" He rang the bell, and waited for the butler.

"Bring a couple of sandwiches and a syphon," he said to the man, "and then don't trouble me any more tonight—or let anybody else."

The man went. Gerald turned to Birkin with his eyes lighted.

"And you used to wrestle with a Jap?" he said. "Did you strip?"

"Sometimes."

"You did! What was he like then, as a wrestler?"

"Good, I believe. I am no judge. He was very quick and slippery and full of electric fire. It is a remarkable thing, what a curious sort of fluid force they seem to have in them, those people—not like a human grip—like a polyp—"

Gerald nodded.

"I should imagine so," he said, "to look at them. They repel me, rather."

"Repel and attract, both. They are very repulsive when they are cold, and they look grey. But when they are hot and roused, there is a definite attraction—a curious kind of full electric fluid—like eels."

"Well—, yes—, probably."

The man brought in the tray and set it down.

"Don't come in any more," said Gerald.

The door was closed.

"Well then," said Gerald; "shall we strip and begin? Will you have a drink first?"

"No, I don't want one."

"Neither do I."

Gerald fastened the door and pushed the furniture aside. The room was large, there was plenty of space, it was thickly carpeted. Then he quickly threw off his clothes, and waited for Birkin. The latter, white and thin, came over to him. Birkin was more a presence than a visible object; Gerald was aware of him completely, but not really visually. Whereas Gerald himself was concrete and noticeable, a piece of pure final substance.

"Now," said Birkin, "I will show you what I learned, and what I remember. You let me take you so—" And his hands closed on the naked body of the other man. In another moment, he had Gerald swung over lightly and balanced against his knee, head downwards. Relaxed, Gerald sprang to his feet with eyes glittering.

"That's smart," he said. "Now try again."

So the two men began to struggle together. They were very dissimilar. Birkin was tall and narrow, his bones were very thin and fine. Gerald was much heavier and more plastic. His bones were strong and round, his limbs were rounded, all his contours were beautifully and fully moulded. He seemed to stand with a proper, rich weight on the face of the earth, whilst Birkin seemed to have the centre of gravitation in his own middle. And Gerald had a rich, frictional kind of strength, rather mechanical, but sudden and invincible, whereas Birkin was abstract as to be almost intangible. He impinged invisibly upon the other man, scarcely seeming to touch him, like a garment, and then suddenly piercing in a tense fine grip that seemed to penetrate into the very quick of Gerald's being.

They stopped, they discussed methods, they practised grips and throws, they became more accustomed to each other, to each other's rhythm, they got a kind of mutual physical understanding. And then again they had a real struggle. They seemed to drive their white flesh deeper and deeper against each other, as if they would break into a oneness. Birkin had a great subtle energy, that would press upon the other man with an uncanny force, weigh him like a spell put upon him. Then it would pass, and Gerald would heave free, with white, heaving, dazzling movements.

So the two men entwined and wrestled with each other, working nearer and nearer. Both were white and clear, but Gerald flushed smart red where he was touched, and Birkin remained white and tense. He seemed to penetrate into Gerald's more solid, more diffuse bulk, to interfuse his body through the body of the other, as if to bring it subtly into subjection, always seizing with some rapid necromantic foreknowledge every motion of the other flesh, converting and counteracting it, playing upon the limbs and trunk of Gerald like some hard wind. It was as if Birkin's whole physical intelligence interpenetrated into Gerald's body, as if his fine, sublimated energy entered into the flesh of the fuller man, like some potency, casting a fine net, a prison, through the muscles into the very depths of Gerald's physical being.

So they wrestled swiftly, rapturously, intent and mindless at last, two essential white figures ever working into a tighter, closer oneness of struggle, with a strange, octopus-like knotting and flashing of limbs in the subdued light of the room; a tense white knot of flesh gripped in silence between the walls of old brown books. Now and again came a sharp gasp of breath, or a sound like a sigh, then the rapid thudding of movement on the thickly-carpeted floor, then the strange sound of flesh escaping under flesh. Often, in the white, interlaced knot of violent living being that swayed silently, there was no head to be seen, only the swift, tight limbs, the solid white backs, the physical junction of two bodies clinched into oneness. Then would appear the gleaming, ruffled head of Gerald, as the struggle changed, then for a moment the dun-coloured, shadow-like head of the other man would lift up from the conflict, the eyes wide and dreadful and sightless.

At length Gerald lay back inert on the carpet, his breast rising in great slow panting, whilst Birkin kneeled over him, almost unconscious. Birkin was much more exhausted. He caught little, short breaths, he could scarcely breathe any more. The earth seemed to tilt and sway, and a complete darkness was coming over his mind. He did not know what happened. He slid forward quite unconscious, over Gerald, and Gerald did not notice. Then he was half-conscious again, aware only of the strange tilting and sliding of the world. The world was sliding, everything was sliding off into the darkness. And he was sliding endlessly, endlessly away.

He came to consciousness again, hearing an immense knocking outside. What could be happening, what was it, the great hammer-strokes resounding through the house? He did not know. And then it came to him that it was his own heart beating. But that seemed impossible, the noise was outside. No, it was inside himself, it was his own heart. And the beating was painful, so strained, surcharged. He wondered if Gerald heard it. He did not know whether he were standing or lying or falling.

When he realised that he was fallen prostrate upon Gerald's body he wondered, he was surprised. But he sat up, steadying himself with his hand and waiting for his heart to become stiller and less painful. It hurt very much, and took away his consciousness.

Gerald however was still less conscious than Birkin. They waited dimly, in a sort of not-being, for many uncounted, unknown minutes.

"Of course—" panted Gerald, "I didn't have to be rough—with you—I had to keep back—my force—"

Birkin heard the sound as if his own spirit stood behind him, outside him, and listened to it. His body was in a trance of exhaustion, his spirit heard thinly. His body could not answer. Only he knew his heart was getting quieter. He was divided entirely between his spirit, which stood outside, and knew, and his body, that was a plunging, unconscious stroke of blood.

"I could have thrown you—using violence—" panted Gerald. "But you beat me right enough."

"Yes," said Birkin, hardening his throat and producing the words in the tension there, "You're much stronger than I—you could beat me—easily."

Then he relaxed again to the terrible plunging of his heart and his blood.

"It surprised me," panted Gerald, "what strength you've got. Almost—supernatural."

"For a moment," said Birkin.

He still heard as if it were his own disembodied spirit hearing, standing at some distance behind him. It drew nearer however, his spirit. And the violent striking of blood in his chest was sinking quieter, allowing his mind to come back. He realised that he was leaning with all his weight on the soft body of the other man. It startled him, because he thought he had withdrawn. He recovered himself, and sat up. But he was still vague and unestablished. He put out his hand to steady himself. It touched the hand of Gerald, that was lying out on the floor. And Gerald's hand closed warm and sudden over Birkin's, they remained exhausted and breathless, the one hand clasped closely over the other. It was Birkin whose hand, in swift response, had closed in a strong, warm clasp over the hand of the other. Gerald's clasp had been sudden and momentaneous.

The normal consciousness however was returning, ebbing back. Birkin could breathe almost naturally again. Gerald's hand slowly withdrew, Birkin slowly, dazedly rose to his feet and went towards the table. He poured out a whisky and soda. Gerald also came for a drink.

"It was a real set-to, wasn't it?" said Birkin, looking at Gerald with darkened eyes.

"God, yes," said Gerald. He looked at the delicate body of the other man, and added: "It wasn't too much for you, was it?"

"No. One ought to wrestle and strive and be physically close. It makes one sane."

"You do think so?"

"I do. Don't you?"

"Yes," said Gerald, "it's life for me—"

There were long spaces of silence between their words. The wrestling had some deep meaning to them—an unfinished meaning.

"We are mentally, spiritually intimate, therefore we should be more or less physically intimate too—it is more whole."

"Certainly it is," said Gerald. Then he laughed pleasantly, adding: "It's rather wonderful to me."

He stretched out his arms handsomely.

"Yes," said Birkin. "—I don't know why one should have to justify oneself."

"No."

The two men began to dress.

"I think also that you are beautiful," said Birkin to Gerald, "and that is enjoyable too. One should enjoy what is given."

"You think I am beautiful—how do you mean, physically?" asked Gerald, his eyes glistening.

"Yes. You have a northern kind of beauty, like light refracted from snow—and a beautiful plastic form. Yes, that is there to enjoy as well. We should enjoy everything."

Gerald laughed in his throat, and said:

"That's certainly one way of looking at it.—I can say this much, I feel better. It has certainly helped me.—Is this the Brüderschaft you wanted?"

"Perhaps. Do you think this pledges anything?"

"I don't know," laughed Gerald.

"At any rate, one feels freer and more open now—and that is what we want."

"Certainly," said Gerald.

They drew to the fire, with the decanters and the glasses and the food.

"I always eat a little before I go to bed," said Gerald. "I sleep better."

"I should not sleep so well," said Birkin.

"No? There you are, we are not alike.—I'll put a dressing-gown on." Birkin remained alone, looking at the fire. His mind had reverted to Ursula. She seemed to return again into his consciousness. Gerald came down wearing a gown of broad-barred, thick black-and-green silk, brilliant and striking.

"You are very fine," said Birkin, looking at the full robe.

"It was a caftan in Bokhara," said Gerald. "I like it."

"I like it too."

Birkin was silent, thinking how scrupulous Gerald was in his attire, how expensive too. He wore silk socks, and studs of fine workmanship, and silk underclothing, and silk braces. Curious! This was another of the differences between them. Birkin was careless and unimaginative about his own appearance.

"Of course you," said Gerald, as if he had been thinking; "there's something curious about you. You're curiously strong. One doesn't expect it, it is rather surprising."

Birkin laughed. He was looking at the handsome figure of the other man, blond and comely in the rich robe, and he was half thinking of the difference between it and himself—so different; as far, perhaps, apart as man from woman, yet in another direction. But really it was Ursula, it was the woman who was gaining ascendance over Birkin's being, at this moment. Gerald was becoming dim again, lapsing out of him.

"Do you know," he said suddenly, "I went and proposed to Ursula Brangwen tonight, that she should marry me."

He saw the blank shining wonder come over Gerald's face.

"You did?"

"Yes. Almost formally—speaking first to her father, as it should be, in the world—though that was accident—or mischief."

Gerald only stared in wonder, as if he did not grasp.

"You don't mean to say that you seriously went and asked her family to let you marry her?"

"Yes," said Birkin, "I did."

"What, had you spoken to her before about it, then?"

"No, not a word. I suddenly thought I would go there and ask her—and her father happened to come instead of her—so I asked him first."

"If you could have her?" concluded Gerald.

"Ye-es, that."

"And you didn't speak to her?"

"Yes. She came in afterwards. So it was put to her as well."

"It was!—And what did she say then?—You're an engaged man?"

"No,—she only said she didn't want to be bullied into answering."

"She what?"

"Said she didn't want to be bullied into answering."

"'Said she didn't want to be bullied into answering!' Why what did she mean by that?"

Birkin raised his shoulders.—"Can't say," he answered. "Didn't want to be bothered just then, I suppose."

"But is this really so?—And what did you do then?"

"I walked out of the house and came here."

"You came straight here?"

"Yes."

Gerald stared in amazement and amusement. He could not take it in.

"But is this really true, as you say it now?"

"Word for word."

"It is?"

He leaned back in his chair, filled with delight and amusement.

"Well that's good," he said. "And so you came here to wrestle with your good angel, did you?"

"Did I?" said Birkin.

"Well it looks like it. Isn't that what you did?"

Now Birkin could not follow Gerald's meaning.

"And what's going to happen?" said Gerald. "You're going to keep open the proposition, so to speak?"

"I suppose so. I vowed to myself I would see them all to the devil. But I suppose I shall ask her again, in a little while."

Gerald watched him steadily.

"So you're fond of her then?" he asked.

"I think—I love her," said Birkin, his face going very still and fixed.

Gerald glistened for a moment with pleasure, as if it were something done specially to please him. Then his face assumed a fitting gravity, and he nodded his head slowly.

"You know," he said, "I always believed in love—true love.—But where does one find it, nowadays?"

"I don't know," said Birkin.

"Very rarely," said Gerald. Then, after a pause, "I've never felt it myself—not what I should call love. I've gone after women—and been keen enough over some of them. But I've never felt *love*. I don't believe I've ever felt as much *love* for a woman, as I have for you—not *love*. You understand what I mean?"

"Yes. I'm sure you've never loved a woman."

"You feel that, do you?—And do you think I ever shall? You understand what I mean?" He put his hand to his breast, closing his fist there, as if he would draw something out. "I mean that—that——I can't express what it is, but I know it."

"What is it, then?" asked Birkin.

"You see, I can't put it into words. I mean, at any rate, something abiding, something that can't change——"

His eyes were bright and puzzled.

"Now do you think I shall ever feel that for a woman?" he asked, anxiously.

Birkin looked at him, and shook his head.

"I don't know," he said. "I could not say."

Gerald had been on the *qui vive*, as awaiting his fate. Now he drew back in his chair.

"No," he said, "and neither do I, and neither do I."

"We are different, you and I," said Birkin. "I can't tell your life."

"No," said Gerald, "no more can I. But I tell you—I begin to doubt it."

"That you will ever love a woman?"

"Well—yes—what you would truly call *love*—"

"You doubt it?"

"Well—I begin to."

There was a long pause.

"Life has all kinds of things," said Birkin. "There isn't only one road."

"Yes, I believe that too. I believe it.—And mind you, I don't care how it is with me—I don't care how it is—so long as I don't feel—" he paused, and a blank, barren look passed over his face, to express his feeling—"so long as I feel I've *lived*, somehow—and I don't care how it is—but I want to feel that—"

"Fulfilled," said Birkin.

"We-ell, perhaps it is, fulfilled;—I don't use the same words as you."

"It is the same."

Chapter XXI

Threshold

Gudrun was away in London, having a little show of her work, with a friend, and looking round, preparing for flight from Beldover. Come what might, she would be on the wing in a very short time. She received a letter from Winifred Crich, ornamented with drawings.

"Father also has been to London, to be examined by the doctors. It made him very tired. They say he must rest a very great deal, so he is mostly in bed. He brought me a lovely tropical parrot in faïence, of Dresden ware, also a man ploughing, and two mice climbing up a stalk, also in faïence. The mice are Copenhagen ware. They are the best, but mice don't shine so much, otherwise they are very good, their tails are slim and long. They all shine nearly like glass. Of course it is the glaze, but I don't like it. Gerald likes the man ploughing the best, his trousers are torn, he is ploughing with an ox, being I suppose a German peasant. It is all grey and white, white shirt and grey trousers, but very shiny and clean. Mr Birkin likes the girl best, under the hawthorn blossom, with a lamb, and with daffodils painted on her skirts, in the drawing room. But that is silly, because the lamb is not a real lamb, and she is silly too.

"Dear Miss Brangwen are you coming back soon, you are very much missed here. I enclose a drawing of father sitting up in bed. He says he hopes you are not going to forsake us. Oh dear Miss Brangwen, I am sure you won't. Do come back and draw the ferrets, they are the most lovely noble darlings in the world. We might carve them in holly-wood, playing against a background of green leaves. Oh do let us, for they are most beautiful.

"Father says we might have a studio. Gerald says we could easily have a beautiful one over the stables, it would only need windows to be put in the slant of the roof, which is a simple matter. Then you could stay here all day and work, and we could live in the studio, like two real artists, like the man in the picture in the hall, with the frying-pan and the walls all covered with drawings. I long to be free, to live the free life of an artist. Even Gerald told father that only an artist is free, because he lives in a creative world of his own.———"

Gudrun caught the drift of the family intentions, in this letter. Gerald wanted her to be attached to the household at Shortlands, he was using Winifred as his stalking-horse. The father thought only of his child, he saw a rock of salvation in Gudrun. And Gudrun admired him for his perspicacity. The child, moreover, was really exceptional. Gudrun was quite content. She was quite willing, given a studio, to spend her days at

Shortlands. She disliked the Grammar School already thoroughly, she wanted to be free. If a studio were provided, she would be free to go on with her work, she would await the turn of events with complete serenity. And she was really interested in Winifred, she would be quite glad to understand the girl.

So there was quite a little festivity on Winifred's account, the day Gudrun returned to Shortlands.

"You should make a bunch of flowers to give to Miss Brangwen when she arrives," Gerald said smiling to his sister.

"Oh no," cried Winifred, "it's silly."

"Not at all. It is a very charming and ordinary attention."

"Oh, it *is* silly," protested Winifred, with all the extreme *mauvaise honte* of her years. Nevertheless, the idea appealed to her. She wanted very much to carry it out. She flitted round the green-houses and the conservatory looking wistfully at the flowers on their stems. And the more she looked, the more she *longed* to have a bunch of the blossoms she saw, the more fascinated she became with her little vision of ceremony, and the more consumedly shy and self-conscious she grew, till she was almost beside herself. She could not get the idea out of her mind. It was as if some haunting challenge prompted her, and she had not enough courage to take it up. So again she drifted into the green-houses, looking at the lovely roses in their pots, and at the virginal cyclamens, and at the mystic white clusters of a creeper. The beauty, oh the beauty of them, and oh the paradisal bliss, if she should have a perfect bouquet and could give it to Gudrun the next day. Her passion and her complete indecision almost made her ill.

At last she slid to her father's side.

"Daddy—" she said.

"What my precious?"

But she hung back, the tears almost coming to her eyes, in her sensitive confusion. Her father looked at her, and his heart ran hot with tenderness, an anguish of poignant love.

"What do you want to say to me, my love?"

"Daddy—!" her eyes smiled laconically—"isn't it silly if I give Miss Brangwen some flowers when she comes?"

The sick man looked at the bright, knowing eyes of his child, and his heart burned with love.

"No, darling, that's not silly. It's what they do to queens."

This was not very reassuring to Winifred. She half suspected that queens in themselves were a silliness. Yet she so wanted her little romantic occasion.

"Shall I then?" she asked.

"Give Miss Brangwen some flowers? Do, Birdie. Tell Wilson I say you are to have what you want."

The child smiled a small, subtle, unconscious smile to herself, in anticipation of her way.

"But I won't get them till tomorrow," she said.

"Not till tomorrow, Birdie.—Give me a kiss then—"

Winifred silently kissed the sick man, and drifted out of the room. She again went the round of the green-houses and the conservatory, informing the gardener, in her high, peremptory, simple fashion, of what she wanted, telling him all the blooms she had selected.

"What do you want these for?" Wilson asked her.

"I want them," she said. She wished servants did not ask questions.

"Ay, you've said as much. But what do you want them for, for decoration, or to send away, or what?"

"I want them for a presentation bouquet."

"A presentation bouquet! Who's coming then?—the Duchess of Portland?"

"No."

"Oh, not her?—Well you'll have a rare poppy-show if you put all the things you've mentioned into your bouquet."

"Yes, I want a rare poppy-show."

"You do! Then there's no more to be said."

The next day Winifred, in a dress of silvery velvet, and holding a gaudy bunch of flowers in her hand, waited with keen impatience in the schoolroom, looking down the drive for Gudrun's arrival. It was a wet morning. Under her nose was the strange fragrance of hot-house flowers, the bunch was like a little fire to her, she seemed to have a strange new fire in her heart. This slight sense of romance stirred her like an intoxicant.

At last she saw Gudrun coming, and she ran downstairs to warn her father and Gerald. They, laughing at her anxiety and gravity, came with her into the hall. The man-servant came hastening to the door, and there he was, relieving Gudrun of her umbrella, and then of her raincoat. The welcoming party hung back till their visitor entered the hall.

Gudrun was flushed with the rain, her hair was blown in loose little curls, she was like a flower just opened in the rain, the heart of the blossom just newly visible, seeming to emit a warmth of retained sunshine. Gerald winced in spirit, seeing her so beautiful and unknown. She was wearing a soft blue dress, and her stockings were of dark red.

Winifred advanced with odd, stately formality.

"We are so glad you've come back," she said. "These are your flowers." She presented the bouquet.

"Mine!" cried Gudrun. She was suspended for a moment, then a vivid flush went over her, she was as if blinded for a moment with a flame of pleasure. Then her eyes, strange and flaming, lifted and looked at the father, and at Gerald. And again Gerald shrank in spirit, as if it would be more than he could bear, as her hot, exposed eyes rested on him. There was something so revealed, she was revealed beyond bearing, to his eyes. He turned his face aside. And he felt he would not be able to avert her. And he writhed under the imprisonment.

Gudrun put her face into the flowers.

"But how beautiful they are!" she said, in a muffled voice. Then, with a strange, suddenly revealed passion, she stooped and kissed Winifred.

Mr Crich went forward with his hand held out to her.

"I was afraid you were going to run away from us," he said, playfully.

Gudrun looked up at him with a luminous, roguish, unknown face.

"Really!" she replied. "No, I didn't want to stay in London."

Her voice seemed to imply that she was glad to get back to Shortlands, her tone was warm and subtly caressing.

"That is a good thing," smiled the father. "You see you are very welcome here among us."

Gudrun only looked into his face with dark-blue, warm, shy eyes. She was unconsciously carried away by her own power.

"And you look as if you came home in every possible triumph," Mr Crich continued, holding her hand.

"No," she said, glowing strangely. "I haven't had any triumph till I came here."

"Ah come come! We're not going to hear any of those tales. Haven't we read notices in the paper, Gerald?"

"You came off pretty well," said Gerald to her, shaking hands. "Did you sell anything?"

"No," she said, "not much."

"Just as well," he said.

She wondered what he meant. But she was all aglow with her reception, carried away by this little flattering ceremonial on her behalf.

"Winifred," said the father, "have you a pair of shoes for Miss Brangwen?—You had better change at once—"

Gudrun went out with her bouquet in her hand.

"Quite a remarkable young woman," said the father to Gerald, when she had gone.

"Yes," replied Gerald briefly, as if he did not like the observation.

Mr Crich liked Gudrun to sit with him for half an hour. Usually he was ashy and wretched, with all the life gnawed out of him. But as soon as he rallied, he liked to make-belief that he was just as before, quite well and in the midst of life—not of the outer world, but in the midst of a strong essential life. And to this belief, Gudrun contributed perfectly. With her, he could get by stimulation those precious half-hours of strength and exaltation and pure freedom, when he seemed to live more than he had ever lived.

She came to him as he lay propped up in the library. His face was like yellow wax, his eyes darkened, as it were sightless. His black beard, now streaked with grey, seemed to spring out of the waxy flesh of a corpse. Yet the atmosphere about him was energetic and playful. Gudrun subscribed to this, perfectly. To her fancy, he was just an ordinary man. Only his rather terrible appearance was photographed upon her soul, away beneath her consciousness. She knew that, in spite of his playfulness, his eyes could not change from their darkened vacancy, they were the eyes of a man who is dead.

"Ah, this is Miss Brangwen," he said, suddenly rousing as she entered, announced by the man-servant. "Thomas, put Miss Brangwen a chair here—that's right." He looked at her soft, fresh face with pleasure. It gave him the illusion of life. "Now, you will have a glass of sherry and a little piece of cake.—Thomas——"

"No thank you," said Gudrun. And as soon as she had said it, her heart sank horribly. The sick man seemed to fall into a gap of death, at her contradiction. She ought to play up to him, not to contravene him. In an instant she was smiling her rather roguish smile.

"I don't like sherry very much," she said. "But I like almost anything else."

The sick man caught at this straw instantly.

"Not sherry! No! Something else! What then? What is there Thomas?"

"Port wine—curaçao——"

"I would love some curaçao—" said Gudrun, looking at the sick man confidingly.

"You would. Well then Thomas, curaçao—and a little cake, or a biscuit?"

"A biscuit," said Gudrun. She did not want anything, but she was wise.

"Yes."

He waited till she was settled with her little glass and her biscuit. Then he was satisfied.

"You have heard the plan," he said with some excitement, "for a studio for Winifred, over the stables?"

"No!" exclaimed Gudrun, in mock wonder.

"Oh!—I thought Winnie wrote it to you, in her letter?"

"Oh—yes—of course.—But I thought perhaps it was only her own little idea—" Gudrun smiled subtly, indulgently.

The sick man smiled also, elated.

"Oh no. It is a real project. There is a good room under the roof of the stables—with sloping rafters. We had thought of converting it into a studio."

"How *very* nice that would be!" cried Gudrun with excited warmth. The thought of the rafters stirred her.

"You think it would? Well, it can be done."

"But how perfectly splendid for Winifred! Of course, it is just what is needed, if she is to work at all seriously. One must have one's workshop, otherwise one never ceases to be an amateur."

"Is that so? Yes.—Of course.—Of course, I should like you to share it with Winifred."

"Thank you *so* much."

Gudrun knew all these things already, but she must look shy and very grateful, as if overcome.

"Of course, what I should like best, would be if you could give up your work at the Grammar School, and just avail yourself of the studio, and work there—well, as much or as little as you liked—"

He looked at Gudrun with dark, vacant eyes. She looked back at him as if full of gratitude. These phrases of a dying man were so complete and natural, coming like echoes through his dead mouth.

"And as to your earnings—you don't mind taking from me what you have taken from the Education Committee, do you? I don't want you to be a loser."

"Oh," said Gudrun, "if I can have the studio and work there, I can earn money enough, really I can."

"Well," he said, pleased to be the benefactor, "we can see about all that.—You wouldn't mind spending your days here?"

"If there were a studio to work in," said Gudrun, "I could ask for nothing better."

"Is that so?"

He was really very pleased. But already he was getting tired. She could see the grey, awful semi-consciousness of mere pain and dissolution coming over him again, the torture coming into the vacancy of his darkened eyes. It was not over yet, this process of death. She rose softly, saying:

"Perhaps you will sleep. I must look for Winifred."

She went out, telling the nurse that she had left him. Day by day the tissue of the sick man was further and further reduced, nearer and nearer the process came, towards the last knot which held the human being in its unity. But this knot was hard and unrelaxed, the will of the dying man never gave way. He might be dead in nine-tenths, yet the remaining tenth remained unchanged, till it too was torn apart. With his will he held the unit of himself firm, but the circle of his power was ever and ever reduced, it would be reduced to a point at last, then swept away.

To adhere to life, he must adhere to human relationships, and he caught at every straw. Winifred, the butler, the nurse, Gudrun, these were the people who meant all to him, in these last resources. Gerald, in his father's presence, stiffened with repulsion. It was so, to a less degree, with all the other children except Winifred. They could not see anything but the death, when they looked at their father. It was as some subterranean dislike overcame them. They could not see the familiar face, hear the familiar voice. They were overwhelmed by the antipathy of visible and audible death. Gerald could not breathe in his father's presence. He must get out at once. And so, in the same way, the father could not bear the presence of his son. It sent a final irritation through the soul of the dying man.

The studio was made ready, Gudrun and Winifred moved in. They enjoyed so much the ordering and the appointing of it. And now they need hardly be in the house at all. They had their meals in the studio, they lived there safely. For the house was becoming dreadful. There were two nurses in white, flitting silently about, like heralds of death. The father was confined to his bed, there was a come and go of sotto-voce sisters and brothers and children.

Winifred was her father's constant visitor. Every morning, after break-fast, she went into his room when he was washed and propped up in bed, to spend half an hour with him.

"Are you better, Daddy?" she asked him invariably.

And invariably he answered:

"Yes, I think I'm a little better, pet."

She held his hand in both her own, lovingly and protectively. And this was very dear to him.

She ran in again as a rule at lunchtime, to tell him the course of events, and every evening, when the curtains were drawn, and his room was cosy, she spent a long time with him. Gudrun was gone home, Winifred was alone in the house, she liked best to be with her father. They talked and prattled at random, he always as if he were well, just the same as when he was going about. So that Winifred, with a child's subtle instinct for avoiding the painful things, behaved as if nothing serious was the matter. Instinctively, she withheld her attention, and was happy. Yet in her remoter soul, she knew as well as the adults knew: perhaps better.

Her father was quite well in his make-belief with her. But when she went away, he relapsed under the misery of his dissolution. But still there were these bright moments, though as his strength waned, his faculty for attention grew weaker, and the nurse had to send Winifred away, to save him from exhaustion.

He never admitted that he was going to die. He knew it was so, he knew it was the end. Yet even to himself he did not admit it. He hated the fact, mortally. His will was rigid. He could not bear being overcome by death. For him, there was no death. And yet, at times, he felt a great need to cry out and to wail and complain. He would have liked to cry aloud to Gerald, so that his son should be horrified out of his composure. Gerald was instinctively aware of this, and he recoiled, to avoid any such thing. This uncleanness of death repelled him too much. One should die quickly, like the Romans, one should be master of one's fate in dying as in living. He was convulsed in the clasp of this death of his father's, as in the coils of the great serpent of Laocoön. The great serpent had got the father, and the son was dragged into the embrace of horrifying death along with him. He resisted always. And in some strange way, he was a tower of strength to his father.

The last time the dying man asked to see Gudrun he was grey with near death. Yet he must see someone, he must, in the intervals of consciousness, catch into connection with the living world, lest he should have to accept his own situation. Fortunately he was most of his time dazed and half gone. And he spent many hours dimly thinking of the past, as it were, dimly re-living his old experiences. But there were times even to the end when he was capable of realising what was happening to him in the present, the death that was on him. And these were the times when he called in outside help, no matter whose. For to realise this death that he was dying was a death beyond death, never to be borne. It was an admission never to be made.

Gudrun was shocked by his appearance, and by the darkened, almost disintegrated eyes, that still were unconquered and firm.

"Well," he said in his weakened voice, "and how are you and Winifred getting on?"

"Oh, very well indeed," replied Gudrun.

There were slight dead gaps in the conversation, as if the ideas called up were only elusive straws floating on the dark chaos of the sick man's dying.

"The studio answers all right?" he said.

"Splendid. It couldn't be more beautiful and perfect," said Gudrun. She waited for what he would say next.

"And you think Winifred has the makings of a sculptor?"

It was strange how hollow the words were, meaningless.

"I'm sure she has. She will do good things one day."

"Ah! Then her life won't be altogether wasted, you think?"

Gudrun was rather surprised.

"Sure it won't!" she exclaimed softly.

"That's right."

Again Gudrun waited for what he would say.

"You find life pleasant, it is good to live, isn't it?" he asked, with a pitiful faint smile that was almost too much for Gudrun.

"Yes," she smiled—she would lie at random—"I get a pretty good time I believe."

"That's right. A happy nature is a great asset."

Again Gudrun smiled, though her soul was dry with repulsion. Did one have to die like this, having the life extracted forcibly from one, whilst one smiled and made conversation to the end? Was there no other way? Must one go through all the horror of this victory over death, the triumph of the integral will, that would not be broken till it disappeared utterly? One must, it was the only way. She admired the self-possession and the control of the dying man exceedingly. But she loathed the death itself. She was glad the everyday world held good, and she need not recognise anything beyond.

"You are quite all right here?—nothing we can do for you?—nothing you find wrong in your position?"

"Except that you are too good to me," said Gudrun.

"Ah, well, the fault of that lies with yourself," he said, and he felt a little exultation, that he had made this speech. He was still so strong and living! But the nausea of death began to creep back on him, in reaction.

Gudrun went away, back to Winifred. Mademoiselle had left, Gudrun stayed a good deal at Shortlands, and a tutor came in to carry on Winifred's education. But he did not live in the house, he was connected with the Grammar School.

One day, Gudrun was to drive with Winifred and Gerald and Birkin to town, in the car. It was a dark, showery day. Winifred and Gudrun were ready and waiting at the door. Winifred was very quiet, but Gudrun had not noticed. Suddenly the child asked, in a voice of unconcern:

"Do you think my father is going to die, Miss Brangwen?"

Gudrun started.

"I don't know," she replied.

"Don't you truly?"

"Nobody knows for certain. He *may* die, of course."

The child pondered a few moments, then she asked:

"But do you *think* he will die?"

It was put almost like a question in geography or science, insistent, as if she would force an admission from the adult. The watchful, slightly triumphant child was almost diabolical.

"Do I think he will die?" repeated Gudrun. "Yes, I do."

But Winifred's large eyes were fixed on her, and the girl did not move.

"He is very ill," said Gudrun.

A small smile came over Winifred's face, subtle and sceptical.

"*I* don't believe he will," the child asserted mockingly, and she moved away into the drive. Gudrun watched the isolated figure, and her heart stood still. Winifred was playing with a little rivulet of water, absorbedly, as if nothing had been said.

"I've made a proper dam," she cried, out of the moist distance.

Gerald came to the door from out of the hall behind.

"It is just as well she doesn't choose to believe it," he said.

Gudrun looked at him. Their eyes met; and they exchanged a sardonic understanding.

"Just as well," said Gudrun.

He looked at her again, and a fire flickered up in his eyes.

"Best to dance while Rome burns, since it must burn, don't you think?" he said.

She was rather taken aback. But, gathering herself together, she replied:

"Oh—better dance than wail, certainly."

"So I think."

And they both felt the subterranean desire to let go, to fling away everything, and lapse into a sheer unrestraint, brutal and licentious. A strange black passion surged up pure in Gudrun. She felt strong. She felt her hands so strong, as if she could tear the world asunder with them. She remembered the abandonments of Roman licence, and her heart grew hot. She knew she wanted this herself also—or something, something equivalent. Ah, if that which was unknown and suppressed in her were once let loose, what an orgiastic and satisfying event it would be. And she wanted it, she trembled slightly from the proximity of the man, who stood just behind her, suggestive of the same black licentiousness that rose in herself. She wanted it with him, this unacknowledged frenzy. For a moment the clear perception of this preoccupied her, distinct and perfect in its final reality. Then she shut it off completely, saying:

"We might as well go down to the lodge after Winifred—we can get in the car there."

"So we can," he answered, going with her.

They found Winifred at the lodge admiring the litter of pure-bred white puppies. The girl looked up, and there was a rather ugly, unseeing cast in her eyes as she turned to Gerald and Gudrun. She did not want to see them.

"Look!" she cried. "Three new puppies! Marshall says this one seems perfect. Isn't it a sweetling? But it isn't so nice as its mother." She turned to caress the fine white bull-terrier bitch that stood uneasily near her.

"My dearest Lady Crich," she said, "you are beautiful as an angel on earth. Angel—angel—*don't* you think she's good enough and beautiful enough to go to heaven, Gudrun?—They will be in heaven, won't they—and *especially* my darling Lady Crich!—Mrs Marshall,—I say!"

"Yes Miss Winifred?" said the woman, appearing at the door.

"Oh do call this one Lady Winifred, if she turns out perfect, will you? Do tell Marshall to call it Lady Winifred."

"I'll tell him—but I'm afraid that's a gentleman puppy, Miss Winifred."

"Oh *no*!" There was the sound of a car. "There's Rupert!" cried the child, and she ran to the gate.

Birkin, driving his car, pulled up outside the lodge gate.

"We're ready!" cried Winifred. "I want to sit in front with you, Rupert. May I?"

"I'm afraid you'll fidget about and fall out," he said.

"No I won't. I do want to sit in front next to you. It makes my feet so lovely and warm, from the engines."

Birkin helped her up, amused at sending Gerald to sit by Gudrun in the body of the car.

"Have you any news, Rupert?" Gerald called, as they rushed along the lanes.

"News?" exclaimed Birkin.

"Yes." Gerald looked at Gudrun, who sat by his side, and he said, his eyes narrowly laughing, "I want to know whether I ought to congratulate him, but I can't get anything definite out of him."

Gudrun flushed deeply.

"Congratulate him on what?" she asked.

"There was some mention of an engagement—at least, he said something to me about it."

Gudrun flushed darkly.

"You mean with Ursula?" she said, in challenge.

"Yes. That is so, isn't it?"

"I don't think there's any engagement," said Gudrun coldly.

"That so?—Still no developments, Rupert?" he called.

"Where? Matrimonial? No."

"How's that?" called Gudrun.

Birkin glanced quickly round. There was irritation in his eyes also.

"Why?" he replied. "What do you think of it, Gudrun?"

"Oh," she cried, determined to fling her stone also into the pool, since they had begun, "I don't think she wants an engagement. Naturally, she's a bird that prefers the bush." Gudrun's voice was clear and gong-like. It reminded Rupert of her father's, so strong and vibrant.

"And I," said Birkin, his face playful but yet determined, "I want a binding contract, and am not keen on love, particularly free love."

They were both amused. *Why* this public avowal? Gerald seemed suspended a moment, in amusement.

"Love isn't good enough for you?" he called.

"No!" shouted Birkin.

"Ha, well that's being over-refined," said Gerald, and the car ran on through the mud.

"What's the matter, really?" said Gerald, turning to Gudrun.

This was an assumption of a sort of intimacy that irritated Gudrun almost like an affront. It seemed to her that Gerald was deliberately insulting her, and infringing on the decent privacy of them all.

"What is it?" she said, in her high, repellant voice. "Don't ask me!—I know nothing about *ultimate* marriage, I assure you: or even penultimate."

"Only the ordinary unwarrantable brand!" replied Gerald. "Just so—same here. I am no expert on marriage, and degrees of ultimateness. It seems to be a bee that buzzes loudly in Rupert's bonnet."

"Exactly! But that is his trouble, exactly! Instead of wanting a woman for herself, he wants his *ideas* fulfilled. Which, when it comes to actual practice, is not good enough."

"Oh no. Best go slap for what's womanly in woman, like a bull at a gate." Then he seemed to glimmer in himself. "—You think love is the ticket, do you?" he asked.

"Certainly, while it lasts—you only can't insist on *permanency*," came Gudrun's voice, strident above the noise.

"Marriage or no marriage, ultimate or penultimate or just so-so?—take the love as you find it."

"As you please, or as you don't please," she echoed. "Marriage is a social arrangement, I take it, and has nothing to do with the question of love."

His eyes were flickering on her all the time. She felt as if he were kissing her freely and malevolently. It made the colour burn in her cheeks, but her heart was quite firm and unfailing.

"You think Rupert is off his head a bit?" Gerald asked.

Her eyes flashed with acknowledgement.

"As regards a woman, yes," she said, "I do. There *is* such a thing as two people being in love for the whole of their lives—perhaps. But marriage is neither here nor there, even then.—If they are in love, well and good. If not—why break eggs about it!"

"Yes," said Gerald. "That's how it strikes me. But what about Rupert?"

"I can't make out—neither can he nor anybody. He seems to think that if you marry you can get through marriage into a third heaven, or something—all very vague."

"Very! And who wants a third heaven?—As a matter of fact, Rupert has a great yearning to be *safe*—to tie himself to the mast."

"Yes. It seems to me he's mistaken there too," said Gudrun. "I'm sure a mistress is more likely to be faithful than a wife—just because she is her *own* mistress. No—he says he believes that a man and wife can go further than any other two beings—but *where*, is not explained. They can know each other, heavenly and hellish, but particularly hellish, so perfectly that they go beyond heaven and hell—into—there it all breaks down—into nowhere—"

"Into Paradise, he says," laughed Gerald.

Gudrun shrugged her shoulders.

"*Je m'en fiche* of your Paradise!" she said.

"Not being a Mohammedan," said Gerald. Birkin sat motionless, driving the car, quite unconscious of what they said. And Gudrun, sitting immediately behind him, felt a sort of ironic pleasure in thus exposing him.

"He says," she added, with a grimace of irony, "that you can find an eternal equilibrium in marriage, if you accept the unison, and still leave yourself separate, don't try to fuse."

"Doesn't inspire me," said Gerald.

"That's just it," said Gudrun.

"I believe in love, in a real *abandon*, if you're capable of it," said Gerald.

"So do I," said she.

"And so does Rupert, too—though he is always shouting."

"No," said Gudrun. "He won't abandon himself to the other person. You can't be sure of him. That's the trouble, I think."

"Yet he wants marriage!—Marriage—*et puis?*"

"Le paradis!" mocked Gudrun.

Birkin, as he drove, felt a creeping of the spine, as if somebody was threatening his neck. But he shrugged with indifference. It began to rain. Here was a change. He stopped the car and got down to put up the hood.

Chapter XXII

Woman to Woman

They came to the town, and left Gerald at the railway station. Gudrun and Winifred were to come to tea with Birkin, who expected Ursula also. In the afternoon, however, the first person to turn up was Hermione. Birkin was out, so she went in the drawing-room, looking at his books and papers, and playing on the piano. Then Ursula arrived. She was surprised, unpleasantly so, to see Hermione, of whom she had heard nothing for some time.

"It is a surprise to see you," she said.

"Yes," said Hermione—"I've been away at Aix—"

"Oh, for your health?"

"Yes."

The two women looked at each other. Ursula resented Hermione's long, grave, downward-looking face. There was something of the stupidity and the unenlightened self-esteem of a horse in it. "She's got a horse-face," Ursula said to herself, "she runs between blinkers." It did seem as if Hermione, like the moon, had only one side to her penny. There was no obverse. She stared out all the time on the narrow, but to her, complete world of the extant consciousness. In the darkness, she did not exist. Like the moon, one half of her was lost to life. Her self was all in her head, she did not know what it was spontaneously to run or move, like a fish in the water, or a weasel on the grass. She must always *know*.

But Ursula only suffered from Hermione's one-sidedness. She only felt Hermione's cool confidence, which seemed to put her down as nothing. Hermione, who brooded and brooded till she was exhausted with the ache of her effort at consciousness, spent and ashen in her body, who gained so slowly and with such effort her final and barren conclusions of knowledge, was apt, in the presence of other women, whom she thought simply female, to wear the conclusions of her bitter assurance like jewels which conferred on her an unquestionable distinction, established her in a higher order of life. She was apt, mentally, to condescend to women such as Ursula, whom she regarded as purely emotional. Poor Hermione, it was her one possession, this aching certainty of hers, it was her only justification. She must be confident here, for God knows, she felt rejected and deficient enough elsewhere. In the life of thought, of the spirit, she was one of the elect. And she wanted to be universal. But there was a devastating cynicism at the bottom of her. She did not believe in her own universals—they were sham. She did not believe in the inner life—it was a trick, not a reality. She did not believe in the spiritual world—it was an affectation. In the last resort, she believed in Mammon, the flesh, and the devil—these at least were not sham. She was a priestess without belief, without conviction, suckled in a creed outworn, and condemned to the reiteration of mysteries that were not divine to her. Yet there was no escape. She was a leaf upon a dying tree. What help was there then, but to fight still for the old, withered truths, to die for the old, outworn belief, to be a sacred and inviolate priestess of desecrated mysteries? The old great truths *had* been true. And she was a leaf of the old great tree of knowledge, that was withering now. To the old and last truth then she must be faithful, even though cynicism and mockery took place at the bottom of her soul.

"I am so glad to see you," she said to Ursula, in her slow voice, that was like an incantation. "—You and Rupert have become quite friends?"

"Oh yes," said Ursula. "He is always somewhere in the background."

Hermione paused before she answered. She saw perfectly well the other woman's vaunt: it seemed truly vulgar.

"Is he!" she said slowly, and with perfect equanimity. "And do you think you will marry?"

The question was so calm and mild, so simple and bare and dispassionate that Ursula was somewhat taken aback, rather attracted. It pleased her almost like a wickedness. There was some delightful naked irony in Hermione.

"Well," replied Ursula, "*he* wants to, awfully, but I'm not so sure."

Hermione watched her with slow calm eyes. She noted this new expression of vaunting. How she envied Ursula a certain unconscious positivity! even her vulgarity!

"Why aren't you sure?" she asked, in her easy sing-song. She was perfectly at her ease, perhaps even rather happy in this conversation. "You don't really love him?"

Ursula flushed a little at the mild impertinence of this question. And yet she could not definitely take offence. Hermione seemed so calmly and sanely candid. After all, it was rather great to be able to be so sane.

"He says it isn't love he wants," she replied.

"What is it then?" Hermione was slow and level.

"He wants me really to accept him in marriage."

Hermione was silent for some time, watching Ursula with slow, pensive eyes.

"Does he," she said at length, without expression. Then, rousing, "And what is it you don't want? You don't want marriage?"

"No—I don't—not really. I don't want to give the sort of *submission* he insists on. He wants me to give myself up—and I simply don't feel that I *can* do it."

Again there was a long pause, before Hermione replied:

"Not if you don't want to." Then again there was silence. Hermione shuddered with a strange desire. Ah, if only he had asked *her* to subserve him, to be his slave! She shuddered with desire.

"You see I can't—"

"But exactly in what does—"

They had both begun at once, they both stopped. Then Hermione, assuming priority of speech, resumed as if wearily:

"To what does he want you to submit?"

"He says he wants me to accept him non-emotionally, and finally——I really don't know *what* he means. He says he wants the demon part of himself to be mated—physically—not the human being.—You see he says one thing one day, and another the next—and he always contradicts himself—"

"And always thinks about himself, and his own dissatisfaction," said Hermione slowly.

"Yes," cried Ursula. "As if there were no-one but himself concerned.—That makes it so impossible."

But immediately she began to retract.

"He insists on my accepting God knows what in *him*," she resumed. "He wants me to accept *him* as—as an absolute—But it seems to me he doesn't want to *give* anything. He doesn't want real warm intimacy—he won't have it—he rejects it. He won't let me think, really, and he won't let me *feel*—he hates feelings."

There was a long pause, bitter for Hermione. Ah, if only he would have made this demand of her! Her he *drove* into thought, drove inexorably into knowledge—and then execrated her for it.

"He wants me to sink myself in him," Ursula resumed, "not to have any being of my own——"

"Then why doesn't he marry an odalisk?" said Hermione in her mild sing-song, "if it is that he wants." Her long face looked sardonic and amused.

"Yes," said Ursula vaguely.—After all, the tiresome thing was, he did *not* want an odalisk, he did not want a slave. Hermione would have been his slave—there was in her a horrible desire to prostrate herself before a man—a man who worshipped her, however, and admitted her as the supreme thing.—He did not want an odalisk. He wanted a woman to *take* something from him, to give herself up so much that she could take the last realities of him, the last facts, the last physical facts, physical and unbearable.

And if she did, would he acknowledge her? Would he be able to acknowledge her through everything, or would he use her just as an instrument, use her for his own private satisfactions, not admitting her? That was what the other men had done. They had wanted their own show, and they would not admit her, they turned all she was into nothingness. Just as Hermione now betrayed herself as a woman. Hermione was like a man, she believed only in men's things. She betrayed the woman in herself.—And Birkin, would he acknowledge, or would he deny her?

"Yes," said Hermione, as each woman came out of her own separate reverie. "It would be a mistake—I think it would be a mistake—"

"To marry him?" asked Ursula.

"Yes," said Hermione slowly—"I think you need a man—soldierly, strong-willed—" Hermione held out her hand and clenched it with rhapsodic intensity. "You should have a man like the old heroes—you need to stand behind him as he goes into battle, you need to *see* his strength, and to *hear* his shout— —You need a man physically strong, and *virile* in his will, *not* a sensitive man— —" there was a break, as if the pythoness had uttered the oracle, and now the woman went on, in a rhapsody-wearied voice: "And you see, Rupert isn't this, he isn't. He is frail in health and body, he needs great, great care. Then he is so changeable and unsure of himself—it requires the greatest patience and understanding to help him. And I don't think you are patient. You would have to be prepared to suffer—dreadfully. I can't *tell* you how much suffering it would take to make him happy. He lives an *intensely* spiritual life, at times—too, too wonderful. And then come the reactions.—I can't speak of what I have been through with him.— —We have been together so long, I really do know him, I *do* know what he is.— —And I feel I must say it; I feel it would be perfectly *disastrous* for you to marry him—for you even more than for him."—Hermione lapsed into bitter reverie.—"He is so uncertain, so unstable—he wearies, and then reacts. I couldn't *tell* you what his reactions are. I couldn't *tell* you the agony of them.— —That which he affirms and loves one day—a little later he turns on it in a fury of destruction.——He is never constant, always this awful, dreadful reaction.——Always the quick change from good to bad, bad to good—And nothing is so devastating, nothing——"

"Yes," said Ursula humbly, "you must have suffered."

An unearthly light came on Hermione's face. She clenched her hand like one inspired.

"And one must be willing to suffer—willing to suffer for him hourly, daily—if you are going to help him, if he is to keep true to anything at all——"

"And I don't *want* to suffer hourly and daily," said Ursula. "I don't, I should be ashamed. I think it is degrading not to be happy."

Hermione stopped and looked at her a long time.

"Do you," she said at last. And this utterance seemed to her a mark of Ursula's far distance from herself. For to Hermione suffering was the greatest reality, come what might. Yet she too had a creed of happiness.

"Yes," she said. "One *should* be happy—." But it was a matter of will.

"Yes," said Hermione, listlessly now, "I can only feel that it would be disastrous, disastrous——at least, to marry in a hurry. Can't you be together without marriage? Can't you go away and live somewhere without marriage?—I do feel that marriage would be fatal, for both of you. I think for you even more than for him—and I think of his health——"

"Of course," said Ursula, "*I* don't care about marriage—it isn't really important to me—it's he who wants it."

"It is his idea for the moment," said Hermione, with that weary finality, and a sort of *si jeunesse savait* infallibility.

There was a pause. Then Ursula broke into faltering challenge.

"You think I'm merely a physical woman, don't you?"

"No indeed," said Hermione. "No indeed! But I think you are vital and *young*—it isn't a question of years, or even of experience—it is almost a question of race. Rupert is race-old, he comes of an old race—and you seem to me so young, you come of a young, inexperienced race."

"Do I!" said Ursula.—"But I think he is awfully young, on one side."

"Yes, perhaps—childish in many respects. Nevertheless——"

They both lapsed into silence. Ursula was filled with deep resentment and a touch of hopelessness. "It isn't true," she said to herself, silently addressing her adversary. "It isn't true. And it is *you* who want a physically strong, bullying man, not I. It is you who want an unsensitive man, not I. You *don't* know anything about Rupert, not really, in spite of the years you have had him. You don't give him a woman's love, you give him an ideal love, and that is why he reacts away from you. You *don't* know. You only know the dead things. Any kitchen maid would know something about him, you don't know. What do you think your knowledge is but dead understanding, that doesn't mean a thing. You are so false, and untrue, how could you know anything? What is the good of your talking about love—you untrue spectre of a woman! How can you know anything, when you don't believe? You don't believe in yourself and your own womanhood, so what good is your conceited, shallow cleverness—!"

The two women sat on in antagonistic silence. Hermione felt injured, that all her good intention, all her offering, only left the other woman in vulgar antagonism. But then, Ursula could not understand, never would understand, could never be more than the usual jealous and unreasonable female, with a good deal of powerful female emotion, female attraction, and a fair amount of female understanding, but no mind. Hermione had decided long ago that where there was no mind, it was useless to appeal for reason—one had merely to ignore the ignorant. And Rupert—he had now reacted towards the strongly female, healthy, selfish woman—it was his reaction for the time being—there was no helping it all. It was all a foolish backward and forward, a violent oscillation that would at length be too violent for his coherency, and he would smash and be dead. There was no saving him. This violent and directionless reaction between animalism and spiritual truth would go on in him till he tore himself in two between the opposite directions, and disappeared meaninglessly out of life. It was no good——he too was without unity, without *mind*, in the ultimate stages of living; not quite man enough to make a destiny for a woman.

They sat on till Birkin came in and found them together. He felt at once the antagonism in the atmosphere, something radical and insuperable, and he bit his lip. But he affected a bluff manner.

"Hello, Hermione, are you back again? How do you feel?"

"Oh, better. And how are you—you don't look well—"

"Oh?—I believe Gudrun and Winnie Crich are coming in to tea. At least they said they were. We shall be a tea-party. What train did you come by, Ursula?"

It was rather annoying to see him trying to placate both women at once. Both women watched him, Hermione with deep resentment and pity for him, Ursula very impatient. He was nervous and apparently in quite good spirits, chattering the conventional commonplaces. Ursula was amazed and indignant at the way he made small-talk; he was adept as any *fat* in Christendom. She became quite stiff, she would not answer. It all seemed to her so false and so belittling. And still Gudrun did not appear.

"I think I shall go to Florence for the winter," said Hermione at length.

"Will you?" he answered. "But it is so cold there."

"Yes, but I shall stay with Palestra. It is quite comfortable."

"What takes you to Florence?"

"I don't know," said Hermione slowly. Then she looked at him with her slow, heavy gaze. "Barnes is starting his school of aesthetics, and Olandese is going to give a set of discourses on the Italian national policy—"

"Both rubbish," he said.

"No, I don't think so," said Hermione.

"Which do you admire, then?"

"I admire both. Barnes is a pioneer.—And then I am interested in Italy, in her coming to national consciousness."

"I wish she'd come to something different from national consciousness, then," said Birkin; "especially as it only means a sort of commercial-industrial consciousness. I hate Italy and her national rant.—And I think Barnes is an amateur."

Hermione was silent for some moments, in a state of hostility. But yet, she had got Birkin back again into her world! How subtle her influence was, she seemed to start his irritable attention into her direction exclusively, in one minute. He was her creature.

"No," she said, "you are wrong." Then a sort of tension came over her, she raised her face like the pythoness inspired with oracles, and went on, in rhapsodic manner: "il Sandro mi scrive che ha accolto il più grande entusiasmo, tutti i giovani, e fanciulle e ragazzi, sono appassionati, appassionati per l'Italia, e vogliono assolutamente imparare tutto———" She went on in Italian, as if, in thinking of the Italians she thought in their language.

He listened with a shade of distaste to her rhapsody, then he said:

"For all that, I don't like it. Their nationalism is just industrialism,—that, and a shallow jealousy I detest so much."

"I think you are wrong—I think you are wrong—" said Hermione. "It seems to me purely spontaneous and beautiful, the modern Italian's *passion*, for it is a passion, for Italy, L'Italia—"

"Do you know Italy well?" Ursula asked of Hermione. Hermione hated to be broken in upon in this manner. Yet she answered mildly:

"Yes, pretty well.——I spent several years of my girlhood there, with my mother.——My mother died in Florence."

"Oh."

There was a pause, painful to Ursula and to Birkin. Hermione however seemed abstracted and calm. Birkin was white, his eye glowed as if he were in a fever, he was far too overwrought. How Ursula suffered in this tense atmosphere of strained wills! Her head seemed bound round by iron bands.

Birkin rang the bell for tea. They would not wait for Gudrun any longer. When the door was opened, the cat walked in.

"Micio! Micio!" called Hermione, in her slow, deliberate sing-song. The young cat turned to look at her, then, with his slow and stately walk he advanced to her side.

"Vieni—vieni qua," Hermione was saying, in her strange caressive, protective voice, as if she were always the elder, the mother superior. "Vieni dire Buon Giorno alla zia. Mi ricorde, mi ricorde bene—non è vero, piccolo? È vero che mi ricordi? È vero?" And slowly she rubbed his head, slowly and with ironic indifference.

"Does he understand Italian?" said Ursula, who knew nothing of the language.

"Yes," said Hermione at length. "His mother was Italian. She was born in my waste-paper basket, in Florence, on the morning of Rupert's birthday. She was his birthday present."

Tea was brought in. Birkin poured out for them. It was strange how inviolable was the intimacy which existed between him and Hermione. Ursula felt that she was an outsider. The very tea-cups and the old silver was a bond between Hermione and Birkin. It seemed to belong to an old, past world which they inhabited together, and in which Ursula was a foreigner. She was almost a parvenue in their old cultured milieu. Her convention was not their convention, their standards were not her standards. But theirs were established, they had the sanction and the grace of age. He and she together, Hermione and Birkin, were people of the same old tradition, the same withered, deadening culture. And she, Ursula, was an intruder. So they always made her feel.

Hermione poured a little cream into a saucer. The simple way she assumed her rights in Birkin's room maddened and discouraged Ursula. There was a fatality about it, as if it were bound to be. Hermione lifted the cat and put the cream before him. He planted his two paws on the edge of the table and bent his graceful young head to drink.

"Siccuro che capisce italiano," sang Hermione, "non l'avrà dimenticato, la lingua della Mamma."

She lifted the cat's head with her long, slow, white fingers, not letting him drink, holding him in her power. It was always the same, this joy in power she manifested, peculiarly in power over any male being. He blinked forbearingly, with a male, bored expression, licking his whiskers. Hermione laughed in her short, grunting fashion.

"Ecco, il bravo ragazzo, come è superbo, questo!"

She made a vivid picture, so calm and strange with the cat. She had a true static impressiveness, she was a social artist in some ways.

The cat refused to look at her, indifferently avoided her fingers, and began to drink again, his nose down to the cream, perfectly balanced, as he lapped with his odd little click.

"It's bad for him, teaching him to eat at table," said Birkin.

"Yes," said Hermione, easily assenting.

Then, looking down at the cat, she resumed in her old, mocking, humorous sing-song:

"Ti imparano fare brutte cose, brutte cose— —"

She lifted the Mino's white chin on her fore-finger, slowly. The young cat looked round with a supremely forbearing air, avoided seeing anything, withdrew his chin, and began to wash his face with his paw. Hermione grunted her laughter, pleased.

"Bel giovanotto—" she said.

The cat reached forward again and put his fine white paw on the edge of the saucer. Hermione lifted it down with delicate slowness. This deliberate, delicate carefulness of movement reminded Ursula of Gudrun.

"No! Non è permesso di mettere il zampino nel tondinetto. Non piace al babbo. Un signor gatto così selvatico—!"

And she kept her finger on the softly planted paw of the cat, and her voice had the same whimsical, humorous note of bullying.

Ursula had her nose out of joint. She wanted to go away now. It all seemed no good. Hermione was established for ever, she herself was ephemeral and had not yet even arrived.

"I will go now," she said suddenly.

Birkin looked at her almost in fear—he so dreaded her anger.

"But there is no need for such hurry," he said.

"Yes," she answered. "I will go." And turning to Hermione, before there was time to say any more, she held out her hand and said: "Goodbye."

"Goodbye—" sang Hermione, detaining the hand. "Must you really go now?"

"Yes, I think I'll go," said Ursula, her face set, and averted from Hermione's eyes.

"You think you will— —"

But Ursula had got her hand free. She turned to Birkin with a quick, almost jeering: "Goodbye," and she was opening the door before he had time to do it for her.

When she got outside the house she ran down the road in fury and agitation. It was strange, the unreasoning rage and violence Hermione roused in her, by her very presence. Ursula knew she gave herself away to the other woman, she knew she looked ill-bred, uncouth, exaggerated. But she did not care. She only ran up the road, lest she should go back and jeer in the faces of the two she had left behind. For they outraged her.

Chapter XXIII

Excurse

Next day Birkin sought Ursula out. It happened to be the half-day at the Grammar School. He appeared towards the end of the morning, and asked her, would she drive with him in the afternoon. She consented. But her face was closed and unresponding, and his heart sank.

The afternoon was fine and dim. He was driving the motor-car, and she sat beside him. But still her face was closed against him, unresponding. When she became like this, like a wall against him, his heart contracted.

His life now seemed so reduced, that he hardly cared any more. At moments it seemed to him he did not care a straw whether Ursula or Hermione or anybody else existed or did not exist. Why bother! Why strive for a coherent, satisfied life? Why not drift on in a series of accidents—like a picaresque novel? Why not? Why bother about human relationships? Why take them seriously—male or female? Why form any serious connections at all? Why not be casual, drifting along, taking all for what it was worth?

And yet, still, he was damned and doomed to the old effort at serious living.

"Look," he said, "what I bought." The car was running along a broad white road, between autumn trees.

He gave her a little bit of screwed-up paper. She took it and opened it.

"How lovely!" she cried.

She examined the gift.

"How perfectly lovely!" she cried again. "But why do you give them me?" She put the question offensively.

His face flickered with bored irritation. He shrugged his shoulders slightly.

"I wanted to," he said, coolly.

"But why? Why should you?"

"Am I called on to find reasons?" he asked.

There was a silence, whilst she examined the rings that had been screwed up in the paper.

"I think they are *beautiful*," she said, "especially this. This is wonderful—"

It was a round opal, red and fiery, set in a circle of tiny rubies.

"You like that best?" he said.

"I think I do."

"I like the sapphire," he said.

"This?"

It was a rose-shaped, beautiful sapphire, with small brilliants.

"Yes," she said, "it *is* lovely." She held it in the light. "Yes, perhaps it *is* the best—"

"The blue—" he said.

"Yes, wonderful—"

He suddenly swung the car out of the way of a farm-cart. It tilted on the bank. He was a careless driver, yet very quick. But Ursula was frightened. There was always that something regardless in him which terrified her. She suddenly felt he might kill her, by making some dreadful accident with the motor-car. For a moment she was stony with fear.

"Isn't it rather dangerous, the way you drive?" she asked him.

"No, it isn't dangerous," he said. And then, after a pause: "Don't you like the yellow ring at all?"

It was a squarish topaz set in a frame of steel, or some other similar mineral, finely wrought.

"Yes," she said, "I do like it. But why did you buy three rings?"

"I wanted them. They are second-hand."

"You bought them for yourself?"

"No. Rings look wrong on my hands."

"Why did you buy them then?"

"I bought them to give to you."

"But why? Surely you ought to give them to Hermione! You belong to her."

He did not answer. She remained with the jewels shut in her hand. She wanted to try them on her finger, but something in her would not let her. And moreover, she was afraid her hands were too large, she shrank from the mortification of a failure to put them on any but her little finger. They travelled in silence through the empty lanes.

Driving in a motor-car excited her, she forgot his presence even.

"Where are we?" she asked suddenly.

"Not far from Worksop."

"And where are we going?"

"Anywhere."

It was the answer she liked.

She opened her hand to look at the rings. They gave her *such* pleasure, as they lay, the three circles, with their knotted jewels, entangled in her palm. She would have to try them on. She did so secretly, unwilling to let him see, so that he should not know her finger was too large for them. But he saw nevertheless. He always saw, if she wanted him not to. It was another of his hateful, watchful characteristics.

Only the opal, with its thin wire loop, would go on her ring finger. And she was superstitious. No, there was ill-portent enough, she would not accept this ring from him in pledge.

"Look," she said, putting forward her hand, that was half-closed and shrinking. "The others don't fit me."

He looked at the red-glinting, soft stone, on her over-sensitive skin.

"Yes," he said.

"But opals are unlucky, aren't they?" she said wistfully.

"No. I prefer unlucky things. Luck is vulgar. Who wants what *luck* would bring? I don't."

"But why?" she laughed.

And, consumed with desire to see how the other rings would look on her hand, she put them on her little finger.

"They can be made a little bigger," he said.

"Yes," she replied, doubtfully. And she sighed. She knew that, in accepting the rings, she was accepting a pledge. Yet fate seemed more than herself. She looked again at the jewels. They were very beautiful to her eyes—not as ornament, or wealth, but as tiny fragments of loveliness.

"I'm glad you bought them," she said, putting her hand, half unwillingly, gently on his arm.

He smiled, slightly. He wanted her to come to him. But he was angry at the bottom of his soul, and indifferent. He knew she had a passion for him, really. But he was not finally interesting. There were depths of passion where one became impersonal and indifferent, unemotional. Whereas Ursula was still at the emotional personal level—always so abominably personal.—He had taken her as he had never been taken himself. He had taken her at the roots of her darkness and shame—like a demon, laughing over the fountain of mystic corruption which was one of the sources of her being, laughing, shrugging, accepting, accepting finally.—As for her, when would she so much go beyond herself as to accept him at the quick of death?

She now became quite happy. The motor-car ran on, the afternoon was soft and dim, she talked with lively interest, analysing people and their motives—Gudrun, Gerald. He answered vaguely. He was not very much interested any more in personalities and in people—people were all different, but they were all enclosed nowadays in a definite limitation he said; there were only about two great ideas, two great streams of activity remaining, with various forms of reaction therefrom. The reactions were all varied in various people, but they followed a few great laws, and intrinsically there was no difference. They acted and re-acted involuntarily according to a few great laws, and once the laws, the great principles, were known, people were no longer mystically interesting. They were all essentially alike, the differences were only variations on a theme. None of them transcended the given terms.

Ursula did not agree—people were still an adventure to her—but—perhaps not as much as she tried to persuade herself. Perhaps there was something mechanical, now, in her interest. Perhaps also her interest was destructive, her analysing was a real tearing to pieces. There was an under-space in her where she did not care for people and their idiosyncrasies, even to destroy them. She seemed to touch for a moment this undersilence in herself, she became still, and she turned for a moment purely to Birkin.

"Won't it be lovely to go home in the dark?" she said. "We might have tea rather late—shall we?—and have high tea?—wouldn't that be rather nice?"

"I promised to be at Shortlands for dinner," he said.

"But—it doesn't matter—you can go tomorrow—."

"Hermione is there," he said, in rather an uneasy voice. "She is going away in two days. I suppose I ought to say goodbye to her—I shall never see her again."

Ursula drew away, closed in a violent silence. He knitted his brows, and his eyes began to sparkle again in anger.

"You don't mind, do you?" he asked irritably.

"No, I don't care—why should I—Why should I mind?"

Her tone was jeering and offensive.

"That's what I ask myself," he said; "why *should* you mind! But you seem to." His brows were tense with violent irritation.

"I *assure* you I don't, I don't mind in the least. Go where you belong—it's what I want you to do."

"Ah you fool!" he cried, "with your 'go where you belong.' It's finished between Hermione and me. She means much more to *you*, if it comes to that, than she does to me. For you can only revolt in pure reaction from her—and to be her opposite is to be her counterpart."

"Ah, opposite!" cried Ursula. "I know your dodges. I am not taken in by your word-twisting. You belong to Hermione and her dead show.—Well, if you do, you do. I don't blame you. But then you've nothing to do with me."

In his inflamed, overwrought exasperation, he stopped the car, and they sat there, in the middle of the country lane, to have it out. It was a crisis of war between them, so they did not see the ridiculousness of their situation.

"If you weren't a fool, if only you weren't a fool," he cried in bitter despair, "you'd see that one could be decent, even where one has been wrong. I *was* wrong to go on all those years with Hermione—it was a deathly process. But after all, one can have a little human decency.—But no, you would tear my soul out with your jealousy, at the very mention of Hermione's name."

"I jealous! *I*—jealous! You *are* mistaken if you think that. I'm not jealous in the least of Hermione, she is nothing to me, not *that*!" And Ursula snapped her fingers. "No, it's you who are a liar. It's you who must return, like a dog to his vomit. It is what Hermione *stands for* that I *hate*, I *hate* it, it is lies, it is false, it is death.—But you want it, you can't help it, you can't help yourself. You belong to that old, deathly way of living—then go back to it.—But don't come to me, for I've nothing to do with it."

And in the stress of her violent emotion, she got down from the car and went to the hedgerow, picking unconsciously some flesh-pink spindle berries, some of which were burst, showing their orange seeds.

"Ah, you are a fool," he cried, bitterly, with some contempt.

"Yes, I am. I *am* a fool. And thank God for it. I'm too big a fool to swallow your clevernesses, God be praised. You go to your women—go to them—they are your sort. You've always had a string of them trailing after you—and you always will. Go to your spiritual brides—but don't come to me as well, because I'm not having any, thank you.—You're not satisfied, aren't you? Your spiritual brides can't give you what you want, they aren't common and fleshly enough for you, aren't they? So you come to me, and keep them in the background! You will marry me, for daily use. But you'll keep yourself well provided with spiritual brides, in the background.—I know your dirty little game." Suddenly a flame ran over her, and she stamped her foot madly on the road, and he winced, afraid she would strike him. "And *I*, *I'm* not spiritual enough, *I'm* not as spiritual as that Hermione—!" Her brows knitted, her eyes blazed like a tiger's. "Then *go* to her, that's all I say, *go* to her, *go*.—Ha, she spiritual—*spiritual*, she! A dirty materialist as she is. *She* spiritual?—What does she care for, what *is* her spirituality? What *is* it?" Her fury seemed to blaze out and burn his face. He shrank a little. "I tell you it's *dirt*, *dirt*, and nothing *but* dirt.—And it's dirt you want, you crave for it.—Spiritual! Is *that* spiritual, her bullying, her conceit, her sordid materialism? She's a fishwife, a fishwife, she is such a materialist. And all so sordid. What does she work out to, in the end, with all her social passion, as you call it. Social passion—what social passion has she?—show it me!—where is it? She wants petty, immediate *power*, she wants the illusion that she is a great woman, that is all.—In her soul she's a devilish unbeliever, common as dirt. That's what she is at the bottom. And all the rest is *pretence*—but you love it. You love the sham spirituality, it's your food. And why?—Because of the dirt underneath.—Do you think I don't know the foulness of your sex life—and hers?—I do. And it's that foulness you want, you liar. Then have it, have it.—You're such a liar."

She turned away, spasmodically tearing the twigs of spindle berry from the hedge, and fastening them, with vibrating fingers, in the bosom of her coat.

He stood watching in silence. A wonderful tenderness burned in him, at the sight of her quivering, so sensitive fingers: and at the same time he was full of rage and callousness.

"This is a degrading exhibition," he said coolly.

"Yes, degrading indeed," she said. "But more to me than to you."

"Since you choose to degrade yourself," he said. Again the flash came over her face, the yellow lights concentrated in her eyes.

"*You!*" she cried. "You! You truth-lover! you purity-monger! It *stinks*, your truth and your purity. It stinks of the offal you feed on, you scavenger dog, you eater of corpses.—You are foul, *foul*—and you must know it. Your purity, your candour, your goodness—yes thank you, we've had some. What you are is a foul, deathly thing, that's what you are, obscene and perverse.—You, and love! You may well say you don't want love. No, you want *yourself*, and dirt, and death—that's what you want. You are so *perverse*, so death-eating. And then—"

"There's a bicycle coming," he said, writhing under her loud denunciation.

She glanced down the road.

"I don't care," she cried.

Nevertheless she was silent. The cyclist, having heard the voices raised in altercation, glanced curiously at the man, and the woman, and at the standing motor-car, as he passed.

"—Afternoon," he said, cheerfully.

"Good-afternoon," replied Birkin coldly.

They were silent as the man passed into the distance.

A clearer look had come over Birkin's face. He knew she was in the main right. He knew he was perverse, so spiritual on the one hand, and in some strange way, degraded, on the other. But was she herself any better? Was anybody any better?

"It may all be true, lies and stink and all," he said. "But Hermione's spiritual intimacy is no rottener than your emotional-jealous intimacy.— One can preserve the decencies, even to one's enemies: for one's own sake. Hermione is my enemy—to her last breath. That's why I must bow her off the field."

"You! You and your enemies and your bows! A pretty picture you make of yourself. But it takes nobody in but yourself. I, *jealous*! *I*! What I say," her voice sprang into flame, "I say because it is *true*, do you see, because you are *you*, a foul and false liar, a whited sepulchre. That's why I say it. And *you*, hear it."

"And be grateful," he added, with a satirical grimace.

"Yes," she cried, "and if you have a spark of decency in you, be grateful."

"Not having a spark of decency, however—" he retorted.

"No," she cried, "you haven't a *spark*. And so you can go your way, and I'll go mine. It's no good, not the slightest.—So you can leave me now, I don't want to go any further with you—leave me—."

"You don't even know where you are," he said.

"Oh, don't bother, I assure you I shall be all right. I've got ten shillings in my purse, and that will take me back from anywhere *you* have brought me to." She hesitated. The rings were still on her fingers, two on her little finger, one on her ring finger. Still she hesitated.

"Very good," he said. "The only hopeless thing is a fool."

"You are quite right," she said.

Still she hesitated. Then an ugly, malevolent look came over her face, she pulled the rings from her fingers, and tossed them at him. One touched his face, the others hit his coat, and they scattered into the mud.

"And take your rings," she said, "and go and buy yourself a female elsewhere—there are plenty to be had, who will be quite glad to share your spiritual mess,—or to have your physical mess, and leave your spiritual mess to Hermione."

With which she walked away, desultorily, up the road. He stood motionless, watching her sullen, rather ugly walk. She was sullenly picking and pulling at the twigs of the hedge as she passed. She grew smaller, she seemed to pass out of his sight. A darkness came over his mind. Only a small, mechanical speck of consciousness hovered near him.

He felt tired and weak. Yet also he was relieved. He gave up his old position. He went and sat on the bank. No doubt Ursula was right. It was true, really, what she said. He knew that his spirituality was concomitant of a process of depravity, a sort of pleasure in self-destruction. There really *was* a certain stimulant in self-destruction, for him—especially when it was translated spiritually.—But then he knew it—he knew it, and had done. And was not Ursula's way of emotional intimacy, emotional and physical, was it not just as dangerous as Hermione's abstract spiritual intimacy? Fusion, fusion, this horrible fusion of two beings, which every woman, and most men insisted on, was it not nauseous and horrible anyhow, whether it was a fusion of the spirit or of the emotional body? Hermione saw herself as the perfect Idea, to which all men must come: and Ursula was the perfect Womb, the bath of birth, to which all men must come! And both were horrible. Why could they not remain individuals, limited by their own limits? Why this dreadful all-comprehensiveness, this hateful tyranny? Why not leave the other being free, why try to absorb, or melt, or merge? One might abandon oneself utterly to the *moment*, but not to any other being.

He could not bear to see the rings lying in the pale mud of the road. He picked them up, and wiped them unconsciously on his hands. They were the little tokens of the reality of beauty, the reality of happiness in warm creation.—But he had made his hands all dirty and gritty.

There was a darkness over his mind. The terrible knot of consciousness that had persisted there like an obsession was broken, gone, his life was dissolved in darkness over his limbs and his body. But there was a point of anxiety in his heart now. He wanted her to come back. He breathed lightly and regularly like an infant, that breathes innocently, beyond the touch of responsibility.

She was coming back. He saw her drifting desultorily under the high hedge, advancing towards him slowly. He did not move, he did not look again. He was as if asleep, at peace, slumbering and utterly relaxed.

She came up and stood before him, hanging her head.

"See what a flower I found you," she said, wistfully, holding a piece of purple-red bell-heather under his face. He saw the clump of coloured bells, and the tree-like, tiny branch: also her hands, with their over-fine, over-sensitive skin.

"Pretty!" he said, looking up at her with a smile, taking the flower. Everything had become simple again, quite simple, the complexity gone into nowhere. But he badly wanted to cry: except that he was weary and bored by emotion.

Then a hot passion of tenderness for her filled his heart. He stood up and looked into her face. It was new and oh, so delicate in its luminous wonder and fear. He put his arms round her, and she hid her face on his shoulder.

It was peace, just simply peace, as he stood folding her quietly there on the open lane. It was peace at last. The old, detestable world of tension had passed away at last, his soul was strong and at ease.

She looked up at him. The wonderful yellow light in her eyes now was soft and yielded, they were at peace with each other. He kissed her, softly, many, many times. A laugh came into her eyes.

"Did I abuse you?" she asked.

He smiled too, and took her hand, that was so soft and given.

"Never mind," she said, "it is all for the good."

He kissed her again, softly, many times.

"Isn't it?" she said.

"Certainly," he replied. "Wait! I shall have my own back."

She laughed suddenly, with a wild catch in her voice, and flung her arms round him.

"You are mine, my love, aren't you?" she cried, straining him close.

"Yes," he said, softly.

His voice was so soft and final, she went very still, as if under a fate which had taken her. Yes, she acquiesced—but it was accomplished without her acquiescence. He was kissing her quietly, repeatedly, with a soft, still happiness that almost made her heart stop beating.

"My love!" she cried, lifting her face and looking with frightened, gentle wonder of bliss. Was it all real? But his eyes were beautiful and soft and immune from stress or excitement, beautiful and smiling lightly to her, smiling with her. She hid her face on his shoulder, hiding before him, because he could see her so completely. She knew he loved her, and she was afraid, she was in a strange element, a new heaven round about her. She wished he were passionate, because in passion she was at home. But this was so still and frail, as space is more frightening than force.

Again, quickly, she lifted her head.

"Do you love me?" she said, quickly, impulsively.

"Yes," he replied, not heeding her motion, only her stillness.

She knew it was true. She broke away.

"So you ought," she said, turning round to look at the road. "Did you find the rings?"

"Yes."

"Where are they?"

"In my pocket."

She put her hand into his pocket and took them out.

She was restless.

"Shall we go," she said.

"Yes," he answered. And they mounted the car once more, and left behind them this memorable battle-field.

They drifted through the mild, late afternoon, in a beautiful motion that was smiling and transcendent. His mind was sweetly at ease, the life flowed through him as from some new fountain, he was as if born out of the cramp of a womb.

"Are you happy?" she asked him, in her strange, delighted way.

"Yes," he said.

"So am I," she cried in sudden ecstasy, putting her arm round him and clutching him violently against her, as he steered the motor-car.

"Don't drive much more," she said. "I don't want you to be always doing something."

"No," he said. "We'll finish this little trip, and then we'll be free."

"We will, my love, we will," she cried in delight, kissing him as he turned to her.

He drove on in a strange new wakefulness, the tension of his consciousness broken. He seemed to be conscious all over, all his body awake with a simple, glimmering awareness, as if he had just come awake, like a thing that is born, like a bird when it comes out of an egg, into a new universe.

They dropped down a long hill in the dusk, and suddenly Ursula recognised on her right hand, below in the hollow, the form of Southwell Minster.

"Are we here!" she cried with pleasure.

The rigid, sombre, ugly cathedral was settling under the gloom of the coming night, as they entered the narrow town, the golden lights showed like slabs of revelation, in the shop-windows.

"Father came here with mother," she said, "when they first knew each other. He loves it—he loves the minster. Do you?"

"Yes. It looks like quartz crystals sticking up out of the dark hollow. We'll have our high tea at the Saracen's Head."

As they descended, they heard the Minster bells playing a hymn, when the hour had struck six.

> "Glory to thee my God this night
> For all the blessings of the light——"

So, to Ursula's ear, the tune fell out, drop by drop, from the unseen sky on to the dusky town. It was like dim, bygone centuries sounding. It was all so far off. She stood in the old yard of the inn, smelling of straw and stables and petrol. Above, she could see the first stars. What was it all? This was no actual world, it was the dream-world of one's childhood—a great circum-scribed reminiscence. The world had become unreal. She herself was a strange, transcendent reality.

They sat together in a little parlour by the fire.

"Is it true?" she said, wondering.

"What?"

"Everything—is everything true?"

"The best is true," he said, grimacing at her.

"Is it?" she replied, laughing, but unassured.

She looked at him. He seemed still so separate. New eyes were opened in her soul, she saw a strange creature from another world, in him. It was as if she were enchanted, and everything were metamorphosed. She recalled again the old magic of the Book of Genesis, where the Sons of God saw the daughters of men, that they were fair. And he was one of these, one of these strange creatures from the beyond, looking down at her, and seeing she was fair.

He stood on the hearth-rug looking at her, at her face that was upturned exactly like a flower, a fresh, luminous flower, glinting faintly golden with the dew of the first light. And he was smiling faintly as if there were no speech in the world, save the silent delight of flowers in each other. Smilingly they delighted in each other's presence, pure presence, not to be thought of, even known. But his eyes had a faintly ironical contraction.

And she was drawn to him strangely, as in a spell. Kneeling on the hearth-rug before him, she put her arms round his loins, and put her face against his thighs. Riches! Riches? She was overwhelmed with a sense of a heavenful of riches.

"We love each other," she said in delight.

"More than that," he answered, looking down at her with his glim-mering, easy face.

Unconsciously, with her sensitive finger-tips, she was tracing the back of his thighs, following some mysterious life-flow there. She had dis-covered something, something more than wonderful, more wonderful than life itself. It was the strange mystery of his life-motion, there, at the back of the thighs, down the flanks. It was a strange reality of his being, the very stuff of being, there in the straight downflow of the thighs. It was here she discovered him one of the Sons of God such as were in the beginning of the world, not a man, something other, something more.

This was release at last. She had had lovers, she had known passion. But this was neither love nor passion. It was the daughters of men coming back to the Sons of God, the strange inhuman Sons of God who are in the beginning.

Her face was now one dazzle of released, golden light, as she looked up at him, and laid her hands full on his thighs, behind, as he stood before her. He looked down at her with a rich bright brow like a diadem above his eyes. She was beautiful as a new marvellous flower opened at his knees, a paradisal flower she was, beyond womanhood, such a flower of luminousness. Yet something was tight and unfree in him. He did not like this crouching, this radiance—not altogether.

It was all achieved, for her. She had found one of the Sons of God from the Beginning, and he had found one of the first most luminous daughters of men.

She traced with her hands the line of his loins and thighs, at the back, and a living fire ran through her, from him, darkly. It was a dark flood of electric passion she released from him, drew into herself. She had established a rich new circuit, a new current of passional electric energy, between the two of them, released from the darkest poles of the body and established in perfect circuit. It was a dark fire of electricity that rushed from him to her, and flooded them both with rich peace, satisfaction.

"My love," she cried, lifting her face to him, her eyes, her mouth open in transport.

"My love," he answered, bending and kissing her, always kissing her.

She closed her hands over the full, rounded body of his loins, as he stooped over her, she seemed to touch the quick of the mystery of darkness that was bodily him. She seemed to faint beneath, and he seemed to faint, stooping over her. It was a perfect passing away for both of them, and at the same time the most intolerable accession into being, the marvellous fulness of immediate gratification, overwhelming, outflooding from the Source of the deepest life-force, the darkest, deepest, strangest life-source of the human body, at the back and base of the loins.

After a lapse of stillness, after the rivers of strange dark fluid richness had passed over her, flooding, carrying away her mind and flooding down her spine and down her knees, past her feet, a strange flood, sweeping away everything and leaving her an essential new being, she was left quite free, she was free in complete ease, her complete self. So she rose, stilly and blithe, smiling at him. He stood before her, glimmering, so awfully real, that her heart almost stopped beating. He stood there in his strange, whole body, that had its marvellous fountains, like the bodies of the Sons of God who were in the beginning. There were strange fountains of his body, more mysterious and potent than any she had imagined or known, more satisfying, ah, finally, mystically-physically satisfying. She had thought there was no source deeper than the phallic source. And now, behold, from the smitten rock of the man's body, from the strange marvellous flanks and thighs, deeper, further in mystery than the phallic source, came the floods of ineffable darkness and ineffable riches.

They were glad, and they could forget perfectly. They laughed, and went to the meal provided. There was a venison pasty, of all things, a large broad-faced cut ham, eggs and cresses and red beet-root, and medlars and apple-tart, and tea.

"What *good* things!" she cried with pleasure. "How noble it looks!— Shall I pour out the tea?—"

She was usually nervous and uncertain at performing these public duties, such as giving tea. But today she forgot, she was at her ease, entirely forgetting to have misgivings. The tea-pot poured beautifully from a proud slender spout. Her eyes were warm with smiles as she gave him his tea. She had learned at last to be still and perfect.

"Everything is ours," she said to him.

"Everything," he answered.

She gave a queer little crowing sound of triumph.

"I'm so glad!" she cried, with unspeakable relief.

"So am I," he said. "But I'm thinking. We'd better get out of our responsibilities as quick as we can."

"What responsibilities?" she asked, wondering.

"We must drop our jobs, like a shot."

A new understanding dawned into her face.

"Of course," she said, "there's that."

"We must get out," he said. "There's nothing for it but to get out, quick."

She looked at him doubtfully across the table.

"But where?" she said.

"I don't know," he said. "We'll just wander about for a bit."

Again she looked at him quizzically.

"I should be perfectly happy at the Mill," she said.

"It's very near the old thing," he said. "Let us wander a bit."

His voice could be so soft and happy-go-lucky, it went through her veins like an exhilaration. Nevertheless she dreamed of a valley, and wild gardens, and peace. She had a desire too for splendour—an aristocratic extravagant splendour. Wandering seemed to her like restlessness, dissatisfaction.

"Where will you wander to?" she asked.

"I don't know. I feel as if I would just meet you and we'd set off—just towards the distance."

"But where can one go?" she asked, anxiously. "After all, there *is* only the world, and none of it is very distant."

"Still," he said, "I should like to go with you—nowhere. It would be rather wandering just to nowhere. That's the place to get to—nowhere. One wants to wander away from the world's somewheres, into our own nowhere."

Still she meditated.

"You see, my love," she said, "I'm so afraid that while we are only people, we've got to take the world that's given—because there isn't any other."

"Yes there is," he said. "There's somewhere where we can be free—somewhere where one needn't wear much clothes—none even— —where one meets a few people who have gone through enough, and can take things for granted—where you be yourself, without bothering. There is somewhere—there are one or two people—"

"But where—?" she sighed.

"Somewhere—anywhere. Let's wander off. That's the thing to do—let's wander off."

"Yes—" she said, thrilled at the thought of travel. But to her it was only travel.

"To be free," he said. "To be free, in a free place, with a few other people!"

"Yes," she said wistfully. Those "few other people" depressed her.

"It isn't really a locality, though," he said. "It's a perfected relation between you and me, and others—the perfection relation—so that we are free together."

"It is, my love, isn't it," she said. "It's you and me. It's you and me, isn't it?" She stretched out her arms to him. He went across, and stooped to kiss her face. Her arms closed round him again, her hands spread upon his shoulders, moving slowly there, moving slowly on his back, down his back slowly, with a strange recurrent, rhythmic motion, yet moving slowly down, pressing mysteriously over his loins, over his flanks. The sense of the awfulness of riches that could never be impaired flooded her mind like a swoon, a death in most marvellous possession, mystic-sure. She possessed him so utterly and intolerably, that she herself lapsed out. And yet she was only sitting still in the chair, with her hands pressed upon him, and lost.

Again he softly kissed her.

"We shall never go apart again," he murmured quietly.

And she did not speak, but only pressed her hands firmer down upon the source of darkness in him.

They decided, when they woke again from the pure swoon, to write their resignations from the world of work there and then. She wanted this.

He rang the bell, and ordered note-paper without a printed address. The waiter cleared the table.

"Now then," he said, "yours first. Put your home address, and the date—then 'Director of Education, Town Hall—Sir—' Now then!—I don't know how one really stands—I suppose one could get out of it in less than a month—Anyhow 'Sir—I beg to resign my post as class-mistress in the Willey Green Grammar School. I should be very grateful if you would liberate me as soon as possible, without waiting for the expiration of the month's notice.'—That'll do. Have you got it? Let me look. 'Ursula Brangwen.' Good! Now I'll write mine. I ought to give them three months, but I can plead health. I can arrange it all right."

He sat and wrote out his formal resignation.

"Now," he said, when the envelopes were sealed and addressed, "shall we post them here, both together?—I know Jackie will say 'Here's a coincidence!', when he receives them in all their identity. Shall we let him say it, or not?"

"I don't care," she said.

"No—?" he said, pondering.

"It doesn't matter, does it?" she said.

"Yes," he replied. "Their imaginations shall not work on us. I'll post yours here, mine after.—I cannot be implicated in their imaginings."

He looked at her with his strange, non-human singleness.

"Yes, you are right," she said.

She lifted her face to him, all shining and open. It was as if he might enter straight in to the source of her radiance. His face became a little distracted.

"Shall we go?" he said.

"As you like," she replied.

They were soon out of the little town, and running through the uneven lanes of the country. Ursula nestled near him, into his constant warmth, and watched the pale-lit revelation racing ahead, the visible night. Sometimes it was a wide old road, with grass-spaces on either side, flying magic and elvin in the greenish illumination, sometimes it was trees looming overhead, sometimes it was bramble bushes, sometimes the walls of a crew-yard and the butt of a barn.

"Are you going to Shortlands to dinner?" Ursula asked him suddenly. He started.

"Good God!" he said. "Shortlands. Never again. Not that.—Besides we should be too late."

"Where are we going then—to the Mill?"

"If you like.—Pity to go anywhere on this good dark night. Pity to come out of it, really. Pity we can't stop in the good darkness. It is better than anything ever would be—this good immediate darkness."

She sat wondering. The car lurched and swayed. She knew there was no leaving him, the darkness held them both and contained them, it was not to be surpassed. Besides she had a full mystic knowledge of his suave loins of darkness, dark-clad and suave, and in this knowledge there was some of the inevitability and the beauty of fate, fate which one asks for, which one accepts in full.

He sat still like an Egyptian Pharaoh, driving the car. He felt as if he were seated in immemorial potency, like the great carven statues of real Egypt, as real and as fulfilled with subtle strength, as these are, with a vague inscrutable smile on the lips. He knew what it was to have the strange and magical current of force in his back and loins, and down his legs, force so perfect that it stayed him immobile, and left his face subtly, mindlessly smiling. He knew what it was to be awake and potent in that other basic mind, the deepest physical mind. And from this source he had a pure and magic control, magical, mystical, a force in darkness, like electricity.

It was very difficult to speak, it was so perfect to sit in this pure living silence, subtle, full of unthinkable knowledge and unthinkable force, upheld immemorially in timeless force, like the immobile, supremely potent Egyptians, seated forever in their living, subtle silence.

"We need not go home," he said. "This car has seats that let down and make a bed, and we can lift the hood."

She was glad and frightened. She cowered near to him.

"But what about them at home?" she said.

"Send a telegram."

Nothing more was said. They ran on in silence. But with a sort of second consciousness he steered the car towards a destination. For he had the free intelligence to direct his own ends. His arms and his breast and his head were rounded and living like those of the Greek, he had not the unawakened straight arms of the Egyptian, nor the sealed, slumbering head. A lambent intelligence played secondarily above his pure Egyptian concentration in darkness.

They came to a village that lined along the road. The car crept slowly along, until he saw the post-office. Then he pulled up.

"I will send a telegram to your father," he said. "I will merely say 'spending the night in town,' shall I?"

"Yes," she answered. She did not want to be disturbed into taking thought.

She watched him move into the post-office. It was also a shop, she saw. Strange, he was. Even as he went into the lighted, public place he remained dark and magic, the living silence seemed the body of reality in him, subtle, potent, indiscoverable. There he was! In a strange uplift of elation she saw him, the being never to be revealed, awful in its potency, mystic and real. This dark, subtle reality of him, never to be translated, liberated her into perfection, her own perfected being. She too was dark and fulfilled in silence.

He came out, throwing some packages into the car.

"There is some bread, and cheese, and raisins, and apples, and hard chocolate," he said, in his voice that was as if laughing, because of the unblemished stillness and force which was the reality in him. She would have to touch him. To speak, to see, was nothing. It was a travesty to look and to comprehend the man there. Darkness and silence must fall perfectly on her, then she could know mystically, in unrevealed touch. She must lightly, mindlessly connect with him, have the knowledge which is death of knowledge, the reality of surety in not-knowing.

Soon they had run on again into the darkness. She did not ask where they were going, she did not care. She sat in a fulness and a pure potency that was like apathy, mindless and immobile. She was next to him, and hung in a pure rest, as a star is hung, balanced unthinkably.—Still there remained a dark lambency of anticipation. She would touch him. With perfect fine finger-tips of reality she would touch the reality in him, the suave, pure, untranslateable reality of his loins of darkness. To touch, mindlessly in darkness to come in pure touching upon the living reality of him, his suave perfect loins and thighs of darkness, this was her sustaining anticipation.

And he too waited in the magical steadfastness of suspense, for her to take this knowledge of him as he had taken it of her. He knew her darkly, with the fulness of dark knowledge. Now she would know him, and he too would be liberated. He would be night-free, like an Egyptian, steadfast in perfectly suspended equilibrium, pure mystic nodality of physical being. They would give each other this star-equilibrium which alone is freedom.

She saw that they were running among trees—great old trees with dying bracken undergrowth. The palish, gnarled trunks showed ghostly, and like old priests in the hovering distance, the fern rose magical and mysterious. It was a night all darkness, with low cloud. The motor-car advanced slowly.

"Where are we?" she whispered.

"In Sherwood Forest."

It was evident he knew the place. He drove softly, watching. Then they came to a green road between the trees. They turned cautiously round, and were advancing between the oaks of the forest, down a green lane. The green lane widened into a little circle of grass, where there was a small trickle of water at the bottom of a sloping bank. The car stopped.

"We will stay here," he said, "and put out the lights."

He extinguished the lamps at once, and it was pure night, with shadows of trees like realities of other, nightly being. He threw a rug on to the bracken, and they sat in stillness and mindless silence. There were faint sounds from the wood, but no disturbance, no possible disturbance, the world was under a strange ban, a new mystery had supervened.

They threw off their clothes, and he gathered her to him, and found her, found the pure lambent reality of her forever invisible flesh. Quenched, inhuman, his fingers upon her unrevealed nudity were the fingers of silence upon silence, the body of mysterious night upon the body of mysterious night, the night masculine and feminine, never to be seen with the eye, or known with the mind, only known as a palpable revelation of living otherness.

She had her desire of him, she touched, she received the maximums of unspeakable communication in touch, dark, subtle, positively silent, a magnificent gift and give again, a perfect acceptance and yielding, a mystery, the reality of that which can never be known, vital, sensual reality that can never be transmuted into mind content, but remains outside, living body of darkness and silence and subtlety, the mystic body of reality. She had her desire fulfilled, he had his desire fulfilled. For she was to him what he was to her, the immemorial magnificence of mystic, palpable, real otherness.

They slept the chilly night through under the hood of the car, a night of unbroken sleep. It was already high day when he awoke. They looked at each other and laughed, then looked away, filled with darkness and secrecy. Then they kissed and remembered the magnificence of the night. It was so magnificent, such an inheritance of a universe of dark reality, that they were afraid to seem to remember. They hid away the remembrance and the knowledge.

Chapter XXIV

Death and Love

Thomas Crich died slowly, terribly slowly. It seemed impossible to everybody, that the thread of life could be drawn out so thin, and yet not break. The sick man lay unutterably weak and spent, kept alive by morphia and by drinks, which he sipped slowly. He was only half conscious—a thin strand of consciousness linking the darkness of death with the light of day. Yet his will was unbroken, he was integral, complete. Only he must have perfect stillness about him.

Any presence but that of the nurses, was a strain and an effort to him now. Every morning, Gerald went into the room, hoping to find his father passed away at last. Yet always he saw the same transparent face, the same weary dark hair on the waxen forehead, and the awful, inchoate dark eyes, which seemed to be decomposing into formless darkness, having only a tiny grain of vision within them.

And always, as the dark, inchoate eyes turned to him, there passed through Gerald's bowels a burning stroke of revolt, that seemed to resound through his whole being, threatening to break his mind with its clangour, and make him mad.

Every morning, the son stood there, erect and taut with life, gleaming in his blondness. The gleaming blondness of his strange, imminent being put the father into a fever of fretful irritation. He could not bear to meet the uncanny, downward look of Gerald's blue eyes. But it was only for a moment. Each on the brink of departure, the father and son looked at each other, then parted.

For a long time Gerald preserved a perfect sang froid, he remained quite collected. But at last, fear undermined him. He was afraid of some horrible collapse in himself. He had to stay and see this thing through. Some perverse will made him watch his father drawn over the borders of life. And yet, now, every day, the great red-hot stroke of horrified fear through the bowels of the son struck a further inflammation, Gerald went about all day with a tendency to cringe, as if there were the point of a sword of Damocles pricking the nape of his neck.

There was no escape—he was bound up with his father, he had to see him through. And the father's will never relaxed or yielded to death. It would have to snap when death at last snapped it,—if it did not persist after physical death. In the same way, the will of the son never yielded. He stood firm and immune, he was outside this death and this dying.

It was a trial by ordeal. Could he stand and see his father slowly dissolve and disappear in death, without once yielding his will, without once relenting before the omnipotence of death. Like a Red Indian undergoing torture, Gerald would experience the whole process of slow death without wincing or flinching. He even triumphed in it. He somehow *wanted* this death, even forced it. It was as if he himself were dealing the death, even when he most recoiled in horror. Still, he would deal it, he would triumph through death.

But in the stress of this ordeal, Gerald too lost his hold on the outer, daily life. That which was much to him, came to mean nothing. Work, pleasure—it was all left behind. He went on more or less mechanically with his business, but this activity was all extraneous. The real activity was this ghastly wrestling for death, in his own soul. And his own will should triumph. Come what might, he would not bow down or submit or acknowledge a master. He had no master in death.

But as the fight went on, and all that he had been and was continued to be destroyed, so that life was a hollow shell all round him, roaring and clattering like the sound of the sea, a noise in which he participated externally, and inside this hollow shell was all the darkness and fearful space of death, he knew he would have to find reinforcements, otherwise he would collapse inwards upon the great dark void which circled at the centre of his soul. His will held his outer life, his outer mind, his outer being unbroken and unchanged. But the pressure was too great. He would have to find something to make good the equilibrium. Something must come with him into the hollow void of death in his soul, fill it up, and so equalise the pressure within to the pressure without. For day by day he felt more and more like a bubble filled with darkness, round which whirled the iridescence of his consciousness, and upon which the pressure of the outer world, the outer life, roared vastly.

In this extremity his instinct led him to Gudrun. He threw away everything now—he only wanted the relation established with her. He would follow her to the studio, to be near her, to talk to her. He would stand about the room, aimlessly picking up the implements, the lumps of clay, the little figures she had cast—they were whimsical and grotesque— looking at them without perceiving them. And she felt him following her, dogging her heels like a doom. She held away from him, and yet she knew he drew always a little nearer, a little nearer.

"I say," he said to her one evening, in an odd, unthinking, uncertain way, "won't you stay to dinner tonight?—I wish you would."

She started slightly. He spoke to her like a man making a request of another man.

"They'll be expecting me at home," she said.

"Oh, they won't mind, will they?" he said. "I should be awfully glad if you'd stay."

Her long silence gave consent at last.

"I'll tell Thomas, shall I?" he said.

"I must go almost immediately after dinner," she said.

It was a dark, cold evening. There was no fire in the drawing-room, they sat in the library. He was mostly silent, absent, and Winifred talked little. But when Gerald did rouse himself, he smiled and was pleasant and ordinary with her. Then there came over him again the long blanks, of which he was not aware.

She was very much attracted by him. He looked so pre-occupied, and his strange, blank silences, which she could not read, moved her and made her wonder over him, made her feel reverential towards him.

But he was very kind. He gave her the best things at the table, he had a bottle of slightly sweet, delicious golden wine brought out for dinner, knowing she would prefer it to the burgundy. She felt herself esteemed, needed almost.

As they took coffee in the library, there was a soft, very soft knocking at the door. He started, and called "Come in." The timbre of his voice, like something vibrating at high pitch, unnerved Gudrun. A nurse in white entered, half hovering in the doorway like a shadow. She was very good-looking, but strangely enough, shy and self-mistrusting.

"The doctor would like to speak to you, Mr Crich," she said, in her low, discreet voice.

"The doctor!" he said, starting up. "Where is he?"

"He is in the dining room."

"Tell him I'm coming."

He drank up his coffee, and followed the nurse, who had dissolved like a shadow.

"Which nurse was that?" asked Gudrun.

"Miss Inglis—I like her best," replied Winifred.

After a while Gerald came back, looking absorbed by his own thoughts, and having some of that tension and abstraction which is seen in a slightly drunken man. He did not say what the doctor had wanted him for, but stood before the fire, with his hands behind his back, and his face open and as if rapt. Not that he was really thinking—he was only arrested in pure suspense inside himself, and thoughts wafted through his mind without order.

"I must go now and see Mama," said Winifred, "and see Dadda before he goes to sleep."

She bade them both goodnight.

Gudrun also rose to take her leave.

"You needn't go yet, need you?" said Gerald, glancing quickly at the clock. "It is early yet. I'll walk down with you when you go. Sit down, don't hurry away."

Gudrun sat down, as if, absent as he was, his will had power over her. She felt almost mesmerised. He was strange to her, something unknown. What was he thinking, what was he feeling, as he stood there rapt, saying nothing? He kept her—she could feel that. He would not let her go. She watched him in humble submissiveness.

"Had the doctor anything new to tell you?" she asked softly, at length, with that gentle, timid sympathy which touched a keen fibre in his heart.

He lifted his eyebrows with a negligent, indifferent expression.

"No—nothing new," he replied, as if the question were quite casual, trivial. "He says the pulse is very weak indeed, very intermittent—but that doesn't necessarily mean much, you know."

He looked down at her. Her eyes were dark and soft and unfolded, with a stricken look that roused him.

"No," she murmured at length. "—I don't understand anything about these things."

"Just as well not," he said.—"I say, won't you have a cigarette?—do!" He quickly fetched the box, and held her a light. Then he stood before her on the hearth again.

"No," he said, "we've never had much illness in the house, either—not till father." He seemed to meditate a while. Then, looking down at her, with strangely communicative blue eyes, that filled her with dread, he continued: "It's something you don't reckon with, you know, till it is there. And then you realise that it was there all the time—it was always there—you understand what I mean?—the possibility of this incurable illness, this slow death."

He moved his feet uneasily on the marble hearth, and put his cigarette to his mouth, looking up at the ceiling.

"I know," murmured Gudrun; "it is dreadful."

He smoked without knowing. Then he took the cigarette from his lips, bared his teeth, and putting the tip of his tongue between his teeth, spat off a grain of tobacco, turning slightly aside, like a man who is alone, or who is lost in thought.

"I don't know what the effect actually *is*, on one," he said, and again he looked down at her. Her eyes were dark and stricken with knowledge, looking into his. He saw her submerged, and he turned aside his face. "But I absolutely am not the same. There's nothing left, if you understand what I mean. You seem to be clutching at the void—and at the same time you are void yourself.—And so you don't know what to *do*."

"No," she murmured. A heavy thrill ran down her nerves, heavy, almost pleasure, almost pain. "What can be done?" she added.

He turned, and flipped the ash from his cigarette on to the great marble hearth-stone, that lay bare to the room, without fender or bar.

"I don't know, I'm sure," he replied. "But I do think you've got to find some way of resolving the situation—not because you want to, but because you've *got* to, otherwise you're done. The whole of everything, and yourself included, is just on the point of caving in, and you are just holding it up with your hands.—Well, it's a situation that obviously can't continue. You can't stand holding the roof up with your hands, for ever. You know that sooner or later you'll *have* to let go.—Do you understand what I mean?—And so something's got to be done, or there's a universal collapse—as far as you yourself are concerned."

He shifted slightly on the hearth, crunching a cinder under his heel. He looked down at it. Gudrun was aware of the beautiful old marble panels of the fireplace, swelling softly carved, round him and above him. She felt as if she were caught at last by fate, imprisoned in some horrible and fatal trap.

"But what *can* be done?" she murmured humbly. "You must use me if I can be of any help at all—but how can I? I don't see how I *can* help you."

He looked down at her critically.

"I don't want you to *help*," he said, slightly irritated, "because there's nothing to be *done*. I only want sympathy, do you see: I want somebody I can talk to sympathetically. That eases the strain. And there *is* nobody to talk to sympathetically. That's the curious thing. There *is* nobody. There's Rupert Birkin. But then he *isn't* sympathetic, he wants to *dictate*. And that is no use whatsoever."

She was caught in a strange snare. She looked down at her hands.

Then there was the sound of the door softly opening. Gerald started. He was chagrined. It was his starting that really startled Gudrun. Then he went forward, with quick, graceful, intentional courtesy.

"Oh, mother!" he said. "How nice of you to come down. How are you?"

The elderly woman, loosely and bulkily wrapped in a purple gown, came forward silently, slightly hulked, as usual. Her son was at her side. He pushed her up a chair, saying:

"You know Miss Brangwen, don't you?"

The mother glanced at Gudrun indifferently.

"Yes," she said. Then she turned her wonderful, forget-me-not blue eyes up to her son, as she slowly sat down in the chair he had brought her.

"I came to ask you about your father," she said, in her rapid, scarcely-audible voice. "I didn't know you had company."

"No? Didn't Winifred tell you?—Miss Brangwen stayed to dinner, to make us a little more lively—"

Mrs Crich turned slowly round to Gudrun, and looked at her, but with unseeing eyes.

"I'm afraid it would be no treat to her." Then she turned again to her son. "Winifred tells me the doctor had something to say about your father. What is it?"

"Only that the pulse is very weak—misses altogether a good many times—so that he might not last the night out," Gerald replied.

Mrs Crich sat perfectly impassive, as if she had not heard. Her bulk seemed hunched in the chair, her fair hair hung slack over her ears. But her skin was clear and fine, her hands, as she sat with them forgotten and folded, were quite beautiful, full of potential energy. A great mass of energy seemed decaying up in that silent, hulking form.

She looked up at her son, as he stood, keen and soldierly, near to her. Her eyes were most wonderfully blue, bluer than forget-me-nots. She seemed to have a certain confidence in Gerald, and to feel a certain motherly mistrust of him.

"How *are* you?" she muttered, in her strangely quiet voice, as if nobody should hear but him. "You're not getting into a state, are you? You're not letting it make you hysterical?"

The curious challenge in the last words startled Gudrun.

"I don't think so, mother," he answered, rather coldly cheery. "Somebody's got to see it through, you know."

"Have they? Have they?" answered his mother rapidly. "Why should *you* take it on yourself? What have *you* to do, seeing it through? It will see itself through. You are not needed."

"No, I don't suppose I can do any good," he answered. "It's just how it affects us, you see."

"You like to be affected—don't you? It's quite nuts for you? You would have to be important. You have no need to stop at home. Why don't you go away?"

These sentences, evidently the ripened grain of many dark hours, took Gerald by surprise.

"I don't think it's any good going away now, mother, at the last minute," he said, coldly.

"You take care," replied his mother. "You mind *yourself*, that's your business. You take too much on yourself.—You mind *yourself*, or you'll find yourself in Queer Street, that's what will happen to you. You're hysterical, always were."

"I'm all right, mother," he said. "There's no need to worry about *me*, I assure you."

"Let the dead bury their dead—don't go and bury yourself along with them—that's what I tell you. I know you well enough."

He did not answer this, not knowing what to say. The mother sat bunched up in silence, her beautiful white hands, that had no rings whatsoever, clasping the pommels of her arm-chair.

"You can't do it," she said, almost bitterly. "You haven't the nerve. You're as weak as a cat, really—always were.—Is this young woman staying here?"

"No," said Gerald. "She is going home tonight."

"Then she'd better have the dog-cart. Does she go far?"

"Only to Beldover."

"Ah." The elderly woman never looked at Gudrun, yet she seemed to take knowledge of her presence.

"You are inclined to take too much on yourself, Gerald," said the mother, pulling herself to her feet, with a little difficulty.

"Will you go, mother?" he asked politely.

"Yes, I'll go up again," she replied. Turning to Gudrun, she bade her "Goodnight." Then she went slowly to the door, as if she were unaccustomed to walking. At the door she lifted her face to him, implicitly. He kissed her.

"Don't come any farther with me," she said, in her barely audible voice. "I don't want you any farther."

He bade her goodnight, watched her cross to the stairs and mount slowly. Then he closed the door and came back to Gudrun. Gudrun rose also, to go.

"A queer being, my mother," he said.

"Yes," replied Gudrun.

"She has her own thoughts."

"Yes," said Gudrun.

Then they were silent.

"You want to go?" he asked. "Half a minute, I'll just have a horse put in—"

"No," said Gudrun, "I want to walk."

He had promised to walk with her down the long, lonely mile of drive, and she wanted this.

"You might *just* as well drive," he said.

"I'd *much rather* walk," she asserted, with emphasis.

"You would?—Then I will come along with you.—You know where your things are?—I'll put boots on."

He put on a cap, and an overcoat over his evening dress. They went out into the night.

"Let us light a cigarette," he said, stopping in a sheltered angle of the porch. "You have one too."

So, with the scent of tobacco on the night air, they set off down the dark drive, that ran between close-cut hedges through sloping meadows.

He wanted to put his arm round her. If he could put his arm round her, and draw her against him as they walked, he would equilibrate himself. For now he felt like a pair of scales, the half of which tips down and down into an infinite void. He must recover some sort of balance. And here was the hope and the perfect recovery.

Blind to her, thinking only of himself, he slipped his arm softly round her waist, and drew her to him. Her heart fainted, feeling herself taken. But then, his arm was so strong, she quailed under its powerful close grasp. She died a little death, and was drawn against him as they walked down the stormy darkness. He seemed to balance her perfectly in opposition to himself, in their dual motion of walking. So, suddenly, he was liberated and perfect, strong, heroic.

He put his hand to his mouth and threw his cigarette away, a gleaming point, into the unseen hedge. Then he was quite free to balance her.

"That's better," he said, with exultancy.

The exultation in his voice was like a sweetish, poisonous drug to her. Did she then mean so much to him? She sipped the poison.

"Are you happier?" she asked, wistfully.

"Much better," he said, in the same exultant voice, "and I *was* rather far gone."

She nestled against him. He felt her all soft and warm, she was the rich, lovely substance of his being. The warmth and motion of her walk suffused through him wonderfully.

"I'm *so* glad if I help you," she said.

"Yes," he answered. "There's nobody else could do it, if you wouldn't."

"That is true," she said to herself, with a thrill of strange, fatal elation.

As they walked, he seemed to lift her nearer and nearer to himself, till she moved upon the firm vehicle of his body. He was so strong, so sustaining, and he could not be opposed. She drifted along in a wonderful interfusion of physical motion, down the dark, blowy hill-side. Across, shone the little yellow lights of Beldover, many of them, spread in a thick patch on another dark hill. But he and she were walking in perfect, isolated darkness, outside the world.

"But how much do you care for me?" came her voice, almost querulous. "You see, I don't know, I don't understand."

"How much!" His voice rang with a painful elation. "I don't know either—but everything." He was startled by his own declaration. It was true. So, he stripped himself of every safeguard, in making this admission to her. He cared everything for her—she was everything.

"But I can't believe it," said her low voice, amazed, trembling. She was trembling with doubt and exultance. This was the thing she wanted to hear, only this. Yet now she heard it, heard the strange clapping vibration of truth in his voice as he said it, she could not believe. She could not believe—she did not believe. Yet she believed, triumphantly, with fatal exultance.

"Why not?" he said. "Why don't you believe it?—It's true. It is true, as we stand at this moment—" he stood still with her in the wind; "I care for nothing on earth, or in heaven, outside this spot where we are. And it isn't my own presence I care about, it is all yours. I'd sell my soul a hundred times—but I couldn't bear not to have you here. I couldn't bear to be alone. My brain would burst. It is true."

He drew her closer to him, with definite movement.

"No," she murmured, afraid. Yet this was what she wanted. Why did she so lose courage?

They resumed their strange walk. They were such strangers—and yet they were so frightfully, unthinkably near. It was like a madness. Yet it was what she wanted, it was what she wanted.

They had descended the hill, and now they were coming to the square arch where the road passed under the colliery railway. The arch, Gudrun knew, had walls of squared stone, mossy on one side with water that trickled down, dry on the other side. She had stood under it to hear the train rumble thundering over the logs overhead. And she knew that under this dark and lonely bridge the young colliers stood in the darkness with their sweethearts, in rainy weather. And so she wanted to stand under the bridge with *her* sweetheart, and be kissed under the bridge in the invisible darkness. Her steps dragged as she drew near.

So, under the bridge, they came to a standstill, and he lifted her upon his breast. His body vibrated taut and powerful as he closed upon her and crushed her, breathless and dazed and destroyed, crushed her upon his breast. Ah, it was terrible, and perfect. Under this bridge, the colliers pressed their lovers to their breast. And now, under the bridge, the master of them all pressed her to himself! And how much more powerful and terrible was his embrace, than theirs, how much more concentrated and supreme his love was, than theirs, in the same sort! She felt she would swoon, die, under the vibrating, inhuman tension of his arms and his body—she would pass away. Then the unthinkable, high vibration slackened and became more undulating, he slackened and drew her with him to stand with his back to the wall.

She was almost unconscious. So, the colliers' lovers would stand with their backs to the walls, holding their sweethearts and kissing them as she was being kissed.—Ah, but would their kisses be fine and powerful as the kisses of the firm-mouthed master? Even the keen, short-cut moustache—the colliers would not have that.

And the colliers' sweethearts would, like herself, hang their heads back limp over their shoulder, and look out from the dark archway, at the close patch of yellow lights on the unseen hill in the distance, or at the vague form of trees, and at the buildings of the colliery wood-yard, in the other direction.

His arms were fast round her, he seemed to be gathering her into himself, her warmth, her softness, her adorable weight, drinking in the suffusion of her physical being, avidly. He lifted her, and seemed to pour her into himself, like wine into a cup.

"This is worth everything," he said, in a strange, penetrating voice.

So she relaxed, and seemed to melt, to flow into him, as if she were some infinitely warm and precious suffusion filling into his veins, like an intoxicant. Her arms were round his neck, he kissed her and held her perfectly suspended, she was all slack and flowing in to him, and he was the firm, strong cup that receives the wine of her life. So she lay cast upon him, stranded, lifted up against him, melting and melting under his kisses, melting into his limbs and bones, as if he were soft iron becoming surcharged with her electric life.

Till she seemed to swoon, gradually her mind went, and she passed away, everything in her was melted down and fluid, and she lay still, become contained by him, sleeping in him as lightning sleeps in a pure, soft stone. So she was passed away and gone in him, and he was perfected.

When she opened her eyes again, and saw the patch of lights in the distance, it seemed to her strange that the world still existed, that she was standing under the bridge resting her head on Gerald's breast. Gerald—who was he? He was the exquisite adventure, the desirable unknown to her.

She looked up, and in the darkness saw his face above her, his shapely, male face. There seemed a faint, white light emitted from him, a white aura, as if he were visitor from the unseen. She reached up, like Eve reaching to the apples on the tree of knowledge, and she kissed him, though her passion was a transcendent fear of the thing he was, touching his face with her infinitely delicate, encroaching, wondering fingers. Her fingers went over the mould of his face, over his features. How perfect and foreign he was—ah how dangerous! Her soul thrilled with complete knowledge. This was the glistening, forbidden apple, this face of a man. She kissed him, putting her fingers over his face, his eyes, his nostrils, over his brows and his ears, to his neck, to know him, to gather him in by touch. He was so firm and shapely, with such satisfying, inconceivable shape-liness, strange yet unutterably clear. He was such an unutterable enemy, yet glistening with uncanny white fire. She wanted to touch him and touch him and touch him, till she had him all in her hands, till she had strained him into her knowledge. Ah, if she could have the precious *knowledge* of him, she would be filled, and nothing could deprive her of this. For he was so unsure, so risky in the common world of day.

"You are so *beautiful*," she murmured in her throat.

He wondered, and was suspended. But she felt him quiver, and come down involuntarily nearer upon her. He could not help himself. Her fingers had him under their power. The fathomless, fathomless desire they could evoke in him was deeper than death, where he had no choice.

But she knew now, and it was enough. For the time, her soul was destroyed with the exquisite shock of his invisible fluid lightning. She knew. And this knowledge was a death from which she must recover. How much more of him was there to know? Ah much, much, many days harvesting for her large, yet perfectly subtle and intelligent hands, upon the field of his living, radio-active body. Ah, her hands were eager, greedy for knowledge. But for the present it was enough, enough, as much as her soul could bear. Too much, and she would shatter herself, she would fill the fine vial of her soul too quickly, and it would break. Enough now—enough for the time being. There were all the afterdays when her

hands, like birds, could feed upon the fields of his mystical plastic form.
Till then enough.

And even he was glad to be checked, rebuked, held back. For to desire is
better than to possess, the finality of the end was dreaded as deeply as it
was desired.

They walked on towards the town, towards where the lamps threaded
singly, at long intervals down the dark high-road of the valley. They came
at length to the gate of the drive.

"Don't come any further," she said.

"You'd rather I didn't?" he asked, relieved. He did not want to go up the
public streets with her, his soul all naked and alight as it was.

"Much rather—goodnight." She held out her hand. He grasped it, then
touched the perilous, potent fingers with his lips.

"Goodnight," he said. "Tomorrow."

And they parted. He went home full of the strength and the power of
living desire.

But the next day, she did not come, she sent a note, that she was kept
indoors by a cold. Here was a torment! But he possessed his soul in some
sort of patience, writing a brief answer, telling her how sorry he was not to
see her.

The day after this, he stayed at home—it seemed so futile to go down to
the offices. His father could not live the week out. And he wanted to be at
home, suspended.

Gerald sat on a chair by the window in his father's room. The landscape
outside was black and winter-sodden. His father lay grey and ashen on the
bed, a nurse moved silently in her white dress, neat and elegant, even
beautiful. There was a scent of eau-de-cologne in the room. The nurse
went out of the room, Gerald was alone with death, facing the winter-black
landscape.

"Is there much more water in Denley?" came the faint voice, determined and querulous, from the bed. The dying man was asking about a
leakage from Willey Water into one of the pits.

"Some more—we shall have to run off the lake," said Gerald.

"Will you—?" The faint voice filtered to extinction.

There was dead stillness. The grey-faced, sick man lay with eyes closed,
more dead than death. Gerald looked away. He felt his heart was seared, it
would perish if this went on much longer.

Suddenly he heard a strange noise. Turning round, he saw his father's
eyes wide open, strained and rolling in a frenzy of inhuman struggling.
Gerald started to his feet, and stood transfixed in horror.

"Wha—a—ah-h-h—" came a horrible choking rattle from his father's throat, the fearful, frenzied eye, rolling awfully in its wild fruitless search for help, passed blindly over Gerald, then up came the dark blood and mess pumping over the face of the agonised being, the tense body relaxed, the head fell aside, down the pillow.

Gerald stood transfixed, his soul echoing in horror. He would move, but he could not. He could not move his limbs. His brain seemed to re-echo, like a pulse.

The nurse in white softly entered. She glanced at Gerald, then at the bed.

"Ah!" came her soft, whimpering cry, and she hurried forward to the dead man. "Ah—h!" came the slight sound of her agitated distress, as she stood bending over the bedside. Then she recovered, turned, and came for towel and sponge. She was wiping the dead face carefully, and murmuring, almost whimpering, very softly: "Poor Mr Crich!—Poor Mr Crich!—Oh poor Mr Crich!"

"Is he dead?" clanged Gerald's sharp voice.

"Oh yes, he's gone," replied the soft, moaning voice of the nurse, as she looked up at Gerald's face. She was young and beautiful and quivering. A strange sort of grin went over Gerald's face, over the horror. And he walked out of the room.

He was going to tell his mother. On the landing he met his brother Basil.

"He's gone, Basil," he said, scarcely able to subdue his voice, not to let an unconscious, frightening exultation sound through.

"What?" cried Basil, going pale.

Gerald nodded. Then he went on to his mother's room.

She was sitting in her purple gown, sewing, very slowly sewing, putting in a stitch, then another stitch. She looked up at Gerald with her blue, undaunted eyes.

"Father's gone," he said.

"He's dead? Who says so?"

"Oh, you know, mother, if you see him."

She put her sewing down, and slowly rose.

"Are you going to see him?" he asked.

"Yes," she said.

By the bedside the children already stood in a weeping group.

"Oh mother—!" cried the daughters, almost in hysterics, weeping loudly.

But the mother went forward. The dead man lay in repose, as if gently asleep, so gently, so peacefully, like a young man sleeping in purity. He was still warm.

She stood looking at him in gloomy, heavy silence, for some time.

"Ay," she said bitterly, at length, speaking as if to the unseen witnesses of the air. "You're dead." She stood for some minutes in silence, looking down. "Beautiful," she asserted, "beautiful as if life had never touched you—never touched you.—God send I look different.—I hope I shall look my years, when I am dead.—Beautiful, beautiful," she crooned over him. "You can see him in his teens, with his first beard on his face.—A beautiful soul, beautiful—" Then there was a tearing in her voice as she cried: "None of you look like this, when you are dead! Don't let it happen again." It was a strange, wild command from out of the unknown. Her children moved unconsciously together, in a nearer group, at the dreadful command in her voice. The colour was flushed bright in her cheek, she looked awful and wonderful. "Blame me, blame me if you like, that he lies there like a lad in his teens, with his first beard on his face. Blame me if you like. But you none of you know." She was silent in intense silence. Then there came, in a low, tense voice: "If I thought that the children I bore would lie looking like that in death, I'd strangle them when they were infants, yes—"

"No mother," came the strange, clarion voice of Gerald from the background, "we are different, we don't blame you."

She turned and looked full in his eyes. Then she lifted her hands in a strange half-gesture of mad despair.

"Pray!" she said strongly. "Pray for yourselves to God, for there's no help for you from your parents."

"Oh mother!" cried her daughters wildly.

But she had turned and gone, and they all went quickly away from each other.

When Gudrun heard that Mr Crich was dead, she felt rebuked. She had stayed away lest Gerald should think her too easy of winning. And now, he was in the midst of trouble, whilst she was cold.

The following day she went up as usual to Winifred, who was glad to see her, glad to get away into the studio. The girl had wept, and then, too frightened, had turned aside to avoid any more tragic eventuality. She and Gudrun resumed work as usual, in the isolation of the studio, and this seemed an immeasurable happiness, a pure world of freedom, after the aimlessness and misery of the house—Gudrun stayed on till evening. She and Winifred had dinner brought up to the studio, where they ate in freedom, away from all the people in the house.

After dinner Gerald came up. The great high studio was full of shadow and a fragrance of coffee, Gudrun and Winifred had a little table near the fire at the far end, with a white lamp whose light did not travel far. They were a tiny world to themselves, the two girls, surrounded by lovely shadows, the beams and rafters shadowy overhead, the benches and implements shadowy down the studio.

"You are cosy enough here," said Gerald, going up to them.

There was a low brick fireplace full of fire, an old blue turkish rug, the little oak table with the lamp and the white-and-blue cloth and the dessert, and Gudrun making coffee in an odd brass coffee-maker, and Winifred scalding a little milk in a tiny saucepan.

"Have you had coffee?" said Gudrun.

"I have—but I'll have some more with you," he replied.

"Then you must have it in a glass—there are only two cups," said Winifred.

"It is the same to me," he said, taking a chair and coming into the charmed circle of the girls. How happy they were, how cosy and glamorous it was with them, in a world of lofty shadows! The outside world, in which he had been transacting funeral business all the day, was completely wiped out. In an instant he snuffed glamour and magic.

They had all their things very dainty, two odd and lovely little cups, scarlet and solid gilt, and a little black jug with scarlet discs, and the curious coffee-machine, whose spirit-flame flowed steadily, almost invisible. There was the effect of rather sinister richness, in which Gerald at once escaped himself.

They all sat down, and Gudrun carefully poured out the coffee.

"Will you have milk?" she asked, calmly, yet nervously poising the little black jug with its big red dots. She was always so completely controlled, yet so bitterly nervous.

"No, I won't," he replied.

So, with a curious humility, she placed him the little cup of coffee, and herself took the awkward tumbler. She seemed to want to serve him.

"Why don't you give me the glass—it is so clumsy for you," he said. He would much rather have had it, and seen her daintily served. But she was silent, pleased with the disparity, with her self-abasement.

"You are quite *en ménage*," he said.

"Yes. We aren't really at home to visitors," said Winifred.

"You're not? Then I'm an intruder."

For once he felt his conventional dress was out of place, he was an outsider.

Gudrun was very quiet. She did not feel drawn to talk to him. At this stage, silence was best—or mere light words. It was best to leave serious things aside. So they talked gaily and lightly, till they heard the man below lead out the horse, and call it to "back—back!" into the dog-cart that was to take Gudrun home. So she put on her things, and shook hands with Gerald, without once meeting his eyes. And she was gone.

The funeral was detestable. Afterwards, at the tea-table, the daughters kept saying—"He was a good father to us—the best father in the world"—or else "We shan't easily find another man as good as father was."

Gerald acquiesced in all this. It was the right conventional attitude, and, as far as the world went, he believed in the conventions. He took it as a matter of course. But Winifred hated everything, and hid in the studio, and cried her heart out, and wished Gudrun would come.

Luckily everybody was going away. The Criches never stayed long at home. By dinner-time, Gerald was left quite alone. Even Winifred was carried off to London for a few days, with her sister Laura.

But when Gerald was really left alone, he could not bear it. One day passed by, and another. And all the time he was like a man hung in chains over the edge of an abyss. Struggle as he might, he could not turn himself to the solid earth, he could not get footing. He was suspended on the edge of a void, writhing. Whatever he thought of, was the abyss—whether it were friends or strangers, or work or play, it all showed him only the same bottomless void, in which his heart swung perishing. There was no escape, there was nothing to grasp hold of. He must writhe on the edge of the chasm, suspended in chains of invisible physical life.

At first he was quiet, he kept still, expecting the extremity to pass away, expecting to find himself released into the world of the living, after this extremity of penance. But it did not pass, and a crisis gained upon him.

As the evening of the third day came on, his heart rang with fear. He could not bear another night. Another night was coming on, for another night he was to be suspended in chains of physical life, over the bottomless pit of nothingness. And he could not bear it. He could not bear it. He was frightened deeply, and coldly, frightened in his soul. He did not believe in his own strength any more. He could not fall into this infinite void, and rise again. If he fell, he would be gone for ever. He must withdraw, he must seek reinforcements. He did not believe in his own single self, any further than this.

After dinner, faced with the ultimate experience of his own nothingness, he turned aside. He pulled on his boots, put on his coat, and set out to walk in the night.

It was dark and misty. He went through the wood, stumbling and feeling his way, to the Mill. Birkin was away. Good—he was half glad. He turned up the hill, and stumbled blindly over the wild slopes, having lost the path in the complete darkness. It was boring. Where was he going? No matter. He stumbled on till he came to a path again. Then he went on through another wood. His mind became dark, he went on automatically. Without thought or sensation, he stumbled unevenly on, out into the open again, fumbling for stiles, losing the path, and going along the hedges of the fields till he came to the outlet.

And at last he came to a high-road. It had distracted him to struggle blindly through the maze of darkness. But now, he must take a direction. And he did not even know where he was. But he must take a direction now. Nothing would be resolved by merely walking, walking away. He had to take a direction.

He stood still on the road, that was high in the utterly dark night, and he did not know where he was. It was a strange sensation: his heart beating, and ringed round with the utterly unknown darkness. So he stood for some time.

Then he heard footsteps, and saw a small, swinging light. He immediately went towards this. It was a miner.

"Can you tell me," he said, "where this road goes?"

"Road?—Ay, it goos ter Whatmore."

"Whatmore! Oh thank you, that's right. I thought I was wrong. Goodnight."

"Goodnight," replied the broad voice of the miner.

Gerald guessed where he was. At least, when he came to Whatmore, he would know. He was glad to be on a high-road. He walked forward as in a sleep of decision.

That was Whatmore village—? Yes, the Kings Head—and there the hall gates. He descended the steep hill almost running. Winding through the hollow, he passed the Grammar School, and came to Willey Green Church. The churchyard! He halted.

Then in another moment he had clambered up the wall and was going among the graves. Even in this darkness he could see the heaped pallor of old white flowers at his feet. This then was the grave. He stooped down. The flowers were cold and clammy: there was a raw scent of chrysanthemums and tube-roses, deadened. He felt the clay beneath, and shrank, it was so horribly cold and sticky. He stood away in revulsion.

Here was one centre then, here in the complete darkness beside the unseen, raw grave. But there was nothing for him here. No, he had nothing to stay here for. He felt as if some of the clay were sticking cold and unclean, on his heart. No, enough of this.

Where then?—home? Never! It was no use going there. That was less than no use. It could not be done. There was somewhere else to go. Where?

A dangerous resolve formed in his heart, like a fixed idea. There was Gudrun.—She would be safe in her home.—But he could get at her—he *would* get at her. He would not go back tonight till he had come to her, if it cost him his life. He staked his all on this throw.

He set off walking straight across the fields towards Beldover. It was so dark, nobody could ever see him. His feet were wet and cold, heavy with clay. But he went on persistently, like a wind, straight forward, as if to his fate. There were great gaps in his consciousness. He was conscious that he was at Winthorpe hamlet, but quite unconscious how he had got there. And then, as in a dream, he was in the long street of Beldover, with its street-lamps.

There was a noise of voices, and of a door shutting loudly, and being barred, and of men talking in the night. The "Lord Nelson" had just closed, and the drinkers were going home. He had better ask one of these where she lived—for he did not know the side streets at all.

"Can you tell me where Somerset Drive is?" he asked of one of the uneven men.

"Where what?" replied the tipsy miner's voice.

"Somerset Drive."

"Somerset Drive!—I've heerd o' such a place, but I couldn't for my life say wheer it is.—Who might you be wanting?"

"Mr Brangwen—William Brangwen."

"William Brangwen—?—?"

"Who teaches at the Grammar School, at Willey Green—his daughter teaches there too."

"OO—O—O—Oh, Brangwen! *Now* I've got you. Of *course*, William Brangwen! Yes, Yes, he's got two lasses as teaches, aside hisself. Ay, that's him!—that's him!—Why certainly I know where he lives, back your life I do! Yi—*what* place do they ca' it?"

"Somerset Drive," repeated Gerald patiently. He knew his own colliers fairly well.

"Somerset Drive, for certain!" said the collier, swinging his arm as if catching something up. "Somerset Drive—yi!—I couldn't for my life lay hold o' the lercality o' the place. Yis, I know the place, to be sure I do—"

He turned unsteadily on his feet, and pointed up the dark, nigh-deserted road.

"You go up theer—an' you ta'e th' first—yi, th' first turnin' on your left—o' that side—past Withamses tuffy shop—"

"*I* know," said Gerald.

"Ay! You go down a bit, past wheer th' water-man lives—and then Somerset Drive, as they ca' it, branches off on 't right-hand side—an' there's nowt but three houses in it, no more than three, I believe—an' I'm a'most certain as theirs is th' last—th' last o' th' three—you see—"

"Thank you very much," said Gerald. "Goodnight."

And he started off, leaving the tipsy man there standing rooted.

Gerald went past the dark shops and houses, most of them sleeping now, and twisted round to the little blind road that ended on a field of darkness. He slowed down, as he neared his goal, not knowing how he should proceed. What if the house were closed in darkness?

But it was not. He saw a big lighted window, and heard voices, then a gate banged. His quick ears caught the sound of Birkin's voice, his keen eyes made out Birkin, with Ursula standing in a pale dress on the step of the garden path. Then Ursula stepped down, and came along the road, holding Birkin's arm.

Gerald went across into the darkness and they dawdled past him, talking happily, Birkin's voice low, Ursula's high and distinct. Gerald went quickly to the house.

The blinds were drawn before the big, lighted window of the dining-room. Looking up the path at the side, he could see the door left open, shedding a soft, coloured light from the hall lamp. He went quickly and silently up the path, and looked up into the hall. There were pictures on the walls, and the antlers of a stag—and the stairs going up on one side—and just near the foot of the stairs the half-opened door of the dining-room.

With heart drawn fine, Gerald stepped into the hall, whose floor was of coloured tiles, went quickly and looked into the large, pleasant room. In a chair by the fire, the father sat asleep, his head tilted back against the side of the big oak chimney piece, his ruddy face seen foreshortened, the nostrils open, the mouth fallen a little. It would take the merest sound to wake him.

Gerald stood a second suspended. He glanced down the passage behind him. It was all dark. Again he was suspended. Then he went swiftly upstairs. His senses were so finely, almost supernaturally keen, that he seemed to cast his own will over the half-unconscious house.

He came to the first landing. There he stood, scarcely breathing. Again, corresponding to the door below, there was a door ajar. That would be the mother's room. He could hear her moving about in the candle-light. She would be expecting her husband to come up. He looked along the dark landing.

Then silently, on infinitely careful feet, he went along the passage, feeling the wall with the extreme tips of his fingers. There was a door. He stood and listened. He could hear two people's breathing. It was not that. He went stealthily forward. There was another door, slightly open. The room was in darkness. Empty. Then there was the bathroom, he could smell the soap and the heat. Then at the end was another bedroom—one soft breathing. This was she.

With an almost occult carefulness he turned the door handle, and opened the door an inch. It creaked slightly. Then he opened it another inch—then another. His heart did not beat, he seemed to create a silence about himself, an obliviousness.

He was in the room. Still the sleeper breathed softly. It was very dark. He felt his way forward inch by inch, with his feet and hands. He touched the bed, he could hear the sleeper. He drew nearer, bending close as if his eyes would disclose whatever there was. And then, very near his face, to his fear, he saw the round, dark head of a boy.

He recovered, turned round, saw the door afar, a faint light revealed. And he retreated swiftly, drew the door to without fastening it, and passed rapidly down the passage. At the head of the stairs he hesitated. There was still time to flee.

But it was unthinkable. He would maintain his will. He turned past the door of the parental bedroom like a shadow, and was climbing the second flight of stairs. They creaked under his weight—it was exasperating. Ah what disaster, if the mother's door opened just beneath him, and she saw him! It would have to be, if it were so. He held the control still.

He was not quite up these stairs when he heard a quick running of feet below, the outer door was closed and locked, he heard Ursula's voice, then the father's sleepy exclamation. He pressed on swiftly to the upper landing.

Again a door was ajar, a room was empty. Feeling his way forward, with the tips of his fingers, travelling rapidly, like a blind man, anxious lest Ursula should come upstairs, he found another door. There, with his preternaturally fine senses alert, he listened. He heard someone moving in bed. This would be she.

Softly now, like one who has only one sense, the tactile sense, he turned the latch. It clicked. He held still. The bed-clothes rustled. His heart did not beat. Then again he drew the latch back, and very gently pushed the door. It made a sticking noise as it gave.

"Ursula?" said Gudrun's voice, frightened. He quickly opened the door and pushed it behind him.

"Is it you, Ursula?" came Gudrun's frightened voice. He heard her sitting up in bed. In another moment she would scream.

"No, it's me," he said, feeling his way towards her. "It is I, Gerald."

She sat motionless in her bed in sheer astonishment. She was too astonished, too much taken by surprise, even to be afraid.

"Gerald!" she echoed, in blank amazement.

He had found his way to the bed, and his outstretched hand touched her warm breast, blindly. She shrank away.

"Let me make a light," she said, springing out.

He stood perfectly motionless. He heard her touch the match-box, he heard her fingers in their movement. Then he saw her in the light of a match, which she held to the candle. The light rose in the room, then sank to a small dimness, as the flame sank down on the candle, before it mounted again.

She looked at him, as he stood near the other side of the bed. His cap was pulled low over his brow, his black overcoat was buttoned close up to his chin. His face was strange and luminous. He was inevitable as a supernatural being. When she had seen him, she knew. She knew there was something fatal in the situation, and she must accept it. Yet she must challenge him.

"How did you come up?" she asked.

"I walked up the stairs—the door was open." She looked at him.

"I haven't closed this door, either," he said. She walked swiftly across the room, and closed her door, softly, and locked it. Then she came back.

She was wonderful, with startled eyes and flushed cheeks, and her plait of hair rather short and thick down her back, and her long, fine white night-dress falling to her feet.

She saw that his boots were all clayey, even his trousers were plastered with clay. And she wondered if he had made footprints all the way up. He was a very strange figure, standing in her bedroom, near the tossed bed.

"Why have you come?" she asked, almost querulous.

"I wanted to," he replied.

And this she could see, from his face. It was fate.

"You are so muddy," she said, in distaste, but gently.

He looked down at his feet.

"I was walking in the dark," he replied. But he felt vividly elated. There was a pause. He stood on one side of the tumbled bed, she on the other. He did not even take his cap from his brows.

"And what do you want of me," she challenged.

He looked aside, and did not answer. Save for the extreme beauty and mystic attractiveness of his distinct, strange face, she would have sent him away. But his face was too wonderful and undiscovered to her. It fascinated her with the fascination of pure beauty, cast a spell on her, like nostalgia, an ache.

"What do you want of me?" she repeated, in an estranged voice.

He pulled off his cap, in a movement of dream-liberation, and went across to her. But he could not touch her, because she stood barefoot in her night-dress, and he was muddy and damp. Her eyes, wide and large and wondering, watched him, and asked him the ultimate question.

"I came—because I must," he said. "Why do you ask?"

She looked at him in doubt and wonder.

"I must ask," she said.

He shook his head slightly.

"There is no answer," he replied, with strange vacancy.

There was about him a curious, and almost godlike air of simplicity and naive directness. He reminded her of an apparition, the young Hermes.

"But why did you come to me?" she persisted.

"Because—it has to be so.—If there weren't you in the world, then *I* shouldn't be in the world, either."

She stood looking at him, with large, wide, wondering, stricken eyes. His eyes were looking steadily into hers all the time, and he seemed fixed in an odd supernatural steadfastness. She sighed. She was lost now. She had no choice.

"Won't you take off your boots," she said. "They must be wet."

He dropped his cap on a chair, unbuttoned his overcoat, lifting up his chin to unfasten the throat buttons. His short, keen hair was ruffled. He was so beautifully blond, like wheat. He pulled off his overcoat.

Quickly he pulled off his jacket, pulled loose his black tie, and was unfastening his studs, which were headed each with a pearl. She listened, watching, hoping no one would hear the starched linen crackle. It seemed to snap like pistol-shots.

He had come for vindication. She let him hold her in his arms, clasp her close against him. He found in her an infinite relief. Into her he poured all his pent-up darkness and corrosive death, and he was whole again. It was wonderful, marvellous, it was a miracle. This was the ever-recurrent miracle of his life, at the knowledge of which he was lost in an ecstasy of relief and wonder. And she, subject, received him as a vessel filled with his bitter potion of death. She had no power at this crisis to resist. The terrible frictional violence of death filled her, and she received it in an ecstasy of subjection, in throes of acute, violent sensation.

As he drew nearer to her, he plunged deeper into her enveloping soft warmth, a wonderful creative heat that penetrated his veins and gave him life again. He felt himself dissolving and sinking to rest in the bath of her living strength. It seemed as if her heart in her breast were a second unconquerable sun, into the glow and creative strength of which he plunged further and further. All his veins, that were murdered and lacerated, healed softly as life came pulsing in, stealing invisibly in to him as if it were the all-powerful effluence of the sun. His blood, which seemed to have been drawn back into death, came ebbing on the return, surely, beautifully, powerfully.

He felt his limbs growing fuller and flexible with life, his body gained an unknown strength. He was a man again, strong and rounded. And he was a child, so soothed and restored and full of gratitude.

And she, she was the great bath of life, he worshipped her. Mother and substance of all life she was. And he, child and man, received of her and was made whole. His pure body was almost killed. But the miraculous, soft effluence of her breast suffused over him, over his seared, damaged brain, like a healing lymph, like a soft, soothing flow of life itself, perfect as if he were bathed in the womb again.

His brain was hurt, seared, the tissue was as if destroyed. He had not known how hurt he was, how his tissue, the very tissue of his brain was damaged by the corrosive flood of death. Now, as the healing lymph of her effluence flowed through him, he knew how destroyed he was, like a plant whose tissue is burst from inwards by a frost.

He buried his small, hard head between her breasts, and pressed her breasts against him with his hands. And she with quivering hands pressed his head against her, as he lay suffused out, and she lay fully conscious. The lovely, creative warmth flooded through him like a sleep of fecundity within the womb. Ah if only she would grant him the flow of this living effluence, he would be restored, he would be complete again. He was afraid she would deny him before it was finished. Like a child at the breast, he cleaved intensely to her, and she could not put him away. And his seared, ruined membrane relaxed, softened, that which was seared and stiff and blasted yielded again, became soft and flexible, palpitating with new life. He was infinitely grateful, as to God, or as an infant is at its mother's breast. He was glad and grateful like a delirium, as he felt his own wholeness come over him again, as he felt the full, unutterable sleep coming over him, the sleep of complete exhaustion and restoration.

But Gudrun lay wide awake, destroyed into perfect consciousness. She lay motionless, with wide eyes staring motionless into the darkness, whilst he was sunk away in sleep, his arms round her.

She seemed to lie hearing waves break on a hidden shore, long, slow, gloomy waves breaking with the rhythm of fate, so monotonously that it seemed eternal. This endless breaking of slow, sullen waves of fate held her like a possession, whilst she lay with dark, wide eyes looking into the darkness. She could see so far, as far as eternity—yet she saw nothing. She was suspended in perfect consciousness—and of what was she conscious?

This mood of extremity, when she lay staring into eternity, utterly suspended, and conscious of everything, to the last limits, passed, and left her uneasy. She had lain so long motionless. She moved, she became self-conscious. She wanted to look at him, to see him.

But she dared not make a light, because she knew he would wake, and she did not want to break his perfect sleep, that she knew he had got of her.

She disengaged herself, softly, and rose up a little to look at him. There was a faint light, it seemed to her, in the room. She could just distinguish his features, as he slept the perfect sleep. In this darkness, she seemed to see him so distinctly. But he was far off, in another world. Ah, she could shriek with torment, he was so far off, and perfected, in another world. She seemed to look at him as at a pebble far away under clear, dark water. And here was she, left with all the anguish of consciousness, whilst he was sunk deep into the other element of mindless, remote, living shadow-gleam. He was beautiful, far-off, and perfected. They would never be together. Ah, this awful, inhuman distance which would always be interposed between her and the other being!

There was nothing to do but to lie still and endure. She felt an overwhelming tenderness for him, and a dark understirring of jealous hatred, that he should lie so perfect and immune, in an otherworld, whilst she was tormented with violent wakefulness, cast out in the outer darkness.

She lay in intense and vivid consciousness, an exhausting superconsciousness. The church clock struck the hours, it seemed to her, in quick succession. She heard them distinctly in the tension of her vivid consciousness. And he slept as if time were one moment, unchanging and unmoving.

She was exhausted, wearied. Yet she must continue in this state of violent active superconsciousness. She was conscious of everything—her childhood, her girlhood, all the forgotten incidents, all the unrealised influences and all the happenings she had not understood, pertaining to herself, to her family, to her friends, her lovers, her acquaintances, everybody. It was as if she drew a glittering rope of knowledge out of the sea of darkness, drew and drew and drew it out of the fathomless depths of the past, and still it did not come to an end, there was no end to it, she must haul and haul at the rope of glittering conscious, pull it out phosphorescent from the endless depths of the unconsciousness, till she was weary, aching, exhausted, and fit to break, and yet she had not done.

Ah, if only she might wake him! She turned uneasily. When could she rouse him and send him away? When could she disturb him? And she relapsed into her activity of automatic consciousness, that would never end.

But the time was drawing near when she could wake him. It was like a release. The clock had struck four, outside in the night. Thank God the night had passed almost away. At five he must go, and she would be released. Then she could relax and fill her own place. Now she was driven up against his perfect sleeping motion like a knife white-hot on a grindstone. There was something monstrous about him, about his juxta-position against her.

The last hour was the longest. And yet, at last, it passed. Her heart leapt with relief—yes, there was the slow, strong stroke of the church clock—at last, after this night of eternity. She waited to catch each slow, fatal reverberation—"Three———four———*five*!" There, it was finished. A weight rolled off her.

She raised herself, leaned over him tenderly, and kissed him. She was sad to wake him. After a few moments, she kissed him again. But he did not stir. The darling, he was so deep in sleep! What a shame to take him out of it. She let him lie a little longer. But he must go—he must really go.

With full over-tenderness she took his face between her hands, and kissed his eyes. The eyes opened, he remained motionless, looking at her. Her heart stood still. To hide her face from his dreadful opened eyes, in the darkness, she bent down and kissed him, whispering:

"You must go, my love."

But she was sick with terror, sick.

He put his arms round her. Her heart sank.

"But you must go, my love. It's late."

"What time is it?" he said.

Strange, his man's voice. She quivered. It was an intolerable oppression to her.

"Past five o'clock," she said.

But he only closed his arms round her again. Her heart cried within her in torture. She disengaged herself firmly.

"You really must go," she said.

"Not for a minute," he said.

She lay still, nestling against him, but unyielding.

"Not for a minute," he repeated, clasping her closer.

"Yes," she said, unyielding. "I'm afraid if you stay any longer."

There was a certain coldness in her voice that made him release her, and she broke away, rose and lit the candle. That then was the end.

He got up. He was warm and full of life and desire. Yet he felt a little bit ashamed, humiliated, putting on his clothes before her, in the candle-light. For he felt revealed, exposed to her, at a time when she was in some way against him. It was all very difficult to understand. He dressed himself quickly, without collar or tie. Still he felt full and complete, perfected.— She thought it humiliating to see a man dressing: the ridiculous shirt, the ridiculous trousers and braces. But again an idea saved her.

"It is like a workman getting up to go to work," thought Gudrun. "And I am like a workman's wife." But an ache like nausea was upon her: a nausea of him.

He pushed his collar and tie into his overcoat pocket. Then he sat down and pulled on his boots. They were sodden, as were his socks and trouser-bottoms. But he himself was quick and warm.

"Perhaps you ought to have put your boots on downstairs," she said.

At once, without answering, he pulled them off again, and stood holding them in his hand. She had thrust her feet into slippers, and flung a loose robe round her. She was ready. She looked at him as he stood waiting, his black coat buttoned to the chin, his cap pulled down, his boots in his hand. And the passionate almost hateful fascination revived in her for a moment. It was not exhausted. His face was so warm-looking, wide-eyed and full of newness, so perfect. She felt old, old. She went to him heavily, to be kissed. He kissed her quickly. She wished his warm, expressionless beauty did not so fatally put a spell on her, compel her and subjugate her. It was a burden upon her, that she resented but could not escape. Yet when she looked at his straight, man's brows, and at his rather small, well-shapen nose, and at his blue, indifferent eyes, she knew her passion for him was not yet satisfied, perhaps never to be satisfied. Only now she was weary, with an ache like nausea. She wanted him gone.

They went downstairs quickly. It seemed they made a prodigious noise. He followed her as, wrapped in her vivid green wrap, she preceded him with the light. She suffered badly with fear, lest her people should be roused. He hardly cared. He did not care now who knew.—And she hated this in him. One *must* be cautious: one must preserve oneself.

She led the way to the kitchen. It was neat and tidy, as the woman had left it. He looked up at the clock—twenty minutes past five! Then he sat down on a chair to put on his boots. She waited, watching his every movement. She wanted it to be over, it was a great nervous strain on her.

He stood up—she unbolted the back door, and looked out. A cold, raw night, not yet dawn, with a piece of a moon in the vague sky. She was glad she need not go out.

"Goodbye then," he murmured.

"I'll come to the gate," she said.

And again she hurried on in front, to warn him of the steps. And at the gate, once more she stood on the step whilst he stood below her.

"Goodbye," she whispered.

He kissed her, dutifully, and turned away. She suffered torments hearing his firm tread going so distinctly down the road. Ah, the insensitiveness of that firm tread!

She closed the gate, and crept quickly and noiselessly back to bed. When she was in her room, and the door closed, and all safe, she breathed freely, and a great weight fell off her. She nestled down in bed, in the groove his body had made, in the warmth he had left. And, excited, worn-out, yet still satisfied, she fell soon into a deep, heavy sleep.

Gerald walked quickly through the raw darkness of the coming dawn. He met nobody. His mind was beautifully still and thoughtless, like a still pool, and his body full and warm and rich. He went quickly along towards Shortlands, in a grateful self-sufficiency.

Chapter XXV

Marriage or Not

The Brangwen family was going to move from Beldover. It was necessary now for the father to be in town.

Birkin had taken out a marriage licence, yet Ursula deferred from day to day. She would not fix any definite time—she still wavered. Her month's notice to leave the Grammar School was in its third week. Christmas was not far off.

Gerald waited for the Ursula–Birkin marriage. It was something crucial to him.

"Shall we make it a double-barrelled affair?" he said to Birkin one day.

"Who for the second shot?" asked Birkin.

"Gudrun and me," said Gerald, the venturesome twinkle in his eyes.

Birkin looked at him steadily, as if somewhat taken aback.

"Serious—or joking?" he asked.

"Oh, serious.—Shall I? Shall Gudrun and I rush in along with you?"

"Do by all means," said Birkin.—"I didn't know you'd got that length."

"What length?" said Gerald, looking at the other man, and laughing. "Oh yes, we've gone all the lengths."

"There remains to put it on a broad social basis, and to achieve a high moral purpose," said Birkin.

"Something like that: the length and breadth and height of it," replied Gerald, smiling.

"Oh well," said Birkin, "it's a very admirable step to take, I should say."

Gerald looked at him closely.

"Why aren't you enthusiastic?" he asked. "I thought you were such dead nuts on marriage."

Birkin lifted his shoulders.

"One might as well be dead nuts on noses.—There are all sorts of noses, snub and otherwise—"

Gerald laughed.

"And all sorts of marriage, also snub and otherwise?" he said.

"That's it."

"And you think if I marry, it will be snub?" asked Gerald quizzically, his head a little on one side.

322

Birkin laughed quickly.

"How do I know what it will be!" he said. "Don't lambaste me with my own parallels—"

Gerald pondered a while.

"But I should like to know your opinion, exactly," he said.

"On your marriage?—or marrying?—why should you want my opinion? I've got no opinions. I'm not interested in legal marriage, one way or another.—It's a mere question of convenience."

Still Gerald watched him closely.

"More than that, I think," he said seriously. "However you may be bored by the ethics of marriage, yet really to marry, in one's own personal case, is something critical, final—"

"You mean there is something final in going to the registrar with a woman?"

"If you're coming back with her, I do," said Gerald. "It is in some way irrevocable."

"Yes, I agree," said Birkin.

"No matter how one regards legal marriage, yet to enter into the married state, in one's own personal instance, is final—"

"I believe it is," said Birkin, "somewhere."

"The question remains then, should one do it," said Gerald.

Birkin watched him narrowly, with amused eyes.

"You are like Lord Bacon, Gerald," he said. "You argue it like a lawyer—or like Hamlet's to-be-or-not-to-be.—If I were you I would *not* marry: but ask Gudrun, not me. You're not marrying me, are you?"

Gerald did not heed the latter part of this speech.

"Yes," he said, "one must consider it coldly.—It is something critical.—One comes to the point where one must take a step in one direction or another. And marriage is one direction—"

"And what is the other?" asked Birkin quickly.

Gerald looked up at him with hot, strangely-conscious eyes, that the other man could not understand.

"I can't say," he replied. "If I knew *that*—." He moved uneasily on his feet, and did not finish.

"You mean if you knew the alternative?" asked Birkin. "And since you don't know it, marriage is a *pis aller*."

Gerald looked up at Birkin with the same hot, constrained eyes.

"One does have the feeling that marriage is a *pis aller*," he admitted.

"Then don't do it," said Birkin. "I tell you," he went on, "the same as I've said before, marriage in the old sense seems to me repulsive. *Egoïsme à deux* is nothing to it. It's a sort of tacit hunting in couples: the world all in couples, each couple in its own little house, watching its own little interests, and stewing in its own little privacy—it's the most repulsive thing on earth."

"I quite agree," said Gerald. "There's something inferior about it. But as I say, what's the alternative."

"One should avoid this *home* instinct. It's not an instinct, it's a habit of cowardliness. One should never have a *home*."

"I agree really," said Gerald. "But there's no alternative."

"We've got to find one.—I do believe in a permanent union between a man and a woman. Chopping about is merely an exhaustive process.—But a permanent relation between a man and a woman isn't the last word—it certainly isn't."

"Quite," said Gerald.

"In fact," said Birkin, "because the relation between man and woman is made the supreme and exclusive relationship, that's where all the tightness and meanness and insufficiency comes in."

"Yes, I believe you," said Gerald.

"You've got to take down the love-and-marriage ideal from its pedestal. We want something broader.—I believe in the *additional* perfect relationship between man and man—additional to marriage."

"I can never see how they can be the same," said Gerald.

"Not the same—but equally important, equally creative, equally sacred, if you like."

Gerald moved uneasily.—"You know, I can't feel that," said he. "Surely there can never be anything as strong between man and man as sex love is between man and woman. Nature doesn't provide the basis."

"Well, of course, I think she does. And I don't think we shall ever be happy till we establish ourselves on this basis. You've got to get rid of the *exclusiveness* of married love. And you've got to admit the unadmitted love of man for man. It makes for a greater freedom for everybody, a greater power of individuality both in men and women."

"I know," said Gerald, "you believe something like that. Only I can't *feel* it, you see." He put his hand on Birkin's arm, with a sort of deprecating affection. And he smiled as if triumphantly.

He was ready to be doomed. Marriage was like a doom to him. He was willing to condemn himself in marriage, to become like a convict condemned to the mines of the underworld, living no life in the sun, but having a dreadful subterranean activity. He was willing to accept this. And marriage was the seal of his condemnation. He was willing to be sealed thus in the underworld, like a soul damned but living forever in damnation.—But he would not make any pure relationship with any other soul. He could not. Marriage was not the committing of himself into a relationship with Gudrun. It was a committing of himself in acceptance of the established world, he would accept the established order, in which he did not livingly believe, and then he would retreat to the underworld for his life. This he would do.

The other way was to accept Rupert's offer of love, to enter into the bond of pure trust and love with the other man, and then subsequently with the woman. If he pledged himself with the man he would later be able to pledge himself with the woman: not merely in legal marriage, but in absolute, mystic marriage.

Yet he could not accept the offer. There was a numbness upon him, a numbness either of unborn, absent volition, or of atrophy. Perhaps it was the absence of volition. For he was strangely elated at Rupert's offer. Yet he was still more glad to reject it, not to be committed.

Chapter XXVI

A Chair

There was a jumble market every Monday afternoon in the old market-place in town. Ursula and Birkin strayed down there one afternoon. They had been talking of furniture, and they wanted to see if there was any fragment they would like to buy, amid the heaps of rubbish collected on the cobble-stones.

The old market square was not very large, a mere bare patch of granite setts, usually, with a few fruit-stalls under a wall. It was in a poor quarter of the town. Meagre houses stood down one side, there was a hosiery factory, a great blank with myriad oblong windows, at the end, a street of little shops with flagstone pavement down the other side, and, for a crowning monument, the public baths, of new red brick, with a clock-tower. The people who moved about seemed stumpy and sordid, the air seemed to smell rather dirty, there was a sense of many mean streets ramifying off into warrens of meanness. Now and again a great chocolate-and-yellow tram-car ground round a difficult bend under the hosiery factory.

Ursula was superficially thrilled when she found herself out among the common people, in the jumbled place piled with old bedding, heaps of old iron, shabby crockery in pale lots, muffled lots of unthinkable clothing. She and Birkin went unwillingly down the narrow aisles between the rusty wares. He was looking at the goods, she at the people.

She excitedly watched a young woman, who was going to have a baby, and who was turning over a mattress and making a young man, down-at-heel and dejected, feel it also. So secretive and active and anxious the young woman seemed, so reluctant, slinking, the young man. He was going to marry her because she was having a child.

When they had felt the mattress, the young woman asked the old man seated on a stool among his wares, how much it was. He told her, and she turned to the young man. The latter was ashamed and self-conscious, he turned his face away, though he left his body standing there, and muttered aside. And again the young woman anxiously and actively fingered the mattress and added up in her mind and bargained with the old, unclean man. All the while, the young man stood by, shamefaced and down-at-heel, submitting.

"Look," said Birkin, "there is a pretty chair."

"Charming!" cried Ursula. "Oh charming."

It was an arm-chair of simple wood, probably birch, but of such fine delicacy of grace, standing there on the sordid stones, it almost brought tears to the eyes. It was square in shape, of the purest, slender lines, and four short lines of wood in the back, that reminded Ursula of harp-strings.

"It was once," said Birkin, "gilded—and it had a cane seat. Somebody has nailed this wooden seat in.—Look, here is a trifle of the red that underlay the gilt. The rest is all black, except where the wood is worn pure and glossy.—It is the fine unity of the lines that is so attractive—look, how they run and meet and counteract.—But of course the wooden seat is wrong—it destroys the perfect lightness and unity in tension the cane gave.—I like it though—"

"Ah yes," said Ursula, "so do I."

"How much is it?" Birkin asked the man.

"Ten shillings."

"And you will send it—?"

It was bought.

"So beautiful, so pure!" Birkin said. "It almost breaks my heart." They walked along between the heaps of rubbish. "My beloved country—it had something to express even when it made that chair."

"And hasn't it now?" asked Ursula. She was always angry when he took this tone.

"No, it hasn't.—When I see that clear, beautiful chair, and I think of England, even Jane Austen's England—it had living thoughts to unfold even then, and pure happiness in unfolding them. And now, we can only fish among the rubbish heaps for the remnants of their old expression. There is no production in us now, only sordid and foul mechanicalness."

"It isn't true," cried Ursula. "Why must you always praise the past, at the expense of the present?—*Really*, I don't think so much of Jane Austen's England. It was materialistic enough, if you like—"

"It could afford to be materialistic," said Birkin, "because it had the power to be something other—which we haven't. We are materialistic because we haven't the power to be anything else—try as we may, we can't bring off anything but materialism: mechanism, the very soul of materialism."

Ursula was subdued into angry silence. She did not heed what he said. She was rebelling against something else.

"And I hate your past—I'm sick of it," she cried. "I believe I even hate that old chair, though it *is* beautiful.—It isn't *my* sort of beauty.—I wish it had been smashed up when its day was over, not left to preach the beloved past at us—I'm sick of the beloved past."

"Not so sick as I am of the accursed present," he said.

"Yes—just the same. I hate the present—but I don't want the past to take its place—I don't want that old chair."

He was rather angry for a moment. Then he looked at the sky shining beyond the tower of the public baths, and he seemed to get over it all. He laughed.

"All right," he said, "then let us not have it. I'm sick of it all, too. At any rate one can't go on living on the old bones of beauty."

"One can't," she cried. "I *don't* want old things."

"The truth is, we don't want things at all," he replied. "The thought of a house and furniture of my own is hateful to me."

This startled her, for a moment. Then she replied:

"So it is to me.—But one must live somewhere."

"Not somewhere—anywhere," he said. "One should just live anywhere—not have a definite place. I don't want a definite place.—As soon as you get a room, and it is *complete*, you want to run from it.—Now my rooms at the Mill are quite complete, I want them at the bottom of the sea. It is a horrible tyranny of a fixed milieu, where each piece of furniture is a commandment-stone."

She clung to his arm as they walked away from the market.

"But what are we going to do," she said. "We must live somehow. And I do want some beauty in my surroundings. I want a sort of natural *grandeur* even, *splendour*."

"You'll never get it in houses and furniture—or even clothes. Houses and furniture and clothes, they are all terms of an old base world, a detestable society of man. And if you have a Tudor house and old, beautiful furniture, it is only the past perpetuated on top of you, horrible.—And if you have a perfect modern house done for you by Poiret, it is something else perpetuated on top of you. It is all horrible. It is all possessions, possessions, bullying you and turning you into a general-isation.—You have to be like Rodin, Michael Angelo, and leave a piece of raw rock unfinished to your figure. You must leave your surroundings sketchy, unfinished, so that you are never contained, never confined, never dominated from the outside."

She stood in the street contemplating.

"And we are never to have a complete place of our own—never a home?" she said.

"Pray God, in this world, no," he answered.

"But there's only this world," she objected.

He spread out his hands with a gesture of indifference.

"Meanwhile, then, we'll avoid having things of our own," he said.

"But you've just bought a chair," she said.

"I can tell the man I don't want it," he replied.

She pondered again. Then a queer little movement twitched her face.

"No," she said, "we don't want it. I'm sick of old things."

"New ones as well," he said.

They retraced their steps.

There, in front of some furniture, stood the young couple, the woman who was going to have a baby, and the narrow-faced youth. She was fair, rather short, stout. He was of medium height, attractively built. His dark hair fell sideways over his brow, from under his cap, he stood strangely aloof, like one of the damned.

"Let us give it to *them*," whispered Ursula. "Look, they are getting a home together."

"*I* won't aid and abet them in it," he said petulantly, instantly sympathising with the aloof, furtive youth, against the active, procreant female.

"Oh yes," cried Ursula. "It's right for them—there's nothing else, for them."

"Very well," said Birkin, "you offer it them—I'll watch."

Ursula went rather nervously to the young couple, who were discussing an iron washstand—or rather, the man was glancing furtively and wonderingly, like a prisoner, at the abominable article, whilst the woman was arguing.

"We bought a chair," said Ursula, "and we don't want it. Would you have it? We should be glad if you would."

The young couple looked round on her, not believing that she could be addressing them.

"Would you care for it?" repeated Ursula. "It's really *very* pretty—but—but—" she smiled rather dazzlingly.

The young couple only stared at her, and looked significantly at each other, to know what to do. And the man curiously obliterated himself, as if he could make himself invisible, as a rat can.

"We wanted to *give* it you," explained Ursula, now overcome with confusion and dread of them. She was attracted by the young man. He was a still, mindless creature, hardly a man at all, a creature that the towns have produced, strangely pure-bred and fine in one sense, furtive, quick, subtle. His lashes were dark and long and fine over his eyes, that had no mind in them, only a dreadful kind of subject, inward consciousness, glazed and dark. His dark brows, and all his lines, were finely drawn. He would be a dreadful, but wonderful lover to a woman, so marvellously contributed. His legs would be marvellously subtle and alive, under the shapeless trousers, he had some of the fineness and stillness and silkiness of a dark-eyed, silent rat.

Ursula had apprehended him with a fine *frisson* of attraction. The full-built woman was staring offensively. Again Ursula forgot him.

"Won't you have the chair?" she said.

The man looked at her with a sideways look of appreciation, yet far-off, almost insolent. The woman drew herself up. There was a certain coster-monger richness about her. She did not know what Ursula was after, she was on her guard, hostile. Birkin approached, smiling wickedly at seeing Ursula so nonplussed and frightened.

"What's the matter?" he said, smiling.

His eyelids had dropped slightly, there was about him the same suggestive, mocking secrecy that was in the bearing of the two city creatures.—The man jerked his head a little on one side, indicating Ursula, and said, with curious amiable, jeering warmth:

"What she warnt?—Eh!" An odd smile writhed his lips.

Birkin looked at him from under his slack, ironical eyelids.

"To give you a chair—that—with the label on it," he said, pointing.

The man looked at the object indicated. There was a curious hostility in male, outlawed understanding between the two men.

"What's she warnt to give it *us* for, guvnor," he replied, in a tone of free intimacy that insulted Ursula.

"Thought you'd like it—it's a pretty chair. We bought it, and don't want it. No need for you to have it, don't be frightened," said Birkin, with a wry smile.

The man glanced up at him, half inimical, half recognising.

"Why don't you want it for yourselves, if you've just bought it?" asked the woman coolly. "'Taint good enough for you, now you've had a look at it.—Frightened it's got something in it, eh?"

She was looking at Ursula, admiringly, but with some resentment.

"I'd never thought of that," said Birkin. "But no, the wood's too thin everywhere."

"You see," said Ursula, her face luminous and pleased. "*We* are just going to get married, and we thought we'd buy things. Then we decided, just now, that we wouldn't have furniture, we'd go abroad."

The full built, slightly blowsy city girl looked at the fine face of the other woman, with appreciation. They appreciated each other. The youth stood aside, his face expressionless and timeless, the thin line of the black moustache drawn strangely suggestive over his rather wide, closed mouth. He was impassive, abstract, like some dark suggestive presence, a gutter-presence.

"It's all right to be some folks," said the city girl, turning to her own young man. He did not look at her, but he smiled with the lower part of his face, putting his head aside in an odd gesture of assent. His eyes were unchanging, glazed with darkness.

"Cawsts something to chynge your mind," he said, in an incredibly low accent.

"Only ten shillings this time," said Birkin.

The man looked up at him with a grimace of a smile, furtive, unsure.

"Cheap at 'arf a quid, guvnor," he said. "Not like getting divawced."

"We're not married yet," said Birkin.

"No, no more aren't we," said the young woman loudly. "But we shall be, a Saturday."

Again she looked at the young man with a determined, protective look, at once overbearing and very gentle. He grinned sickily, turning away his head. She had got his manhood, but Lord, what did he care! He had a strange furtive pride and slinking singleness.

"Good luck to you," said Birkin.

"Same to you," said the young woman. Then, rather tentatively: "When's yours coming off, then?"

Birkin looked round at Ursula.

"It's for the lady to say," he replied. "We go to the registrar the moment she's ready."

Ursula laughed, covered with confusion and bewilderment.

"No 'urry," said the young man, grinning suggestive.

"Oh, don't break your neck to get there," said the young woman. "'Slike when you're dead—you're a long time married."

The young man turned aside as if this hit him.

"The longer the better, let us hope," said Birkin.

"That's it, guvnor," said the young man admiringly. "Enjoy it while it larsts—niver whip a dead donkey."

"Only when he's shamming dead," said the young woman, looking at her young man with caressive tenderness of authority.

"Aw, there's a difference," he said satirically.

"What about the chair?" said Birkin.

"Yes, all right," said the woman.

They trailed off to the dealer, the handsome but abject young fellow hanging a little aside.

"That's it," said Birkin. "Will you take it with you, or have the address altered?"

"Oh, Fred can carry it. Make him do what he can for the dear old 'ome."

"Mike use of 'im," said Fred, grimly humorous, as he took the chair from the dealer. His movements were graceful, yet curiously abject, slinking.

"'Ere's mother's cosy chair," he said. "Warnts a cushion."

And he stood it down on the market stones.

"Don't you think it's pretty?" laughed Ursula.

"Oh, I do," said the young woman.

"'Ave a sit in it, you'll wish you'd kept it," said the young man.

Ursula promptly sat down in the middle of the market-place.

"Awfully comfortable," she said. "But rather hard.—You try it." She invited the young man to a seat. But he turned uncouthly, awkwardly aside, glancing up at her with quick bright eyes, oddly suggestive, like a quick, live rat.

"Don't spoil him," said the young woman. "He's not used to arm-chairs, 'e isn't."

The young man turned away, and said, with averted grin:

"Only warnts legs on 'is."

The four parted. The young woman thanked them.

"Thank you for the chair—it'll last till it gives way."

"Keep it for an ornyment," said the young man.

"Good afternoon—good afternoon," said Ursula and Birkin.

"Goo'—luck to you," said the young man, glancing and avoiding Birkin's eyes, as he turned aside his head.

The two couples went asunder, Ursula clinging to Birkin's arm. When they had gone some distance, she glanced back and saw the young man going beside the full, easy young woman. His trousers sank over his heels, he moved with a sort of slinking evasion, more crushed with odd self-consciousness now he had the slim old arm-chair to carry, his arm over the back, the four fine, square, tapering legs swaying perilously near the granite setts of the pavement. And yet he was somewhere indomitable and separate, like a quick, vital rat. He had a queer, subterranean beauty, repulsive too.

"How strange they are!" said Ursula.

"Children of men," he said. "They remind me of Jesus' 'The meek shall inherit the earth.'"

"But they aren't the meek," said Ursula.

"Yes, I don't know why, but they are," he replied.

They waited for the tram-car. Ursula sat on top and looked out on the town. The dusk was just dimming the hollows of crowded houses.

"And are they going to inherit the earth?" she said.

"Yes—they."

"Then what are we going to do?" she asked. "We're not like them—are we?—We're not the meek?"

"No.—We've got to live in the chinks they leave us."

"How horrible!" cried Ursula. "I don't want to live in chinks."

"Don't worry," he said. "They are the children of men, they like market-places and street-corners best. That leaves plenty of chinks."

"All the world," she said.

"Ah no—but some room."

The tram-car mounted slowly up the hill, where the ugly winter-grey masses of houses looked like a vision of hell that is cold and angular. They sat and looked. Away in the distance was an angry redness of sunset. It was all cold, somehow small, crowded, and like the end of the world.

"I don't mind it even then," said Ursula, looking at the repulsiveness of it all. "It doesn't concern me."

"No more it does," he replied, holding her hand. "One needn't see. One goes one's way. In my world it is sunny and spacious—"

"It is, my love, isn't it," she cried, hugging near to him on the top of the tram-car, so that the other passengers stared at them.

"And we will wander about on the face of the earth," he said, "and we'll look at the world beyond just this bit."

There was a long silence. Her face was radiant like gold, as she sat thinking.

"I don't want to inherit the earth," she said. "I don't want to inherit anything."

He closed his hand over hers.

"Neither do I. I want to be disinherited."

She clasped his fingers closely.

"We won't care about *anything*," she said.

He sat still, and laughed.

"And we'll be married, and have done with them," she added.

—Again he laughed.

"It's one way of getting rid of everything," she said, "to get married."

"And one way of accepting the whole world," he added.

"A whole other world, yes," she said happily.

"Perhaps there's Gerald—and Gudrun—" he said.

"If there is there is, you see," she said. "It's no good our worrying. We can't really alter them, can we?"

"No," he said. "One has no right to try—not with the best intentions in the world."

"Do you try to force them?" she asked.

"Perhaps," he said. "Why should I want him to be free, if it isn't his business?"

She paused for a time.

"We can't *make* him happy, anyhow," she said. "He'd have to be it of himself."

"I know," he said. "But we want other people with us, don't we?"

"Why should we?" she asked.

"I don't know," he said uneasily. "One has a hankering after a sort of further fellowship."

"But why?" she insisted. "Why should you hanker after other people? Why should you need them?"

This hit him right on the quick. His brows knitted.

"Does it end with just our two selves?" he asked, tense.

"Yes—what more do you want? If anybody likes to come along, let them. But why must you run after them?"

His face was tense and unsatisfied.

"You see," he said, "I always imagine our being really happy with some few other people—a little freedom with people."

She pondered for a moment.

"Yes, one does want that. But it must *happen*. You can't do anything for it with your will. You always seem to think you can *force* the flowers to come out. People must love us because they love us—you can't *make* them."

"I know," he said. "But must one take no steps at all? Must one just go as if one were alone in the world—the only creature in the world?"

"You've got me," she said. "Why should you *need* others? Why must you *force* people to agree with you? Why can't you be single by yourself, as you are always saying?—You try to bully Gerald—as you tried to bully Hermione.—You must learn to be alone.—And it's so horrid of you. You've got me. And yet you want to force other people to love you as well. You do try to bully them to love you.—And even then, you don't want their love."

His face was full of real perplexity.

"Don't I?" he said. "It's the problem I can't solve. I *know* I want a perfect and complete relationship with you: and we've nearly got it—we really have.—But beyond that. *Do* I want a real, ultimate relationship with Gerald. Do I want a final, almost extra-human relationship with him—a relationship in the ultimates of me and him—or don't I?"

She looked at him for a long time, with strange bright eyes, but she did not answer.

Chapter XXVII

Flitting

That evening Ursula returned home very bright-eyed and wondrous—which irritated her people. Her father came home at supper-time, tired after the evening class, and the long journey home. Gudrun was reading, the mother sat in silence.

Suddenly Ursula said, to the company at large, in a bright voice:

"Rupert and I are going to be married tomorrow."

Her father turned round, stiffly.

"You what?" he said.

"Tomorrow!" echoed Gudrun.

"Indeed!" said the mother.

But Ursula only smiled wonderfully, and did not reply.

"Married tomorrow!" cried her father harshly. "What are you talking about!"

"Yes," said Ursula. "Why not?" Those two words, from her, always drove him mad. "Everything is all right—we shall go to the registrar's office—"

There was a second's hush in the room, after Ursula's blithe vagueness.

"*Really*, Ursula!" said Gudrun.

"Might we ask why there has been all this secrecy?" demanded the mother, rather superbly.

"But there hasn't," said Ursula. "You knew."

"Who knew?" now cried her father. "Who knew? What do you mean, by your '*you knew*'?" He was in one of his stupid rages, she instantly closed against him.

"Of course you knew," she said coolly. "You knew we were going to get married."

There was a dangerous pause.

"We knew you were going to get married, did we? Knew! Why when does anybody know anything about *you*, you shifty bitch!"

"Father!" cried Gudrun, flushing deep in violent remonstrance. Then, in a cold, but gentle voice, as if to remind her sister to be tractable. "But isn't it a *fearfully* sudden decision, Ursula?" she asked.

"No, not really," replied Ursula, with the same maddening cheerfulness. "He's been *wanting* me to agree, for weeks—he's had the licence ready. Only I—I wasn't ready in myself. Now I am ready—is there anything to be disagreeable about?"

"Certainly not," said Gudrun, but in a tone of cold reproof. "You are perfectly free to do as you like."

"'Ready in yourself'—*yourself*, that's all that matters, isn't it! 'I wasn't ready in myself,'" he mimicked her phrase offensively. "You and *yourself*, you're of some importance, aren't you?"

She drew herself up and set back her throat, her eyes shining yellow and dangerous.

"I am to myself," she said, wounded and mortified. "I know I am not to anybody else. You only wanted to *bully* me—you never cared for my happiness."

He was leaning forward watching her, his face intense like a spark.

"Ursula, what are you saying? Keep your tongue still," cried her mother. Ursula swung round, and the lights in her eyes flashed.

"No I won't," she cried. "I won't hold my tongue and be bullied.—What does it matter which day I get married—what does it *matter*! It doesn't affect anybody but myself."

Her father was tense and gathered together like a cat about to spring.

"Doesn't it?" he cried, coming nearer to her. She shrank away.

"No, how can it?" she replied, shrinking but stubborn.

"It doesn't matter to *me* then, what you do—what becomes of you—?" he cried, in a strange voice like a cry.

The mother and Gudrun stood back as if hypnotised.

"No," stammered Ursula. Her father was very near to her. "You only want to— —"

She knew it was dangerous, and she stopped. He was gathered together, every muscle ready.

"What—?" he challenged.

"Bully me," she muttered, and even as her lips were moving, his hand had caught her smack at the side of the face and she was sent up against the door.

"Father!" cried Gudrun in a high voice—"It is *impossible*!"

He stood unmoving. Ursula recovered, her hand was on the door handle. She slowly drew herself up. He seemed doubtful now.

"It's true," she declared, with brilliant tears in her eyes, her head lifted up in defiance. "What has your love meant—what did it ever mean?—bullying, and denial—it did—"

He was advancing again with strange, tense movements, and clenched fist, and the face of a murderer. But swift as lightning she had flashed out of the door, and they heard her running upstairs.

He stood for a moment looking at the door. Then, like a defeated animal, he turned and went back to his seat by the fire.

Gudrun was very white. Out of the intense silence, the mother's voice was heard saying, cold and angry:

"Well, you shouldn't take so much notice of her."

Again the silence fell, each followed a separate set of emotions and thoughts.

Suddenly the door opened again: Ursula, dressed in hat and furs, with a small valise in her hand:

"Goodbye!" she said, in her maddening, bright, almost mocking tone. "I'm going."

And in the next instant the door was closed, they heard the outer door, then her quick steps down the garden path, then the gate banged, and her light footfall was gone. There was a silence like death in the house.

Ursula went straight to the station, hastening heedlessly, on winged feet. There was no train, she must walk on to the junction. As she went through the darkness, she began to cry, and she wept bitterly, with a dumb, heart-broken, child's anguish, all the way on the road, and in the train. Time passed unheeded and unknown, she did not know where she was, nor what was taking place. Only she wept from fathomless depths of hopeless, hopeless grief, the terrible grief of a child, that knows no extenuation.

Yet her voice had the same defensive brightness as she spoke to Birkin's landlady at the door.

"Good evening! Is Mr Birkin in? Can I see him?"

"Yes, he's in. He's in his study."

Ursula stepped past the woman. His door opened. He had heard her voice.

"Hello!" he exclaimed in surprise, seeing her standing there with the valise in her hand, and marks of tears on her face. She was one who wept without showing many traces, like a child.

"Do I look a sight?" she said, shrinking.

"No—why? Come in," he took the bag from her hand and they went into the study.

There, immediately, her lips began to tremble like those of a child that remembers again, and the tears came rushing up.

"What's the matter?" he asked, taking her in his arms. She sobbed violently on his shoulder, whilst he held her still, waiting.

"What's the matter?" he said again, when she was quieter. But she only pressed her face further into his shoulder, in pain, like a child that cannot tell.

"What is it, then?" he asked.

Suddenly she broke away, wiped her eyes, regained her composure, and went and sat in a chair.

"Father hit me," she announced, sitting bunched up, rather like a ruffled bird, her eyes very bright.

"What for?" he said.

She looked away, and would not answer. There was a pitiful redness about her sensitive nostrils, and her quivering lips.

"Why?" he repeated, in his strange, soft, penetrating voice.

She looked round at him, rather defiantly.

"Because I said I was going to be married tomorrow, and he bullied me."

"Why did he bully you?"

Her mouth dropped again, she remembered the scene once more, the tears came up.

"Because I said he didn't care—and he doesn't, it's only his domineer-ingness that's hurt—" she said, her mouth pulled awry by her weeping, all the time she spoke, so that he almost smiled, it seemed so childish. Yet it was not childish, it was a mortal conflict, a deep wound.

"It isn't quite true," he said. "And even so, you shouldn't *say* it."

"It *is* true—it *is* true," she wept. "And I won't be bullied by his pretending it's love—when it *isn't*—he doesn't care, how can he—no, he can't—."

He sat in silence. She moved him beyond himself.

"Then you shouldn't rouse him, if he can't," replied Birkin quietly.

"And I *have* loved him, I have," she wept, "I've loved him always, and he's always done this to me, he has—."

"It's been a love of opposition, then," he said. "Never mind—it will be all right. It's nothing desperate."

"Yes," she wept, "it is, it is."

"Why?"

"I shall never see him again——"

"Not immediately—Don't cry, you had to break with him, it had to be—don't cry."

He went over to her and kissed her fine, fragile hair, touching her wet cheeks gently.

"Don't cry," he repeated, "don't cry any more."

He held her head close against him, very close and quiet.

At last she was still. Then she looked up, her eyes wide and frightened. "Don't you want me?" she asked.

"Want you?" His darkened, steady eyes puzzled her and did not give her play.

"Do you wish I hadn't come?" she asked, anxious now again, for fear she might be out of place.

"No," he said. "I wish there hadn't been the violence—so much ugliness—but perhaps it was inevitable."

She watched him in silence. He seemed deadened.

"But where shall I stay?" she asked, feeling humiliated.

He thought for a moment.

"Here, with me," he said. "We're married as much today as we shall be tomorrow."

"But—"

"I'll tell Mrs Varley," he said. "Never mind now."

He sat looking at her. She could feel his darkened, steady eyes looking at her all the time. It made her a little bit frightened. She pushed her hair off her forehead nervously.

"Do I look ugly?" she said.

And she blew her nose again.

A small smile came round his eyes.

"No," he said, "fortunately."

And he went across to her, and gathered her like a belonging in his arms. She was so tenderly beautiful, he could not bear to see her, he could only bear to hide her against himself. Now, washed all clear by her tears, she was new and frail like a flower just unfolded, a flower so new, so tender, so made perfect by inner light, that he could not bear to look on her, he must hide her against himself, cover his eyes against her. She had the perfect candour of creation, something translucent and simple, like a radiant, shining flower that moment unfolded in primal blessedness. She was so new, so wonder-clear, so undimmed. And he was so old, so steeped in heavy memories. Her soul was new, undefined and glimmering with the unseen. And his soul was dark and gloomy, it had only one grain of living hope, like a grain of mustard seed. But this one living grain in him matched the perfect youth in her.

"I love you," he whispered as he kissed her, and trembled with pure hope, like a man who is born again to a wonderful, lovely hope far exceeding the bounds of death.

She could not know how much it meant to him, how much he meant by the few words. Almost childish, she wanted proof, and statement, even overstatement. For everything seemed still uncertain, unfixed to her.

But the passion of gratitude with which he received her into his soul, the extreme, unthinkable gladness of knowing himself living and fit to unite with her, he, who was so nearly dead, who was so near to being gone with the rest of his race down the slope of mechanical death, could never be understood by her. He worshipped her as age worships youth, he gloried in her because, in his one grain of faith, he was young as she, he was her proper mate. This marriage with her was his resurrection and his life.

All this she could not know. She wanted to be made much of, to be adored. There were infinite distances of silence between them. How could he tell her of the immanence of her beauty, that was not form or weight or colour, but something like a strange golden light! How could he know himself what her beauty lay in, for him. He said "Your nose is beautiful, your chin is adorable." But it sounded like lies, and she was disappointed, hurt. Even when he said, whispering with truth, "I love you, I love you," it was not the real truth. It was something beyond love, such a gladness of having surpassed oneself, of having transcended the old existence. How could he say 'I', when he was something new and unknown, not himself at all? This I, this old formula of the ego, was a dead letter.

In the new, superfine bliss, a peace superseding knowledge, there was no I and you, there was only the third, unrealised wonder, the wonder of existing not as oneself, but in a consummation of my being and of her being in a new One, a new, paradisal unit regained from the duality. How can I say "I love you", when I have ceased to be, and you have ceased to be, we are both caught up and transcended into a new oneness where everything is silent, because there is nothing to answer, all is perfect and at one. Speech travels between the separate parts. But in the perfect One there is perfect silence of bliss.

They were married by law on the next day, and she did as he bade her, she wrote to her father and mother. Her mother replied, not her father.

She did not go back to school. She stayed with Birkin in his rooms, or at the Mill, moving with him as he moved. But she did not see anybody, save Gudrun and Gerald. She was all strange and wondering as yet, but relieved as by dawn.

Gerald sat talking to her one afternoon, in the warm study down at the Mill. Rupert had not yet come home.

"You are happy?" Gerald asked her, with a smile.

"Very happy!" she cried, shrinking a little in her brightness.

"Yes, one can see it."

"Can one?" cried Ursula, in surprise.

He looked up at her with a communicative smile.

"Oh yes, plainly."

She was pleased. She meditated a moment.

"And can you see that Rupert is happy as well?"

He lowered his eyelids, and looked aside.

"Oh yes," he said.

"Really?"

"Oh yes."

He was very quiet, as if it were something not to be talked about by him. He seemed sad.

She was very sensitive to suggestion. She asked the question he wanted her to ask.

"Why don't you be happy as well?" she said. "You could be just the same."

He paused a moment.

"With Gudrun?" he asked.

"Yes!" she cried, her eyes glowing. But there was a strange tension, an emphasis, as if they were asserting their wishes, against the truth.

"You think Gudrun would have me, and we should be happy?" he said.

"Yes, I'm *sure*!" she cried.

Her eyes were round with delight. Yet underneath she was constrained, she knew her own insistence.

"Oh, I'm *so* glad," she added.

He smiled.

"What makes you glad?" he said.

"For *her* sake," she replied. "I'm sure you'd—you're the right man for her."

"You are?" he said. "And do you think she would agree with you?"

"Oh yes!" she exclaimed hastily. Then, upon reconsideration, very uneasy: "Though Gudrun isn't so very simple, is she? One doesn't know her in five minutes, does one? She's not like me in that."

She laughed at him with her strange, open, dazzled face.

"You think she's not much like you?" Gerald asked.

She knitted her brows.

"Oh, in many ways she is.—But I never know what she will do when anything new comes."

"You don't?" said Gerald. He was silent for some moments. Then he moved tentatively. "I was going to ask her, in any case, to go away with me at Christmas," he said, in a very small, cautious voice.

"Go away with you? For a time, you mean?"

"As long as she likes," he said, with a deprecating movement.

They were both silent for some minutes.

"Of course," said Ursula at last, "she *might* just be willing to rush into marriage. You can see."

"Yes," smiled Gerald, "I can see.—But in case she won't—do you think she would go abroad with me for a few days—or for a fortnight?"

"Oh yes," said Ursula. "I'd ask her."

"Do you think we might all go together?"

"All of us?" Again Ursula's face lighted up. "It would be rather fun, don't you think?"

"Great fun," he said.

"And then you could see," said Ursula.

"What?"

"How things went.—I think it is best to take the honeymoon before the wedding—don't you?"

She was pleased with this *mot*. He laughed.

"In certain cases," he said. "I'd rather it were so in my own case."

"Would you!" exclaimed Ursula. Then doubtingly, "Yes, perhaps you're right.—One should please oneself."

Birkin came in a little later, and Ursula told him what had been said.

"Gudrun!" exclaimed Birkin. "She's a born mistress, just as Gerald is a born lover—*amant en titre*. If as somebody says all women are either wives or mistresses, then Gudrun is a mistress."

"And all men either lovers or husbands?" cried Ursula. "But why not both?"

"The one excludes the other," he laughed.

"Then I want a lover," cried Ursula.

"No you don't," he said.

"But I do," she wailed.

He kissed her, and laughed.

It was two days after this that Ursula was to go to fetch her things from the house in Beldover. The removal had taken place, the family had gone. Gudrun had rooms in Willey Green.

Ursula had not seen her parents since her marriage. She wept over the rupture, yet what was the good making it up! Good or not good, she could not go to them. So her things had been left behind, and she and Gudrun were to walk over for them, in the afternoon.

It was a wintry afternoon, with red in the sky, when they arrived at the house. The windows were dark and blank, already the place was frightening. A stark, void entrance-hall struck a chill to the hearts of the girls.

"I don't believe I dare have come in alone," said Ursula. "It frightens me."

"Ursula!" cried Gudrun. "Isn't it amazing? Can you believe you lived in this place and never felt it? How I lived here a day without dying of terror, I cannot conceive!"

They looked in the big dining-room. It was a good-sized room, but now, a cell would have been lovelier. The large bay windows were naked, the floor was stripped, and a border of dark polish went round the tract of pale boarding. In the faded wall-paper were dark patches where furniture had stood, where pictures had hung. The sense of walls, dry, thin, flimsy-seeming walls, and a flimsy flooring, pale with its artificial black edges, was neutralising to the mind. Everything was null to the senses, there was enclosure without substance, for the walls were dry and papery. Where were they standing, on earth, or suspended in some cardboard box? In the hearth was burnt paper, and scraps of half-burnt paper.

"Imagine that we passed our days here!" said Ursula.

"I know," cried Gudrun. "It is too appalling. What *must* we be like, if we are the contents of *this*!"

"Vile!" said Ursula. "It really is."

And she recognised half-burnt covers of "Vogue"—half-burnt representations of women in gowns—lying under the grate.

They went to the drawing-room. Another piece of shut-in air, without weight or substance, only a sense of intolerable papery imprisonment in nothingness. The kitchen did look more substantial, because of the red-tiled floor and the stove, but it was cold and horrid.

The two girls tramped hollowly up the bare stairs. Every sound re-echoed under their hearts. They tramped down the bare corridor. Against the wall of Ursula's bedroom were her things—a trunk, a work-basket, some books, loose coats, a hat-box, standing desolate in the universal emptiness of the dusk.

"A cheerful sight, aren't they?" said Ursula, looking down at her forsaken possessions.

"Very cheerful," said Gudrun.

The two girls set to, carrying everything down to the front door. Again and again they made the hollow, re-echoing transit. The whole place seemed to resound about them with a noise of hollow, empty futility. In the distance the empty, invisible rooms sent forth a vibration almost of obscenity. They almost fled with the last articles, into the out-of-doors.

But it was cold. They were waiting for Birkin, who was coming with the car. They went indoors again, and upstairs to their parents' front bedroom, whose windows looked down on the road, and across the country at the black-barred sunset, black and red barred, without light.

They sat down in the window-seat, to wait. Both girls were looking over the room. It was void, with a meaninglessness that was almost dreadful.

"Really," said Ursula, "this room *couldn't* be sacred, could it?"

Gudrun looked over it with slow eyes.

"Impossible," she replied.

"When I think of their lives—father's and mother's—their love, and their marriage, and all us children, and our bringing-up—would you have such a life, Prune?"

"I wouldn't, Ursula."

"It all seems so *nothing*—their two lives—there's no *meaning* in it.— Really, if they had *not* met, and *not* married, and *not* lived together—it wouldn't have mattered, would it?"

"Of course—you can't tell," said Gudrun.

"No.—But if I thought my life was going to be like it—Prune," she caught Gudrun's arm, "I should run."

Gudrun was silent for a few moments.

"As a matter of fact, one cannot contemplate the ordinary life—one cannot contemplate it," replied Gudrun. "With you, Ursula, it is quite different. You will be out of it all, with Birkin. He's a special case.—But with the ordinary man, who has his life fixed in one place, marriage is just impossible.—There may be, and there *are*, thousands of women who want it, and could conceive of nothing else. But the very thought of it sends me *mad*.—One must be free, above all, one must be free. One may forfeit everything else, but one must be free—one must not become 7 Pinchbeck Street—or Somerset Drive—or Shortlands.—No man will be sufficient to make that good—no man!—To marry, one must have a free lance, or nothing, a comrade-in-arms, a Glücksritter. A man with a position in the social world—well, it is just impossible, impossible!"

"What a lovely word—a Glücksritter!" said Ursula. "So much nicer than a soldier of fortune."

"Yes, isn't it!" said Gudrun. "I'd tilt the world with a Glücksritter. But a home, an establishment—Ursula, what would it mean?—*think*!"

"I know," said Ursula. "We've had one home—that's enough for me."

"Quite enough," said Gudrun.

"The little grey home in the west," quoted Ursula ironically.

"*Doesn't* it sound grey, too!" said Gudrun grimly.

They were interrupted by the sound of the car. There was Birkin—Ursula was surprised that she felt so lit up, that she became suddenly so free from the problems of grey homes in the west.

They heard his heels click on the hall pavement below.

"Hello!" he called, his voice echoing alive through the house. Ursula smiled to herself. *He* was frightened of the place too.

"Hello! Here we are," she called downstairs.

And they heard him quickly running up.

"This is a ghostly situation," he said.

"These houses don't have ghosts—they've never had any personality, and only a place with personality can have a ghost," said Gudrun.

"I suppose so. Are you both weeping over the past?"

"We are," said Gudrun grimly.

Ursula laughed.

"Not weeping that it's gone—but weeping that it ever *was*," she said.

"Oh," he replied, relieved.

He sat down for a moment. There was something in his presence, Ursula thought, lambent and alive. It made even the impertinent structure of this null house disappear.

"Gudrun says she could not bear to be married and put into a house," said Ursula, meaningful—they knew this referred to Gerald.

He was silent for some moments.

"Well," he said, "if you know beforehand you couldn't stand it, you're safe."

"Quite!" said Gudrun.

"Why *does* every woman think her aim in life is to have a hubby and a little grey home in the west? Why is this the goal of life? Why should it be?" asked Ursula.

"Il faut avoir le respect de ses bêtises," said Birkin.

"But you needn't have the respect for the bêtise before you've committed it," laughed Ursula.

"Ah then: 'il faut avoir le respect des bêtises du papa'."

"Et de la maman," added Gudrun satirically.

"Et des voisins," said Ursula.

They all laughed, and rose. It was getting dark. They carried the things to the car. Gudrun locked the door of the empty house. Birkin had lighted the lamps of the automobile. It all seemed very happy, as if they were setting out.

"Do you mind stopping at Coulsons. I have to leave the key there," said Gudrun.

"Right," said Birkin, and they moved off.

They stopped in the main street. The shops were just lighted, the last miners were passing home along the causeways, half-visible shadows in their grey pit-dirt, moving through the blue air. But their feet rang harshly, in manifold sound, along the pavement.

How pleased Gudrun was to come out of the shop, and enter the car, and be borne swiftly away into the down-hill of palpable dusk, with Ursula and Birkin! What an adventure life seemed at this moment! How deeply, how suddenly she envied Ursula! Life for her was so quick, and an open door—so reckless, as if not only this world, but the world that was gone and the world to come were nothing to her. Ah, if she could be *just like that*, it would be perfect.

For always, except in her moments of excitement, she felt a want within herself, she was unsure. She had felt that now, at last, in Gerald's strong and violent love, she was living fully and finally. But when she compared herself with Ursula, already her soul was jealous, unsatisfied. She was not satisfied—she was never to be satisfied.

What was she short of now? It was marriage—it was the wonderful stability of marriage. She did want it, let her say what she might. She had been lying. The old idea of marriage was right even now—marriage and the home. Yet her mouth gave a little grimace at the words. She thought of Gerald and Shortlands—marriage and the home! Ah well, let it rest! He meant a great deal to her—but—! Perhaps it was not in her to marry. She was one of life's outcasts, one of the drifting lives that have no root. No, no—it could not be so. She suddenly conjured up a rosy room, with herself in a beautiful gown, and a handsome man in evening dress who held her in his arms in the firelight, and kissed her. This picture she entitled "Home." It would have done for the Royal Academy.

"Come with us to tea—*do*," said Ursula, as they ran nearer to the cottages of Willey Green.

"Thanks awfully—but I *must* go in—" said Gudrun. She wanted very much to go on with Ursula and Birkin. That seemed like life indeed to her. Yet a certain perversity would not let her.

"Do come—yes, it would be so nice," pleaded Ursula.

"I'm awfully sorry—I should love to—but I can't—really—"

She descended from the car in trembling haste.

"Can't you really!" came Ursula's regretful voice.

"No, really I can't," responded Gudrun's pathetic, chagrined words out of the dusk.

"All right, are you?" called Birkin.

"Quite!" said Gudrun. "Goodnight!"

"Goodnight," they called.

"Come whenever you like, we shall be glad," called Birkin.

"Thank you very much," called Gudrun, in the strange, twanging voice of lonely chagrin that was very puzzling to him. She turned away to her cottage gate, and they drove on. But immediately she stood to watch them, as the car ran vague into the distance. And as she went up the path to her strange house, her heart was full of incomprehensible bitterness.

In her parlour was a long-case clock, and inserted into its dial was a ruddy, round, slant-eyed, joyous-painted face, that wagged over with the most ridiculous ogle when the clock ticked, and back again with the same absurd glad eye at the next tick. All the time the absurd smooth, brown-ruddy face gave her an obtrusive "glad eye." She stood for minutes, watching it, till a sort of maddened disgust overcame her, and she laughed at herself, hollowly. And still it rocked, and gave her the glad eye from one side, then from the other, from one side, then from the other. Ah, how unhappy she was! In the midst of her most active happiness, ah, how unhappy she was! She glanced at the table. Gooseberry jam, and the same home-made cake with too much soda in it! Still, gooseberry jam was good, and one so rarely got it.

All the evening she wanted to go to the Mill. But she coldly refused to allow herself. She went the next afternoon instead. She was happy to find Ursula alone. It was a lovely, intimate, secluded atmosphere. They talked endlessly and delightedly. "Aren't you *fearfully* happy here?" said Gudrun to her sister, glancing at her own bright eyes in the mirror. She always envied, almost with resentment, the strange positive fulness that subsisted in the atmosphere around Ursula and Birkin.

"How really beautifully this room is done," she said aloud. "This hard plaited matting—what a lovely colour it is, the colour of cool light!"

And it seemed to her perfect.

"Ursula," she said at length, in a voice of question and detachment, "did you know that Gerald Crich had suggested our going away all together at Christmas?"

"Yes, he's spoken to Rupert."

A deep flush dyed Gudrun's cheek. She was silent a moment, as if taken aback, and not knowing what to say.

"But don't you think," she said at last, "it is *amazingly cool*!"

Ursula laughed.

"I liked him for it," she said.

Gudrun was silent. It was evident that, whilst she was almost mortified by Gerald's taking the liberty of making such a suggestion to Birkin, yet the idea itself attracted her strongly.

"There's a rather lovely simplicity about Gerald, I think," said Ursula. "So defiant, somehow!—Oh, I think he's *very* lovable."

Gudrun did not reply for some moments. She had still to get over the feeling of insult at the liberty taken with her freedom.

"What did Rupert say—do you know?" she asked.

"He said it would be most awfully jolly," said Ursula.

Again Gudrun looked down, and was silent.

"Don't you think it would?" said Ursula, tentatively. She was never quite sure how many defences Gudrun was having round herself.

Gudrun raised her face with difficulty, and held it averted.

"I think it *might* be awfully jolly, as you say," she replied. "But don't you think it was an unpardonable liberty to take—to talk of such a thing to Rupert—who after all—You see what I mean, Ursula—they might have been two men arranging an outing with some little *type* they'd picked up. Oh, I think it's unforgiveable, quite!"—She used the French word, '*type*.'

Her eye flashed, her soft face was flushed and sullen. Ursula looked on, rather frightened, frightened most of all because she thought Gudrun seemed rather common, really like a little *type*. But she had not the courage quite to think this—not right out—

"Oh no," she cried, stammering. "Oh no—not at all like that—oh no!—No, I think it's rather beautiful, the friendship between Rupert and Gerald. They just are simple—they say anything to each other, like brothers."

Gudrun flushed deeper. She could not *bear* it that Gerald gave her away—even to Birkin.

"But do you think even brothers have any right to exchange confidences of that sort?" she asked, with deep anger.

"Oh yes," said Ursula. "There's never anything said that isn't perfectly straightforward.—No, the thing that's amazed me most in Gerald—how perfectly simple and direct he can be!—And you know, it takes rather a big man. Most of them *must* be indirect, they are such cowards."

But Gudrun was still silent with anger. She wanted the absolutest secrecy kept, with regard to her movements.

"Won't you go?" said Ursula. "Do, we might all be so happy!—There is something I *love* about Gerald—he's *much* more lovable than I thought him. He's free, Gudrun, he really is."

Gudrun's mouth was still closed sullen and ugly. She opened it at length.

"Do you know where he proposes to go?" she asked.

"Yes—to the Tyrol, where he used to go when he was in Germany—a lovely place where students go, small and rough and lovely, for winter sport!"

Through Gudrun's mind went the angry thought—"they know everything."

"Yes," she said aloud, "about forty kilometers from Innsbruck, isn't it?"

"I don't know exactly where—but it would be lovely, don't you think, high in the perfect snow—?"

"Very lovely!" said Gudrun, sarcastically.

Ursula was put out.

"Of course," she said, "I think Gerald spoke to Rupert so that it *shouldn't* seem like a little outing with a *type*—"

"I know, of course," said Gudrun, "that he quite commonly does take up with that sort."

"Does he!" said Ursula. "Why how do you know?"

"I know of a model in Chelsea," said Gudrun coldly.

Now Ursula was silent.

"Well," she said at last, with a doubtful laugh, "I hope he has a good time with her." At which Gudrun only looked more glum.

Chapter XXVIII

Gudrun in the Pompadour

Christmas drew near, all four prepared for flight. Birkin and Ursula were busy packing their few personal things, making them ready to be sent off, to whatever country and whatever place they might choose at last. Gudrun was very much excited. She loved to be on the wing.

She and Gerald, being ready first, set off via London and Paris to Innsbruck, where they would meet Ursula and Birkin. In London they stayed one night. They went to a music-hall, and afterwards to the Pompadour Café.

Gudrun hated the Café, yet she always went back to it, as did most of the artists of her acquaintance. She loathed its atmosphere of petty vice and petty jealousy and petty art. Yet she always called in again, when she was in town. It was as if she *had* to return to this small, slow, central whirlpool of disintegration and dissolution: just give it a look.

She sat with Gerald drinking some sweetish liqueur, and staring with black, sullen looks at the various groups of people at the tables. She would greet nobody, but young men nodded to her frequently, with a kind of sneering familiarity. She cut them all. And it gave her pleasure to sit there, cheeks flushed, eyes black and sullen, seeing them all objectively, as put away from her, like creatures in some menagerie of apish, degraded souls. God, what a foul crew they were! Her blood beat black and thick in her veins with rage and loathing. Yet she must sit and watch, watch. One or two people came to speak to her. From every side of the Café, eyes turned half furtively, half jeeringly at her, men looking over their shoulders, women under their hats.

The old crowd was there, Carlyon in his corner with his pupils and his girl, Halliday and Libidnikov and the Pussum—they were all there. Gudrun watched Gerald. She watched his eyes linger a moment on Halliday, on Halliday's party. These last were on the look-out—they nodded to him, he nodded again. They giggled and whispered among themselves. Gerald watched them with the steady twinkle in his eyes. They were urging the Pussum to something.

She at last rose. She was wearing a curious dress of dark silk splashed and spattered with different colours, a curious motley effect. She was thinner, her eyes were perhaps hotter, more disintegrated. Otherwise she was just the same. Gerald watched her with the same steady twinkle in his eyes as she came across.

She held out her thin brown hand to him.

"How are you?" she said.

He shook hands with her, but remained seated, and let her stand near him, against the table. She nodded blackly to Gudrun, whom she did not know to speak to, but well enough by sight and reputation.

"I am very well," said Gerald. "And you—?"

"Oh I'm all wight.—What about Wupert?"

"Rupert?—He's very well too."

"Yes, I don't mean that. What about him being married?"

"Oh—yes, he is married."

The Pussum's eyes had a hot flash.

"Oh, he's weally bwought it off then, has he? When was he married?"

"A week or two ago."

"Weally! He's never written."

"No."

"No.—Don't you think it's too bad?"

This last was in a tone of challenge. The Pussum let it be known, by her tone, that she was aware of Gudrun's listening.

"I suppose he didn't feel like it," replied Gerald.

"But why didn't he?" pursued the Pussum.

This was received in silence. There was an ugly mocking persistence in the small, beautiful figure of the short-haired girl, as she stood near Gerald.

"Are you staying in town long?" she asked.

"Tonight only."

"Oh, only tonight.—Are you coming over to speak to Julius?"

"Not tonight."

"Oh very well. I'll tell him then." Then came her touch of diablerie. "You're looking awf'lly fit."

"Yes—I feel it." Gerald was quite calm and easy, a spark of satiric amusement in his eye.

"Are you having a good time?"

This was a direct blow for Gudrun, spoken in a level, toneless voice of callous ease.

"Yes," he replied, quite colourlessly.

"I'm awf'lly sorry you aren't coming round to the flat.—You aren't very faithful to your fwiends."

"Not very," he said.

She nodded them both 'Goodnight', and went back slowly to her own set. Gudrun watched her curious walk, stiff and jerking at the loins. They heard her level, toneless voice distinctly.

"He won't come over;—he is otherwise engaged," it said.

There was more laughter and lowered voices and mockery at the table.

"Is she a friend of yours?" said Gudrun, looking calmly at Gerald.

"I've stayed at Halliday's flat with Birkin," he said, meeting her slow, calm eyes. And she knew that the Pussum was one of his mistresses—and he knew she knew.

She looked round, and called for the waiter. She wanted an iced cocktail, of all things. This amused Gerald—he wondered what was up.

The Halliday party was tipsy, and malicious. They were talking out loudly about Birkin, ridiculing him on every point, particularly on his marriage.

"Oh, *don't* make me think of Birkin," Halliday was squealing. "He makes me perfectly sick. He is as bad as Jesus. 'Lord, *what* must I do to be saved'."

He giggled to himself tipsily.

"Do you remember," came the quick voice of the Russian, "the letters he used to send. 'Desire is holy—'"

"Oh yes!" cried Halliday. "Oh, how perfectly splendid! Why, I've got one in my pocket. I'm sure I have."

He took out various papers from his pocket book.

"I'm sure I've—*hic!*—*Oh dear!*—got one."

Gerald and Gudrun were watching absorbedly.

"Oh yes, how perfectly—*hic!*—splendid!—Don't make me laugh, Pussum, it gives me the hiccup. Hic!—" They all giggled.

"What did he say in that one?" the Pussum asked, leaning forward, her dark, soft hair falling and swinging against her face. There was something curiously indecent, obscene, about her small, longish, dark skull, particularly when the ears showed.

"Wait—oh do wait! No—o, I won't give it you, I'll read it aloud. I'll read you the choice bits—*hic!* Oh dear! Do you think if I drank water it would take off this hiccup? *Hic!* Oh, I feel perfectly helpless."

"Isn't that the letter about uniting the dark and the light—and the Flux of Corruption?" asked Maxim, in his precise, quick voice.

"I believe so," said the Pussum.

"Oh is it? I'd forgotten—*hic!*—it was that one," Halliday said, opening the letter. "*Hic!*—Oh yes. How perfectly splendid! This is one of the best.—'There is a phase in every race—'" he read in the sing-song, slow, distinct voice of a clergyman reading the Scriptures, "'when the desire for destruction overcomes every other desire. In the individual, this desire is ultimately a desire for destruction in the self'—*hic!*—" he paused and looked up.

"I hope he's going ahead with the destruction of himself," said the quick voice of the Russian. Halliday giggled, and lolled his head back, vaguely.

"There's not much to destroy in him," said the Pussum. "He's so thin already, there's only a fag-end to start on."

"Oh, isn't it beautiful! I love reading it! I believe it has cured my hiccup!" squealed Halliday. "Do let me go on.—'It is a desire for the reduction process in oneself, a reducing back to the origins, a return along the Flux of Corruption, to the original rudimentary conditions of being—' Oh, but I *do* think it is wonderful. It *almost* supersedes the Bible—"

"Yes—Flux of Corruption," said the Russian. "I remember that phrase."

"Oh, he was always talking about Corwuption," said the Pussum. "He must be corwupt himself, to have it so much on his mind."

"Exactly!" said the Russian.

"Do let me go on! Oh, this is a perfectly wonderful piece! But do listen to this. 'And in the great retrogression, the reducing back of the created body of life, we get knowledge, and beyond knowledge, the phosphorescent ecstasy of acute sensation.'—Oh, I do think those phrases are too absurdly wonderful. Oh but don't you think they *are*—they're nearly as good as Jesus.—'—and if, Julius, you want this ecstasy of reduction with the Pussum, you must go on till it is fulfilled. But surely there is in you also, somewhere, the living desire for positive creation, relationships in ultimate faith, when all this process of active corruption, with all its flowers of mud, is transcended, and more or less finished—'—I do wonder what the flowers of mud are. Pussum, you are a flower of mud."

"Thank you—and what are you?"

"Oh, I'm another, surely, according to this letter! We're all flowers of mud.—Fleurs—*hic!*—du mal!—It's perfectly wonderful, Birkin harrowing Hell—harrowing the Pompadour—*Hic!*"

"Go on—go on," said Maxim. "What comes next. It's really very interesting."

"I think it's awful cheek to write like that," said the Pussum.

"Yes—yes, so do I," said the Russian. "He is a megalomaniac, of course—it is a form of religious mania. He thinks he is the saviour of man—go on reading."

"Surely," Halliday intoned, "Surely goodness and mercy hath followed me all the days of my life—" he broke off, and giggled. Then he began again, intoning like a clergyman. "Surely there will come an end in us to this desire—for the constant going apart,—this passion for putting asunder—everything—ourselves, reducing ourselves part from part,—reacting in intimacy only for destruction,—using sex as a great reducing agent, by friction between the two great elements of male and female obtaining a frenzy of sensual satisfaction—reducing the old ideas, going back to the savages for our sensations, always seeking to *lose* ourselves in some ultimate black sensation, mindless and infinite— burning only with destructive fires, raging on with the hope of being burnt out utterly—"

"I want to go," said Gudrun to Gerald, as she signalled the waiter. Her eyes were flashing, her cheeks were flushed. The strange effect of Birkin's letter read aloud in a perfect clerical sing-song, clear and resonant, phrase by phrase, made the blood mount into her head as if she were mad.

She rose, whilst Gerald was paying the bill, and walked over to Halliday's table. They all glanced up at her.

"Excuse me," she said. "Is that a genuine letter you are reading?"

"Oh yes," said Halliday. "Quite genuine."

"May I see?"

Smiling foolishly he handed it to her, as if hypnotised.

"Thank you," she said.

And she turned and walked out of the Café with the letter, all down the brilliant room, between the tables, in her measured fashion. It was some moments before anybody realised what was happening.

From Halliday's table came half articulate cries, then somebody booed, then all the far end of the place began booing after Gudrun's retreating form. She was fashionably dressed in blackish-green and silver, her hat was brilliant green, like the sheen on an insect, but the brim was soft dark green, a falling edge with fine silver, her coat was dark green, lustrous, with a high collar of grey fur, and great fur cuffs, the edge of her dress showed silver and black velvet, her stockings and shoes were silver grey. She moved with slow, fashionable indifference to the door. The porter opened obsequiously for her, and, at her nod, hurried to the edge of the pavement and whistled for a taxi. The two lights of a vehicle almost immediately curved round towards her, like two eyes.

Gerald had followed in wonder, amid all the booing, not having caught her misdeed. He heard the Pussum's voice saying:

"Go and get it back from her! I never heard of such a thing! Go and get it back from her.—Tell Gerald Crich—there he goes—go and make him give it up."

Gudrun stood at the door of the taxi, which the man held open for her.

"To the hôtel?" she asked, as Gerald came out, hurriedly.

"Where you like," he answered.

"Right!" she said. Then, to the driver: "Wagstaff's—Barton Street."

The driver bowed his head, and put down the flag.

Gudrun entered the taxi, with the deliberate, cold movement of a woman who is well-dressed and contemptuous in her soul. Yet she was frozen with overwrought feeling. Gerald followed her.

"You've forgotten the man," she said coolly, with a slight nod of her hat. Gerald gave the porter a shilling. The man saluted. They were in motion.

"What was all the row about?" asked Gerald, in wondering excitement.

"I walked away with Birkin's letter," she said, and he saw the crushed paper in her hand.

His eyes glittered with satisfaction.

"Ah!" he said. "Splendid!—A set of jackasses!"

"I could have *killed* them!" she cried in passion. "*Dogs*!—they *are* dogs!—Why is Rupert such a *fool* as to write such letters to them? *Why* does he give himself away to such canaille? It's a thing that *cannot be borne*—"

Gerald wondered over her strange passion.

And she could not rest any longer in London. They must go by the morning train from Charing Cross. As they drew over the bridge, in the train, having glimpses of the river between the great iron girders, she cried:

"I feel I could *never* see this *foul* town again—. I couldn't *bear* to come back to it."

Chapter XXIX

Continental

Ursula went on in an unreal suspense, the last weeks before going away. She was not herself—she was not anything. She was something that is going to be—soon—soon—very soon. But as yet, she was only imminent.

She went to see her parents. It was a rather stiff, sad meeting, more like a verification of separateness than a reunion. But they were all vague and indefinite with one another, stiffened in the fate that moved them apart.

She did not really come to, until she was on the ship crossing from Dover to Ostend. Dimly she had come down to London with Birkin, London had been a vagueness, so had the train-journey to Dover. It was all like a sleep.

And now, at last, as she stood in the stern of the ship, in a pitch-dark, rather blowy night, feeling the motion of the sea, and watching the small, rather desolate little lights that twinkled on the shores of England, as on the shores of nowhere, watched them sinking smaller and smaller on the profound and living darkness, she felt her soul stirring to awake from its anaesthetic sleep.

"Let us go forward, shall we?" said Birkin. He wanted to be at the tip of their projection. So they left off looking at the faint sparks that glimmered out of nowhere, in the far distance, called England, and turned their faces to the unfathomed night in front.

They went right to the bows of the softly plunging vessel. In the complete obscurity, Birkin found a comparatively sheltered nook, where a great rope was coiled up. It was quite near the very point of the ship, near the black, unpierced space ahead. Here they sat down, folded together, folded round with the same rug, creeping in nearer and ever nearer to one another, till it seemed they had crept right in to each other, and become one substance. It was very cold, and the darkness was palpable.

One of the ship's crew came along the deck, dark as the darkness, not really visible. They then made out the faintest pallor of his face. He felt their presence, and stopped, unsure—then bent forward. When his face was near them, he saw the faint pallor of their faces. Then he withdrew, like a phantom. And they watched him without making any sound.

They seemed to fall away into the profound darkness. There was no sky, no earth, only one unbroken darkness, into which, with a soft, sleeping motion, they seemed to fall, like one closed seed of life falling through dark, fathomless space.

They had forgotten where they were, forgotten all that was and all that had been, conscious only in their heart, and there conscious only of this pure trajectory through the surpassing darkness. The ship's prow cleaved on, with a faint noise of cleavage, into the complete night, without knowing, without seeing, only surging on.

In Ursula the sense of the unrealised world ahead triumphed over everything. In the midst of this profound darkness, there seemed to glow on her heart the effulgence of a paradise unknown and unrealised. Her heart was full of the most wonderful light, golden like honey of darkness, sweet like the warmth of day, a light which was not shed on the world, only on the unknown paradise towards which she was going, a sweetness of habitation, a delight of living quite unknown, but hers infallibly.

In her transport she lifted her face suddenly to him, and he touched it with his lips. So cold, so fresh, so sea-clear her face was, it was like kissing a flower that grows near the surf.

But he did not know the ecstasy of bliss in foreknowledge, that she knew. To him, the wonder of this transit was overwhelming. He was falling through a gulf of infinite darkness, like a meteorite plunging across the chasm between the worlds. The world was torn in two, and he was plunging like an unlit star through the ineffable rift. What was beyond was not yet for him. He was overcome by the trajectory.

In a trance he lay enfolding Ursula round about. His face was against her fine, fragile hair, he breathed its fragrance with the sea and the profound night. And his soul was at peace; yielded, as he fell into the unknown. This was the first time that an utter and absolute peace had entered his heart, now, in this final transit out of life.

When there came some stir on the deck, they roused. They stood up. How stiff and cramped they were, in the night-time! And yet the paradisal glow on her heart, and the unutterable peace of darkness in his, this was the all-in-all.

They stood up and looked ahead. Low lights were seen down the darkness. This was the world again. It was not the bliss of her heart, nor the peace of his. It was the superficial unreal world of fact. Yet not quite the old world. For the peace and the bliss in their hearts was enduring.

Strange, and desolate above all things, like disembarking from the Styx into the desolated underworld, was this landing at night. There was the raw, half-lighted, covered-in vastness of the dark place, boarded and hollow underfoot, with only desolation everywhere. Ursula had caught sight of the big pallid, mystic letters "OSTEND," standing in the darkness. Everybody was hurrying with a blind, insect-like intentness through the dark grey air, porters were calling in unEnglish English, then trotting with heavy bags, their colourless blouses looking ghostly as they disappeared; Ursula stood at a long, low, zinc-covered barrier, along with hundreds of other spectral people, and all the way down the vast, raw darkness was this low stretch of open bags and spectral people, whilst, on the other side of the barrier, pallid officials in peaked caps and moustaches were turning the underclothing in the bags, then scrawling a chalk-mark.

It was done. Birkin snapped the hand bags, off they went, the porter coming behind. They were through a great doorway and in the open night again—ah, a railway platform! Voices were still calling in inhuman agitation through the dark-grey air, spectres were running along the darkness between the trains.

"Köln—Berlin—" Ursula made out on the boards hung on the high train on one side.

"Here we are," said Birkin. And on her side she saw:

"ELSASS—LOTHRINGEN—Luxembourg, Metz—BASEL."

That was it, Basle!

The porter came up:

"A Bâle—deuxième classe?—Voilà."

And he clambered into the high train. They followed. The compartments were already some of them taken. But many were dim and empty. The luggage was stowed, the porter was tipped.

"Nous avons encore—?" said Birkin, looking at his watch and at the porter.

"Encore une demi-heure." With which, in his blue blouse, he disappeared. He was ugly and insolent.

"Come," said Birkin. "It is cold. Let us eat."

There was a coffee-wagon on the platform. They drank hot, watery coffee, and ate the long rolls, split, with ham between, which were such a wide bite that it almost dislocated Ursula's jaw; and they walked beside the high trains. It was all so strange, so extremely desolate, like the underworld, grey, grey, dirt-grey, desolate, forlorn, nowhere—grey, dreary nowhere.

At last they were moving through the night. In the darkness Ursula made out the flat fields, the wet flat dreary darkness of the continent. They pulled up surprisingly soon—Bruges! Then on through the level darkness, with glimpses of sleeping farms and thin poplar trees and deserted high-roads. She sat dismayed, hand in hand with Birkin. He, pale, immobile, like a *revenant* himself, looked sometimes out of the window, sometimes closed his eyes. Then his eyes opened again, dark as the darkness outside.

A flash of a few lights on the darkness—Ghent station! A few more spectres moving outside on the platform—then the bell—then motion again through the level darkness.

Ursula saw a man with a lantern come out of a farm by the railway, and cross to the dark farm-buildings. She thought of the Marsh, the old, intimate farm-life at Cossethay. My God, how far was she projected from her childhood, how far was she still to go! In one life-time one travelled through aeons. The great chasm of memory, from her childhood in the intimate country surroundings of Cossethay and the Marsh Farm—she remembered the servant Tilly, who used to give her bread and butter sprinkled with brown sugar, in the old living-room where the grandfather clock had two pink roses in a basket painted above the figures on the face—and now, when she was travelling into the unknown with Birkin, an utter stranger—was so great, that it seemed she had no identity, that the child she had been, playing in Cossethay churchyard, was a little creature of history, not really herself.

They were at Brussels—half an hour for breakfast. They got down. On the great station clock it said six o'clock. They had coffee and rolls and honey in the vast, desert refreshment room, so dreary, always so dreary, dirty, so spacious, such desolation of space. But she washed her face and hands in hot water, and combed her hair—that was a blessing.

Soon they were in the train again and moving on. The greyness of dawn began. There were several people in the compartment, large, florid Belgian business-men with long brown beards, talking incessantly in an ugly French she was too tired to follow.

It seemed the train ran by degrees out of the darkness into a faint light, then beat after beat into the day. Ah, how weary it was! Faintly, the trees showed, like shadows. Then a house, white, had a curious distinctness. How was it? Then she saw a village—there were always houses passing.

This was an old world she was still journeying through, winter-heavy and dreary. There was plough-land and pasture, and copses of bare trees, copses of bushes, and homesteads naked and work-bare. No new earth had come to pass.

She looked at Birkin's face. It was white and still and eternal, too eternal. She linked her fingers imploringly in his, under the cover of her rug. His fingers responded, his eyes looked back at her. How dark, like a night, his eyes were, like another world beyond! Oh, if he were the world as well, if only the world were he! If only he could call a world into being, that should be their own world!

The Belgians left, the train ran on, through Luxembourg, through Alsace-Lorraine, through Metz. But she was blind, she could see no more. Her soul did not look out.

They came at last to Basle, to the hotel. It was all a drifting trance, from which she never came to. They went out in the morning, before the train departed. She saw the streets, the river, she stood on the bridge. But it all meant nothing. She remembered some shops—one full of pictures, one with orange velvet and ermine. But what did these signify?—nothing.

She was not at ease till they were in the train again. Then she was relieved. So long as they were moving onwards, she was satisfied. They came to Zürich, then, before very long, ran under the mountains, that were deep in snow. At last she was drawing near. This was the other world, now.

Innsbruck was wonderful, deep in snow, and evening. They drove in an open sledge over the snow: the train had been so hot and stifling. And the hotel, with the golden light glowing under the porch, seemed like a home.

They laughed with pleasure when they were in the hall. The place seemed full and busy.

"Do you know if Mr and Mrs Crich—English—from Paris, have arrived?" Birkin asked in German.

The porter reflected a moment, and was just going to answer, when Ursula caught sight of Gudrun sauntering down the stairs, wearing her dark glossy coat, with grey fur.

"Gudrun! Gudrun!" she called, waving up the well of the staircase: "Yu-hu!"

Gudrun looked over the rail, and immediately lost her sauntering, diffident air. Her eyes flashed.

"Really—Ursula!" she cried.

And she began to move downstairs as Ursula ran up. They met at a turn and kissed with laughter and exclamations inarticulate and stirring.

"But!" cried Gudrun, mortified. "We thought it was *tomorrow* you were coming! I wanted to come to the station."

"No, we've come today!" cried Ursula. "Isn't it lovely here!"

"Adorable!" said Gudrun. "Gerald's just gone out to get something.—Ursula, aren't you *fearfully* tired?"

"No, not so very. But I look a filthy sight, don't I?"

"No, you don't. You look almost perfectly fresh.—I like that fur cap *immensely*!"

She glanced over Ursula, who wore a big soft coat with a collar of deep, soft, blond fur, and a soft blond cap of fur.

"And you!" cried Ursula. "What do you think *you* look like!"

Gudrun assumed an unconcerned, expressionless face.

"Do you like it?" she said.

"It's *very* fine!" cried Ursula, perhaps with a touch of satire.

"Go up—or come down," said Birkin.

For there the sisters stood, Gudrun with her hand on Ursula's arm, on the turn of the stairs half way to the first landing, blocking the way, and affording full entertainment to the whole of the hall below, from the door porter to the plump Jew in black clothes.

The two young women slowly mounted, followed by Birkin and the porter.

"First floor?" asked Gudrun, looking back over her shoulder.

"Second madam—the lift—!" the porter replied, and he darted to the elevator, to forestall the two women. But they ignored him, as, chattering without heed, they set to mount the second flight. Rather chagrined, the porter followed.

It was curious, the delight of the sisters in each other, at this meeting. It was as if they met in exile, and united their solitary forces against all the world. Birkin looked on with some mistrust and wonder.

When they had bathed and changed, Gerald came in. He looked shining like the sun on frost.

"Go with Gerald and smoke," said Ursula to Birkin. "Gudrun and I want to talk."

Then the sisters sat in Gudrun's bedroom, and talked clothes, and experiences. Gudrun told Ursula the experience of the Birkin letter in the café, Ursula was shocked and frightened.

"Where is the letter?" she asked.

"I kept it," said Gudrun.

"You'll give it me, won't you?" she said. But Gudrun was silent for some moments, before she replied:

"Do you really want it, Ursula?"

"I want to read it," said Ursula.

"Certainly," said Gudrun.

Even now, she could not admit, to Ursula, that she wanted to keep it, as a memento, or a symbol. But Ursula knew, and was not pleased. So the subject was switched off.

"What did you do in Paris?" asked Ursula.

"Oh," said Gudrun laconically—"the usual things. We had a *fine* party one night in Fanny Rath's studio."

"Did you? And you and Gerald were there! Who else? Tell me about it."

"Well," said Gudrun. "There's nothing particular to tell. You know Fanny is *frightfully* in love with that painter, Billy Macfarlane. *He* was there—so Fanny spared nothing, she spent *very* freely.—It was really remarkable! Of course, everybody got fearfully drunk—but in an interesting way, not like that filthy London crowd. The fact is, these were all people that matter, which makes all the difference. There was a Roumanian, a fine chap. He got completely drunk, and climbed to the top of a high studio ladder, and gave the most marvellous address—really, Ursula, it was wonderful! He began in French—La vie, c'est une affaire d'âmes impériales—in a most beautiful voice—he was a fine-looking chap—but he had got into Roumanian before he had finished, and not a soul understood. But Donald Gilchrist was worked to a frenzy. He dashed his glass to the ground, and declared, by God, he was glad he had been born, by God, it was a miracle to be alive.—And do you know, Ursula, so it was—" Gudrun laughed rather hollowly.

"But how was Gerald among them all?" asked Ursula.

"Gerald! Oh, my word, he came out like a dandelion in the sun! *He's* a whole Saturnalia in himself, once he is roused. I shouldn't like to say whose waist his arm did not go round.—Really, Ursula, he seems to reap the women like a harvest: there wasn't one that would have resisted him. It was too amazing! Can you understand it?"

Ursula reflected, and a dancing light came into her eyes.

"Yes," she said, "I can. He is such a whole-hogger."

"Whole-hogger!—I should think so!" exclaimed Gudrun. "But it is true, Ursula, every woman in the room was ready to surrender to him—Chanticleer isn't in it—even Fanny Rath, who is genuinely in love with Billy Macfarlane! I never was more amazed in my life!—And you know, afterwards—I felt I was a whole *roomful* of women. I was no more myself to him, than I was Queen Victoria. I was a whole roomful of women at once. It was most astounding!—But my eye, I'd caught a Sultan that time—"

Gudrun's eyes were flashing, her cheek was hot, she looked strange, exotic, satiric. Ursula was fascinated at once—and yet uneasy.

They had to get ready for dinner. Gudrun came down in a daring gown of vivid green silk and tissue of gold, with green velvet bodice, and a strange black-and-white band round her hair. She was really brilliantly beautiful, and everybody noticed her. Gerald was in that full-blooded, gleaming state when he was most handsome. Birkin watched them with quick, laughing, half-sinister eyes, Ursula quite lost her head. There seemed a spell, almost a blinding spell, cast round their table, as if they were lighted up more strongly than the rest of the dining-room.

"Don't you love to be in this place?" cried Gudrun. "Isn't the snow wonderful! Do you notice how it exalts everything? It is simply marvelous. One really does feel übermenschlich—more than human."

"One does," cried Ursula. "But isn't that partly the being out of England?"

"Oh, of course," cried Gudrun. "One could never feel like this in England, for the simple reason that the damper is *never* lifted off one, there. It is quite impossible really to let go, in England, of that I am assured."

And she turned again to the food she was eating. She was fluttering with vivid intensity.

"It's quite true," said Gerald, "it never is *quite* the same in England.— But perhaps we don't want it to be—perhaps it's like bringing the light a little too near the powder-magazine, to let go altogether, in England. One is afraid what might happen, if *everybody else* let go."

"My God!" cried Gudrun. "But wouldn't it be wonderful, if all England *did* suddenly go off like a display of fireworks."

"It couldn't," said Ursula. "They are all too damp, the powder is damp in them."

"I'm not so sure of that," said Gerald.

"Nor I," said Birkin. "When the English really begin to go off, *en masse*, it'll be time to shut your ears, and run."

"They never will," said Ursula.

"We'll see," he replied.

"Isn't it marvellous," said Gudrun, "how thankful one can be, to be out of one's country. I cannot believe myself, I am so transported, the moment I set foot on a foreign shore. I say to myself 'here steps a new creature into life.'"

"Don't be too hard on poor old England," said Gerald. "Though we curse it, we love it really."

To Ursula, there seemed a fund of cynicism in these words.

"We may." said Birkin. "But it's a damnably uncomfortable love: like a love for an aged parent who suffers horribly from a complication of diseases, for which there is no hope."

Gudrun looked at him with dilated dark eyes.

"You think there is no hope?" she asked, in her pertinent fashion.

But Birkin backed away. He would not answer such a question.

"Any hope of England's becoming real? God knows. It's a great actual unreality now, an aggregation into unreality.—It might be real, if there were no Englishmen."

"You think the English will have to disappear?" persisted Gudrun. It was strange, her pointed interest in his answer. It might have been her own fate she was inquiring after. Her dark, dilated eyes rested on Birkin, as if she could conjure the truth of the future out of him, as out of some instrument of divination.

He was pale. Then, reluctantly, he answered:

"Well—what else is in front of them, but disappearance?—They've got to disappear from their own special brand of Englishness, anyhow."

Gudrun watched him as if in a hypnotic state, her eyes wide and fixed on him.

"But in what way do you mean, disappear?—" she persisted.

"Yes, do you mean a change of heart?" put in Gerald.

"I don't mean anything, why should I?" said Birkin. "I'm an Englishman, and I've paid the price of it. I can't talk about England—I can only speak for myself."

"Yes," said Gudrun slowly, "You love England immensely, *immensely*, Rupert."

"And leave her," he replied.

"No, not for good. You'll come back," said Gerald, nodding sagely.

"They say the lice crawl off a dying body," said Birkin, with a glare of bitterness. "So I leave England."

"Ah, but you'll come back," said Gudrun, with a sardonic smile.

"*Tant pis pour moi*," he replied.

"Isn't he angry with his mother country!" laughed Gerald, amused.

"Ah, a patriot!" said Gudrun, with something like a sneer.

Birkin refused to answer any more.

Gudrun watched him still for a few seconds. Then she turned away. It was finished, her spell of divination in him. She felt already purely cynical. She looked at Gerald. He was wonderful like a piece of radium to her. She felt she could consume herself and know *all*, by means of this fatal, living metal. She smiled to herself at her fancy. And what would she do with herself, when she had destroyed herself? For if spirit, if integral being is destructible, Matter is indestructible.

He was looking bright and abstracted, puzzled, for the moment. She stretched out her beautiful arm, with its fluff of green tulle, and touched his chin with her subtle, artist's fingers.

"What are they then?" she asked, with a strange, knowing smile.

"What?" he replied, his eyes suddenly dilating with wonder.

"Your thoughts."

Gerald looked like a man coming awake.

"I think I had none," he said.

"Really!" she said, with grave laughter in her voice.

And to Birkin, it was as if she killed Gerald, with that touch.

"Ah but," cried Gudrun, "let us drink to Britannia—let us drink to Britannia."

It seemed there was wild despair in her voice. Gerald laughed, and filled the glasses.

"I think Rupert means," he said "that *nationally* all Englishmen must die, so that they can exist individually and—"

"Super-nationally—" put in Gudrun, with a slight ironic grimace, raising her glass.

Chapter XXX

Snow

The next day, they descended at the tiny railway station of Hohenhausen, at the end of the tiny valley railway. It was snow everywhere, a white, perfect cradle of snow, new and frozen, sweeping up up on either side, black crags and white sweeps of silver towards the blue pale heavens.

As they stepped out on to the naked platform, with only snow around and above, Gudrun shrank as if it chilled her heart.

"My God, Jerry," she said, turning to Gerald with sudden intimacy, "you've done it now."

"What?"

She made a faint gesture, indicating the world on either hand.

"Look at it!"

She seemed afraid to go on. He laughed.

They were in the heart of the mountains. From high above, on either side, swept down the white fold of snow, so that one seemed small and tiny in a valley of pure concrete heaven, all strangely radiant and changeless and silent.

"It makes one feel so small and alone," said Ursula, turning to Birkin and laying her hand on his arm.

"You're not sorry you've come, are you?" said Gerald to Gudrun.

She looked doubtful. They went out of the station between banks of snow.

"Ah," said Gerald, sniffing the air in elation, "this is perfect.—There's our sledge.—We'll walk a bit—we'll run up the road."

Gudrun, always doubtful, dropped her heavy coat on the sledge, as he did his, and they set off. Suddenly she threw up her head and set off scudding along the road of snow, pulling her cap down over her ears. Her blue, bright dress fluttered in the wind, her thick scarlet stockings were brilliant above the whiteness. Gerald watched her: she seemed to be rushing towards her fate, and leaving him behind. He let her get some distance, then, loosening his limbs, he went after her.

Everywhere was deep and silent snow. Great snow-eaves weighed down the broad-roofed Tyrolese houses, that were sunk to the window-sashes in snow. Peasant-women, full-skirted, wearing each a cross-over shawl, and thick snowboots, turned in the way to look at the soft, determined girl running with such heavy fleetness from the man, who was overtaking her, but not gaining any power over her.

They passed the inn with its painted shutters and balcony, a few cottages half buried in the snow; then the snow-buried silent saw-mill by the roofed bridge, which crossed the hidden stream, over which they ran into the very depth of the untouched sheets of snow. It was a silence and a sheer whiteness exhilarating to madness. But the perfect silence was most terrifying, isolating the soul, surrounding the heart with frozen air.

"It's a marvellous place, for all that," said Gudrun, looking into his eyes with a strange, meaning look. His soul leapt.

"Good!" he said.

A fierce, electric energy seemed to flow over all his limbs, his muscles were surcharged, his hands felt hard with strength. They walked along rapidly up the snow-road, that was marked by withered branches of trees stuck in at intervals. He and she were separate, like opposite poles of one fierce energy. But they felt powerful enough to leap over the confines of life into the forbidden places, and back again.

Birkin and Ursula were running along also, over the snow. He had disposed of the luggage, and they had a little start of the sledges. Ursula was excited and happy, but she kept turning suddenly to catch hold of Birkin's arm, to make sure of him.

"This is something I never expected," she said. "It is a different world, here."

They went on into a snow meadow. There they were overtaken by the sledge, that came tinkling through the silence. It was another mile before they came upon Gudrun and Gerald, on the steep up-climb, beside the pink, half-buried shrine.

Then they passed into a gulley, where were walls of black rock, and a river filled with snow, and a still blue sky above. Through a covered bridge they went, drumming roughly over the boards, crossing the snow-bed once more, then slowly up and up, the horses walking swiftly, the driver cracking his long whip as he walked beside, and calling his strange wild *heu-heu*!, the walls of rock passing slowly by, till they emerged again between slopes and masses of snow. Up and up, gradually, they went, through the cold shadow-radiance of the afternoon, silenced by the imminence of the mountains, the luminous, dazing sides of snow that rose above them and fell away beneath.

They came forth at last in a little high table-land of snow, where stood the last peaks of snow like the heart petals of an open rose. In the midst of the last deserted valleys of heaven stood a lonely building with brown wooden walls and white-heavy roof, deep and deserted in the waste of snow, like a dream. It stood like a rock that had rolled down from the last steep slopes, a rock that had taken the form of a house, and was now half buried. It was unbelievable that one could live there uncrushed by all this terrible waste of whiteness and silence and clear, upper, ringing cold.

Yet the sledges ran up in fine style, people came to the door laughing and excited, the floor of the hostel rang hollow, the passage was wet with snow, it was a real, warm interior.

The new-comers tramped up the bare wooden stairs, following the serving woman. Gudrun and Gerald took the first bedroom. In a moment they found themselves alone in a bare, smallish, close-shut room that was all of golden-coloured wood, floor, walls, ceiling, door, all of the same warm-gold panelling of oiled pine. There was a window opposite the door, but low down, because the roof sloped. Under the slope of the ceiling were the table with wash-hand bowl and jug, and across, another table with mirror. On either side the door were two beds piled high with an enormous blue-checked overbolster, enormous.

This was all—no cupboard, none of the amenities of life. Here they were shut up together in this cell of golden-coloured wood, with two blue-checked beds. They looked at each other and laughed, frightened by this naked nearness of isolation.

A man knocked and came in with the luggage. He was a sturdy fellow with flattish cheek-bones, rather pale, and with coarse fair moustache. Gudrun watched him put down the bags, in silence, then tramp heavily out.

"It isn't too rough, is it?" Gerald asked.

The bedroom was not very warm, and she shivered slightly.

"It is wonderful," she equivocated. "Look at the colour of this panelling—it's wonderful, like being inside a nut."

He was standing watching her, feeling his short-cut moustache, leaning back slightly and watching her with his keen, undaunted eyes, dominated by the constant passion, that was like a doom upon him.

She went and crouched down in front of the window, curious.

"Oh, but this—!" she cried involuntarily, almost in pain.

In front was a valley shut in under the sky, the last huge slopes of snow and black rock, and at the end, like the navel of the earth, a white-folded wall, and two peaks glimmering in the late light. Straight in front ran the cradle of silent snow, between the great slopes, that were fringed with a little roughness of pine-trees, like hair, round the base. But the cradle of snow ran on to the eternal closing-in, where the walls of snow and rock rose impenetrable, and the mountain peaks above were in heaven immediate. This was the centre, the knot, the navel of the world, where the earth belonged to the skies, pure, unapproachable, impassable.

It filled Gudrun with a strange rapture. She crouched in front of the window, clenching her face in her hands, in a sort of trance. At last she had arrived, she had reached her place. Here at last she folded her venture and settled down like a crystal in the navel of snow, and was gone.

Gerald bent above her and was looking out over her shoulder. Already he felt he was alone. She was gone. She was completely gone, and there was icy vapour round his heart. He saw the blind valley, the great cul de sac of snow and mountain peaks, under the heaven. And there was no way out. The terrible silence and cold and the glamorous whiteness of the dusk wrapped him round, and she remained crouching before the window, as at a shrine, a shadow.

"Do you like it?" he asked, in a voice that sounded detached and foreign. At least she might acknowledge he was with her. But she only averted her soft, mute face a little from his gaze. And he knew that there were tears in her eyes, her own tears, tears of her strange religion, that put him to nought.

Quite suddenly, he put his hand under her chin and lifted up her face to him. Her dark blue eyes, in their wetness of tears, dilated as if she was startled in her very soul. They looked at him through their tears in terror and a little horror. His light blue eyes were keen, small-pupilled and unnatural in their vision. Her lips parted, as she breathed with difficulty.

The passion came up in him, stroke after stroke, like the ringing of a bronze bell, so strong and unflawed and indomitable. His knees tightened to bronze, as he hung above her soft face, whose lips parted and whose eyes dilated in a strange violation. In the grasp of his hand her chin was unutterably soft and silken. He felt strong as winter, his hands were living metal, invincible and not to be turned aside. His heart rang like a bell clanging inside him.

He took her up in his arms. She was soft and inert, motionless. All the while her eyes, in which the tears had not yet dried, were dilated as if in a kind of swoon of fascination and helplessness. He was superhumanly strong, and unflawed, as if invested with supernatural force.

He lifted her close and folded her against him. Her softness, her inert, relaxed weight lay against his own surcharged, bronze-like limbs in a heaviness of desirability that would destroy him, if he were not fulfilled. She moved convulsively, recoiling away from him. His heart went up like a flame of ice, he closed over her like steel. He would destroy her rather than be denied.

But the overweening power of his body was too much for her. She relaxed again, and lay loose and soft, panting in a little delirium. And to him, she was so sweet, she was such bliss of release, that he would have suffered a whole eternity of torture rather than forego one second of this pang of unsurpassable bliss.

"My God," he said to her, his face drawn and strange, transfigured, "what next?"

She lay perfectly still, with a still, child-like face and dark eyes, looking at him. She was lost, fallen right away.

"I shall always love you," he said, looking at her.

But she did not hear. She lay looking at him as at something she could never understand, never: as a child looks at a grown-up person, without hope of understanding, only submitting.

He kissed her, kissed her eyes shut, so that she should not look any more. He wanted something now, some recognition, some sign, some admission. But she only lay silent and child-like and remote, like a child that is overcome and cannot understand, only feels lost. He kissed her again, giving up.

"Shall we go down and have coffee and Kuchen?" he asked.

The twilight was falling slate-blue at the window. She closed her eyes, closed away the monotonous level of dead wonder, and opened them again to the everyday world.

"Yes," she said briefly, regaining her will with a click.

She went again to the window. Blue evening had fallen over the cradle of snow and over the great pallid slopes. But in the heaven the peaks of snow were rosy, glistening like transcendent, radiant spikes of blossom in the heavenly upper-world, so lovely and beyond.

Gudrun saw all their loveliness, she *knew* how immortally beautiful they were, great pistils of rose-coloured, snow-fed fire in the blue twilight of the heaven. She could *see* it, she knew it, but she was not of it. She was divorced, debarred, a soul shut out.

With a last look of remorse, she turned away, and was doing her hair. He had unstrapped the luggage, and was waiting, watching her. She knew he was watching her. It made her a little hasty and feverish in her precipitation.

They went downstairs, both with a strange, other-world look on their faces, and with a glow in their eyes. They saw Birkin and Ursula sitting at the long table in a corner, waiting for them.

"How good and simple they look together," Gudrun thought, jealously. She envied them some spontaneity, a childish sufficiency to which she herself could never approach. They seemed such children to her.

"Such *good* Kranzkuchen!" cried Ursula greedily. "So *good*!"

"Right," said Gudrun. "Can we have Kaffee mit Kranzkuchen?" she added, to the waiter.

And she seated herself on the bench, beside Gerald. Birkin, looking at them, felt a pain of tenderness for them.

"I think the place is really wonderful, Gerald," he said; "prachtvoll and wunderbar and wunderschön and unbeschreiblich and all the other German adjectives."

Gerald broke into a slight smile.

"*I* like it," he said.

The tables, of white scrubbed wood, were placed round three sides of the room, as in a Gasthaus. Birkin and Ursula sat with their backs to the wall, which was of oiled wood, and Gerald and Gudrun sat in the corner next them, near to the stove. It was a fairly large place, with a tiny bar, just like a country inn, but quite simple and bare, and all of oiled wood, ceilings and walls and floor, the only furniture being the tables and benches going round three sides, the great green stove, and the bar and the doors on the fourth side. The windows were double, and quite uncurtained. It was early evening.

The coffee came—hot and good—and a whole ring of cake.

"A whole Kuchen!" cried Ursula. "They give you more than us! I want some of yours."

There were other people in the place, ten altogether, so Birkin had found out: two artists, three students, a man and wife, and a Professor and two daughters,—all Germans. The four English people, being new-comers, sat in their coign of vantage to watch. The Germans peeped in at the door, called a word to the waiter, and went away again. It was not meal-time, so they did not come into this dining-room, but betook themselves, when their boots were changed, to the Reunionsaal.

The English visitors could hear the occasional twanging of a zither, the strumming of a piano, snatches of laughter and shouting and singing, a faint vibration of voices. The whole building being of wood, it seemed to carry every sound, like a drum, but instead of increasing each particular noise, it decreased it, so that the sound of the zither seemed tiny, as if a diminutive zither were playing somewhere, and it seemed the piano must be a small one, like a little spinet.

The host came when the coffee was finished. He was a Tyrolese, broad, rather flat-cheeked, with a pale, pock-marked skin and flourishing moustaches.

"Would you like to go to the Reunionsaal and be introduced to the other ladies and gentlemen?" he asked, bending forward and smiling, showing his large, strong teeth. His blue eyes went quickly from one to the other—he was not quite sure of his ground with these English people. He was unhappy too because he spoke no English, and he was not sure whether to try his French.

"Shall we go to the Reunionsaal and be introduced to the other people?" repeated Gerald, laughing.

There was a moment's hesitation.

"I suppose we'd better—better break the ice," said Birkin.

The women rose, rather flushed. And the Wirt's black, beetle-like, broad-shouldered figure went on ignominiously in front, towards the noise. He opened the door and ushered the four strangers into the play-room.

Instantly a silence fell, a slight embarrassment came over the company. The new-comers had a sense of many blond faces looking their way. Then the host was bowing to a short, energetic-looking man with large moustaches, and saying in a low voice:

"Herr Professor, darf ich Sie vorstellen—"

The Herr Professor was prompt and energetic. He bowed low to the English people, smiling, and began to be a comrade at once.

"Nehmen die Herrschaften teil an unserer Unterhaltung?" he said, with a vigorous suavity, his voice curling up in the question.

The four English people smiled, lounging with an attentive uneasiness in the middle of the room. Gerald, who was spokesman, said that they would willingly take part in the entertainment. Gudrun and Ursula, laughing, excited, felt the eyes of all the men upon them, and they lifted their heads and looked nowhere, and felt royal.

The Professor announced the names of those present, sans cérémonie, there was a bowing to the wrong people and to the right people. Everybody was there, except the man and wife. The two tall, clear-skinned, athletic daughters of the professor, with their plain-cut, dark blue blouses and loden skirts, their rather long, strong necks, their clear blue eyes and carefully banded hair, and their blushes, bowed and stood back; the three students bowed very low, in the humble hope of making an impression of extreme good-breeding; then there was a small, dark-skinned man with full eyes, an odd creature, like a child, and like a troll, quick, detached: he bowed slightly; his companion, a large fair young man, stylishly dressed, blushed to the eyes and bowed very low.

It was over.

"Herr Loerke was giving us a recitation in the Cologne dialect," said the Professor.

"He must forgive us for interrupting him," said Gerald, "we should like very much to hear it."

There was instantly a bowing and an offering of seats. Gudrun and Ursula, Gerald and Birkin sat in the deep sofas against the wall. The room was of naked oiled panelling, like the rest of the house. It had a piano, sofas and chairs, and a couple of tables with books and magazines. In its complete absence of decoration, save for the big blue stove, it was cosy and pleasant.

Herr Loerke was the little man with the boyish figure, and the round, full, sensitive-looking head, and the quick, full eyes, like a mouse's. He glanced swiftly from one to the other of the strangers, and held himself aloof.

"Please, go on with the recitation," said the Professor, suavely, with his slight authority. Loerke, who was sitting hunched on the piano stool, blinked and did not answer.

"It would be a great pleasure," said Ursula, who had been getting the sentence ready, in German, for some minutes.

Then suddenly, the small, unresponding man swung aside, towards his previous audience, and broke forth, exactly as he had broken off, in a controlled, mocking voice, giving an imitation of a quarrel between an old Cologne woman and a railway guard.

His body was slight and unformed, like a boy's, but his voice was mature, sardonic, its movement had the flexibility of essential energy, and of a mocking, penetrating understanding. Gudrun could not understand a word of his monologue, but she was spell-bound watching him. He must be an artist: nobody else could have such fine adjustment and singleness. The Germans were doubled up with laughter, hearing his strange, droll words, his droll phrases of dialect. And in the midst of their paroxysms, they glanced with deference at the four English strangers, the elect. Gudrun and Ursula were forced to laugh. Then the room rang with shouts of laughter, the blue eyes of the Professor's daughters were swimming over with laughter-tears, their clear cheeks were flushed crimson with mirth, their father broke out in the most astonishing peals of hilarity, the students bowed their heads on their knees in excess of joy. Ursula looked round amazed, the laughter was bubbling out of her involuntarily. She looked at Gudrun, Gudrun looked at her: and the two sisters burst out laughing, carried away. Loerke glanced at them swiftly, with his full eyes. Birkin was sniggering involuntarily, Gerald Crich sat erect, with a glistening look of amusement on his face. And the laughter crashed out again, in wild paroxysms, the Professor's daughters were reduced to shaking helplessness, the veins in the Professor's neck were swollen, his face was purple, he was strangled in ultimate silent spasms of laughter, the students were shouting half-articulated words that tailed off in helpless explosions. Then suddenly the rapid patter of the artist ceased, there were little whoops of subsiding mirth, Ursula and Gudrun were wiping their eyes, and the Professor was crying loudly:

"Ja, das war merkwürdig, das war famos—"

"Wirklich famos!" echoed his exhausted daughters, faintly.

"And we couldn't understand it," cried Ursula.

"Oh leider, leider," cried the Professor.

"You couldn't understand it?" cried the students, let loose at last in speech with the new-comers. "Ja, das ist wirklich schade, das ist schade, gnädige Frau. Wissen Sie———"

The mixture was made, the new-comers were stirred into the party, like new ingredients, the whole room was alive. Gerald was in his element, he talked freely and excitedly, his face glistened with a strange amusement. Perhaps even Birkin, in the end, would break forth. He was shy and withheld, though full of attention.

Ursula was prevailed upon to sing "Annie Lowrie," as the Professor called it. There was a hush of *extreme* deference. She had never been so flattered in her life. Gudrun accompanied her on the piano, playing from memory.

Ursula had a beautiful ringing voice, but usually no confidence, she spoiled everything. This evening she felt conceited and untrammelled. Birkin was well in the background, she shone almost in reaction, the Germans made her feel fine and infallible, she was liberated into overweening self-confidence. She felt like a bird flying in the air, as her voice soared out, enjoying herself extremely in the balance and flight of the song, like the motion of a bird's wings that is up in the wind, sliding and playing on the air, she played with sentimentality, supported by rapturous attention. She was very happy, singing that song by herself, full of a conceit of emotion and power, working upon all those people, and upon herself, exerting herself with gratification, giving immeasurable gratification to the Germans.

At the end, the Germans were all touched with admiring, delicious melancholy, they praised her in soft, reverent voices, they could not say too much.

"Wie schön, wie rührend! Ach, die Schottischen Lieder, sie haben so viel Stimmung! Aber die gnädige Frau hat eine *wunderbare* Stimme; die gnädige Frau ist wirklich eine Künstlerin, aber wirklich!"

She was dilated and brilliant, like a flower in the morning sun. She felt Birkin looking at her, as if he were jealous of her, and her breasts thrilled, her veins were all golden. She was as happy as the sun that has just opened above clouds. And everybody seemed so admiring and radiant, it was perfect.

After dinner she wanted to go out for a minute, to look at the world. The company tried to dissuade her—it was so terribly cold. But just to look, she said.

They all four wrapped up warmly, and found themselves in a vague, unsubstantial outdoors of dim snow and ghosts of an upper-world, that made strange shadows before the stars. It was indeed cold, bruisingly, frighteningly, unnaturally cold. Ursula could not believe the air in her nostrils. It seemed conscious, malevolent, purposive in its intense, murderous coldness.

Yet it was wonderful, an intoxication, a silence of dim, unrealised snow, of the invisible intervening between her and the visible, between her and the flashing stars. She could see Orion sloping up. How wonderful he was, wonderful enough to make one cry aloud.

And all around was this cradle of snow, and there was firm snow underfoot, that struck with heavy cold through her boot-soles. It was night, and silence. She imagined she could hear the stars. She imagined distinctly she could hear the celestial, musical motion of the stars, quite near at hand. She seemed like a bird flying amongst their harmonious motion.

And she clung close to Birkin. Suddenly, she realised she did not know what he was thinking. She did not know where he was ranging.

"My love!" she said, stopping to look at him.

His face was pale, his eyes dark, there was a faint spark of starlight on them. And he saw her face soft and upturned to him, very near. He kissed her softly.

"What then?" he asked.

"Do you love me?" she asked.

"Too much," he answered, quietly.

She clung a little closer.

"Not too much," she pleaded.

"Far too much—" he said, almost sadly.

"And does it make you sad, that I am everything to you?" she asked, wistful.

He held her close, kissing her, and saying, scarcely audible:

"No, but I feel like a beggar—I feel poor."

She was silent, looking at the stars now. Then she kissed him.

"Don't be a beggar," she pleaded, wistfully. "It isn't ignominious, that you love me."

"It is ignominious to feel poor, isn't it?" he replied.

"Why?—why should it be?" she asked. He only stood still, in the terribly cold air that moved invisibly over the mountain tops, folding her round with his arms.

"I couldn't bear this cold, eternal place without you," he said. "I couldn't bear it, it would kill the quick of my life."

She kissed him again, suddenly.

"Do you hate it?" she asked, puzzled, wondering.

"If I couldn't come near to you, if you weren't here, I should hate it, I couldn't bear it," he answered.

"But the people are nice," she said.

"I mean the snow, the stillness, the cold, the frozen eternality," he said.

She wondered. Then her spirit came home to him, nestling unconscious in him.

"Yes, it is good we are warm and together," she said.

And they turned home again. They saw the golden lights of the hotel glouring out in the night of snow-silence, small in the hollow, like a cluster of yellow berries. It seemed like a bunch of sun-sparks, tiny and orange in the midst of the snow-darkness. Behind, was a high shadow of a peak, blotting out the stars, like a ghost.

They drew near to their home. They saw a man come from the dark building, with a lighted lantern which swung golden, and made that his dark feet walked in a halo of snow. He was a small, dark figure in the darkened snow. He unlatched the door of an outhouse. A smell of cows, hot, animal, almost like beef, came out on the heavily cold air. There was a glimpse of two cattle in their dark stalls, then the door was shut again, and not a chink of light showed. It had reminded Ursula again of home, of the Marsh, of her childhood, and of the journey to Brussels, and, strangely enough, of Anton Skrebensky.

Oh God, could one bear it, this past which was gone down the abyss? Could she bear, that it ever had been! She looked round this silent, upper world of snow and stars and powerful cold. There was another world, like views on a magic lantern: the Marsh, Cossethay, Ilkeston, lit up with a common, unreal light. There was a shadowy, unreal Ursula, a whole shadow-play of an unreal life. It was as unreal, and circumscribed, as a magic-lantern show. She wished the slides could all be broken. She wished it could be gone for ever, like a lantern-slide which is broken. She wanted to have no past. She wanted to have come down from the slopes of heaven to this place, with Birkin, not to have toiled out of the murk of her childhood and her upbringing, slowly, all soiled. She felt that memory was a dirty trick played upon her. What was this decree, that she should 'remember'! Why not a bath of pure oblivion, a new birth, without any recollections or blemish of a past life. She was with Birkin, she had just come into life, here in the high snow, against the stars. What had she to do with parents and antecedents? She knew herself new and unbegotten, she had no father, no mother, no anterior connections, she was herself, pure and silvery, she belonged only to the oneness with Birkin, a oneness that struck deeper notes, sounding into the heart of the universe, the heart of reality, where she had never existed before.

Even Gudrun was a separate unit, separate, separate, having nothing to do with this self, this Ursula, in her new world of reality. That old shadow-world, the actuality of the past—ah, let it go! She rose free on the wings of her new condition.

Gudrun and Gerald had not come in. They had walked up the valley straight in front of the house, not like Ursula and Birkin, on to the little hill at the right. Gudrun was driven by a strange desire. She wanted to plunge on and on, till she came to the end of the valley of snow. Then she wanted to climb the wall of white finality, climb over, into the peaks that sprang up like sharp petals in the heart of the frozen, mysterious navel of the world. She felt that there, over the strange, blind, terrible wall of rocky snow, there in the navel of the mystic world, among the final cluster of peaks, there, in the infolded navel of it all, was her consummation. If she could but come there, alone, and pass into the infolded navel of eternal snow and of uprising, immortal peaks of snow and rock, she would be a oneness with all, she would be herself the eternal, infinite silence, the sleeping, timeless, frozen centre of the All.

They went back to the house, to the Reunionsaal. She was curious to see what was going on. The men there made her alert, roused her curiosity. It was a new taste of life for her, they were so prostrate before her, yet so full of life.

The party was boisterous; they were dancing all together, dancing the Schuhplatteln, the Tyrolese dance of the clapping hands and tossing the partner in the air at the crisis. The Germans were all proficient—they were from Munich chiefly. Gerald also was quite passable. There were three zithers twanging away in a corner. It was a scene of great animation and confusion. The professor was initiating Ursula into the dance, stamping, clapping, and swinging her high, with amazing force and zest, when the crisis came. Birkin was behaving manfully with one of the professor's fresh, strong daughters, who was exceedingly happy. Everybody was dancing, there was the most boisterous turmoil.

Gudrun looked on with delight. The solid wooden floor resounded to the knocking heels of the men, the air quivered with the clapping hands and the zither music, there was a golden dust about the hanging lamps.

Suddenly the dance finished, Loerke and the students rushed out to bring in drinks. There was an excited clamour of voices, a chinking of mug-lids, a great crying of "Prosit—Prosit!" Loerke was everywhere at once, like a gnome—suggesting drinks for the women, making an obscure, slightly risky joke with the men, confusing and mystifying the waiter.

He wanted very much to dance with Gudrun. From the first moment he had seen her, he wanted to make a connection with her. Instinctively she felt this, and she waited for him to come up. But a kind of sulkiness kept him away from her, so she thought he disliked her.

"Will you schuhplattern, gnädige Frau?" said the large, fair youth, Loerke's companion. He was too soft, too humble for Gudrun's taste. But she wanted to dance, and the fair youth, who was called Leitner, was handsome enough, in his uneasy, slightly abject fashion, a humility that covered a certain fear. She accepted him as a partner.

The zithers sounded out again, the dance began. Gerald led them, laughing, with one of the Professor's daughters. Ursula danced with one of the students, Birkin with the other daughter of the Professor, the Professor with Frau Kramer, and the rest of the men danced together, with quite as much zest as if they had had women partners.

Because Gudrun had danced with the well-built, soft youth, his companion, Loerke was more pettish and exasperated than ever, and would not even notice her existence in the room. This piqued her, but she made up to herself by dancing with the professor, who was strong as a mature, well-seasoned bull, and as full of coarse energy. She could not bear him, critically, and yet she enjoyed being rushed through the dance, and tossed up into the air, on his coarse, powerful impetus. The professor enjoyed it too, he eyed her with strange, large blue eyes, full of galvanic fire. She hated him for the seasoned, semi-paternal animalism with which he regarded her, but she admired his weight of strength.

The room was charged with excitement and strong, animal emotion. Loerke was kept away from Gudrun, to whom he wanted to speak, as by a hedge of thorns, and he felt a sardonic, ruthless hatred for his young love-companion, Leitner, who was his penniless dependent. He mocked the youth, with an acid ridicule, that made Leitner red in the face and impotent with resentment.

Gerald, who had now got the dance perfectly, was dancing again with the younger of the Professor's daughters, who was almost dying of virgin excitement, because she thought Gerald so handsome, so superb. He had her in his power, as if she were a palpitating bird, a fluttering, flushing, bewildered creature. And it made him smile, as she shrank convulsively between his hands, violently, when he must throw her into the air. At the end, she was so overcome with prostrate love for him, that she could scarcely speak sensibly at all.

Birkin was dancing with Ursula. There were odd little fires playing in his eyes, he seemed to have turned into something wicked and flickering, mocking, suggestive, quite impossible. Ursula was frightened of him, and fascinated. Clear, before her eyes, as in a vision, she could see the sardonic, licentious mockery of his eyes, he moved towards her with subtle, animal, indifferent approach. The strangeness of his hands, which came quick and cunning, inevitably to the vital place beneath her breasts, and, lifting with mocking, suggestive impulse, carried her through the air as if without strength, through black-magic, made her swoon with fear. For a moment she revolted, it was horrible. She would break the spell. But before the resolution had formed she had submitted again, yielded to her fear. He knew all the time what he was doing, she could see it in his smiling, concentrated eyes. It was his responsibility, she would leave it to him.

When they were alone in the darkness, she felt the strange licentiousness of him hovering upon her. She was troubled and repelled. Why should he turn like this?

"What is it?" she asked in dread.

But his face only glistened on her, unknown, horrible. And yet she was fascinated. Her impulse was to repel him violently, break from this spell of mocking brutishness. But she was too fascinated, she wanted to submit, she wanted to know. What would he do to her?

He was so attractive, and so repulsive at once. The sardonic suggestivity that flickered over his face and looked from his narrowed eyes, made her want to hide, to hide herself away from him, and watch him from somewhere unseen.

"Why are you like this?" she demanded again, rousing against him with sudden force and animosity.

The flickering fires in his eyes concentrated as he looked into her eyes. Then the lids drooped with a faint motion of satiric contempt. Then they rose again to the same remorseless suggestivity. And she gave way, he might do as he would. His licentiousness was repulsively attractive. But he was self-responsible, she would see what it was.

They might do as they liked—this she realised as she went to sleep. How could anything that gave one satisfaction be excluded? What was degrading?—Who cared? Degrading things were real, with a different reality. And he was so unabashed and unrestrained. Wasn't it rather horrible, a man who could be so soulful and spiritual, now to be so—she balked at her own thoughts and memories: then she added—so bestial? So bestial, they two!—so degraded! She winced.—But after all, why not? She exulted as well. Why not be bestial, and go the whole round of experience? She exulted in it. She was bestial. How good it was to be really shameful! There would be no shameful thing she had not experienced.—Yet she was unabashed, she was herself. Why not?—She was free, when she knew everything, and no dark shameful things were denied her.

Gudrun, who had been watching Gerald in the Reunionsaal, suddenly thought:

"He should have all the women he can—it is his nature. It is absurd to call him monogamous—he is naturally promiscuous. That is his nature."

The thought came to her involuntarily. It shocked her somewhat. It was as if she had seen some new Mene! Mene! upon the wall. Yet it was merely true. A voice seemed to have spoken it to her so clearly, that for the moment she believed in inspiration.

"It is really true," she said to herself again. ·

She knew quite well she had believed it all along. She knew it implicitly. But she must keep it dark—almost from herself. She must keep it completely secret. It was knowledge for her alone, and scarcely even to be admitted to herself.

The deep resolve formed in her, to combat him. One of them must triumph over the other. Which should it be? Her soul steeled itself with strength. Almost she laughed within herself, at her confidence. It woke a certain keen, half contemptuous pity, tenderness for him: she was so ruthless.

Everybody retired early. The professor and Loerke went into a small lounge to drink. They both watched Gudrun go along the landing, by the railing, upstairs.

"Ein schönes Frauenzimmer," said the Professor.

"Ja!" assented Loerke, shortly.

Gerald walked with his queer, long wolf-steps across the bedroom to the window, stooped and looked out, then rose again, and turned to Gudrun, his eyes sharp with an abstract smile. He seemed very tall to her, she saw the glisten of his whitish eyebrows, that met between his brows.

"How do you like it?" he said.

He seemed to be laughing inside himself, quite unconsciously. She looked at him. He was a phenomenon to her, not a human being: a sort of creature, greedy.

"I like it very much," she replied.

"Who do you like best downstairs?" he asked, standing tall and glistening above her, with his glistening stiff hair erect.

"Who do I like best?" she repeated, wanting to answer his question, and finding it difficult to collect herself. "Why I don't know, I don't know enough about them yet, to be able to say. Whom do *you* like best?"

"Oh I don't care—I don't like or dislike any of them. It doesn't matter about me. I wanted to know about you."

"But why?" she asked, going rather pale.

The abstract, unconscious smile in his eyes was intensified.

"I wanted to know," he said.

She turned aside, breaking the spell. In some strange way, she felt he was getting power over her.

"Well I can't tell you already," she said.

She went to the mirror to take out the hairpins from her hair. She stood before the mirror every night for some minutes, brushing her fine dark hair. It was part of the inevitable ritual of her life.

He followed her, and stood behind her. She was busy, with bent head, taking out the pins and shaking her warm hair loose. When she looked up, she saw him in the glass, standing behind her, watching unconsciously, not consciously seeing her, and yet watching, with fine-pupilled eyes that *seemed* to smile, and which were not really smiling.

She started. It took all her courage for her to continue brushing her hair, as usual, for her to pretend she was at her ease. She was far, far from being at her ease with him. She beat her brains wildly for something to say to him.

"What are your plans for tomorrow?" she asked, nonchalant, whilst her heart was beating so furiously, her eyes were so bright with strange nervousness, she felt he could not but observe. But she knew also that he was completely blind, blind as a wolf looking at her. It was a strange battle between her ordinary consciousness and his uncanny, black-art consciousness.

"I don't know," he replied; "what would you like to do?"

He spoke emptily, his mind was sunk away.

"Oh," she said, with easy protestation, "I'm ready for anything—anything will be fine for *me*, I'm sure."

And to herself she was saying:

"God, why am I so nervous,—why are you so *nervous*, you fool. If he sees it I'm done for for ever—you *know* you're done for for ever, if he sees the absurd state you're in."

And she smiled to herself as if it were all child's play. Meanwhile her heart was plunging, she was almost fainting. She could see him, in the mirror, as he stood there behind her, tall and over-arching—blond and terribly frightening. She glanced at his reflection with furtive eyes, willing to give anything to save him from knowing she could see him. He did not know she could see his reflection. He was looking unconsciously, glisteningly down at her head, from which the hair fell loose, as she brushed it with wild, nervous hand. She held her head aside and brushed and brushed her hair madly. For her life, she could not turn round and face him. For her life, *she could not*. And the knowledge made her almost sink to the ground in a faint, helpless, spent. She was aware of his frightening, impending figure standing close behind her, she was aware of his hard, strong, unyielding chest, close upon her back. And she felt she could not bear it any more, in a few minutes she would fall down at his feet, grovelling at his feet, and letting him destroy her.

The thought pricked up all her sharp intelligence and presence of mind. She dared not turn round to him—and there he stood motionless, unbroken. Summoning all her strength, she said in a full, resonant, nonchalant voice, that was forced out with all her remaining self-control:

"Oh would you mind looking in that bag behind there and giving me my————"

Here her power fell inert. "My what—my what—?" she screamed in silence to herself.

But he had started round, surprised and startled that she should ask him to look in her bag, which she always kept so *very* private to herself. She turned now, her face white, her dark eyes blazing with uncanny, over-wrought excitement. She saw him stooping to the bag, undoing the loosely buckled strap. She had conquered him, he was stooping down, servile.

"Your what?" he asked.

"Oh, a little enamel box—yellow—with a design of a cormorant plucking her breast—"

She went towards him, stooping her beautiful, bare arm, and deftly turned some of her things, disclosing the box, which was exquisitely painted.

"That is it, see," she said, taking it from under his eyes.

And he was baffled now. He was left to fasten up the bag, whilst she swiftly did up her hair for the night, and sat down to unfasten her shoes. She would not turn her back to him any more.

He was baffled, frustrated, but unconscious. She had the whip hand over him now. She knew he had not realised her terrible panic. Her heart was beating heavily still. Fool, fool that she was, to get into such a state! How she thanked God for Gerald's obtuse blindness. Thank God he could see nothing.

She sat slowly unlacing her shoes, and he too commenced to undress. Thank God that crisis was over. She felt almost fond of him now, almost in love with him.

"Ah Gerald," she laughed, caressively, teasingly, "Ah, what a fine game you played with the Professor's daughter—didn't you now?"

"What game?" he asked, looking round.

"*Isn't* she in love with you—oh *dear*, isn't she in love with you!" said Gudrun, smiling in her gayest, most attractive mood.

"I shouldn't think so," he said.

"'Shouldn't think so!'" she teased. "Why the poor girl is lying at this moment overwhelmed, dying with love for you. She thinks you're *wonderful*—oh marvellous, beyond what man has ever been.—*Really*, isn't it funny?"

"Why funny, what is funny?" he asked.

"Why to see you working it on her," she said, with a half reproach that confused the male conceit in him. "Really Gerald, the poor girl——!"

"I did nothing to her," he said.

"Oh, it was too shameful, the way you simply swept her off her feet."

"That was Schuhplatteln," he replied, with a bright grin.

"Ha—ha—ha!" laughed Gudrun.

Her mockery quivered through his muscles with curious re-echoes. When he slept he seemed to crouch down in the bed, lapped up in his own strength, that yet was hollow.

And Gudrun slept strongly, a victorious sleep. Suddenly, she was almost fiercely awake. The small timber room glowed with the dawn, that came upwards from the low window. She could see down the valley when she lifted her head: the snow with a pinkish, half-revealed magic, the fringe of pine-trees at the bottom of the slope. And one tiny figure moved over the vaguely-illumined space.

She glanced at his watch: it was seven o'clock. He was still completely asleep. And she was so hard awake, it was almost frightening—a hard, metallic wakefulness. She lay looking at him.

He slept in the subjection of his own health and defeat. She was overcome by a sincere regard for him. Till now, she was afraid before him. She lay and thought about him, what he was, what he represented in the world. A fine, independent will, he had. She thought of the revolution he had worked in the mines, in so short a time. She knew that, if he were confronted with any problem, any hard actual difficulty, he would overcome it. If he laid hold of any idea, he would carry it through. He had the faculty of making order out of confusion. Only let him grip hold of a situation, and he would bring to pass an inevitable conclusion.

For a few moments she was borne away on the wild wings of ambition. Gerald, with his force of will and his power for comprehending the actual world, should be set to solve the problems of the day, the problem of industrialism in the modern world. She knew he would, in the course of time, effect the changes he desired, he could re-organise the industrial system. She knew he could do it. As an instrument, in these things, he was marvellous, she had never seen any man with his potentiality. He was unaware of it, but she knew.

He only needed to be hitched on, he needed that his hand should be set to the task, because he was so unconscious. And this she could do. She would marry him, he would go into Parliament in the Conservative interest, he would clear up the great muddle of labour and industry. He was so superbly fearless, masterful, he knew that every problem could be worked out, in life as in geometry. And he would care neither about himself nor about anything but the pure working out of the problem. He was very pure, really.

Her heart beat fast, she flew away on wings of elation, imagining a future. He would be a Napoleon of peace, or a Bismarck—and she the woman behind him. She had read Bismarck's letters, and had been deeply moved by them. And Gerald would be freer, more dauntless than Bismarck.

But even as she lay in fictitious transport, bathed in the strange, false sunshine of hope in life, something seemed to snap in her, and a terrible cynicism began to gain upon her, blowing in like a wind. Everything turned to irony with her: the last flavour of everything, was ironical. When she felt her pang of undeniable reality, this was when she knew the hard irony of hopes and ideas.

She lay and looked at him, as he slept. He was sheerly beautiful, he was a perfect instrument. To her mind, he was a pure, inhuman, almost superhuman instrument. His instrumentality appealed so strongly to her, she wished she were God, to use him as a tool.

And at the same instant, came the ironical question: "What for?" She thought of the colliers' wives, with their linoleum and their lace curtains and their little girls in high-laced boots. She thought of the wives and daughters of the pit-managers, their tennis-parties, and their terrible struggles to be superior each to the other, in the social scale. There was Shortlands with its meaningless distinction, the meaningless crowd of the Criches. There was London, the House of Commons, the extant social world. My God!

Young as she was, Gudrun had touched the whole pulse of social England, she had no ideals of rising in the world. She knew, with the perfect cynicism of cruel youth, that to rise in the world meant to have one outside show instead of another, the advance was like having a spurious half-crown instead of a spurious penny. The whole coinage of valuation was spurious. Yet of course, her cynicism knew well enough that, in a world where spurious coin was current, a bad sovereign was better than a bad farthing. But rich and poor, she despised both alike.

Already she mocked at herself for her dreams. They could be fulfilled easily enough. But she recognised too well, in her spirit, the mockery of her own impulses. What did she care, that Gerald had created a richly-paying industry out of an old worn-out concern? What did she care? The worn-out concern, and the rapid, splendidly-organised industry, they were alike indifferent to her, they were bad money.—Yet of course, she cared a great deal, outwardly—and outwardly was all that mattered, for inwardly was a bad joke.

Everything was intrinsically a piece of irony to her. She leaned over Gerald and said in her heart, with compassion:

"Oh, my dear, my dear, the game isn't worth even you. You are a fine thing really—why should you be used on such a poor show!"

Her heart was breaking with pity and grief for him. And at the same moment, a grimace came over her mouth, of mocking irony at her own unspoken tirade. Ah, what a farce it was! She thought of Parnell and Katherine O'Shea. Parnell! After all, who can take the nationalisation of Ireland seriously? Who can take political Ireland really seriously, whatever it does? And who can take political England seriously? Who can? Who can care a straw, really, how the old, patched-up Constitution is tinkered at any more? Who cares a button for our national ideals, any more than for our national bowler hat? Aha, it is all old hat, it is all old bowler hat?

That's all it is, Gerald, my young hero. At any rate we'll spare ourselves the nausea of stirring the old broth any more. You be beautiful, my Gerald, and reckless. There *are* perfect moments. Wake up, Gerald, wake up, convince me of the perfect moments, oh convince me, I need it.

He opened his eyes, and looked at her. She greeted him with a mocking, enigmatic smile in which was a poignant gaiety. Over his face went the reflection of the smile, he smiled too, purely unconsciously.

That filled her with extraordinary delight, to see the smile cross his face, reflected from her face. She remembered, that was how a baby smiled. It filled her with extraordinary radiant delight.

"You've done it," she said.

"What?" he asked, dazed.

"Convinced me."

And she bent down, kissing him passionately, passionately, so that he was bewildered. He did not ask her of what he had convinced her, though he meant to. He was glad she was kissing him. She seemed to be feeling for his very heart, to touch the quick of him. And he wanted her to touch the quick of his being, he wanted that most of all.

Outside, somebody was singing, in a manly, reckless, handsome voice:

> "Mach mir auf, mach mir auf, du Stolze,
> Mach mir ein Feuer von Holze
> Vom Regen bin ich nass
> Vom Regen bin ich nass—"

Gudrun knew, that that song would sound through her eternity, sung in a manly, reckless, mocking voice. It marked one of her supreme moments, the supreme pangs of her nervous gratification. There it was, fixed in eternity for her.

The day came fine and bluish. There was a light wind blowing among the mountain-tops, keen as a rapier where it touched, carrying with it a fine dust of snow-powder. Gerald went out with the fine, blind face of a man who is in his state of fulfilment. Gudrun and he were in perfect static unity this morning, both unseeing and unwitting. They went out with a toboggan, leaving Ursula and Birkin to follow.

Gudrun was all scarlet and royal blue—a scarlet jersey and cap, and a royal blue skirt and stockings. She went gaily over the white snow, with Gerald beside her, in white and grey, pulling the little toboggan. They grew small in the distance of snow, climbing the steep slope.

For Gudrun herself, she seemed to pass altogether into the whiteness of the snow, she became a pure, thoughtless crystal. When she reached the top of the slope, in the wind, she looked round, and saw peak beyond peak of rock and snow, bluish, transcendent in heaven. And it seemed to her like a garden, with the peaks for pure flowers, and her heart gathering them. She had no separate consciousness for Gerald.

She held on to him as they went sheering down over the keen slope. She felt as if her senses were being whetted on some fine grindstone, that was keen as flame. The snow sprinted on either side, like sparks from a blade that is being sharpened, the whiteness round about ran swifter, swifter, in pure flame the white slope flew against her, and she fused like one molten, dancing globule, rushed through a white intensity. Then there was a great swerve at the bottom, when they swung as it were in a fall to earth, in the diminishing motion.

They came to rest. But when she rose to her feet, she could not stand. She gave a strange cry, turned and clung to him, sinking her face on his breast, fainting in him. Utter oblivion came over her, as she lay for a few moments abandoned against him.

"What is it?" he was saying. "Was it too much for you?"

But she heard nothing.

When she came to, she stood up and looked round, astonished. Her face was white, her eyes brilliant and large.

"What is it?" he repeated. "Did it upset you?"

She looked at him with her brilliant eyes, that seemed to have undergone some transfiguration, and she laughed, with a terrible merriment.

"No," she cried, with triumphant joy. "It was the complete moment of my life."

And she looked at him with her dazzling, overweening laughter, like one possessed. A fine blade seemed to enter his heart, but he did not care, or take any notice.

But they climbed up the slope again, and they flew down through the white flame again, splendidly, splendidly. Gudrun was laughing and flashing, powdered with snow-crystals, Gerald worked perfectly. He felt he could guide the toboggan to a hair's-breadth, almost he could make it pierce into the air and right into the very heart of the sky. It seemed to him the flying sledge was but his strength spread out, he had but to move his arms, the motion was his own. They explored the great slopes, to find another slide. He felt there must be something better than they had known. And he found what he desired, a perfect long, fierce sweep, sheering past the foot of a rock and into the trees at the base. It was dangerous, he knew. But then he knew also he could direct the sledge between his fingers.

The first days passed in an ecstasy of physical motion, sleighing, ski-ing, skating, moving in an intensity of speed and white light that surpassed life itself, and carried the souls of the human beings beyond into an inhuman abstraction of velocity and weight and eternal, frozen snow.

Gerald's eyes became hard and strange, and as he went by on his skis he was more like some powerful, fateful sigh than a man, his muscles elastic in a perfect, soaring trajectory, his body projected in pure flight, mindless, soulless, whirling along one perfect line of force.

Luckily there came a day of snow, when they must all stay indoors: otherwise, Birkin said, they would all lose their faculties, and begin to utter themselves in cries and shrieks, like some strange, unknown species of snow-creatures.

It happened in the afternoon that Ursula sat in the Reunionsaal talking to Loerke. The latter had seemed unhappy lately. He was lively and full of mischievous humour, as usual. But Ursula had thought he was sulky about something. His partner, too, the big, fair, good-looking youth, was ill at ease, going about as if he belonged to nowhere, and was kept in some sort of subjection, against which he was rebelling.

Loerke had hardly talked to Gudrun. His associate, on the other hand, had paid her constantly a soft, over-deferential attention. Gudrun wanted to talk to Loerke. He was a sculptor, and she wanted to hear his view of his art. And his figure attracted her. There was the look of a little wastrel about him, that intrigued her, and an old man's look, that interested her, and then, beside this, an uncanny singleness, a quality of being by himself, not in contact with anybody else, that marked out an artist to her. He was a chatterer, a mag-pie, a maker of mischievous word-jokes, that were sometimes very clever, but which often were not—And she could see in his brown, gnome's eyes, the black look of inorganic misery, which lay behind all his small buffoonery.

His figure interested her—the figure of a boy, almost of a street arab. He made no attempt to conceal it. He always wore a simple loden suit, with knee breeches. His legs were thin, and he made no attempt to disguise the fact: which was of itself remarkable, in a German. And he never ingratiated himself anywhere, not in the slightest, but kept to himself, for all his apparent playfulness.

Leitner, his companion, was a great sportsman, very handsome with his big limbs and his blue eyes. Loerke would go tobogganing, or ski-ing, or skating, in little snatches, but he was indifferent. And his fine, thin nostrils, the nostrils of a pure-bred street arab, would quiver with contempt at Leitner's splothering gymnastic displays. It was evident that the two men, who had travelled and lived together in the last degree of intimacy, had now reached the stage of loathing. Leitner hated Loerke with an injured, writhing, impotent hatred, and Loerke treated Leitner with a fine-quivering contempt and sarcasm. Soon the two would have to go apart.

Already they were rarely together. Leitner ran attaching himself to somebody or other, always deferring, Loerke was a good deal alone. Out of doors he wore a Westphalian cap, a close brown-velvet head with big brown-velvet flaps down over his ears, so that he looked like a lop-eared rabbit, or a troll. His face was brown-red, with a dry, bright skin, that seemed to crinkle with his mobile expressions. His eyes were arresting—brown, full, like a rabbit's, or like a troll's, or like the eyes of a lost being, having a strange, dumb, depraved look of knowledge, and a quick spark of uncanny fire. Whenever Gudrun had tried to talk to him he had shied away unresponsive, looking at her with his watchful dark eyes, but entering into no relation with her. He had made her feel that her slow French, and her slower German, were hateful to him. As for his own inadequate English, he was much too awkward to try it at all. But he understood a good deal of what was said, nevertheless. And Gudrun, piqued, left him alone.

This afternoon, however, she came into the lounge as he was talking to Ursula. His fine, black hair somehow reminded her of a bat, thin as it was on his full, sensitive-looking head, and worn away at the temples, he sat hunched up, as if his spirit were bat-like. And Gudrun could see he was making some slow confidence to Ursula, unwilling, a slow, grudging, scanty self-revelation. She went and sat by her sister.

He looked at her, then looked away again, as if he took no notice of her. But as a matter of fact, she interested him deeply.

"Isn't it interesting, Prune," said Ursula, turning to her sister, "Herr Loerke is doing a great frieze for a factory in Cologne, for the outside, the street."

She looked at him, at his thin, brown, nervous hands, that were prehensile, and somehow like talons, like 'griffes,' inhuman.

"What in?" she asked.

"*Aus was?*" repeated Ursula.

"*Granit*," he replied.

It had become immediately a laconic series of question and answer between fellow craftsmen.

"What is the relief?" asked Gudrun.

"Alto rilievo."

"And at what height?"

It was very interesting to Gudrun, to think of his making the great granite frieze for a great granite factory in Cologne. She got from him some notion of the design. It was a representation of a fair, with peasants and artizans in an orgy of enjoyment, drunk and absurd in their modern dress, whirling ridiculously in roundabouts, gaping at shows, kissing and staggering and rolling in knots, swinging in swing-boats and firing down shooting galleries, a frenzy of chaotic motion.

There was a swift discussion of technicalities. Gudrun was very much impressed.

"But how wonderful, to have such a factory!" cried Ursula. "Is the whole building fine?"

"Oh yes," he replied. "The frieze is part of the whole architecture. Yes, it is a colossal thing."

Then he seemed to stiffen, shrugged his shoulders, and went on:

"Sculpture and architecture must go together. The day for irrelevant statues, as for wall pictures, is over. As a matter of fact sculpture is always part of an architectural conception. And since churches are all museum stuff, since industry is our business, now, then let us make our places of industry our art—our factory-area our Parthenon—ecco!"

Ursula pondered.

"I suppose," she said, "there is no *need* for our great works to be so hideous."

Instantly he broke into motion.

"There you are!" he cried, "there you are! There is not only *no need* for our places of work to be ugly, but their ugliness ruins the work, in the end. Men will not go on submitting to such intolerable ugliness. In the end it will hurt too much, and they will wither because of it. And this will wither the *work* as well. They will think the work itself is ugly: the machines, the very act of labour. Whereas machinery and the acts of labour are extremely, maddeningly beautiful. But this will be the end of our civilisation, when people will not work because work has become so intolerable to their senses, it nauseates them too much, they would rather starve. *Then* we shall see the hammer used only for smashing, then we shall see it.—Yet here we are—we have the opportunity to make beautiful factories, beautiful machine-houses—we have the opportunity—"

Gudrun could only partly understand. She could have cried with vexation.

"What does he say?" she asked Ursula. And Ursula translated, stammering and brief. Loerke watched Gudrun's face, to see her judgment.

"And do you think then," said Gudrun, "that art should serve industry?"

"Art should *interpret* industry, as art once interpreted religion," he said.

"But does your fair interpret industry?" she asked him.

"Certainly. What is man doing, when he is at a fair like this? He is fulfilling the counterpart of labour—the machine works him, instead of he the machine. He enjoys the mechanical motion, in his own body."

"But is there nothing but work—mechanical work?" said Gudrun.

"Nothing but work!" he repeated, leaning forward, his eyes two darknesses, with needle-points of light. "No, it is nothing but this, serving a machine, or enjoying the motion of a machine—motion, that is all.—You have never worked for hunger, or you would know what God governs us."

Gudrun quivered and flushed. For some reason she was almost in tears.

"No, I have not worked for hunger," she replied. "But I have worked?"

"Travaillé—lavorato?" he cried. "E che lavoro—che lavoro? Quel travail est-ce que vous avez fait?"

He broke into a mixture of Italian and French, instinctively using a foreign language when he spoke to her.

"You have never worked as the world works," he said to her, with sarcasm.

"Yes," she said, "I have. And I do—I work now for my daily bread."

He paused, looked at her steadily, then dropped the subject entirely. She seemed to him to be trifling.

"But have *you* ever worked as the world works?" Ursula asked him.

He looked at her untrustful.

"Yes," he replied, with a surly bark. "I have known what it was to lie in bed for three days, because I had nothing to eat."

Gudrun was looking at him with large, grave eyes, that seemed to draw the confession from him as the marrow from his bones. All his nature held him back from confessing. And yet her large, grave eyes upon him seemed to open some valve in his veins, and involuntarily he was telling.

"My father was a man who did not like work, and we had no mother. We lived in Austria, Polish Austria. How did we live? Ha!—somehow! Mostly in a room with three other families—one set in each corner—and the W.C. in the middle of the room—a pan with a plank on it—ha! I had two brothers and a sister—and there might be a woman with my father. He was a free being, in his way—would fight with any man in the town—a garrison town—and was a little man too. But he wouldn't work for anybody—set his heart against it, and wouldn't."

"And how did you live then?" asked Ursula.

He looked at her—then, suddenly, at Gudrun.

"Do you understand?" he asked.

"Enough," she replied.

Their eyes met for a moment. Then he looked away. He would say no more.

"And how did you become a sculptor?" asked Ursula.

"How did I become a sculptor—" he paused. "Dunque—" he resumed, in a changed manner, and beginning to speak French—"I became old enough—I used to steal from the market-place. Later, I went to work—I imprinted the stamp on clay bottles, before they were baked. It was an earthenware-bottle factory. There I began making models. One day, I had had enough. I lay in the sun and did not go to work. Then I walked to Munich—then I walked to Italy—begging, begging everything.

"The Italians were very good to me—they were good and honorable to me. From Bozen to Rome, almost every night, I had a meal and a bed, perhaps of straw, with some peasant. I love the Italian people, with all my heart.

"Dunque, adesso—maintenant—I earn a thousand pounds in a year, or I earn two thousand—."

He looked down at the ground, his voice tailing off into silence.

Gudrun looked at his fine, thin, shiny skin, reddish-brown from the sun, drawn tight over his full temples; and at his thin hair—, and at the thick, coarse, brush-like moustache, cut short above his mobile, rather shapeless mouth.

"How old are you?" she asked.

He looked up at her with his full, elvin eyes, startled.

"*Wie alt?*" he repeated. And he hesitated. It was evidently one of his reticencies.

"How old are *you?*" he replied, without answering.

"I am twenty-six," she answered.

"Twenty-six," he repeated, looking into her eyes. He paused. Then he said:

"Und Ihr Herr Gemahl, wie alt ist er?"

"Who?" asked Gudrun.

"Your husband," said Ursula, with a certain irony.

"I haven't got a husband," said Gudrun in English. In German she answered.

"He is thirty-one."

But Loerke was watching closely, with his uncanny, full, suspicious eyes. Something in Gudrun seemed to accord with him. He was really like one of the "little people" who have no soul, who has found his mate in a human being. But he suffered in his discovery. She too was fascinated by him, fascinated, as if some strange creature, a rabbit or a bat or a brown seal, had begun to talk to her. But also, she knew what he was unconscious of, his tremendous power of understanding, of apprehending her living motion. He did not know his own power. He did not know how, with his full, submerged, watchful eyes, he could look into her and see her, what she was, see her secrets. He would only want her to be herself.—He knew her verily, with a subconscious, sinister knowledge, devoid of illusions and hopes.

To Gudrun, there was in Loerke the rock-bottom of all life. Everybody else had their illusion, must have their illusion, their before and after. But he, with a perfect stoicism, did without any before and after, dispensed with all illusion. He did not deceive himself, in the last issue. In the last issue he cared about nothing, he was troubled about nothing, he made not the slightest attempt to be at one with anything. He existed a pure, unconnected will, stoical and momentaneous. There was only his work.

It was curious too how his poverty, the degradation of his earlier life, attracted her. There was something insipid and tasteless to her, in the idea of a gentleman, a man who had gone the usual course through school and university. A certain violent sympathy, however, came up in her for this mud-child. He seemed to be the very stuff of the underworld of life. There was no going beyond him.

Ursula too was attracted by Loerke. In both sisters he commanded a certain homage. But there were moments when to Ursula he seemed indescribably inferior, false, a vulgarism.

Both Birkin and Gerald disliked him, Gerald ignoring him with some contempt, Birkin exasperated.

"What do the women find so impressive in that little brat?" Gerald asked.

"God above knows," replied Birkin; "unless it's some sort of appeal he makes to them, which flatters them and has such a power over them."

Gerald looked up in surprise.

"*Does* he make an appeal to them?" he asked.

"Oh yes," replied Birkin. "He is the perfectly subjected being, existing almost like a criminal. And the women rush towards that, like a current of air towards a vacuum."

"Funny they should rush to that," said Gerald.

"Makes one mad, too," said Birkin. "But he has the fascination of pity and repulsion for them, a little obscene monster of the darkness that he is."

Gerald stood still, suspended in thought.

"What *do* women want, at the bottom?" he asked.

Birkin shrugged his shoulders.

"God knows," he said. "Some satisfaction in basic repulsion, it seems to me. They seem to creep down some ghastly tunnel of darkness, and will never be satisfied till they've come to the end."

Gerald looked out into the mist of fine snow that was blowing by. Everywhere was blind today, horribly blind.

"And what *is* the end?" he asked.

Birkin shook his head.

"I've not got there yet, so I don't know. Ask Loerke, he's pretty near. He is a good many stages further than either you or I can go."

"Yes, but stages further in what?" cried Gerald, irritated.

Birkin sighed, and gathered his brows into a knot of anger.

"Stages further in social hatred," he said. "He lives like a rat, in the river of corruption, just where it falls over into the bottomless pit. He's further on than we are. He hates the ideal more acutely. He *hates* the ideal utterly, yet it still dominates him. I expect he is a Jew—or part Jewish."

"Probably," said Gerald.

"He is a gnawing little negation, gnawing at the roots of life."

"But why does anybody care about him?" cried Gerald.

"Because they hate the ideal also, in their souls. They want to explore the sewers, and he's the wizard rat that swims ahead."

Still Gerald stood and stared at the blind haze of snow outside.

"I don't understand your terms, really," he said, in a flat, doomed voice. "But it sounds a rum sort of desire."

"I suppose we want the same," said Birkin. "Only we want to take a quick jump downwards, in a sort of ecstasy—and he ebbs with the stream, the sewer stream."

Meanwhile Gudrun and Ursula waited for the next opportunity to talk to Loerke. It was no use beginning when the men were there. Then they could get into no touch with the isolated little sculptor. He had to be alone with them. And he preferred Ursula to be there, as a sort of transmitter to Gudrun.

"Do you do nothing but architectural sculpture?" Gudrun asked him one evening.

"Not now," he replied. "I have done all sorts—except portraits—I never did portraits. But other things—"

"What kind of thing?" asked Gudrun.

He paused a moment, then rose, and went out of the room. He returned almost immediately with a little roll of paper, which he handed to her. She unrolled it. It was a photogravure reproduction of a statuette, signed F. Loerke.

"That is quite an early thing—*not* mechanical," he said, "more popular."

The statuette was of a naked girl, small, finely made, sitting on a great naked horse. The girl was young and tender, a mere bud. She was sitting sideways on the horse, her face in her hands, as if in shame and grief, in a little abandon. Her hair, which was short and must be flaxen, fell forward, divided, half covering her hands.

Her limbs were young and tender. Her legs, scarcely formed yet, the legs of a maiden just passing towards cruel womanhood, dangled childishly over the side of the powerful horse, pathetically, the small feet folded one over the other, as if to hide. But there was no hiding. There she was exposed naked on the naked flank of the horse.

The horse stood stock still, stretched in a kind of start. It was a massive, magnificent stallion, rigid with pent up power. Its neck was arched and terrible, like a sickle, its flanks were pressed back, rigid with power.

Gudrun went pale, and a darkness came over her eyes, like shame, she looked up with a certain supplication, almost slave-like. He glanced at her, and jerked his head a little.

"How big is it?" she asked, in a toneless voice, persisting in appearing casual and unaffected.

"How big?" he replied, glancing again at her. "Without pedestal—so high" he measured with his hand—"with pedestal, so—"

He looked at her steadily. There was a little brusque, turgid contempt for her in his swift gesture, and she seemed to cringe a little.

"And what is it done in?" she asked, throwing back her head and looking at him with affected coldness.

He still gazed at her steadily, and his dominance was not shaken.

"Bronze—green bronze."

"Green bronze!" repeated Gudrun, coldly accepting his challenge. She was thinking of the slender, immature, tender limbs of the girl, smooth and cold in green bronze.

"Yes, beautiful," she murmured, looking up at him with a certain dark homage.

He closed his eyes and looked aside, triumphant.

"Why," said Ursula, "did you make the horse so stiff? It is as stiff as a block."

"Stiff!" he repeated, in arms at once.

"Yes. *Look* how stock and stupid and brutal it is. Horses are sensitive, quite delicate and sensitive, really."

He raised his shoulders, spread his hands in a shrug of slow indifference, as much as to inform her she was an amateur and an impertinent nobody.

"Wissen Sie," he said, with an insulting patience and condescension in his voice, "that horse is a certain *form*, part of a whole form. It is part of a work of art, a piece of form. It is not a picture of a friendly horse to which you give a lump of sugar, do you see—it is part of a work of art, it has no relation to anything outside that work of art."

Ursula, angry at being treated quite so insultingly *de haut en bas*, from the height of esoteric art to the depth of general exoteric amateurism, replied hotly, flushing and lifting her face:

"But it *is* a picture of a horse, nevertheless."

He lifted his shoulders in another shrug.

"As you like—it is not the picture of a cow, certainly."

Here Gudrun broke in, flushed and brilliant, anxious to avoid any more of this, any more of Ursula's foolish persistence in giving herself away.

"What do you mean by 'it is a picture of a horse'?" she cried at her sister. "What do you mean by a horse? You mean an idea you have in *your* head, and which you want to see represented. This is another idea altogether, quite another idea. Call it a horse if you like, or say it is not a horse. I have just as much right to say that *your* horse isn't a horse, that it is a falsity of your own make-up."

Ursula wavered, baffled. Then her words came.

"But why does he have this idea of a horse?" she said. "I know it is his idea. I know it is a picture of himself, really—"

Loerke snorted with rage.

"A picture of myself!" he repeated, in derision. "Wissen Sie, gnädige Frau, that is a Kunstwerk, a work of art. It is a work of art, it is a picture of nothing, of absolutely nothing. It has nothing to do with anything but itself, it has no relation with the everyday world of this and the other, there is no connection between them, absolutely none, they are two different and distinct planes of existence, and to translate one into the other is worse than foolish, it is a darkening of all counsel, a making confusion everywhere. Do you see, you *must not* confuse the relative world of action, with the absolute world of art. That you *must not do*."

"That is quite true," cried Gudrun, let loose in a sort of rhapsody. "The two things are quite and permanently apart, they have nothing to do with one another. *I* and my art, they have *nothing* to do with each other. My art stands in another world, I am in this world."

Her face was flushed and transfigured. Loerke, who was sitting with his head ducked, like some creature at bay, looked up at her swiftly, almost furtively, and murmured:

"Ja—so ist es, so ist es."

Ursula was silent after this outburst. She was furious. She wanted to poke a hole into them both.

"It isn't a word of it true, of all this harangue you have made me," she replied flatly. "The horse is a picture of your own stock stupid brutality, and the girl was a girl you loved and tortured and then ignored."

He looked up at her with a small smile of contempt in his eyes. He would not trouble to answer this last charge. Gudrun too was silent in exasperated contempt. Ursula *was* such an insufferable outsider, rushing in where angels would fear to tread. But there—fools must be suffered, if not gladly.

But Ursula was persistent too.

"As for your world of art and your world of reality," she replied; "you have to separate the two, because you can't bear to know what you are. You can't bear to realise what a stock, stiff, hide-bound brutality you *are* really, so you say 'it's the world of art.' The world of art is only the truth about the real world, that's all—but you are too far gone to see it."

She was white and trembling, intent. Gudrun and Loerke sat in stiff dislike of her. Gerald too, who had come up in the beginning of the speech, stood looking at her in complete disapproval and opposition. He felt she was undignified, she put a sort of vulgarity over the esotericism which gave man his last distinction. He joined his forces with the other two. They all three wanted her to go away. But she sat on in silence, her soul weeping, throbbing violently, her fingers twisting her handkerchief.

The others maintained a dead silence, letting the display of Ursula's obtrusiveness pass by. Then Gudrun asked, in a voice that was quite cool and casual, as if resuming a casual conversation:

"Was the girl a model?"

"Nein, sie war kein Modell. Sie war eine kleine Malschülerin."

"An art-student!" replied Gudrun.

And how the situation revealed itself to her! She saw the girl art-student, unformed and of pernicious recklessness, too young, her straight flaxen hair cut short, hanging just into her neck, curving inwards slightly, because it was rather thick; and Loerke, the well-known master-sculptor, and the girl, probably well-brought-up and of good family, thinking herself so great to be his mistress. Oh how well she knew the common callousness of it all. Dresden, Paris, or London, what did it matter? She knew it.

"Where is she now?" Ursula asked.

Loerke raised his shoulders, to convey his complete ignorance and indifference.

"That is already six years ago," he said; "she will be twenty-three years old, no more good."

Gerald had picked up the picture and was looking at it. It attracted him also. He saw on the pedestal, that the piece was called "Lady Godiva."

"But this isn't Lady Godiva," he said, smiling good-humouredly. "She was the middle-aged wife of some Earl or other, who covered herself with her long hair."

"A la Maud Allan," said Gudrun, with a mocking grimace.

"Why Maud Allan?" he replied. "Isn't it so?—I always thought the legend was that."

"Yes, Gerald dear, I'm quite *sure* you've got the legend perfectly."

She was laughing at him, with a little, mock-caressive contempt.

"To be sure, I'd rather see the woman than the hair," he laughed in return.

"Wouldn't you just!" mocked Gudrun.

Ursula rose and went away, leaving the three together.

Gudrun took the picture again from Gerald, and sat looking at it closely.

"Of course," she said, turning to tease Loerke now, "you *understood* your little Malschülerin."

He raised his eyebrows and his shoulders in a complacent shrug.

"The little girl?" asked Gerald, pointing to the figure. Gudrun was sitting with the picture in her lap. She looked up at Gerald, full into his eyes, so that he seemed to be blinded.

"*Didn't* he understand her!" she said to Gerald, in a slightly mocking, humourous playfulness. "You've only to look at the feet—*aren't* they darling, so pretty and tender—oh, they're really wonderful, they are really—"

She lifted her eyes slowly, with a hot, flaming look into Loerke's eyes. His soul was filled with her burning recognition, he seemed to grow more uppish and lordly.

Gerald looked at the small, sculptured feet. They were turned together, half covering each other in pathetic shyness and fear. He looked at them a long time, fascinated. Then, in some pain, he put the picture away from him. He felt full of barrenness.

"What was her name?" Gudrun asked Loerke.

"Annette von Weck," Loerke replied, reminiscent. "Ja, sie war hübsch.

She was pretty—but she was tiresome. She was a nuisance—not for a minute would she keep still—not until I'd slapped her hard and made her cry—then she'd sit for five minutes."

He was thinking over the work, his work, the all-important to him.

"Did you really slap her?" asked Gudrun, coolly. He glanced back at her, reading her challenge.

"Yes, I did," he said, nonchalant, "harder than I have ever beat anything in my life.—I had to, I had to.—It was the only way I got the work done."

Gudrun watched him with large, dark-filled eyes, for some moments. She seemed to be considering his very soul. Then she looked down, in silence.

"Why did you have such a young Godiva then?" asked Gerald. "She is so small, besides, on the horse—not big enough for it—such a child."

A queer spasm went over Loerke's face.

"Yes," he said, "I don't like them any bigger, any older. Then they are beautiful, at sixteen, seventeen, eighteen—after that, they are no use to me."

There was a moment's pause.

"Why not?" asked Gerald.

Loerke shrugged his shoulders.

"I don't find them interesting—or beautiful—they are no good to me, for my work."

"Do you mean to say a woman isn't beautiful after she is twenty?" asked Gerald.

"For me, no. Before twenty, she is small and fresh and tender and slight. After that—let her be what she likes, she has nothing for me. The Venus of Milo is a bourgeoise—so are they all."

"And you don't care for women at all after twenty?" asked Gerald.

"They are no good to me, they are of no use in my art," Loerke repeated impatiently. "I don't find them beautiful."

"You are an epicure," said Gerald, with a slight sarcastic laugh.

"And what about men?" asked Gudrun suddenly.

"Yes, they are good at all ages," replied Loerke. "A man should be big and powerful—whether he is old or young is of no account, so he has the size, something of massiveness and stupid form."

Ursula went out alone into the world of pure, new snow. But the dazzling whiteness seemed to beat upon her till it hurt her, she felt the cold was slowly strangling her soul. Her head felt dazed and numb.

Suddenly, she wanted to go away. It occurred to her, like a miracle, that she might go away into another world. She had felt so doomed up here in the eternal snow, as if there were no beyond.

Now suddenly, as by a miracle, she remembered that away beyond, below her, lay the dark fruitful earth, that towards the south there were stretches of land dark with orange trees and cypress, grey with olives, that ilex trees lifted wonderful plumy tufts in shadow against a blue sky. Miracle of miracles!—this utterly silent, frozen world of the mountain-tops was not universal! One might leave it and have done with it. One might go away.

She wanted to realise the miracle at once. She wanted at this instant to have done with the snow-world, the terrible static, ice-built mountain-tops. She wanted to see the dark earth, to smell its earthy fecundity, to see the patient wintry vegetation, to feel the sunshine touch a response in the buds.

She went back gladly to the house, full of hope. Birkin was reading, lying in bed.

"Rupert," she said, bursting in on him, "I want to go away."

He looked up at her slowly.

"Do you?" he replied mildly.

She sat by him and put her arms round his neck. It surprised her that he was so little surprised.

"Don't *you*?" she asked, troubled.

"I hadn't thought about it," he said. "But I'm sure I do."

She sat up, suddenly erect.

"I hate it," she said. "I hate this snow, and the unnaturalness of it, the unnatural light it throws on everybody, the ghastly glamour, the unnatural feelings it makes everybody have."

He lay still, and laughed, meditating.

"Well," he said, "we can *go* away—we can go tomorrow. We'll go tomorrow to Verona, and find Romeo and Juliet, and sit in the amphi-theatre—shall we?"

Suddenly she hid her face against his shoulder with perplexity and shyness. He lay so untrammelled.

"Yes," she said softly, filled with relief. She felt her soul had new wings, now he was so uncaring. "I shall love to be Romeo and Juliet," she said.—"My love!"

"Though a fearfully cold wind blows in Verona," he said, "from out of the Alps. We shall have the smell of the snow in our noses."

She sat up and looked at him.

"Are you glad to go?" she asked, troubled. His eyes were inscrutable and laughing. She hid her face against his neck, clinging close to him, pleading:

"Don't laugh at me—don't laugh at me."

"Why—how's that?" he laughed, putting his arms round her.

"Because I don't want to be laughed at," she whispered.

He laughed more, as he kissed her delicate, finely perfumed hair.

"Do you love me?" she whispered, in wild seriousness.

"Yes," he answered, laughing.

Suddenly she lifted her mouth to be kissed. Her lips were taut and quivering and strenuous, his were soft, deep and delicate. He waited a few moments in the kiss. Then a shade of sadness went over his soul.

"Your mouth is so hard," he said, in faint reproach.

"And yours is so soft and nice," she said gladly.

"But why do you always grip your lips?" he asked, regretful.

"Never mind," she said swiftly. "It is my way."

She knew he loved her; she was sure of him. Yet she could not let go a certain hold over herself, she could not bear him to question her. She gave herself up in delight to being loved by him. She knew that, in spite of his joy when she abandoned herself, he was a little bit saddened too. She could give herself up to his activity. But she could not be herself, she *dared* not come forth quite nakedly to his nakedness, abandoning all adjustment, lapsing in pure faith with him. She abandoned herself to *him*, or she took hold of him and gathered her joy of him. And she enjoyed him fully. But they were never *quite* together, at the same moment, one was always a little left out. Nevertheless she was glad in hope, glorious and free, full of life and liberty. And he was still and soft and patient, for the time.

They made their preparations to leave the next day. First they went to Gudrun's room, where she and Gerald were just dressed ready for the evening indoors.

"Prune," said Ursula. "I think we shall go away tomorrow. I can't stand the snow any more. It hurts my skin and my soul."

"Does it really hurt your soul, Ursula?" asked Gudrun in some surprise. "I can quite believe it hurts your skin—it is *terrible*. But I thought it was *admirable* for the soul."

"No, not for mine. It just injures it," said Ursula.

"Really!" cried Gudrun.

There was a silence in the room. And Ursula and Birkin could feel that Gudrun and Gerald were relieved by their going.

"You will go south?" said Gerald, a little ring of uneasiness in his voice.

"Yes," said Birkin, turning away.

There was a queer, indefinable hostility between the two men, lately. Birkin was on the whole dim and indifferent, drifting along in a dim, easy flow, unnoticing and patient, since he came abroad, whilst Gerald, on the other hand, was intense and gripped into white light, agonistes. The two men revoked one another.

Gerald and Gudrun were very kind to the two who were departing, solicitous for their welfare as if they were two children. Gudrun came to Ursula's bedroom with three pairs of the coloured stockings for which she was notorious, and she threw them on the bed. But these were thick silk stockings, vermilion, cornflower blue, and grey, bought in Paris. The grey ones were knitted, seamless and heavy. Ursula was in raptures. She knew Gudrun must be feeling *very* loving, to give away such treasures.

"I can't take them from you Prune," she cried. "I can't possibly deprive you of them—the jewels."

"*Aren't* they jewels!" cried Gudrun, eying her gifts with an envious eye. "*Aren't* they real lambs!"

"Yes, you *must* keep them," said Ursula.

"I don't *want* them, I've got three more pairs. I *want* you to keep them—I want you to have them—they're yours, there—."

And with trembling, excited hands she put the coveted stockings under Ursula's pillow.

"One gets the greatest joy of all out of really lovely stockings," said Ursula.

"One does," replied Gudrun; "the greatest joy of all."

And she sat down in the chair. It was evident she had come for a last talk. Ursula, not knowing what she wanted, waited in silence.

"Do you *feel*, Ursula," Gudrun began, rather sceptically, "that 'you are going away for ever, never to return—' sort of thing?"

"Oh, we shall come back," said Ursula. "It isn't a question of train-journeys."

"Yes, I know. But spiritually, so to speak, you are going away from us all?"

Ursula quivered.

"I don't know a bit what is going to happen," she said. "I only know we are going somewhere."

Gudrun waited.

"And you are glad?" she asked.

Ursula meditated for a moment.

"I believe I am *very* glad," she replied.

But Gudrun read the unconscious brightness on her sister's face, rather than the uncertain tones of her speech.

"But don't you think you'll *want* the old connection with the world— Father and the rest of us, and all that it means, England and the world of thought—don't you think you'll *need* that, really to make a world?"

Ursula was silent, trying to imagine.

"I think," she said at length, involuntarily, "that Rupert is right—one wants a new space to be in, and one falls away from the old."

Gudrun watched her sister with impassive face and steady eyes.

"One wants a new space to be in, I quite agree," she said. "But *I* think that a new world is a development from this world, and that to isolate oneself with one other person, isn't to find a new world at all, but only to secure oneself in one's illusions."

Ursula looked out of the window. In her soul she began to wrestle, and she was frightened. She was always frightened of words, because she knew that mere word-force could always make her believe what she did not believe.

"Perhaps," she said, full of mistrust, of herself and everybody. "But," she added, "I do think that one can't have anything new whilst one cares for the old—do you know what I mean?—even fighting the old is belonging to it.—I know, one is tempted to stop with the world, just to fight it.—But then it isn't worth it."

Gudrun considered herself.

"Yes," she said. "In a way, one is of the world if one lives in it. But isn't it really an illusion, to think you can get out of it? After all, a cottage in the Abruzzi, or wherever it may be, isn't a new world.—No, the only thing to do with the world, is to see it through."

Ursula looked away. She was so frightened of argument.

"But there *can* be something else, can't there?" she said. "One can see it through in one's soul, long enough before it sees itself through in actuality. And then, when one has seen in one's soul, one is something else."

"*Can* one see it through in one's soul?" asked Gudrun. "If you mean that you can see to the end of what will happen, I don't agree.—I really can't agree.—And anyhow, you can't suddenly fly off on to a new planet, because you think you can see to the end of *this*."

Ursula suddenly straightened herself.

"Yes," she said, "yes—one knows. One has no more connections here. One has a sort of other self, that belongs to a new planet, not to this.—You've got to hop off."

Gudrun reflected for a few moments. Then a smile of ridicule, almost of contempt, came over her face.

"And what will happen when you find yourself in space?" she cried in derision. "After all, the great ideas of the world are the same there. You above everybody can't get away from the fact that love, for instance, is the supreme thing, in space as well as on earth."

"No," said Ursula, "it isn't. Love is too human and little. I believe in something inhuman, of which love is only a little part. I believe what we must fulfil comes out of the Unknown to us, and it is something infinitely more than love. It isn't so merely *human*."

Gudrun looked at Ursula with steady, balancing eyes. She admired and despised her sister so much, both. Then suddenly she averted her face, saying coldly, uglily:

"Well, I've got no further than love, yet."

Over Ursula's mind flashed the thought: "Because you never *have* loved, you can't get beyond it."

Gudrun rose, came over to Ursula and put her arm round her neck.

"Go and find your new world, dear," she said, her voice clanging with false benignity. "After all, the happiest voyage is the quest of Rupert's Blessed Isles."

Her arm rested round Ursula's neck, her fingers on Ursula's cheek, for a few moments. Ursula was supremely uncomfortable meanwhile. There was an insult in Gudrun's protective patronage that was really too hurting. Feeling her sister's resistance, Gudrun drew awkwardly away, turned over the pillow and disclosed the stockings again.

"Ha—ha!" she laughed, rather hollowly. "How we do talk indeed—new worlds and old—!"

And they passed to the familiar, worldly subjects.

Gerald and Birkin had walked on ahead, waiting for the sledge to overtake them, conveying the departing guests.

"How much longer will you stay here?" asked Birkin, glancing up at Gerald's very red, almost blank face.

"Oh I can't say," Gerald replied. "Till we get tired of it."

"You're not afraid of the snow melting first?" asked Birkin.

Gerald laughed.

"Does it melt?" he said.

"Things are all right with you then?" said Birkin.

Gerald screwed up his eyes a little.

"All right?" he said. "I never know what those common words mean. All right and all wrong, don't they become synonymous, somewhere?"

"Yes, I suppose.—How about going back?" asked Birkin.

"Oh, I don't know. We may never get back. I don't look before and after," said Gerald.

"*Nor* pine for what is not," said Birkin.

Gerald looked into the distance, with the small-pupilled, abstract eyes of a hawk.

"No. There's something final about this. And Gudrun seems like the end, to me. I don't know—but she seems so soft, her skin like silk, her arms heavy and soft. And it withers my consciousness, somehow, it burns the pith of my mind." He went on a few paces, staring ahead, his eyes fixed, looking like a mask used in ghastly religions of the barbarians. "It blasts your soul's eye," he said, "and leaves you sightless. Yet you *want* to be sightless, you *want* to be blasted, you don't want it any different."

He was speaking as if in a trance, verbal and blank. Then suddenly he braced himself up with a kind of rhapsody, and looked at Birkin with vindictive, cowed eyes, saying:

"Do you know what it is to suffer when you are with a woman? She's so beautiful, so perfect, you find her *so good*, it tears you like a silk, and every stroke and bit cuts hot—ha, that perfection, when you blast yourself, you blast yourself!—And then—" he stopped on the snow and suddenly opened his clenched hands—"it's nothing—your brain might have gone charred as rags—and"—he looked round into the air with a queer histrionic movement—"it's blasting—you understand what I mean—it is a great experience, something final—and then—you're shrivelled as if struck by electricity."

He walked on in silence. It seemed like bragging, but like a man in extremity bragging truthfully.

"Of course," he resumed, "I wouldn't *not* have had it: it's a complete experience. And she's a wonderful woman. But—how I hate her somewhere!—It's curious—"

Birkin looked at him, at his strange, scarcely conscious face. Gerald seemed blank before his own words.

"But you've had enough now?" said Birkin. "You have had your experience. Why work on an old wound?"

"Oh," said Gerald, "I don't know. It's not finished—"

And the two walked on.

"I've loved you, as well as Gudrun, don't forget," said Birkin bitterly. Gerald looked at him strangely, abstractedly.

"Have you?" he said, with icy scepticism. "Or do you think you have?" He was hardly responsible for what he said.

The sledge came. Gudrun dismounted and they all made their farewells. They wanted to go apart, all of them. Birkin took his place, and the sledge drove away leaving Gudrun and Gerald standing on the snow, waving. Something froze Birkin's heart, seeing them standing there in the isolation of the snow, growing smaller and more isolated.

Chapter XXXI

Snowed Up

When Ursula and Birkin were gone, Gudrun felt herself free in her contest with Gerald. As they grew more used to each other, he seemed to press upon her more and more. At first she could manage him, so that her own will was always left free. But very soon, he began to ignore her female tactics, he dropped his respect for her whims and her privacies, he began to exert his own will, blindly, without submitting to hers.

Already a vital conflict had set in, which frightened them both. But he was alone, whilst already she had begun to cast round for external resource.

When Ursula had gone, Gudrun felt her own existence had become stark and elemental. She went and crouched alone in her bedroom, looking out of the window at the big, flashing stars. In front was the faint shadow of the mountain-knot. That was the pivot. She felt strange and inevitable, as if she were centred upon the pivot of all existence, there was no further reality.

Presently Gerald opened the door. She knew he would not be long before he came. She was rarely alone now, he pressed upon her like a frost, deadening her.

"Are you alone in the dark?" he said. And she could tell by his tone he resented it, he resented the isolation she had drawn round herself. Yet, feeling static and inevitable, she was kind towards him.

"Would you like to light the candle?" she asked.

He did not answer, but came and stood behind her, in the darkness.

"Look," she said, "at that lovely star up there. Do you know its name?"

He crouched beside her, to look through the low window.

"No," he said. "It is very fine."

"*Isn't* it beautiful? Do you notice how it darts different coloured fires—it flashes really superbly—"

They remained in silence. With a mute, heavy gesture she put her hand on his knee, and took his hand.

"Are you regretting Ursula?" he asked.

"No, not at all," she said. Then, in a slow mood, she asked:

"How much do you love me?"

He stiffened himself further against her.

"How much do you think I do?" he asked.

"I don't know," she replied.

"But what is your opinion?" he asked.

There was a pause. At length, in the darkness, came her voice, hard and indifferent:

"Very little indeed," she said coldly, almost flippant. His heart went icy at the sound of her voice.

"Why don't I love you?" he asked, as if admitting the truth of her accusation, yet hating her for it.

"I don't know why you don't—I've been good to you. You were in a *fearful* state, when you came to me."

Her heart was beating to suffocate her, yet she was stony and unrelenting.

"When was I in a fearful state?" he asked.

"When you first came to me. I *had* to take pity on you.—But it was never love."

It was that statement 'It was never love,' which sounded in his ears with madness.

"Why must you repeat it so often, that there is no love?" he said in a voice strangled with rage.

"Well you don't *think* you love, do you?" she asked.

He was silent with cold passion of anger.

"You don't think you *can* love me, do you?" she repeated, almost with a sneer.

"No," he said.

"You know you never *have* loved me, don't you?"

"I don't know what you mean by the word 'love'," he replied.

"Yes you do.—You know all right that you have never loved me. Have you, do you think?"

"No," he said, prompted by some barren spirit of truthfulness and obstinacy.

"And you never *will* love me," she said finally. "Will you?"

There was a diabolic coldness in her, too much to bear.

"No," he said.

"Then," she replied, "what have you against me!"

He was silent in cold, frightened rage and despair. "If only I could kill her," his heart was whispering repeatedly. "If only I could kill her—I should be free." It seemed to him that death was the only severing of this Gordian knot.

"Why do you torture me?" he said.

She flung her arms round his neck.

"Ah, I don't want to torture you," she said pityingly, as if she were comforting a child. The impertinence made his veins go cold, he was insensible. She held her arms round his neck, in a triumph of pity. And her pity for him was as cold as stone, its deepest motive was hate of him, and fear of his power over her, which she must always counterfoil.

"Say you love me," she pleaded. "Say you will love me for ever—won't you—won't you?"

But it was her voice only that coaxed him. Her senses were entirely apart from him, cold and destructive of him. It was her overbearing *will* that insisted.

"Won't you say you'll love me always?" she coaxed. "Say it, even if it isn't true—say it Gerald, do."

"I will love you always," he repeated, in real agony, forcing the words out.

She gave him a quick kiss.

"Fancy your actually having said it," she said, with a touch of raillery.

He stood as if he had been beaten.

"Try to love me a little more, and to want me a little less," she said, in a half contemptuous, half coaxing tone.

The darkness seemed to be swaying in waves across his mind, great waves of darkness plunging across his mind. It seemed to him he was degraded at the very quick, made of no account.

"You mean you don't want me?" he said.

"You are so insistent, and there is so little grace in you, so little fineness. You are so crude. You break me—you only waste me—it is horrible to me."

"Horrible to you?" he repeated.

"Yes. Don't you think I might have a room to myself, now Ursula has gone? You can say you want a dressing-room."

"You do as you like—you can leave altogether if you like," he managed to articulate.

"Yes I know that," she replied. "So can you. You can leave me whenever you like—without notice even."

The great tides of darkness were swinging across his mind, he could hardly stand upright. A terrible weariness overcame him, he felt he must lie on the floor. Dropping off his clothes, he got into bed, and lay like a man suddenly overcome by drunkenness, the darkness lifting and plunging as if he were lying upon a black, giddy sea. He lay still in this strange, horrific reeling for some time, purely unconscious.

At length she slipped from her own bed and came over to him. He remained rigid, his back to her. He was all but unconscious.

She put her arms round his terrifying, insentient body, and laid her cheek against his hard shoulder.

"Gerald," she whispered. "Gerald."

There was no change in him. She caught him against her. She pressed her breasts against his shoulders, she kissed his shoulder, through the sleeping-jacket. Her mind wondered, over his rigid, unliving body. She was bewildered and insistent, only her will was set for him to speak to her.

"Gerald, my dear!" she whispered, bending over him, kissing his ear.

Her warm breath playing, flying rhythmically over his ear, seemed to relax the tension. She could feel his body gradually relaxing a little, losing its terrifying, unnatural rigidity. Her hands clutched his limbs, his muscles, going over him spasmodically.

The hot blood began to flow again through his veins, his limbs relaxed.

"Turn round to me," she whispered, forlorn with insistence and triumph.

So at last he was given again, warm and flexible. He turned and gathered her in his arms. And feeling her soft against him, so perfectly and wondrously soft and recipient, his arms tightened on her, she was as if crushed powerless in him. His brain seemed hard and invincible now like a jewel, there was no resisting him.

His passion was awful to her, tense and ghastly and impersonal, like a destruction, ultimate. She felt it would kill her, she was being killed.

"My God, my God!" she cried in anguish, in his embrace, feeling her life being killed within her. And when he was kissing her, soothing her, her breath came slowly, as if she were really spent, dying.

"Shall I die, shall I die?" she repeated to herself.

And in the night, and in him, there was no answer to the question.

And yet, next day, the fragment of her which was not destroyed remained intact and hostile, she did not go away, she remained to finish the holiday, admitting nothing. He scarcely ever left her alone, but followed her like a shadow, he was like a doom upon her, a continual 'thou shalt', 'thou shalt not'. Sometimes it was he who seemed strongest, whilst she was almost gone, creeping near the earth like a spent wind; sometimes it was the reverse. But always it was this eternal see-saw, one destroyed that the other might exist, one ratified because the other was nulled.

"In the end," she said to herself, "I shall go away from him."

"I can be free of her," he said to himself in his paroxysms of suffering.

And he set himself to be free. He even prepared to go away, to leave her in the lurch. But for the first time there was a flaw in his will.

"Where shall I go?" he asked himself.

"Can't you be self-sufficient?" he replied to himself, putting himself upon his pride.

"Self-sufficient?" he repeated.

It seemed to him that Gudrun was sufficient unto herself, closed round and completed, like a thing in a case. In the calm, static reason of his soul, he recognised this, and admitted it was her right, to be closed round upon herself, self-complete, without desire. He realised it, he admitted it, it only needed one last effort on his own part, to win for himself the same completeness. He knew that it only needed one convulsion of his will for him to be able to turn upon himself also, to close upon himself as a stone fixes upon itself, and is impervious, self-completed, a thing isolated.

This knowledge threw him into a terrible chaos. Because, however much he might mentally *will* to be immune and self-complete, the desire for this state was lacking, and he could not create it. He could see that, to exist at all, he must be perfectly free of Gudrun, leave her if she wanted to be left, demand nothing of her, have no claim upon her.

But then, to have no claim upon her, he must stand by himself, in sheer nothingness. And his brain turned to nought at the idea. It was a state of nothingness.—On the other hand, he might give in, and fawn to her.—Or, finally, he might kill her.—Or he might become just indifferent, purpose-less, dissipated, momentaneous.—But his nature was too serious, not gay enough or subtle enough for mocking licentiousness.

A strange rent had been torn in him; like a victim that is torn open and given to the heavens, so he had been torn apart and given to Gudrun. How should he close again? This wound, this strange, infinitely-sensitive opening of his soul, where he was exposed, like an open flower, to all the universe, and in which he was given to his complement, the other, the unknown, this wound, this disclosure, this unfolding of his own covering, leaving him incomplete, limited, unfinished, like an open flower under the sky, this was his cruelest joy. Why then should he forego it. Why should he close up and become impervious, immune, like a partial thing in a sheath, when he had broken forth, like a seed that has germinated, to issue forth in being, embracing the unrealised heavens.

He would keep the unfinished bliss of his own yearning even through the torture she inflicted upon him. A strange obstinacy possessed him. He would not go away from her whatever she said or did. A strange, deathly yearning carried him along with her. She was the determinating influence of his very being. Though she treated him with contempt, repeated rebuffs and denials, still he would never be gone, since in being near her, even, he felt the quickening, the going forth in him, the release, the knowledge of his own limitation and the magic of the promise, as well as the mystery of his own destruction and annihilation.

She tortured the open heart of him even as he turned to her. And she was tortured herself. It may have been her will was stronger. She felt, with horror, as if he tore at the bud of her heart, tore it open, like an irreverent, persistent being. Like a boy who pulls off a fly's wings, or tears open a bud to see what is in the flower, he tore at her privacy, at her very life, he would destroy her as an immature bud, torn open, is destroyed.

She might open towards him, a long while hence, in her dreams, when she was a pure spirit. But now she was not to be violated and ruined. She closed against him fiercely.

They climbed together, at evening, up the high slope, to see the sun set. In the finely breathing, keen wind they stood and watched the yellow sun sink in crimson and disappear. Then in the east the peaks and ridges glowed with living rose, incandescent like immortal flowers against a brown-purple sky, a miracle, whilst down below the world was a bluish shadow, and above, like an annunciation, hovered a rosy transport in mid air.

To her it was so beautiful, it was a delirium, she wanted to gather the glowing, eternal peaks to her breast, and die. He saw them, saw they were beautiful. But there arose no clamour in his breast, only a bitterness that was visionary in itself. He wished the peaks were grey and unbeautiful, so that she should not get her support from them. Why did she betray the two of them so terribly, in embracing the glow of evening? Why did she leave him standing there, with the ice-wind blowing through his heart, like death, to gratify herself among the rosy snow-tips?

"What does the twilight matter?" he said. "Why do you grovel before it? Is it so important to you?"

She winced in violation and in fury.

"Go away," she cried, "and leave me to it. It is beautiful, beautiful," she sang, in strange, rhapsodic tones. "It is the most beautiful thing I have ever seen in my life. Don't try and come between it and me. Take yourself away, you are out of place—"

He stood back a little, and left her standing there, statue-like, transported into the mystic glowing east. Already the rose was fading, large white stars were flashing out. He waited. He would forego everything but the yearning.

"That was the most perfect thing I have ever seen," she said in cold, brutal tones, when at last she turned round to him. "It amazes me that you should want to destroy it. If you can't see it yourself, why try to debar me?" But in reality, he had destroyed it for her, she was straining after a dead effect.

"One day," he said, softly, looking up at her, "I shall destroy *you*, as you stand looking at a sunset; because you are such a liar."

There was a soft, voluptuous promise to himself in the words. She was chilled, but arrogant.

"Ha!" she said. "I am not afraid of your threats!"

She denied herself to him, she kept her room rigidly private to herself. But he waited on, in a curious patience, belonging to his yearning for her.

"In the end," he said to himself, with real voluptuous promise, "when it reaches that point, I shall do away with her." And he trembled delicately in every limb, in anticipation, as he trembled in his most violent accesses of passionate approach to her, trembling with too-much desire.

She had a curious sort of allegiance with Loerke, all the while, now, something insidious and traitorous. Gerald knew of it. But in the unnatural state of patience, and the unwillingness to harden himself against her, in which he found himself, he took no notice, although her soft kindliness to the other man, whom he hated as a noxious insect, made him shiver again with an access of the strange shuddering that came over him repeatedly.

He left her alone only when he went ski-ing, a sport he loved, and which she did not practise. Then he seemed to sweep out of life, to be a projectile into the beyond. And often, when he went away, she talked to the little German sculptor. They had an invariable topic, in their art.

They were almost of the same ideas. He hated Mestrovic, was not satisfied with the Futurists, he liked the West African wooden figures, the Aztec art, Mexican and Central American. He saw the grotesque, and a curious sort of mechanical motion intoxicated him, a confusion in nature.

They had a curious game with each other, Gudrun and Loerke, of infinite suggestivity, strange and leering, as if they had some esoteric understanding of life, that they alone were initiated into the fearful central secrets, that the world dared not know. Their whole correspondence was in a strange, barely comprehensible suggestivity, they kindled themselves at the subtle lusts of the Egyptians or the Mexicans. The whole game was one of subtle inter-suggestivity, and they wanted to keep it on the plane of suggestion. From their verbal and physical *nuances* they got the highest satisfaction in the nerves, from a queer interchange of half-suggested ideas, looks, expressions and gestures, which were quite intolerable, though incomprehensible, to Gerald. He had no terms in which to think of their commerce, his terms were much too gross.

The suggestion of primitive art was their refuge, and the inner mysteries of sensation their object of worship. Art and Life were to them the Reality and the Unreality.

"Of course," said Gudrun, "life doesn't *really* matter—it is one's art which is central. What one does in one's life has *peu de rapport*, it doesn't signify much."

"Yes, that is so, exactly," replied the sculptor. "What one does in one's art, that is the breath of one's being. What one does in one's life, that is a bagatelle for the outsiders to fuss about."

It was curious what a sense of elation and freedom Gudrun found in this communication. She felt established for ever. Of course Gerald was *bagatelle*—love was one of the temporal things in her life, except in so far as she was an artist. She thought of Cleopatra—Cleopatra must have been an artist; she reaped the essential from a man, she harvested the ultimate sensation, and threw away the husk; and Mary Stuart, and Eleonora Duse, panting with her lovers after the theatre, these were the exoteric exponents of love. After all, what was the lover but fuel for the transport of this subtle knowledge, for a female art, the art of pure, perfect knowledge in sensuous understanding.

One evening Gerald was arguing with Loerke about Italy and Tripoli. The Englishman was in a strange, inflammable state, the German was excited. It was a contest of words, but it meant a conflict in spirit between the two men. And all the while Gudrun could see in Gerald an arrogant, English contempt for a foreigner. Although Gerald was quivering, his eyes flashing, his face flushed, in his argument there was a brusqueness, a savage contempt in his manner, that made Gudrun's blood flare up, and made Loerke keen and mortified. For Gerald came down like a sledge-hammer with his assertions, anything the little German said was merely contemptible rubbish.

At last Loerke turned to Gudrun, raising his hands in helpless irony, a shrug of ironical dismissal, something appealing and child-like:

"Sehen Sie, Gnädige Frau—" he began.

"Bitte sagen Sie nicht immer gnädige Frau," cried Gudrun, her eyes flashing, her cheeks burning. She looked like a vivid Medusa. Her voice was loud and clamorous, the other people in the room were startled.

"Please don't call me Mrs Crich," she cried aloud.

The name, in Loerke's mouth particularly, had been an intolerable humiliation and constraint upon her, these many days.

The two men looked at her in amazement. Gerald went white at the cheek-bones.

"What shall I say, then?" asked Loerke, with soft, mocking insinuation.

"Sagen Sie nur nicht das," she muttered, her cheeks flushed crimson. "Not that, at least."

She saw, by the dawning look on Loerke's face, that he had understood. She was *not* Mrs Crich! So-o-o, that explained a great deal.

"Soll ich Fräulein sagen?" he asked, malevolently.

She looked at him with some aversion.

"I am not married," she said, with some hauteur.

Her heart was fluttering now, beating like a bewildered bird. She knew she had dealt a cruel wound, and she could not bear it.

Gerald sat erect, perfectly still, his face pale and calm, like the face of a statue. He was unaware of her, or of Loerke, or anybody. He sat perfectly still, in an unalterable calm. Loerke, meanwhile, was crouching and glancing up from under his ducked head.

Gudrun was tortured for something to say, to relieve the suspense. She twisted her face in a smile, and glanced knowingly, almost sneering, at Gerald.

"Truth is best," she said to him, with a grimace.

But now again, she was under his domination; now, because she had dealt him this blow, because she had destroyed him, and she did not know how he had taken it. She watched him. He was interesting to her. She had lost her interest in Loerke.

Gerald rose at length, and went over, in a leisurely, still movement, to the professor. The two began a conversation on Goethe.

She was rather piqued by the simplicity of Gerald's demeanour this evening. He did not seem angry or disgusted, only he looked curiously innocent and pure, really beautiful. Sometimes it came upon him, this look of clear distance, and it always fascinated her.

She waited, troubled, throughout the evening. She thought he would avoid her, or give some sign. But he spoke to her simply and unemotionally, as he would to anyone else in the room. A certain peace, an abstraction possessed his soul.

She went to his room, hotly, violently in love with him. He was so beautiful and inaccessible. He kissed her, he was a lover to her. And she had extreme pleasure of him. But he did not come to, he remained remote and candid, unconscious. She wanted to speak to him. But this innocent beautiful state of unconsciousness that had come upon him prevented her. She felt tormented and dark.

In the morning, however, he looked at her with a little aversion, some horror and some hatred darkening into his eyes. She withdrew on to her old ground. But still he would not gather himself together, against her.

Loerke was waiting for her now. The little artist, isolated in his own complete envelope, felt that here at last was a woman from whom he could get something. He was uneasy all the while, waiting to talk with her, subtly contriving to be near her. Her presence filled him with keenness and excitement, he gravitated cunningly towards her, as if she had some unseen force of attraction.

He was not in the least doubtful of himself, as regards Gerald. Gerald was one of the outsiders. Loerke only hated him for being rich and proud and of fine appearance. All these things, however, riches, pride of social standing, handsome physique, were externals. When it came to the relation with a woman such as Gudrun, he, Loerke, had an approach and a power that Gerald never dreamed of.

How should Gerald hope to satisfy a woman of Gudrun's calibre? Did he think that pride or masterful will or physical strength would help him? Loerke knew a secret beyond these things. The greatest power is the one that is subtle and adjusts itself, not the one which blindly attacks. And he, Loerke, had understanding where Gerald was a calf. He, Loerke, could penetrate into depths far out of Gerald's knowledge, Gerald was left behind like a postulant in the ante-room of this temple of mysteries, this woman. But he, Loerke, could he not penetrate into the inner darkness, find the spirit of the woman in its inner recess, and wrestle with it there, the central serpent that is coiled at the core of life.

What was it, after all, that a woman wanted? Was it mere social effect, fulfilment of ambition in the social world, in the community of mankind? Was it even a union in love and goodness? Did she want "goodness"? Who but a fool would accept this of Gudrun? This was but the street view of her wants. Cross the threshold, and you found her completely, completely cynical about the social world and its advantages. Once inside the house of her soul, and there was a pungent atmosphere of corrosion, an inflamed darkness of sensation, and a vivid, subtle, critical consciousness, that saw the world distorted, horrific.

What then, what next? Was it sheer blind force of passion that would satisfy her now? Not this, but the subtle thrills of extreme sensation in reduction. It was an unbroken will reacting against her unbroken will in a myriad subtle thrills of reduction, the last subtle activities of analysis and breaking-down carried out in the darkness of her, whilst the outside form, the individual, was utterly unchanged, even sentimental in its poses.

But between two particular people, any two people on earth, the range of pure sensational experience is limited. The climax of sensual reaction, once reached in any direction, is reached finally, there is no going on. There is only repetition possible, or the going apart of the two protagonists, or the subjugating of the one will to the other, or death.

Gerald had penetrated all the outer places of Gudrun's soul. He was to her the most crucial instance of the existing world, the ne plus ultra of the world of man as it existed for her. In him she knew the world, and had done with it. Knowing him finally she was the Alexander seeking new worlds.— But there *were* no new worlds, there were no more *men*, there were only creatures, little, ultimate *creatures* like Loerke. The world was finished now, for her. There was only the inner, individual darkness, sensation within the ego, the obscene religious mystery of ultimate reduction, the mystic frictional activities of diabolic reducing down, disintegrating the vital organic body of life.

All this Gudrun knew in her subconsciousness, not in her mind. She knew her next step—she knew what she should move on to, when she left Gerald. She was afraid of Gerald, that he might kill her. But she did not intend to be killed. A fine thread still united her to him. It should not be *her* death which broke it.—She had further to go, a further, slow, exquisite experience to reap, unthinkable subtleties of sensation to know, before she was finished.

Of the last series of subtleties Gerald was not capable. He could not touch the quick of her. But where his ruder blows could not penetrate, the fine, insinuating blade of Loerke's insect-like comprehension could. At least, it was time for her now to pass over to the other, the creature, the final craftsman. She knew that Loerke, in his innermost soul, was detached from everything, for him there was neither heaven nor earth nor hell. He admitted no allegiance, he gave no adherence anywhere. He was single and, by abstraction from the rest, absolute in himself.

Whereas in Gerald's soul there still lingered some attachment to the rest, to the whole. And this was his limitation. He was limited, *borné*, subject to his necessity, in the last issue, for goodness, for righteousness, for oneness with the ultimate purpose. That the ultimate purpose might be the perfect and subtle experiencing of the process of death, the will being kept unimpaired, that was not allowed in him. And this was his limitation.

There was a hovering triumph in Loerke, since Gudrun had denied her marriage with Gerald. The artist seemed to hover like a creature on the wing, waiting to settle. He did not approach Gudrun violently, he was never ill-timed. But, carried on by a sure instinct in the complete darkness of his soul, he corresponded mystically with her, imperceptibly, but palpably.

For two days, he talked to her, continued the discussions of art, of life, in which they both found such pleasure. They praised the by-gone things, they took a sentimental, childish delight in the achieved perfections of the past. Particularly they liked the late eighteenth century, the period of Goethe and of Shelley, and Mozart.

They played with the past, and with the great figures of the past, a sort of little game of chess, or marionettes, all to please themselves. They had all the great men for their marionettes, and they two were the god of the show, working it all. As for the future, that they never mentioned except one laughed out some mocking dream of the destruction of the world by a ridiculous catastrophe of man's invention: a man invented such a perfect explosive that it blew the earth in two, and the two halves set off in different directions through space, to the dismay of the inhabitants: or else the people of the world divided into two halves, and each half decided *it* was perfect and right, the other half was wrong and must be destroyed; so another end of the world. Or else, Loerke's dream of fear, the world went cold, and snow fell everywhere, and only white creatures, polar-bears, white foxes, and men like awful white snow-birds, persisted in ice cruelty.

Apart from these stories, they never talked of the future. They delighted most either in mocking imaginations of destruction, or in sentimental, fine marionette-shows of the past. It was a sentimental delight to reconstruct the world of Goethe at Weimar, or of Schiller and poverty and faithful love, or to see again Jean Jacques in his quakings, or Voltaire at Ferney, or Frederick the Great reading his own poetry.

They talked together for hours, of literature and sculpture and painting, amusing themselves with Flaxman and Blake and Fuseli, with tenderness, and with Feuerbach and Böcklin. It would take them a life-time, they felt, to live again, in petto, the lives of the great artists. But they preferred to stay in the eighteenth and the nineteenth centuries.

They talked in a mixture of languages. The groundwork was French, in either case. But he ended most of his sentences in a stumble of English and a conclusion of German, she skilfully wove herself to her end in whatever phrase came to her. She took a peculiar delight in this conversation. It was full of odd, fantastic expression, of double meanings, of evasions, of suggestive vagueness. It was a real physical pleasure to her to make this thread of conversation out of the different-coloured strands of three languages.

And all the while they two were hovering, hesitating round the flame of some invisible declaration. He wanted it, but was held back by some inevitable reluctance. She wanted it also, but she wanted to put it off, to put it off indefinitely. She still had some pity for Gerald, some connection with him. And the most fatal of all, she had the reminiscent sentimental compassion for herself in connection with him. Because of what *had* been, she felt herself held to him by immortal, invisible threads—because of what *had* been, because of his coming to her that first night, into her own house, in his extremity, because——.

Gerald was gradually overcome with a revulsion of loathing for Loerke. He did not take the man seriously, he despised him merely, except as he felt in Gudrun's veins the influence of the little creature. It was this that drove Gerald wild, the feeling in Gudrun's veins of Loerke's presence, Loerke's being, flowing dominant through her.

"What makes you so smitten with that little vermin?" he asked, really puzzled. For he, man-like, could not see anything attractive or important *at all* in Loerke. Gerald expected to find some handsomeness or nobleness, to account for a woman's subjection. But he saw none here, only an insect-like repulsiveness.

Gudrun flushed deeply. It was these attacks she would never forgive.

"What do you mean?" she replied. "My God, what a mercy I am *not* married to you!"

Her voice of flouting and contempt scotched him. He was brought up short. But he recovered himself.

"Tell me, only tell me," he reiterated, in a dangerous, narrowed voice—"tell me what it is" that fascinates you in him."

"I am not fascinated," she said, with cold, repelling innocence.

"Yes you are. You are fascinated by that little dry snake, like a bird gaping ready to fall down its throat."

She looked at him with black fury.

"I don't choose to be discussed by you," she said.

"It doesn't matter whether you choose or not," he replied, "that doesn't alter the fact that you are ready to fall down and kiss the feet of that little insect. And I don't want to prevent you—do it, fall down and kiss his feet. But I want to know, what it is that fascinates you—what is it?"

She was silent, suffused with black rage.

"How *dare* you come brow-beating me," she cried, "how dare you, you little squire, you bully. What right have you over me, do you think?"

His face was white and gleaming, she knew by the light in his eyes that she was in his power—the wolf. And because she was in his power, she hated him with a power that she wondered did not kill him. In her will she killed him as he stood, effaced him.

"It's not a question of right," said Gerald, sitting down on a chair. She watched the change in his body: she saw his clenched, mechanical body moving there like an obsession. Her hatred of him was tinged with fatal contempt. "It's not a question of my right over you—though I *have* some right, remember. I want to know, I only want to know what it is that subjugates you to that little scum of a sculptor downstairs, what it is that brings you down like a humble maggot, in worship of him. I want to know what you creep after."

She stood over against the window, listening. Then she turned round.

"Do you?" she said, in her most easy, most cutting voice. "Do you want to know what it is in him? It's because he has some understanding of a woman, because he is not stupid, that's why it is."

A queer, sinister, animal-like smile came over Gerald's face.

"But what understanding is it?" he said. "The understanding of a flea, a hopping flea with a proboscis. Why should you crawl abject before the understanding of a flea?"

There passed through Gudrun's mind Blake's representation of the soul of a flea. She wanted to fit it to Loerke. Blake was a clown too. But it was necessary to answer Gerald.

"Don't you think the understanding of a flea is more interesting than the understanding of a fool—?" she asked.

"A fool?" he repeated—

"A fool, a conceited fool—a Dummkopf," she replied, adding the German word.

"Do you call me a fool?" he replied. "Well, wouldn't I rather be the fool I am, than that flea downstairs?"

She looked at him. A certain blunt, blind stupidity in him palled on her soul, limiting her.

"You give yourself away by that last," she said.

He sat and wondered.

"I shall go away soon," he said.

She turned on him.

"Remember," she said, "I am completely independent of you—completely. You make your arrangements, I make mine."

He pondered this.

"You mean we are strangers from this minute?" he asked.

She halted and flushed. He was putting her in a trap, forcing her hand. She turned round on him.

"Strangers," she said, "we can never be. But if you *want* to make any movement apart from me, then I wish you to know you are perfectly free to do so. Do not consider me in the slightest."

Even so slight an implication that she needed him and was depending on him still was sufficient to rouse his passion. As he sat, a change came over his body, the hot, molten stream mounted involuntarily through his veins. He groaned inwardly, under its bondage, but he loved it. He looked at her with clear eyes, waiting for her.

She knew at once, and was shaken with cold revulsion. *How* could he look at her with those clear, warm, waiting eyes, waiting for her, even now? What had been said between them, was it not enough to put them worlds asunder, to freeze them forever apart? And yet he was all transfused and roused, waiting for her.

It confused her. Turning her head aside, she said:

"I shall always *tell* you, whenever I am going to make any change—"

And with this she moved out of the room.

He sat suspended in a fine recoil of disappointment, that seemed gradually to be destroying his understanding. But the unconscious state of patience persisted in him. He remained motionless, without thought or knowledge, for a long time. Then he rose, and went downstairs, to play at chess with one of the students. His face was open and clear, with a certain innocent *laisser-aller* that troubled Gudrun most, made her almost afraid of him, whilst she disliked him deeply for it.

It was after this that Loerke, who had never yet spoken to her personally, began to ask her of her state.

"You are not married at all, are you?" he asked.

She looked full at him.

"Not in the least," she replied, in her measured way.

Loerke laughed, wrinkling up his face oddly. There was a thin wisp of his hair straying on his forehead, she noticed that his skin was of a clear brown colour, his hands, his wrists. And his hands seemed closely prehensile. He seemed like topaz, so strangely brownish and pellucid.

"Good," he said.

Still it needed some courage for him to go on.

"Was Mrs Birkin your sister?" he asked.

"Yes."

"And was *she* married?"

"She was married."

"Have you parents, then?"

"Yes," said Gudrun, "we have parents."

And she told him, briefly, laconically, her position. He watched her closely, curiously all the while.

"So!" he exclaimed with some surprise. "And the Herr Crich, is he rich?"

"Yes, he is rich, a coal-owner."

"How long has your friendship with him lasted?"

"Some months."

There was a pause.

"Yes, I am surprised," he said at length. "The English, I thought they were so—cold.—And what do you think to do when you leave here?"

"What do I think to do?" she repeated.

"Yes. You cannot go back to the teaching. No—" he shrugged his shoulders—"that is impossible. Leave that to the *canaille* who can do nothing else. You, for your part—you know, you are a remarkable woman, *eine seltsame Frau*. Why deny it—why make any question of it? You are an extraordinary woman, why should you follow the ordinary course, the ordinary life?"

Gudrun sat looking at her hands, flushed. She was pleased that he said, so simply, that she was a remarkable woman. He would not say that to flatter her—he was far too self-opinionated and objective by nature. He said it as he would say, a piece of sculpture was remarkable, because he knew it was so.

And it gratified her to hear it from him. Other people had such a passion to make everything of one degree, of one pattern. In England it was chic to be perfectly ordinary. And it was a relief to her to be acknowledged extraordinary. Then she need not fret about the common standards.

"You see," she said, "I have no money whatsoever."

"Ach, money!" he cried, lifting his shoulders. "When one is grown up, money is lying about at one's service. It is only when one is young that it is rare. Take no thought for money—that always lies to hand."

"Does it?" she said, laughing.

"Always. The Gerald will give you a sum, if you ask him for it—"

She flushed deeply.

"I will ask anybody else," she said, with some difficulty—"but not him."

Loerke looked closely at her.

"Good," he said. "Then let it be somebody else. Only don't go back to that England, that school. No, that is stupid."

Again there was a pause. He was afraid to ask her outright to go with him, he was not even quite sure he wanted her; and she was afraid to be asked. He begrudged his own isolation, was *very* chary of sharing his life, even for a day.

"The only other place I know is Paris," she said, "and I can't stand that."

She looked with her wide, steady eyes full at Loerke. He lowered his head and averted his face.

"Paris, no!" he said. "Between the *religion d'amour*, and the latest 'ism', and the new turning to Jesus, one had better ride on a carrousel all day. But come to Dresden. I have a studio there—I can give you work—Oh, that would be easy enough. I haven't seen any of your things, but I believe in you. Come to Dresden—that is a fine town to be in, and as good a life as you can expect of a town. You have everything there, without the foolishness of Paris or the beer of Munich."

He sat and looked at her, coldly. What she liked about him was that he spoke to her simple and flat, as to himself. He was a fellow craftsman, a fellow being to her, first.

"No—Paris," he resumed, "it makes me sick. Pah—l'amour. I detest it. L'amour, l'amore, die Liebe—I detest it in every language. Women and love, there is no greater tedium," he cried.

She was slightly offended. And yet, this was her own basic feeling. Men, and love—there was no greater tedium.

"I think the same," she said.

"A bore," he repeated. "What does it matter, whether I wear this hat or another. So love! I needn't wear a hat at all, only for convenience. Neither need I love, except for convenience.—I tell you what, gnädige Frau—" and he leaned towards her—then he made a quick, odd gesture, as of striking something aside—"gnädiges Fräulein, never mind.—I tell you what, I would give everything, everything, all your love, for a little companionship in intelligence—" his eyes flickered darkly, evilly at her.—"You understand?" he asked, with a faint smile. "It wouldn't matter if she was a hundred years old, a thousand—it would be all the same to me, so that she can *understand*." He shut his eyes with a little snap.

Again Gudrun was rather offended. Did he not think her good-looking, then? Suddenly she laughed.

"I shall have to wait about eighty years to suit you, at that," she said. "I am ugly enough, aren't I?"

He looked at her with an artist's sudden, critical, estimating eye.

"You are beautiful," he said, "and I am glad of it. But it isn't that—it isn't that," he cried, with emphasis that flattered her. "It is that you have a certain wit, it is the kind of understanding. For me, I am little, chétif, insignificant. Good! Do not ask me to be strong and handsome, then. But it is the *me*—" he put his fingers to his mouth, oddly—"it is the *me* that is looking for a mistress, and my *me* is waiting for the *thee* of the mistress, for the match to my particular intelligence—You understand?"

"Yes," she said. "I understand."

"As for the other, this amour—" he made a gesture, dashing his hand aside, as if to dash away something troublesome—"it is unimportant, unimportant. Does it matter, whether I drink white wine this evening, or whether I drink nothing? It *does not matter*, it does not matter. So this love, this amour, this *baiser*. Yes or no, soit ou soit pas, today, tomorrow, or never, it is all the same, it does not matter—no more than the white wine."

He ended with an odd dropping of the head in a desperate negation. Gudrun watched him steadily. She had gone pale.

Suddenly she stretched over and seized his hand in her own.

"That is true," she said, in rather a high, vehement voice, "that is true for me too. It is the understanding that matters."

He looked up at her almost frightened, furtive. Then he nodded, a little sullenly. She let go his hand: he had made not the slightest response. And they sat in silence.

"Do you know," he said, suddenly looking at her with dark, self-important, prophetic eyes, "your fate and mine, they will run together, till—" and he broke off in a little grimace.

"Till when?" she asked, blenched, her lips going white. She was terribly susceptible to these evil prognostications. But he only shook his head.

"I don't know," he said, "I don't know."

Gerald did not come in from his ski-ing until night-fall, he missed the coffee and cake that she took at four o'clock. The snow was in perfect condition, he had travelled a long way, by himself, among the snow ridges, on his skis. He had climbed high, so high that he could see over the top of the pass, five miles distant, could see the Marienhütte, the hostel on the crest of the pass, half buried in snow, and over into the deep valley beyond, to the dark of the pine-trees. One could go that way home; but he shuddered with nausea at the thought of home;—one could travel on skis down there, and come to the old Imperial road, below the pass. But why come to any road? He revolted at the thought of finding himself in the world again. He must stay up there in the snow forever. He had been happy by himself, high up there alone, travelling swiftly on skis, taking far flights, and skimming past the dark rocks veined with brilliant snow.

But he felt something icy gathering at his heart. This strange mood of patience and innocence which had persisted in him for some days, was passing away, he would be left again a prey to the horrible passions and tortures.

So he came down reluctantly, snow-burned, snow-estranged, to the house in the hollow, between the knuckles of the mountain-tops. He saw its lights shining yellow, and he held back, wishing he need not go in, to confront those people, to hear the turmoil of voices and to feel the confusion of other presences. He was isolated as if there were a vacuum round his heart, or a sheath of pure ice.

The moment he saw Gudrun, something jolted in his soul. She was looking rather lofty and superb, smiling slowly and graciously to the Germans. A sudden desire leapt in his heart, to kill her. He thought, what a perfect voluptuous fulfilment it would be, to kill her. His mind was absent all the evening, estranged by the snow and his passion. But he kept the idea constant within him, what a perfect voluptuous consummation it would be to strangle her, to strangle every spark of life out of her, till she lay completely inert, soft, relaxed for ever, a soft heap lying dead between his hands, utterly dead. Then he would have had her finally and for ever, there would be such a perfect voluptuous finality.

Gudrun was unaware of what he was feeling, he seemed so quiet and amiable, as usual. His amiability even made her feel brutal towards him.

She went into his room where he was partially undressed. She did not notice the curious, glad gleam of pure hatred, with which he looked at her. She stood near the door, with her hand behind her.

"I have been thinking, Gerald," she said, with an insulting nonchalance, "that I shall not go back to England."

"Oh," he said. "Where will you go then?"

But she ignored his question. She had her own logical statement to make, and it must be made as she had thought it.

"I can't see the use of going back," she continued. "It is over between me and you—"

She paused for him to speak. But he said nothing. He was only talking to himself, saying 'Over, is it? I believe it is over. But it isn't finished. Remember, it isn't finished. We must put some sort of a finish on it. There must be a conclusion, there must be finality.'

So he talked to himself, but aloud, he said nothing whatever.

"What has been has been," she continued. "There is nothing that I regret. I hope you regret nothing—"

She waited for him to speak.

"Oh, I regret nothing," he said, accommodatingly.

"Good then," she answered, "good then. Then neither of us cherishes any regrets, which is as it should be."

"Quite as it should be," he said aimlessly.

She paused, to gather up her thread again.

"Our attempt has been a failure," she said. "But we can try again, elsewhere."

A little flicker of rage ran through his blood. It was as if she were rousing him, goading him. Why must she do it?

"Attempt at what?" he asked.

"At being lovers, I suppose," she said, a little baffled, yet so trivial she made it all seem.

"Our attempt at being lovers has been a failure?" he repeated aloud.

To himself, he was saying: 'I ought to kill her here. There is only this left, for me to kill her.' A heavy, overcharged desire, to bring about her death, possessed him.

She was unaware.

"Hasn't it?" she asked. "Do you think it has been a success?"

Again the insult of the flippant question ran through his blood like a current of fire.

"It had some of the elements of success, our relationship," he replied. "It—might have come off."

But he paused before concluding the last phrase. Even as he began the sentence, he did not believe in what he was going to say. He knew it never could have been a success.

"No," she replied. "You cannot love."

"And you?" he asked.

Her wide, dark-filled eyes were fixed on him, like two moons of darkness.

"I couldn't love *you*," she said, with stark cold truth.

A blinding flash went over his brain, his body jolted. His heart had burst into flame. His consciousness was gone into his wrists, into his hands. He was one blind, incontinent desire, to kill her. His wrists were bursting, there would be no satisfaction, till his hands had closed on her.

But even before his body swerved forward on her, a sudden, cunning comprehension was expressed on her face, and in a flash she was out of the door. She ran in one flash to her room and locked herself in. She was afraid, but confident. She knew her life trembled on the edge of an abyss. But she was curiously sure of her footing. She knew her cunning could outwit him.

She trembled, as she stood in her room, with excitement and awful exhilaration. She knew she could outwit him. She could depend on her presence of mind, and on her wits. But it was a fight to the death, she knew it now. One slip, and she was lost. She had a strange, tense, exhilarated sickness in her body, as one who is in peril of falling from a great height, but who does not look down, does not admit the fear.

"I will go away the day after tomorrow," she said.

She only did not want Gerald to think that she was afraid of him, that she was running away because she was afraid of him. She was not afraid of him, fundamentally. She knew it was her safeguard to avoid his physical violence. But even physically she was not afraid of him. She wanted to prove it to him. When she had proved it, that, whatever he was, she was not afraid of him; when she had proved *that*, she could leave him forever. But meanwhile the fight between them, terrible as she knew it to be, was inconclusive. And she wanted to be confident in herself. However many terrors she might have, she would be unafraid, uncowed by him. He could never cow her, nor dominate her, nor have any right over her; this she would maintain until she had proved it. Once it was proved, she was free of him for ever.

But she had not proved it yet, neither to him nor to herself. And this was what still bound her to him. She was bound to him, she could not live beyond him. She sat up in bed, closely wrapped up, for many hours, thinking endlessly to herself. It was as if she would never have done weaving the great provision of her thoughts.

"It isn't as if he really loved me," she said to herself. "He doesn't. Every woman he comes across, he wants to make her in love with him. He doesn't even know that he is doing it. But there he is, before every woman he unfurls his male attractiveness, displays his great desirability, he tries to make every woman think how wonderful it would be to have him for a lover. His very ignoring of the women is part of the game: he is never *unconscious* of them. He should have been a cockerel, so he could strut before fifty females, all his subjects. But really, his Don Juan does *not* interest me. I could play Doña Juanita a million times better than he plays Juan. He bores me, you know. His maleness bores me. Nothing is so boring as the phallus, so inherently stupid and stupidly conceited. Really, the fathomless conceit of these men, it is ridiculous—the little strutters.

"They are all alike. Look at Birkin. Built out of the limitation of conceit they are, and nothing else. Really, nothing but their ridiculous limitation and intrinsic insignificance could make them so conceited.

"As for Loerke, there is a thousand times more in him than in a Gerald.

Gerald is so limited, there is a dead end to him. He would grind on at the old mills forever. And really, there is no corn between the mill-stones any more. They grind on and on, when there is nothing to grind—saying the same things, believing the same things, acting the same things—Oh my God, it would wear out the patience of a stone.

"I don't worship Loerke, but at any rate, he is a free individual. He is not stiff with conceit of his own maleness. He is not grinding dutifully at the old mills. Oh God, when I think of Gerald, and his work—those offices at Beldover, and the mines—it makes my heart sick. What *have* I to do with it—and him thinking he can be a lover to a woman! One might as well ask it of a self-satisfied lamp-post.—These men, with their eternal jobs—and their eternal mills of God that keep on grinding at nothing! It is too boring, just boring. However did I come to take him seriously at all!

"At least, in Dresden, one will have one's back to it all. And there will be amusing things to do. It will be amusing to go to these eurythmic displays, and the German opera, the German theatre. It *will* be amusing to take part in German Bohemian life. And Loerke *is* an artist, he is a free individual. One will escape from so much—that is the chief thing—escape so much hideous boring repetition of vulgar actions, vulgar phrases, vulgar postures. I don't delude myself that I shall find an elixir of life in Dresden. I know I shan't. But I shall get away from people who have their own homes and their own children and their own acquaintances and their own this and their own that. I shall be among people who *don't* own things and who *haven't* got a home and a domestic servant in the back-ground, who *haven't* got a standing and a status and a degree and a circle of friends of the same. Oh God, the wheels within wheels of people—it makes one's head tick like a clock, with a very madness of dead mechanical monotony and meaninglessness. How I *hate* life, how I hate it. How I hate the Geralds, that they can offer one nothing else.

"Shortlands!—Heavens! Think of living there, one week, then the next, and *then the third*— —

"No, I won't think of it—it is too much— —"

And she broke off, really terrified, really unable to bear any more. The thought of the mechanical succession of day following day, day following day, ad infinitum, was one of the things that made her heart palpitate with a real approach of madness. The terrible bondage of this tick-tack of time, this twitching of the hands of the clock, this eternal repetition of hours and days,—Oh God, it was too awful to contemplate. And there was no escape from it, no escape.

She almost wished Gerald were with her, to save her from the terror of her own thoughts. Oh, how she suffered, lying there alone, confronted by the terrible clock, with its eternal tick-tack. All life, all life resolved itself into this: tick-tack, tick-tack, tick-tack; then the striking of the hour; then the tick-tack, tick-tack, and the twitching of the clock-fingers.

Gerald could not save her from it. He, his body, his motion, his life—it was the same ticking, the same twitching across the dial, a horrible, mechanical twitching forward over the face of the hours. What were his kisses, his embraces. She could hear their tick-tack, tick-tack.

Ha—ha—she laughed to herself, so frightened that she was trying to laugh it off—ha—ha, how maddening it was, to be sure, to be sure!

Then, with a fleeting self-conscious motion, she wondered if she would be very much surprised, on rising in the morning, to realise that her hair *had* turned white. She had *felt* it turning white so often, under the intolerable burden of her thoughts and her sensations. Yet there it remained, brown as ever, and there she was herself, looking a picture of health.

Perhaps she was healthy. Perhaps it was only her unabateable health that left her so exposed to the truth. If she were sickly she would have illusions, imaginations. As it was, there was no escape. She must always see and know and never escape. She could never escape. There she was, placed before the clock-face of life. And if she turned round, as in a railway station, to look at the book-stall, still she could see, with her very spine she could see the clock, always the great white clock-face. In vain she fluttered the leaves of books, or made statuettes in clay. She knew she was not *really* reading, she was not *really* working. She was watching the fingers twitch across the eternal, mechanical, monotonous clock-face of time. She never really lived, she only watched. Indeed, she was like a little, twelve-hour clock, vis-à-vis with the enormous clock of eternity—there she was, like Dignity and Impudence, or Impudence and Dignity.

The picture pleased her. Didn't her face really look like a clock-dial—rather roundish, and often pale, and impassive. She would have got up to look, in the mirror, but the thought of the sight of her own face, that was like a twelve-hour clock-dial, filled her with such deep terror, that she hastened to think of something else.

Oh, why wasn't somebody kind to her? Why wasn't there somebody who would take her in their arms, and hold her to their breast, and give her rest, pure, deep, healing rest. Oh why wasn't there somebody to take her in their arms and fold her safe and perfect, for sleep. She wanted so much this perfect enfolded sleep. She lay always so unsheathed in sleep. She would lie always unsheathed in sleep, unrelieved, unsaved. Oh how could she bear it, this endless unrelief, this eternal unrelief.

Gerald! Could *he* fold her in his arms and sheathe her in sleep? Ha! He needed putting to sleep himself—poor Gerald. That was all he needed. What did he do, he made the burden for her greater, the burden of her sleep was the more intolerable, when he was there. He was an added weariness upon her unripening nights, her unfruitful slumbers. Perhaps he got some repose from her. Perhaps he did. Perhaps this was what he was always dogging her for, like a child that is famished crying for the breast. Perhaps this was the secret of his passion, his forever unquenched desire for her—that he needed her to put him to sleep, to give him repose.

What then! Was she his mother? Had she asked for a child, whom she must nurse through the nights, for her lover. She despised him, she despised him, she hardened her heart. An infant crying in the night, this Don Juan.

Yes, but how she hated the infant crying in the night. She would murder it gladly. She would stifle it and bury it, like Hetty Sorrell did. No doubt Hetty Sorrell's infant cried in the night—no doubt Arthur Donnithorne's infant would. Ha—the Arthur Donnithornes, the Geralds of this world. So manly by day, yet all the while, such a crying of infants in the night. Let them turn into mechanisms, let them. Let them become instruments, pure machines, pure wills that work like clock-work, in perpetual repetition. Let them be this, let them be taken up entirely in their work, let them be perfect parts of a great machine, having a slumber of constant repetition. Let Gerald manage his firm. There he would be satisfied, as satisfied as a wheel-barrow that goes backwards and forwards along a plank all day—she had seen it.

The wheel-barrow—the one humble wheel—the unit of the firm. Then the cart, with two wheels; then the truck, with four; then the donkey-engine, with eight; then the winding-engine, with sixteen, and so on, till it came to the miner, with a thousand wheels, and then the electrician, with three thousand, and the underground manager, with twenty thousand, and the general manager, with a hundred thousand little wheels working away to complete his make-up, and then Gerald, with a million wheels and cogs and axles.

Poor Gerald, such a lot of little wheels to his make-up! He was more intricate than a chronometer-watch. But oh heavens, what weariness! What weariness, God above! A chronometer-watch—a beetle—her soul fainted with utter ennui, from the thought. So many wheels to count and consider and calculate! Enough, enough—there was an end to man's capacity for complications, even. Or perhaps there was no end.

Meanwhile Gerald sat in his room, reading. When Gudrun was gone, he was left stupefied with arrested desire. He sat on the side of the bed for an hour, stupefied, little strands of consciousness appearing and reappearing. But he did not move, for a long time he remained inert, his head dropped on his breast.

Then he looked up and realised that he was going to bed. He was cold. Soon he was lying down in the dark.

But what he could not bear, was the darkness. The solid darkness confronting him drove him mad. So he rose, and made a light. He remained seated for a while, staring in front. He did not think of Gudrun, he did not think of anything.

Then suddenly he went downstairs for a book. He had all his life been in terror of the nights that should come, when he could not sleep. He knew that this would be too much for him, to have to face nights of sleeplessness and of horrified watching the hours.

So he sat for hours in bed, like a statue, reading. His mind, hard and acute, read on rapidly, his body understood nothing. In a state of rigid unconsciousness, he read on through the night, till morning, when, weary and disgusted in spirit, disgusted most of all with himself, he slept for two hours.

Then he got up, hard and full of energy. Gudrun scarcely spoke to him, except at coffee she said:

"I shall be leaving tomorrow."

"We will go together as far as Innsbruck, for appearances sake?" he asked.

"Perhaps," she said.

She said 'Perhaps' between the sips of her coffee. And the sound of her taking her breath in the word, was nauseous to him. He rose quickly, to be away from her.

He went and made arrangements for the departure on the morrow. Then, taking some food, he set out for the day on the skis. Perhaps, he said to the Wirt, he would go up to the Marienhütte, perhaps to the village below.

To Gudrun, this day was full of a promise like spring. She felt an approaching release, a new fountain of life rising up in her. It gave her pleasure to dawdle through her packing, it gave her pleasure to dip into books, to try on her different garments, to look at herself in the glass. She felt a new lease of life was come upon her, and she was happy like a child, very attractive and beautiful to everybody, with her soft, luxuriant figure and her happiness. Yet underneath was death itself.

In the afternoon she had to go out with Loerke. Her tomorrow was perfectly vague before her. This was what gave her pleasure. She might be going to England with Gerald, she might be going to Dresden with Loerke, she might be going to Munich, to a girl-friend she had there. Anything might come to pass on the morrow. And today was the white, snowy, iridescent threshold of all possibility. All possibility—that was the charm to her, the lovely, iridescent, indefinite charm—pure illusion. All possibility—because death was inevitable, and *nothing* was possible but death.

She did not want things to materialise, to take any definite shape. She wanted, suddenly, at one moment of the journey tomorrow, to be wafted into an utterly new course, by some utterly unforeseen event, or motion. So that, although she wanted to go out with Loerke for the last time into the snow, she did not want to be serious or business-like.

And Loerke was not a serious figure. In his brown-velvet cap, that made his head as round as a chestnut, with the brown-velvet flaps loose and wild over his ears, and a wisp of elf-like, thin black hair blowing above his full, elf-like dark eyes, the shiny, transparent brown skin crinkling up into odd grimaces on his small-featured face, he looked an odd little boy-man, a bat. But in his figure, in the greeny loden suit, he looked chétif and puny, though still strangely different from the rest.

He had taken a little toboggan, for the two of them, and they trudged between the blinding slopes of snow, that burned their now hardening faces, laughing in an endless sequence of quips and jests and polyglot fancies. The fancies were the reality to both of them, they were both so happy, tossing about the little coloured balls of verbal humour and whimsicality. Their natures seemed to sparkle in full interplay, they were enjoying a pure game. And they wanted to keep it on the level of a game, their relationship: *such* a fine game.

Loerke did not take the tobogganing very seriously. He put no fire and intensity into it, as Gerald did. Which pleased Gudrun. She was weary, oh so weary of Gerald's gripped intensity of physical motion. Loerke let the sledge go wildly and gaily, like a flying leaf, and when, at a bend, he pitched both her and him out into the snow, he only waited for them both to pick themselves up unhurt off the keen white ground, to be laughing and pert as a pixie. She knew he would be making ironical, playful remarks as he wandered in hell—if he were in the humour. And that pleased her immensely. It seemed like a rising above the dreariness of actuality, the monotony of contingencies.

They played till the sun went down, in pure amusement, careless and timeless. Then, as the little sledge twirled riskily to rest at the bottom of the slope,

"Wait!" he said suddenly, and he produced from somewhere a large thermos flask, a packet of Kekse, and a bottle of Schnapps.

"Oh Loerke," she cried, "what an inspiration! What a comble de joie indeed! What is the Schnapps?"

He looked at it, and laughed.

"Heidelbeer!" he said.

"No! From the bilberries under the snow. Doesn't it look as if it were distilled from snow. Can you—" she sniffed, and sniffed at the bottle— "can you smell bilberries? *Isn't* it wonderful! It is exactly as if one could smell them through the snow."

She stamped her foot lightly on the ground. He kneeled down and whistled, and put his ear to the snow. As he did so his black eyes twinkled up.

"Ha! Ha!" she laughed, warmed by the whimsical way in which he mocked at her verbal extravagances. He was always teasing her, mocking her ways. But as he in his mockery was even more absurd than she in her extravaganzas, what could one do but laugh and feel liberated.

She could feel their voices, hers and his, ringing silvery like bells in the frozen, motionless air of the first twilight. How perfect it was, how *very* perfect it was, this silvery isolation and interplay.

She sipped the hot coffee, whose fragrance flew around them like bees murmuring around flowers, in the snowy air, she drank tiny sips of the Heidelbeerwasser, she ate the cold, sweet, creamy wafers. How good everything was! How perfect everything tasted and smelled and sounded, here in this utter stillness of snow and falling twilight.

"You are going away tomorrow?" his voice came at last.

"Yes."

There was a pause, when the evening seemed to rise in its silent, ringing pallor infinitely high, to the infinite which was near at hand.

"*Wohin?*"

That was the question—*wohin?* where to? *wohin?* What a lovely word! She *never* wanted it answered. Let it chime for ever.

"I don't know," she said, smiling at him.

He caught the smile from her.

"One never does," he said.

"One never does," she repeated.

There was a silence, wherein he ate biscuits rapidly, as a rabbit eats leaves.

"But," he laughed, "where will you take a ticket to?"

"Oh heaven!" she cried. "One must take a ticket!"

Here was a blow. She saw herself at the wicket, at the railway station. Then a relieving thought came to her. She breathed freely.

"But one needn't go," she said.

"Certainly not," he said.

"I mean one needn't go where one's ticket says."

That struck him. One might take a ticket, so as not to travel to the destination it indicated. One might break off, and avoid the destination. A point located. That was an idea!

"Then take a ticket to London," he said. "One should never go there."

"Right," she answered.

He poured a little coffee into a tin can.

"You won't tell me where you will go?" he asked.

"Really and truly," she said, "I don't know. It depends which way the wind blows."

He looked at her quizzically, then he pursed up his lips, like Zephyrus, blowing across the snow.

"It goes towards Germany," he said.

"I believe so," she laughed.

Suddenly, they were aware of a vague white figure near them. It was Gerald. Gudrun's heart leapt in sudden terror, profound terror. She rose to her feet.

"They told me where you were," came Gerald's voice, like a judgment in the whitish air of twilight.

"*Maria!*—you come like a ghost," exclaimed Loerke.

Gerald did not answer. His presence was unnatural and ghostly to them.

Loerke shook the flask—then he held it inverted over the snow. Only a few brown drops trickled out.

"All gone!" he said.

To Gerald, the smallish, odd figure of the German was distinct and objective, as if seen through field glasses. And he disliked the small figure exceedingly, he wanted it removed.

Then Loerke rattled the box which held the biscuits.

"Biscuits there are still," he said.

And reaching from his seated posture in the sledge, he handed them to Gudrun. She fumbled, and took one. He would have held them to Gerald, but Gerald so definitely did not want to be offered a biscuit, that Loerke, rather vaguely, put the box aside. Then he took up the small bottle, and held it to the light.

"Also there is some Schnapps," he said to himself.

Then suddenly, he elevated the bottle gallantly in the air, a strange grotesque figure leaning towards Gudrun, and said:

"Gnädiges Fräulein," he said, "wohl—."

There was a crack, the bottle was flying, Loerke had started back, the three stood quivering in violent emotion.

Loerke turned to Gerald, a devilish leer on his bright-skinned face.

"Well done!" he said, in a satirical, demoniac frenzy. "C'est le sport, sans doute."

The next instant he was sitting ludicrously in the snow, Gerald's fist having rung against the side of his head. But Loerke pulled himself together, rose, quivering, looking full at Gerald, his body weak and furtive, but his eyes demoniacal with satire.

"Vive le héros, vive—"

But he flinched, as, in a black flash Gerald's fist came upon him, banged into the other side of his head, and sent him aside like a broken straw.

But Gudrun had moved forward. She raised her clenched hand high, and brought it down, with a great downward stroke, over the face and on to the breast of Gerald.

A great astonishment burst upon him, as if the air had broken. Wide, wide his soul opened, in wonder, feeling the pain. Then it laughed, turning, with strong hands outstretched, at last to take the apple of his desire. At last he could finish his desire.

He took the throat of Gudrun between his hands, that were hard and indomitably powerful. And her throat was beautifully, so beautifully soft. Save that, within, he could feel the slippery chords of her life. And this he crushed, this he could crush. What bliss! Oh what bliss, at last, what satisfaction, at last! The pure zest of satisfaction filled his soul. He was watching the unconsciousness come into her swollen face, watching her eyes roll back. How ugly she was! What a fulfilment, what a satisfaction! How good this was, oh how good it was, what a god-given gratification, at last! He was unconscious of her fighting and struggling. That struggling was her reciprocal lustful passion in this embrace, the more violent it became, the greater the frenzy of delight, till the zenith was reached, the crisis, the struggle was overborne, her movement became softer, appeased.

Loerke roused himself on the snow, too dazed and hurt to get up. Only his eyes were conscious.

"Monsieur!" he said, in his thin, roused voice: "Quand vous aurez fini—"

A revulsion of contempt and disgust came over Gerald's soul. The disgust went to the very bottom of him, a nausea. Ah, what was he doing, to what depths was he letting himself go! As if he cared about her enough to kill her, to have her life on his hands!

A weakness ran over his body, a terrible relaxing, a thaw, a decay of strength. Without knowing, he had let go his grip, and Gudrun had fallen to her knees. Must he see, must he know?

A fearful weakness possessed him, his joints were turned to water. He drifted, as on a wind, veered, and went drifting away.

"I didn't want it, really," was the last confession of disgust in his soul, as he drifted up the slope, weak, finished, only sheering off unconsciously from any further contact. "I've had enough—I want to go to sleep. I've had enough." He was sunk under a sense of nausea.

He was weak, but he did not want to rest, he wanted to go on and on, to the end. Never again to stay, till he came to the end, that was all the desire that remained to him. So he drifted on and on, unconscious and weak, not thinking of anything, so long as he could keep in action.

The twilight spread a weird, unearthly light overhead, bluish-rose in colour, the cold blue night sank on the snow. In the valley below, behind, in the great bed of snow, were two small figures, Gudrun dropped on her knees, like one executed, and Loerke sitting propped up near her. That was all.

Gerald stumbled on up the slope of snow, in the bluish darkness, always climbing, always unconsciously climbing, weary though he was. On his left was a steep slope with black rocks and fallen masses of rock and veins of snow slashing in and about the blackness of rock, veins of snow slashing vaguely in and about the blackness of rock. Yet there was no sound, all this made no noise.

To add to his difficulty, a small bright moon shone brilliantly just ahead, on the right, a painful brilliant thing that was always there, unremitting, from which there was no escape. He wanted so to come to the end—he had had enough. Yet he did not sleep.

He surged painfully up, sometimes having to cross a slope of black rock, that was blown bare of snow. Here he was afraid of falling, very much afraid of falling. And high up here, on the crest, moved a wind that almost overpowered him with a sleep-heavy iciness. Only it was not here, the end, he must still go on. His indefinite nausea would not let him stay.

Having gained one ridge, he saw the vague shadow of something higher, in front. Always higher, always higher. He knew he was following the track towards the summit of the slopes, where was the Marienhütte, and the descent on the other side. But he was not really conscious. He only wanted to go on, to go on whilst he could, to move, to keep going, that was all, to keep going, until it was finished. He had lost all his sense of place. And yet, in the remaining instinct of life, his feet sought the track where the skis had gone.

He slithered down a sheer snow-slope. That frightened him. He had no alpenstock, nothing. But having come safely to rest, he began to walk on, in the illuminated darkness. It was as cold as sleep. He was between two ridges, in a hollow. So he swerved. Should he climb the other ridge, or wander along the hollow. How frail the thread of his being was stretched!

He would perhaps climb the ridge. The snow was firm and simple. He went along. There was something standing out of the snow. He approached, with dimmest curiosity.

It was a half-buried crucifix, a little Christ under a little sloping hood, at the top of a pole. He sheered away. Somebody was going to murder him. He had a great dread of being murdered. But it was a dread which stood outside him, like his own ghost.

Yet why be afraid. It was bound to happen. To be murdered! He looked round in terror at the snow, the rocking, pale-shadowy slopes of the upper world. He was bound to be murdered, he could see it. This was the moment when the death was uplifted, and there was no escape.

Lord Jesus, was it then bound to be—Lord Jesus? He could feel the blow descending, he knew he was murdered. Vaguely wandering forward, his hands lifted as if to feel what would happen, he was waiting for the moment when he would stop, when it would cease. It was not over yet.

He had come to the hollow basin of snow, surrounded by sheer slopes and precipices, out of which rose a track that brought one to the top of the mountain. But he wandered on unconsciously, till he slipped and fell down, and as he fell something broke in his soul, and immediately he went to sleep.

Chapter XXXII

Exeunt

When they brought the body home, the next morning, Gudrun was shut up in her room. From her window she saw men coming along with a burden, over the snow. She sat still and let the minutes go by.

There came a tap at her door. She opened. There stood a woman, saying softly, oh, far too reverently:

"They have found him, madame?"

"Il est mort?"

"Yes—hours ago."

Gudrun did not know what to say. What should she say? What should she feel? What should she do? What did they expect of her? She was coldly at a loss.

"Thank you," she said, and she shut the door of her room. The woman went away mortified. Not a word, not a tear—ha, Gudrun was cold, a cold woman.

Gudrun sat on in her room, her face pale and impassive. What was she to do? She could not weep and make a scene. She could not alter herself. She sat motionless, hiding from people. Her one motive was to avoid actual contact with events. She only wrote out a long telegram to Ursula and Birkin.

In the afternoon, however, she rose suddenly, to look for Loerke. She glanced with apprehension at the door of the room that had been Gerald's. Not for worlds would she enter there.

She found Loerke sitting alone in the lounge. She went straight up to him.

"It isn't true, is it?" she said.

He looked up at her. A small smile of misery twisted his face. He shrugged his shoulders.

"True?" he echoed.

"We haven't killed him?" she asked. He disliked her coming to him in such a manner. He raised his shoulders wearily.

"It has happened," he said.

She looked at him. He sat crushed and frustrated for the time being, quite as emotionless and barren as herself. My God, this was a barren tragedy, barren, barren.

She returned to her room to wait for Ursula and Birkin. She wanted to get away, only to get away. She could not think or feel until she had got away, till she was loosed from this position.

The day passed, the next day came. She heard the sledge, saw Ursula and Birkin alight. And she shrank from these also.

Ursula came straight up to her.

"Gudrun!" she cried, the tears running down her cheeks. And she took her sister in her arms. Gudrun hid her face on Ursula's shoulder, but still she could not escape the cold devil of irony that froze her soul.

"Ha—ha!" she thought, "this is the right behaviour."

But she could not weep, and the sight of her cold, pale, impassive face soon stopped the fountain of Ursula's tears. In a few moments, the sisters had nothing to say to each other.

"Was it very vile to be dragged back here again?" Gudrun asked at length.

Ursula looked up in some bewilderment.

"I never thought of it," she said.

"I felt a beast, fetching you," said Gudrun. "But I simply couldn't see people. That is too much for me."

"Yes," said Ursula, chilled.

Birkin tapped and entered. His face was white and expressionless. She knew he knew. He gave her his hand, saying:

"The end of *this* trip, at any rate." Gudrun glanced at him, afraid.

There was silence between the three of them, nothing to be said. At length Ursula asked, in a small voice:

"Have you seen him?"

He looked back at Ursula with a hard, cold look, and did not trouble to answer.

"Have you seen him?" she repeated.

"I have," he said, coldly.

Then he looked at Gudrun.

"Have you done anything?" he said.

"Nothing," she replied, "nothing."

She shrank in cold disgust from making any statement.

"Loerke says that Gerald came to you when you were sitting on the sledge at the bottom of the Rudelbahn, that you had words, and Gerald walked away.—What were the words about?—I had better know so that I can satisfy the authorities, if necessary."

Gudrun looked up at him, white, child-like, mute with trouble.

"There weren't even any words," she said. "He knocked Loerke down and stunned him, he half strangled me, then he went away."

To herself she was saying: "A pretty little sample of the eternal triangle!" And she turned ironically away, because she knew that the fight had been between Gerald and herself, and that the presence of the third party was a mere contingency—an inevitable contingency perhaps, but a contingency none the less. But let them have it as an example of the eternal triangle, the trinity of hate. It would be simpler for them.

Birkin went away, his manner cold and abstracted. But she knew he would do things for her, nevertheless, he would see her through. She smiled slightly to herself, with contempt. Let him do the work, since he was so extremely *good* at looking after other people.

Birkin went again to Gerald. He had loved him. And yet he felt chiefly disgust at the inert body lying there. It was so inert, so coldly dead, a carcase, Birkin's bowels seemed to turn to ice. He had to stand and look at the frozen dead body that had been Gerald.

It was the frozen carcase of a dead male. Birkin remembered a rabbit which he had once found frozen like a board on the snow. It had been rigid like a dried board when he picked it up. And now this was Gerald, stiff as a board, curled up as if for sleep, yet with the horrible hardness somehow evident. It filled him with horror. The room must be made warm, the body must be thawed. The limbs would break like glass or like wood if they had to be straightened.

He reached and touched the dead face. And the sharp, heavy bruise of ice bruised his living bowels. He wondered if he himself were freezing too, freezing from the inside.—In the short blond moustache the life-breath was frozen into a block of ice, beneath the silent nostrils. And this was Gerald!

Again he touched the sharp, almost glittering fair hair of the frozen body. It was icy-cold, hair icy-cold, almost venomous. Birkin's heart began to freeze. He had loved Gerald. Now he looked at the shapely, strange-coloured face, with the small, fine, pinched nose and the manly cheeks, saw it frozen like an ice-pebble—yet he had loved it. What was one to think or feel?—His brain was beginning to freeze, his blood was turning to ice-water. So cold, so cold, a heavy, bruising cold pressing on his arms from outside, and a heavier cold congealing within him, in his heart and in his bowels.

He went over the snow-slopes, to see where the death had been. At last he came to the great shallow among the precipices and slopes, near the summit of the pass. It was a grey day, the third day of greyness and stillness. All was white, icy, pallid, save for the scoring of black rocks that jutted like roots sometimes, and sometimes were in naked faces. In the distance a slope sheered down from a peak, with many black rock-slides.

It was like a shallow pot lying among the stone and snow of the upper world. In this pot Gerald had gone to sleep. At the far end, the guides had driven iron stakes deep into the snow-wall, so that, by means of the great rope attached, they could haul themselves up the massive snow-front out on to the jagged summit of the pass, naked to heaven, where the Marienhütte hid among the naked rocks. Round about, spiked, slashed snow-peaks pricked the heaven.

Gerald might have found this rope. He might have hauled himself up to the crest. He might have heard the dogs in the Marienhütte, and found shelter. He might have gone on, down the steep, steep fall of the south side, down into the dark valley with its pines, on to the great Imperial road leading south to Italy.

He might! And what then? The Imperial road! The south? Italy? What then? Was it a way out?—It was only a way in again. Birkin stood high in the painful air, looking at the peaks, and the way south. Was it any good going south, to Italy? Down the old, old Imperial road?

He turned away. Either the heart would break, or cease to care. Best cease to care. Whatever the mystery which has brought forth man and the universe, it is a non-human mystery, it has its own great ends, man is not the criterion. Best leave it all to the vast, creative, non-human mystery. Best strive with oneself only, not with the universe.

"God cannot do without man." It was a saying of some great French religious teacher.—But surely this is false. God can do without man. God could do without the ichthyosauri and the mastodon. These monsters failed creatively to develop, so God, the creative mystery, dispensed with them. In the same way the mystery could dispense with man, should he too fail creatively to change and develop. The eternal creative mystery could dispose of man, and replace him with a finer created being: just as the horse has taken the place of the mastodon.

It was very consoling to Birkin, to think this. If humanity ran into a cul de sac, and expended itself, the timeless creative mystery would bring forth some other being, finer, more wonderful, some new, more lovely race, to carry on the embodiment of creation. The game was never up. The mystery of creation was fathomless, infallible, inexhaustible forever. Races came and went, species passed away, but ever new species arose, more lovely, or equally lovely, always surpassing wonder. The fountain-head was incorruptible and unsearchable. It had no limits. It could bring forth miracles, create utter new races and new species, in its own hour, new forms of consciousness, new forms of body, new units of being. To be man was as nothing compared to the possibilities of the creative mystery. To have one's pulse beating direct from the mystery, this was perfection, unutterable satisfaction. Human or inhuman mattered nothing. The perfect pulse throbbed with indescribable being, miraculous unborn species.

Birkin went home again to Gerald. He went into the room, and sat down on the bed. Dead, dead and cold!

> "Imperial Ceasar dead, and turned to clay
> Would stop a hole to keep the wind away."

There was no response from that which had been Gerald. Strange, congealed, icy substance—no more. No more!

Terribly weary, Birkin went away, about the day's business. He did it all quietly, without bother. To rant, to rave, to be tragic, to make situations—it was all too late. Best be quiet, and bear one's soul in patience and in fulness.

But when he went in again, at evening, to look at Gerald between the candles, because of his heart's hunger, suddenly his heart contracted, his own candle all but fell from his hand, as, with a strange whimpering cry, the tears broke out. He sat down in a chair, shaken by a sudden access. Ursula, who had followed him, recoiled aghast from him, as he sat with sunken head and body convulsively shaken, making a strange, horrible sound of tears.

"I didn't want it to be like this—I didn't want it to be like this," he cried to himself.

Ursula could but think of the Kaiser's: "Ich habe es nicht gewollt." She looked almost with horror on Birkin.

Suddenly he was silent. But he sat with his head dropped, to hide his face. Then furtively he wiped his face with his fingers. Then suddenly he lifted his head, and looked straight at Ursula, with dark, almost vengeful eyes.

"He should have loved me," he said. "I offered him."

She, afraid, white, with mute lips answered:

"What difference would it have made!"

"It would!" he said. "It would."

He forgot her, and turned to look at Gerald. With head oddly lifted, like a man who draws his head back from an insult, half haughtily, he watched the cold, mute, material face. It had a bluish cast. It sent a shaft like ice through the heart of the living man. Cold, mute, material! Birkin remembered how once Gerald had clutched his hand, with a warm, momentaneous grip of final love. For one second—then let go again, let go for ever. If he had kept true to that clasp, death would not have mattered. Those who die, and dying still can love, still believe, do not die. They live still in the beloved. Gerald might still have been living in the spirit with Birkin, even after death. He might have lived with his friend, a further life.

But now he was dead, like clay, like bluish, corruptible ice. Birkin looked at the pale fingers, the inert mass. He remembered a dead stallion he had seen: a dead mass of maleness, repugnant. He remembered also the beautiful face of one whom he had loved, and who had died still having the faith to yield to the mystery. That dead face was beautiful, no one could call it cold, mute, material. No one could remember it without gaining faith in the mystery, without the soul's warming with new, deep life-trust.

And Gerald! The denier! He left the heart cold, frozen, hardly able to beat. Gerald's father had looked wistful, to break the heart: but not this last terrible look of cold, mute Matter. Birkin watched and watched.

Ursula stood aside watching the living man stare at the frozen face of the dead man. Both faces were unmoved and unmoving. The candle-flames flickered in the frozen air, in the intense silence.

"Haven't you seen enough?" she said.

He got up.

"It's a bitter thing to me," he said.

"What—that he's dead?" she said.

His eyes just met hers. He did not answer.

"You've got me," she said.

He smiled, and kissed her.

"If I die," he said, "you'll know I haven't left you."

"And me?" she cried.

"And you won't have left me," he said. "We shan't have any need to despair, in death."

She took hold of his hand.

"But need you despair over Gerald?" she said.

"Yes," he answered.

They went away. Gerald was taken to England, to be buried. Birkin and Ursula accompanied the body, along with one of Gerald's brothers. It was the Crich brothers and sisters who insisted on the burial in England. Birkin wanted to leave the dead man in the Alps, near the snow. But the family was strident, loudly insistent.

Gudrun went to Dresden. She wrote no particulars of herself. Ursula stayed at the Mill with Birkin for a week or two. They were both very quiet.

"Did you need Gerald?" she asked one evening.

"Yes," he said.

"Aren't I enough for you?" she asked.

"No," he said. "You are enough for me, as far as woman is concerned. You are all women to me. But I wanted a man friend, as eternal as you and I are eternal."

"Why aren't I enough?" she said. "You are enough for me. I don't want anybody else but you. Why isn't it the same with you?"

"Having you, I can live all my life without anybody else, any other sheer intimacy. But to make it complete, really happy, I wanted eternal union with a man too: another kind of love," he said.

"I don't believe it," she said. "It's an obstinacy, a theory, a perversity."

"Well—" he said.

"You can't have two kinds of love. Why should you!"

"It seems as if I can't," he said. "Yet I wanted it."

"You can't have it, because it's false, impossible," she said.

"I don't believe that," he answered.

NOTE ON THE TEXT

Lawrence began this novel as 'The Sisters' in the spring of 1913 and after several drafts split it the next year into *The Rainbow*, published 1915, and *Women in Love*, on which he continued work in 1916. *Rainbow* was suppressed by court order in Britain a month and a half after publication, and one result was that Lawrence could not find a publisher for the second novel until November 1920 when Thomas Seltzer brought out a private edition in the USA; he published a trade edition two years later after defending the novel successfully in court. Martin Secker published *Women in Love* in England in June 1921 after censoring passages, some with Lawrence's reluctant consent and some without, but had to withdraw it and make alterations after Philip Heseltine threatened a libel suit.

Lawrence typed 368 pp. in two copies of *Women in Love* in July–October 1916; both copies were heavily and differently revised with some further alterations made by his wife Frieda, before Lawrence turned over the rest of the typing to his agent J. P. Pinker's office. From one copy of that typescript, a second was made in February–March 1917 which Lawrence revised immediately and continued to revise until he sent it to Seltzer in September 1919. He received proofs too late from Seltzer, but did make corrections for Secker's printing.

The text of this Grafton Edition is reproduced from that of the Cambridge Edition of the Works of D. H. Lawrence, edited by David Farmer, Lindeth Vasey, and John Worthen, which uses as its base-text the revised second typescript which has been emended from both copies of the first typescript (and manuscript of the part typed for Pinker) and those corrections in proofs for Secker's edition which were not the result of external pressure on the author; the text has also been emended lightly to standardise spelling and hyphenation.

CHRONOLOGY

11 September 1885	Born in Eastwood, Nottinghamshire
September 1898–July 1901	Pupil at Nottingham High School
1902–1908	Pupil teacher; student at University College, Nottingham
7 December 1907	First publication: 'A Prelude', in *Nottinghamshire Guardian*
October 1908	Appointed as teacher at Davidson Road School, Croydon
November 1909	Publishes five poems in *English Review*
3 December 1910	Engagement to Louie Burrows; broken off on 4 February 1912
9 December 1910	Death of his mother, Lydia Lawrence
19 January 1911	*The White Peacock* published in New York (20 January in London)
19 November 1911	Ill with pneumonia; resigns his teaching post on 28 February 1912
March 1912	Meets Frieda Weekley; they elope to Germany on 3 May
23 May 1912	*The Trespasser*
September 1912–March 1913	At Gargnano, Lago di Garda, Italy
February 1913	*Love Poems and Others*
29 May 1913	*Sons and Lovers*
June–August 1913	In England
August 1913–June 1914	In Germany, Switzerland and Italy
13 July 1914	Marries Frieda Weekley in London
July 1914–December 1915	In London, Buckinghamshire and Sussex
26 November 1914	*The Prussian Officer*
30 September 1915	*The Rainbow*; suppressed by court order on 13 November
June 1916	*Twilight in Italy*
July 1916	*Amores*
15 October 1917	After twenty-one months' residence in Cornwall, ordered to leave by military authorities

October 1917–November 1919	In London, Berkshire and Derbyshire
December 1917	*Look! We Have Come Through!*
October 1918	*New Poems*
November 1919–February 1922	To Italy, then Capri and Sicily
20 November 1919	*Bay*
November 1920	Private publication of *Women in Love* (New York), *The Lost Girl*
10 May 1921	*Psychoanalysis and the Unconscious* (New York)
12 December 1921	*Sea and Sardinia* (New York)
March–August 1922	In Ceylon and Australia
14 April 1922	*Aaron's Rod* (New York)
September 1922–March 1923	In New Mexico
23 October 1922	*Fantasia of the Unconscious* (New York)
24 October 1922	*England, My England* (New York)
March 1923	*The Ladybird, The Fox, The Captain's Doll*
March–November 1923	In Mexico and USA
27 August 1923	*Studies in Classic American Literature* (New York)
September 1923	*Kangaroo*
9 October 1923	*Birds, Beasts and Flowers* (New York)
December 1923–March 1924	In England, France and Germany
March 1924–September 1925	In New Mexico and Mexico
August 1924	*The Boy in the Bush* (with Mollie Skinner)
10 September 1924	Death of his father, John Arthur Lawrence
14 May 1925	*St Mawr together with The Princess*
September 1925–June 1928	In England and mainly Italy
7 December 1925	*Reflections on the Death of a Porcupine* (Philadelphia)
January 1926	*The Plumed Serpent*
June 1927	*Mornings in Mexico*
24 May 1928	*The Woman Who Rode Away and Other Stories*
June 1928–March 1930	In Switzerland and, principally, in France

July 1928	*Lady Chatterley's Lover* privately published (Florence)
September 1928	*Collected Poems*
July 1929	Exhibition of paintings in London raided by police. *Pansies* (manuscript earlier seized in the mail)
September 1929	*The Escaped Cock* (Paris)
2 March 1930	Dies at Vence, Alpes Maritimes, France

ON TOP OF THE WORLD

CLIMBING THE WORLD'S 14 HIGHEST MOUNTAINS

RICHARD SALE & JOHN CLEARE

CollinsWillow

An Imprint of HarperCollins*Publishers*

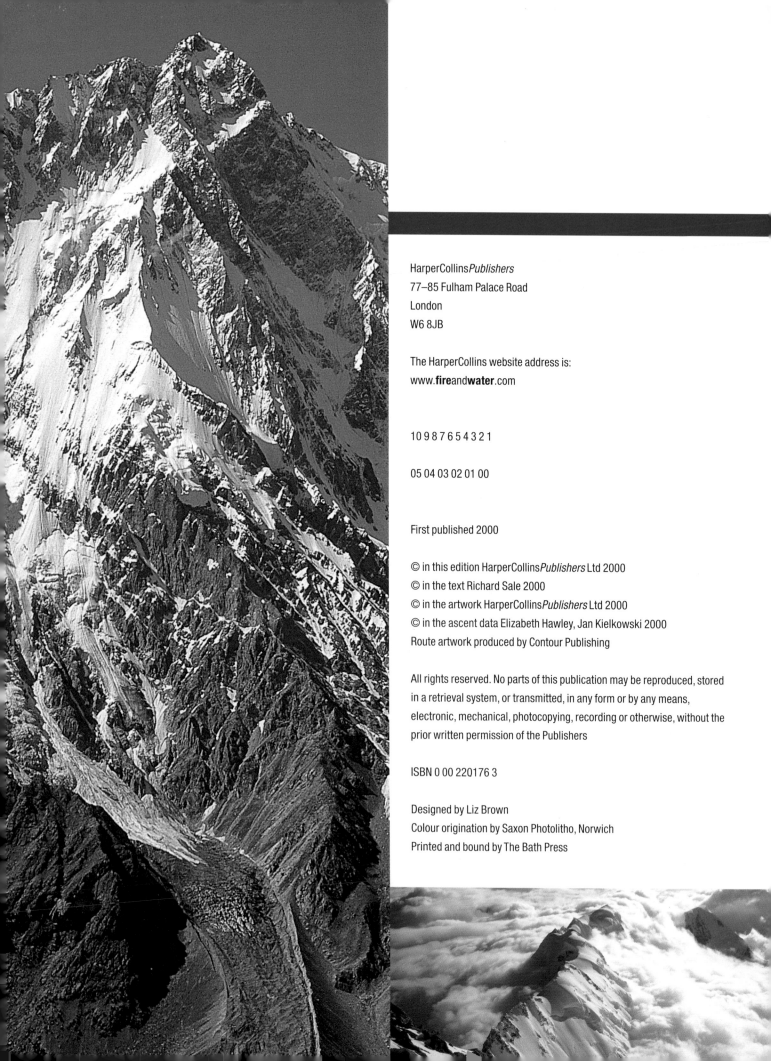

HarperCollins*Publishers*
77–85 Fulham Palace Road
London
W6 8JB

The HarperCollins website address is:
www.**fire**and**water**.com

10 9 8 7 6 5 4 3 2 1

05 04 03 02 01 00

First published 2000

ISBN 0 00 220176 3

Designed by Liz Brown
Colour origination by Saxon Photolitho, Norwich
Printed and bound by The Bath Press

contents

Foreword

As a boy I was a drain on the resources of my local library, reading every book they had or that I could persuade them to find or buy on climbing. There were few books on the European Alps, even fewer on British climbing. Most were on the Himalaya – Kamet, Nanda Devi, Mason's *Abode of Snow*. And there were the accounts of the first ascents of the highest mountains on Earth. But despite my love of the hills and enthusiasm for climbing I was a climber of relatively modest accomplishment. Not good enough for the sponsored teams to the high peaks and, when they became available, not rich enough to join the commercial trips, I could afford only to go to the Himalaya to gaze at the great peaks and dream. When, finally, I did acquire some personal sponsorship for an expedition to an 8,000m peak I had a nightmare trip, illness preventing me from discovering if I had the potential to join the 8,000m club.

There will be some who will question the right of anyone who does not list the ascent on an 8,000m peak in his list of climbing achievements to write a history of the first 50 years of climbing on them. But that is flawed logic which would see books on art written only by artists, those on sport only by players. Books on climbing by climbers can bring an immediacy that cannot be matched by non-practitioners. But they can also bring a subjectivity which can mask much that is worthwhile. I bring, I hope, enough climbing knowledge to understand the climbs and the objectivity of one who is a step back from the real heat. I also bring a love of high hills. I hope that is enough.

Richard Sale

Above Everest from the south, with the south-west face rising from the Western Cwm **Main picture** *Gasherbrum I* **Far Right** *Summit day on Everest's south-east ridge. In the background, to the right of the climber, is Makalu*

In 1793, just months after the execution of Louis XVI and with the Reign of Terror about to start, the French Revolutionary Council appointed the scientist Joseph Lagrange, Italian-born but of French ancestry, to head a commission charged with the creation of a new system of weights and measures. The system was destined, as the Council had hoped, to gain world-wide acceptance.

The commission decided that its unit of length should be one ten-millionth of the length of the quadrant from the equator to the north pole which passed through Dunkirk, France's most northerly town, a unit which had been first proposed a century earlier by Gabriel Mouton. As the surveyors of the Great Trigonometric Survey in India during the next century were to discover, measuring the length of a quadrant was not easy.

Having obtained an approximate value the commission abandoned its plan and adopted instead a length (equal to that of the approximate value) defined by two marks scratched on a bar of platinum-iridium alloy held in Paris. This length was called a metre (the French for 'measure', deriving from the Greek metron – measure), a unit which has now received world-wide acceptance in the scientific community and acceptance in many countries, with the notable exceptions of Britain and the USA.

Half a century after the definition of the metre the world's highest mountains were discovered in the Himalaya and Karakoram ranges. Conversion of the imperial measurements of the British survey's heights of these peaks into the metric system showed that of the vast numbers of huge peaks that form the 2,400km (1,500 mile) Himalayan ranges just 14 were more than 8,000m (26,240ft) high. This book concerns itself with those 14.

On the scale of difficulty of climbing on lower peaks – say those of the European Alps where climbing as a sport is usually said to have developed – the easiest routes to the summits of the 8,000ers are at the lower end, certainly no more difficult than routes which were being climbed in the late 19th century or the early years of the 20th century. The problem of climbing the great peaks was altitude, which fatigued the climber, making clumsiness and errors of judgement more likely and forcing him or her to spend longer on the climb. The longer a climb takes the more vulnerable the climber is to changes in weather, the risk of avalanches and the effects of the cold. At sea level a fit man can climb 300m (1,000ft) up a hillside of reasonable steepness in 30 minutes or so. Most of the 8,000ers rise 3,000–3,500m (10,000–11,500ft) above the base camps used by climbers. Applying the same ascent rule suggests a climb of 5–6 hours. While no one would be foolish enough to suggest that such an ascent time is possible (though the fastest times, on the 'easiest' routes are now making the conversion much less outrageous than it would have seemed even 20 years ago) it is interesting to compare this ascent time with the time allocated for an ascent of Cho Oyu, one of the 'easiest' 8,000ers, on a commercial climb – about 40 days. The difference is the slowing effect of altitude with its attendant need for a series of camps, each of which must be stocked, and the period of acclimatisation of the climbers.

Before climbing began as a sport, humans had climbed above 5,350m (17,500ft) for religious and trade purposes and,

Ed Webster jumarring up the 'Fourth Cauliflower Tower' on Everest's Kangshung Face

Summit day on a commercial expedition to Everest's south-east ridge

general conclusion. As more than one climber has noted, at great altitudes everything can go well – and you can still die. When the actual environment of the climber is considered – probably dehydrated, certainly mildly (at least) malnourished and exhausted – it is no surprise that deaths occur, these factors adding to the effects of anoxia. Newspapers, ever anxious for a sensational headline to boost sales, have referred to heights above 8,000m as the 'Death Zone'. While it is easy, not to say worthwhile, to sneer at such easy copy, the papers have it about right, though it might be argued that it is an error to pick 8,000m rather than 7,500m or 7,000m. The only difference is in the speed of corpse-creation and the scarcity of 8,000m peaks.

probably, for hunting, but there were no permanent settlements above that height. Above 5,350m there is insufficient oxygen in the air (about 50 per cent of that at sea level, though the actual situation for the climber is made worse by the fact that the diffusion process of oxygen from the air into the blood is less efficient when the oxygen partial pressure is reduced) to maintain life indefinitely. By the time a man reaches 6,000m (20,000ft) deterioration of bodily functions has begun. As altitude increases further this deterioration accelerates. Acclimatisation seeks to reduce the effect of the decrease in available oxygen by increasing the number of red blood cells. At sea level the average number of red cells is about 5 million per 1 cc (0.6 cubic in) of blood. Proper acclimatisation to 5,350m might raise this to about 6 million per cc (compared to 7 million per cc plus for a person born and raised at a comparable altitude). Above that height further acclimatisation is not possible: the body's capability, in terms of adjusting to the lack of oxygen, has reached a limit.

At altitudes above 7,000m (23,000ft), and particularly beyond 8,000m (26,247ft), the survival time for a human being reduces dramatically. As always, there is a spread of abilities between individual climbers, but in general, a well-acclimatised climber placed at 8,000m in warm conditions with an adequate supply of food and drink will die in a few days. At the summit of Everest this survival time reduces to a very few days. In 1999 the Sherpa Babu Chire spent almost 24 hours on the summit of Everest without supplementary (ie. bottled) oxygen. Though impressive (if somewhat bizarre), this feat in no way negates the

Since climbing above 8,000m is, therefore, to look death in the face it begs the question of why anyone should want to. Faced with this question many choose to trot out the tired response attributed (probably incorrectly, but that's another story) to George Leigh Mallory who, when asked why he wanted to climb Everest, on which he was killed in 1924, replied 'because it's there'. The phrase has been used so often it has acquired near mythical status, its apparent profundity able to put an end to further discussion. But strip away the quasi-philosophical gloss from this mantra and the phrase is irritatingly banal, the sort of comment you might expect from someone caught vandalising a bus shelter. Mountains are there for everyone, but not everyone chooses to climb them or even cares whether they are climbed or not. The same is true of any human endeavour. To answer the question 'Why?' probably takes more understanding of the human psyche than we will ever possess. Jerzy Kukuczka, the second man to climb all 14 8,000ers, stated – 'There is no answer … to the endless question about the point of expeditions to the Himalayan giants. I never found a need to explain this. I went to the mountains and climbed them. That is all.'

Yet despite the illogicality of the activity (Lionel Terray, one of the finest climbers France has ever produced, entitled his autobiography *Les Conquérants de l'Inutile – Conquistadors of the Useless*) and the dangers – both of high altitude and the objective dangers of climbing in the Himalaya (poor weather, avalanches) there has never been any shortage of those willing to try. These aspirants ensured that the history of 8,000m

Makalu from the First Step on Everest's north-east ridge

climbing was a retracing of that of climbing in the European Alps, but on a much compressed timescale. On the great peaks the era of first ascents took a decade (1950–1960: Shisha Pangma was not climbed until 1964 but there seems little doubt that had it been in Nepal or Pakistan rather than closed Tibet its first ascent would have been much earlier). The face era – in the Himalaya it is the south rather than the north faces which usually command the climber's interest – also took about ten years, but did not start until 1970, in part because of access difficulties to the peaks. By the 1980s climbers were already talking of 'last great problems' and shifting their interest to much steeper faces on lower peaks. The third stage, what had been disparagingly termed 'easy day for a lady' in the Alps, had arrived by the late 1980s (a good case could be made for an even earlier date) with commercial expeditions leading clients to the summits, clients who might have limited, even no, experience.

Many of the climbing elite, and a good few others, decried the advent of commercialism, but it was inevitable for two reasons. The first was economic: the great peaks lie in the territories of China, Nepal and Pakistan, very poor countries by western standards. Given the desire of these countries for hard currency any idea for increasing the number of climbers (and therefore income as each climber pays a peak fee) was bound to be greeted with enthusiasm and encouraged. This situation causes loud lamenting occasionally from individuals and organisations in the wealthier countries. Much of this lamenting smacks of elitism and should be listened to with scepticism: climbing is a sport with a huge potential for egotism, and self-importance and elitism are symbiotic. Some of the lamenting is plainly naïve, an expectation that the great peaks are too noble to be sullied with commercialism, but if Everest was in one of the world's developed countries is there anyone who seriously believes it would not have been exploited in a similar, or even more hard-nosed, way? But there are good reasons why some of the protestations should be listened to with care. A case

Nearing the summit on Makalu

probably more crowded than Everest's summit ridge and on more days in a year – yet no credible voice is raised in complaint (though it is, of course, true that guiding does not – nor ever has by virtue of the relatively small numbers involved in its earliest period – involve the cultural and environmental problems in the European Alps that it does in, say, Nepal).

Within the ranks of those climbers who did not join the commercial expeditions – and there are few who have not taken this option at least occasionally – the competition for the limited available sponsorship has

could be made for maintaining that in the Alps of the 19th century affluent British climbers were exploiting a poorer native population in a way that echoed the imperialism of British foreign policy. Calling this racially based pseudo-slavery would probably be stretching the point, but there are some who would go that far in describing the current western approach to climbing the great peaks. The effect of large numbers of rich Westerners on poor Himalayan and Karakoram communities has been significant, both in terms of cultural upheaval and environmental damage. The government ministers of the countries involved enjoy the dollar-earning potential of expeditions, but are not directly affected by the havoc wrought by them.

always been high. The era of national sponsorship of expeditions to the great peaks did not last long, though the sponsorship of single nation teams by national corporations continues: indeed, it remains a significant way of raising funds for major projects for certain high-profile climbers. For individuals such sponsorship has always been haphazard, the likelihood of being included in such a team being dependent on factors outside the control of most climbers. And though such expeditions allowed individuals to raise their own profiles, the publicity (and therefore potential for future sponsorship) was diluted if sizeable teams were involved. This was especially the case in climbing as most of the publicity went to the team leader and the climbers who reached the summit. In that sense

The second reason for the inevitability of commercial climbing has to do with climbers themselves. The climbing scene has its own magazines, each crammed with advertisements. None of these offer paid employment to climbers. Although climbing is the profession of some individuals it is not a profession *per se*. Many climbers who wish to do their own climbs on the 8,000m peaks – which can demand large expenditure in both time and equipment – or just want to reach the top of them must become guides, just as they do in the Alps. On a good summer's day in the Alps the Matterhorn's Hörnli Ridge will be crowded with guided climbers –

Commercial expedition on Gasherbrum I

climbing differed from most other team sports: in large expeditions team success was invested in individuals and it was their names, not that of the team, that won the plaudits. Half the world has heard of Hillary and Tenzing: how many of those people could name two other team members? It is surprising that there were not more problems on large expeditions than there appear to have been, especially as one frequent effect of high altitude is to make people fractious: Frank Smythe noted that happy teams in the Himalaya were 'as much of a miracle as a happy marriage' and that was before the advent of full-time climbers (though it is worth recalling that Smythe had a reputation as a difficult man at the best of times).

Publicity was important, at least for some climbers, because a high media profile guaranteed success in the book lists, on the lecture circuit or with sponsors willing to cover the costs of travel and equipment. There were those who treated the idea with disdain, but played the media

Langtang Himal from Pungpa Ri during an unsuccessful attempt on Shisha Pangma in 1987

game anyway: often those who dismissed the suggestion of sponsorship by an equipment manufacturer could afford to because of their book sales or lecture income. But to sell more books or encourage a larger audience more audacious climbs were required. Out of this arose, in parallel with the growth of commercial expeditions, the 'race' to climb all 14 of the 8,000ers; the record fast ascents; the ascents of several 8,000ers in a season; and the soloing of the peaks, occasionally by new hard routes.

The challenge to complete all 14 peaks is, in many ways, the most interesting of these because it, too, is in part dependent on history. Had the metre been a little longer then there would be fewer peaks above the magic figure and the climbing of all of them would have been a simpler task. Had there been just two, or three, or four many climbers would have climbed them all and in relatively short periods, and the completion may not have raised many eyebrows. Had the metre been a little shorter

Looking west from Shisha Pangma towards the peaks around Manaslu there would have been more peaks. Had there been 30 or 40 then it is doubtful whether anyone would have felt the need to climb them all (or been able to). Fourteen peaks is almost exactly the right number. To climb them all takes a very special commitment over a long period of time.

Reinhold Messner was the first climber to reach the top of all 14 8,000ers. He claims the idea of climbing them all grew over time rather than being his objective from an early stage and it is certainly the case that his early climbs seemed to be intent on pushing at the borders of the possible on the great peaks rather than peak-bagging: Nanga Parbat's Rupal Face, Gasherbrum I in pure alpine style with Peter Habeler, Everest without bottled oxygen (again with Habeler), Nanga Parbat and then Everest solo. His late rush to complete the climbs even allowed further advances – the Gasherbrum I and II traverse, a new route on Annapurna by a small team – though mostly he climbed the original routes (always, it must be said, without supplementary oxygen and usually in lightweight expeditions). It took Messner 16 years to complete the 14, starting with Nanga Parbat in 1970 and finishing with Lhotse in 1986. A year later Jerzy Kukuczka became the second man to complete the 14. It had taken him eight years and on 12 of the peaks he had completed either a new route or the first winter ascent. The only exceptions were Dhaulagiri (Kukuczka completed the first 'official' winter ascent, but the summit had been reached in winter three years before by a team which had started climbing before the official winter season) and Lhotse, his first 8,000er in 1979. Ironically, during an attempt at a new route on Lhotse in 1989 he was killed just short of the summit. The third to complete the 14 was the Swiss Erhard Loretan, but by then the quest had become a clear competition. Frenchman Benôit Chamoux was on Kangchenjunga, Loretan's 14th peak, at the same time and was also seeking to be the third to complete the set. Many have said that the race between them caused (or, at least, contributed) to Chamoux's death on the mountain. There was a French media team at Kangchenjunga's base ready to relay news of Chamoux's ascent (had he made it) to the world. Chamoux might have followed Loretan to the top, as he would have done had he survived, but he would have been first to broadcast the news: the climbing world would have known the truth, but in today's world the first with the news is the first, inconvenient facts rarely being allowed to get in the way of a good story. By the time the truth had emerged the news would have moved on.

The climbing world would also have questioned the validity of Chamoux's claims as he had not reached the true summit of Shisha Pangma but a slightly lower subsidiary summit. This was a problem that was to resurface later and continues to create correspondence in climbing journals. Fausto De Stefani admitted not reaching the summit of Lhotse when he became the sixth 'all-14' climber, but just how close he came is disputed. Was it just a few metres, as he claimed, or was it 150m (500ft)? How close is close – when is a summit not a summit? As the millennium draws to a close there is a queue forming to be next to complete the set, but question marks hang above many – did they reach Cho Oyu's summit or just the edge of the summit plateau? Broad Peak's top or the fore-summit? Shisha

Shisha Pangma from the Pang La, Tibet

Pangma's top or a subsidiary point on the long summit edge?

To the non-climbing world those allegations may seem trivial, but to a sponsor-led and, therefore, media-concerned (if not obsessed) sport they are vital. The issue is even more stark when solo ascents are considered. Messner provided a panorama of shots on Nanga Parbat's summit and himself plus Chinese tripod on Everest, but later soloists, because of poor visibility, lack of time or lack of media savvy have not. Climbing is no more immune to fraud than other activities involving ambitious human beings and has its share of known deceptions (the claimed first ascent of Denali (McKinley) for instance) and claims which are still debated – Maestri's first climb on Cerro Torre as an example. As a consequence it is perhaps no surprise that some of the more outrageous claims are treated with caution. But occasionally these outrageous

Lhotse (left), the South Col and Everest from Makalu

claims are true. Several Sherpas doubted Habeler and Messner's bottled oxygen-free ascent of Everest, particularly in the time they claimed, and there might have been doubters of Messner's solo climb too without the summit shots. Sometimes the doubts raised are legitimate, but, it seems, some claims are doubted for more than technical reasons – did the Sherpas resent not having made the first bottled gas-free ascent of Everest because it usurped their position of physical pre-eminence in high altitude climbing? Can we be sure that none of the doubts over Tomo Cesen's claimed solo ascent of Lhotse's south face in 1990 were untouched by envy or the problems it raised for future sponsorship, the 'last great problem' having been solved?

By coincidence the fiftieth anniversary of the ascent of Annapurna coincides with the end of the millennium (more or less: remarkably it lies almost exactly half-way between the popular millennial end – 31 December 1999 – and the pedantically correct one – 31 December 2000). In The White Spider, his book on the history of the Eiger's north wall, Heinrich Harrer chose, as an arbitrary endpoint for updating the story, the 50th ascent. He had a point: in the early years of the wall's history it was possible for most climbers to list the names of the ascentionists, they were the famous names of the sport. But then, inevitably, progress means a general increase in standards: the list of ascents grows longer, the rate of ascents increases and the names of the ascentionists become

and most of the names are virtually unknown. There might be arguments about K2, perhaps even about Annapurna, but it could be said with justification that the sun has now come out for all the great peaks.

As the second millennium ends it is reasonable to ask what the third one will bring. It would be easy to fall into the trap of assuming that equipment will not improve, that one-piece down suits, lightweight step-in crampons on plastic boots, ice axes which weigh almost nothing and all the rest is as advanced as it can ever be. They doubtless thought the same on Annapurna in 1950. Equipment will improve, it always does. Personal fitness will too and, because they are climbing on the shoulders of their predecessors, the confidence of climbers will also increase. The supremely fit Messner took 2½ days to solo Everest from the north: it has now been done in a day. Conditions might have been easier, but they cannot explain all of the near 300 per cent improvement. So, ascent times will come down. Many will join of the 'all-14' club. Climbs of several, probably all, of the 14 will be completed in 12 months, in a calendar year, in less than a year. Someone will climb Everest a dozen times, two dozen times. The Everest horseshoe – Nuptse, Lhotse, Everest – will be climbed. Other last great problems will be identified and quickly dispatched.

Climbers will strive. They will succeed. They will die.
And the peaks will be indifferent to it all.
Nothing changes.

less well-known. As Don Whillans, the great British climber said of the rock climbs he and partner Joe Brown had put up, climbs which had such an aura of invincibility that at first few even attempted them – 'everyone will be doing them when the sun comes out'.

The sun came out for the Eiger's north wall. Then it came out for Everest: in 1975 there had been about 50 ascents and the names of the climbers were famous ones. Twenty-five years later there have been 1,200 ascents

Makalu from Base Camp. To the left is the south face, with the south-east ridge to the right of the summit

discovery

Sir George Everest

In Sanskrit, the language of the ancient civilisations of the Indus and the Ganges, the language of the Vedas, the Upanishads and the Bhagavad Gita, the vast mountains which separated the plain of the Ganges from the Tibetan Plateau were the Hima alaya, the abode of snow.

Though obviously known to the earliest nomads and settlers of Tibet and northern India, the Himalaya was unknown to Europe until the expedition of Alexander the Great reached the Hindu Kush. Later, trade between the countries of the eastern Mediterranean and Asia doubtless brought news of the great peaks further east, but the barbarian invasions from the 3rd century AD cut the old silk route and brought trade and communication to a virtual standstill. Not for another 700 years would trade links be re-established. Marco Polo made his journeys in 1271 and 1295, but only in the 16th century does the Himalaya appear on a map of European provenance, drawn by a Spanish Jesuit who visited Hindustan.

In the mid-18th century both the British and French established trading centres on the east coast of India and sought to expand their spheres of influences over the sub-continent. Though their interests were nominally commercial – the British were represented by the East India Company rather than the Crown, but the difference was technical rather than real – both countries were seeking eastern empires. This led, inevitably, to conflict and the British won a decisive battle at Plassey in 1757. After the battle Britain controlled Bengal, extending its control to the whole eastern coast of India by 1805 and to the entire sub-continent by about 1815.

Although limited trade can be carried out along learned routes, real commerce requires maps. Government also needs maps, particularly as taxation is often based on landholdings. Maps have been in existence since the civilisations of Babylon and Egypt, and regular surveys have probably been carried out over the same period, even if, as with the Domesday Book of post-invasion Norman Britain, they were based on ad hoc measurements of area such as the land which could be ploughed by an ox-team in one day. After the battle of Plassey the commander of the victorious army, Robert Clive, was appointed Governor of the new British holding of Bengal and created Baron Clive of Plassey. One of Clive's first acts was to appoint Capt. James Rennell to survey his governorate. Rennell's survey took him north to the borders of Bhutan. There, within sight of the Himalaya he was stopped by the descendants of the Mongols who still hold that kingdom. Rennell surveyed an area of 3,800km² (1,500 sq. miles) and published, in 1783, a Map of Hindoostan, though the representation of the unsurveyed Himalaya was based on early travellers' maps.

Rennell's work was continued by later surveyors, but they headed south towards Madras. Then, in 1800, William Lambton, who had been captured – as an Ensign in the Infantry – at Yorktown in 1781, before serving under Col Arthur Wellesley (later to be the Duke of Wellington) in India, proposed a survey of the whole sub-continent. Lambton called the work the Great Trigonometrical Survey (it was known as the GTS for short) and ordered the construction of a half-ton theodolite almost 1m (3ft) across which was christened the Great Theodolite. Lambton also proposed the measurement of a Great Meridional Arc, a survey of the 78° line of longitude.

Lambton was a man of vision and one whose use of the word 'great' as an adjective implies that he was also perfectly aware of the status of his vision. The GTS would survey a country almost 30 times the size of Britain to the same accuracy as the Ordnance Survey of 1791. The measurement of the Great Meridional Arc would allow a calculation of the extent to which the Earth deviated, if it did at all, from a perfect sphere. The 78° meridian was the longest on accessible land, stretching for 2,500km (over 1,500 miles) from east of Cape Comorin, at India's southern tip, to the Himalaya. Lambton began work in 1802. For his survey he used a network of triangles, a thorough, but slow

technique. In 1818 Lambton took on a new chief assistant, Lt George Everest whose contribution to the work was to be fundamental when he became Superintendent of the GTS in January 1823. At that time Everest succeeded Lambton, who was at work until the end, dying during the working day at the age of 70.

But before considering the work of Everest, it is worth noting that although accepted heights of Himalayan peaks were not available until after the new Superintendent's death, measurements were being made much earlier. Sketch maps showing the routes through the difficult country around the India-Nepal border, and into Nepal, had been made by British army officers from the late 1760s, though it was not until 1804 that Charles Crawford, the commander of the military escort which accompanied the first British Resident to the Nepalese king's court in Kathmandu, suggested that the peaks of the Nepal Himalaya (or the Indian Caucasus as he called them) could be among the highest in the world, perhaps even higher

A survey team during the early surveying of the Himalaya

than the Andes of South America. In 1808 Lt WS Webb set out to explore the upper reaches of the Ganges. On his return journey he could see some of the high peaks noted by Crawford and took sightings of them from survey stations on the plain. Back at his base Webb calculated the height of one particular peak – Dhawala Gira – and was astonished by his results. Crawford's suggestion that these peaks were among the world's highest was much less than the truth – they were the actual highest. In 1809 Webb returned to validate his measurements: there was no doubt, and he published the result, Dhawala Gira (which we would spell Dhaulagiri) was 26,862ft high. This height, 8,190m, is only 23m (75ft) higher than the currently accepted figure of 8,167m, an indication of the accuracy of Webb's survey. But rather than marvelling at this colossal height, the geographers of Europe scoffed at this crazy army man who could not do even the simplest calculations. For them Chimborazo in the Ecuadorean Andes was the world's highest mountain and would officially remain so for many years. One interesting exception to this official line was the publication, in 1842, of an article which gave the comparative heights of the world's tallest peaks. Chimboraco [sic] is listed as 21,464ft, but four peaks in the Himalaya are also given. Dhawala Gira in Thibet [sic] is 26,462ft. The height is curious as it does not agree with Webb's, but is identical with that shown on an engraving of 1817 of unknown provenance. There are also two illustrations published between 1817 and 1842 which show 'Dhawala Gira' but give differing heights. Equally interesting is the fact that measured from the geocentre (the centre of mass of the earth, that is the point about which it rotates) Chimborazo is actually the furthest summit. The earth's rotation causes it to flatten at the poles: Everest is 28° north, while Chimborazo is on the equator (more or less). Despite being 2,600m (8,530ft) lower than Everest it is actually 2,200m (7,220ft) further from the geocentre.

The limited, tentative journeys into Nepal of Crawford and others were the last for over 140 years. By 1814 the East India Company had finally had enough of raids on its trading routes and centres and began the two-year Nepalese War. This ended with a re-defining of Nepal's western border, bringing the Kumaun Himalaya (the mountains around Nanda Devi) into India, but closing the Nepalese borders to foreigners. Surveys to the highest peaks would, for the present, have to be carried out from India.

George Everest was born on 4 July 1790, probably at Gwernvale, a beautiful house (now a hotel, and extended in less splendid style) near Crickhowell, a small town nestling beside the River Usk and below the Black Mountains of southern Wales, where his father, Tristram, was a solicitor.

George was the third child of six of Tristram (who also had an office in Greenwich) and Lucetta Mary, née Smith. In view of the now common pronunciation of the name of the world's highest mountain as Ever-est, it is interesting to note that George would have been appalled. Throughout his life he followed his family's preferred pronunciation of Eve-rest.

George became a Gentleman Cadet at 14 and joined the Royal Military Academy, Woolwich soon after. He left Woolwich in November 1805 and the following year, just seven days after his 16th birthday, he arrived in India having been gazetted as a Lieutenant in the Bengal Artillery. Little is known of his early military career, but he was certainly engaged in survey work by 1811 when he was temporarily stationed on Java. He became Lambton's chief assistant in 1818 and took over as Superintendent of the GTS in 1823. He was made Surveyor General of India in 1830. He retired from both posts in 1843. In 1846 he married 23 year old Emma Wing and fathered six children between 1849 and 1859. George was knighted in 1861 and died on 1 December 1866. He is buried in the churchyard of St Andrew's Church, Hove on England's south coast. Sir George had only two grandchildren, both born to his eldest son: neither had children of their own, the Everest line dying out in 1935.

In his capacity as senior surveyor in India Everest replaced Lambton's system with a gridiron of triangular chains, speeding the work on the meridian, and improved the design of theodolites with a consequent improvement in the precision of the survey. Everest completed the measurement of the Great Meridional Arc in 1841, but had not progressed the survey of the country to the borders of Nepal before his retirement. In the years that followed, the 'North-Eastern Himalaya' and 'North-Western' series of triangulations completed the task. In 1849, during surveys from the Ganges plain around Bihar observations were made of a previously unsurveyed peak in forbidden Nepal. On a numbering system that started to the east of Darjeeling, with Kangchenjunga's southern and main summits being Peaks VIII and IX, and Makalu Peak XIII, this newly surveyed mountain was Peak XV. The computations of the height of the peak were begun in 1852, but not until 1856 did Andrew Waugh, who had succeeded Everest as Surveyor General, feel justified in publishing the calculated height and the fact that Peak XV was probably the highest mountain in the world.

It is usually said that not until 1865, after an exhaustive search for a local name for Peak XV, was it given the name Everest, but in fact the name was in use from the first time the peak's height and probable status were published. In March 1856 Andrew Waugh wrote to Maj Thuillier, the Deputy

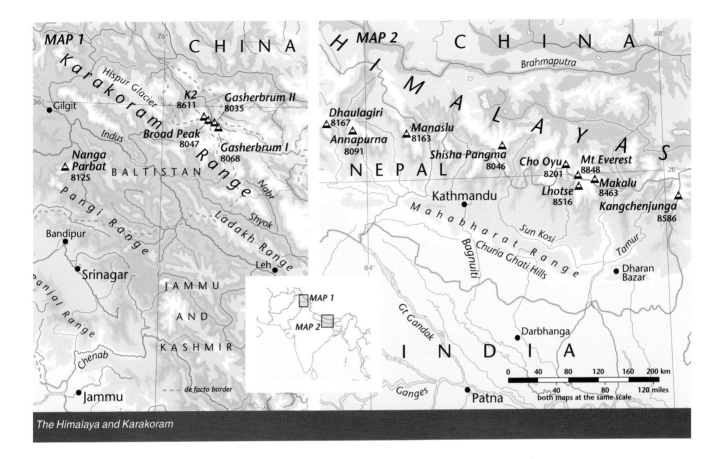

The Himalaya and Karakoram

Surveyor-General, in Calcutta (and later, as Gen. Sir Henry Thuillier, to succeed Waugh as Surveyor General) – 'I was taught by my respected chief and predecessor, Col. George Everest, to assign to every geographical object its true local or national appellation … But here we have a mountain, most probably the highest in the world, without any local name that we can discover, whose native appellation, if it has any, will not very likely be ascertained before we are allowed to penetrate Nepal, and to approach very close to this stupendous mass. In the meantime, the privilege, as well as the duty, devolves on me to assign to this lofty pinnacle … a name whereby it may be known among geographers, and become a household word … In testimony of my affectionate respect for a revered chief – in conformity with what I believe to be the wish of all the members of the scientific department over which I have the honour to preside – and to perpetuate the memory of that illustrious master of accurate geographical research – I have determined to name this noble peak … Mont Everest'. The height was given as 29,002ft (8,842m).

Later this height was increased to 29,028ft (8,848m), which is the currently accepted altitude. In 1999 a Boston Museum of Science GPS system attached to Bishop's Ledge, the outcrop just below the summit – and so-called because it is visible in the famous shot of Lute Jerstad taken by Barry Bishop

during the American 1963 expedition – suggested a height of no more than 8,830m (28,970ft): just a few days later the National Geographic Society, co-sponsors of the experiment, announced that the correct height was actually 8,850m (29,035ft).

Thuillier used Waugh's letter to formally announce the findings of the world's highest mountain in August 1856 at a meeting of the Asiatic Society of Bengal. Apart from the use of the French 'mont' (used either to denote a single peak rather than a massif or an affectation by the alpine-travelling British – and dropped in 1857 in favour of Mount, which has itself now been dropped altogether) the name of the world's highest mountain had been fixed. In August 1856 in a letter to the Asiatic Society following Thuillier's announcement, Brian Hodgson, a former political resident of Kathmandu, and then resident of Darjeeling, claimed the peak was actually called Devadhunga or Bhairathan. As a result of this letter, in early 1857 Waugh set up a committee to investigate the peak's name. This concluded that Devadhunga (meaning God's Seat) was applied to many places and that there was no evidence to support Bhairathan. This was fortunate as in January 1857 an official letter from the Secretary of State for India (written in reply to one from Waugh in July 1856) accepted the name Everest.

early climbs

The Diamir Face of Nanga Parbat. Mummery attempted the face up the prominent ribs

The 'discovery' of the highest mountain in the world coincided with the beginning of the 'Golden Age' of climbing in the European Alps.

Mont Blanc had been climbed in 1786, and though other peaks had also been ascended (Piz Bernina and the Jungfrau for instance) it was not until the arrival of the British in the mid-19th century that there was any real impetus for the climbing of the remaining 4,000m (13,123ft) peaks. The highest summit of Monte Rosa was climbed in 1855 – by five Britons, one of whom, Charles Hudson, was to die in the Matterhorn's first ascent tragedy, and three guides – and in the following ten years virtually all the remaining 4,000m peaks were climbed, culminating in the ascent of the Matterhorn by Whymper, Croz

and their team in 1865. The pace of exploration increased during the ten years, something approaching 100 peaks being climbed between 1863 and 1865. The equipment of these early pioneers was rudimentary. A type of crampon had been produced soon after the ascent of Mont Blanc, but was infrequently used, most climbers relying on nailed boots and steps cut into steep snow or ice. The steps were cut with a long handled ice axe, many still with the blade set hatchet-like rather than today's design. Rope was made from hemp which was heavy when wet and hawser-like when frozen. Rope handling was rudimentary with few real belays and little belay technique: the rope's value was more comfort than reality, a slip by one member often resulting in the whole team falling. Clothing was little more than old street clothes, heavy tweed coats and trousers, a hat or cap pulled down tight over the head. A sustained period of bad weather would have been extremely serious to these early climbers and it says much for their endurance, speed over (albeit straightforward) mixed terrain and good weather forecasting that so few accidents occurred: even with modern equipment these earliest routes can still trouble, even kill, the unwary or unlucky.

After the Golden Age climbing changed. The ascent of Mont Blanc had been for scientific (and later aesthetic) as much as adventurous reasons. In the Golden Age the sport had been the preserve of gentlemen – clergymen, noblemen and the leisured merchant class – climbing with local guides. Whymper had been different, a humble engraver motivated by a more modern approach. After the Matterhorn the use of guides by pioneers declined and any pretext of science/exploration was dropped: the climbing now was solely for the sport. The change was personified by Albert Mummery, a British climber who, after a long period climbing with the Swiss guide Alexander Burgener, began to climb hard routes

The first team to attempt K2 – Wesseley, Eckenstein, Jacot-Guillarmod, Crowley, Pfannl and Knowles

simply for the joy of it rather than as a means to reach a particular summit. The Mummery era, the last 20 years of the 19th century, also saw improvements in technique. Abseiling was first used in about 1879 and in the Eastern Alps pitons began to be used to supplement natural belays on the compact rock walls of the Tyrol and Dolomites. Mummery was also an early pioneer of climbing on ranges outside the Alps. Unsurprisingly, the aim of the early explorations was to repeat the development of the Alps – first the tops had to be reached by the easiest route available, only then would climbers turn to harder variations.

After Mummery the improvement in techniques and equipment accelerated. In the early years of the 20th century Oscar Eckenstein manufactured lightweight crampons which could be carried on a rucsac and short-handled ice axes, while in the Eastern Alps pitons with an eye (rather than a ring through which the rope could be threaded) and karabiners were invented. With these inventions climbers could more easily climb mixed, and steeper, ground, and could protect themselves with running belays, allowing standards to be pushed forward. Rock climbing standards were further improved with the invention of lightweight boots with felt soles and advanced rope techniques such as the tension traverse.

Mallory and Norton at about 8,200m (26,900ft), the highest point reached during the 1922 expedition

The 1914–18 War brought developments to a halt. When the conflict ended the order in the Alps changed. The Britain which gave birth to the early pioneers was in decline and losing its confidence. Though its climbers were still in the forefront of Himalayan exploration – India (and dreams of empire) would still be British for another 25 years – in the Alps they had lost their position of pre-eminence. Now the nations which possessed the mountains produced the climbers, Armand Charlet from France, Hans Lauper from Switzerland, Emilio Comici from Italy, Willo Welzenbach from Germany. In the wake of the advances by these new

Vittorio Sella's photograph of the west face of K2 taken in 1909 during the Duke of the Abruzzi's expedition

'modern' era. It is almost a reflex action to smile and shake the head at the Victorian mountaineer's clothing and equipment, yet there is really very little difference between it and that worn and carried by the Schmid brothers who first climbed the Matterhorn's north wall. Fifty years on again, the modern climber, encased in man-made fabrics that are light, warm, wind and waterproof and virtually indestructible, and carrying equipment of new alloys of superior strength and design, seems to inhabit a completely different world. Yet the inherent challenge of climbing remains the same, the advances in equipment and technique being mirrored by equal advances in the standard of the climbs completed by the best. On the first ascent of the Eiger's north face Heinrich Harrer did not have crampons (though this was by design rather than through lack of availability: it is not a decision today's climbers would contemplate) while Fritz Kasparek had 10-points, though Andreas Heckmair and Ludwig Vörg had sets of the new 12-points. None of the four had boots shod with Vibram (Vitale Bramani's revolutionary sole – named after him – did not appear until 1939) or were clad in clothes that shed water. Instead their jackets became sodden wet and then

Edward Norton approaching the Great (Norton)Couloir at about 8,500m (28,000ft) in 1924, probably the highest point reached, and the highest photograph taken, for almost 30 years

pioneers the great faces of the Alps were attempted; the 'six great north faces' of the Matterhorn, Cima Grande di Lavaredo, Petit Dru, Piz Badile, Grandes Jorasses and Eiger were all climbed in the 1930s. It is illuminating to compare the photographs of the Alpine pioneers of Mummery's era with those of 50 years later – the 1930s, the period of north face climbing – and then with those from a half century later, the

Members of the 1921 Everest reconnaissance expedition – Woolaston, Howard-Bury, Heron and Raeburn (back row), Mallory, Wheeler, Bullock, Morshead (front row)

cold when water from the upper face drenched them. Yet for all that the photographs of the four seem to place them in an era as remote as that of Mummery their achievement was considerable, the face retaining a reputation as the ultimate Alpine test piece for half a century and still being no easy day. When, not so many years ago, after a lecture in Britain Heckmair was asked how he had managed the climb with an old-fashioned ice axe, one without the modern inclined pick he famously responded that whether one climbed the Eiger or not did not depend on the droop of your ice pick.

The Sikkim side of Kangchenjunga, seen from the forepeak of Siniolchu. The expeditions of the 1930s attempted the north-east spur (facing the photographer) a route not finally climbed until 1977

Early Climbs in the Himalaya

Note: Explorations and early climbs on the 8,000m (26,247ft) peaks are detailed in the chapters on each peak. Below they are cross-referenced only.

The history of the early exploration of the Himalaya is studded with occasional claims to have reached a higher point or summit than any previous human. The recent discovery of the frozen corpses of children close to the summit of Llullaillaco, a 6,723m (22,057ft) mountain in northern Argentina renders most such claims redundant. The three children are believed to have been human sacrifices by the Inca priesthood, killed perhaps 500 years ago. It is likely that this was as high as men reached in South America, the Andes rarely rising above the

6,000m (19,700ft) contour. On the north (Tibetan) side of the Himalaya the summer snow line can be as high as 6,500m (21,300ft) and though vegetation at such a height is scarce, yaks and snow leopards have been reported from 6,100m (20,000ft) and the Tibetan gazelle (or goa) at over 5,500m (18,000ft). It is likely that man reached equivalent heights in search of game, perhaps even higher when exploring trade routes, but did not live at such heights: Gorak Shep, well-known to Everest trekkers because of the superb view of the Everest massif from nearby Kala Pattar, is at

The ridge camp at about 6,000m (19,750ft) during one of the early German attempts on Kangchenjunga's north-east spur

Mallory and Irvine about to leave the North Col camp for their final assault in 1924

Nanga Parbat seen over the Fairy Meadow

choose one peak rather than another, or choose to press on to the summit when a lower shoulder would be adequate for his purposes? One of the most striking examples of a figure reconnoitring this grey area was William Johnson who, though a member of the GTS, seems to have climbed as much for the thrill as to place triangulation stations. In 1865 on an unsanctioned journey into China's Kunlun Shan (a journey which led to his resignation from the GTS) he claimed to have climbed a 7,284m (23,898ft) peak. More recent surveys give the peak's height as 6,710m (22,014ft) and some, both at the time and today, question Johnson's claim, though it is beyond doubt that Johnson did achieve such altitudes elsewhere.

It is now generally agreed that the first pure climber to visit the Himalaya was WW Graham in the spring of 1883. At that time Bhutan and Nepal were off limits, Sikkim vaguely hostile

5,190m (17,000ft). The early surveyors in the Indian Himalaya climbed several dozen peaks over 6,100m (20,000ft) and several over 6,400m (21,000ft). There is also a famous incident from 1862, when a khalasi (an Indian assistant of the survey staff) reached a summit to the north of the Spiti River in Himachal Pradesh claimed to be over 7,000m (22,950ft) high. The man's name is not recorded, but the peak's name is given as Shilla. More recent surveys have fixed its height at 6,111m (20,049ft), sadly dismantling a myth it would have been nicer to maintain. As an aside here, a delightful insight into the methods of the India survey is gained by asking just how such khalasis checked the heights of their stations. Triangulation used theodolites from fixed platforms – and many of these were dotted around the northern India highlands – but such instruments were too expensive to be handed out to everyone (and, probably, were most definitely not entrusted by British members of the survey to local helpers). Instead the helpers were given thermometers, no less fragile perhaps, but a great deal cheaper, and told to boil water, measuring the boiling point allowing a measure of the local air pressure and, therefore, height.

Exactly when climbers, rather than explorers or map makers, came to the Himalaya is a matter of opinion – when does an explorer become a climber? Why does a map maker

Uli Wieland making trail towards the Moor's Head with the ridge to the Silver S beyond during the 1934 German expedition to Nanga Parbat

and the Karakoram both remote and politically sensitive, the borders of Russia, Afghanistan and British Indian having still to be defined. Of the Himalaya only Himachal Pradesh and northern Uttar Pradesh (Garhwal and Kumaun) were easily and safely accessible. It is therefore surprising that Graham, accompanied by his Swiss guide Joseph Imboden, chose to go to Sikkim. The pair explored the southern approaches to Kangchenjunga, but then Imboden fell ill and had to return to Switzerland. Graham next employed two Swiss guides. Emil Boss and Ulrich Kauffmann and headed for Garhwal. The trio arrived in July and completed two climbs which, if true, were astonishing. Graham claims to have reached 6,900m (over 22,600ft) on Dunagiri (7,070m/

Kamet, seen from a peak on the ridge between the East Kamet Glacier and Banke Plateau

23,196ft and not climbed until 1929), then climbed Changabang (6,864m/22,520ft) the peak whose fierce granite spire dominates the Ramani Glacier. The ascent of Changabang is now given no credence: indeed, it was being questioned within 15 years of Graham's trip. The accepted first ascent of Changabang did not take place until 1974 when the peak was climbed by an Anglo-Indian team. The claimed height on Dunagiri is also disputed: many believe it likely he got no higher than 6,100m (20,000ft) on a subsidiary ridge.

After his Garhwal climb Graham returned to Sikkim with Boss and claimed to have climbed Kabru (7,349m/24,111ft) to the south of Kangchenjunga. If true Graham and Boss would have been the first men known to have gone above 24,000ft (7,315m), but that ascent is also discounted by most authorities who believe that Graham actually climbed a peak about 1,220m (4,000ft) lower. It is not thought that Graham was a liar, his explorations being well documented. More likely his obvious inability to tell north from south and east from west, and to make assumptions about what he was looking at which owed more to wishful thinking than geography, meant he was genuinely mistaken about which mountain he was actually on. It would be a few more years yet before man definitely passed the 24,000ft contour.

In the 1880s FE Younghusband, a young British army officer stationed at Meerut met (at Dharmsala, now famous as the home of the Dalai Lama, the exiled Tibetan spiritual leader) men who had accompanied RB Shaw, Younghusband's uncle, the first Englishman to cross the Himalaya. Perhaps fired by this meeting, Younghusband explored the Indus Valley and what is now Afghanistan, and then joined an expedition to Manchuria. Returning from Peking (now Beijing) he became the first European to cross the Gobi Desert. In expeditions in 1887 and 1889 he explored the Karakoram, crossing the Muztagh Pass, a feat which still arouses the admiration of climbers. Then, in 1890 he explored the Pamirs meeting a Cossack patrol under Col. Yonoff who told him he was trespassing on soil that Russia had annexed. Yonoff escorted Younghusband south and expelled him from 'Russian' territory. This was the era of the 'Great Game' when the empires of Britain and Russia were expanding their influence in the Asian heartland. The incident caused a political storm and led to the defining of the borders of Britain, Russia and China. The British secured the Karakoram, Russia the Pamirs, and to ensure that the two great powers did not share a border, that being seen as a potential source of conflict, a long finger of Afghanistan was poked out between the two, reaching the border of China, a geographical oddity which still remains. Defining the borders meant the Karakoram could now be safely explored.

Following Younghusband's trips to the Karakoram, Conway took his influential expedition to the Baltoro, naming Broad Peak and Hidden Peak (the early name for Gasherbrum I) and Concordia, but from a point of view of climbing the next significant expedition was that of Mummery, Collie and Hastings, together with Bruce and two Gurkhas, to Nanga Parbat in 1895, a trip which ended in the what can probably be claimed as the first deaths of climbers in the Himalaya. The loss of Mummery was also a significant blow both to the British, and the world climbing scene, as he was arguably the most competent and experienced climber of the period.

Holdsworth on the summit of Kamet, pipe still firmly clenched between his teeth

he was unable to find a reasonable route before he ran out of supplies. After restocking the expedition headed north-west, away from Nanda Devi: it was now nearing the end of June and Longstaff preferred Kamet to Nanda Devi as it was further from the approaching monsoon and so offered a better chance of good weather. But that year's monsoon was severe and its effects reached the Garhwal, forcing the expedition to retreat.

In 1909 the Duke of the Abruzzi's expedition to the Baltoro reached a height of 7,500m (24,600ft) on Chogolisa, an altitude record which was to stand until the Everest expedition of the 1920s, though there were to be further increases in the height record for summits. The first was as a by-product of the 1930 International Expedition to Kangchenjunga led by the Swiss geologist Gunther Dyhrenfurth. The attempt on the big peak was abandoned after the death of a Sherpa, but the team stayed on in the area to climb a number of 6,000m and 7,000m peaks. One of the latter, Jonsong, 7,420m (24,343ft), was the highest and was climbed by six members of the team together with two Sherpas in early June 1930.

The new height record was to last just a year. Following Longstaff's initial look at Kamet the peak was attempted several times in the years before the 1914–18 War. In 1913 Charles Meade, who had already tried the peak in previous years, reached Meade's Col (between Kamet and Abi Gamin) with the French guide Pierre Blanc. The pair had found the route to the summit, but bad weather and the fact that they had not fully acclimatised stopped them from going further. After the war there was a further attempt to climb the peak in 1920 after which it was left alone until 1931. That year a team under Frank Smythe, and including the young Eric Shipton, reached the top by way of Meade's Col. The summit was reached by five of the six expedition members, together with two Sherpas, climbing as two teams on 21 and 23 June 1931. The climb not only established a peak height record – Kamet is 7,756m (25,446ft) – but the book of the expedition was a model of its kind, establishing a template which was to be used for the next 50 years. It included a list of sponsors – a list which was to expand and so form a significant part of later books – which noted not only the assistance of the steamship company which took the expedition to India, the food and film companies, but

Shipton on the summit of Kamet

Two years after Mummery's disappearance on Nanga Parbat Matthias Zurbriggen, who had been with Conway in the Baltoro in 1892, climbed Aconcagua in Argentina. Zurbriggen, who had been employed as a guide by the Briton Edward Fitzgerald, soloed the last section of the mountain, reaching the top on 14 January. The climb was repeated soon after by other members of the expedition. Aconcagua, at 6,960m (22,835ft) was probably the highest summit to have been reached at that time.

It was ten years before this peak height was surpassed, Dr Tom Longstaff and the Brocherel brothers Henri and Alexis – or Enrico and Alessio, as they were French guides from Italian Courmayeur – reaching the summit of Trisul, a 7,120m (23,360ft) peak close to Nanda Devi on 12 June 1907. It had been Longstaff's intention to climb Nanda Devi after Trisul but

Nanda Devi in early morning light, seen from Changabang. The north face is in sun, with the north ridge dividing light from shade

1936 a British-American team co-led by Graham Brown and Charles Houston climbed the mountain, Tilman and Noel Odell (the last man to see Mallory and Irvine alive) reaching the summit on 29 August 1936.

The ascent of Nanda Devi was memorable for reasons other than it being the highest peak climbed until 1950. The small well-knit team was a model for the democratic groups which would operate in the Himalaya after the era of the first ascents: the team even declined, at first, to release the names of the summiteers. The expedition book, by Tilman, is, arguably, the finest of its kind ever produced, Tilman's laconic style and elegant wit making it a joy to read. The climb also represented the last days of Empire: Tilman notes that when he and Odell reached the summit 'I believe we so far forgot ourselves as to shake hands on it'. Although something of this gentlemanly behaviour can be detected in the 1950s, particularly on the 1953 Everest expedition, it had disappeared by the time of the summit rushes and overt competitiveness of the late and post-8,000m era.

the Gramophone Co Ltd of Calcutta who supplied a gramophone and records. This delightful touch, totally of its time, but a forerunner of today's CD and cassette players (and radios and satellite phones), is complemented by an equally dated (but equally delightful) aspect of the book's photographs. On the pre-climb group shot Holdsworth (who, as with the other team members, is never referred to by, or even given, his Christian name throughout the book) is shown with a pipe clenched between his teeth. The pipe is still there in the shot of Holdsworth at the summit.

The peak height was to be raised once more before the 1939–45 War halted further exploration of the Himalaya. Nanda Devi was, at 7,816m (25,643ft), the highest peak in the British Empire and had inspired climbers since Longstaff had photographed it in 1905. It is a magnificent, beautiful mountain, but one as well protected as the legend of its name would suggest. Nanda was the daughter of the king of Kumaun (part of Garhwal). She was very beautiful and much desired, and a stronger king demanded her as his wife. Nanda's father refused, but was defeated in battle by her suitor. Nanda fled to a mountain sanctuary, taking refuge on its highest peak. Nanda Devi means Princess, or Goddess, Nanda, and other peaks of the sanctuary are named for the legend – Trisul, for example, means 'trident', the weapon threatening the suitor king.

Nanda Devi's sanctuary, an almost continuous circle of peaks (including Changabang) and huge mountain walls prevented access to the peak for many years. Then, in 1934, Eric Shipton and Bill Tilman, together with three Sherpas, forced a way through the gorge of the Rishi Ganga, reaching the inner sanctuary and identifying a route to the summit. In

A climber at about 7,000m (23,000ft) during the successful 1936 expedition to Nanda Devi

annapurna 8,047m

‘ **Do you think it is worth it?** ’

LOUIS LACHENAL TO
MAURICE HERZOG
on the summit climb during
the first ascent of Annapurna

The 1939–45 War brought an end to Himalayan climbing, the major nations participating in the exploration and climbs of the 1930s being those most actively involved in the conflict. In the immediate post-war years exhausted nations recuperated, but it was not long before man's restlessness overcame the austerity and relative disorganisation.

The demands of war meant that British influence in Tibet waned between 1939 and 1945. Then, in 1947 the Dalai Lama's horoscope prophesied that Tibet would be threatened by foreigners and the country closed its borders to all outsiders. Before the British had a chance to re-assert their influence – they were, technically, still the guarantors of Tibetan autonomy – or the Tibetans had calculated that the advantages of outside friends in limiting the colonial ambitions of its vast neighbour outweighed the horoscope's predictions, the Chinese invaded, closing access to the northern side of Everest and other great peaks for decades. In the face of such a formidable opponent the British quietly forgot their obligations.

With Tibet closed interest might have shifted to the western end of the Himalaya, but the great peaks of the Karakoram were also off-limits as the newly established nations of India and Pakistan quarrelled over border lines. Then, in 1948 the formerly closed, secretive nation of Nepal, concerned over the longer term intentions of China and wanting to acquire powerful friends, tentatively opened its borders, firstly to a group of American ornithologists, then to a team of Swiss climbers who, under René Dittert, explored the north-east of the country. In 1949 the French Fédération Française de la Montagne began negotiations with the Nepalese government for permission to climb one of the great peaks that stood wholly within Nepal.

France was in an excellent position to mount a determined attempt, many of the leading climbers of the late 1940s/early 1950s being French, a situation due, in large part, to the unfortunate circumstances of the war. Although some French men escaped German-occupied France to form the Free French battalions, most were trapped in the country. Military service was abolished, but the French civilian authorities introduced Les Chantiers de la Jeunesse, an organisation aimed at giving idle young men something to do, with a view to promoting the ideas of honest toil and citizenship, fearful that otherwise the fabric of the nation would rot away. A parallel organisation, Jeunesse et Montagne, was set up in mountain areas. Here officers from the French armed services helped civilian instructors to train young men in skiing and mountaineering. The JM, as it was known, helped maintain the officer corps' fitness and expertise while teaching mountaincraft to a generation of climbing enthusiasts. Lionel Terray, arguably the greatest alpinist of the immediate post-war era, was a product of the JM and notes the rigours of the training and the later work the trainees did in helping the maquis liberate the French Alps. Terray records one day when, carrying 20kg (44lb) packs, his troop climbed almost 3,000m (nearly 9,000ft) and descended almost the same height with little food. The JM training and partisan battles took place in both summer and winter, giving the French an almost unrivalled understanding of snow conditions and of climbing and survival techniques in the harshest conditions. When the war ended France had a group of young men capable of repeating the great alpine climbs of the Germans, Austrians and Italians and of pushing standards even higher. Gaston

Annapurna I (the main summit) from Poon Hill

Annapurna's northern flank is seen over the Annapurna North Glacier. Annapurna East rises on the left skyline

Above South Face
1 *British (1970)*
2 *Japanese (1981)*
3 *Polish (1981) to Central Summit*
4 *Spanish (1981) to Central Summit*

Below North Face
A *East Summit*
B *Main Summit*
1 *French (1950)*
2 *Dutch (1977)*
3 *Polish (1996)*
4 *East Ridge (skyline from left), Loretan and Joos (1984) over East and Central (hidden in cloud) Summits to Main Summit*

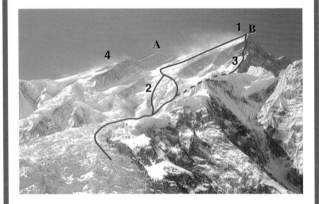

Left West Face
1 *Messner/Kammerlander (1985)*

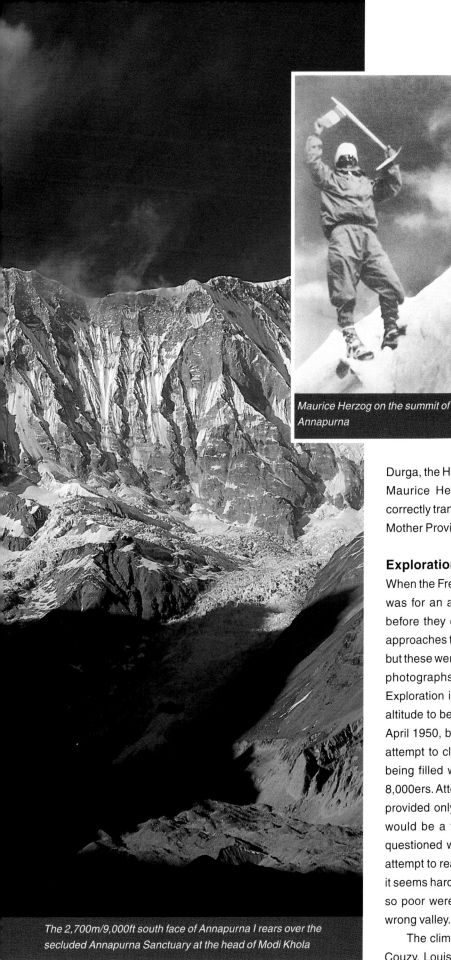

Maurice Herzog on the summit of Annapurna

The 2,700m/9,000ft south face of Annapurna I rears over the secluded Annapurna Sanctuary at the head of Modi Khola

Rébuffat made the second ascents of the Walker Spur and the north face of the Piz Badile, as well as early ascents of the other great north faces. Louis Lachenal and Lionel Terray made the second ascent of the Eiger's north wall and reduced the fastest time on the Piz Badile's face from 19 hours to 7½ hours, a tribute to their astonishing fitness as well as their climbing abilities. These men were to form the core of the French 1950 Himalayan expedition.

Name

Annapurna was Peak XXXIX of the Indian survey, its local name being a combination of two Sanskrit words whose literal meaning is 'filled with food'. However, the name also contains the root of another name for Durga, the Hindu Divine Mother, consort of Lord Shiva, and, as Maurice Herzog was told during his expedition, is more correctly translated as 'Goddess of the Harvests', ie. the Divine Mother Provider.

Exploration and First Ascent

When the French arrived in the spring of 1950 their permission was for an attempt on either Dhaulagiri or Annapurna, but before they could set foot on either they needed to explore approaches to the peaks. Maps from the Indian survey existed, but these were soon shown to be highly inaccurate, while aerial photographs taken by the Swiss Foundation for Alpine Exploration in 1949, though intriguing, were from too low an altitude to be of great value. The French arrived in Nepal on 5 April 1950, but it was not until 23 May that Herzog decided to attempt to climb Annapurna, much of the intervening period being filled with attempts to reach the base of either of the 8,000ers. Attempts to reach Dhaulagiri from the east and north provided only views of the mountain which suggested that it would be a formidable undertaking (indeed, Lionel Terray questioned whether it would ever be climbed) while the first attempt to reach Annapurna failed to find the mountains at all: it seems hardly credible that an 8,000m peak could be lost, but so poor were the maps that the French were actually in the wrong valley.

The climbing team which turned to Annapurna was Jean Couzy, Louis Lachenal, Gaston Rébuffat, Marcel Schatz and

Lionel Terray. Jacques Oudot was the team doctor, Marcel Ichac the photographer and Francis de Noyelle, a young diplomat, the liaison officer. The team was led by Maurice Herzog, General Secretary of the Groupe de Haute Montagne and supported by eight Sherpas under sirdar Angtharkay.

The team left Paris on 30 March 1950 with 3½ tons of equipment, including nylon anoraks, overtrousers and ropes: spin-off from the 1939–45 War made this the first major expedition to be equipped with synthetic materials. The French had down jackets and lightweight climbing equipment (crampons etc.). They also had improved oxygen equipment, though this was actually only used for physiological tests low on the mountain, none of the climbers going high (including the summit pair) using it. Though the use of new materials and the lightest equipment was a recognition of the arduousness of climbing on the great peaks, the attempt to minimise weight was to have disastrous consequences: the lightweight boots meant that all the climbers suffered from cold feet and the summit climbers were frostbitten.

Maurice Herzog's account of the expedition is one of the greatest mountaineering books of all time, a multi-faceted diamond of a book. With it the reader can feel compassion, marvel at heroism, grimace at horror. It is epic tale, grand tragedy, a perfection of schadenfreude. The early chapters on Nepal (and, to a lesser extent, India) before the tourist invasions of later years are fascinating: the acetylene lamps lighting the customs office in Old Delhi; the old Nepalese seeing white men for the first time and eyeing them suspiciously while the children crowded around bug-eyed with curiosity; caravans of joyful Tibetan traders arriving from a country which would soon change for ever, replacing joy with sorrow.

Climbers on the 'handle' of the Sickle Glacier

Herzog's description of the exploration of the approaches to Dhaulagiri and Annapurna are equally fascinating. The team members took an oath of allegiance to the leader before departure. That, and the boyish nature of the dialogue Herzog quotes verbatim – though many of the exchanges must have been invented later their 'feel' and context are presumably real – conjure up an air of innocence, a

Annapurna from the west. The north-west face, first climbed by Kammerlander and Messner, lies furthest from the photographer

group of naive, young men on a great adventure: it is no surprise when members ride in and out of camp on horseback. The much more recent publication of the unabridged version of Louis Lachenal's diaries (the earlier version of them had been edited by Herzog's brother and Lucien Davies, who omitted sections which did not reflect Maurice's view of the expedition) and those of Gaston Rébuffat (quoted in a biography of him) suggest that things were not quite as idyllic as Herzog makes them seem. But whatever the case, the innocence was soon to be lost.

After spending many weeks exploring Herzog finally decided that Annapurna's north face offered the best chance of success (a decision perhaps aided by a conversation with a Buddhist lama who visited the team's camp and told them that 'Dhaulagiri is not propitious to you ... give up and turn your thoughts towards the other side ... towards Muktinath' – the town near Annapurna).

The French first attempted the north-west ridge (the Cauliflower Ridge as they called it), but soon realised that even if they could climb it there was no chance of the Sherpas being able to carry loads up it. They therefore abandoned it in favour of the north face, choosing a route across the relatively easy-angled face to the foot of the Sickle, a prominent snow-field/glacier (named for the shape of its icewall edge) descending from the summit. The route to the Sickle, at the base of which Camp V was established on 2 June, took only ten days from Camp I, an exploration camp of the North Annapurna Glacier. That is an astonishingly quick time for so big and unknown a mountain, made even more remarkable when the weather the French experienced is recalled. Though they had a run of fine mornings, the afternoons invariably brought thick snow which required the routes between camps to be broken almost daily. The snow also brought the threat of avalanches. Annapurna's north face is now known to be avalanche prone, the weight of new snow in 1950 (30–50cm/12–20in fell most afternoons) adding to the ever present risk. But, of course, time was valuable – the monsoon was due to arrive on 5 June.

On the northern flank the great serac wall of The Sickle hangs over Camp II of the 1970 Expedition

Herzog's account notes that those Sherpas with pre-war experience said the climbing on Annapurna was much harder. He notes too the inexperience of the Sherpas in ice climbing and their resulting disinclination to take a lead in developing the route. How things change, today's Sherpas often being more experienced and skilled than their clients. Herzog's account also displays the lack of understanding of the best method of acclimatisation. The strongest climbers pushed ahead until they were exhausted, then descended for rest, a strategy now discarded in favour of a phased gain in altitude. The consequence was that on 2 June it was Herzog and Lachenal who occupied Camp V, not Lachenal and Terray as had been expected. Herzog offered Angtharkay the chance of continuing to the summit on 3 June, but he declined as his feet were frozen and descended.

Herzog and Lachenal had no sleep on the night of 2 June, being kept awake by the wind – which threatened to blow the tent down – and the build up of snow on the fabric. In the morning they were so worn out they failed to make any drinks. Dehydration is now recognised as a major contributor to frostbite, blood thickening due to the increase in red cell numbers being aggravated by a thinning of plasma. The pair were also taking a mix of pills prescribed by the team doctor. These included Maxiton which suppresses feeling of fatigue, in part by creating a sense of euphoria. Herzog's book shows that he enjoyed every aspect of the early expedition – the thrill of being in the Himalaya and being with some of the world's best climbers – but his occasional unbounded joy was as nothing to the almost permanent sense of euphoria on the summit climb. While Lachenal stopped periodically to massage his frozen feet, Herzog climbed in a world seemingly remote from reality. Eventually Lachenal asked Herzog what he would do if he (Lachenal) descended. Herzog said he would continue alone and so Lachenal agreed to accompany him. Herzog's book implies that the pair were climbing for the glory of France, but Lachenal's unabridged diaries show he did not share this view. He felt that if Herzog continued alone he would not return – 'this summit climb was not a matter of national prestige. It was une affaire de cordée.' Une affaire de cordée, a matter of the rope, the obligation one man on a rope has for the man on the other

end – the more so, perhaps, as Lachenal was a far more experienced climber and a professional guide, while Herzog was an 'amateur'. Elsewhere Lachenal states that for him Annapurna was no more important than any other mountain and that he did not owe his feet to the youth of France. When the pair reached the summit at about 2pm Herzog was utterly overjoyed, almost oblivious to Lachenal's insistence that they go down immediately. Lachenal clearly sensed how close to the limit they were.

On the summit photo most often published a snow slope rises beyond the triumphant Herzog, a fact which led some to

Gerry Owens makes the last stride to the summit during the second ascent. A few days later Dougal Haston and Don Whillans stood on the left-hand hump after climbing the south face

question (and still to question) whether the true summit had been reached. Herzog dismissed the objections by saying that there was a cornice at the summit and that the angle the photograph had been taken at gave a distorted view of it. With the snow fall and winds of the days before the top was reached, it is hardly surprising that a significant cornice had formed and when all the shots of Herzog are examined it is definitely the case that as Lachenal changed his position, the apparent snow slope beyond Herzog diminishes. Given Herzog's strange mental state it is easy to see why doubters distrust his insistence, but those who knew Lachenal point to the fact that his diary states simply that they had reached the summit and that he would not have said so had it not been the case. On later climbs there has been a less distinct cornice, or no cornice at all: subsequent photos show that the summit, the highest bump on a ridge which is the culmination of the mountain's south face, can be a narrow point on which two or three people can stand.

In Herzog's account of the descent from the summit he is pursuing Lachenal who, fearful of frostbite, has descended at speed. Herzog recalls losing his gloves when he opened his rucsac, though he does not know why he opened it or why he did not use his spare socks as makeshift gloves. Clearly he was still euphoric. He claims to have followed Lachenal until mist enveloped them both. However, Lachenal's version is that Herzog was in front and that, unable to catch his team leader, he was constantly shouting and pointing to his hands in an attempt to draw Herzog's attention to his lack of gloves. Lachenal being behind Herzog would also explain why Herzog arrived at Camp V first, with Lachenal's cry for help after his fall being heard by Herzog, and by Terray and Rébuffat who had come up to the camp to meet them. Lachenal fell on relatively easy ground and was brought back to the camp by Terray though he was by now frantic to get down so that Oudot could attend to his frozen feet.

Herzog's frozen hands were probably already beyond saving, but his and Lachenal's feet might have been saved if 4 June had been fine. Terray and Rébuffat treated them in the then-approved method of lashing the bare, frozen flesh with knotted rope. Today it is recognised that body warmth is the best treatment, the whipping technique having been relegated to dubious massage parlours. After a night of poor sleep and pain – with the summit pair having their first liquid for some 24 hours – the four climbers started out for Camp IV in a snowstorm. All day they tried to reach the camp, failing because of poor visibility and deep snow. The night spent in a fortuitously-found crevasse – Lachenal fell into it – was fearful

Climbers pause for rest during the second ascent in 1970

Gerry Owens just below the summit furing the second ascent

and probably caused the permanent damage to the summit pair's feet. The four climbers were buried by an avalanche the following morning and had the monsoon arrived on time would almost certainly have died, but 5 June was fine. Terray and Rébuffat were snow-blinded, having spent much of the previous day without goggles trying to peer through the storm. Lachenal, seeing the chance of salvation slipping away shouted towards Camp IV – and was heard at Camp II 1,260m (4,100ft) below. The distraught occupants of II – many hours climbing away – were relieved to see a search party from IV arrive soon after: the crevasse had been only 200m (650ft) from the camp.

Herzog's account of the retreat from the mountain is harrowing. He had given up hope in the crevasse and asked to be allowed to die, and was then caught in an avalanche on the treacherous lower face, he and two Sherpas being carried down 150m (500ft) and saved from death by a miraculous snagging of the rope. The rest of the descent and the march out from the mountain through the monsoon, with pauses for excruciating injections and, eventually, the casual amputation of Herzog's fingers and toes and Lachenal's toes, is as gripping an evocation of horror as could be imagined. Herzog spares nothing, of himself or the situation: he overhears Oudot fearing that gas gangrene would kill him in appalling fashion; the sweeping away of black amputated digits with a twig broom; and the fact that red-bellied flies lay eggs on his open stumps, the doctor allowing maggots to hatch so they would consume the dead flesh, cleaning the wound. In Paris 225g (½lb) of maggots were extracted from his mutilated extremities.

Herzog's account of the climb is factual rather than lyrical, yet his style allows the beauty of the mountains to shine through. His inclusion of team conversations, warts and all, set a standard followed, usually much less successfully, by later writers. His final sentence, after thoughts on an expedition which almost killed him and which maimed both summit climbers, that 'there are other Annapurnas in the lives of men' is as profound an explanation for man's exploratory zeal as could be written.

Later Ascents

The returning French were greeted by a nation hysterical with joy and pride, its self-worth restored, its prestige renewed. For the team members the Annapurna experience was more traumatic, and only two would answer the call when four years later, the French returned to the high peaks.

After Annapurna the 'Golden Age' of 8,000m peak climbing occupied the world's leading climbers for a decade. Political difficulties then made travel to Nepal impossible for several years. By the time travel problems eased again in the late 1960s a new generation of climbers, some barely of school age when Annapurna was climbed, had arrived. The French ascent of Jannu in 1962 had pointed the way to a new era of climbing on lower, but technically difficult, peaks, though the impetus had still been the first ascent. Next came the German attempts at Nanga Parbat's Rupal face which they tried several times during the 1960s. Another early indication of the new outlook came on Annapurna in 1969 when a German expedition failed in an ambitious project to climb the 7.5km (4½ mile) ridge from Glacier Dome to main summit. Then, in 1970 a British expedition arrived on the south side of the mountain to attempt the vast south face. This expedition, together with the German Rupal face climbs, heralded a new era in Himalayan climbing, a deliberate attempt at a difficult line to a previously climbed summit. Development in the Himalaya was thus taking the same path as in the Alps, but with the timescales hugely compressed. Ironically, at the same time a British-Nepalese Army expedition was on the north side of the

Climbing fixed ropes above Camp V during the British south face climb in 1970

mountain, repeating the French line, but using oxygen. Simultaneously, therefore, the old (some would argue retrograde) and new styles were at work, separated by a vast mountain of snow and ice and an equally large difference in attitude.

From its base Annapurna's south face rises almost 3,000m (about 9,500ft), making it twice the height of the north wall of the Eiger – but the base of the wall is 1,000m (3,300ft) higher than the Eiger's summit. From the start of the major difficulties the face has an angle of 55°, about the same as the ice-fields and Ramp on the Eiger. The comparison with sections on the Eiger are a feature of the expedition book by Chris Bonington, the team leader, who had completed the British ascent of the north wall's 1938 route with Ian Clough, another team member. The other climbers were Martin Boysen, Mick Burke, Nick Escourt, Dougal Haston, Mike Thompson and Don Whillans – as strong a team as had been assembled at that time in the Himalaya – together with the American Tom Frost. The latter was included for sponsorship reasons, his presence helping to sell the climb in the US. Such overt commercialism was another new feature in the Himalaya. The team was completed by Dave

Annapurna from the west, showing the peak's well-defined rock strata

north side of the mountain was. Taking turns, the pair climbed to the narrow summit bump, the tracks of Henry Day and Gerry Owens – who had made the second ascent of Annapurna on 20 May – being just discernible. Two days later Burke and Frost attempted to repeat the climb, Burke getting no higher than Camp VI, Frost continuing alone to about 7,700m (just over 25,000ft).

After the attempt by Burke and Frost, Bonington ordered the team to clear the mountain, aware that with the monsoon due, with regular avalanches on the face and falling stones threatening to injure climbers and cut the fixed ropes, the climbers' luck might be running out. Ironically it was during this final phase that an ice tower collapsed, killing Ian Clough. But despite this tragedy the expedition had been a major success, the first 'modern' climb of an 8,000er. It was a business success too, Bonington's astute commercial sense preparing the way for later expeditions of his own and others.

There were further deaths on the mountain in 1973. Having failed on the north-east buttress a Japanese team transferred their interest to the original route. On this two teams climbed to within 150m (500ft) of the top before being forced to retreat by high winds and exhaustion. During the descent four Japanese and a Sherpa were killed by an avalanche. Later in the year an Italian team failed on the north-west ridge, two members being killed by an avalanche during the descent.

In 1974 a Spanish team climbed Annapurna East, the 8,012m (26,280ft) point that represents the eastern end of the long, summit ridge, by a route to the east of the French route, continuing up the north ridge, but an attempt on the main summit via the south-east ridge in 1975 by an Austrian team failed when their Sherpas went home, claiming that their clothing, food and equipment was inadequate. The Austrians continued, but abandoned the attempt when one team member was killed by an avalanche. The Spanish route was followed again in 1980 when a German team used it to gain the upper north face which they climbed to the central summit.

The fourth ascent of the main peak came in 1977 when a Dutch team, celebrating the 75th anniversary of the Royal Dutch Alpine Club (an organisation which sounds as unlikely as the Saharan Canoe Club, but one which has produced some notable climbers), completed the first post-monsoon climb. The Dutch route, to the left of the French route, along what is now termed the Dutch Rib, had the advantage of being less prone

Lambert as doctor and Kelvin Kent as Base Camp Manager. The team's equipment was much improved over that of the French, with warmer clothing, lighter climbing gear (though problems with crampons coming off are a recurrent theme of the ascent – step-in crampons would help in later years, as would droop pick ice axes) and better tents.

One other detail should not be overlooked: as Bonington noted, the French had first to find their mountain, whereas his team didn't even need a map to find the face.

The climb (up the face's left buttress) was straightforward to Camp III at 6,100m (just over 20,100ft) but then a narrow ice ridge, which had to be turned on the left, required seven days of hard climbing. Further up a 300m (1,000ft) rock band was overcome with climbing which was equally difficult. Towards the end of May, with deteriorating weather perhaps predicating the early arrival of the monsoon, Dougal Haston and Don Whillans occupied Camp VI at 7,300m (about 24,000ft). The intention had been to establish another camp 300m (1,000ft) higher, but with exhaustion affecting virtually the entire team and, consequently, limited food and equipment reaching the lead climbers, the pair left the camp on 27 May on what, in retrospect, was a make or break bid for the summit. Climbing ropes they had fixed earlier – the last of the 4.5km (almost 3 miles or 15,000ft) of rope which had been fixed on the face to aid load carrying – then climbing unroped they reached the summit ridge just 10m (33ft) below the summit. Haston was surprised, after many weeks on the face, at just how flat the to avalanches and, therefore, the preferred option for later parties on the north side of the peak. The summiteers used oxygen.

1978 brought a notable success when a team of American women (but including one British woman in a mirror-image of the 1970 south face team) repeated the Dutch route, claiming several firsts. The team, led by Arlene Blum, needed to raise US $80,000 to finance the climb. Of this three-quarters was realised by the sale of T-shirts bearing the legend 'A Woman's Place is On Top ... Annapurna'. Blum wanted to employ Sherpanis rather than Sherpas for the climb, but discovered that they were only interested in helping with the cooking and laundry, a somewhat chastening position in view of the overtly feminist aims of the expedition. In the event the team was supported by Sherpas – hardly a body blow to the feminist ideal as the woman did the lead climbing and the use of Sherpas has never been seen as diminishing the achievements of male teams. The expedition was post-monsoon and used oxygen, claiming the first female ascent when Irene Miller and Vera Komarkova, together with two Sherpas reached the summit. Sadly a second summit attempt failed, with Alison Chadwick-Onyszkiewicz, the British team member, and Vera Watson being killed.

A French team followed the original route in 1979 but during an attempted ski descent Yves Morin skied into the loose end of a fixed rope and was killed. There was further

Dougal Haston on the fixed ropes between Camps V and VI during the 1970 British south face expedition

success on the Dutch route in 1980, then significant climbs in 1981, a Polish team climbing a new route on the south face to the right of the British route, with climbing of a similar standard to that of the north face of the Matterhorn. The route led directly to the middle top (Annapurna Central) of the summit ridge (at 8,051m/26,538ft). The summit climbers, Maciej Berbeka and Boguslav Probulski reached the top in a severe storm and did not continue to the main summit. That was reached by two members of a Japanese team which completed a hard route, post-monsoon, on the south face between the British and Polish routes (the central buttress). A Japanese climber died in a second summit attempt. Meanwhile, on the north-west ridge four climbers (two French and two Sherpas) died attempting a new route.

In 1982 the south face was again the centre of attraction, a three-man team attempting an alpine style ascent of a route to the right of the Polish route. The climb was abandoned when the Briton Alex McIntyre was killed by stonefall. The route was climbed (to the middle summit) in alpine style in 1984 by the Spaniards Nil Bohigas and Enric Lucas. That year also saw the ascent of the east ridge by a six-man team under Frank Tschirky. The summit pair of Erhard Loretan and Norbert Joos. In just three days they climbed the ridge from close to Glacier Dome to the east summit, continuing over the middle and main summits and descending the north face. Also in 1984 a Korean team claimed to have climbed the peak in winter. This claim was denied by their Sherpas and also by a French team on the mountain at the same time. The French stated that the Korean claim was not consistent with French observations, nor with the state of the mountain which was dangerous due to heavy snow fall. General opinion now suggests that the Koreans stopped about two hours short of the summit.

Late in 1985 the Japanese failed in a winter attempt on the British south face route (a Bulgarian team having no more success on the Polish route in early 1986), but 1985 was most notable for the first ascent of the north-west face by Reinhold Messner and Hans Kammerlander, Messner claiming his eleventh of the 14 8,000ers. The vast concave north-west face was one of the last unclimbed faces on the great peaks and proved difficult, requiring Messner's small team to set up two fixed camps, with two bivouacs above that. The final climb was into the teeth of gale-force winds, the summit ridge testing both climbers. In his account of the climb Messner claims it was only Kammerlander's drive that kept the pair going and only his presence that allowed Messner to believe in his own survival. During the descent the pair had to contend with new snow and were glad of the assistance of other members of the team, Reinhard Patscheider and Reinhard Schiestl. During the night

Ian Clough on fixed ropes during the 1970 British south face expedition

only Patscheider's constant clearing of fresh snow from the tent prevented the exhausted pair from suffocating. A few days later Patscheider, Schiestl and Swami Prem Darshano (the fifth member of the team) attempted to repeat the climb, but were forced back by deep snow. During the descent Patscheider survived a 400m (1,300ft) fall.

Maurice Herzog returned to the north side base camp with a French expedition in 1986. The emotional return did not ensure success, the French failing on the north ridge, though an Italian team followed Herzog's original route in just six days (base to summit and return). The first winter ascent of Annapurna was finally made in 1987 by a small Polish team, Jerzy Kukuczka (climbing his thirteenth 8,000er) and Artur Hajzer following the French route to reach the top on 3 February. Kukuczka, a man seemingly immune to cold and suffering, referred to the climb as 'cold hell' as, being on the northern side of the peak, the climbers did not see the sun after leaving base camp, climbing in a perpetual shade on ice so

The summit of Annapurna (the second ascent)

climbing illegally (ie. without a permit), claimed a solo ascent during the post-monsoon period.

During the 1990s Annapurna's south face continued to exercise a fascination for those seeking very hard climbing at altitude. Post-monsoon in 1992 the French climbers Pierre Beghin and Jean-Christophe Lafaille attempted a new line to the right of the British route. Climbing in part at night for better snow conditions the pair reached 7,500m (24,600ft) before deciding to retreat. During the descent Beghin fixed an abseil from a Friend, saving a piton for lower down. The Friend pulled and Beghin fell to his death, leaving Lafaille to downclimb solo over extremely difficult terrain. He reached a bivouac at about 7,000m (23,000ft) and continued down, now using tent pegs as pitons and a 20m (70ft) 6mm rope. Nearing an early camp at 6,500m (21,300ft) a stonefall broke Lafaille's right arm. As he is right-handed his position was now serious. He shouted to Slovenian climbers on the British route, but was not heard and so was forced to put a makeshift splint on his arm and to abseil down the face using his good arm and his teeth. He eventually reached the base of the wall and walked to the Slovene base camp from where he was helicoptered to Kathmandu. In 1996 Lafaille returned to the face, attempting to solo the British route. He failed due to deep snow, but claimed 'It's a very nice route, not very dangerous – an interesting route'.

In 1993 Annapurna and Dhaulagiri became the first peaks climbed by the 'Chinese Tibetan Expedition to 14 Mountains of 8,000m of the World' whose aim is to put a Tibetan (hopefully, but not necessarily, the same one) on all 14 summits by 2002. Post-monsoon in 1994 the south face was again the main attraction, a South Korean team climbing the British route, but an attempt at a new route to the right by Catherine Destivelle and Eric Decamp failing. The pair than attempted to follow the Korean ropes but gave up at 7,700m (25,250ft).

Later ascents have filled in some of the 'missing' firsts on the peak. In April 1995 the Slovenians Andrej and Davorin Karnicar climbed the French route on the north side, reaching the top at 8.25am. After a stay of about an hour they descended by ski, reaching base camp at 6pm. In spring 1996 the French climber André Georges soloed the French route, the first confirmed solo. Just eleven days earlier Georges had soloed Dhaulagiri. Post monsoon in 1996 a Polish-Ukrainian team made the first ascent of the north-west ridge, reaching it by following the early stages of the original route. The ridge required the fixing of 2km (1¼miles) of rope. The summit was reached on 20 October by the Pole Andrzej Marciniak and the Ukrainian Vladyslav Terzyul.

It seemed as though the mountain, renowned for its avalanches and notorious for the deaths during early climbs,

hard crampons barely bit into it. In the post-monsoon period of the same year a Spanish team completed the first alpine-style ascent of the French route, while in December the Japanese completed the first winter ascent of the south face following the British route (with some minor variations). Two of the four summiteers were killed during the descent.

In 1988 Annapurna came of age with its twenty-first ascent. That year also saw the second ascent of the north-west face by a Czech/Italian team. The following year Reinhard Patscheider returned to solo the face, finding that his luck, both good and bad, had not changed. Retreating by paraglider after an avalanche had destroyed his camp he crash-landed and dislocated a shoulder. On his next attempt a piton pulled and he fell 15m (50ft), escaping with an injured back. He retreated, vowing to return. In 1991 a semi-solo ascent was made up the British south face route by Gabriel Denamur of a Belgian/Polish team. Denamur certainly made the top – his tracks were later followed to the summit by Kryzysztof Wielicki. Wielicki saw Denamur's tracks heading down the north side of the peak, but he was not seen by expeditions on that side. Denamur's climb followed a disputed solo by the Italian Giancarlo Gazzola who, had, in the face of modern equipment, techniques and levels of fitness, been tamed. But in the Himalaya that never happens. On Christmas Day 1997 Anatoli Boukreev, one of the world's finest high-altitude climbers, famous for his involvement in the 1996 Everest tragedy, was killed together with Dimitri Sobolev when they were avalanched from the south face of Fang, having chosen to climb the main summit via the south-west ridge. Simone Moro, who was climbing with the pair, was carried 800m (2,600ft) down the face, landing only 50m (160ft) from the team's first camp, his hands badly injured, his clothes torn, all his equipment except his crampons lost. He re-equipped himself, climbed 1,500m (almost 5,000ft) down the face to base camp from where he was helicoptered out after the team's Nepalese cook had walked through the night to raise the alarm.

Two years later, on 29 April 1999 the Spaniard Juan Oiarzábal climbed Annapurna to complete the set of all 14 8,000ers, a quest which had taken him 14 years. The immediate question following his climb was whether he had become the sixth or seventh man to complete the set, given the problem of Fausto di Stefani's ascent of Lhotse. The general feeling in the climbing world seems now to favour the Spaniard being sixth. Finding the French route too dangerous, Oiarzábal's team, funded by Spanish TV, followed the Spanish 1974 East Summit route, then the German 1980 Central Summit route, before climbing the Sickle to the main summit. On the descent the Sherpa Kami Dorje, who had just completed his second ascent of Annapurna, and a female Korean climber fell to their deaths.

At the time of writing there have been fewer ascents of Annapurna than on any other of the 8,000ers. The peak has a fierce reputation, second only to K2 in terms of the ratio of summiteers dying on the descent to successful climbs. It is also the 8,000er with the highest ratio of deaths to successful ascents: for every two climbers who reach the summit one climber dies. These statistics explain why there has been no genuinely commercial expedition to the peak so far: the avalanche-prone north face and the difficult south and north-west faces are likely to ensure that there will be no change to this during the early years of the new millennium, the first 8,000er to have been climbed remaining an elusive, committing summit.

The west face of Annapurna from Kalopani. The main summit (Annapurna I) is to the left, with Fang on the right

> **Many climbers approach Everest with a do ir die attitude. Some of them do, some of them die, and some of them do both.**
>
> ANON

everest 8,848m

everest

Everest was Peak XV of the Indian Survey, named by Surveyor-General Sir Andrew Waugh for his predecessor. Waugh had noted that no local name seemed to exist for the peak – though the search for one had not, at that stage, stretched as far as Nepal and Tibet, both closed to foreigners.

By the time a name could be sought 'Everest' had become a fixture among British mountaineers. As the British were the only nation to approach/attempt the peak in the years prior to the 1939–45 War the name was internationalised by the 1950s when the Swiss and French sought permission for attempts from Nepal.

In later years the search for a local name began again. The most likely candidate is Chomolungma, of which there are several spelling options. This was the name used by the Tibetan authorities in the official document for the 1921 British expedition and was used by team members when talking to locals. The name, meaning 'Mother Goddess of the Country' (with country used in its local sense), seems to have been applied to the Everest massif, ie. including Lhotse, Nuptse and other, smaller, peaks, rather than the main peak itself. Though the name was discovered in Tibet, it seems to have been used in the Khumbu region of Nepal too – no great surprise in view of the trading links across the Himalaya. Interestingly, though, in his autobiography when Tenzing notes the name he claims he was told by his mother that it meant 'the mountain so high that no bird can fly over it' which, if true, suggests a remarkably economical use of syllables. After the Chinese invasion of Tibet, Nepal nervous that the Chinese might attempt to annexe the peak, sought its own local name and came up with Sagarmatha meaning 'Sky Mother' or 'Mother of the Universe' in the Sherpa language. This name has now been applied to a National Park covering the Khumbu region. The Chinese responded to this by producing their own – Qomolangma (sometimes Qomolangma Feng), what might be termed a Sino-local version – claimed to be based on a Tibetan legend of five goddesses (qomo) of whom the most beautiful, the one with a face of emerald green, was Qomo Langsangma or Qomo Langma.

Though there are many who would like to see Chomolungma adapted as the peak's official name, Everest has now been accepted by custom and practice and is very unlikely to be supplanted.

Exploration

Although there had been suggestions about expeditions to reach (and climb) Everest in the years before the 1914–18 War, they had all fallen through for one reason or another, and not until 1921 was an expedition approved. It was led by Charles Howard-Bury and included George Leigh Mallory whose name has become associated with the mountain in a way rivalled only by those of Hillary and Tenzing. The expedition was purely reconnaissance, exploring the north, north-west and eastern sides of the peak. Mallory saw the Khumbu icefall and named the west (now, usually,

The summit pyramid from the Second Step

The mountains of the Everest horseshoe, Everest (left), Lhotse (centre) and Nuptse (right)

western) cwm beyond it – and dismissed as unlikely the possibility of a route going through it and ascending via the col between Everest and the 'south peak' (Lhotse). The expedition also saw the east (Kangshung) face, dismissing it out of hand and climbed to the Chang La, which they renamed the North Col. Mallory, Wheeler and Bullock reached the Col, and Mallory was prepared to push on, believing that in the time available to them they could explore another 600m (2,000ft), but the wind forced him to reconsider. Nevertheless, the team had seen enough to prove that a route to the summit via the North Col and north ridge was feasible. It had been a successful trip, though marred by the death of Alexander Kellas, arguably the most experienced Himalayan climber of the time, whose heart failed

High on the north face. This shot is from much the same position as that of Norton on the 1924 expedition (see Early Climbs)

EVEREST: ASCENT ROUTES

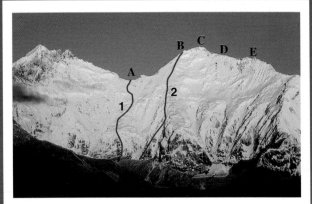

Above East Face

A *South Col*
B *South Summit*
C *Main Summit*
D *North Ridge*
E *Pinnacles*
1 *UK/US 1988*
2 *US 1983*

Above North Face

A *Great or Northern Couloir (in shadowed area), first climbed by the Australians 1984*
1 *Hornbein Couloir, Japanese (1980)*
2 *North Ridge route, Chinese (1960). The face below the ridge has been climbed*
using many variants of the classic route
3 *West Ridge, partial ascent by the Americans via Hornbein Couloir (1963); complete ascent by the Yugoslavians (1979)*

Above From West

A *North (NE) Ridge*
B *Great Couloir*
C *Hornbein Couloir*
D *Summit*
E *South Summit*
F *South Col*
G *Western Cwm*
H *West Ridge*
1 *SE Ridge, first ascent/standard route (1953)*
2 *SW Pillar, Russians (1982)*
3 *SW Face, British (1975)*
4 *South Pillar, Polish (1980)*

due to exhaustion after a prolonged bout of dysentery.

The British returned in 1922, this time led by General Charles Granville Bruce, a giant of a man with a character to match and an enviable knowledge of the Himalaya. Learning from the 1921 trip, the expedition had better food and boots, but the rest of their equipment was much the same – the heavy woollen trousers and jackets which had been used in the Alps for years, though the Australian-born George Finch had a duvet jacket of his own design. Finch was also responsible for the expedition's oxygen equipment, though few of the climbers had any faith in oxygen, and even less in the equipment. The team reached the North Col in mid-May and from it set a number of height records. During the first attempt Mallory, Morshead, Norton and Somervell moved up to a point higher than men had previously reached – and camped there. Next day, Mallory, Norton and Somervell passed the 8,000m (26,240ft) contour for the first time, eventually reaching about 8,200m (about 26,900ft). The trio did not use oxygen, but the second attempt, by Finch and Geoffrey Bruce (the leader's nephew), did. They reached 8,320m (27,300ft), a world record and one especially significant for Geoffrey Bruce: it was his first climb. Later, during a third attempt in early June, with the monsoon already arrived, four climbers and thirteen Sherpas climbed back towards the North Col. The deep fresh snow avalanched and seven Sherpas were killed.

The British returned in 1924, again under General Bruce, though a bout of malaria on the approach march caused him to leave the expedition: Edward Norton took over the leadership. Equipment was much as it had been in 1922, the lesson of Finch's duvet jacket not having been learnt. It is instructive to look at just what the climbers were wearing. For the first summit attempt in 1924 Norton lists his clothing – 'Personally I wore a

The Chinese ladder on the Second Step. Note the snow build up in the crack to the left of the ladder

The Western Cwm from the air showing Everest's south-west face (left), the South Col and Lhotse (ahead), Makalu (beyond), and Nuptse (right)

Climbing the Khumbu Icefall to reach the Western Cwm

thick woollen vest and drawers, a thick flannel shirt and two sweaters under a lightish knickerbocker suit of windproof gaberdine the knickers of which were lined with light flannel, a pair of soft elastic Kashmir putties and a pair of boots of felt, bound and soled with leather and lightly nailed with the usual Alpine nails. Over all I wore a very light pyjama suit of Messrs Burberry's 'Shackleton' windproof gaberdine. On my hands I wore a pair of long fingerless woollen mits inside a similar pair made of gaberdine; though when step-cutting necessitated a sensitive hold on the axe-haft. I sometimes substituted a pair of silk mits for the inner woollen pair. On my head I wore a fur-lined leather motor-cycling helmet, and my eyes and nose were protected by a pair of goggles of Crooke's glass, which were sewn into a leather mask that came well over the nose and covered any part of my face which was not naturally protected by my beard. A huge woollen muffler completed my costume.' When Mallory's body was found in 1999 he was wearing

In the Western Cwm a Sherpa team traverse below Nuptse. To the left is Everest, with Lhotse and the South Col ahead

seven, eight or nine (it was difficult to be exact) layers of clothing, clearly a similar 'costume'. The American climbers noted that Mallory's clothing was equivalent to about two layers of modern fleece – much less than they were wearing. As they pointed out, the clothing was adequate, but left virtually no margin for bad weather or being benighted: Mallory and his comrades were not only skilled climbers, but very brave men.

Norton planned for summit attempts in mid-May, fearful of an early arrival of the monsoon, but a severe and prolonged storm disrupted his plans and it was not until 4 June that the first attempt, by Howard Somervell and Norton himself was made. The pair, neither using bottled oxygen, climbed the rocks of the Yellow Band then moved on to the north face, climbing below the north-east ridge to avoid the First and

A mountaineering icon: Tenzing photographed by Hillary on the summit of Everest

Second Steps, the latter of which was thought to be a formidable obstacle. Somervell had been troubled with high altitude cough, his throat injured by the thin, cold, dry air, and gave up, Norton continuing across the obvious couloir (the Great – or, occasionally, Norton – Couloir) towards ground which, he believed would offer him easy access to the summit pyramid. But the terrain became more difficult and, at 1pm, realising he did not have the time to reach the summit and return safely, he stopped. He had reached 8,570m (about 28,100ft) a height record which would not be broken, with certainty, for almost 30 years and one that would remain unbroken for 54 years for a climber without bottled oxygen. On the descent Somervell's cough grew worse, one coughing fit dislodging the mucous membrane of his larynx which threatened to choke him. Only by pressing his chest violently did he manage to cough up the obstruction, freeing his windpipe.

The second summit attempt was made on 8 June by George Mallory and Andrew (Sandy) Irvine, the youngest and least experienced member of the team. Much has been made of Mallory's choice of companion: his stated reason was Irvine's familiarity with the oxygen equipment the pair would use – but Noel Odell was just as familiar and a more experienced climber. Numerous possible explanations for Mallory's choice have been put forward over the years, many seeing a homoerotic reason, though there is no evidence to

support the claim of Mallory's homosexuality: he was married with a son (though this, in itself, is not, of course, evidence). The most likely explanation seems to be the obvious, banal one – Mallory had become friendly with Irvine, liked his company and was impressed by his fitness and understanding of the delicate oxygen equipment they would be taking. It is true that by the time of the attempt, Odell was probably the best acclimatised and fittest member of the team – but Mallory's choice of Irvine was made on 22 April, not in June. Whatever the reason, it was Mallory and Irvine who occupied Camp VI on 7 June. Sometime on the morning of 8 June they left the camp and climbed into legend.

The known facts of the climb are limited: at 12.50pm Odell, climbing up to Camp VI and having reached about 7,960m (26,100ft), saw, through a break in the clouds, the two climbers on the north-east ridge. Where exactly he saw them would stoke the fires of speculation. Later, at about 2pm when Odell was in Camp VI, a storm broke, lasting for about two hours. When it cleared the mountain was bathed in sunshine, but Odell saw no sign of the summit pair anywhere above him. They did not return to Camp VI and the expedition returned to Britain. In 1933, an ice axe believed to have belonged to Irvine was found below the crest of the ridge near the First Step, lying on shallow-angled slabs.

The discovery of the axe was followed by 60 years of speculation about whether the pair had reached the summit. Then, in 1975 during a Chinese expedition Wang Hongbao claimed to have found an 'English dead', a body with old-fashioned clothing and a wound on its face at about 8,200m (26,900ft), directly below the point where the axe was found. Unfortunately Wang's story was not made public until 1979 when he told a Japanese climber during a subsequent Sino-Japanese expedition. The next day, before further details could be obtained, Wang was killed in an avalanche. In May 1999 George Mallory's body was found on the north face. It, too, was below the point at which the ice axe was found, but the fact that the body was face down, solid frozen into the rocks and was undisturbed has lead to speculation that the body Wang saw was that of Irvine. The pair were clearly descending together – Mallory still had a climbing rope attached to his waist – and there had clearly been an accident: Mallory had broken his lower right leg during a fall – he was several hundred feet below the ice axe – dying of shock and exposure.

The finding of the body was claimed by some to solve the mystery – but it does no such thing. The possible success or probable failure of the Mallory/Irvine attempt still largely rests on Odell's sighting. He first claimed to have seen the pair just below the final pyramid (that is, at least at the Second Step, possibly even higher). If that is so, they could have reached the summit and fallen on their descent. Mallory's snow goggles were in his pocket which might imply a descent in darkness, consistent with a late afternoon arrival at the top. Against this are the difficulties of the Second Step, that no anchor was found at the top of it (implying no abseil, while others who have climbed the step say it would be difficult to downclimb – but Hans Kammerlander skied around the bottom of the Step, so there is a way of bypassing it, and the fact that Odell saw no sign of the pair during the rest of a perfect day.

Odell later changed his mind, believing his sighting was much lower, perhaps at, or just above, the First Step. In that case it is likely the pair were caught by the storm en route to the Second Step and retreated, falling during the height of the

Climbers on the final ridge above the Hillary Step; South Summit in the foreground

storm (with Mallory, perhaps, having removed his goggles because of poor visibility). If that is the case then when Odell saw the mountain again the pair would have only just fallen. Though the likelihood is that the pair failed to reach the top, until Irvine's body is discovered (re-discovered ?) and the film in his camera (if it is found and the film is still processable) unlocks the secret, the real story will remain a mystery.

The next British attempt did not take place for nine years, the Tibetans having taken exception to aspects of the early British expeditions: in 1921 Dr Heron, a geologist with the team, dug into the plateau for samples, convincing the locals he was releasing demons from the earth. Then, in 1924 John Neil filmed one Tibetan delousing another and killing the offending creatures between his teeth. The Tibetans saw this as implying they ate lice and were outraged.

When diplomacy finally smoothed the way, Hugh Ruttledge led an expedition in 1933. It discovered the Irvine ice axe and during two attempts Wyn Harris and Wager, and Frank Smythe climbing alone reached about the same point as Norton had in 1924. During the years that followed, before the 1939–45 War put an end to further attempts, the British came back three more times but never bettered the height record. The 1935 trip, led by Eric Shipton, was notable for including a 19 year old Sherpa on his first expedition. His name was Tenzing.

In 1934 an eccentric Briton, Maurice Wilson, attempted the North Col route solo, dying at about 6,400m (21,000ft), and there were two further solo bids after the war. In 1947 the Canadian Earl Denman, accompanied by Tenzing and another Sherpa, failed to reach the North Col and in 1950 the Dane Klaus Larsen retreated from the North Col. Then, in October 1950 the Chinese invaded Tibet and all foreign expeditions to the northern side of the mountain stopped for 30 years.

Interest in the world's highest mountain did not stop however. The Nepalese opened their borders and in 1950, with the French on Annapurna, Charles Houston, Bill Tilman and others approached the Khumbu icefall, though they did not see into the Western Cwm. In 1951 an expedition under Eric Shipton (including Michael Ward, Tom Bourdillon and Ed Hillary) climbed to a point on Pumori from where they could see that a route existed by way of the Western Cwm, the South Col and south-east ridge. Later they climbed the icefall to the entrance to the Cwm. Though they were shaken by the dangers of the fall and by the risk of load carrying up it, they concluded that the southern route was climbable.

Back in London the British Himalayan Committee appointed Shipton leader of a planned 1952 expedition only to discover, to their astonishment, that the Nepalese had granted

The Hillary Step. The climber is Israeli Doron Erel

permission to the Swiss. The British therefore approached the Swiss making them an offer which amounted, in effect, to allowing them to send a group of climbers on a British expedition. The Swiss declined, hardly surprisingly. The British therefore decided that the Swiss could try pre-monsoon and that they would try post-monsoon. But the Nepalese said no. The British were being required to learn, and quickly, that in the post-war world a glorious past was no passport to a dependable future.

The Swiss pre-monsoon expedition under Ed Wyss-Dunant was exploratory as well as a real attempt: no one had come this way before. Considering that, and the appalling weather which plagued them, they made remarkable progress. They found the Lhotse Face steeper than expected (about the same as Mont Blanc's Brenva Face), and chose to climb the Geneva Spur, a rib of rock on its left edge, which led to the South Col. In screaming winds and perishing cold three Swiss, Tenzing and three other Sherpas camped on the Col. The next day the three Sherpas descended while Lambert, Tenzing, Flory and Aubert continued up the south-east ridge. At about 8,380m (27,500ft) a tent was pitched. Here Raymond Lambert and Tenzing stayed while Flory and Aubert retreated to the Col. The following day, despite using oxygen Lambert and Tenzing managed only some 200m (650ft) up the ridge in five hours of climbing. Their attempt had ended, but their estimated height of about 8,600m (28,200ft) was probably a little higher than that reached on the north side. A second attempt got no higher than the South Col.

The Swiss returned post-monsoon, aware that the British had permission for 1953 and the French for 1954. This time they were led by Gabriel Chevalley who, with Lambert, was the only survivor from the pre-monsoon team. Tenzing went again, but now as a member of the climbing team rather than just Sherpa sirdar. The expedition was dogged by ill-health and a Sherpa, Mingma Dorje, died after being hit by falling ice on the Lhotse Face. The delays these problems caused meant that by the time the South Col was reached winter had come. A token few metres of the south-east ridge were climbed and then the team retreated.

First Ascent

Just as the Swiss had been in the summer of 1952, the British were aware that 1953 might be their last chance for success. Not only had the French been given permission for 1954, but the Swiss had been granted another go in 1955. What they

Don Whillans leaving Camp IV during the attempt on the south-west face in 1971

needed, therefore, was a determined, decisive leader and Eric Shipton, for all his experience and abilities, was a cautious man and one not over-fond of large expeditions. On Cho Oyu in 1952 Shipton had demonstrated all his undoubted abilities as an explorer but, equally, all his failings as a single-minded leader. The British Himalayan Committee therefore appointed John Hunt, an army officer with an impressive Alpine and Himalayan record who had narrowly failed to make the 1936 Everest expedition, as leader.

Hunt's team was a large one and included several who had been with Shipton on Cho Oyu in 1952. It comprised George Band, Tom Bourdillon, Charles Evans, Alf Gregory, Edmund Hillary, George Lowe, Wilfred Noyce, Griffith Pugh (expedition physiologist), Michael Ward (expedition doctor: Evans was

The Khumbu Icefall pours out of the Western Cwm

also a surgeon), Michael Westmacott and Charles Wylie. James Morris of The Times went to write dispatches for the paper and Tom Stobart was there to make a film of the attempt: Alf Gregory, an expert photographer was an 'official' stills photographer. Tenzing was invited to join the climbing team as well as being sirdar of the Sherpas.

Hunt's planning for the expedition was meticulous, his military background clearly evident. The British public offered advice, too, much of it eccentric, some downright bizarre. One idea involved the use of a mortar to fire oxygen cylinders from the Western Cwm to the South Col, obviating the need for tiring load carrying. This even seems to have been considered seriously for a while and the expedition did indeed take a two-inch mortar, intending to fire it at avalanche-prone slopes. In

the event is was not used, but led to a remark which firmly sets the expedition in place and time. On hearing that a newspaper had reported that the 'assault' on the mountain would start with a bombardment by the mortar George Band wondered if, at the same time, Spitfires would circle the South Col. In an age of cruise missiles the remark dates the expedition more than any photograph of climbers not clad in the now-obligatory one-piece down suit.

The expedition established a series of closely spaced camps between the base of the Icefall and that of the Lhotse face. Hunt then outlined his plan for the summit attempts. The expedition had two types of oxygen equipment, the 'open-circuit' in which bottled oxygen is mixed with the surrounding air, enhancing the climber's oxygen supply and the 'closed-circuit', which used a soda-lime canister to extract oxygen from the carbon-dioxide exhaled by the climber and recycled it, topped up with bottled oxygen. The advantage of the latter is that a richer supply of oxygen is produced, allowing the user to climb faster. The drawback is that the user is cut off from the outside world, a claustrophobic situation and one which, if the system fails, causes a much sharper decrease in oxygen supply than users of the open-circuit system experience. The closed circuit system is also much more complex, making problems more likely. As a consequence the open-circuit is now used exclusively by those climbers who choose to use bottled gas at all.

Hunt decided that the first attempt on the peak would be by Bourdillon and Evans using closed-circuit equipment from the South Col, the second by Hillary and Tenzing using open-circuit systems and starting from a camp high on the south-east ridge.

The make-up of the first party was understandable: Bourdillon was the expedition's oxygen equipment expert, and, as a scientist, had helped develop the closed-circuit system; Evans had been his climbing partner during the early stages of the expedition. But why were they to start from the South Col when their chances of success were clearly higher if they started from higher up? Hunt's stated view is that the faster climb rate of users of the closed-circuit system would overcome the problem of a lower start, but it is likely that other unstated factors also played a part. Establishing a camp above the South Col was extremely difficult, supplying it twice might prove impossible. It therefore made sense to supply it once, and man it with the pair who had the best chance of success. Hunt seems to have mistrusted the closed-circuit system, and so probably felt that Hillary and Tenzing stood more chance of reaching the top. If Bourdillon and Evans did succeed – excellent, but even

The east or 'Kangshung' faces of Everest (right) and Lhotse reflected in a pond on the Kharta Glacier

their failure was likely to provide information valuable to the second team. It is probably overstating it to suggest that Hunt's military background was evident again – using the first wave of troops to clear the minefield, one way or another, and the so provide the second wave with an easier passage – but there have been some since who have used it.

The choice of Hillary and Tenzing was less controversial. The pair had gelled well, matching each other for speed and drive. Before Hunt's arrival at Base Camp, Hillary had pushed the route through the Icefall to the Cwm, and the pair had proved far faster than any other team on the mountain. In his latest published look back over an eventful life Hillary states that the partnership was not entirely fortuitous. Realising that Hunt was unlikely to chose a pair of New Zealanders for the summit attempt (and George Lowe was his usual climbing partner) Hillary had deliberately distanced himself from Lowe: it is an admission of startling honesty and one at apparent odds with the idea of Hillary being a lucky innocent. The fact that Hillary was a New Zealander and that Tenzing was Nepalese (or Indian – he was given passports by both nations after the climb) and the only Sherpa who had any desire to reach the summit, has also been used to suggest that Hunt had other motives for his choice – Empire man and local man, a very British choice. There is certainly some evidence to suggest Tenzing was indeed seen as a symbol of the Sherpas in the quest for success on Everest.

Hunt made his announcement of 7 May, but 10 days later it looked premature – the South Col was still an elusive target and the expedition's timetable was going wrong. Not until 21 May was the Col reached, though the pace of the climb then accelerated. On 26 May Bourdillon and Evans set out from the Col at 7am, with Hunt and the Sherpa Da Namgyal following to establish Camp IX on the ridge. Though Bourdillon and Evans made good progress at first, problems with Evans' oxygen set and poor snow conditions slowed them as they got higher. Not until 1am did they reach the South Summit. Reaching it was an achievement, the highest point reached to date, but on Everest it was only a point on the journey. For 30 minutes the pair discussed their options. They had enough oxygen for another two or three hours climbing which, they estimated, should get them to the top. Would they survive a bottled gas-free descent? What if Evans' faulty set failed going up the final ridge? Should Bourdillon go on alone? Finally, they turned to descend.

After the expedition Tom Bourdillon is said to have regretted the decision (or, at least, his own decision) not to continue. Down on the Col the Sherpas, seeing the pair on the South Summit had cheered loudly, believing it to be the true summit. Tenzing, by contrast, was less ecstatic – the sight of

the pair disappearing from view, probably on their way to the true top, meant his own dreams were dashed and he felt the loss keenly.

On their return Bourdillon and Evans were utterly exhausted. The next day the weather was bad, but so poor was

Approaching the summit, climbers toil up the final few rope lengths of the south-east ridge

Bourdillon's condition that he had to be taken down despite it. On 28 May Hillary and Tenzing, supported by Lowe and Ang Nyima moved up to Camp IX. On 29 May Hillary and Tenzing started up at 6.30am, quickly reaching the poor snow below the South Summit which had troubled the first pair. Hillary tackled it head on (Bourdillon and Evans had skirted it on poor rock to the left) and was soon frightened by its condition. He pressed on, knowing a slip would be fatal for them both and knowing the slope could avalanche, but knowing, too, that this was Everest and his only chance of the top. By 9am they had overcome the

High on the first pinnacle of the north-east (Pinnacle) ridge

comfortably. After the congratulations, Hillary took summit shots of Tenzing and then peered down the north side for a sign of Mallory and Irvine. This he mentions in his account, but does not say what he later confided in Ruttledge, that he believed that the last 275m (900ft) of the north ridge looked unclimbable. The pair then ate a bar of Kendal mint cake and started down. At the South Col they were met by George Lowe, Hillary's countryman. Hillary gave him the great news – 'Well', he said 'we knocked the bastard off'.

The north face from the head of the Rongbuk Glacier, with the west ridge on the right and the North Col on the left

slope and reached the South Summit. The final ridge looked hard, but went straightforwardly, the only difficulty being the now-famous Hillary Step. Hillary's later description of the step caused Tenzing deep offence. Hillary first said that after he had climbed the step he was 'gasping like a fish'. In the official expedition book he transferred the (much elaborated) metaphor to Tenzing and implied he had all but hauled the Sherpa up. Tenzing was very offended by both suggestions (and also thought the step was only a third or so the height claimed by Hillary). Hillary omitted fish references from his autobiography, Tenzing mentioned them verbatim in his.

The pair then continued over easier ground to the summit. The discovery of Mallory's body in 1999 led to interviews with Hillary during which, several newspapers claimed, he finally admitted who had been the first to reach the top. Since Tenzing had already admitted this in his ghosted autobiography several decades before, this 'new' information seemed surprisingly dated. Below the summit the pair paused. Hillary was concerned that the apparent top might be a cornice overhanging the stupendous east face and so made Tenzing take a belay while he continuously probed his way up to a table-sized summit on which half-a-dozen men could stand

Later Ascents

The news of the climbing of Everest reached Britain by way of a coded message in time for *The Times* to announce it on 2 June, the day Queen Elizabeth II was crowned. The French, who had 'booked' the mountain for 1954 abandoned their plan, but the Swiss, due to return, in 1955 merely slipped a year and went for the double, not only repeating the South Col route twice but making the first ascent of Lhotse. Thereafter, there was a steady stream of expeditions to the peak, a stream that grew to something more akin to a river once cheaper travel, better equipment, familiarity and the increased number of experienced Sherpas and climbers allowed mere mortals (wealthy mere mortals that is) to realise their ambitions. To date the mountain has had over 1,000 ascents by more than 800 climbers, some climbers chalking up multiple ascents: the Sherpa Ang Rita was the first to have climbed Everest ten times, all without bottled gas (though there are persistent rumours that he sometimes used bottled gas for sleeping before his summit climbs, rumours he denies) – he retired from high altitude climbing in 1999 saying he was 'sick and tired and old enough to retire' at 51, the same year that his record of ten ascents was equalled (by Apa Sherpa) and several Sherpas were threatening to break it. Several Sherpas have completed five or more ascents of the peak, and in May 1999 the American Pete Athans made his sixth ascent, a record (at present) for a non-Sherpa.

Everest has also given rise to a plethora of books, perhaps more than for all other mountains combined. Such a library makes a detailed account of the numerous climbs here superfluous, and below only the key ascents are noted.

In 1960 the Chinese claimed to have climbed the north side of the mountain, following the classic 'Mallory' line over the First and Second Steps. The Second Step proved to be very difficult, taking several hours to climb and requiring the leader to take off his boots in order to climb on the shoulders of a team-mate without inflicting too much damage to him. Three of the four climbers then continued to the summit, climbing through the night to arrive in the early hours of 25 May. On top they claimed to have left a bust of Mao. The rest of the world viewed the claim with scepticism – climbing barefoot? reaching the summit at night? – but later evidence, of the bootless climber's frost-bitten feet (he was never able to climb again) and a photograph almost certainly taken above the Second Step suggest that Wang Fuzhou (often written Wang Fu-Chou in the west), Qu Yinhua (Chu Yin-hua) and the Tibetan Gongbu (Gonpa) probably did make the first ascent of the north/north-east ridge (the Mallory route) in 1960. In 1975 the Chinese repeated the climb and installed a ladder at the crucial section of the Second Step. Only Chinese climbers had therefore climbed the step before 1999 when the American Conrad Anker ignored the ladder to test the grade of the climb: the lack of Chinese climbers in the West, and vice versa did not allow the time taken on the step by the Chinese (amounting to many hours on the first ascent) to be translated into a formal grade. Anker thought it is about 5.8 (British 4c/HVS, French 5, Australian 16), but rightly noted that sea-level 5.8 and 5.8 at 8,580m (over 28,150ft) were quite different propositions. Anker's climb suggests that Mallory and Irvine did not climb the step, and certainly not in the five minutes Odell saw them take over a rock step on the ridge (though Anker took only a few minutes over the climb), but as the climbing is almost certainly affected by the extent of snow banking it is impossible to be certain. If the snow was banked high enough the rock climbing required would be much reduced.

On the Kangshung Face during the first ascent of the Anglo-American route

In 1963 an American team not only put four men on top along the original route, but followed a shoulder of the mountain from the Western Cwm to the west ridge which they followed to the summit. At one point the summiteers, Tom Hornbein and Willy Unsoeld were forced on to the north face, following a prominent snow gully now known as the Hornbein Couloir. Hornbein and Unsoeld descended the original route, making a traverse of the peak. The Indians climbed the mountain in 1965, after which Nepal closed its borders for three years. When the next expedition arrived, the Japanese in 1969, they were assessing the chances of climbing the south-west face. The Japanese tried, and abandoned, the face in 1970 and 1973 (though placing men on the summit along the classic route on both occasions: the 1973 climb was the first post-monsoon ascent), and the face also repulsed an international team in 1971, an Anglo-German team in spring 1972 and a British attempt in autumn 1972. The first two expeditions were notable for their attempts at cross-nation co-operation, attempts foiled by poor weather, poor planning, personal ambition and, it must be said, a degree of cross-nation antagonism.

EVEREST

57

Approaching the South Col, with the south-east ridge and the South Summit beyond

Everest's first female ascent came in 1975 when the Japanese Junko Tabei summitted: just eleven days later the Tibetan woman Panduo (Phantog) summitted on a second Chinese ascent of the north ridge. The main event of 1975 was, however, the ascent of the south-west face by a British team under Chris Bonington. The team, many of whom had been on the Annapurna South Face expedition, climbed the rock band, the face's main obstacle, on its left side (all other attempts had sought a route on the right), then traversed to the South Summit, following the classic route from there to the top. Dougal Haston and Doug Scott reached the summit, followed by Peter Boardman and Sherpa Pertemba, and, in all likelihood, Mick Burke who disappeared near the top, probably breaking through a cornice during his lone descent in a storm. The first pair, Haston and Scott, survived a bivouac without bottled oxygen in a snowhole dug at the South Summit when benighted during their descent.

In 1978 the Italian (Tyrolean) Reinhold Messner and the Austrian Peter Habeler became the first men to climb Everest without bottled oxygen. The pair were attached to an Austrian expedition and when a solo attempt by Messner (after Habeler had gone down with food poisoning) was cut short by a storm which almost killed him, Habeler had second thoughts about the project. He asked to join the Austrian team officially but was turned down. Furious at the refusal he rejoined Messner and the pair climbed to the South Col. From there they followed the classic route, utilising the steps of Austrians who had summitted five days earlier. They reached the South Summit in 6½ hours, the summit an hour later. Habeler descended to the South Col, in part glissading and at one point falling, in one hour. Messner took only a few minutes longer. The times astonished the world, especially the Sherpa community who doubted whether anyone could outperform them at altitude. But Messner and Habeler were very fit and very fast, a fact they had already proved on Gasherbrum I and, in Messner's case, would prove again. Everest was Messner's fourth 8,000er.

The following year a Yugoslavian team climbed the West Ridge from the Lho La, four members (Nejc Zaplotnik, Andrej Stremfelj, Stane Belak and Stipe Bozik) and the Sherpa Ang Phu reaching the top. Ang Phu was killed on the descent. Then, on 17 February 1980, the Poles Leszek Cichy and Kryzysztof Wielicki, using bottled oxygen, completed the first winter ascent of the peak, following the classic line. 1980 also saw the first non-Chinese ascent of the north side of Everest, the Japanese Yasuo Kato soloing the Mallory line from the top camp when his companion stopped, while two of his countrymen followed a direct line up the north face and Hornbein Couloir to the summit. At the same time a Polish team climbed the South Pillar (which flanks the south-west face, leading directly to the South Summit). One of the two who reached the summit on 19 May 1980 was Jerzy Kukuczka, climbing his second 8,000er: the other climber was Andrzej Czok. The two Poles used bottled oxygen as far as the South Summit, continuing to the summit without bottled gas when their supply ran out. During the 1980 monsoon Reinhold Messner returned to the mountain, climbing a route on the north face solo. Although the last stage of the mountain had been soloed before (by Burke on the south side and Kato on the north) those climbers had been with full teams and each had started out with a colleague. Messner was completely alone on the mountain (in itself a situation unlikely ever to be repeated) making his achievement an astonishing exercise in both ability and control. He camped above the North Col on his first night, than traversed the north face (the Mallory route was deep in snow) to a camp at 8,200m (26,900ft). The next day he continued below the ridge, then climbed up to the summit, reaching it at 3pm. He regained his camp that night and descended to the East Rongbuk Glacier the next day. The climb remains one of the great achievements of mountaineering.

In 1982 a Russian team climbed a pillar at the left edge of the south-west face, a very hard route, probably the hardest line to the highest summit: eleven climbers reached the top. In the winter of 1982/83 a French attempt on the west ridge failed, but a Belgian climber who disappeared on 7 January 1983 turned up in Kathmandu on 14 January. He had slipped down the Tibetan side of the Lho La and walked out via the Rongbuk glacier (being

Litter on the South Col. Beyond is the south-east ridge leading up to the South Summit

The tiny figure of a climber on the Rongbuk Glacier (bottom right) is dwarfed by Everest's north face. The right skyline is the west ridge, the left skyline is the classic north-side route

mistaken for a yeti in a Tibetan village en route), a remarkable escape. Later in 1983 an American team made the first ascent of the east face via the central pillar direct to the South Summit, six members reaching the summit, a very under-rated climb on a formidable face. In 1984 the Australians Tim McCartney-Snape and Greg Mortimer climbed the Great (Norton) Couloir up the north face. Later McCartney-Snape returned to the mountain: he walked in from the shore of the Bay of Bengal and climbed to the summit, the first 'full' ascent. An even more 'full' ascent occurred in 1996 when Göran Kropp cycled to Nepal from his Swedish home, climbed the peak without bottled oxygen and cycled home again.

In December 1987, the Sherpa Ang Rita became the first person to summit Everest in winter without bottled oxygen when he summitted as part of a South Korean expedition. It was his fourth ascent of the peak. In the spring season of the following year the peak was traversed by a Chinese/Japanese/Nepalese team, climbers on the Mallory and original routes meeting at the summit and some descending each way so that the traverse was completed in both directions. The same spring Stephen Venables reached the top via a new route on the east face (to the South Col, continuing along the classic route) he had made with two American colleagues. In the post-monsoon period of 1988 the Frenchman Marc Batard soloed the classic route from Base Camp to summit in 22½ hours (following a trail made by previous climbers) and the New Zealander Lydia Bradey made the first female ascent without bottled oxygen, though her ascent has been questioned by some experts, based on timings from others on the final climb on the same day. (The first

Climbers approach the South Summit at about 8,500m (28,000ft) on the south-east ridge. Beyond lies the frontier peak of Shartse (7,444m/24,423ft) with Makalu standing in the distance

undisputed female, bottled oxygen-free ascent was made in 1995 by the Briton Alison Hargreaves following the Mallory route on the Tibetan side.) Also in 1988 a four-man Czech team completed an alpine-style, bottled oxygen-free ascent of the south-west face (British route). Only one man reached the summit, though at least three made the South Summit. Tragically all four died during the descent. 1988 also saw the fastest descent of the peak, Frenchman Jean-Marc Boivin parapenting from the summit to Camp II (at 6,700m/22,000ft) in just eleven minutes.

By 1990 the first commercial expeditions were climbing the mountain (the actual first commercial climb was in 1985 when American Dick Bass was guided to the top by David Breashers) the rate of successful ascents accelerating. Some variants to existing routes were climbed and there were still significant achievements. In 1993 the Japanese climbed the south-west face in winter, but Fernando Garrido failed at 7,750m (25,400ft) in an attempt at a winter solo. The Japanese fixed 3.6km (2¼miles) of rope in temperatures as low as minus 36°C and six men reached the top in three pairs between 18 and 22 December.

In 1995 a Japanese expedition completed the full north-east ridge. This, the 'pinnacle ridge', had been attempted several times and had cost the lives of the British climbers Peter Boardman and Joe Tasker. It had been climbed as far as the junction with the north ridge in 1986 by Briton Harry Taylor and New Zealander Russell Brice, but bad weather prevented them from continuing to the top. Also in 1995, the Sherpa Babu Chhire (or Tshering) made two ascents of the Mallory route separated by just 12 days as part of a commercial expedition. Between Babu's two ascents the Italian (Tyrolean) Reinhard Patscheider climbed the same route from the base of the North Col to the summit in 21 hours. More poignantly, on the same day as Patscheider's ascent George Mallory, grandson of the British Everest pioneer, completed the route on which his grandfather had disappeared 51 years before. In 1996 Patscheider's time on the classic north face route was reduced to 16¾ hours by another Tyrolean, Hans Kammerlander. Kammerlander intended a ski descent of the Great Couloir, but finding it too icy skied his ascent route instead, finding a way around the base of the Second Step. As the wind had stripped much of the snow from the north face he was forced to downclimb short sections, but could claim a nearly-ski descent.

Dougal Haston on the summit, photographed by Doug Scott after the first ascent of the south-west face

The north face from the Rongbuk Glacier

But just as ascents of Everest were appearing to have become routine – not since 1993 has there been a year without a successful ascent – with tens of climbers reaching the summit on the same day, just how fragile a man's existence is at the summit was illustrated when a sudden storm on 10 May 1996 caught the members of two commercial expeditions on the way down from the summit killing several, including the two expedition leaders Rob Hall and Scott Fischer, and maiming another through frostbite. It was a cruel reminder that 8,000m peaks are not to be taken for granted, but only a comma in the Everest story. On 16 October 1998 the Sherpa Kaji climbed the southern original route in 20 hours 24 minutes, his fifth ascent. He would have been quicker but lost an hour on the Lhotse face due to high winds and another hour near the South Summit waiting for a rope to be fixed by his assisting party of Sherpas. He also rested for 30 minutes. It was an impressive achievement, though Japanese climbers on the peak at the same time have raised doubts over whether he actually

summitted. Another, more curious, time record was established in 1999 when Sherpa Babu Chhire (or Tshering) camped on the summit, remaining there for 21½ hours. He arrived at 9am on 6 May with two other Sherpas and stayed until 7.30am on the 7 May, returning to a hero's welcome on the South Col. A fortnight later Apa Sherpa completed his tenth ascent (all with bottled oxygen) from the north side. On that same day Sergio Martini finally climbed Everest and would have joined the 'all-14' club but for the disputed ascent of Lhotse with partner Fausto de Stefani.

Everest has now been climbed about 1,200 times, but such is its draw that many of these have been multiple ascents: fewer than 900 climbers have their names on the summit roll. It has been climbed by 60 year olds and a 17 year old, and in 1998 had its first ascent by a disabled climber, Welsh-born, but US-naturalised, Tom Whittaker who had lost a foot in car crash. He was accompanied to top by Jeff Rhoads and Sherpa Tashi Tshering. On his first try he had to retreat, the other two reaching the top. A week later Whittaker tried again and made it. His co-climbers thus reached the top twice in seven days.

It might be assumed that as the fiftieth anniversary of the first ascent approaches the Everest story has few remaining chapters to write, but that is a rash suggestion to make. The draw of the world's highest mountain will remain and its records will always be broken.

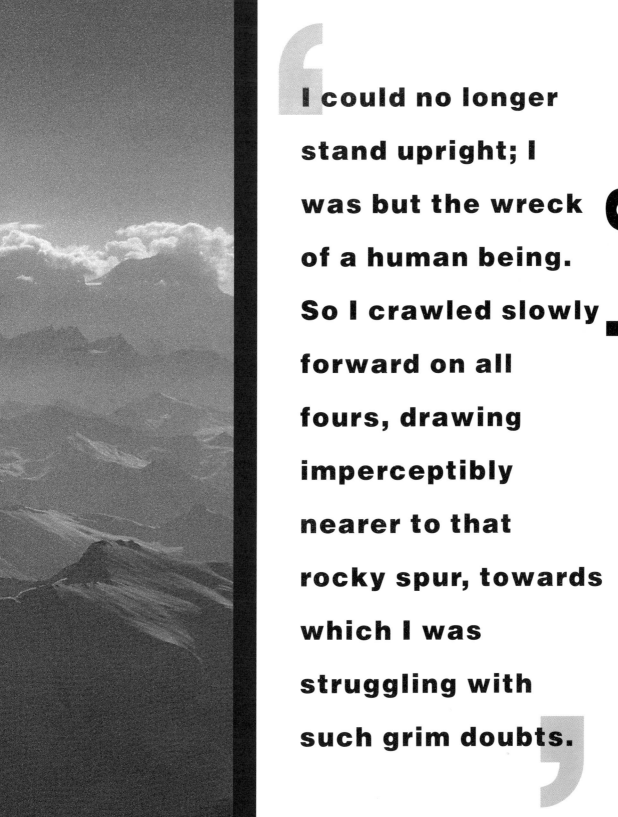

Nanga Parbat 8,125m

"I could no longer stand upright; I was but the wreck of a human being. So I crawled slowly forward on all fours, drawing imperceptibly nearer to that rocky spur, towards which I was struggling with such grim doubts."

HERMANN BUHL on the final steps to the summit

nanga parbat

Nanga Parbat is the most westerly of the 8,000m peaks standing in massive isolation about 125km (80 miles) north of the Kashmiri capital of Srinigar. Though geographically close to the Karakoram peaks it is actually the western bastion of the Greater Himalaya, overlooking the Indus River which forms the range's western border.

Though geographically close to the Karakoram peaks it is actually the western bastion of the Greater Himalaya, overlooking the Indus river which forms the range's western border. In the winter of 1840/41 an earthquake caused a huge rock slide from the northern Nanga Parbat massif blocking the Indus valley and creating a vast lake stretching almost to Gilgit over 60km (40 miles) away. The natural dam eventually broke in the summer of 1841, the resultant tidal wave causing massive damage and loss of life. It is said that a Sikh army camped in the lower valley was completely annihilated.

The mountain's name derives from the Sanskrit Nanga Parvata, 'naked mountain', probably from its isolation. The Kashmiri name Diamir, meaning King of Mountains, has been popularly overtaken by the Sanskrit version, though it is applied to the peak's western flank. Many believe the peak to be the most beautiful of all the great peaks which would make Diamir a fitting name, though the longer version does seem more appropriate, its lyricism reflecting the mountain's magnificent presence, if not its brutal history.

Exploration

The peak was probably first seen, by western eyes, by the British explorer and artist GT Vigne who explored Kashmir in 1835, seeing the 'stupendous peak' from a pass to the north of Srinigar. It was visited by the three Germans brothers Von Schlagintweit in 1856, then by the doctor/missionary Dr Arthur Neve in 1887. Neve was probably the first westerner to see the peak's Rupal flank, the tallest mountain wall in the world. Over the next few years the peak was sketched and photographed several more times, the very fact of its isolation from other major peaks meaning that its base was relatively easy to

The Mazeno Ridge, one of the last great problems on Nanga Parbat

The Diamir Face of Nanga Parbat from the Diamir Valley

NANGA PARBAT: ASCENT ROUTES

Above North-east Face
1 *First ascent, Buhl (1953)*

2 *Japanese 1995*

Above Rupal Face
1 *German 'Schell Route' (1976)*
2 *German/Italian (1970)*

3 *Polish/Mexican (1985)*

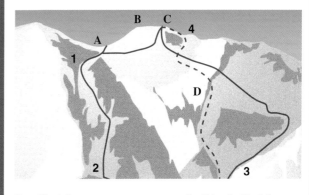

Above Diamir Face
A *Bazhin Gap*
B *Shoulder*
C *Main Summit*
D *Mummery Ribs*
1 *Germans (1962) climbed to Bazhin Gap and followed Buhl (1953) line to summit. Now climbers traverse below the summit*

pyramid and take a direct line to the summit
2 *German (1962) 'Kinshofer Route'*
3 *Messner solo (1978); dotted line is descent route*
4 *'Schell Route' follows upper part of this ridge (see above)*

approach on all sides. It is likely that the photographs of EF Knight, taken in 1891, and Conway's view of the peak from near Gilgit before his Baltoro expedition, were among the reasons for the interest in the peak shown by three of Britain's finest alpinists in 1895.

Albert Mummery was, arguably, the best climber of the time. Born in 1855, he was a very unlikely mountaineer, being slightly hunchbacked because of a spinal birth defect and very short-sighted. But firstly in the company of the guide Alexander Burgener (with whom he did the first ascent of the Zmutt ridge on the Matterhorn) and then climbing guideless (notably on the Grépon) he established a reputation for bold, difficult ascents. In 1895, together with Geoffrey Hastings and J Norman Collie, Mummery went to Nanga Parbat intending to explore it thoroughly and, if possible, to climb it.

The Britons first looked at the gigantic Rupal Face which they thought unclimbable, then crossed the Mazeno Pass to look at the Diamir Face which looked much more promising. The three were now joined by the young Major Charles Bruce who, as General Bruce, was later to lead expeditions to Everest, and two of his Gurkhas, Ragobir and Goman Singh, though Bruce soon left the expedition, mumps and the impending end of his leave forcing his withdrawal.

Though Mummery's enthusiasm for the climbing was high throughout the trip, the expedition record makes it clear that the Britons had little understanding of what they were involved in (at least at first – Collie later commented ruefully on the difference in scale of Himalayan and alpine peaks). The party often ran low on food – rarely a problem in the European Alps with their studding of farms and villages – and Mummery firmly believed that a single day was all that was needed to reach the summit from a height of about 6,100m (20,000ft). With Hastings off getting supplies Mummery, together with Collie,

The Rakhiot flank of Nanga Parbat

the two Gurkhas and a local hunter called Lor Khan, attacked what is now called the Mummery Rib, a complex of rock spurs leading up the Diamir Face towards the main summit. After an initial retreat Mummery tried again accompanied only by Ragobir. At a height

of about 6,100m (20,000ft) they were forced to turn back when Ragobir, who appears only to have eaten when told to, fell ill.

Abandoning the Diamir Face Mummery next decided to explore the northern side of the peak. Unimpressed by Hastings' and Collie's idea of taking the long route around the north-west ridge, Mummery and the two Gurkhas set off to cross the Diama Pass. On the far side of the ridge Hastings and Collie waited in vain: Mummery, Ragobir and Goman Singh probably died in an avalanche on the Diamir side of the pass.

Not until 1930 did climbers consider returning to Nanga Parbat, and again it was one of the foremost alpinists of the time who had the dream. Wilhelm (Willo) Welzenbach was born in Munich in 1900, taking an engineering degree at the city's university and working as an architect for Munich City Council. He was a good rock climber, but is famous as an innovative ice climber, inventing the ice piton and pushing the use of 10-point crampons and step-cutting to their limits on steep ice: not until

Hermann Buhl looks across to the final ridge

Buhl's classic shot from the summit, looking back down his ascent route

the arrival of front-point crampons and short ice axes were ice climbing standards advanced. Welzenbach used his improved techniques to climb north faces in the eastern Alps (and, later, the western Alps) which had been thought unclimbable. His ascents of the north faces of the Gross Weissbachhorn, the Grands Charmoz and some Bernese Oberland faces were the hardest climbs of the late 1920s/early 1930s. But some of the climbs were not only hard but risky, the faces swept by avalanches or stones, and climbers of the old school thought them completely unjustified. Welzenbach, the leader of the new developments, climbed mostly with others from Munich, the 'Munich School' producing climbers who went on to climb some of the great north faces including the Matterhorn and the

Eiger. Their apparent 'death or glory' attitude to climbing appealed to Germany's new rulers, the Nazi party enjoying the reflected glory of handsome, blond youths risking death to bring famous victories back to the Fatherland, a fact which only served to increase the polarisation between the old and new schools. Today it is clear that the Bavarians were just advancing the standards of the sport, as is inevitable, but at the time the movement was seen to have more sinister overtones. Doubtless some of the young German climbers were not opposed to the fame their exploits brought – but that is equally true today.

There is no evidence that Welzenbach's desire to extend his climbing horizons beyond the Alps were motivated by anything other than an interest in the next challenge. In 1928 Munich School climbers went to the Caucasus and the Pamirs and in 1929 Paul Bauer led an expedition to Kangchenjunga. Illness stopped Welzenbach from going to the Pamirs, business commitments from joining Bauer. In 1930 he applied for permission to go to Nanga Parbat, but though the British were willing for him to go, the Germans were not, giving state backing to another Kangchenjunga attempt. When that failed Welzenbach tried again for Nanga Parbat in 1931 – but Bauer, with whom Welzenbach had fallen out, convinced the authorities to back him on Kangchenjunga again. This they did, though when the expedition failed they gave Welzenbach their blessing for 1932. But that year Munich City Council refused Welzenbach's request for leave and so it was his partner on the Grands Charmoz, Willy Merkl, who led the expedition.

Merkl's expedition, which included an American, Rand Herron, Fritz Wiessner, who was later to become a naturalised American and was almost to climb K2 in 1939, and the Austrian Peter Aschenbrenner, included no climbers who had been with Bauer (a clear indication of the needle between Welzenbach and Bauer) and no one who spoke the local language. Because of possible problems with a difficult local tribe, the Germans were required to approach from the south, having to cross numerous high and heavily snowed-up passes to reach their preferred, north-east face. From its base, and a marvellously pastoral camp site Merkl named the Marchenwiese, Fairy Meadow – all climbs on Nanga Parbat start low and, consequently, in pleasant surroundings: as Jerzy Kukuczka put it, it is the only mountain on which you climb through all the seasons, from real summer to -40° – the team forged a long route up the face of the Rakhiot Peak, aiming to cross the Silver Saddle and Silver Plateau to reach the peak's northern ridge. The weather, and sheer inexperience, stopped them at Camp VII, placed on the east ridge beyond the Rakhiot Peak at about 7,000m (23,000ft). As a reconnaissance the expedition had

The mountain from the Rupal Valley

been a success, but a shadow was cast over it during the return: stopping over at Cairo Rand Herron climbed the Pyramids at Giza. Descending from the second at a run he tripped, fell and was killed.

In 1934 the Germans returned, now with the full backing of the Nazi regime which ensured that the best of equipment and Sherpas were available. Welzenbach went too, but the leader was, again, Willy Merkl despite the misgivings of many who had been in the 1932 team. Steady progress was made along the route pioneered in 1932 until one of the climbers, Alfred Drexel, died quite suddenly, probably of pulmonary oedema. The retreat to the Fairy Meadow which followed cost the expedition 17 days, a loss that was to cost it victory and create a tragedy.

The route was eventually pushed out again, crossing the face of the Rakhiot Peak to reach the east ridge and a rock pillar the Germans called the Mohrenkopf (literally the Moor's Head, but actually named for a chocolate-covered cream cake popular in Germany at the time). From there the ridge dipped 120m (400ft) then rose to the Silver Saddle. The Germans placed Camp VII beyond the dip and from it on 6 July five climbers and eleven Sherpas climbed upwards.

The Austrians Aschenbrenner and Erwin Schneider broke trail, reaching the Saddle at 10.30am. They waited until noon when the others arrived, then started across the wide, flat Silver Plateau towards the summit. At around 2pm they arrived below the Subsidiary Summit, at a height of about 7,830m (25,700ft). They were only about 300m (1,000ft) below the summit, but still over 1½ km (more than a mile) horizontally from it. They found a good campsite, but when the three Germans and the Sherpas did not arrive Schneider went back to see what the delay was. After another 1½ hours Aschenbrenner trudged after him. Merkl, Welzenbach and Uli Wieland had stopped at the Saddle, deciding to camp there despite Schneider's attempts to persuade them across the plateau. It seemed a trivial point, however, as the team thought it certain that the following they would all make it to the top.

The expedition was now dangerously extended. There were 16 men at Camp VIII, but no one between them and Camp IV over 1,500m (5,000ft) below and some 4km (2½ miles) away horizontally. Worse still, bad weather at Camp IV – quite unlike the sunshine on the plateau – prevented supplies being carried higher. Had the weather stayed fine those details might not have mattered, but on the night of 6 July a fierce storm broke. Nanga Parbat, as with the Karakoram peaks, is sufficiently far west to avoid the monsoon which makes summer climbing in Nepal dangerous, but occasionally storms from severe monsoons do creep as far as the Punjab Himalaya and the Karakoram.

The storm of early July 1934 lasted many days. By the morning of the 8 July the 16 men on the plateau were in a poor state. Poles had snapped, semi-collapsing their tents, allowing in blown snow which soaked and froze them. With daylight came the decision to retreat despite the continuing storm: it was a stark choice – stay and die, descend and probably die. Aschenbrenner and Schneider, still the fittest, set off to break trail with three Sherpas, but an early fall by one Sherpa lost the Austrians' sleeping bags. Knowing there were spares only at Camp V the Austrians unroped from the Sherpas and ploughed down through the storm. At 7pm the pair collapsed, exhausted into Camp IV. They assumed the others, following their trail, would soon follow.

The other three Germans and the remaining Sherpas, exhausted by the storm, the lack of food and drink, and affected by the altitude, did not even make Camp VII on 8 July, spending

On the 'Kinshofer Wall', Diamir Face

Approaching the 'Kinshofer Wall' on the Kinshofer Route, Diamir Face

a night in the open. During it one Sherpa died. The next day the remaining climbers descended, but Wieland died just metres from the camp. Over the next five days a tragedy of increasing agony was played out on the ridge. Welzenbach died in Camp VII, Merkl some time on 14 or 15 July near the Moor's Head. Of the Sherpas, five more died, a second at the bivouac above Camp VII, three between Camps V and IV and one, Gaylay, who chose to stay with Merkl.

Looking into the Diamir Valley from the summit at dusk

On the expedition's return Aschenbrenner and Schneider were ordered before a 'Court of Honour' of Munich climbers and declared to be 'without honour' for having abandoned the three Sherpas (and, implicitly, the Germans). Given the desperate fight for life on the mountain the decision, taken in warmth and comfort, was harsh, though the circumstances of the Austrian decision to unrope from the Sherpas is still debated.

The tragedy was a blow to the pride of nationalist German, one which they immediately sought to rectify. Paul Bauer was given state aid to found the Deutsche Himalaja-Stiftung (German Himalayan Foundation) but it was not until 1936 that he was able to raise a team. But rather than Nanga Parbat Bauer went to Sikkim: his claimed reason was that '1934 had destroyed everything and we had to begin again', but was there a remnant of the old animosity with Welzenbach in the decision?

In 1936 Angerer, Hinterstoisser, Kurz and Rainer died in a drawn-out tragedy on the public stage of the Eiger's North Wall, glorious deaths, perhaps, but a further blow to nationalist pride. There could be no further delay in the demand to 'vindicate (1934's) tragic blow' on Nanga Parbat: in 1937 the Germans returned to the mountain though, significantly, under the leadership of Karl Wein (who had been on the 1936 Sikkim expedition) not Paul Bauer.

Following the line of the 1934 route the Germans established Camp IV, an Advanced Base Camp, beneath the Rakhiot Peak. On 14 July it was occupied by seven Germans and nine Sherpas. The Germans represented the entire climbing team, only the team doctor and a cartographer being left lower on the mountain. Just after midnight a serac broke high on the ridge above the camp causing an avalanche which overwhelmed the camp. All sixteen men were buried beneath tons of ice, dying instantly.

Now Paul Bauer had no choice and he led the fourth German expedition in 1938. An interesting sidelight on the extent to which Germany felt it owned Nanga Parbat, having paid for it in blood (eleven Germans, together with 15 Sherpas now lay dead on its flanks – as well as Mummery and his two Gurkhas) is revealed by the response to a suggestion by the British climbers Smythe and Shipton that they might try the peak: they received many outraged letters from Germans claiming that it was improper for Britons to attempt Germany's mountain. Bauer's team followed the 'standard' route, discovering the bodies of Merkl and Gaylay near the Mohrenkopf (Merkl's body had on it a poignant note from Welzenbach asking for aid), but were defeated by bad weather before the Silver Saddle was reached.

In 1939, with war clouds gathering over Europe, the Germans returned, this time with a four-men reconnaissance team to see if the long, avalanche-swept route past the Rakhiot Peak was actually the best line. The four men explored the Diamir Face – finding remains of Mummery's 1895 attempt – and decided that a route existed there. They sent a letter of their findings back to Germany and preparations were made for an attempt on the Diamir Face in 1940. But war intervened: back in British India the four Germans were interred. The escape of one of the four, Heinrich Harrer (who had been one of the first team to climb the Eiger's North Wall), into Tibet, formed the basis of his book Seven Years in Tibet, recently the basis of a successful film. Unfortunately for Harrer the film re-opened the question of the links between the Nazi party and the German climbers of the later 1930s and, in particular, his own position on National Socialism.

First Ascent

In November 1950 three young Britons (Crace, Marsh and Thornley), together with four Sherpas, including Tenzing, approached Nanga Parbat. They were poorly equipped for winter climbing, more intent on an adventure than a real

On the south-east pillar of the Rupal Face

attempt at the peak. Against the advice of Tenzing and the other Sherpas the three Britons climbed along the Rakhiot Glacier. Marsh soon retreated suffering from frostbite, but the other two continued. On 1 December they were seen at about 5,500m (18,000ft), but after a snow storm no trace of them was seen again.

Two years later the Germans, recovered from the devastation of the 1939–45 War, were considering a return to 'their' mountain. There was, however, no unanimity of purpose between the German Himalayan and Alpine Clubs, and, eventually, a physician of limited climbing experience decided to mount his own expedition. Dr Karl-Maria Herrligkoffer was the step-brother of Willy Merkl and, as a youth of 17 in 1934, had hero-worshipped his older brother. He was determined that his expedition would climb Nanga Parbat as a memorial to Merkl. The unknown Herrligkoffer's single mindedness and confrontational style led to serious dissent in Germany, much of the climbing establishment and, due to their influence, the press being against his expedition. Despite this he assembled a strong team. Peter Aschenbrenner, veteran of the 1932 and 1934 expeditions, was the climbing leader, Herrligkoffer's lack of experience preventing him from going much beyond base camp, and with him were Fritz Aumann, Albert Bitterling, Hermann Buhl, Hans Ertl (who was also the expedition photographer), Walter Frauenberger, Otto Kempter, Hermann Köllensperger and Kuno Rainer, a mix of Austrians and Germans. Of these the best known was Buhl, who could perhaps be best described as the German-speaking rival of great French post-war climbers – Lachenal, Rébuffat and Terray. He had completed an early ascent of the Eiger's north wall in a large team – created when appalling weather forced an amalgamation of three separate ropes – with Rébuffat. Buhl specialised in solo and winter climbs, climbs which required amazing resolve and self-control, these climbs including the first solo of the Watzmann's east face which he completed in winter and at night. He was also phenomenally quick, completing an early, and solo (the first solo), ascent of the Piz Badile's north face in less than half the best time to date. Kuno Rainer, another Tyrolean, was Buhl's partner on many of his best climbs, including the fourth ascent of the Dru's north face, an early ascent of the Walker spur on the Grandes Jorasses and the first winter ascent of the Marmolada's south-west face.

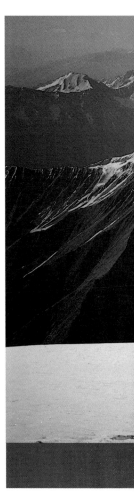

Perhaps in deference to his step-brother Herrligkoffer chose the 1930s route rather than the Diamir Face, but progress in establishing camps was slow because of the lack of Sherpas. Herrligkoffer's explanation for this was that the half-dozen who had been hired were not allowed into Pakistan, but Buhl's account of the climb suggests that because they were not met at the border they were turned away. The Germans therefore used Hunza porters, finding them less willing to carry heavy loads across steep ice, a fact which slowed the build up. The weather, too, was poor, but on 30 June it changed, the first half of July being almost perfect. On 30 June Buhl, Ertl, Frauenberger and Kempter were in Camp III at 6,150m (20,180ft) below the Rakhiot Peak preparing to push towards the Silver Saddle for a summit attempt. The expected summit pair had been Buhl and Rainer, but Rainer had developed phlebitis and Kempter was to be Buhl's partner. Herrligkoffer's official account of the expedition notes nothing of interest on that day, but the four at Camp III are adamant that they received repeated demands by radio to return to base camp. The reasons were vague – the monsoon was expected (yet the weather was now glorious), everyone needed to rest (yet

Climbing fluted ice on the south-east pillar

On the Mazeno Ridge

An aerial view of the Rakhiot face with the Diamir flank on the right hand side

In the Great Couloir on the south-east pillar, Rupal Face

progress had been so slow any further delay would result in almost certain defeat), Aschenbrenner was leaving the expedition early and the team should assemble to say goodbye. The four at Camp III refused to descend, and after a long period Herrligkoffer eventually relented.

The four now returned to Camp IV and pushed on to place Camp V just beyond the Mohrenkopf. There, on the night of 2 July Buhl and Kempter slept ready for an attempt on the summit the following day. With hindsight it is easy to see that Camp V was too low. Set at about 6,900m (22,640ft), it was over 1,200m (about 4,000ft) below the summit, and with the descent into the Bazhin Gap closer to 1,400m (4,600ft) below. It was also over 6km (nearly 4 miles) away horizontally. The reasons for not putting another camp on the Silver Saddle are not clear. It is probable that the four climbers at Camp III, the only part of the expedition now operating, just did not have the resources to do so, but it is also possible that the experience of Aschenbrenner and Schneider in 1934, reaching the base of the Subsidiary Summit by noon and believing themselves only an hour or so from the top played a part. In reality, the final climb to the main

summit took Buhl ten hours and involved the hardest climbing on the final day.

Unable to sleep Buhl dressed at 1am and left the tent at 2.30am, intending to break trail so that Kempter, who followed about 30 minutes later, could easily catch him. Climbing without bottled oxygen Buhl reached the Silver Saddle at 7am and began to cross the plateau beyond in heat that was 'merciless, parching my body'. He left his rucsac on the plateau, convinced he would return to it by nightfall, taking only what he could carry in his pockets. As he climbed towards the Subsidiary Summit (which he did not reach, traversing some 40m/130ft – below it) he saw that Kempter had given up. Buhl reached the Bazhin Gap at 2pm absolutely exhausted and racked by hunger and thirst.

At the Gap Buhl took Pervitin, a stimulant developed by the Luftwaffe to combat exhaustion in air-crews, and began the climb to the Shoulder, the last hump of the ridge before the main summit. The climbing was now hard, with steep, iced and loose rock, dangerous cornices and an uninviting drop down the Rupal Face to the side. Buhl had thought the climb from the Bazhin Gap would take about an hour: it took five. Not until 7pm did he reach the summit – he had been climbing for 16½ hours. Buhl stayed on the summit – a raised dome on which several climbers could gather – for 30 minutes. He took some photos, then with the light fading fast, he started to descend.

Buhl had left his ice axe, with a Pakistani flag attached, on the summit. Soon after starting the descent he lost a strap from his left crampon. With one crampon and two ski sticks his progress slowed – he had hoped to reach the Bazhin Gap before darkness fell, but was forced to bivouac standing on a ledge, holding the ski sticks in one hand and a small hold with the other. Utterly exhausted he dozed occasionally,

High on the south-east pillar, Rupal Face

miraculously maintaining his balance when he did. Equally amazingly the night was calm, so that although the temperature plunged he was not wind chilled. He hoped to continue by moonlight, but his stance was in moon shadow and he was forced to wait until dawn. The day was beautiful, the sun warming him – but then roasting his dehydrated body.

On the final descent to the Bazhin Gap and the climb towards the Subsidiary Summit and Silver Plateau, Buhl's emaciated condition led him to hallucinate. He had conversations (two-way conversations) with an imagined colleague and distinctly heard voices calling him. When he recovered his rucsac his mouth was so dry he could not swallow glucose tablets and was forced to eat snow. On the plateau realising that night was approaching and knowing he was unlikely to survive a second bivouac he took more Pervitin – he had also taken Padutin, an anti-frostbite drug – and with its help reached the Silver Saddle. It was 5.30pm. The sight of the tent and other expedition members now buoyed him as he descended to the camp. He reached it at 7pm 40½ hours after leaving. His first words were 'Yesterday was the finest day of my life'. It was no understatement, Buhl's climb ranking among the greatest feats in the history of mountaineering.

When Buhl came in to view on the Silver Saddle Walter Frauenberger was fixing a memorial tablet to Merkl, Welzenbach and Wieland on the Mohrenkopf. The question which immediately comes to mind was why none of the climbers at Camp V went out to look for Buhl on the Silver Plateau at any time on 4 July. Rainer had waited on the Silver Saddle for most of 3 July, not returning to camp until 7pm. He was too exhausted to go up again on 4 July, but what of the other two? There was a plan, apparently, to go up to the plateau with oxygen equipment on 5 July if Buhl had not returned. The lack of oxygen to administer to the possibly exhausted Buhl is cited as the reason for there being no rescue attempt on 4 July, but to have waited until the 5th would have meant looking for a man who had spent over 48 hours alone and ill-equipped above 7,800m (25,600ft). But whatever view is taken today, so many years after the event, it is clear that Burl had no hard feelings about Frauenberger and Ertl. His own account of the climb records the three becoming firm friends and meeting on 3 July 1954 to celebrate the anniversary of the climb.

Events surrounding the retreat from the mountain led to bitter wrangling back in Germany. Herrligkoffer claims that on Buhl's return to Base Camp there were celebrations (the official expedition includes a photograph of clearly-staged cheering), but Buhl recalls only a cool, joyless reception. Herrligkoffer claims that treatment of Buhl's frostbite would have been pointless as the damage was already too far advanced. Buhl states that the expedition's medical supplies had already left base camp en route for Germany when he arrived and notes that 'there was no Dr Oudot among my team-mates', a bitter comparison to the treatment of Lachenal and Herzog after Annapurna's first ascent. Buhl's feelings were obviously even more bitter, but he had by then learned, as others would later, that Herrligkoffer was both litigious and tenacious when crossed. In the event Buhl lost the ends of two toes on his right foot, an injury was caused him pain for the rest of his climbing life.

Rakhiot Peak from the south-east pillar

Later Ascents

In 1961 Karl-Maria Herrligkoffer organised another team and returned to Nanga Parbat to look at the Diamir Face. Taking a line between Mummery's Rib and the suggested route of the 1938 reconnaissance his team hoped to reach the Bazhin Gap from where they would follow Buhl's route to the summit. Bad weather forced a retreat from a height of about 7,100m (23,300ft), but Herrligkoffer returned the following year. A summit attempt by a team of five climbers on 22 June was reduced to a team of three – Toni Kinshofer and Anderl Mannhardt (who had been on the first winter ascent of the Eiger's north wall) and Siegi Löw – when two stopped as a result of exhaustion. In poor weather the three took seven hours to climb to the summit from the Bazhin Gap (Buhl had taken five hours) reaching the summit at 5pm. At the top they found the small cairn Hermann Buhl had constructed in 1953. The three bivouaced only 70m (230ft) below the summit – all being frostbitten in the extreme cold – and continued their descent, unroped the following day. Löw had taken a heavy dose of Pervitin and, badly affected by frostbite and the drug, fell on the descent to the Gap. He died of his injuries. Kinshofer (who waited with Löw until he died and spent two nights bivouaced above the last camp with no sleeping bag or tent) and Mannhardt climbed down, but each suffered subsequent amputations due to frostbite.

After success on the Diamir Face Herrligkoffer turned his attention to the Rupal Face, the highest mountain wall in the world. With sections almost as steep as the south face of Annapurna, though not as sustained as that face, the Rupal was a formidable challenge. The Germans reconnoitred the route in June 1963 Toni Kinshofer, recovered from frostbite injuries, favouring a line along the face's left edge (later climbed by a team under Hanns Schell), but others feeling a direct line was feasible. It was the later line that was attempted by the first full expedition in January 1964. To attempt a new route on a long, steep face in winter was highly ambitious, but Herrligkoffer's reasons were not pioneering – he had an Antarctic trip planned for the autumn of 1964 and so could not go in the summer. Before the Germans had set foot on the face Herrligkoffer had named various features, attaching Wieland's name to those at the base, Welzenbach's to the central features and Merkl's to those at the top. In 1964 the team barely climbed beyond 'Wieland' before difficulties with their Pakistani liaison officer caused their permit to be cancelled.

Political problems prevented Herrligkoffer returning to the Rupal Face until 1968 when he brought a team built around three of the four Germans who had completed the John Harlin Route on the Eiger's north wall. The team reached the foot of the 'Merkl'

A phoenix cloud formation over a cloud sea obscuring the sun, seen from high on the south-east pillar

Herrligkoffer came back again in 1970. Only one of the 1964 team came with him, but he still had a strong team, including the young Italian Tyrol climber Reinhold Messner. In 1968 Messner had made the first solo ascents of the Philipp-Flamm route on the Civetta and the Les Droites north face, and had a reputation as a brilliant and fast climber. The team also included Reinhold's brother Günther. For six weeks the team fixed route up the face, finally establishing a camp (Camp V) at 7,350m (24,100ft) at the foot of the Merkl Gully. There was no radio at Camp V, but it had been agreed earlier that Base Camp would fire a flare on the evening of 26 June to tell V's occupants (the Messner brothers and Gerhard Baur) what the weather forecast was for the 27th. A red flare meant bad weather, a blue one good. With the weather apparently set fair Camp V was surprised to see a red flare. The events which followed the flare ended – as so many of Herrligkoffer's trips – in the German courts with ugly accusations on all sides. The facts are that Reinhold Messner left Camp V early on 27 June climbing solo, followed later by Günther Messner and Baur who were to fix ropes in the Merkl Gully. The rope fixing went badly and Baur, troubled by an altitude cough, returned to camp. Günther

section of the face – at about 7,100m (23,300ft) – at which point Günther Strobel sustained a badly broken leg. Strobel's rescue from the face brought antagonisms between the climbers and Herrligkoffer to the surface and the expedition broke up.

On the Mazeno Ridge

climbed off to catch his brother which, using his trail, he managed. The two continued to the summit reaching it at about 5pm. Reinhold states his brother was now suffering from altitude sickness and hallucinating, and was incapable of soloing back down the difficult ascent route. The pair therefore retreated along the south-west (Mazeno) ridge, bivouacing in a hollow (the Merkl Gap) below the mountain's south shoulder.

Early on 28 June Felix Kuen and Peter Scholz started up from Camp V. At around 6am they heard shouts – apparently calls for help – as did Gerd Mändl in the camp below. At about 10am they reached a point 80m (250ft) or so from the ridge and had a shouted conversation with Reinhold Messner. Messner claims that during this conversation he asked for a rope, as Günther could not descend without one, and told Kuen and Scholz to climb across to him as the route from him to the summit was easier than the face. Kuen and Scholz claim Reinhold did not ask for a rope, denied calling for help and said that all was well. The pair say they did not see Günther Messner and that at the end of the conversation Reinhold bent down to pick up something which was clearly heavy: they assumed this was a rucsac. But neither of the Messner brothers had taken a rucsac.

Kuen and Scholz continued to the summit, bivouacing near the south shoulder on their descent. On returning to Camp V

they discovered that the Messner brothers had not arrived. In fact the Messners had descended the easier-angled Diamir Face, bivouacing on 28 June and descending again the next day. Reinhold was climbing faster than Günther and at some time on 29 June Günther disappeared, presumably killed by an avalanche. Reinhold spent 30 June searching for his brother, then continued alone, rejoining the surprised expedition with the help of the Pakistani army. Messner subsequently lost six toes and several finger joints to frostbite.

Back in Germany Messner made a number of accusations against Herrligkoffer, chiefly over the red and blue flares, which resulted in court cases which found in the expedition leader's favour. There was also an unpleasant accusation that what Messner had stooped to pick up at the end of his conversation with Kuen and Scholz was his brother. This he

Kinshofer Route, Diamir Face

Late evening shot towards the Mazeno Ridge from close to the summit on the Kinshofer Route

vehemently denied. The court cases silenced the parties (at least in public) but have not resolved the issues raised by the incidents of 26–28 June. Why was a red flare fired? The leader claimed that all the 'blue' flares were actually red by accident – how could this be? and how was it known without firing them? What were the cries (of help) heard early on 28 June? What exactly was said during the exchange between Reinhold Messner and Kuen and Scholz? Why did Reinhold not simply climb back on to the south shoulder to meet the other two and

so obtain help for his brother? What, if anything, did Reinhold bend to pick up? It is unlikely now that a satisfactory answer will ever be obtained to these questions, and to speculate runs the risk of court proceedings. The only undebated matters from the expedition are that the first ascent of the Rupal Face and the first traverse of an 8,000m peak were achieved, and that Reinhold Messner put his foot on the first rung of a remarkable ladder. Sadly, the aftermath of the climb completely overshadowed its achievement. Though less difficult than the

British Annapurna south face route completed just a few weeks before (in subsequent years it has been the Annapurna face rather than the Rupal which has attracted the top climbers), the ascent of the Rupal face was a significant milestone in the history of climbing on the great peaks.

In 1971 a Czechoslovakian team repeated the Buhl route (having failed in their first attempt in 1969) placing two members on top. This is the only repeat to date of the long line of the first ascent and makes Nanga Parbat one of only two 8,000ers on which the usually favoured route is not the line of the first ascent: the other is Gasherbrum I (though here the reason for the change is very different). The Czechs also made the first ascent of the Subsidiary Summit which Buhl had traversed below. Herrligkoffer returned in 1975 to try three separate routes with one team. The climbers made most progress on the south/south-west ridge (at the left edge of the Rupal Face), but failed at 7,550m (24,7756ft). The route was climbed the following year by a team of four (Hanns Schell, as leader, with Siegi Gimpel, Robert Schauer and Hilmar Sturm) which placed three camps on the ridge before being forced to retreat by a storm. On their return they discovered Camp III to be under 2m (6½ft) of fresh snow. They placed a fourth camp at 7,450m (24,450ft) and started from it early on 9 August. They bivouaced at 7,700m (25,300ft) that night and at 8,020m (26,300ft) on the 10th. On 11 August they reached the summit after an hour's climb and descended to Camp IV. Though Schell

was now very ill, probably from a minor pulmonary embolism, the four safely reached their base camp. The team had made limited use of porters (only on one section low on the mountain to gain time lost on the walk-in) and had achieved a near-alpine ascent of a new route, a superb achievement, but one which was to be eclipsed within two years.

In 1977 two Americans were killed during an attempt on the Diamir Face and a Polish expedition failed to repeat the Schell route (often called the Kinshofer route as Toni Kinshofer was the first to point out its feasibility, a fact which causes confusion as the 'standard' line on the Diamir Face is also usually called the Kinshofer). Then in 1978 Reinhold Messner returned to the mountain. In 1971 Messner had searched the base of the Diamir face for signs of his brother and had come again in 1973, attempting to solo the face: he retreated from a point about one-third of the way up. Now he was determined to complete the climb. Setting out from a bivouac at the foot of the wall be climbed a new route on its right side, bivouacing at 6,400m (21,000ft) and again at 7,400m (24,300ft). From this second bivouac he climbed directly to the summit rather than taking the ridge from the Merkl Gap (and therefore avoiding the point where he bivouaced with his brother). He reached the summit at 4pm on 9 August, then returned to his top bivouac (just a few weeks after his ascent an Austrian team climbed the left side of the face, finding the tin Messner had left at the summit). On the following day avalanches following an earthquake destroyed his ascent route, forcing him to descend the Mummery Rib: Messner had completed the seventh ascent of the peak, having already completed the third, the climb establishing him as probably the finest high-altitude mountaineer in the world. Indeed, a strong case could be argued for Messner being one of the greatest, all the major innovations on 8,000m peaks being his – first true alpine ascent (of Gasherbrum I), first solo ascent from base camp (here on Nanga Parbat), first ascent of Everest without bottled oxygen, first solo of Everest (also without bottled gas) and first man to climb all 14 8,000m peaks. It is a phenomenal record: one is forced to wonder to what extent the achievements were initiated by the trauma of his brother's death in 1970.

Sunset at Camp II on the Kinshofer Route, Diamir Face

Left-hand side of the Diamir Face. The Kinshofer Route threads a way through the cliff line

Also in August 1978 a six-man Austrian team climbed the Kinshofer route on the Diamir Face, five of the six reaching the summit. (Though usually called the Kinshofer, the now standard line deviates from that of Kinshofer, Löw and Mannhardt, crossing the upper face directly to the summit rather than climbing to the Bazhin Gap.) There were then no further successful climbs until 1981 when an Italian team climbed a variant of the Kinshofer route (on the Diamir Face) and a Dutch team climbed a variant of the Schell route. The four Dutch climbers, Ger Friele, Bas Gresnigt, Ronald Naar and Gerard van Strang, reached the south-west (Mazeno) ridge and decided to cross the Diamir Face to reach the top. They bivouaced on the ridge at 7,516m (24,660ft) on 3 August, but the next day three of them (Gresnigt descending exhausted) progressed by only 35m (115ft) on the face, taking the wrong line several times. They bivouaced again at 7,550m (24,775ft). Friele was now too sick to continue, the other two continuing to 7,800m (25,600ft) where van Strang was forced to abandon. Naar continued alone to the top. After the climb Friele lost two joints from each of his fingers.

In 1982 Herrligkoffer returned, intent on climbing the south-east pillar, to the right of the German Rupal face route.

Seen in profile on photographs from the Buhl route this line is steep, averaging 65°–70°, but has the advantage of being relatively avalanche free. In May 1982 a strong team under Yannick Seigneur had attempted the line, but had abandoned it after a porter had slipped to his death off a fixed rope and Seigneur had been caught in an avalanche – ironically in view of the line's supposed safety – and was lucky to escape with broken ribs and a cracked pelvis. The team had reached about 7,100m (23,300ft). Herrligkoffer's team arrived in July and by mid-August had established Camp V at 7,500m (24,600ft). From it, on 16 August, four climbers set out, climbing the near-vertical pillar. Three retreated, but the Swiss Ueli Bühler continued alone. He bivouaced without equipment and at noon on 17 August reached the South Summit (8,042m/26,385ft), but was unable to continue to the main summit and retreated to Camp V. His companions abandoned a summit attempt to bring him down – a journey he was lucky to survive. Bühler later lost the last joint of several fingers and half his toes to frostbite. In 1985 a predominately Polish team completed the route, the main summit being reached by Jerzy Kukuczka and Carlos Carsolio (each on their way to completing the 14 8,000ers) together with Zygmunt Heinrich and Slavomir Lobodzinski, the summit climb involving two days without food or water. During this expedition the climbers found that one of their lower camps had been blown away by the blast from a vast avalanche falling over 1km (over ½ mile) away and at one point, during a violent storm, Kukuczka noticed sparks jumping between the piton he was belayed to and the rock. There can be few better motives for getting away from a place, but he was forced to stay attached for 30 long minutes.

In October 1984 Tsuneo Hasegawa, having been part of a Japanese expedition which failed on the Schell route in the summer, returned to attempt the first winter and first solo ascents. He chose the Rupal Face for this audacious plan, but was forced to abandon. The summer of 1984 saw Liliane and Maurice Barrard on the summit. They were part of a porter-less four person team on the Diamir Face and achieved the first French, first female and first married couple ascents. Any married couple ascent might be thought of as a likely unique achievement, but Nanga Parbat has been climbed several more times by couples. A year after Liliane Barrard's ascent three Poles from an all-woman expedition repeated the climb.

1988 saw the German Sigi Hupfauer complete his seventh ascent of an 8,000er by way of the now standard Diamir Face route. It was an ascent notable for the cold, the wind and a dramatic descent in worsening weather, but Hupfauer's account is dismissive of these 'minor' problems, noting, in a laconic, but clearly hurt way, that 'we had difficult relations with

The Rupal face of Nanga Parbat

the Pakistani authorities. We also found the Chilas people deceitful.'

In 1992 the Britons Mark Miller and Jon Tinker led a semi-commercial team attempting a new route. The aim was to climb the Rakhiot Peak from the east, than to follow the Buhl route to the summit. The attempt was abandoned low on the mountain due to huge snowfalls. Later that year the French pair Eric Monier and Monique Loos failed in a winter attempt on the Schell route. 1992 also saw the first of several attempts on the Mazeno Ridge by British climber Doug Scott. The ridge is about 15km (9 miles) long from the Mazeno Pass, the longest ridge to any 8,000er. It had been attempted in 1979 by a French team who spent 30 days in bad weather on it before retreating. Scott's team (British and Russian climbers with Sherpa support) used the Schell route to place supplies above 7,000m (23,000ft), but during that period several climbers were injured by rock falls. The remaining members then climbed from the Pass, reaching Pt6,970 (22,280ft) just less than half-way along the ridge. Scott tried again in 1993 with Wojciech Kurtyka and Richard Cowper. Though they climbed the Mazeno Spire (a probable first ascent) they were less successful on the ridge than in '92. An avalanche carried Scott almost 400m (1,200ft) down the mountain – he was lucky to escape with a damaged ankle – and the climb was abandoned. Another attempt in 1995 (by Scott, Kurtyka, Rick Allen and Andrew Lock, though Scott was ill and forced to retire) reached 7,000m (23,000ft) about two-thirds of the way along the ridge. Kurtyka and Erhard Loretan tried again in 1997, failing at about one-third distance.

A Japanese team opened a new route on the north side of the mountain in 1995, taking a direct route to the Silver Saddle where they placed a camp at 7,350m (24,100ft). The first summit attempt was abandoned due to the cold and one climber's chest pains, but a second attempt was made on 23 July. Starting at 3am after a night breathing bottled oxygen, Yukio Yabe, Takeshi Akiyama and Hiroshi Saito followed Buhl's route to the top, reaching it at 5pm. They left the summit after an hour, but failed to reach the Bazhin Gap before nightfall, bivouacing at 7,700m (25,250ft). They finally reached the Silver Saddle camp on 24 August 39 hours after leaving it. The climb was yet another demonstration of the phenomenal performance of Hermann Buhl. A year later Krzysztof Wielicki soloed the Diamir Face (Kinshofer line) to become the fifth 'all-14' climber at the age of 46. Wielicki arrived in base camp after completing an ascent of K2, but found that he was too late to join his prospective team as they had already left. He therefore decided to solo the mountain, a climb delayed by 24 hours by an abscess which erupted on his face. He spent the time high on the mountain in a tent he fortuitously found left from an earlier expedition, suffering hallucinations from an antibiotic he took to combat the abscess. He eventually reached the top on 1 September 1996. Wielicki's record of ascents included the first winter ascents of Everest in 1980, Kangchenjunga (1986) and Lhotse (part solo, 1988), first solo of Broad Peak in 1984, new routes on Manaslu (1984), Dhaulagiri (1990 – the new route on the east face reached the original route and Wielicki did not continue tot he summit having already sumitted along the original) and Shisha Pangma (solo, 1993). Only on Everest during the first winter ascent did Wielicki use bottled oxygen.

Attempts to claim the first winter ascent in late 1996 and early 1997 again failed. In February 1997 two Poles reached a point just 250m (800ft) from the top, but retreated with severe frostbite. Their expedition subsequently notched up an unwanted first – first helicopter rescue from the Diamir base camp. In February 1998 another Polish team returned, determined to complete Nanga Parbat's first winter ascent. After battling winds up to 140km/h (90mph) the team were forced to abandon the climb when one member fell and broke a leg. There has been no winter ascent of Nanga Parbat to date and the long Mazeno Ridge remains one of the great peaks' outstanding problems.

To date there have been around 170 ascents of Nanga Parbat, but the mountain's position means that summit climbers usually have to contend with extreme cold. This slows progress and a large number of summiteers have been forced to bivouac on the way down. With its high number of fatal accidents – more climbers have died on the peak than on any 8,000er apart from Everest which, of course, has had a great deal more traffic – Nanga Parbat has long had a reputation as a killer mountain. But the accidents of the 1930s have distorted the statistics which suggest that Nanga Parbat is second only to Annapurna in the ratio of deaths to successful ascent. Now a summiteer is as likely to survive a descent from Nanga Parbat as from any other 8,000er apart from the 'dangerous five' peaks – K2, Annapurna, Makalu, Kangchenjunga and Everest. Despite this comforting fact Nanga Parbat remains a very serious undertaking, climbers drawn by the romance of its name and history sustaining a higher-than-average number of frostbite injuries. Even with improvements in equipment the intense cold on Nanga Parbat and the usually long summit days are likely to ensure that this grim statistic remains true.

Looking north-east towards the Rakhiot Peak from the south-east pillar

K2 8,611m

"It was one of those sights which impress a man forever, and produce a permanent effect upon the mind, a lasting sense of the greatness and grandeur of Nature's work, which he can never lose or forget."

FRANCIS YOUNGHUSBAND
on seeing K2 from the north

K2

In 1856 Capt. TG Montgomerie, a British army survey officer working in what is now northern Pakistan but was then British India, surveyed a number of peaks in the Baltoro region of the Karakoram from a distance of about 200km. (125 miles). He catalogued the peaks he surveyed by number, giving each the prefix 'K', for Karakoram.

In 1861, the area was explored and resurveyed by parties under Col. HH Godwin-Austen. They discovered that the second peak of Montgomerie's list, K2, was actually the highest in the area. Godwin-Austen's men produced the first map of the area and also described the route to the peak. Later, when it was discovered that K2 was the second highest mountain in the world, the British tried to name it Mount Godwin-Austen, a name which can still be found in very old books on the Karakoram or climbing. The Indian authorities were very much against this naming of peaks for prominent members of the ruling classes and objected strongly. Indeed, the Indian protests over the use of such commemorative names were sufficient to prevent their use on any mountain except the world's highest. Godwin-Austen had a much better claim to be recognised in the name of K2 than Sir George

Everest had with the highest peak, but the protests were heeded and the name quietly dropped. Later, when the official numbering of Karakoram peaks was undertaken the decision was made to renumber them so as to conform to current convention (from east to west, as in the Himalaya). K2 became K13, a name used in an official publication of 1879. But by then the older designation had become so ingrained that the new one soon disappeared. In view of the reputation that the peak has gathered it is perhaps a good thing that the superstitious number 13 did not find favour.

A later search for a local name for the peak revealed that there was none. Latterly the Pakistan authorities have attempted to rename the peak using names 'discovered' among local peoples, but these have all failed. Dapsang gained some credence and is occasionally still heard, but it seems to

Camp II on the Abruzzi Spur. Masherbrum dominates the south-western skyline

derive from a plateau some distance from the peak and is unknown to the Hunzas. Mount Akbar was also tried, the name meaning Great Mountain, but seemed to have nationalistic overtones and was ignored. Pakistan also tried to impose Lamba Pahar, a Kashmiri name, also meaning Great Mountain, but that had the disadvantages of being clearly (and overtly) tied up with the border dispute with India over Kashmir and also of being completely unknown to the Kashmiris, the latter fact being deemed positive proof of its unsuitability. In Baltistan the name Chogori (which also means Great Mountain) does appear to have been applied to the peak and would probably have been accepted had not the peak been known as K2 for decades before Chogori came to light. Chogori is a very beautiful name (and is probably the basis for a Chinese attempt to rename the peak Mount Qogir, an attempt which has, thankful, failed), but the clipped and impersonal nature of K2 seems just so appropriate for a mountain with a reputation for difficulty and danger which exceeds that of any other 8,000m peak.

Exploration

In 1892 the base of the peak was reached for the first time by the British mountaineer Martin Conway. Conway explored the Baltoro, naming Concordia (either after Konkordiaplatz, a junction on Switzerland's Aletsch Glacier, or the Place de la Concorde in Paris – though the former seems more likely there is evidence to suggest the latter: it is, for instance, quoted in Desio's book on the first ascent) and discovering the Godwin-Austen and Vigne Glaciers. Conway also named Broad Peak and Hidden Peak (Gasherbrum I). Conway's team made an attempt on a peak he called Golden Throne (Baltoro Kangri) reaching a subsidiary summit. Although Conway's expedition did little actual climbing, in terms of exploration it was a major success. Conway also logged the effects of altitude on pulse rate and general health, the effects of different diets and the behaviour and value of equipment, all of which were very important for later expeditions. Ten years after Conway's trip a small team of British and Austrian climbers and a Swiss doctor under Oscar Eckenstein arrived to climb K2. Alfred Mummery had attempted Nanga Parbat in 1895, but as yet no one had any idea of the difficulties of attempting 8,000m peaks. Eckenstein had been with Conway during the early stages of his trip, but had left after a disagreement, possibly over differing views of the aims of the expedition (climbing or exploration), but more likely over personal matters, Eckenstein being a radical, Conway an establishment man. Eckenstein clearly believed that the peak was just a bigger version of those in the Alps, but the two Austrian climbers, Heinrich Pfannl and V Wessely, who

K2: ASCENT ROUTES

North Face
1 *NE Ridge. Lower section followed by Americans (1978) before traverse of East Face to Abruzzi Spur*

2 *Japanese (1982)*
3 *Japanese (1990)*
4 *Beghin/Profit (1991), approach from NW Ridge*

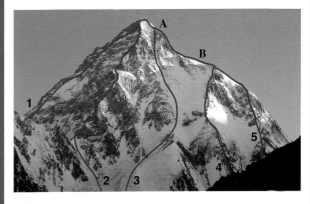

South and West Faces
A *Bottleneck*
B *Shoulder*
1 *West Ridge/West Face Japanese (1981); variation Japanese (1997)*
2 *SSW Ridge Polish (1986)*

3 *Kukuczka/Pietrowski (1986)*
4 *SSE Spur Basques (1994); but lower section earlier by International team (1983) and Cesen (1986)*
5 *Abruzzi Spur (and ESE Ridge) Italians (1953); the classic route*

were among the best in Europe, seem to rapidly have come to the conclusion that K2 was too big a mountain for the small team to attempt. They suggested abandoning the attempt in favour of climbing Skyang Kangri. Had they done this they might well have succeeded, establishing a summit record that would have lasted for decades – Skyang Kangri is 7,545m (24,750ft) – and completing one of the great feats of mountaineering. But despite their warnings Eckenstein doggedly refused to deflect from his objective, with the result that the team did not get higher than 6,600m (21,650ft) and then had to retreat hastily when Pfannl contracted pulmonary oedema. That he survived was due to the presence of the Swiss

Climbing House's Chimney on the Abruzzi Spur

Dr Jacot-Guillarmod who recognised the symptoms – the European Alps being high enough for some climbers to contract the condition on rapid ascents – and to evacuate him to lower ground. The expedition was also notable for including Edward Alexander (Alesteir) Crowley, the self-proclaimed Great Beast 666 etc, whose abilities as a climber have been completely overshadowed by those as a self-publicist, though they actually seem to have been far greater than his abilities to conjure up the Devil.

In 1909 K2 was attempted by an Italian team led by the Duke of the Abruzzi who correctly identified the south-east ridge – now often referred to as the Abruzzi Ridge or Spur – as the most straightforward way to the summit. The Duke's team included Vittorio Sella, arguably the greatest mountain photographer of all time whose shots still inspire new generations of climbers. Ironically in view of this, the most famous photograph taken by the expedition – of K2 from Windy Gap (Skyang La) to the north-east – was actually taken by Abruzzi himself, though it is frequently credited to Sella. Abruzzi's team did not get high – only to about 6,000m (19,700ft) – but they established, in their own eyes at least, the Italian 'ownership' of the peak, a fact reinforced by another Italian expedition which arrived in the area in 1929. This trip,

Gary Ball abseiling down House's Chimney

under the leadership of the Duke of Spoleto was for scientific and exploratory purposes and made no attempt to climb the peak. One member of the team was the geologist Ardito Desio.

Today, almost a century after these early struggles on the peak and half-a-century after the first ascent – the idea of K2 being an Italian mountain seems ludicrous, but at the time the national pride engendered by the expeditions and in anticipation of success was very real. British influence over Tibet meant that all of the early attempts on Everest were by British teams. By the time Nepal opened its borders in the early 1950s Everest was established as a British mountain and the issuing of a permit to the Swiss in 1952 was met by a mixture of outrage and fear: Britons had died on Everest – what right had these newcomers to attempt our mountain? By the same logic the Germans 'owned' Nanga Parbat, a peak on whose flank eleven Germans (together with 15 locals) lay buried. The Italians were therefore aggrieved to discover that an American expedition had set out for K2 in the early summer of 1938. (There had been further exploration in 1937 when a small British team under Eric Shipton visited the Shaksgam Valley and photographed the northern flank of K2.) Mussolini's ill-considered invasion of Ethiopia had ended, though the invasion of Albania must have been at the planning stage, but despite these distractions it is strange that an expedition to K2, Italy's mountain, did not fire the nationalistic imagination of Il Duce.

The Americans, under Charles Houston solved the problems set by the lower section of the Abruzzi Ridge, Bill House climbing the chimney which now bears his name, probably the hardest single pitch climbed at that time in the Karakoram or Himalaya. The Americans set seven camps along the ridge and from the top one Houston and Paul Petzoldt climbed up to the Shoulder. There the exhausted Houston stopped, Petzoldt continuing up to about 7,925m (26,000ft). The summit looked so close, but Petzoldt could go no further.

The following year, while Europe was distracted by the prelude to war, the Americans tried again, this time with a team led by the German-born, American-naturalised Fritz Wiessner. Wiessner was a brilliant rock climber, but his team was not in the same league and included a deputy with limited experience and one member, Dudley Wolfe, who was apparently taken because he was rich enough to buy his way on to the trip despite having no experience at all. With Wiessner lead climbing virtually the whole time and taking Wolfe with him (the young man's ambition seemingly over-riding Wiessner's mountain judgement) the team established eight camps, Camp VIII being just below a prominent change of angle on the ridge, a feature now known as the Shoulder. Here Wolfe was finally forced to stop, overcome by exhaustion, but Wiessner and Sherpa Pasang Dawa Lama continued, placing another camp at about 8,000m (26,247ft). From it they set out for the top, but Wiessner, being a rock climber, chose to tackle the headwall above the Shoulder rather than the now-used route (the Bottleneck Couloir). The pair reached about 8,370m (27,450ft) with just a one more short section of difficult climbing before they would reach easy ground. Wiessner wanted to push on but Pasang Dawa Lama refused to move. Some have suggested he was afraid of the mountain gods who would kill them if (as was inevitable) they reached the summit or were descending when night fell. Others have suggested the Sherpa showed good sense, realising the two would either not survive a night out or, if they did, the difficult descent of the headwall. Wiessner reluctantly retreated planning to try again the following day. On the descent the pair's crampons were dislodged from Pasang's rucsac. After a rest day (it is now known that there is really no such thing above 8,000m, physical

deterioration outweighing any perceived benefit) they did go up again, this time trying the Bottleneck Couloir, but without crampons the step cutting was too arduous and they were forced to retreat.

Wiessner now planned to go down to Camp VIII to collect crampons, supplies and someone to replace the exhausted Pasang Dawa Lama, but on arriving he found that no one had arrived to resupply the camp or help Dudley Wolfe. He was therefore forced to continue down taking Wolfe as far as Camp VII. On the way an accident resulted in the loss of Wolfe's sleeping bag, leaving the three men with just one between them, Wiessner having left his at Camp VIII. After a grim night Wolfe was too exhausted to descend so Wiessner and Pasang continued alone. To their horror they found the mountain had been stripped – on whose orders would be the subject of debate for years. Wiessner and Pasang spent another bagless night at Camp II and continued to Base Camp. Wiessner nor any of the Americans were fit to attempt a rescue of Dudley Wolfe, but four Sherpas set out. They reached him at Camp VII, finding him in a dreadful state: he had not even had the strength to leave the tent to relieve himself and had had nothing to eat or drink for some time. The Sherpas tried to get him down to Camp VI but he did not have the energy. Forced to retreat, three of the Sherpas – Pasang Kikuli, Pasang Kitar and Phinsoo – set out from Camp VI again the following day. Neither they nor Dudley Wolfe were seen again. K2 had exacted its first blood sacrifice.

Back in America an attempt was made to blame Wiessner

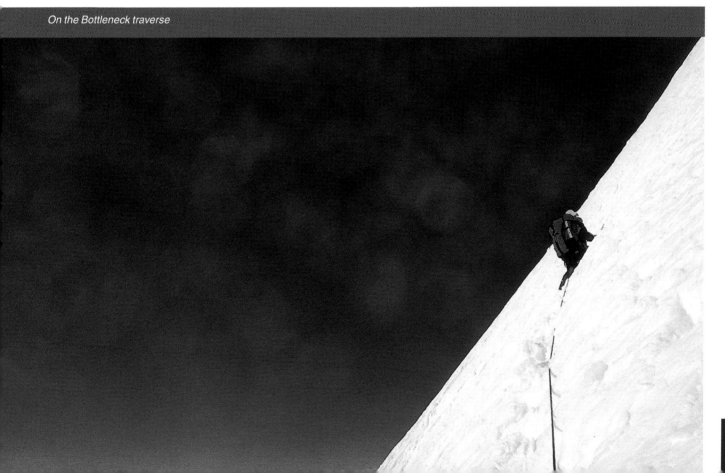

On the Bottleneck traverse

87

for the tragedy, something made easier by the fact that he was German born. History has largely vindicated him, the American Alpine Club, from which he had resigned in protest at his treatment, eventually making him an Honorary Member. Wiessner may not have been a good team leader and seems to

Compagnoni and Lacedelli on the summit after the first ascent

have had a definite blindspot over Wolfe's abilities, but the unsavoury nature of some of the attacks on his character are a slur on the name of mountaineering.

War prevented either the Americans, who now also saw K2 as their mountain, or the Italians from attempting the peak for several years. In 1953 permission was given for the Americans to try again, the Italians being given a permit for 1954. Realising that this might be their last chance the Americans prepared a strong team of eight under the leadership of Charles Houston, but a ten day storm destroyed all hope of success and put the men – all eight caught in a camp just below the Shoulder – in jeopardy. Art Gilkey developed thrombosis and when the weather finally cleared could not climb down. The others therefore lowered him in a stretcher, a remarkable feat. But during a traverse of an icy section of mountain to the site of an earlier camp one man slipped, dragging away his rope-mate and knocking another rope of two off. The four falling men became entangled with the ropes from Gilkey's stretcher, to which another climber was attached, and six men were suddenly falling. Pete Schoening, later to be in the first team to climb Gasherbrum I, stopped all six plummeting to their deaths. The accident exhausted the men, and Gilkey's stretcher was fixed with pitons while the others retreated to the

camp. While erecting the tents they could hear Gilkey's muffled shouts from across the slope, shouts they assumed were of encouragement. When they returned for him the slope had been swept bare by an avalanche: Gilkey could have been shouting in warning, a desperate thought that could make strong men weep.

The Americans had not been allowed to bring Sherpas into Pakistan making it necessary to carry all their own loads. They had reached the Shoulder and then also safely evacuated themselves down one of the most dangerous mountains in the world in appalling conditions. True, Art Gilkey had died, but to mountaineers everywhere the expedition had been outstanding.

First Ascent

The Italians returned to K2 in 1954 and,

Early morning sun catches K2, as seen from Concordia

K2 from Concordia. The classic view from the junction of the Baltoro and Godwin-Austen Glaciers, with Broad Peak to the right and Marble Peak to the left

knowing that the Americans too would come back to a mountain knew they had to succeed. The expedition was jointly sponsored by the Italian National Council for Research, a scientific body, and the Italian Alpine Club and had a dual purpose: not only was K2 to be climbed but a whole series of geographic, geological and natural history studies were to be carried out. The National Council, backed by funds from the government, were the major sponsors and their man, Prof Ardito Desio (who had been with Spoleto in 1929) was to be overall leader. The Italian Alpine Club suggested Ricardo Cassin, Italy's greatest climber, as head of the climbing team. When the two men went on a reconnaissance in 1953 the difference not only in funding but in perceived class was obvious. Desio travelled around Pakistan by air, Cassin by drawn-out, exhausting train journeys: Desio went to the posh receptions, Cassin did not. Back in Italy Desio engineered Cassin's resignation from the expedition. Later, to add to this injustice, Cassin was declared unfit for the rigours of the trip by the Desio-headed expedition committee, a dubious decision which left him understandably bitter.

With a free-hand Desio now organised a series of medical tests and a training camp to whittle down the list of 23 candidates to a final team. This comprised Enrico Abram, Ugo Angelino, Walter Bonatti, Achille Compagnoni, Cirillo Floreanini, Pino Gallotti, Lino Lacedelli, Mario Puchoz, Ubaldo Rey, Gino Soldà and Sergio Viotto. Dr Guido Pagani was the team doctor and there were four scientists – Paolo Graziosi, Antonio Marussi, Bruno Zanettin and Francesco Lombardi – as

well as Mario Fantin who was to make a film of the climb. The Pakistani 'observer' was Ata Ullah and there was a team of ten high-altitude Hunza porters. Desio also published a plan for the expedition. In part this was excellent, referring to the need for correct acclimatisation and the need to minimise time spent above 7,500m (24,600ft), but also included the suggestion that all members 'should conform to a diet and a hygiene regime calculated to maintain them in a state of maximum physical efficiency. This is an obligation which devolves on all ... the indisposition of one or more members ... due to over-eating or drinking may jeopardise the whole undertaking.' The 57 year old Desio clearly believed the young climbers needed to be treated as schoolboys. Desio also issued a four-phase plan for the climb which amounted to no more than reach mountain;

Marble Peak from Concordia, K2 is on the right

climb up, establishing camps; gain summit; go home. While undeniably correct the plan was wholly unhelpful. Desio added timings to the phases and, not surprisingly, they all turned out to be wrong.

On the walk-in, during a bout of horse-play between Bonatti and Lacedelli, two of the youngest team members, Bonatti rolled down a slope and was concussed and badly bruised. Anxious that the headmasterly Desio did not know about the incident Bonatti spent several days in his tent with 'stomach trouble', a fact which might have influenced team selection later on. The Italians made good progress on the Abruzzi Ridge assisted, in part, by a detailed route description from Charles Houston who also told

Rob Hall on a fixed rope below House's Chimney

them about camp sites and what food the Italians might find there, a typically generous gesture by the American: an interesting detail of this information was the quantity of marmalade the Americans had left behind. The Italians used a winch to haul loads low on the mountain and another for the same purpose on House's Chimney (Compagnoni being less impressed by its difficulty than later climbers have been), but progress was halted when Mario Puchoz died. His sudden death was put down to pneumonia, but was almost certainly oedema. In the expedition book Desio notes his death 'after a very brief agony'. After bringing the body down for burial climbing began again, but was now slowed by bad weather. Desio, whose age and lack of experience kept him low on the mountain, had sent regular, numbered message of exhortation to the climbers, many of them couched in eyebrow-raising tones of nationalistic fervour. Now he sent another pointing out the 'moral responsibility' of the climbers to succeed and noting that success would lead them to be hailed throughout the world 'as champions of your race' and that 'your fame will endure throughout your lives and long after you are dead'. He added 'even if you never achieve anything else of note you will be able to say that you have not lived in vain'.

Despite Desio's plan, the bad weather meant that when Camp VIII was established (at 7,820m/25,650ft – at the edge of the Shoulder) it was already late July and the Italians were in a poor position to mount a summit bid. They had decided to use bottled oxygen from their top camp (Camp IX) but minimum supplies only had reached Camp VII. Only six climbers were still capable of going high and now Bonatti, arguably the strongest, went down with a real stomach upset. Desio had put Compagnoni, the second-oldest team member and the one the leader seemed to find the most agreeable, in charge of the summit bid: it is likely that this latest Bonatti illness, together with the (non-existent) earlier one coloured Compagnoni's view of his suitability for the final team, but whatever the reason Compagnoni chose Lacedelli to accompany him to the top. However, to make a summit bid a superhuman effort was required from the others. While the summit pair climbed up to establish Camp IX Bonatti and the others descended from VIII to VII to collect the oxygen and other supplies and carry them all the way to IX, clearly a plan of last resort. What happened next became the subject of arguments for years and even reached the law courts.

Having brought the oxygen sets to Camp VIII only Bonatti and the Hunza Mahdi had the energy to continue. But it was now mid-afternoon. Bonatti claimed Compagnoni had agreed to re-site Camp IX 100m (330ft) lower to help those carrying the sets, Compagnoni states the intention was to place it as high as possible. As a result night had fallen before Bonatti and Mahdi reached the camp. Bonatti claims that his cries for help were ignored, the only interest the summit pair had during a

On the Bottleneck section of the first ascent route

shouted conversation being whether the oxygen had been brought up. Compagnoni claims that the two were told to dump the oxygen and return to Camp VIII when it became clear that they could not reach Camp IX. Unable to downclimb in the dark Bonatti and Mahdi were forced to spend a night in the open at 8,000m (26,247ft). Bonatti survived unscathed, but Mahdi, whose boots were inferior, subsequently lost both toes and fingers to his frostbite injuries.

On 30 July Compagnoni and Lacedelli had first to climb down to retrieve the oxygen sets (which supports Bonatti's views that the camp should have been lower), then set out for the summit. The snow in the Bottleneck Couloir was rotten, so

Joe Tasker on the west ridge, with Masherbrum in the background

Sunrise over the Gasherbrum peaks and Broad Peak from the Abruzzi Spur

they climbed the rocks to the left (but not as far left as Wiessner in 1939), Compagnoni taking a short fall. They then traversed below a band of ice cliffs. Their oxygen ran out, but they continued upwards still carrying the sets (which weighed over 20kg – 45lbs), eventually reaching the summit of the most beautiful, most difficult 8,000m peak on earth at 6pm. It had been a fine, committing climb and one which had taken a heavy

toil on Compagnoni particularly: on the descent to Camp VIII he fell three times, the last a 16m (50ft) fall he was lucky to survive uninjured. The next day, on the descent from Camp VIII he fell again, sliding 200m (650ft) down the mountain and stopping in a snow drift on the edge of oblivion.

When the expedition book was published Bonatti was appalled at the way his and Mahdi's bivouac was downplayed. He

Bonatti successfully sued a newspaper which claimed his manoeuvring on the mountain was in order to reach the summit first, a clearly ludicrous suggestion, though there is little doubt that he felt cheated of the summit. He claims that Compagnoni suggested that, as the strongest, he might replace either himself or Lacedelli, and almost certainly wanted to reach Camp IX so that might happen. But after the bivouac survival came before ambition. That Bonatti felt cheated is evident from the fact that in 1955 he tried to raise sponsorship for a solo repeat of the climb, planning to carry a 25kg rucsac and to spend one week on the route using equipment left behind in 1954. His attempt to raise the money failed, but it is interesting to speculate what might have happened had he returned to K2. After K2 Bonatti became the greatest alpinist of the day with a string of remarkable climbs which showed not only great ability but a phenomenal willpower. Perhaps he might have succeeded on K2 in which case the whole history of climbing on the great peaks would have been rewritten. As it was, Bonatti only returned once to the high peaks, making the first ascent of Gasherbrum IV on an Italian expedition in 1958.

Later Ascents

As with the other 8,000ers, after the first ascent K2 was left alone for many years, though in the case of the Karakoram peaks this had less to do with lack of interest than lack of access. Border tensions between Pakistan and India over Kashmir and border discussions between Pakistan and China persuaded the Pakistani authorities to close the area. The tensions have continued, sometimes easing but, at the time writing, increasing, while the discussions resulted in the northern side of K2 becoming Chinese territory, two of the mountain's ridges defining the border between the two countries, a summiteer having a foot in each.

Not until 1975 was permission for a major expedition given (though in 1960 a German-American expedition reached about 7,250m/23,800ft on the first ascent route). The 1975 expedition was American, led by Jim Whittaker, the first American to reach Everest's summit, and attempted a new route on the north-west ridge. But tensions between factions in the team mirrored, on a smaller scale, those over Kashmir and the climb was abandoned at 6,700m (22,000ft). The various disputes were aired in Galen Rowell's book In the Throne Room of the Mountain Gods. By covering issues which other expedition books had ignored or brushed aside, the book, was a complete contrast to those which preceded it and set a trend for many which followed. Also in 1975 a strong Polish team (19 climbers, seemingly a large number until it is remembered that poverty meant the Poles did not employ high-altitude porters,

wrote his own version and tried for years to secure an apology from the Italian Alpine Club. When he got one, on the 40th anniversary of the climb, Compagnoni, by then 80 years old, was incensed, though no one was inclined to listen to him as he had lost the respect of his team mates by suing the Club for a share of the film profits on the grounds that he had lost several fingers to frostbite which, he claimed, was caused by filming at the summit.

carrying their own loads) attempted to climb the north-east ridge, the one Eckenstein's team had looked at in 1902. The Poles fixed rope up the ridge and eventually established Camp VI at around 8,000m (26,250ft). Using oxygen above the camp Cichy and Holnicki failed at 8,250m (27,000ft) in the summit bid, while the next day Chrobak and Wróz reached 8,400m (27,550ft). Their oxygen then ran out and reluctantly they retreated. Illness in the team prevented any further attempt.

While the Poles were on the north-east ridge a Japanese team was reconnoitring the Abruzzi ridge prior to a full-scale attempt in 1977. The 1977 expedition was vast, 50 Japanese and 1,500 porters: given these resources it is no surprise the expedition succeeded. On 8 August Shoji Nakamura, Tsuneo Shigehiro and Takayoshi Takatsuka made the second ascent of K2 following the Italian line. The following day three more Japanese and the Pakistani Ashraf Aman repeated the climb.

The following year Pakistan gave permission to two expeditions, but gave a British team led by Chris Bonington first choice of route and first go. The British tried the west ridge, but had reached only about 6,700m (22,000ft) when Nick Estcourt was swept away by an avalanche and killed. The attempt was then abandoned. The second team, of Americans again under Jim Whittaker, had also wanted to attempt the west ridge, but were forced to try the north-east ridge instead. Some of the 1975 team returned and again factions formed. One comprised those climbers who believed they could and should reach the top, the other those who the first group thought couldn't and shouldn't. The factions were nicknamed A and B and when one member of the 'shouldn't' team was naive enough to ask a

'should' man what A and B meant he was told 'Best and Asshole', a comment unlikely to guarantee maximum harmony and co-operation. Despite this the Americans made steady progress up the 1976 Polish line. But with a camp established below the final, difficult headwall, Whittaker realised he had neither the time nor an adequate supply line to finish the climb. Lou Reichardt and Jim Wickwire therefore traversed the east face to the Shoulder above the Abruzzi Ridge and continued along the original route to the top, reaching it late on 6 September. The pair carried oxygen equipment but intended to

Camp I on the Abruzzi Ridge with the Godwin-Austen Glacier already far below

use it high on the climb. When he tried to use it Reichardt found his equipment was faulty. He continued without it, becoming the first man to climb K2 without supplementary gas. Wickwire stayed for 40 minutes on the summit and consequently was overtaken by night on the descent and forced to bivouac. He was found by Rick Ridgeway and John Roskelley, but had survived well enough to descend unaided as they continued to the top. Neither of the second pair used supplementary oxygen.

In 1979 Reinhold Messner led a team of six to attempt the south-south-west ridge (which he dubbed the 'Magic

K2 from the Baltoro Glacier. The Abruzzi Ridge is to the right

Broad Peak (left) and K2 from Gasherbrum I

Line'), but rapidly concluded it was too dangerous for the team's porters and probably too much for such a small party. To the disgust of several members (notably Renato Casarotto) Messner therefore transferred to the original route, reaching the summit with Michl Dacher. It was Messner's fifth 8,000er. After Messner's team withdrew from the south-south-west ridge a large French team (including Pierre Beghin and Yannick Seigneur) attempted it, reaching a height of 8,400m (27,550ft) before bad weather forced a retreat. During the expedition Jean-Marc Boivin set a world record for hang gliders by using one to descend from Camp IV, at 7,600m (24,900ft), to Base Camp. The following year a four-man British team (Peter Boardman, Dick Renshaw, Doug Scott and Joe Tasker) returned to the west ridge, but at about 7,000m (23,000ft) time pressures and internal disputes led to Scott leaving the team and the other three attempting an alpine-style ascent of the original route. At 8,100m (26,600ft), poised for a summit bid, their camp was destroyed by avalanches: they were lucky to survive these and the nightmare descent which followed.

Early in the 1981 season the Pakistani permit system allowed a four man Franco-German team to try the south face – the team, led by Yannick Seigneur reached 7,400m (24,300ft) – before a large Japanese team arrived to attempt the west ridge. The Japanese followed the 1980 British line, continuing along the ridge to reach about 8,200m (26,900ft). From there they followed a snow band across the west face to the top of the south-west ridge. The route, which was fixed with 5,500m

(almost 3 1/2 miles) of rope, had taken 52 days to climb. On 6 August Eiho Otani, Matsushi Yamashita and Nazir Sabir climbed the fixed ropes to the south-west ridge and started for the summit. The three climbers had helped fix the last ropes on 5 August using bottled oxygen, but now, at 8,300m (27,250ft), dumped their sets in the face of extremely difficult climbing where the flow of gas did not compensate for the weight of the equipment. By 6pm they had climbed to about 8,470m (27,750ft) where they decided to bivouac without any equipment or food, using a candle to warm a hastily dug snow hole. Next morning, 7 August, they climbed another 100m (328ft) to arrive at the end of the difficulties, just 50m (160ft) from the top. Here Otani and Yamashita radioed the team leader and were told to descend as they were too tired to continue. Sabir, a Hunza high-altitude porter who had become a leading mountaineer and was ambitious to climb K2, was appalled. After 45 minutes of sometimes heated argument the leader eventually agreed they could continue. Yamashita was by now too exhausted to continue, but Otani and Sabir climbed on, reaching the top an hour later. Despite a nightmare descent the three, tired and badly dehydrated, reached base camp safely.

Another Japanese expedition attempted K2 in 1982, choosing to attempt the north ridge on the Chinese side of the mountain, having reconnoitred the route the previous year. The approach was epic, the last place camels (!) could reach being 15km (10 miles) from the peak. The absence of a local

Avalanche on the south face, seen from Base Camp

The Japanese north ridge route was repeated in 1983 by an Italian team, their climb being the only success of the year, though an international team led by Doug Scott climbed the south-south-east spur (to the left of the Abruzzi Spur) to within a few metres of the Shoulder. There were no successes in 1984, and 1985's eleven summiteers all climbed the original route: one of the eleven died descending. Then came 1986 a year about which much (some objectionable, some probably actionable) has been written. The facts are that nine expeditions were given permission for K2, many of them for the original route, and some of the others transferring to that route when their intended climb proved too difficult. Two Americans Alan Pennington and John Smolich were killed by an avalanche on 21 June, but two days later six people reached the top. Wanda Rutkiewicz made the first female ascent followed shortly after by Liliane Barrard making the second. Liliane climbed with her husband Maurice, but the pair were killed during their descent. On 5 July eight more climbers summitted, all along the original route, these including Benôit Chamoux who climbed the route in 23 hours, and Josef Rakoncaj, climbing K2

population meant the Japanese had two teams, one of high altitude climbers, the other of support climbers who ferried loads to the mountain. The lead climbers followed the 45° north ridge, setting camps and fixing ropes, but deviated from the ridge towards the summit, climbing an obvious snow field to the left. High on the peak they met a Polish team which was attempting the north-west ridge from Pakistan, but had been forced into China by the difficulties of their route. The encounter led to a high-level protest by the Chinese: the Poles failed to reach the top which is, perhaps, just as well. The Japanese did summit, Naoé Sakashita, Yukihiro Yanagisawa and Hiroshi Yoshino reaching the top on 14 August with four more Japanese following them the next day. All the Japanese climbed solo and without bottled oxygen. All seven were forced to bivouac on their descent and sadly Yanagisawa, after a bivouac without a down jacket or sleeping bag, fell and was killed.

for the second time. To date he is the only climber to have sumitted more than once. Given the reputation of the mountain it is likely that those who do achieve multiple ascents will remain a select band.

On 8 July Jerzy Kukuczka and Tadeusz Piotrowski summitted having completed an astonishing climb on the south face. The two Poles had been members of Dr Karl-Maria Herrligkoffer's international expedition, the other members of which (apart from the German Toni Freudig) had decided the face was too hard and too dangerous and had gone off to climb the original route, two Swiss members summitting on 5 July. It was this expedition which prompted Kukuczka's famous comparison of western and Polish expeditions, claiming they were similar to their cars: the western vehicle is better on good roads, but the old Polish model keeps going when the road gets rough. Most of those who have quoted the remark see it as a

The Gasherbrum peaks and Broad Peak from high on the Abruzzi Spur

comment on expeditions in general, but Kukuczka actually meant it as applying to the climbers not the organisation, being scathing of prima donna western climbers who retreat at the first sign of danger, extreme difficulties or bad weather. It is a very controversial view, which may explain why it has been so frequently mis-assigned, but the fact that most of the very hard climbs at high altitude are now accomplished by teams from ex-eastern bloc countries would seem to support it. Of the western nations, only Japan consistently produces climbers which operate at the highest levels of difficulty rather than making very fast ascents of explored lines. There are exceptions, of course (and it must be said that most of the pioneering climbs on the peaks were completed by western climbers), but these are notable chiefly because of their scarcity.

With Freudig's help the Poles climbed the face to just below a serac barrier that had frightened off previous expeditions and their own team-mates. Then, without Freudig they established an equipment dump at 7,000m (23,000ft). After a ten-day delay due to bad weather Kukuczka and Piotrowski returned to the face. It took two days to reach their dump, two more to reach the final headwall. On this they also spent two days, on the first of which Kukuczka, in the lead, climbed only 30m (100ft) of what he later described as the hardest climbing he had ever done at altitude. At their bivouac the Poles dropped their last gas cylinder, but used a candle to melt a mug of water. The next day they summitted and descended towards the shoulder, but were forced to bivouac again. Now, in appalling weather and badly dehydrated they continued to descend towards the camps on the original route, but Piotrowski lost his crampons and immediately slipped off the mountain. Kukuczka made it down safely: K2 had been his eleventh 8,000er and the one which took him closest to the limit.

A few days after the Poles completed their climb the Italian Renato Casarotto fell into a crevasse and died while descending from an attempted solo of the 'Magic Line'. The number of deaths on the peak had risen from 12 to 18, but 1986 was not over yet. A few weeks later a group of climbers gathered in a camp (Camp IV) on the Shoulder. On 1 August three Austrians, Willy Bauer, Alfred Imitzer and Hannes Wieser arrived at the camp and on 2 August they made a summit bid, being forced to retreat from 8,400m (27,600ft). On return to the camp they met three Koreans (Chang Bong-Wan, Chang Byong-Ho, and Kim Chang-Sun), Austrian Kurt Diemberger and Briton Julie Tullis (from an Italian expedition), Alan Rouse (sole remaining member of an expedition he had led) and a Polish woman, Dobroslawa Wolf, known as Mrówka (Ant), from a team that was attempting to climb the south-south-west ridge (Magic Line). The ten climbers shared three tents which should have accommodated just seven. On 3 August the three Koreans climbed to the summit, two returning to Camp IV, one being forced to bivouac at the Bottleneck. The others at Camp IV decided to rest, a dubious decision since it is known that above 8,000m (26,247ft) rest cannot compensate for the body's deterioration. To make matters worse the nine at Camp IV (one Korean bivouacing higher) were joined by two other climbers.

On 3 August the Poles Przemyslaw Piasecki and Wojciech Wröz and the Czech Peter Bozik had completed the Magic Line, an under-rated climb whose completion was overshadowed by the subsequent tragedy. Wröz fell to his

The Chinese (north) side of K2

Nick Escourt leads two other team mebers on the west ridge during the 1978 British expedition

Battling through deep snow on the west ridge

death as the three descended the original route, but the surviving pair made a total of eleven in Camp IV which had been overcrowded with 10. On 4 August the two Poles and the three Koreans descended, while Bauer, Imitzer, Diemberger, Tullis, Rouse and Wolf (Mrówka) went for the summit. Wieser, who was not strong enough for another summit bid, declined to descend with the Poles, preferring to wait for his team-mates. Of the six, all but Mrówka summitted, but Diemberger and Tullis, who were lucky to survive a long fall on the descent, were forced to bivouac above Camp IV. A storm now trapped the seven climbers at Camp IV for five days during which time Julie Tullis died. On 10 August, knowing that further delay would be fatal, five climbers set out to descend during a break in the weather: the delirious Rouse was left at Camp IV. On the descent Imitzer and Wieser stopped and died close to Camp IV, Mrówka on the fixed ropes lower down. Only the frostbitten Bauer and Diemberger made it to Base Camp. The accusations and counter-accusations over this tragedy rumble on. (For Diemberger's account see *K2 – The Endless Knot*.)

If the Polish ascent of the Magic Line was overshadowed by the tragedy so too was the claimed solo ascent by Tomo Cesen of the south-south-east spur. Cesen climbed the route to the Shoulder, reaching it on 4 August, but did not attempt to reach either the summit or Camp IV before descending the Abruzzi Spur. The climb was controversial because Cesen claimed a new route, though virtually (actually?) all of it had been climbed by Scott's team in 1983, and many doubted his claim. His unseen descent of the original route was possible

(no one was moving on it that day) and supported his story (why claim decent of a well-known route, risking possible non-sightings by other climbers, when he could claim a descent of his deserted ascent route?), but though Cesen's claim is now accepted by many it is still classed as dubious by some.

During the next four years there were no further ascents of K2, but there were many failures. A Swiss-Polish team failed on the west face, two teams failed on the east face and a Polish team failed in a winter attempt of the original route. Then in 1990 a Japanese team climbed a new route on the north side while a four man Australian-American team put three men on the summit along the 1982 Japanese north ridge route, a fine effort. The next year Pierre Beghin and Christophe Profit completed the Polish north-west ridge/north-west face/north ridge route in an epic 40-day climb. The pair reached the summit as night fell on 15 August, the flash bulbs of their ritual photos being seen by trekkers at Concordia.

1992 and 1993 were more successful years, seven climbers following the original route to the top in 92, 14 in 93. The total to the top in 1993 was 16, the Briton Jonathan Pratt and American Dan Mazur following the Japanese west ridge route in an epic climb: the summit climb and descent took 32 hours from their top camp. In 1994 a Basque team completed the south-south-east spur route to the top, but they used fixed ropes on a route which Scott and, probably, Cesen, climbed without. There were successes on the original route and the north ridge too, but tragedy struck three Ukrainians on the original. Two weeks after their summit bid the remains of one were found below the Bottleneck and the other two were found dead in a bivouac at 8,400m (27,600ft). It is assumed that they were on their way down – bivouacs on the way to the summit are rare – but did they reach the top?

There was further tragedy in 1995. After successful climbs

in July, six climbers summitted late on 13 August, their ascents confirmed by radio. As they descended a vicious wind strafed the peak and, it is assumed, blew the Spaniards Javier Escartin, Javier Olivar and Lorenzo Ortiz, the Briton Alison Hargreaves, the American Rob Slater and the Canadian Bruce Grant to their deaths. The same year a German commercial expedition failed to climb the north ridge.

In 1996 Japanese climber Masafumi Todaka soloed the original route (though there were several teams on the line at the same time and on the summit on the same day) after he had failed to solo the 1986 Kukuczka/Piotrowski route and a Japanese team repeated of the 1994 Basque route on the south-south-east spur, twelve Japanese reaching the top after fixing 4km (2½ miles) of rope. The Japanese reached the summit in two groups of six on 12 and 14 August, a team of four Chileans who had also climbed the route summitting on 13 August. The Japanese were back in 1997, this time fixing 3km (2 miles) of rope in completing a variant to the west face route.

Seven Japanese and four Sherpas – using oxygen above 7,500m (24,600ft) for reasons of safety – reached the summit. It was the first time Sherpas had climbed in the Karakoram since 1939 and were only allowed into Pakistan because they were added to the Japanese permit as climbers. It was also to be the last climb of the century. In 1998 and 1999 K2 repulsed everyone who had made the long trip along the Baltoro, though there was a significant attempt by Hans Kammerlander in 1999. He reached about 8,400m (27,000) on the Basque route with the intention of skiing down from the summit. He vowed to return.

By the end of the century the number of successful summiteers on K2 was approaching 200, a remarkable number for so difficult and dangerous a mountain, one which illustrates the unique fascination of this beautiful peak. But the statistics go on to show that the chances of being killed on the descent from the summit are about 1 in 7, a frighteningly high ratio, but one which is unlikely to dissuade future climbers.

The summit of K2 looking north east

cho oyu 8,201m

"In the red glow of the setting sun I reached the summit. Doing so I experienced a wonderful feeling, as one step took me into another world. The steep walls and the knife-edged ridges vanished, it was as if I had stepped out of a dark and dangerous canyon onto a plateau bathed in purple light."

JERZY KUKUCZKA

cho oyu

Despite its vast bulk – it is the sixth highest mountain in the world – the British India Survey did not at first assign Cho Oyu a peak number. Though it was eventually assigned T45 (later changed to M1) it must have originally seemed a minor peak among the giants that spread across the Nepalese horizon from Makalu to Dhaulagiri.

The name is now invariably stated to mean 'Goddess of Turquoise', the peak glowing turquoise when seen from Tibet in the light of an afternoon sun (and, as any visitor to Tibet soon realises, turquoise is a favourite stone of the Tibetans). As goddess is chomo in Tibetan, and turquoise is yu, the contraction of chomo yu to Cho Oyu seems conclusive, but it is worth noting that this derivation is by no means certain. A lama at Namche Bazar told Herbert Tichy that the name meant 'Mighty Head' and Heinrich Harrer claimed that the real name was cho-i-u meaning 'god's head'. Harrer's suggestion is interesting because many early books have the peak's name as Cho Uyo which would be a

good phonetic approximation of the three Tibetan syllables. Harrer's name is also close to the alternative Tibetan translation of the name as 'bald god'. In Tibetan legend Cho Oyu, the bald god, has his back turned to Chomolungma, the mother goddess, because she refused to marry him.

Exploration

Prior to 1921 little notice was taken of the mountain even though it had certainly been observed many times. In that year Howard-Bury's Everest reconnaissance, heading south from Tingri, reached the Nangpa La, to the west of the peak and obtained several good photographs of it from both the west and

Above Cho Oyu from the Tibetan plateau near Tingri. *Right* Camp II on the classic route

Above From West
A Point 7570
1 First ascent/'classic' route (1954)
2 SW Ridge, first climbed (in part) by the Polish (1986), but in its entirety by an

international team (1993)
Below From North
1 Yugoslavians (1988)
2 Kotov/Pierson (1997)
3 Spanish (1996)

Above From South 1 Poles (winter 1985)
2 East Ridge (skyline to right of summit), Soviets (1991)
Below South-west Face
A Summit **B** Gyabrag Lho Glacier

C Point 7570 **1** First ascent (1954)
2 SW ridge, Polish (1986), international team (1993) **3** Yamanoi solo (1994)
4 Kurtyka/Loretan/Troillet (1990)

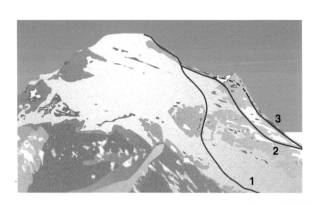

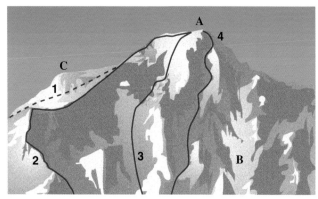

the north-west. It was also photographed on the Houston Everest flight of 1933. However with access through Nepal denied it was not until 1951 that the approaches to the mountain were explored. The main objective of the 1951 British reconnaissance under Eric Shipton was an exploration of the Nepalese side of Everest as a prelude to an assumed British expedition in 1952. Shipton's team included several who were to take part in the 1953 British Expedition – including Edmund Hillary. The team tried, but failed, to reach the Nup La to the east of Cho Oyu, but from close to it saw no easy route from that side.

In 1952 Shipton returned with a stronger team intent on continuing the exploration of Cho Oyu (the Swiss being on Everest) and, if possible, climbing it. The main purpose of the expedition, however, was to test oxygen, equipment

Pasang Dawa Lama on the summit after the first ascent

and personnel for the 1953 Everest attempt. This time the Nup La was climbed, but the view of Cho Oyu reinforced the opinion formed in 1951. The expedition then went to the west side of the peak, climbing the Nangpa La. From here it was clear that a route existed from the north-west. But on that side of the mountain lay an undefined border between Nepal and Tibet. The Chinese were now occupying Tibet and, rumour had it, were already just a short distance to the north. If his team were discovered by Chinese soldiers in an area that might form part of a border dispute Shipton was fearful that the Nepalese might react by cancelling the British 1953 permit for Everest. By contrast Hillary was of the view that as the climbers would at all times be above 5,700m (18,700ft) there was no possibility of detection. In the end Hillary and George Lowe (who was also on Everest in 1953) made an attempt, reaching a height of about 6,800m (22,400ft) where they were stopped by an ice fall. Realising that to overcome this, and to fix it with ropes so that Sherpas could carry loads through it, would take greater resources than they had at their disposal, they retreated.

First Ascent

Herbert Tichy was born in 1912 and studied geology at

Early morning sun illuminates the southern flanks of Cho Oyu, seen over Gokyo Tsho beside the Ngozumpa Glacier

Cho Oyu from the north on the Tibetan plateau

university, completing his doctorate at Vienna with a thesis on Himalayan geology, with practical work carried out in Tibet in 1936. During the winter of 1953/54 he went on a private expedition to western Nepal accompanied by the Sherpas Pasang Dawa Lama (who had almost climbed K2 with Wiessner in 1939), Adjiba and Gyalsen. The four climbed several 6,100m peaks (20,000ft) and discussed the possibility of climbing something bigger. On his return to Austria in January 1954 Tichy applied for permission to attempt Cho Oyu and this was granted in April. With two friends, Sepp Jochler, a

brilliant climber who had accompanied Hermann Buhl on the Eiger's north wall, and Helmut Heuberger, a geographer from the University of Innsbruck, Tichy returned to Nepal in late August. The three-man, nominally leaderless, team were accompanied by seven Sherpas – Tichy's three west Nepal companions plus four others – with Pasang Dawa Lama as sirdar. The team carried two oxygen cylinders for emergency use and limited medical equipment: though Tichy and Heuberger were Dr Tichy and Dr Heuberger, neither was a medic. In his book of the expedition Tichy notes the advice given to him by a surgeon before the trip on the use of a scalpel for the amputation of severely frost-bitten fingers or toes – 'press hard and then make as clean a cut as possible'.

Though he was an oil geologist, Tichy had worked for a short time as a journalist and despite his self-deprecating view of his literary abilities his expedition book is a marvellous read, a fairy-tale of a story. While later books have tended to concentrate on the drudgery of approach marches Tichy found the walk-in a joy. Indeed, the climb is the middle, almost incidental, section of a book that explores eastern Nepal. There are profound insights – the difference between porters and Sherpas is that the former live longer, the latter more proudly – and unexpected hilarity – the team bought a sheep which they walked (dog-like on a lead, the Sherpas vying with each other for the privilege of holding its rope and everyone looking for good grass patches for it to feed on) for several days before it changed from companion to evening meal.

As with Shipton, Tichy was concerned about trespassing into Tibet from the Nangpa La, but took the view that discovery was unlikely. From a Base Camp at about 5,500m (18,000ft) the team rapidly climbed up to the ice cliffs which had stopped

Approaching Camp II

Camp II below the classic route on Cho Oyu

Hillary and Lowe, Tichy doing much of the work as Jochler was slow in acclimatising and Heuberger seems content to have played a supporting role. To Tichy's amazement he, Pasang and Adjiba climbed through the ice fall in an hour. Deciding that a fixed rope was necessary the trio tried to fix long wooden pegs at the top of the fall, but found the snow beneath the ice too rotten to hold them. The problem was solved by the three urinating on the pegs, the cold rapidly creating a solid, and presumably yellow, anchor. The next day Tichy and five Sherpas climbed up and established a camp (Camp IV) at about 6,930m (22,750ft). Here Tichy and three of the Sherpas stayed, intending to make a summit bid the following day.

The following morning it was cloudless but bitingly cold, with a fierce wind threatening to sweep tents and climbers from the mountains. The four climbers dressed and left the tents which were immediately blown flat by the wind. The Sherpas were convinced they would all die, Pasang repeating this view over and over. Then, as the wind threatened to blow one tent away, Tichy flung himself across it burying his hands in the snow as an anchor. He was gloveless and within seconds his fingers were frozen. He thrust his hands between the thighs of Pasang and Adjiba, but the pain was so bad he could barely think rationally. Fortunately the accident galvanised the Sherpas who packed the tents and began an epic descent. Tichy was lowered down the ice cliffs and the team successfully reached Camp III where Sepp Jochler, now fully fit, met them. The team retreated to Base Camp, sending Pasang off to Namche Bazar for supplies.

As they rested at base two figures were seen approaching. Tichy nervously assumed that they were Chinese soldiers, but it was Mde Claude Kogan and another member of a Swiss team, led by Raymond Lambert, that the Austrians had met in Kathmandu. The Swiss had intended to climb Gauri Sankar, but finding it too hard they had decided to climb Cho Oyu instead. Tichy was appalled and pointed out that he, not they, had the permit for the mountain. During discussions that became increasingly acrimonious the Swiss refused to back down and the Austrians refused to join forces. Sepp Jochler was particularly adamant over the latter: they had come as a small team to climb the peak and he preferred failure to compromise. Tichy suggested that the Austrians be allowed one attempt before the Swiss tried, but Lambert declined: it was late autumn, winter's storm would start soon, delays were out of the question. Eventually an unsatisfactory arrangement was reached, the Austrians being given a few days start on the climb. This gave Tichy his first try, but with the Swiss preparing their route as he did.

With no time for the healing of his frost-bitten hands and no time to wait for Pasang's return with supplies the Austrians started up again. They climbed up to their old Camp III below the ice cliffs and excavated a snow cave in case the wind increased again. In the cave Heuberger practised his injection skills on Tichy, hoping to reduce the final frostbite damage, while Jochler and the Sherpas re-established Camp IV. On their return they discovered that the Swiss had placed their own fixed rope on the ice fall – the race had become serious. The next day Pasang reached the cave, grey with the fatigue of a long, fast climb. The team, including Tichy despite his inability to use his hands, now climbed towards Camp IV. To their relief the vicious wind had cleared loose snow from the mountain leaving a hard snow base that made cramponing easy. They moved Camp IV a little higher – to about 6,980m (22,900ft) – but fearing a change in the weather and the Swiss, who could not be far behind, they decided to attempt a long climb for the summit rather than establishing another camp. The plan was for Jochler and Pasang to make the attempt, but late in the evening Tichy decided to join them. The three left camp at 6am, finding the snow still perfect for rapid movement. Despite being 1,220m (4,000ft) from the summit they arrived just below it at 3pm. Pasang Dawa Lama, who was leading at the time, stopped and the three, arm in arm, walked up on to the vast snow dome top – large enough to accommodate ball games – that is the culmination of the huge summit plateau. It was the first post-monsoon ascent of an 8,000er and the first by such a small team.

Pasang Dawa Lama's climb was remarkable: in three days he had climbed from 4,250m (14,000ft) to the summit. On the descent it became clear why: Pasang had bartered a bride in Lukla, agreeing with her father that there would be no price for her (bridegrooms pay compensation to the father for the loss of a daughter in Nepal) if he climbed Cho Oyu, but would pay 1,000 rupees, a vast sum, if he failed. The final chapter of

High on the classic route

Tichy's book deals with Pasang's wedding. Tichy later maintained that for several weeks on their return from the peak the whole team, Austrians and Sherpas alike, were 'either tipsy or completely plastered'. This sustained re-hydration also helped his frostbite injuries which were less serious than he had feared. Ironically in view of the race they had precipitated, the Swiss attempt on Cho Oyu failed, Lambert and Mde Kogan being defeated by high winds at about 7,500m (24,600ft).

Later Ascents

Pasang Dawa Lama climbed Cho Oyu again in 1958, this time as sirdar of an Indian expedition, making the second ascent with Sonam Gyatso. This expedition resulted in the first death on the mountain, Maj ND Jayal, the first Director of the Himalayan Mountaineering Institute in Darjeeling (an organisation set up by Nehru to capitalise on Tenzing's fame after Everest: Tenzing coveted the directorship but was made Chief Instructor, an appointment he resented) dying of pulmonary oedema low on the mountain.

In 1959 an International Woman's Expedition (French, British, Belgium, Swiss and Nepalese) led by Mde Claude Kogan attempted to repeat the original route. Kogan, the Belgian climber Claudine van der Stratten and Sherpa Ang Norbu established Camp IV at 7,100m (23,300ft) but were then pinned down by a storm. In trying to reach them two Sherpas (Wangdi and Chhowang) were hit by an avalanche. Wangdi managed to dig himself out, but was unable to reach his colleague. Subsequently another avalanche destroyed Camp IV killing the three inhabitants. There were further deaths five years later during an expedition which has a much-disputed claim to Cho Oyu's third ascent. The German Fritz Stammberger claimed to have reached the summit alone on 25 April 1964, but the Sherpa Phu Dorje claims to have been with him. The 'summit' photographs were almost certainly not taken at the top, nor at the time Stammberger claims to have reached it. Two other team members, after failing in their summit attempt reached the top camp exhausted and unable to descend. A rescue attempt found one dead, the other dying on the descent.

Snow picked up by high winds obscure the view of the classic route

For more than a decade Cho Oyu remained undisturbed, but then in 1978 two Austrians (Furtner and Koblmüller), visiting the region on a trekking permit, claimed to have climbed a new route on the south-east face. This unsanctioned ascent was discounted by many, but not by the Nepalese who banned the pair for several years. Only in 1981, 17 years after the disputed third ascent was a team granted a permit to attempt the peak again, a Nepalese/Japanese team attempting (and failing) on the east face and, subsequently, on the south ridge. The following year an attempt to complete a legitimate ascent of the south-east face ended when Reinhard Karl, one of Germany's foremost climbers (the first German to climb Everest) was killed by an avalanche.

In 1983, having failed in a bid to climb Cho Oyu in winter via the south-east face (in December 1982), Reinhold Messner successfully completed a part-new route on the south-west side reaching the summit with Hans Kammerlander and Michl Dacher. The trio climbed the peak in alpine style, reaching the

Dawn light catches the neighbouring frontier peak of Cho Aui (7,352m/24,121ft); view is to the south west from about 7,600m (25,000ft) on Cho Oyu

top on 5 May after three bivouacs. They were back at Base Camp on 7 May, five days after leaving it. Cho Oyu was Messner's tenth 8,000er. Messner's line was repeated in 1984 by the Czechs Vera Komarkova and Margita Dina Sterbova making the first women's ascent. 1984 also saw a failed attempt to climb the east ridge by a semi-commercial team and a post-monsoon attempt on the south-east buttress, a Yugoslavian team reaching 7,600m (24,900ft) on the latter. This route involved 1,400m (4,600ft) of climbing on a pillar of rock at an average angle of 60°. The team – all Slovenes, a fact which is much more important in today's Balkans than it was at the time – overcame all the difficulties, but were then defeated by winds gusting to 130km/h (80mph). The route was completed on February 1985, a Polish team claiming not only its first winter ascent, but the first winter ascent of Cho Oyu, the first ever winter first ascent of an 8,000er, if a sentence can be allowed to have so many 'firsts' in it. The summit was reached by Maciej Berbeka and Maciej Pawlikowski, then by Zygmunt Heinrich and Jerzy Kukuczka. Kukuczka was successfully claiming his eighth 8,000er and finally admitting that he was in

a race with Messner for first man to climb all 14 peaks. However, Kukuczka had no interest in repeating the easy lines to claim the prize, wanting to complete either new routes or first winter ascents. This, and the fact that Messner was already a couple of peaks ahead having begun his campaign almost a decade earlier (he had climbed five before Kukuczka's first), meant Kukuczka's challenge was never very realistic, though at one stage he had climbed eleven peaks to Messner's 12.

Later in 1985 there were several more ascents, including one by a Chinese team. They followed the original route, reversing the trespass of Tichy's team by climbing into Nepal. In December of the same year the second winter ascent was accomplished alpine style by two Czechs (Jaromir Stejskal and Dusan Becik) from an American-Canadian-Czech team, the first alpine style winter ascent of an 8,000er. A new route was established in 1986, a Polish team climbing the lower section of the south-west buttress, joining the normal route at about 7,750m (25,400ft). An

international team climbed a variation of this route soon after, Peter Habeler and Marcel Rüedi being the first of seven climbers to reach the summit.

Over subsequent years Cho Oyu became popular with climbers seeking high altitude experience, its reputation as the 'easiest' 8,000er being firmly established by the mid-1980s. It was also an early candidate for fully commercial expeditions, one led by the Austrian Marcus Schmuck climbing a partially new route from the Tibetan side in 1987. Not all the hazards met by climbers were weather or mountain-based however, members of American and Chilean teams which followed the original route, and therefore crossed into Tibet, having their equipment, passports and permits confiscated.

In February 1988 Fernando Garrido climbed the original route solo, the first winter solo of an 8,000er. Despite the mountain being (relatively) easy, Garrido's climb was a remarkable achievement, the Spaniard braving high winds, temperatures down to minus 40°C and being forced to bivouac on his descent. Equally remarkable was Frenchman Marc Batard's ascent with the Sherpa Sungdare in the early

September 1988, the pair reaching the summit in 18 hours from Base Camp despite having to break trail throughout the climb, theirs being the first post-monsoon ascent. On the same expedition Bruno Gouvy on snowboard, Véronique Périllat on monoski and Michel Vincent and Eric Decamp on skis descended from summit to base camp. At the same time Bruno Cormier paraglided down, the first descent from such a height without the aid of people to help him open the canopy. Cormier had next planned to parachute on to the summit of Everest and snowboard down to base camp. He was killed before this ambitious, not to say unlikely, scheme could be put into action.

Climbers at around 7,500m (24,600ft) on the classic route

Soon after the ski descents a Yugoslavian team climbed a new and very hard route on the north face, while seven teams were successful on the original route. In the final stages of the climb the Yugoslavs split into two teams, some taking a direct route to the top, the others traversing on to the original route. Iztok Tomazin, who made the direct climb, climbed down the original route, thus making the first traverse. Another first, one

Cho Oyu from the north in evening light

of more dubious merit, occurred in the winter of 89/90 when two teams given permits for the south-east face ended up fighting each other over priority on the route.

Post-monsoon in 1990 the Swiss pair Erhard Loretan and Jean Troillet, together with the Pole Wojciech Kurtyka, climbed a new route on the south-west face, to the right of the Polish buttress. Starting at 6pm they climbed though the night reaching a point 100m below the summit by the following night. They bivouaced, then continued to the summit at first light and descended the original route, a masterpiece of sustained climbing. The following year, also post-monsoon, a Russian/Ukrainian team succeeded in climbing the east ridge, the 'last great problem' which had resisted several attempts. Five members of a 20 strong party reached the top on 20 October 1991, the sixth member of the summit party stopping when he became concerned over his frostbitten fingers. After his colleagues rejoined him he was unfortunately killed by rockfall.

In February 1993 the peak was climbed by a Spanish team which included one Argentinian and the Swiss woman

Marianne Chapuisat. The team used neither Sherpas nor bottled oxygen, Chapuisat claiming the first winter female ascent of any 8,000er. Also in 1993 the south-west buttress, first attempted and partially climbed in 1986, was climbed by an Italian/Polish/Portugeuse team approaching from the north. They found the route easier than they had anticipated. The team, which included Krzysztof Wielicki, then went on to climb Shisha Pangma.

A sign of the times was a winter ascent of the original route in January 1994 by a team organised by advertising in the climbing press. Two reached the top, but the teams also suffered two deaths. Later in 1994, while most climbers were attempting the normal route there were two fine climbs on the south-west face. Two Japanese women, Taeko Nagao and Yuka Endo, climbed the Loretan/Kurtyka/Troillet 1990 route alpine-style in four days, while at the same time Yasushi Yamanoi soloed a route to the left in two days. Less fortunate were two Serbian climbers who crossed the Nangpa La into Tibet to climb the W ridge. Chinese officials attempted to arrest them, but they climbed rapidly upwards. The Serbians failed to reached the top and were arrested when they descended. The standard practice on the mountain was now to buy a Nepalese permit, approach from Kathmandu, which virtually allows a drive to base camp, then to cross the border into Tibet to climb the easiest route. But from June 1994 the Chinese stationed an official at Nangpa La and charged $2,000 per climber for the border crossing. The first teams to arrive declined to pay, but many later climbers did.

In 1995 Ang Rita summitted for the fourth time (at that time he had also climbed Everest nine times – now ten – Dhaulagiri four times and Kangchenjunga once). The same year the New Zealand guide Guy Cotter was arrested in Lhasa after sending a fax in which he said he had heard a bomb explode and seen speeding army vehicles. He was held in prison for several days, then forced to confess to his 'crime' and deported to Nepal. This may have been the most spectacular aspect of a Cho Oyu expedition of the year, but the undoubted highlight was the ascent by the Briton Norman Croucher who, as a teenager had both legs amputated below the knee by a train after an accident on a railway line. Croucher climbs with artificial legs, his ascent being the first ascent of an 8,000er by so disabled a climber. On the descent he was forced to bivouac, his disability understandably slowing his progress, but was able to do so in his rucsac by removing his lower limbs!

The summit was reached in eleven hours from base camp in 1996 by the New Zealander Russell Brice: he was back in base camp within 24 hours. Then, in the post-monsoon season of the same year, a Spanish/Austrian team climbed a new route along the north-north-west ridge from the Palung La, the Spaniard Oscar Cadiach and the Austrian Sebastian Ruckensteiner climbing in alpine style and reaching the summit on 28 September. Another new route was climbed in 1997 when the Russian Georgi Kotov and the American Bill Pierson, a client climber on a commercial expedition, who climbed a line close to that of Cadiach and Ruckensteiner.

Cho Oyu is now firmly established as the favourite mountain for commercial expedition clients wanting to add an 8,000er to their list of achievements. Only Everest has received more ascents, but interestingly Cho Oyu has had more climbers reach its summit, the multiple ascents of Everest by many climbers distorting the true picture. It would be interesting to speculate how many of these ascents have been by climbers who reach the edge of the huge summit plateau and turn around, not wishing to spend the long time necessary to reach the true summit which is just a few metres higher. It is rumoured that there are those among the aspirants for all 14 8,000ers who have done exactly that. The test, apparently, is to look for the Everest massif: if you cannot see it then you have not reached the top. Of course if the weather is bad …

Last light on the final slopes of Cho Oyu I. The classic route heads up the centre of the this face to reach a wide summit plateau

makalu 8,463m

'The shattered granite offered plenty of holds and, no doubt due to the force and frequency of the wind, there was astonishingly little snow or verglas.'

LIONEL TERRAY

makalu

Makalu was Peak XIII of the Indian Survey, the survey suggesting, in 1884, that its name was Khamba Lung. This seems to have derived from the local area being called Khamba, though the valley to the north of the peak was called Kama Lung (the valley of the River Kama).

Some have suggested that Makalu derives from Kama Lung, the first word having its syllabus transposed. This is a very unconvincing argument and it is far more likely to derive from the Sanskrit Maha Kala, meaning 'great weather' from the mountain's isolated and dominant position in an area renowned for its winds. The Hindu god Shiva, the destroyer, is associated with extremes of weather and the mountain may have been named in deference to him. Interestingly Maha Kala (with an exact or very similar spelling) is Tibetan for 'great black' which is an excellent description of the huge rock pyramid after it has been scoured clean of snow by the wind.

Exploration

The peak was seen and photographed by Howard-Bury's 1921 Everest reconnaissance which explored the Kama Valley and the Kangshung Glacier, heading south from Kharta in Tibet. Wanting to see into Nepal Howard-Bury climbed from the Kangshung on to the ridge below Pethangtse, reaching a height which he estimated at 6,550m (21,500ft). As Pethangtse is only a little over 6,700m (22,000ft) this seems unlikely, more recent research suggesting Howard-Bury probably did not quite reach 6,000m (20,000ft). Nonetheless he had a good view of Makalu's north face (the route of the final part of the first ascent) and glimpsed the west face. In 1933 the Houston flight obtained good photographs of the south and west faces. The west face was also photographed in 1951 and 1952 by Eric Shipton's Everest reconnaissance and Cho Oyu expeditions. In 1952 Shipton, Hillary, Lowe and Evans followed the Barun Glacier to the base of Pethangtse getting a close up view of the west face.

The French has negotiated permission for an attempt on Makalu from Tibet as early as 1934 but the Tibetans had changed their minds before any significant planning was underway. When the British climbed Everest in 1953 the French, who had permission for an attempt in 1954, again turned their attention to the peak. To their surprise and dismay they discovered that Nepal had already given permits to two other groups, one American, the other a New Zealand team under Ed (by then Sir Edmund) Hillary. The French therefore applied for permission for 1955, but also accepted an offer to reconnoitre the peak post-monsoon in 1954.

The Americans – a ten-man group from the Californian Sierra Club led by Dr William Siri and including Dr William Unsoeld who later made the first ascent of Everest's west ridge – arrived on the Barun Glacier in early April. They prospected the south-east and north-

Camp III on the south-east ridge, Californian 1954 Expedition. Baruntse (7,220m/23,688ft) beyond

west ridges, favouring the former along which they placed several camps, but bad weather prevented them from getting above 7,150m (23,460ft). The New Zealand team arrived later, but without Hillary who had broken several ribs during the rescue of another team member from a crevasse. The team explored the northern Barun Glacier towards Pethangtse and also climbed towards the Makalu La (the col between the main summit and Makalu II – also known as Kangchungtse). On this latter climb Hillary, now back with his team, became suddenly, and seriously, ill, the whole team being required to organise his evacuation.

When the French arrived in September, therefore, Makalu was only marginally better explored than it had been pre-war. The French team reached the Makalu La and climbed both Kangchungtse (7,640m/25,066ft) and Chomo Lonzo, both offering a good view of the north face. The climb of Chomo Lonzo, a 7,790m (25,558ft) peak, was a notable achievement, particularly as it was climbed in the teeth of a gale with temperatures down to minus 35°C. In his autobiography Lionel Terray, who made the climb with Jean Couzy, claims it was one of his toughest, most intense, yet memorable and wonderful days, and certainly gives the impression that Chomo Lonzo was climbed for the fun of it rather than as a viewpoint. Nevertheless, the post-monsoon expedition identified the route which would be taken on the first ascent.

First Ascent

As with the post-monsoon team of 1954, the spring 1955 French team was led by Jean Franco. Jean Couzy and Lionel Terray, veterans of Annapurna as well as the 1954 trip, were joined by Jean Bouvier, Serge Coupé, Pierre Leroux. Guido Magnone (who, with Terray, had

MAKALU: ASCENT ROUTES

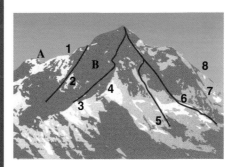

From West

From South-east

West Face

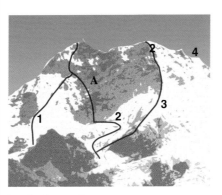

From South

From Makalu La

From West
A *Makalu Col*
B *West face*
1 *NW Ridge, Kukuczka (1981)*
2 *Polish/Brazilian (1982)*
3 *Russians (1997)*
4 *West Ridge/Pillar, French (1971)*
5 *Yugoslavians (1975)*
6 *Beghin (1989)*
7 *South Pillar, Czech (1976)*
8 *SE Ridge, Japanese (1970)*

From South-east
A *South Face*
1 *SE Ridge, Japanese (1970)*
2 *E Ridge, Japanese (1995)*

West Face
1 *Polish/Brazilian (1982)*
2 *Russians (1997)*
3 *West Pillar, French (1971)*
4 *NW Ridge, Kukuczka solo (1981)*

From South
1 *Yugoslavians (1975)*
2 *Beghin (1989)*
3 *S Pillar, Czechs (1976)*
4 *SE Ridge, Japanese (1970)*

From Makalu La
1 *First ascent, French; 'classic' route (1955)*
2 *NW Ridge, Kukuczka solo (1981)*

Jean Couzy on the summit, photographed by Lionel Terray

climbed Fitzroy in Patagonia in 1952, heralding an advance in difficulty for routes on remote peaks, and had also been in the team which climbed the west face of the Dru) and André Vialatte. André Lapras was the team doctor and two geologists, Pierre Bordet and Michel Latreille, accompanied the expedition. The team had no less than 23 Sherpas under sirdar Gyalzen Norbu and a Gurkha soldier, Kindjock Tsering, who acted as a high-altitude porter. The team's equipment showed a step change from that of previous expeditions to the great peaks. Though the base layers were knitted jersey rather than man-made fibre, the one-piece down suits (weighing 800g/1¾lb) were very similar to modern suits, though they needed to be covered with a windproof nylon shell. The French also had improved oxygen sets, based on the British Everest design, but lighter. The vast number of oxygen bottles they took allowed them to use supplementary oxygen from low on the mountain and at high flow rates, and to sleep on bottled gas too, facts which doubtless contributed to the final outcome. The weather also played its part. Though the early stages of the climb were pushed through in indifferent weather, the days of the summit attempts were near perfect, cloudless and almost

still. Snow conditions were equally good, with hard, but cramponable snow, rather than the deep stuff which requires arduous trail-making, or bare ice.

The route to the base of the Makalu La was straightforward, but was much harder to the col. Using, in part, ropes they had placed in 1954 the French fixed ropes all the way to the col where they set Camp V. The ropes helped the Sherpas, several carries with large teams establishing a well-equipped camp at the base of the north-west ridge. The ridge was not attempted, a rising traverse being made across the north face to a last camp, Camp VI, at 7,800m (25,600ft). From it, at 7am on 15 May Terray and Couzy set out. They crossed relatively easy ground to the base of a spur which led up to the east ridge. The spur, which had looked formidable from a distance, was straightforward, the pair reaching the summit at about 11am, having taken only four hours over the mountain's final 660m (2,150ft). The summit was amazing, three almost symmetrical ridges (east, south and north-west) meeting at a pencil-sharp point which could be covered by the palm of a climber's hand and on which a man could sit, but barely stand. (As an aside, the map of the peak, its ridges and the route in Franco's book of the expedition places the summit at the wrong place, at the east end of a short north-south route running ridge: it is at the west end of this – the east – ridge.)

On the following day (16 May) Franco, Magnone and sirdar Gyalzen Norbu repeated the climb, also arriving before noon, and on next day (17 May) Bouvier, Coupé, Leroux and Vialatte reached the summit, again before noon. It was the first time that an entire climbing had reached the summit of an 8,000m peak.

After the climb both Terray and Franco noted the anti-climax they felt at the success. Terray stated that 'victory must be bought at a price of suffering and effort, and the clemency of the weather combined with the progress of technique had sold us this one too cheaply for us to appreciate it at its true value'. Similarly, Franco thought that 'in our hearts we felt a little bit let down. Given the perfection of our tools and the continuity of our good luck, one might even have wished for a slightly tougher adversary'. These seem remarkable sentiments. True, the French had great good fortune with the weather – no wind on the hard climb to Makalu La and perfect conditions on each of the three summit climbs: Franco notes that the knife-sharp summit ridge would have been a much stiffer test if it had carried 0.5m (1½ft) of fresh snow or a significant cornice – good equipment, a small army of Sherpas and almost no sickness among the team members (in part due to the abundant use of bottle oxygen from quite low on the peak). But they also had a strong team and excellent organisation, and they had, after all, climbed the fifth highest mountain in the world, virtually at their first attempt. It seems almost as if, after the trauma of Annapurna, with Herzog and Lachenal barely recovered from their injuries, the team were suffering from the guilt that survivors often experience after major disasters. They had wanted to succeed, but were embarrassed by the ease of the success.

Later Ascents

In 1961 Ed Hillary returned to Makalu on an expedition which, starting in the summer of 1960, had, as objectives, a thorough exploration of the Mingbo region, a search for the yeti and a bottled gas-free ascent of the world's fifth highest peak. The expedition climbed Ama Dablam in March 1961, their permit for Makalu being immediately withdrawn by the Nepalese who claimed the climb was illegal. Hillary spent time in Kathmandu arguing (successful) his case and this may have been the reason why, on climbing to Camp III on Makalu on his return, he suffered a stroke and had to be evacuated. The expedition continued, reaching the Makalu La and establishing a top camp at 8,100m (26,600ft). From here Peter Mulgrew, Dr Tom Nevison and the Sherpa Annullu started for the top. Just 110m (360ft) from it Mulgrew suffered a pulmonary embolism necessitating instant evacuation. Lower on the mountain, with Annullu seeking help, Nevison and Mulgrew were forced to bivouac. As Nevison dug a snow cave he contracted pulmonary oedema, The expedition's second doctor – Michael Ward, who had been

The complex south-east ridge of Makalu

on the British Everest team – fell on his way to render help and contracted pneumonia as a complication to his injuries. The retreat now turned to a near rout, Mulgrew eventually being air-lifted to Kathmandu: he subsequently lost both feet and several fingers to frostbite and had other, serious, complications. So bad were his injuries that his name became a by-word for suffering back in New Zealand. In his book on the climb Mulgrew recalls a stranger, not realising who he was, commiserating with him on his injuries and ending by saying '… it could be worse – look at the rough time that bloke Mulgrew had'.

The rarely-seen Tibetan north-east face of Makalu above the Sakyetang Glacier

117

Not until 1970 was the mountain climbed again. In that year a massive Japanese expedition – 20 climbers, 32 Sherpas and over 400 porters – pushed a route up the long south-east ridge. The 'Black Gendarme', the hardest section of the ridge was climbed, but then bypassed on the west face for ease of load carrying. The first attempt on the summit failed in a

On Chamlang a climber looks north east towards Makalu

snowstorm at about 8,380m (27,500ft), the two climbers being forced to bivouac, but returning safely to camp. The second attempt by Yuichi Ozaki and Hajime Tanaka did reach the summit, but required 17 hours of climbing, the pair continuing to the top after their bottled oxygen had been exhausted. They descended safely by moonlight.

The next ascent, in 1971, pioneered another new route to the top, a French team led by Robert Paragot climbing the west ridge which separates the west and south faces. The ridge is more usually called the west pillar after the near vertical section of rock from 7,350m (24,100ft) to 7,700m (25,250ft). This section required climbing of Grade V+ and A2, very hard at sea level, but an advance in difficulty for an altitude of 7,500m (24,600ft). The weather added to the problems, spring 1971 being the worst of the century with heavy snow, very low temperatures and winds of over 150km/h (almost 100mph). Much of the lead climbing was done by Yannick Seigneur and Bernard Mellet, and it was they, using bottled oxygen from the top of the pillar, who reached the summit after two other summit attempts had failed and the third member of their own party had retreated from about 8,300m (27,200ft). For the time, just a year after the ascent of the south face of Annapurna, this was a remarkable climb, one which has not received the credit it deserves.

Over the next four years there were a series of failures on Makalu's south face by strong teams from Austria (a team which included Reinhold Messner), Czechoslovakia (that team reaching over 8,000m/26,247ft) and Yugoslavia. Finally, post-monsoon in 1975 a Yugoslavian team under Ales Kunaver (who had led the earlier attempt) was successful, seven climbers reaching the summit over a five day period in early October. All the summiteers used supplementary oxygen, though one was forced to abandon his set when it failed well below the top. In 1976 the Czechs also returned and completed their south face line, climbing the south-west buttress to the right of the

Yugoslav route. At the same time a Spanish team was attempting the south-east ridge. The teams decided to combine, with the intention of climbing up the Czech line and down the Spanish. The first summit attempt failed in dreadful weather, but the second succeeded, Milan Krissak, Michal Orolin and Karel Schubert being joined by the Spaniard Jorge Camprubi. Orolin retreated when his oxygen set failed, the other three summitting. On the descent they were caught by a storm. The exhausted Schubert insisted on bivouacing, the other two struggling down. Schubert was never seen again.

In 1977 a British/American/Yugoslav team attempted a

Arial view from the north west shows little Kngchungtse, the Makalu La and the north west ridge and face. Chomo Lonzo on the left (7,790m/25,558ft), is actually in Tibet

Sherpa and bottled oxygen free ascent of the west face. The expedition ended after a series of disasters which, because no one was seriously harmed, seem almost comic: there were illnesses and injuries due to rockfalls, one (unoccupied) camp was destroyed by an avalanche and another by fire when a stove blew up. Without having reached 7,000m (22,950ft) the team retreated. A planned traverse of the peak in 1978 (up the south-east ridge and down the original route) also failed, though the reasons were more to do with the logistics of the climb than bad luck, but seven members of the international team summitted. One of these was Kurt Diemberger who, at 46, was climbing his first 8,000er since his first ascents of Broad Peak and Dhaulagiri. One of the seven, the Sherpa Ang Chappal, became the first man to summit without bottled oxygen.

The French west pillar route was repeated in 1980 by a four man

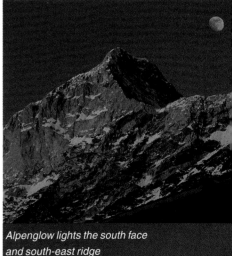

Alpenglow lights the south face and south-east ridge

Attempts to complete the first winter ascent were resumed in 1984/85, a Japanese team failing at 7,520m (24,670ft) and Reinhold Messner and Hans Kammerlander reaching a point just above the Makalu La. In September 1986 Messner and Kammerlander returned with Fritz Mutschlechner and completed the original route. This was Messner's thirteenth 8,000er completed at his fourth attempt on the mountain. Two days before Messner's team summitted Krzysztof Wielicki reached the top along a variant of the French west pillar route. Wielicki had been a member of a Polish expedition, but had been asked by Marcel Ruedi to join him in a two-man alpine style ascent. Concerned that he had not acclimatised, and that Reudi's arrival by helicopter implied that he, too, was not properly acclimatised, Wielicki only agreed with reluctance, stressing that at the first sign of trouble the pair should descend. Wielicki took Diamox and performed beyond his wildest hopes. He pulled ahead of Reudi and summitted alone. On his descent he met Reudi who was climbing slowly, but insisted on continuing, despite the fact that it would mean a bivouac. The next day Wielicki saw Reudi descending from the summit as he made his own way down, but later Messner and his colleagues found Reudi sitting in the snow, dead.

Rob Hall approaching the summit

Makalu seen in the early morning by climbers starting towards the summit of Everest up the south-east ridge

American team climbing without oxygen and in alpine style, John Roskelley reaching the summit alone, the others having stopped for a variety of reasons. In December of the same year an attempted winter ascent of the south-east ridge, an ambitious climb, failed. The next year, climbing post-monsoon, Wojciech Kurtyka, Jerzy Kukuczka and Alex McIntyre failed in an attempt on a new line on the west face, Kukuczka then climbing the north-west ridge solo and without supplementary oxygen in four days. This first true solo (several climbers had climbed the final section of the mountain alone previously) was Kukuczka's third ascent of an 8,000er. In May 1982 a Korean team climbing a variant of the south-east ridge route found the small wooden toy which Kukuczka had placed in a crack just below the top. The Anglo-Polish line on the west face was also completed in 1982 by a Polish-Brazilian team, Andrzej Czok soloing to the top, the final section of climbing being along Kukuczka's north-west ridge route.

In 1984, during an attempt at a new route on the east face of Makalu, which failed less than 100m (330ft) from the top, Jean Affanassieff, Doug Scott and Steve Sustad found the body of Karel Schubert in his final bivouac, a sobering experience which may have influenced the decision to retreat down the difficult ascent route rather than continuing to the top and descending the easier original line.

In 1988 Marc Batard soloed the west pillar and descended the original route, completing the first traverse. With two Sherpas Batard had fixed rope to 7,750m (25,400ft) and then descended. Then, leaving an equipment dump in the evening of 26 April he climbed to the summit, reaching it at 9.45am on 27th, a fine achievement. Equally noteworthy was Pierre Beghin's virtual solo in the post-monsoon period of 1989. With three friends Beghin climbed a new route on the south face to a height of 7,200m (23,600ft). From a camp at that height Beghin continued alone, climbing up to reach the Yugoslav route which he followed, with two bivouacs, to the summit. He descended the original route, but was avalanched, the snow slide leaving him unharmed within a short distance of the camp of a Catalan expedition. The next day he was avalanched again, but was once more unharmed and continued safely to the base of the peak.

1990 saw the first female ascent of Makalu, the American

Alan Hinkes on the summit

face when he was struck by stonefall and forced to retreat from a height of 7,300m (24,000ft), but in spring 1997 a Russian team succeeded in adding a new route to the face. The 'true' west face route, a line directly up the headwall, would involve very hard rock climbing at very high altitude but is dangerous, being swept by stonefall from the upper headwall. The Russians did not take that line, favouring one to the left of the west pillar which offered some shelter from the stonefall. Nonetheless it was a hard route – one of the hardest to date on the great peaks and a notable achievement – difficulties only easing when the top of the west pillar route was reached – at 8,000m (26,250ft) – by a rising traverse. Above 7,300m (24,000ft) the climb was alpine-style by a team of six, but at 8,200m (26,900ft) Salavat Habibulin, who had done much of the leading and as a result was exhausted, was forced to stop. Alexei Bolotov, Igor Bugachevski, Yuri Ermachek, Dmitri Pavlenko and Nikolai Zhilin continued to the summit, reaching it on 24 May. When they returned they found Habibulin had died. On the descent Bugachevski was struck by stonefall and killed.

The true west face route – which has been attempted by several teams though no one has reached higher than 7,300m (24,000ft) – remains to be climbed: it is arguably the latest 'last great problem' of the 8,000ers and as such is sure to be climbed early in the next century. Makalu is also the only Nepalese 8,000er without a winter ascent, another target climb for the next millenium (assuming, wrongly if pedantic truth is sought, that this will begin on 1 January 2000). Makalu is a beautiful, elegant mountain, but it is also a dangerous peak, second only to Annapurna (of the Nepalese peaks – both are less dangerous than K2) in the death rate of climbers descending from the summit, a fact that is likely to limit the interest of commercial teams for a while.

Kitty Calhoun Grissom reaching the top with John Schutt, the two being members of a small team which made an alpine ascent of the French west pillar route. In 1994 an attempt to climb the peak directly from Makalu La by the Russian Anatoli Boukreev and the Bolivian Bernardo Guarachi failed 30m (100ft) from the top. Later Boukreev and Neil Beidleman completed the route in a continuous push, starting at 6.30pm on 13 May and reaching the top at 4.30pm on 15 May. The following year a Japanese team climbed a new route on the north-east side of the peak. Starting in Tibet the route follows the east ridge, a 10km (6¼ mile) ridge beginning at just 3,920m (12,850ft) where they set their base camp. The team climbed the southern face of the ridge to reach the north-west ridge and the original route which they then followed to the top. Eight Japanese reached the summit in two teams of four on 21 and 22 May.

Post monsoon in 1996 the Japanese Yasushi Yamanoi failed in his ambitious attempt to solo a new route on the west

Difficult ground on Makalu's classic route from Makalu La

kangchenjunga 8,586m

'Above 23,000 feet the climber quickly loses weight and grows weak. He is like a sick man, always tired. To turn over in bed, to reach for a boot or a box of matches, brings an attack of breathlessness; every exertion calls for an effort'

CHARLES EVANS

Kangchenjunga, Peak IX of the Indian survey, is the most easterly of the 8,000m peaks, standing on the border between Nepal and Sikkim. From almost any direction the peak looks like a vast tent, the massif being created by four ridges radiating virtually on the cardinal points from the summit.

Kangchenjunga, Peak IX of the Indian survey, is the most easterly of the 8,000m peaks, standing on the border between Nepal and Sikkim. From almost any direction the peak looks like a vast tent, the massif being created by four ridges radiating virtually on the cardinal points from the summit. Strung out along these ridges (which do not meet at the main summit, the east ridge meeting the north-south ridge at the south summit) are a series of tops, the ridges being saw-toothed rather than declining steadily in height. There are, therefore, a number of subsidiary summits, three (at least) over 8,000m (26,247ft): the south summit – occasionally called Kangchenjunga II – was given a unique designation (Peak VIII) by the Indian survey. The central (between the south and main tops) and west summits are both over 8,400m (27,560ft), the west (Yalung Kang) having been the specific object of several expeditions. Some have suggested that Yalung Kang should be added to the list of 8,000ers, but this is unlikely, the peak being insufficiently distinct to be realistically termed a separate mountain.

Kangchenjunga's name is something of a mystery. One Sanskrit scholar claimed it derived from Kancan Jangha, golden thigh, though quite why this should have been is a mystery as there is no physical resemblance (to colour or body part, unless aided by strange, evening light and a vivid imagination), or any obvious legend associated with the area. Most experts now agree a Tibetan origin, deriving from Kang-chen-dzo-nga which would be pronounced (more or less) as Kangchenjunga. One 19th century explorer claimed the name was given to a local Sikkim god who rode a white lion and waved a banner, believing that the lion was the peak, the banner the clouds or snow plume at the summit. The god was believed to live on the summit and early climbers on the peak were asked not to go to the very top to avoid annoying him, causing him to unleash his fury on the locals. This was scrupulously observed by early climbers, but it seems that summiteers have for several years been ignoring the custom. The story of the god is both delightful and plausible, but the actual meaning of the Tibetan words is 'snow-big-treasury-five' which would make the peak the Five Treasures of the Great Snow.

But to what does the five refer? Five summits can be picked out, but more (or less) can just as easily be counted. Some have suggested that the 'five' refers to glaciers, but ten glaciers radiate from the Kangchenjunga massif and it is not easy to unambiguously define any group of just five. The name remains an enigma.

Exploration

In 1848/49 the British botanist Joseph Hooker made two long – and, for the time, remarkable – journeys in Sikkim, travelling to within a few kilometres of Kangchenjunga and sketching it. On his return south from the second trip, accompanied by a Dr. Campbell, an official from Darjeeling, the two men were arrested by the Sikkimese. As Sikkim had become a British protectorate in the wake of Sir David Ochterlony's defeat of a Gurkha army in the Kathmandu valley in March 1816 (which ended the Nepalese war) the British were outraged, the event precipitating the annexing of the southern part of Sikkim by the East India Company. With order, of a sort, restored, travel to the eastern and southern sides of Kangchenjunga became straightforward again. Between 1852 and the end of the century there were at least ten explorations of northern Sikkim,

George Band on the day of the first ascent, crossing slabby rocks about 120m (390ft) below the summit

The north-west flank of Kangchenjunga is seen over the upper reaches of the Kangchenjunga glacier from high above Pangpema. North Col far left, Yalung Lang (Kangchenjunga West) and Kambachen on the right

George Band about 60m (200ft) below the summit on the west ridge during the first ascent. In the background is Yalung Kang, Kangchenjunga's west peak

the area being thoroughly mapped. In 1883 the first true climbing expedition was active in the area, William Graham and his Swiss guides (Josef Imboden on the first trip, Ulrich Kaufmann and Emile Boss on the second) making several first ascents, including the disputed climb of Kabru. Then, in 1899 Douglas Freshfield and a small team including the Italian mountain photographer Vittorio Sella made a complete circuit of the Kangchenjunga massif, involving a few days trek through 'closed' eastern Nepal. Freshfield's book (accurately, if unromantically, called Round Kangchenjunga) illustrated with Sella's photographs not only inspired others, but gave a detailed break-down of the possible routes to the main summit.

Perhaps inspired by Freshfield's book, though he would almost certainly never have admitted such a thing, Aleister Crowley arrived in Sikkim in August 1905 determined to climb the mountain. With the diabolist were Dr. Jacot-Guillarmod who, like Crowley, had been on Eckenstein's 1902 K2 trip, two other Swiss climbers, Alexis Pache and Charles Reymond, an Italian hotelier from Darjeeling called de Righi the team had somehow managed to collect along the way, and a number of porters. The party approached the south-western side of the mountain along the Yalung Glacier, eventually establishing a high camp at about 6,250m (20,500ft). From it Pache explored up to about 6,400m (21,000ft) perhaps a little higher. Faced with the inevitability of defeat – the party was neither experienced enough nor large enough for a serious try – there

was now an argument about what to do next. Crowley had insisted on early morning climbs to reduce the likelihood of avalanches, a sensible precaution, but one to which Guillarmod in particular took exception. Guillarmod now decided to descend from the top camp in the afternoon. Crowley was opposed, claiming later that he should have broken the doctor's leg with his ice axe so as to save his life, but Guillarmod, Pache, de Righi and three porters attached themselves to a single rope and started out. Guillarmod led with de Righi behind him, then the porters, the experienced Pache bringing up the rear. The ill-equipped porters (Crowley did not supply them with boots, apparently claiming to have invoked dark forces to protect them while they walking barefoot in snow) slipped continuously, Pache holding them, but eventually, on a traverse, he was unable to stop another slide. All six men fell, their frantic attempts to stop precipitating an avalanche which buried all but Guillarmod and de Righi. Their shouts for help brought Reymond to the scene, but Crowley declined to help. He was drinking tea and writing a newspaper article and, in any event, was, as he said in the article – which appeared on 11 September 1905 – 'not over-anxious in the circumstances ... to render help. A mountain accident of this sort is one of the things for which I have no sympathy whatever'. Crowley descended past the accident site the next day on his way back to Darjeeling: it took two more days to free the four bodies from the snow. The three porters were buried in a crevasse, Pache beneath a rock cairn which was marked (Pache's Grave) on later maps and on the route diagram of Charles Evans' book of the first ascent.

There were further visits to the area both before and after the 1914–18 War, though none could be classed as an attempt on the peak. In 1921 Alexander Kellas photographed Kangchenjunga before his trip to Everest (during which he died), but not until 1929 was there a further attempt to climb it. That year there were two, the first a clandestine attempt by an American, Edgar Francis Farmer, a young man of limited experience and boundless enthusiasm. Having left his porters on the Yalung Glacier he was last seen climbing towards the Talung Saddle, a col on the south ridge.

Farmer disappeared in May. In August a strong German expedition under Paul Bauer arrived on the other side of the mountain, choosing to attack the eastern side from the Zemu

Climbers on the north-east spur during the first ascent of that route in 1977

Glacier and to climb post-monsoon. After a failed attempt to force a route towards the Zemu Gap, the low point on the south-south-east ridge, the team turned their attention to the north-east spur. The climbing was hard and the weather poor, but the Germans doggedly pursued their line, using a series of snow caves as camps high on the spur where tents could not be pitched. By 3 October they had reached about 7,400m (24,300ft) by which time, they judged, they were above the major difficulties. But a five-day storm then kept the team camp-bound. When the weather improved the climbers retreated safely, but a lot of equipment was lost, buried in or swept away by the snow, or discarded by the climbers in an effort to speed up a descent through deep snow. The loss of equipment forced the team to abandon any further attempt.

Strangely, in view of the years Kangchenjunga had been ignored by climbers, two expeditions had sought permission for 1929, the second, under Prof Gunther Dyhrenfurth being offered 1930 as a compensation for losing out to Bauer. Dyhrenfurth, German-born but later a Swiss national, led an international team which included the German Uli Wieland and the Austrian Erwin Schneider (both later involved in the tragic Nanga Parbat expedition of 1934), and the Briton Frank Smythe. Before the trip Dyhrenfurth was contacted by Francis Farmer's mother who, in dreams, had seen her son held captive in the monastery of Detsenroba (occasionally called Dachenrol or Decherol) in the Yalung valley, a vision apparently backed by various clairvoyants. She wanted Dyhrenfurth to visit the monastery, but her hope of seeing her son again was forlorn – Detsenroba was ruinous.

Not wanting to follow in Bauer's crampon marks Dyhrenfurth asked for, and astonishingly, was granted permission for a limited excursion into Nepal. His team followed the Kangchenjunga Glacier to the peak's north-west quadrant and at first attempted a route on to the north ridge. This was abandoned at about 6,100m (20,000ft) when a section of ice cliff collapsed, sweeping away Erwin Scneider and Chettan, a porter, but miraculously leaving three other climbers and

The north-east spur. This line, which can only be approached from Sikkim, was attempted several times in the 1930s, but not climbed until 1977 when an Indian team completed the route and made the second ascent of the main summit

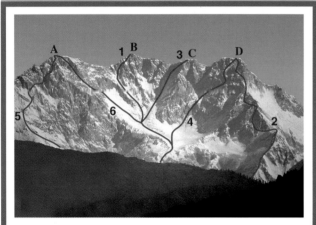

Above South-west Face
A *Yalung Kang* **B** *Main Summit*
C *Central Summit* **D** *South Summit*
1 *First ascent/'classic' route, British (1955)*
2 *South Ridge to S Summit, Prezelj/*
Stremfelj (1991) **3** *Polish to Central*

Summit (1978) **4** *Polish to South Summit*
(1978) **5** *Japanese to Yalung Kang (1973)*
6 *Austro-Germans to Yalung Kang (1975)*
The full traverse of the skyline ridge
(including all four summits) was
accomplished by a Russian team (1989)

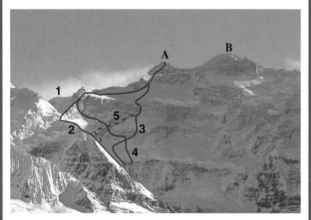

Above North-west Face
A *Main Summit* **B** *Yalung Kang*
1 *NE Spur, Indians (1977)* **2** *Messner/*
Mutschlechner/Ang Dorje (1982)

3 *Japanese (1980)* **4** *British (1979)*
5 *Germans (1983) not to summit*
Variations of these routes have also been
climbed

eleven more porters unscathed. Schneider escaped injury, but Chettan was killed. The team then attempted the north-west spur, aiming to join it beyond Kangbachen, the peak to the west of Yalung Kang. Hard climbing and poor snow and ice conditions limited progress and this attempt, too, was abandoned. The team then concentrated on lower peaks, making ascents of several, including Jonsong.

Post-monsoon in 1931 Paul Bauer returned, this time with a team of eleven – he had nine in 1929 – determined to complete the ascent of the north-east spur. The attempt was overwhelmed by problems – a Sherpa and a porter died of sickness, another Sherpa and one of the German climbers died in a fall, several climbers, including Bauer, went down with illnesses which forced their withdrawal, and the weather was bad. Despite this the team climbed a little higher than their 1929 high point before retreating.

Bauer came back to the area in 1936, but Kangchenjunga was not the intention of his team, which made an attempt on the Twins peak, set where the north ridge divides. It is possible that Bauer was interested in assessing the north ridge as an ascent route, but heavy monsoon snow defeated the team while they were still relatively low. The following year another German team also failed on Twins, while a small British team, including John Hunt, later the leader of the successful British Everest expedition, and his wife, failed to reach the col (the North Col) on the north ridge (between the main summit and the Twins peak) from the Twins Glacier, retreating in the face of rockfalls and difficulties which were too great for the size of the party. Then in 1939 a New Zealand team was given permission for an attempt in 1940: war broke out and the attempt was cancelled.

After the war, the independence granted to India and the decline of British influence caused Sikkim to close its borders, hopeful that a secretive neutrality would allow it to escape the attention of its huge southern and northern neighbours. The attempt was successful for a quarter-century, but in 1975 India, increasingly concerned about Chinese intentions and the relative ease of crossing the Sikkim Himalaya annexed the country.

The loss of a route through Sikkim, together with Nepal's opening of its borders necessitated an enthusiasm for exploring Kangchenjunga's western and southern flanks. In 1953 the Britons John Kempe and Gilmour Lewis explored the Upper Yalung glacier and had a good view of the south-west face. What they saw persuaded the British to send a larger reconnaissance team in 1954 comprising Kempe, Lewis and four others. The team reported that the upper face was clearly climbable and that for the approach to it there were two possibilities, one along the 1905 team's route (past Pache's

Grave), the other by way of a rib now called Kempe's Buttress. A third option via Talung Cwm was dismissed. The success of the 1954 reconnaissance persuaded the British to send a full strength team in 1955: although officially termed a reconnaissance, it was clear from the outset that the organisers hoped for greater things.

First Ascent

The 1955 British expedition was led by Charles Evans, a surgeon, who had been Hunt's deputy on the successful 1953 Everest team (when he had reached the south summit). It comprised George Band, who had also been on Everest in 1953, Joe Brown, Dr John Clegg, the team doctor, the New Zealander Norman Hardie, John Jackson, Tom McKinnon, Neil Mather and Tony Streather. The Sherpa team was led by Dawa Tenzing who had been Evans' personal Sherpa on Everest in 1953. (As a short digression, Evans' book of the expedition – an analytical, unromantic read, what one might perhaps expect from a surgeon – notes an incident on the walk when the breakfasting team were surrounded by curious Nepalese villagers. Anxious to avoid them getting too close, the Sherpas waved the villagers back explaining 'Gently there, not too close, crowding makes them restless and difficult', a rather interesting – and refreshing – change from the standard 'sahibs having trouble with the locals' tale.)

The team followed the Yalung Glacier to the foot of the south-west face, exploring the Kempe's Buttress and Pache's Grave options and choosing the latter. They decided on a route which climbed to a dip in a prominent rock spur (the Western Buttress), then through a valley filled by the upper section of an icefall, that joined the Yalung Glacier, to reach the Great Shelf,

On the north-west face during the first ascent in 1979

a flat/low-angled snow basin beneath the horseshoe-shaped rock wall that forms the summit structure of Yalung Kang and the main summit. From this basin a broad snow slope, The Gangway, leads up to the west ridge. However, the ridge itself was pinnacled and potentially difficult, and it was hoped a route existed on the upper south-west face, bypassing these difficulties.

The route was pushed out in reasonable weather and though heavily crevassed it was relatively safe from the continuous stream of avalanches which fell from high on the face. From Camp III in the upper icefall the route to, and up to the back wall of, the Great Shelf to where Camp V was established, was made by climbers using closed circuit oxygen equipment. This was just a test, however, the rest of the climbers, including the summiteers, using open circuit sets.

From Camp V Evans and Mather led up, Evans clearly anxious about whether The Gangway would be avalanche prone or its snow too rotten to climb: it was perfect and a Camp (Camp VI) was established half-way up at about 8,200m (26,900ft). Here Band and Brown, who had been following the lead pair and two Sherpas, stayed using bottled oxygen to aid their sleep. Back at Camp V Evans received a weather forecast stating that the monsoon would arrive in five days. In the

Doug Scott photographs Peter Boardman climbing the last few steps to Joe Tasker and the summit during the first ascent of the north-west face

expedition book Evans refers to Band and Brown as the first summit-ridge pair, perhaps concerned that the difficulties of the headwall would be so severe they would not have the time to complete the climb. With the monsoon approaching fast he must have had his fingers firmly crossed.

Band and Brown left camp at 8.15am and continued up The Gangway. From lower on the mountain the team had spotted a ledged ramp leading across the headwall to the west ridge, reaching it above the pinnacles. The first attempt to reach this was too low, losing 1½ hours as the pair were forced to backtrack. They chose correctly the second time, following the ramp, which was straightforward, but exposed, to the ridge where they rested and enjoyed a magnificent view. The ridge was also straightforward until a rock tower barred the way. Brown, an expert rock climber who had revolutionised British rock climbing and advanced the top level of difficulty, climbed this on his trademark handjams – the pair had removed their crampons on the ramp and so preferred the rock to a detour on steep snow – and was astonished to discover that he was virtually at the summit, the rock tower ending just a few metres below a snow hump. It was 2.45pm, just 15 minutes from the pair's self-imposed deadline for reaching the top. The summit had been reached ten days after the French ascent of Makalu. As promised, in deference to the local belief that the summit was the home of a god, the pair did not set foot on the actual summit, a shallow snow dome on which a small crowd could congregate. The lack of footprints in the summit snows led Charles Evans to call the expedition book Kangchenjunga: The

Untrodden Peak and has persuaded many to agree with George Band's view that it was better that the summit was left unsullied. Later ascents of the peak also left the summit untrodden at first, but at some stage the promise was broken and the peak is no longer untrodden.

At about 3pm Band and Brown began their descent, reaching Camp VI in darkness at 7pm. The camp was already occupied by Hardie and Streather who, on 26 May, repeated the climb, bypassing the final rock tower by following a snow ramp which lead to the south ridge which they then followed to the summit, reaching it at 12.15pm. They were back in Camp VI by 5pm. The expedition then retreated without incident though on the day of the second summit climb a Sherpa, Pemi Dorje, died at Base Camp, probably from pneumonia: he had become exhausted on an earlier carry up the mountain and had never recovered.

Later Ascents

In 1973 a Japanese expedition climbed Yalung Kang, following the British 1953 route at first, then branching off to follow the south-west ridge. Yutaka Ageta and Takeo Matsuda reached the summit, but were forced to bivouac on the way down. The next day Matsuda fell, probably struck by a falling rock, Ageta being rescued by his team mates. Yalung Kang was climbed again in 1975 by an Austro-German team, following the British route to the Great Shelf then a couloir up the peak's south face. The main summit was not reached again until 1977. That year an Indian Army expedition approached the mountain through Sikkim and followed Paul Bauer's 1930s line along the north-east spur to its junction with the north ridge, and then climbed the north ridge to the top. At 3pm on 31 May Major Prem Chand and the Sherpa Nima Dorje stood on the summit.

The following year the south summit (Kangchenjunga II) was reached by a Polish team which, initially, followed the British route to the Great Shelf. The

Looking down on the North Col during the first ascent of the north-west face route

Poles also climbed the highest and second highest tops of the triple-peaked central summit, a Spanish Yalung Kang expedition which joined forces with them climbing the third top. In the aftermath of these climbs the Polish and Spanish expedition leaders were banned from

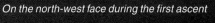
On the north-west face during the first ascent

Battling through jet-stream winds on the upper slopes during the first ascent

Nepal for four years, as each had climbed peaks for which they did not have permission. The Poles were unfortunate – they had always wanted to climb the south summit, but as the Nepalese official who dealt with their application only had the main summit on his list that was written into their permission. The Poles accepted this, not realising the potential implications. The Spaniards had no such excuse – they just did not fancy their peak, and compounded their 'crime' by bypassing Kathmandu on their return so as not to have to face the wrath of officialdom.

In 1979 the main summit was climbed again in fine style. Though Messner and Habeler had climbed Gasherbrum I in alpine style in 1975, then Everest without bottled oxygen in 1978, and Messner had soloed Nanga Parbat, also in 1978, no lightweight, bottled gas-free ascent had yet been made on any of the 'big three peaks'. In early April 1979, after several years persuading the Nepalese to allow an attempt from the west, the Britons Peter Boardman, Doug Scott and Joe Tasker, with Frenchman Georges Bettembourg (who had been on the disputed alpine-style Broad Peak climb in 1978) established a base camp below Kangchenjunga's north-west face, the face

which had defeated Dyhrenfurth's team in 1930. From it a difficult route up the face to the North Col was climbed, three camps being used. A fourth camp was established in a snow cave on the north ridge at 7,440m (24,400ft). A first attempt by Bettembourg, Boardman and Scott (a sick Tasker having retreated) failed in winds estimated at over 140km/h (90mph). A second attempt by Boardman, Scott and the recovered Tasker (Bettembourg not trusting the weather) left the Camp IV snow cave on 15 May, bivouacing that night on the ridge. On 16 May they crossed the north-west face to reach the west ridge close to the line of the first ascent, following that route (the Hardie/Streather variant) to the top, which was reached at 5pm. The trio returned to their bivouac and were safely off the mountain by 19 May. Though not a true alpine style ascent this third ascent of Kangchenjunga was a superb climb.

In 1980 a larger Japanese team, climbing in similar style to the British forced a route up the centre of the north-west face. From a high camp two lightweight summit attempts were made, the first putting four Japanese and a Sherpa on the summit, the second, three days later, also being successful, with two further Japanese and two more Sherpas reaching the top. The Japanese summit climbs were on 14 and 17 May: on 15 May a German climber and two Sherpas from an expedition led by Dr KM Herrligkoffer reached the top along the first ascent route. The following year another Japanese team climbed the main peak, putting five climbers and a Sherpa on the summit, and, in a co-ordinated climb, also placed five climbers on the top of Yalung Kung. The intended traverse between the two was not attempted as it was thought to be more difficult than had been supposed. Later in the year the French pair Jean-Jacques Ricouard and Michel Parmentier repeated the original route in the first post-monsoon ascent. Sadly Ricouard was killed on the descent.

In 1982 Reinhold Messner, Friedl Mutschlechner and the Sherpa Ang Dorje climbed another new route on the north-west face, climbing up to reach the north ridge close to the north col and following the ridge to the top. This was Messner's seventh 8,000er, but not without incident. Messner believes he picked up an amoebic infection on the march in to the peak and was ill during the early part of the climb. He recovered sufficiently to make the summit climb, but during a nightmare descent in a blizzard driven by winds which eventually shredded their tents and intense cold he began to shake and hallucinate. With Mutschlechner frostbitten and Messner seriously ill, the pair escaped only by an effort of will. Messner

was later diagnosed as suffering from an amoebic abscess on his liver.

Pre-monsoon in 1983 the Austrian Georg Bachler soloed the original route from the top camp of the Austrian expedition, but in the post-monsoon period Pierre Beghin completed the first authentic solo by way of the same route. Beghin camped at 6,250m (20,500ft) and 7,700m (25,250ft), reaching the summit on 17 October and descending to 7,200m (23,600ft) on the same day. A Swiss expedition which climbed the north face shortly after found Beghin's altimeter and a note tied to an old oxygen bottle (Beghin climbed without bottled gas) at the summit. In October 1984 Roger Marshall, the British-Canadian

The north-west flank of Kangchenjunga from a camp site at Pangpema

Kangchenjunga from Khesewa Bhanjyang in eastern Nepal

climber repeated Beghin's solo. The same year, and as a complete contrast to these solo climbs, a vast Japanese expedition (22 climbers plus 31 Sherpas) attempted to climb and traverse the massif's four summits. The south, central and main summits were reached, the main summit by two parties, but Yalung Kang was not climbed.

In spring 1985 a Yugoslavian team made the first ascent of the north face of Yalung Kung (the summit team was Borut Bergant and Tomo Cesen, who was later to solo Jannu and then to claim an ascent of Lhotse's south face), then, in 1986 the main peak was climbed in winter for the first time via the original route by a Polish team, Jerzy Kukuczka and Krzysztof Wielicki reaching the summit on 11 January. It was Kukuczka's tenth 8,000er and his third in winter. Wielicki was also now well on his way to climbing all 14 peaks. Sadly this excellent achievement was marred by the death of Andrzej Czok from oedema. His death echoed that of the American

The eastern side of Kangchenjunga from the Goecha La in Sikkim

Chris Chandler who had died in January 1985 during a winter attempt on Yalung Kang's north face with his wife Cherie Bremer-Kemp.

The Indian Army returned to the mountain in 1987 with a

vast team (62 men in total) and ten years after their first ascent of the north-east spur they repeated the climb. This time, however, the summiteers – three rather than two as in 1977 – died on the descent, a prayer flag they had left on the summit being found by the second summit team. On that second attempt, on 31 May, the exact tenth anniversary of their first climb, three more team members reached the top: one of these also died descending. The Indian army had the monopoly of attempts from Sikkim, a fact proved by a non-army Indian team being forced to climb from Nepal in 1988. Their attempt on the north-west face failed, but the Austrian Peter Habeler, once Messner's climbing partner, was successful on a variant of the British north ridge route, climbing alpine style with American Carlos Buhler and Martin Zabeleta of Spain. The following year a huge Soviet team (32 climbers plus 17 Sherpas) succeeded in traversing the four summits (Yalung Kang, main, central and south). In fact separate teams did the traverse in both directions and established new, and very hard, routes to the main and south tops. Given four peaks and 49 climbers a total of almost 200 men-summits was possible and almost half this number was actually achieved, a remarkable record.

By 1991 the peak had still not had an ascent by a woman, and the long south ridge – the border between Nepal and Sikkim – had not been climbed: it was one of the 'last great problems' of the 8,000ers. In that year there were tragedy and success on these outstanding issues. A combined Slovenian/Polish team repeated the original route, two climbers reaching the top with bottled oxygen, but on a subsequent attempt Joze Rozman and Marija Frantar, with just one oxygen bottle between them, reached a point just 150m (less than 500ft) from the top. It was then 4pm and in a radio call to base they said they were cold but that though Ms Frantar was partially snow-blind, she wished to continue despite Rozman's reluctance. Ignoring advice to

The south-west flank of Kangchenjunga is seen up the deep valley of the Yalung Glacier. The main summit is flanked by Yalung Kang and Kangchenjunga South

descend the pair continued up, but at 7pm, night having fallen, reported that they were hopelessly lost. Their bodies were later found near the base of the headwall. In contrast a Slovenian pair, from the same expedition, Marko Prezelj and Andrej Stremfelj succeeded in climbing the south ridge. The pair climbed grade VI, A2 rock and 65°–90° ice to a bivouac at 6,200m (20,350ft) then easier ground to a second bivouac at 7,250m (23,800ft). They were then forced on to the south-west face, but resisted the temptation to traverse to the Great Shelf, climbing up to a third bivouac at 7,600m (24,900ft). The next day they climbed only 300m (1,000ft), bivouacing again at 7,900m (25,900ft) before climbing up through deep snow to join the Soviet route at about 8,100m (26,600ft). They then used the Soviet fixed ropes to move quicker, gaining the south summit. The pair then descended the Polish route to the Great Shelf where the rest of the Slovenian team was attempting the original route. Many observers believe this to be the finest ever alpine-style ascent of the an 8,000er and have even compared it with the Kurtyka/Shauer route on Gasherbrum IV's west face which, though climbed in 1985, is still thought by many to be the finest high-altitude alpine-style ascent to date. The rest of the pair's Polish-Slovenian team succeeded in climbing both the main and central summits.

In 1992 Wanda Rutkiewicz, arguably the leading female high altitude climber of the era with eight 8,000ers to her credit, attempted Kangchenjunga again, having failed to make the summit in 1991. On 12 May her companion Carlos Carsolio, who was climbing faster, summitted and met her still climbing up at 8,250m (27,100ft). He tried to persuade her to go down but she said she would bivouac and continue to the summit the next day. A storm broke during the night and she was never seen again.

There was further tragedy on Kangchenjunga in 1995, a tragedy probably precipitated by the race to be the third person to claim ascents of the 14 8,000ers. The post-monsoon season saw the Swiss Erhard Loretan, who had climbed the other 13 peaks, and Frenchman Benôit Chamoux, who had climbed 12 as well as Shisha Pangma's central summit (Chamoux was claiming this as his thirteenth 8,000er: his ascent of Cho Oyu was also disputed as he and his companions had only reached the edge of the summit plateau) at the base of the mountain. Loretan and his usual partner Jean Troillet, the Italian Sergio Martini (who had climbed ten 8,000ers), Chamoux, Pierre Royer (who was filming Chamoux's fourteenth climb) and three Sherpas (carrying Royer's filming gear as well as other equipment) left together along the normal route, but the Swiss and Martini rapidly drew away from the French and their Sherpas. During a rest period one of the Sherpas

Sunrise over Kangchenjunga from south-south-east on Tiger Hill, Darjeeling

overbalanced and fell to his death. The other two Sherpas descended to him but Chamoux and Royer declined to help. Instead they continued slowly, with Royer now carrying his own film equipment, making frequent radio calls to a French media circus gathered at the mountain's base.

The Swiss ignored the British route above the Great Shelf, continuing up the Gangway to the col between Yalung Kang and the main summit. Sergio Martini, convinced the ridge from the col was too difficult waited for them to return. When they did not he descended. Loretan and Troillet reached the summit at 2.35pm on 5 October and met Chamoux and Royer at 4pm on their descent. At 4.30pm Royer radioed base that he was too tired to continue and was descending, but that Chamoux would continue alone. Chamoux reached the col and bivouaced, radioing at 8am on 6 October that he was continuing up. He was

South-east face of Kangchenjunga (South) is seen over the upper reaches of the Talung Glacier in Sikkim. The South Ridge, left, was climbed by the Slovenians in 1991

not heard from again and neither he nor Royer were seen again. In an unpleasant aftermath the Sherpas refused to search for either climber as they had refused to help their fallen comrade and some saw Chamoux's death as his own fault brought on by poor acclimatisation before the climb in his haste to beat Loretan. The events soured what should have been a good reception to Loretan's achievement: at 36 he was the youngest of the three to have completed the 14 8,000ers.

Not until 1998 was Kangchenjunga climbed by a woman (assuming, of course, that Wanda Rutkiewicz failed to make the summit, which seems highly probable). That year Briton Ginette Harrison, a member of a team led by her American husband Gary Pfisterer, climbed a variant of the British route on the north-west face (which had been pioneered by a German team in 1989). Harrison did not use bottled oxygen. In addition to being the first female ascent, Harrison completed the set for female climbers, Kangchenjunga having been the only 8,000er not to have had a female ascent. While the Anglo-American team was on the mountain a Japanese team was also on the same face. Five climbers reached the top, but two died during the descent and the other three were badly frostbitten. Also in 1998 the Italian Fausto de Stefani climbed Kangchenjunga by the normal route and claimed to be the sixth climber to have completed the 14 peak grand slam. However, de Stefani's claimed ascent of Lhotse remains controversial. He admitted not reaching the summit because of high winds which threatened to blow him and his partner (Sergio Martini) off the rotten snow of the final cornice. But a South Korean who climbed Lhotse shortly after claimed the Italian tracks stopped at least 150m from the top.

Of the 14 8,000ers, only Annapurna and Lhotse have had fewer ascents than Kangchenjunga, a tribute to its formidable size and difficulty. It is also a dangerous mountain, one in twenty of those reaching the summit dying during the descent and the peak claiming a victim for every four climbers who reach the top. But as with K2, despite these grim statistics the lure of the world's third highest mountain and its vast faces will continue to attract the world's leading climbers. If travel to Sikkim becomes acceptable in the next millennium it is likely that teams will soon be heading for the east and south-east faces.

manaslu 8,163m

'Was I lost ? ...
Visibility had by
now dropped to
about ten metres:
there was no
longer any hope
of getting bearings
from distinctive
rock or ice features.
Panic seized me.
I believed I was
simply following a
straight line, but
what if I was going
round in circles?'

REINHOLD MESSNER

manaslu

Manaslu – the accent is on the second syllable: Man-as-loo rather than mana-sloo – was Peak XXX of the Indian Survey and was at first called Kutang I, a name derived from it being the highest peak in the local district of Kutang.

However, as tang is Tibetan for a flat area the name could be from the virtually flat summit plateau, a distinctive feature of the peak when received from the Larkya La, a high pass to the north which would have been crossed by Tibetan traders to reach the valley of the Dudh Khola. The present name is Sanskrit in origin, deriving from manasa meaning the spirit or soul: Manaslu is the mountain of the spirit. The villagers of Sama, a Nepalese village at the north-eastern foot of the peak, refer to it as Kambung, the name of a local god who is believed to reside on the summit, a belief which had serious consequences for an early Japan reconnaissance of the mountain.

Exploration

In 1950, while the French were on Annapurna, a small team under the British explorer/climber Bill Tilman set up camp at Thonje, a village set where the Dudh Khola meets the Marshandi river. From there the team explored the upper Dudh Khola, photographing the western and northern sides

Manaslu's true summit and the sharp East Pinnacle (7,895/25,902ft) are seen from the north east

Above South Face
1 *Austrians (1972)*

Below From North-east
A *East Ridge*

B *East Summit (Pinnacle)*
C *Main Summit*
1 *Hajer/Kukuczka (1986)*
2 *First ascent/standard route, Japanese (1956)*

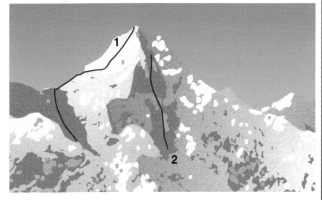

Above From South-east
1 *Polish (1984)*
2 *Kazakh attempt (1990)*

Below From North
1 *Japanese (1971)*
2 *French (1981)*

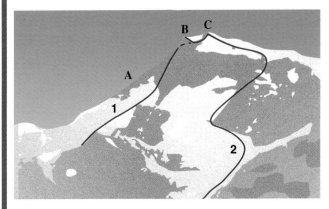

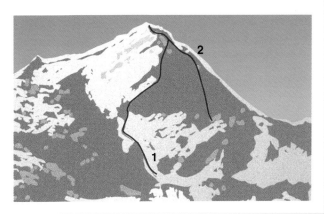

of Manaslu. Tilman knew that his team was not strong enough for a serious attempt on the peak and felt that both the sides he explored offered little chance of success, so turned his attention westward, making an attempt to climb Annapurna IV. When this attempt failed, less than 200m (about 650ft) from the top, the team spent time exploring southern approaches to Manaslu and Himalchuli, the peak to the south-east.

Two years later a small Japanese team arrived intent on exploring all sides of the peak prior to a full-scale attempt in 1953. The team explored the eastern and western sides of the peak, crossing the Larkya La. From Sama they pushed up the east ridge to a height of about 5,250m (17,200ft). From the ridge and later from the Larkya La they identified a feasible route, following the Manaslu Glacier to the peak's North Col then climbing on to the summit plateau. From the Dudh Khola valley they agreed with Tilman's assessment that the western side of the peak was a formidable challenge.

In 1953 the Japanese returned, this time with a full team

(13 climbers plus two scientists) and the intention of climbing of the peak. From Sama they ascended to the edge of the Manaslu Glacier, then placed a series of closely spaced camps on a route over the Naike and North Cols (the Naike Col lies north-east of the North Col and stands between the Manaslu and Larkya Glaciers). From the North Col camp (Camp VIII) – which was connected by a telephone cable strung out across the mountain all the way down to Base Camp – an attempt was made on the summit, but was driven back by bad weather. The weather prevented any further attempt for two weeks, but then a new camp (Camp IX) was established at 7,500m (24,600ft) and a further attempt launched. This failed at about 7,750m (25,400ft) when the climbers realised just how far they were from the summit. Today's climber would have continued, but in 1953, early days on the great peaks, especially for individuals without bottled oxygen or the benefits of modern equipment, the idea of an evening arrival at the summit and a night descent or bivouac was beyond the comprehension of most climbers,

even though Hermann Buhl had completed just such a climb solo the year before on Nanga Parbat.

In the spring of 1954 the Japanese were back, but on this occasion they faced a threat more difficult to overcome than bad weather and technically difficult climbing. At Sama they were met by an angry mob who claimed that the '53 climb had upset the god who lived on the mountain, his anger being shown in a year of appalling weather and an avalanche of

Gyaltsen on the summit, 9 May 1956

unheard of size and direction which had destroyed the local gompa (monastery), one that had stood for 300 years, killing three monks. There had also been epidemics of smallpox and other diseases. The villagers were unwilling to endure more suffering just so the foreigners could amuse themselves on the mountain and were willing, if necessary, to use physical violence if angry shouting was not sufficient to halt the Japanese progress. To prove the point they

Imanishi and Gyaltsen returning from the summit; Muraki and Pemba Sundar go up to meet them

armed themselves with clubs, stones and knives. The Japanese wisely withdrew (one legend has it that several climbers withdrew trouserless, the villagers adding a touch of humiliation to emphasise their point), contenting themselves with an abortive attempt on Ganesh Himal and an exploration of the eastern approaches to Himalchuli.

On their return to Kathmandu the Japanese sought an assurance from the Nepalese government that if they returned to Manaslu at some later date they would not face further intimidation. When they received it they applied for permission for 1955. Unfortunately the Nepalese agreement was sent by sea rather than air mail and did not arrive in Japan until late February 1955, too late to organise a spring expedition. The Japanese therefore sent a delegation to Kathmandu to re-negotiate permissions for the post-monsoon 1955 and spring 1956. They received further assurances on the Sama situation, but to test the validity of these a three-man team visited the area in autumn 1955. There was no problem at Sama, the three climbing to the site of the 1953 base camp and from there exploring alternative approaches to the summit plateau. Despite the team being so small they climbed to the edge of the plateau, at about 7,500m (24,600ft).

First Ascent

On 11 March 1956 another Japanese expedition left Kathmandu for Manaslu. It was led by Yuko Maki, a 62 year-old former president of the Japanese Alpine Club and well-known to European climbers for his first ascent of the Eiger's Mittellegi ridge, with Fritz Amatter, Samuel Brawand and Fritz Steuri, in 1921. His team comprised Sonosuke Chitani, Minoru Higeta, Toshio Imanishi, Kiichiro Kato, Yuichi Matsuda, Junjiro Muraki, Katsuro Ohara, Hiroyoshi Otsuka, Dr. Hirokichi Tatsunuma, Dr. Atsushi Tokunaga (the official expedition doctor though Tatsunuma was also a medical doctor) and Takayoshi Yoda, the expedition photographer. The team was supported by 20 Sherpas under sirdar Gyalzen Norbu. Several members of the team had been on the expeditions of 1953 and 1954. The Japanese used tents with bamboo frames, a more reasonable alternative to metal than at first appears, bamboo being lighter than steel (though more

The summit of Manaslu as seen from Camp II

Bedouin keffiychs or Samurai helmets. With the long sides folded across their shoulders towards their chests the expedition pictures make the climbers look as though they are auditioning for parts as radiation workers in a sci-fi B movie.

Despite assurances, there was some hostility at Sama, but a Nepalese government official rapidly calmed things and the Japanese were allowed to continue. The route followed in 1953 was taken again, but this time fewer camps were used and the summit plateau was approached by a route that stayed south of the North Col, shortening the overall distance. Having established and stocked a camp (Camp IV) to the east of the col by late April, the team used it as an advanced base. The summit plateau was then approached via a broad snow field the Japanese called the Snow Apron. Camp V was placed at the foot of the Apron, Camp VI (at 7,800m/26,000ft) on the plateau edge almost due west of the Pinnacle, the prominent tower of dark rock which lies north-east of the true summit. Imanishi's account of the climb notes that at this stage conversations over the radio with lower camps became heated and 'strong words were exchanged'. He does not elaborate, but the marked difference between this comment and the overly polite tone of the rest of the account suggests a real confrontation. Presumably the lead climbers were concerned over the lack of

brittle than the aluminium-based alloys and carbon fibre of modern tents). They took open-circuit oxygen sets, but for sleeping used 'oxygen candles'. These used potassium chlorate which, with manganese oxide and iron oxide catalysts, undergo an exothermic reaction, the by-product of which is gaseous oxygen. The candles weighed 3.5kg (almost 8lb) but in exchange for this heavy carrying load released 4–5l (about 1 gallon) of oxygen per minute for up to 1½ hours while at the same time producing enough heat to boil water for several mugs. The problem with the candles seems obvious, the oxygen produced dispersing throughout the tent and leaking outside, though at Camp V before their summit climb Imanishi and Gyalzen were fed oxygen by tubes from the next door tent where Dr Tatsunuma spent the night collecting the liberated oxygen and changing candles. However, in the last camp (Camp VI) both summit parties used bottled gas for sleeping before their climbs. As protection against the sun the Japanese wore loose fitting, shoulder-length head covers, looking like

The North Peak of Manaslu viewed from Camp V

progress on the route when the weather became fine, not wishing to squander what might be a narrow weather window.

Camp VI was established on 8 May and the next day Imanishi and Gyalzen Norbu set off for the summit at 8am on a beautiful and virtually windless, though cold, day. The climb up the relatively gently plateau was straightforward, the pair making for the highest snow point which they reached after less than 4 hours climbing. However, on reaching it they discovered that the true summit was a shattered rock tower a short distance away. This they soon climbed reaching the true summit at 12.30pm. The tower's top could accommodate three or four men, but was narrow, leaving little room for photography, Imanishi's dramatic summit

Manaslu with its south-west face is seen from due west near Chame in the Marsyandi gorges

Camp V below the Snow Apron and the East Pinnacle during the first successful expedition

shot of Gyalzen being taken from the nearby snow top. Having already climbed Makalu with the French in 1955 Gyalzen Norbu became the first man to climb two 8,000ers. The pair stayed at the summit for 1½ hours, then climbed down, passing Camp VI to spend the night at Camp V.

The next day Higeta and Kato climbed to Camp VI and on 11 May – another beautiful and windless day – repeated the climb. Utilising the steps cut by the first pair on their descent the two reached the summit in only 3 hours. They filmed the summit with a 16mm movie camera, but unfortunately then dropped it, complete with film, down the south face. Within six days of the second summit climb the expedition had cleared the peak.

Later Ascents

In 1964 a small Dutch expedition climbed Manaslu North Peak (7,157m/23,480ft), the peak between the North and Naike Cols, but the main summit was not attempted again until 1971 when two teams arrived. A Japanese team was to attempt a route from the north-west side – the side deemed unlikely to offer a reasonable route by Tilman and the early Japanese reconnaissances – while a Korean team attempted to repeat the original route. The Koreans were unsuccessful, calling off their attempt when Kim Ki Sup, brother of team leader Kim Ho Sup, was killed by a fall into a crevasse at 7,600m (24,950ft), but the Japanese succeeded in climbing a very difficult route up the north-west face. The team, led by Akira Takahashi, forced a route up the face to the west-north-west ridge in appalling weather (1971 was the worst weather in recorded Nepalese history) where they were confronted with a 250m (800ft) rock step which they called Kasa-Iwa, Umbrella Rock. This part-overhanging cliff at over 7,000m (23,000ft) took four weeks to climb, involving very hard free climbing and some artificial pitches. To service the camp (Camp IV) above it the Japanese set up an aerial ropeway as the cliff was too difficult for laden climbers. The Japanese then discovered that the ridge had a continuous series of difficult, overhanging rock steps. It was now early May and anxious to avoid too much loss of time the team descended from the ridge and forced a route up a difficult ice face to the south, route involving more artificial climbing. Eventually Camp V was set up at the edge of the summit plateau. From it, on 5 May, Kazuharu Kohara and Motoyoshi Tanaka set off at 5am. The summit was 2.5km (1½ miles) away and almost 800m (2,600ft) above, and the plateau was covered in 1m (3ft) of soft snow. Despite this they reached the top at 12.15pm, a phenomenal achievement. From just below the final rock tower the pair retrieved a piton hammered in by Toshio Imanishi, presenting it to Yuko Maki when they returned to Tokyo. The north-west face route was a major advance in difficulty on an 8,000er peak and was accomplished just a year after the British Annapurna south face climb and has never received the international acclaim it deserves, in part, perhaps, because the absence of an English-language book on the route meant it failed to reach the wider audience the British route commanded.

In 1972 the Koreans returned to Manaslu, again attempting to repeat the original route. Kim Ho Sup was once more leader. The team established Camp IA at about 6,500m (21,300ft) and on the night of 10-11 April it was occupied by 5 Koreans, a Japanese climber and 12 Sherpas. Sometime during the night the camp was overwhelmed by an avalanche, 4 Koreans, the Japanese and 10 Sherpas being killed. The remaining Korean, Kim Ye Sup, another brother of the leader, and two Sherpas were left on the surface by the avalanche, having been swept over 750m (2,500ft) down the mountain. As these survivors were trying to organise themselves another avalanche swept them down a further 300m (1,000ft). Again, miraculously, though badly injured, the three survived. The 15 deaths represent one of the worst-ever accidents in the Himalaya.

The storm which precipitated the avalanche on the northern side of the peak also pinned down members of a Tyrolean expedition on the south side. The Tyroleans, led by Wolfgang Nairz were climbing Manaslu's south face, a huge face split by a valley – called Butterfly Valley by the climbers – at about half height. The climbing on the lower face, a 600m

A close-up picture of Manaslu's formidable south-west face, first climbed by a Tyrolean team in 1972

(2,000ft) rock buttress, was as hard as any on the great peaks at that time, requiring fixed ropes and ladders for load carrying. Above the buttress the upper face was avoided by a rising traverse leftwards to the edge of the summit plateau. There a camp (Camp IV) was placed and from it on 25 April, Franz Jäger and Reinhold Messner set off for the summit. The pair had about 2.5km (1½ miles) to cover and 750m (2,500ft) to climb to reach the summit, but conditions were excellent. However, after some hours Jäger decided to return to camp, concerned that to continue would entail a bivouac. Messner continued alone and climbing without bottled oxygen reached the summit at 2pm: Manaslu was his second 8,000er.

During Messner's descent a storm blew up and he was soon engaged in a life-or-death struggle against wind and cold. With visibility down to 10m (30ft or so) he despaired of finding the tent, but could hear occasional shouts from Jäger who, he assumed, was trying to guide him to it. When, hypothermic and exhausted, he finally found the tent he discovered that Jäger was not there, though two other team-mates, Horst Fankhauser and Andi Schlick, were. Fankhauser and Schlick went out to look for Jäger whose shouts could still be heard. They became disorientated and, unable to regain the tent, were forced to dig a snow cave. During the night Schlick left the cave, whether to look for the tent or Jäger will never be known: Fankhauser did not see him again. The morning dawned bright, but the plateau was covered in 2m (6ft) of fresh snow and despite several hours search by Fankhauser and Messner no trace of Jäger or Schlick was found.

The original route was repeated in 1973 by a small German expedition, a Japanese team reconnoitring the east ridge at the same time. The following year a Japanese Ladies expedition also repeated the original route. On 3 May Mieko

Mori, Naoko Nakaseko and Masako Uchida, together with the Sherpa Jangbu, reached the summit, the first female ascent and the first ascent of an 8,000er by an exclusively female team. Sadly Teiko Suzuki died during a second, failed summit attempt. In 1975 a Spanish team repeated the original route, finding the body of either Jäger or Schlick on the summit plateau. The next year the Koreans tried again, the team led by Kim Jung Sup, another brother of Kim Ho Sup. Two climbers, one of them the leader, were seriously injured by falling ice and had to be air-lifted to Kathmandu, and a summit bid failed at about 7,850m (25,750ft). The Koreans, and the Kim family in particular, could be forgiven for feeling that Manaslu was engaged in a dreadful vendetta against them. Finally, in 1980 a Korean team successfully repeated the original route.

In spring 1981 a commercial expedition led by the German Hans von Kaenel placed 15 men on the summit, an Austrian pair, Josef Hillinger and Peter Wörgötter, skiing down from a point about 30m (100ft) below the summit to Camp I over a two day period. Later in the year a four-person French expedition climbed a hard line up Manaslu's west face. The face is over 3,000m (almost 11,000ft) high and included one 1,000m (3,300ft) section of 70° ice and glazed rocks. The face reaches the summit plateau at the same point as the Tyrolean south face traverse. The summit climbers, Pierre Beghin and Bernard Muller bivouaced at the edge of the plateau, continuing to the summit the next day, 7 October, and returning to the bivouac. They were the first to climb the peak in the post-monsoon period. A few days after the French climb a Japanese team completed the original route, three men reaching the summit.

In the post-monsoon period of 1983 a Korean, Huh Young-Ho soloed the peak from 7,200m (23,600ft) having been accompanied by a Sherpa to that height. His presence on the summit was confirmed by a German team who were astonished to meet him there after they had climbed the south face. The Germans had earlier abandoned an attempt on the south ridge. An Austrian attempt on the east ridge also failed. During the winter of 1983/84 a Polish team succeeded in climbing the Tyrolean route on the south side of the mountain,

Manaslu's East Pinnacle catches the dawn light. View to the south west from the Burui Gandaki Valley near Sama Gompa

completing the first winter ascent of Manaslu. The summit was reached on 12 January 1984 by Maciej Berbeka and Ryszard Gajewski, climbing without bottled oxygen. In spring 1984 a small Yugoslavian team climbed the south face in semi-alpine style, while in the autumn a Polish team added another new route on the south side, climbing the south ridge/south-east face. The team first climbed to the Pungen La (between Manaslu and Peak 29) then climbed the left side of the ridge. They were forced on to the south-east face, but regained the ridge, climbing it to the top. The summit was reached in late October by Aleksander Lwow and Krzysztof Wielicki.

In December 1985 a Japanese team made the second winter ascent of the peak following the original line. On the summit they found a (so far unclaimed) cigarette case and lighter which they believed had been left by the first ascent party. The following year a four man team – the Poles Artur Hajzer, Jerzy Kukuczka and Wojciech Kurtyka and the Mexican Carlos Carsolio – tried the east ridge, but were forced to abandon it due to bad weather and dangerous conditions. It was now early November and Kurtyka left the peak, but the other three climbed a new route on the north-east face. After the three had made the first ascent of the East Summit Carsolio was forced to abandon the climb due to frostbite, but Hajzer and Kukuczka continued to the summit. Manaslu was Kukuczka's twelfth 8,000er and while he was on the mountain he heard, by radio, that Messner had climbed Makalu and then, 20 days later, Lhotse, becoming the first man to climb all 14 8,000ers. From his own account of his climbs it is clear that Kukuczka was disappointed to have lost the race, even though he had never been likely to win it given his own strict rules (new route or first winter ascent). He noted after the news about Makalu that as Messner 'goes up the 8,000ers by the normal route as a rule, and is an excellent alpinist ... he would be extremely unlucky not to achieve his aim.' Messner's success on Lhotse proved him right. After Kukuczka's completion of the grand slam Messner sent him a message saying 'You are not second. You are great.' A cynic might argue that there is no better way of reminding someone that they are second than by making a point of telling them that they are not, but Kukuczka was impressed enough to use the message as a 'foreword' in his own book.

The pace of exploration on Manaslu now began to slow, though there were still recognisable 'last great problems'. A Kazakh team abandoned an attempt on the east face in autumn 1990 when three very experienced high altitude climbers died in a fall and an attempt at a winter solo of the south face by Frenchman Eric Monier also failed when be realised that his perceived climbing companion (a 100,000

The north face of Manaslu from near the Larkya La

year old woman) was probably an hallucination and that retreat might therefore be advisable. Clearly a companion of any age or sex would have invalidated a solo climb.

Following the failure of the Kazakh team in 1990 the east face was also the objective of a Ukrainian team in 1991. They, too, failed, but three members succeeded in climbing the south face alpine style. The trio then descended the original route, completing the first traverse of the peak. Manaslu was climbed in winter for the third time in 1995, then on 12 May 1996, the Mexican Carlos Carsolio became the fourth (and at 33 the youngest) to summit the 14 8,000ers when he finally climbed Manaslu having come so close in 1986 with Jerzy Kukuczka and Artur Hajzer.

In 1997, the South Korean Park Young-Seok, who had already climbed five 8,000ers in the previous six months, failed in winter attempt on Manaslu. There was further failure in 1998 for the Japanese husband and wife team of Yasushi Yamanoi and Teako Nagao during their post-monsoon attempt on the north-west face. Despite these failures Manaslu remains one of the most climbed of the Nepalese 8,000ers: only Everest, Cho Oyu and Dhaulagiri having had more ascents. As a contrast it is one of the most dangerous, over 50 climbers having died in their attempts on the peak. Though obviously distorted by the 15 deaths in the dreadful 1972 accident, Manaslu deserves its reputation as a dangerous mountain, the huge summit plateau being no place to be if bad weather envelops the peak.

lhotse 8,516m

"The névé was as tough as sheer ice, and we were determined not to take a single risk in such an exposed position. I cut a row of steps, which necessitated hundreds of strokes of my ice-axe. Just below the crest of the ridge I hacked out a large stance in the snow-cap and leaned my head against the face of the mountain in an effort to recover from my exertions."

ERNST REISS

Lhotse

Lhotse was E1 of the Indian Survey, but appears to have had no local name either in Tibet or Nepal when Charles Howard-Bury's Everest reconnaissance team advanced along the Kama Valley and the northern edge of the Kangshung Glacier in August 1921.

In the absence of an alternative, Howard-Bury christened it Lho-tse, south peak in Tibetan as it lay to the south of Everest, separated from it by the South Col. Because of the name's Tibetan derivation it has stuck.

Exploration

Despite being the fourth highest mountain in the world, Lhotse's closeness to its mighty neighbour meant that it was ignored by early climbers, though the view from the Kangshung side would have dissuaded anyone tempted to try: the east/north-east face is formidable, while the east ridge appears as a coxcomb, a long, high array of ice-glazed rock towers. The ridge has a number of subsidiary summits, that at the eastern end, Lhotse Shar (shar = east), about 1km (⅔mile) from the main summit rising to 8,398m (27,553ft). Between Shar and the main summit there are two central summits, one about 25m (80ft) lower, the other about 25m higher than Shar. As with Yalung Kang (Kangchenjunga's west peak) it has been suggested that Lhotse Shar is an independent peak, but here again the low point on the east ridge is barely 200m (600–650ft) below the main summit, insufficient for the classification of an independent peak in most people's eyes, though in no way reducing the appeal of Lhotse Shar as an objective.

Other than the south face (though this was observed by Tilman during his reconnaissance of the Solo Khumbu area with Charles Houston and party in 1950 and again by Shipton's reconnaissance in 1951) the approaches to Lhotse were explored as a prelude to expeditions to Everest. The Swiss and British Everest expeditions of 1952 and 1953 identified, in passing, that the west face of Lhotse was climbable by way of a narrow couloir which cuts through the rocky face to a point on the summit ridge close to the top. The north ridge, rising from the

Fritz Luchsinger on the summit after the first ascent in 1955

The west face of Lhotse. The Lhotse-Nuptse ridge runs towards the camera; to the right of the main summit is Lhotse Shar

South Col, was obviously a much more difficult climb, barred by a series of steep rock towers which would need to be turned. Those expeditions would also have noticed the difficulties of an attempt along the west (Nuptse) ridge, that ridge also being a narrow sawtooth.

When, in 1955, the first attempt was made on the peak it is not therefore surprising that it was made by way of the Khumbu Icefall, the Western Cwm and the west face. The team was led by the American Norman Dyhrenfurth – son of Prof Gunther Dyhrenfurth – and included both Swiss and American members, as well as Erwin Schneider, a member of the 1934 Nanga Parbat expedition. Climbing post-monsoon, the team established camps through the icefall and Western Cwm, and up to the west face (the Lhotse Face of Everest expeditions) placing the last (Camp V) at about 7,600m (24,900ft). (As an aside, during this trip Schneider and Bruno Spirig skied down the Khumbu Icefall – with two short intervals – an unheralded event which preceded the famed Japanese success by 16 years.) From Camp V, on 16 October Ernst Senn, Arthur Spöhel and two Sherpas continued towards the summit. Spöhel and the Sherpas stopped after about three hours, but Senn continued, reaching the start of the couloir which splits the face, at about 8,100m (26,600ft), before his bottled oxygen ran out. He then retreated to Camp V, but was unable to follow the others down to Camp IV. A storm now marooned Senn at Camp V for five nights though he survived the experience unscathed. A second summit attempt got no higher than Camp V, defeated by another vicious storm.

First Ascent

In 1956 the Swiss returned to Nepal intent upon making the second ascent of Everest, but also with permission to attempt Lhotse. The team was led by Albert Eggler and comprised Wolfgang Diehl, Hans Grimm, Hansrudolf von Gunten, Dr Eduard Leuthold, the expedition doctor, Fritz Luchsinger, Jürg Marmet, Fritz Müller, Ernst Reiss (who had been on the Swiss Everest expedition in Autumn 1952), Adolf Reist and Ernst Schmied. They were supported by a team of 22 Sherpas under sirdar Pasang Dawa Lama (who had climbed Cho Oyu with Jochler and Tichy). When Pasang fell ill at Base Camp Dawa Tenzing took over as sirdar.

While, to the west, the Japanese were forging their route up Manaslu the Swiss team followed the, by now, well-known route through the Khumbu Icefall and along the Western Cwm.

Lhotse (left), Lhotse Shar (centre, and looking the higher of the two summits) and Everest (right, beyond the ridge line) from near the head of the Barun Glacier

The weather was good and by early May they were further up the mountain than the British had been at the same time in 1953. At that time they decided that an attack on both peaks was feasible – though they had permission for both they had waited until they were on the mountain before making a final decision – and that the strongest pair on the day Camp VI was established near the South Col would make an attempt on Lhotse, the rest of the team continuing to build up for attempts on Everest. But now the weather turned bad, pinning the team down for several days. When it cleared, despite the delay the same plan was put into action.

Camp VI was placed close to the top of the Geneva Spur at about 8,000m (26,250ft) and a cable hoist was installed to drag supplies to it. On 17 May Fritz Luchsinger – who had made a remarkable recovery from serious illness early in the trip – and Ernst Reiss moved up to occupy the camp. They left it at 9am the next morning, but lost an hour soon after when Luchsinger's oxygen mask froze. Luckily they had a spare and,

Lhotse's huge south face dwarfs the tiny Island Peak immediately below from the Amphu Lapcha Pass

replacing the malfunctioning one, climbed on. It took them an hour to reach the base of the couloir. This rose at 40°–50°, but the firm snow allowed steady climbing. The couloir was about 5m (16ft) wide and defined by smooth rock ribs. At about half height a rock step almost closed the couloir, but a narrow 60° ice groove allowed it to be bypassed. Eventually the couloir ended at the razor-sharp summit ridge. Rock towers rose on both sides, that on the left being higher. The pair climbed a heavily corniced ridge, then a vertical rock pitch to arrive at a sharp crest, too narrow to stand on, so narrow that they had to hang their rucsacs from ice axes driven into a snow cap so that they could take photographs. It was 2.45pm on 18 May 1956, nine days after the Japanese ascent of Manaslu. The pair stayed 45 minutes on top, discarding their empty oxygen sets before descending. The descent needed great care, but they were back in Camp VI by 6.15pm, taking less than three hours from the top.

Five days after the Lhotse ascent the Swiss team placed two men on Everest's summit, then two more on the next day. The team then retreated from the mountain without incident: the double climb had been a magnificent achievement. Albert Eggler's book on the expedition, Gipfel über den Wolken (Summits above the Clouds) when translated into English was called The Everest-Lhotse Adventure. Though apparently mundane in comparison to the more romantic original, the change did capture the spirit of the expedition – for once, it could be argued, something had been gained in the translation.

Later Ascents

With the main summit climbed, attention passed, briefly, to Lhotse Shar. In 1965 a Japanese team attempted a route up the south-east ridge (the ridge which, beyond a high pass, rises to Island Peak, one of Nepal's most popular trekking peaks). The Japanese established a series of camps up the avalanche-free, but very difficult ridge, but a fall seriously injured one of the team, his evacuation from the mountain taking time and energy. It was over a month before a final camp (Camp V at about 7,300m/23,950ft) was occupied. The camp was almost certainly too low, but a two-man team made a summit attempt, failing at

Approaching the summit

The south face seen from the Imja K Khumbu

just over 8,000m (26,250ft) when it became clear that they had insufficient time to overcome the technical difficulties of the ridge. In 1970 an Austrian team led by Siegfried Aeberli attempted the same ridge. Following a similar line to the Japanese they established a top camp (Camp IV) at 7,620m (25,000ft) and from it Sepp Mayerl and Rolf Walter set out on 12 May. Climbing with oxygen sets, but without using the bottled gas at first, they reached the Japanese high point quite quickly. They then turned on their bottled gas for the final difficult section, reaching the summit just after noon. The top was even more knife-edged than the main summit, the men having to sit astride it as standing was too precarious. A second summit attempt the next day failed when the oxygen set of one of the two climbers stopped working.

With the principal summits climbed and the traverse from Lhotse Shar to the main summit looking futuristic, attention now shifted to the stupendous south face, a 3,300m (over 10,000ft) wall of steep (sometimes vertical, even overhanging, and averaging about 55°) rock and ice. The first attempt was in 1973 by a Japanese team led by Ryochei Uchida. The team made little progress on the south ridge (at the left edge of the face) before the danger from avalanches persuaded them to transfer to the west ridge. On that they reached about 7,300m (23,950ft) before

The classic route up Lhotse's west face from the Western Cwm

the

Ed Viesturs on the classic (west face) route

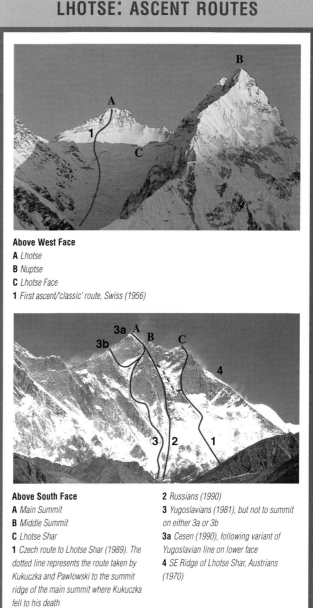

LHOTSE: ASCENT ROUTES

Above West Face

A *Lhotse*

B *Nuptse*

C *Lhotse Face*

1 *First ascent/'classic' route, Swiss (1956)*

Above South Face

A *Main Summit*

B *Middle Summit*

C *Lhotse Shar*

1 *Czech route to Lhotse Shar (1989). The dotted line represents the route taken by Kukuczka and Pawlowski to the summit ridge of the main summit where Kukuczka fell to his death*

2 *Russians (1990)*

3 *Yugoslavians (1981), but not to summit on either 3a or 3b*

3a *Cesen (1990), following variant of Yugoslavian line on lower face*

4 *SE Ridge of Lhotse Shar, Austrians (1970)*

abandoning the attempt. The following year a Polish team attempted a winter ascent of the original route to the main summit, reaching a height of 8,230m (27,000ft) before cold forced them to abandon, one team member dying of exposure. Before any further attempt could be made the Poles discovered that their permit ended on 31 December and had to retreat.

In 1975 an Italian expedition led by Ricardo Cassin, the legendary pre-war climber (who had made the first ascents of the Walker Spur on the Grandes Jorasses, the north-east face of Piz Badile and the north face of the Lavaredo's Cima Ovest) camped below the south face. The team was very strong, including Alessandro Gogna, Ignazio Piussi and Reinhold

Messner (a Tyrolean, but from the Italian Tyrol). This team, too, found a direct route up the face too dangerous and attempted a leftward traverse towards the Lhotse-Nuptse ridge. The Italians had reached about 7,400m (24,300ft) when avalanches destroyed both their base and top camps, injuring – though not seriously – four men. The attempt was then abandoned. A Japanese team trying the same line in 1976 climbed a little higher but were also forced to abandon by the avalanche danger.

When in 1977, the main summit of Lhotse was finally, after 21 years, reached again it was by an Austro-German team led by Dr. Gerhard Schmatz following the original route. The

second ascent was made on 8 May by Johann von Känel, Hermann Warth and the Sherpa Urkien. Two more teams reached the summit – a total of ten summiteers in the three attempts – Michl Dacher completing the first ascent without supplementary oxygen. Sadly, on the third summit climb Max Lutz was killed while descending. The original route was repeated twice in 1979, an Austrian team climbing it in the spring and a Polish team making the first post-monsoon ascent of the peak in October. One of the Poles was Jerzy Kukuczka making his first ascent of an 8,000er.

In 1980 Frenchmen Nicholas Jaegar arrived at the base of the south face with Nicholas Bérardini and Georges Bettembourg apparently with the audacious plan of not only soloing it, but then continuing down to the South Col and climbing Everest. His attempt on the face was soon abandoned because of the avalanche threat and he decided to solo Lhotse Shar and then follow the east ridge to the main summit. He was last seen at a height of about 8,000m (26,250ft) on the south-east ridge. Six days of bad weather then hid the mountain from view. Jaeger's final bivouac was found during a failed attempt to climb Shar in 1983.

A Yugoslav team took up the challenge of the south face in 1981. The team's first camp was a snow cave, the whole area being so constantly swept by avalanches that tents would have been destroyed. The weather was atrocious, with snow daily from noon onwards and descending teams invariably caught in powder snow avalanches. Camp III was placed below a 300m (1,000ft) overhang from which, on one occasion, a vast rock fall hurtled down the route. Thankfully no one was injured. Following further difficult and dangerous climbing the Yugoslav's established Camp V in the U-shaped snow field below the summit headwall. This camp was so vulnerable to avalanches that it was eventually abandoned for one higher on a spur to the east. The final decision to move the camp followed an incident where a tent was so inundated with snow that it was effectively sealed from the outside so that when the climbers began to cook the stove flame exhausted the oxygen and one man fell unconscious. The whole route to the new top camp was fixed with ropes and from it two attempts were made on the headwall, both failing in bad weather. A third attempt was then made, traversing across the snow basin and climbing towards the west ridge. Continuous difficulties finally forced the two climbers – Francek Kenez and Vanja Matijevic – to abandon the attempt, though they did succeed in reaching the ridge. The two finally regained Camp IV 25 hours after starting their climb. It is estimated that the highest point reached was over 8,300m (27,200ft), no more than 200m (650ft) below the top. It had been a remarkable, sensational attempt: the south face had

been climbed, though on the strict rules of Himalayan climbing total success could not be claimed as the summit was not reached.

In the spring of 1984 a Czech team pushed a route up the south face to the right of the Yugoslav line, reaching the summit of Lhotse Shar. The route followed a distinct rock buttress which gave very hard, but relatively avalanche-free, climbing. As with the Yugoslav route, fixed ropes were necessary because of the bad weather and prolonged climb (the Czechs took 51 days over their climb, the Yugoslavs had taken over 60). On 20 May four men left the top camp. Three gave up because of wind and cold but Zoltan Demján continued to the summit. On the next day three more of the team summitted. Post-monsoon in 1985 a Polish team attempted to follow the Czech

Camp on the Lhotse Face – the route to the South Col. The photograph was taken during the 1982 Canadian Everest expedition

line with the intention of bearing west towards the top so as to reach the main summit, but abandoned the attempt when a climber died in a fall.

In the post-monsoon season of 1986, just a week or so after their ascent of Makalu, Reinhold Messner and Hans Kammerlander, together with Friedl Mutschlechner, arrived at Everest base camp for an attempt on Lhotse. Messner had already tried to climb the peak twice in 1975 as part of the Italian south face expedition and in 1980 with one Sherpa. This time his team attached themselves to a commercial Everest expedition, using that party's equipment to reach the Lhotse Face. Here Mutschlechner retreated with toothache, Messner and Kammerlander following the original route to the summit which they reached on 16 October. It was Messner's final climb

of an 8,000er: he had not only climbed all 14, but four to them twice, and all of them without supplementary oxygen, a landmark in Himalayan climbing. Though several of his ascents followed 'normal' routes – while Jerzy Kukuczka, the second man to complete the set, climbed new lines or made first winter ascents on all but one peak – Messner's achievements cannot be underestimated. His ascent of Gasherbrum I with Habeler opened a new era in climbing on the great peaks, while the same pair's bottled gas-free ascent of Everest was an equivalent landmark. Together with his first solo of an 8,000er and solo of Everest when the mountain was free of other climbers these climbs represent a phenomenal CV in climbing on the world's highest mountains.

In the years following Messner grand slam the south face

remained an elusive goal. An international team climbed the face to the summit ridge in the autumn of 1987, but the final 200m (650ft) to the top eluded them as it had the Yugoslavs in 1981. One member of the team was killed in an avalanche. The next year Krzysztof Wielicki (wearing a special part-metal corset following a serious back injury after a fall earlier in the year, an injury which reduced his height by over 1cm (½in), and which made the descent agonising) soloed the original route on the west face from about 7,300m (24,000ft) on 31 December to achieve the first winter ascent. It was not a true solo as the mountain had been prepared to his top camp as part of a Belgian Everest-Lhotse winter expedition, but was still a remarkable climb, Wielicki climbing the final 1,200m (3,950ft) in just 9½ hours. The following year, in attempting to complete the Polish line on the south face, Jerzy Kukuczka and Ryszard Pawlowski, members of an International team, bivouaced at 8,300m (27,200ft), just below the summit ridge. On 24 October Kukuczka climbed on to the ridge, but then fell, probably when a cornice broke. He had fixed a runner and this held, but the 6mm rope – bought cheap in Kathmandu – broke and he fell 3,000m (10,000ft) to the base of the face. The shocked Pawlowski made his way down safely. Kukuczka was a remarkable climber, seemingly immune to suffering and with an insatiable appetite for high altitude climbing. He had climbed all of the 14 8,000ers either by new routes or in winter, all bar one – Lhotse. Success on the south face would have completed the series.

In 1989 French climbers Marc Batard and Christophe Profit each failed in winter solo bids to climb the south face, but the following year the Slovenian Tomo Cesen soloed a line similar to the Polish route, completing the climb by a direct route on the final headwall. Cesen was a phenomenon. In the winter of 1986 he soloed the Eiger, Grandes Jorasses and Matterhorn north faces in a week and had made other extreme solo climbs and some very fast solos of very hard routes. In the Himalaya he summitted during the first ascent of Yalung Kang's north face in 1985 and then in April 1989 he soloed the north face of Jannu, a 2,800m (9,200ft) face which he climbed in 23

On the south face

Everest looms above Lhotse's south face in this view from Ama Dablam's north ridge

hours. On Lhotse in April 1990 he started climbing at 5am on 22nd, on a route to the left of the Yugoslavian 1981 line. He bivouaced at 7,500m (24,600ft) when the sun hit the wall (so avoiding rock falls). His second bivouac was at 8,200m (26,900ft) and from it he reached the summit at 2.20pm on 24th. The final headwall was very hard, Cesen needing three hours to climb one 60m (200ft) section using pitons. Cesen retreated down the same line to about 7,800m (25,600ft), then used the pitons of the Yugslavian route – the ropes having gone – to speed his abseils. He bivouaced at 7,300m (24,000ft) and reached base camp on 25 April.

But then, in autumn 1990 a Soviet team climbed a direct line up the south face using 'old-fashioned' siege tactics and claimed a first ascent, discounting Cesen's claimed solo, adding something new to a whispering campaign that had grown, particularly in France, about the Slovenian's route. Cesen had no photographs to support his claim and the climbing world was soon divided on the issue though, significantly, several who had tried the face backed him. Later the Russians modified their view (they maintained they had been misquoted originally) claiming that Cesen was unlikely to have reached the main summit because of the difficulties of the final ridge, but that he had probably climbed the face, reaching the top of a lower pinnacle. The debate deflected attention from the Soviet climb which was an extraordinary achievement by a team of, mainly, young, inexperienced – but very good – climbers. The summit was reached on 16 October by Sergei

Bershov and Vladimir Karatajev. Supplementary oxygen was used, but the pair reached the top at 7pm long after it had run out. Karatajev later lost almost all his fingers and toes as a result of frostbite. It is unfortunate that the controversy over Cesen's ascent has detracted from a real appreciation of the Soviet climb which many consider to be the hardest route to the top of an 8,000er.

In 1992 Wally Berg and Scott Fischer climbed Lhotse by the normal route and concluded that Cesen had too. His description of the summit agreed with what they saw and they also saw the old orange oxygen bottle he described. They thought it possible he did not climb the last 8m (25ft) to the top as it was an unstable snow cone on which they felt insecure even though they were roped. In 1994 Carlos Carsolio climbed the normal route in under 24 hours on 13 May (having also summitted Cho Oyu on 25 April). He added to the Cesen controversy by noting that part of the Western Cwm was visible from the summit: Cesen had claimed to have looked into the Cwm, a fact seized on by his detractors as others who had definitely reached the summit claimed the Cwm was not visible. Further fuel was added to the Cesen fire in 1996 when photographs of the east ridge taken by other climbers who had summitted that year were published. Cesen claimed to have climbed the ridge on its southern side as that side was much easier, but the photos appeared to show that the northern side was more straightforward. It is also claimed that Reinhold Messner, who had championed Cesen's cause has now changed his opinion on the climb. The debate rumbles on and, in the nature of arguments about solo ascents unsupported by photographic or other evidence, is unlikely to be satisfactorily resolved.

Unfortunately the debate shrouded some very good climbs on Lhotse. In 1994 Erhard Loretan and Jean Troillet also climbed the normal route, but their intended traverse to Lhotse Shar was defeated by bad weather. Then on 10 May 1996 Chantal Mauduit summitted, the first female ascent. However even this climb proved controversial: a Sherpa who had rescued her from near the summit of Everest in 1995 when she was attempting a bottled oxygen free ascent is said to have approached her after her Lhotse climb and said, very simply, 'You lie'.

There was further controversy in 1997 following the claimed ascent by Italians Sergio Martini and Fausto De Stefani. Each had a good reason for wanting to climb Lhotse, Martini then needing only Everest to complete the 14 8,000ers (he subsequently climbed it in 1999), De Stefani needing only Kangchenjunga (which he subsequently climbed in 1998). The pair were honest in admitting that they had not reached the actual summit, claiming the high wind at the top made climbing the final ridge, its cornice of rotten snow, too dangerous. Since it was known that in poor weather the true summit of Lhotse could be difficult to locate the climbing world accepted the ascent. Later however, a South Korean climber, Park Young-Seok (who had climbed five 8,000ers in six months and then failed in a winter bid on Manaslu which would have made it six) reached the true summit and claimed that the Italians' tracks stopped a full 150m (500ft) from the top, rather too far for a minor case of mistaken identity. As De Stefani and Martini are both claimants of the grand slam this debate too is set to run.

The good news in 1998 – the mountain seeming to attract more than its share of bad – was a real climb, a post-monsoon attempt to traverse from Lhotse Shar to the main summit. A Russian team climbed Shar, but were unable to continue because weather and snow conditions were too poor. This traverse, which would include an ascent of Lhotse Middle, the highest unclimbed 'summit' in the world, remains one of the mountain's last great problems. Though Lhotse will always be a poor relative to its huge cousin – it has had fewer ascents than any 8,000er other than Annapurna – the south face, west ridge and Shar-main peak traverse will ensure that it retains the attention of the world's best climbers.

A close up view of Lhotse's formidable south face

gasherbrum II

8,035m

> "He started climbing, while I belayed him from my stance attached to two ice screws. Gradually he moved up. I heard him swearing. There was nowhere to bang in a piton. I watched him struggle, trying once, twice, his calves trembling with the effort ..."

JERZY KUKUCZKA watches Wojciech Kurtyka on the south-east spur

The Gasherbrum group are a series of peaks on a gigantic horseshoe ridge which encloses the South Gasherbrum Glacier. On the eastern side of the glacier is Gasherbrum I, separated by the Gasherbrum La from the pyramidal peaks of Gasherbrum II and III.

To the north-west of these twin peaks another high pass separates them from the trapezoidal Gasherbrum IV. South from here are peaks V and VI, each separated by ridge saddles. In the original classification of the Karakoram peaks Gasherbrum I was K5, Gasherbrum II being K4. The name is from the Balti (a Tibetan dialect) rgasha brum, beautiful mountain (though Dyhrenfurth claimed that he was once told the name meant 'shining wall'). What seems less in doubt than the derivation of the name is that it was originally applied to Gasherbrum IV, the most visible of the peaks. Whether 'beautiful mountain' or 'shining wall' is chosen, the name is appropriate, Gasherbrum IV's elegant shape and sun-catching pale limestone living up to either.

Exploration

The Gasherbrum group lies at the upper end of Baltoro Glacier, close enough to K2 to have shared the early explorations associated with the higher peak. Conway's trip of 1892 saw (and gave the alternative name to) Gasherbrum I, while the Abruzzi expedition of 1909 saw and photographed Gasherbrum I, II and III from what is now called the Sella Pass.

In 1934 the International Himalayan Expedition under Gunther Dyhrenfurth reached the junction of the Abruzzi and South Gasherbrum Glaciers and continued along the latter to the base of Gasherbrum II. From the base Dyhrenfurth could see two obvious lines of ascent to the terrace-like snow-field at the base of the final summit pyramid and was so convinced that from there straightforward climbing would

Larch, Moravec and Willenpart after their summit climb

reach the top that he was tempted to try. Only concerns over the abilities of his Balti porters to establish and support the necessary camps prevented him from doing so.

First Ascent

In 1956 the Austrian Himalayan Society organised an expedition to the Karakoram under Fritz Moravec, the intention being to reconnoitre Gasherbrum II and, if possible, to climb it. In addition to Moravec the expedition included Dr Erich Gattinger, a geologist, Sepp Larch, Hans Ratay, Richard Reinagl, Heinrich Roiss, Dr Georg Weiler, the team doctor, and Hans Willenpart, supported by Cpt Qasim Ali Shah, Hayat Ali Sha and a team of Balti porters. The expedition established a Base Camp near the junction of the Abruzzi and South Gasherbrum Glaciers and Camp I at the base of the south-west spur of the peak. Dyhrenfurth's 1934 reconnaissance had suggested that the easterly of the two spurs (the south spur) rising to the terrace snow-field was the more promising, but the Austrians favoured the other. At its base they found a safe campsite, but after being forced to retreat to Base Camp by a ten-day storm the Austrians discovered that their safe camp had been engulfed by a huge avalanche. Despite two days of digging through debris that was up to 10m (over 30ft) deep they were forced to accept that all their equipment had been lost. Moravec was now forced into an agonising decision – should he abandon the expedition or attempt a rapid ascent with a minimum of camps and support. He decided on the latter.

Ratay and Roiss climbed the ice ridge at the edge of the spur and

Climbers slog up the initial section of the long south-west ridge. The summit, still some 1,500m (5,000ft) above, is seen on the right

established Camp II at 6,700m (22,000ft). Larch and Reinagl then continued up to a shoulder on the spur where they established Camp III at 7,150m (23,500ft). Moravec now hoped to establish a final camp on the terrace snow-field, but the Balti porters were not capable of carrying loads up the spur. As a consequence on 6 July, just four days after abandoning their digging at Camp I, Moravec, Larch and Willenpart left Camp III carrying huge loads, but climbing without bottled oxygen. On dangerous, unstable snow they climbed unroped, as a slip by any one of them could not have been held by the others, and as night fell they reached the terrace. There they were able to find a sheltered spot for a bivouac beneath the cliffs of the summit pyramid's south-east face. They estimated their height at 7,500m (24,600ft). After a bitterly cold night and a meagre

breakfast the three set off along the rising terrace, staying close to the foot of the south-east face. By 9am they had reached the east ridge and could turn along it. Despite deep snow and a final short rock band the ridge was straightforward and at 11.30am on 7 July the three reached the summit, where two man-sized rock pinnacles were set on a small snow dome. The weather was perfect, so warm that the summiteers were able to take off their anoraks and bask in the sun. They built a cairn into which Moravec pushed a film canister with details of their ascent in German and English and an Austrian flag: later summitteers have not mentioned either the cairn or the pinnacles. After an hour the Austrians descended, the descent being without incident. Perhaps because Gasherbrum II is now seen as one of the easiest 8,000ers this first ascent has tended to be ignored by the climbing press, yet it represented an advance in the history of climbing on the great peaks: never before had an 8,000er been climbed by a team which deliberately chose to bivouac during the ascent. The tactic pointed the way forward, though it was almost three decades before the technique became common practice.

Later Ascents

In 1975, 19 years after the first ascent, a French expedition arrived at the base of Gasherbrum II. The French climbed the south spur – that suggested by Dyhrenfurth – to the terrace snow-field, then followed the east ridge, as taken by the Austrians, to the summit. The French intended to establish a Camp III at the top of the spur, but the two lead climbers, Marc Batard and Yannick Seigneur, continued past the intended site and, realising that the ridge climb was straightforward, erected a small tent at a higher level from which they reached the top –

making the second ascent – by 9am the following day. On their way down they met a second pair, Louis Audobert and Bernard Villaret near the tent site. Based on their experience Batard and Seigneur advised stopping at the tent and making an early start. Consequently Audobert and Villaret stopped, making their summit bid at 3am on the next day. By now the weather had deteriorated and eventually Villaret was forced to abandon the attempt in the face of biting cold and high winds. Audobert continued to a point only some 50m (160ft) from the top where he, too, was forced to turn around. Back at the tent the pair waited out the storm for a whole day. When conditions did not improve Audobert decided to descend, but was unable to persuade Villaret to accompany him. After many hours in temperatures estimated at -40°C or lower, with fierce winds and deep snow, Audobert reached Camp II utterly exhausted. Villaret was not seen again.

The day after Batard and Seigneur reached the summit two Polish teams arrived at the base of Gasherbrum II. One was female, led by Wanda Rutkiewicz, and was planning to climb Gasherbrum III, while the other was a male team intent on climbing Gasherbrum II. However, at the time of the arrival of the Poles the men had not been given permission to climb the higher peak and so the two teams combined to attempt Gasherbrum III.

The Poles followed the Austrian (first-ascent) route on the south-west spur, establishing a camp (Camp III) at 7,350m (24,100ft). Permission was now, belatedly, granted for an attempt on Gasherbrum II. On 1 August three men and two women climbed to the col between II and III. The three men felt that the west ridge of Gasherbrum II was too loose to attempt and so traversed around to the north-west face which

High camp on the south-east shoulder of Gasherbrum II. Beyond is the north-western flank of Gasherbrum I

Climbing the classic route on Gasherbrum II

Messner, who was climbing his eighth 8,000er. The same year the French couple Maurice and Liliane Barrard reached the summit. The flurry of activity was due, in large part, to Gasherbrum II rapidly acquiring a reputation as the easiest 8,000er. The French team which included Christine Janin had very limited experience: neither of the men had been higher than Mont Blanc and Janin had almost no climbing experience at all, though she later completed the Seven Summits. Other ascents – alpine style in three days and semi-solo by the Austrian Joseph (Pepo) Trattner – and rumours of illegal ascents persuaded a number of teams to the peak. But the dangers of high altitude climbing should never be underestimated: in 1982 Gasherbrum II claimed three more victims. The body of one of these, the Austrian Norbert Wolf,

they climbed to the summit, completing the third ascent of the peak and establishing the third route to the summit. The women failed in an attempt to climb Gasherbrum III, but two days later a mixed team, 2 men and 2 women, completed the climb. At that time Gasherbrum III was the highest unclimbed mountain in the world. It is also the highest to have had a first ascent by a woman. Halina Krüger-Syrokomska and Anna Okopinska then repeated the original route to the top of Gasherbrum II. Theirs was the first female ascent and the first female ascent of an 8,000m peak without supplementary oxygen.

Over subsequent years Gasherbrum II was climbed many times along the route of the original ascent. In 1981 the French climbers Eric Beaud, Phillippe Grenier and Christine Janin, and the Pakistani Sher Khan climbed the route alpine style in five days. The following year Sher Khan climbed the peak again, this time in the company of Nazir Sabir and Reinhold

Gasherbrum II from Base Camp. To the left is Gasherbrum III

GASHERBRUM II: ASCENT ROUTES

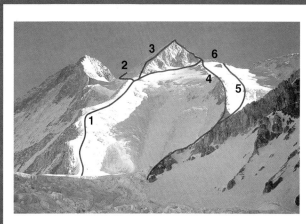

Above South-east Face
1 *First ascent (1956); the 'classic' route*
2 *NW Face, Polish (1975)*
3 *WSW Face, Carsolio (1995)*
4 *French (1975)*

5 *Dutch (1988)*
6 *East Ridge, Kukuczka/Kurtyka (1983)*

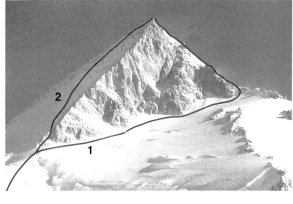

Above South-east Face
1 *First ascent (1956); the 'classic' route*
2 *WSW Face, Carsolio (1995)*

As climbers approach the top of a ridge the view of the high Karakoram peaks opens out

was found by Messner, Khan and Sabir, who attempted a burial. There was a subsequent furore over Messner's willingness to 'climb over bodies' in his pursuit of 8,000m peaks. The comments were both a sign of the times and the result of the jaundiced view of Messner's achievements by some climbers. In later years it has became common practice to camp among bodies on Everest's South Col and the difficulties (some would say impossibility) of retrieving bodies from high altitude have become better understood. As Messner himself has noted, when he climbed Gasherbrum II again in 1984 he found Wolf's body still visible, and at least a dozen other teams had climbed past it in the intervening years. On a happier note, Maurice and Liliane Barrard summitted in 1982, the first husband and wife team, and were accompanied by Liliane's brother for the, to date, only ever ascent of an 8,000er by a brother and sister team.

In 1983 the Poles Jerzy Kukuczka and Wojciech Kurtyka (the pair calling themselves the Alex McIntyre Memorial Expedition) made an alpine ascent of the long, undulating east ridge in three days. The pair descended the original route, thus completing the first traverse of the peak. Gasherbrum II was Kukuczka's fifth 8,000er. The two Poles subsequently climbed

In deep shadow on the classic line

A large team of climbers heads up across a lower section of the classic route

Climber leaving Camp II on the classic route

Gasherbrum I. In 1984 an equally remarkable traverse was achieved by Hans Kammerlander and Reinhold Messner who climbed Gasherbrum II via the original route, then descended south-eastwards before climbing Gasherbrum I.

The following year the peak almost became a circus, Frenchman Pierre Gevaux jumping from the summit beneath a specially designed parachute and Jean-Marc Boivin, another Frenchman, hang-gliding from the top. Boivin climbed the peak on 8 July carrying his 17kg (37½lb) glider. It was too windy to fly, so he descended. Then, on 14 July he climbed the peak again – in 16 hours from base camp – spent four hours digging the glider out of the snow and flew back to base in 20 minutes. Both Gevaux and Boivin established world height records. In the same year the French pair Thierry Renard and Pierre Mure-Ravaud climbed the peak with the intention that Renard should make a ski descent. Mure-Ravaud was unwell and descended with other summiteers, but Michel Metzger accompanied Renard. Renard

claimed the descent was a 'solo descent, extreme ski', Metzger viewing the claim with disdain on the grounds that two men do not constitute a solo and the skiing was hardly extreme.

In 1986 an early commercial expedition placed three members on the summit. Several other teams were also successful, Sher Khan making his third ascent of the peak as a member of one of them, but the dangers of even an easy 8,000er were again emphasised, a Spaniard dying of oedema in a high camp. The following year, prior to making a successful ascent, Jeff Little and Lydia Brady claimed to have had the highest recorded sex on

At sunrise the shadow of Gasherbrum II approaches the sunlit pinnacle of Masherbrum

land at about 7,800m (around 26,000ft). There may, of course, be good reasons why other teams have not broadcast an improvement in this particular height record. In 1988 Henri Albet and Pascal Hittinger, together with Michel Buscail and two Balti porters, climbed the original route to the summit from where Albet snowboarded down, Hittinger using a monoski from a point 10m (33ft) below the top. On the second day of descent Albet fell and was killed: Hittinger immediately abandoned his attempt. One day after Albet and Hittinger reached the top four men from a small Dutch team climbed a variant of the French 1975 route.

The increase in commercial traffic on the peak, and the perceived paucity of available lines, dissuaded many of the top climbers from attempting the peak, though there was (and always will be) a steady stream of climbers intent on completing all the 14 8,000ers and some seeking a Karakoram challenge. In 1995 Carlos Carsolio proved the 'no-new-line'

The Chinese – eastern – flank of Gasherbrum II – a sight few Western climbers have seen

rule by exception, breaking away from the normal route to climb diagonally across the west-south-west face to reach the west ridge, which he followed to the top. The following year the Karakoram challenge was taken up by Frenchman Jean-Christophe Lafaille. Lafaille soloed Gasherbrum II and then Gasherbrum I in a four day climb (see Chapter on Gasherbrum I for fuller details). In 1997 the Russian Anatoli Boukreev, well-known for his involvement in the 1996 Everest tragedy, climbed the peak in 12 hours, although his climb was assisted by ropes fixed by commercial expeditions. The following year an attempt to climb Gasherbrum II from the Chinese side failed due to high winds which threatened to blow the team off the peak. An ascent from that side remains the peak's outstanding problem.

Gasherbrum II is now firmly established as the easiest of the Karakoram's 8,000ers and one of the easiest of all. For some the walk-in along the Baltoro Glacier, with its view of K2, are an advantage, an experience to be savoured, adding to the attraction of the peak. For others, intent only on reaching the summit of an 8,000er the much easier approach to Cho Oyu (and Shisha Pangma now that commercial trips to Tibet have become routine) and its extra metres make that the preferred peak. Only Cho Oyu (and Everest of course) have had more ascents than Gasherbrum II, a situation that is unlikely to change unless politics intervene.

View to the north west from high on Gasherbrum I. Left to right, Gasherbrum IV, Gasherbrum III, Gasherbrum II

broad peak '8,047m

> **'I linked arms with him. He understood immediately what I meant ... At last we were on top ... All I could say was 'Fritz – fantastic'.**

MARCUS SCHMUCK TO FRITZ WINTERSTELLAR on reaching the summit on the first ascent

Broad Peak was not assigned a peak number in the original Karakoram survey, being hidden from the surveyor's view, and was named by Martin Conway during his expedition of 1892.

Broad Peak was not assigned a peak number in the original Karakoram survey, being hidden from the surveyor's view, and was named by Martin Conway during his expedition of 1892. Catching sight of the massif that defines the eastern side of the valley of the Godwin-Austen Glacier, filling the space between the Sella Pass and the Palchan La/Gasherbrum group, Conway noted 'a fine breadth of mountain splendour … a huge Breithorn, as it were, filling the space between K2 and the hidden Gasherbrum'. Conway therefore not only named the peak but was the first to note the similarity of the triple-summitted massif to the alpine peak which forms a section of the back wall of the Zermatt valley. Since that time grateful writers have frequently referred to Broad Peak as the 'Breithorn of the Karakoram'.

Although Broad Peak is now the accepted name both in Pakistan and internationally, efforts have been made to discover an earlier local one. In the absence of any credible candidate, a name was invented by translating Broad Peak into Balti, the local Tibetan dialect. The resulting name is P'alchan Ri or P'alchan Kangri, but the curious 'stop' between the first letter and the second syllable has led to the mis-spelling Phalchan which, in turn, has led to the spelling Falchan. This is very wrong as there is no 'f' sound in Tibetan. Around the time of the peak's first ascent the Pakistani authorities claimed that P'alchan Ri was indeed a name known by the local people: it is, for instance, used by Ardito Desio in his book on the first ascent of K2 (though interestingly the summit climbers, when quoted in that book, use Broad Peak). Was this discovery politically motivated, a result of half-a-century of translation of Conway's name, or a real name? Whatever the truth, it is unlikely that the mountain will now ever be called anything other than Broad Peak, a name descriptive not only of the massif, but of the summit structure of both the main and central peaks.

The central peak rises above the 8,000m-contour but, unlike Yalung Kang and Lhotse Shar, has few advocates for its inclusion as a separate peak, despite having a better – but still hardly adequate – claim than the other two. If the snow in the col between the main and central peaks, accumulated in the

Three of Broad Peak's four summits – North, Central and Main – can be seen in this evening view from the north west

Marcus Schmuck on the summit after the first ascent. Behind him is K2 while the long ridge from the forepeak curves away to his left

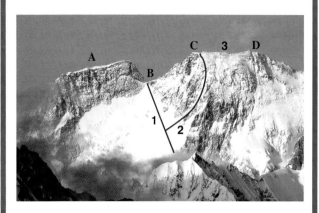

Above From West
A *Broad Peak Central*
B *Broad Col*
C *Forepeak*
D *Main Summit*
1 *Standard route*
2 *Carsolio (1994)*
3 *Long summit ridge. The length of the ridge explains why some climbers, arriving* *at the forepeak, believe they are on the summit, or decide against extending their climb to the main summit. The Kukuczka/Kurtyka (1984) climb followed the skyline ridge from the left. The Polish (1975) route to Broad Peak Central followed the standard route to Broad Col, then the skyline ridge*

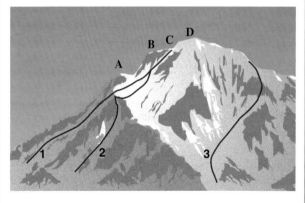

Above From South-west
A *Broad Peak North*
B *Broad Peak Central*
C *Broad Col*
D *Main Summit*
1 *Standard route*
2 *Carsolio (1994)*
3 *Attempts on SSE Spur/South Ridge (1997)*

tight hollow over thousands of years, were to melt, Broad Peak central would qualify as a fifteenth 8,000m peak. Melting might occur if global warming continues. The effect of local glacial and snowfield retreat can be seen in photographs of the summit ridge (between the fore peak and the main summit) taken during the first ascent and more recently. There is a clear reduction in snow cover. It has even been suggested that if the reduction continues, at some point the fore peak might actually overtop the main summit, a fact which would be welcomed by those climbers whose ascentshave finished at the fore peak.

Exploration

After Conway's naming, the mountain's position, on the approach to K2 from Concordia, meant that Broad Peak was well observed on all explorations of the area – by Eckenstein and Abruzzi for instance – and by early expeditions to the higher peak. It was also studied by Gunther Dyhrenfurth's 1934 International Himalayan Expedition to Gasherbrum I. Despite these early sightings, it was not until 1954 that an expedition to Broad Peak was mounted and even then it was only as a second choice. Dr Karl-Maria Herrligkoffer had intended his Austro-German expedition to attempt K2, but finding the Italians had already received permission switched objectives to Gasherbrum I, proposing an audacious approach along the Siachen Glacier. Business commitments delayed Herrligkoffer in Germany and rather than either allowing the expedition to proceed without him or delaying until 1955, he proposed an autumn ascent, eventually arriving in Askole in late September. At that time he was also given permission to attempt Broad Peak and rather than risk difficulties with porters on the Siachen approach he chose the more accessible mountain, taking the familiar route to Concordia.

Herrligkoffer took the view that the obvious ascent route – following the western spur to a snowfield close to the col between the main and central summits, a route proposed by Dyhrenfurth during his 1934 Gasherbrum reconnaissance – would be too difficult for the Balti porters and so chose a longer, less steep route on the eastern side of the south-west ridge. Dyhrenfurth had dismissed this route as too avalanche prone for safety and so it proved, one section – a 300m (1,000ft) couloir – being nicknamed the Kanonenrohr – gun barrel – by

Hermann Buhl below the forepeak during the first ascent. The true summit lies to the left

the climbers. Despite the avalanche dangers and accidents to three members, all of whom escaped major incidents with minor injuries, the team reached about 6,900m (22,650ft) before winter's early storms forced them to abandon the climb.

Hermann Buhl on the summit during the first ascent

First Ascent

In 1957, Hermann Buhl, the lone hero of Nanga Parbat, decided to return to the Karakoram and to try to climb an 8,000er with a small, lightweight expedition. As on Nanga Parbat he intended to dispense with bottled oxygen. When his original team members dropped out he invited Marcus Schmuck to join him. Schmuck wanted to take his normal partner Fritz Wintersteller, and to make up two ropes of two, Hermann Buhl invited the young Kurt Diemberger, after hearing of his ascent of the 'Giant Meringue'. To finance the trip Schmuck persuaded money from the Austrian Alpine Association, of which he was a member, but this was only available on condition that he became the official leader of the expedition. Technically, therefore, Schmuck was the leader, Buhl the climbing leader. In practice the four were a democratic unit.

Buhl's idea was to dispense with porters after Base Camp (at about 5,000m/16,400ft) had been established, using load carrying between camps as a means of acclimatisation. The team arrived at Concordia in May and began work on the west spur – Dyhrenfurth's suggested line – on the 13th. By 21 May they had established and stocked two camps, the first at 5,800m (19,000ft) and the second at 6,400m (21,000ft), intending to use fixed ropes left by Herrligkoffer's 1954 team which they dug out of the ice, as well as some of their own, to establish Camp III. During this work they came across a tin of bacon which the Germans had found in an abandoned Italian camp at K2, and some salami and egg liquor. The meat and drink were still edible despite the curious journey to Broad Peak and the three years high-altitude refrigeration.

Five days of bad weather now pinned the team in Base Camp and not until 28 May did they establish Camp III (6,950m/22,800ft), set at the edge of the snowfield below the col between the main and central peaks. The four abandoned their plan to establish a fourth camp and on 29 May climbed towards the col. Deep snow slowed their progress and it was mid-afternoon before they reached the col, at 7,800m (25,600ft). Believing that the top was the culmination of the ridge above them they continued up, despite the late hour. At 6pm Diemberger and Wintersteller, climbing ahead of Buhl and Schmuck, reached the ridge top, but could then see that the true summit, though only 15–20m (50–60ft) higher, was at least an hour away along a ridge which fell slightly then rose again. As it was too late for a summit bid, reluctantly the four returned to Camp III, reaching it at 9.30pm. Next day they descended to Base Camp in order to rest until their next attempt.

On 8 June they returned to Camp III and at 3.30am the next morning set off for the col again. The weather was good, but the cold intense and Buhl and Diemberger, who took a different line to that of Schmuck and Wintersteller, one that was in shadow for longer, were slowed by fierce pains in Buhl's right foot, the one from which he had lost joints on two toes after his Nanga Parbat climb. Consequently the two reached the col as Schmuck and Wintersteller were leaving it, and then had to wait an hour for Buhl to recover. Not until 2.30pm did Buhl and Diemberger start up the final ridge. Eventually Buhl, exhausted

The first British woman on an 8,000m peak: Julie Tullis on Broad Peak, 1984

by the pain in his foot was forced to stop, but generously allowed Diemberger to climb on alone. Schmuck and Wintersteller reached the true summit at 5.05pm, Diemberger joined them as they were about to leave the summit. The summit was a triangular snow slope backed by a huge cornice which Schmuck and Wintersteller had avoided, but which Diemberger climbed on to in order to take more extensive photographs, a bold, but somewhat risky venture.

On their descent Schmuck and Wintersteller met Buhl on the ridge top, the subsidiary summit, to which he had climbed with difficulty. They told him he would need at least another hour to reach the top and hurried on down. By the time Diemberger had reached the bottom of the dip between the two tops he could see Buhl advancing along the ridge. Diemberger claims their meeting was wordless, Buhl not stopping but climbing slowly towards the top, another monumental display of willpower. Diemberger turned and followed him, the pair reaching the top at about 7pm. Hermann Buhl became the second man to climb two 8,000ers (after Sherpa Gyalzen Norbu) and, if the marginally time lapse between the other three and himself is ignored, the first to be involved in two first ascents. Gyalzen Norbu was on the first ascent of Manaslu, but climbed Makalu the day after its first ascent. Buhl shares with Diemberger (who later climbed Dhaulagiri) the record of two 8,000er first ascents. After watching the setting sun lighting up the surrounding peaks Buhl and Diemberger left the summit, descending to Camp III in the dark.

The four men descended to Base Camp safely, but the expedition was not to have a happy ending: 18 days later while descending Chogolisa's final ridge after their summit attempt had been halted by bad weather Buhl and Diemberger had to feel their way in near zero visibility. Hermann Buhl strayed too close to the edge of a cornice: it collapsed and the greatest mountaineer of the era – one of the greatest of all time – fell to his death.

Later Ascents

In 1975 a Polish team climbed Broad Peak's central summit, a team of six setting out for the summit on 28 July. The route was as for the 1957 climb to the col between the tops, then along the central summit's final ridge. The col was reached in late afternoon and one of the six retreated to the top camp from it. The remaining five climbed on, overcoming two major obstacles to reach a final rock step. Here three men remained while Kazimierz Glazek and Janusz Kulis climbed on, reaching the top at 7.30pm. During the descent the weather worsened, forcing the climbers to move on to the north-east face to avoid a violent blizzard. There, Bohdan Nowaczyk, the last man on an abseil, was killed when the rope anchor failed. Without a rope the four survivors were forced to bivouac. The next morning a search failed to find their companion or the rope and they tied slings together to form a makeshift line. The appalling weather made the descent painfully slow and another bivouac was inevitable. While searching for a suitable spot Andrzej Sikorski slipped, knocking Marek Kesicki and summiteer Kulis off. Only Kulis survived the fall, he and Glazek eventually making camp. Both were frostbitten, Kulis subsequently losing most of his toes.

In 1976 a small French team led by Yannick Seigneur attempted to repeat the original route to the main summit, but failed, and it was not until 1977, 20 years after the first ascent that Broad Peak was climbed again, a large Japanese team following the original route. On 8 August Kazuhisa Noro, Takashi Ozaki and Yoshiyuki Tsuji reached the summit. In 1978 Yannick Seigneur returned and, climbing with Georges Bettembourg, claimed to have repeated the original route in true alpine style, though he reached the summit alone when Bettembourg stopped. However, Bettembourg claims that Seigneur only reached the foresummit, not the true summit, a claim Seigneur denied strenuously despite having admitted only reaching the col between the fore and main summits in an article on the climb.

Subsequent undisputed ascents all took the original line, with minor variations, including that in 1982 of Sher Khan, Reinhold Messner and Nazir Sabir. Broad Peak was Messner's ninth 8,000er (and his third 8,000er of 1982) and was accomplished nine days after the trio had climbed Gasherbrum II. On their way up Messner's team – who climbed the peak alpine style in four days – met Jerzy Kukuczka and Wojciech Kurtyka on their way down. The Poles had completed a similar alpine-style climb of Broad Peak the day before, but were anxious that news of their climb should be kept secret as they were climbing illegally. The pair were on a K2 expedition with permission to acclimatise on neighbouring peaks. They (rightly

On the south ridge during a failed attempt in 1997

before Diemberger's return to the top the Poles Kukuczka and Kurtyka also climbed it for the second time. They began by climbing the North Summit (the 7,600m/24,950ft – third peak of the Karakoram Breithorn – theirs was the first ascent) then climbed over the central summit (making the second ascent, and finding evidence of the Polish 1975 climb on the descent to the col before the main summit) and on to the main summit. This phenomenal climb took just four days. Even quicker was the ascent of Krzysztof Wielicki, a member of a Polish team repeating the original route. He left base camp just after midnight on 14 July and climbing by the light of a full moon reached Camp I at 4am, Camp II at 8am and the col between the central and main summits at 2pm. He was at the top by 4pm (one hour after three other members of the same expedition who had started from the top camp) having completed a 3,150m (10,300ft) climb in 13 hours climbing time. He was back at base camp by 10.30pm, a total time of 22 hours 10 minutes. First solo seems an inadequate description for such a remarkable climb – and there are, of course, those who doubt that 'solo' can be applied to a climb on a prepared mountain, especially as Wielicki rested and took refreshments at the Polish camps. Wielicki's 24-hour climb – the first ascent of an 8,000er in one day – was repeated in 1986 by Benôit Chamoux, then in 1987 Norbert Joos made a 'true' solo reaching the summit on 29 May, the earliest date a Karakoram 8,000er had been climbed.

In March 1988, having failed in a bid to make the first winter ascent of K2, a Polish team transferred its attention to Broad Peak. On 3 March Maciej Berbeka and Aleksander Lwow left base camp and climbed alpine-style through deep snow in intense cold. From a camp at 7,700m (25,250ft) Berbeka continued alone when Lwow was exhausted. He reached what he thought was the top at 6pm on 6 March in appalling weather and was forced to bivouac at 7,900m (25,900ft) on the way down. Though both Berbeka and Lwow suffered frostbite, they reached base camp safely and without permanent injury. Later, when he saw a photograph of the summit area Berbeka acknowledged that because of the bad weather he had not realised he had only reached the foresummit. Technically, therefore, Broad Peak had not been climbed in winter.

1992 saw the first ascent of a Broad Peak summit from the Chinese (east) side, a Spanish team (including one Italian and the Austrian Kurt Diemberger) climbing a hard line to Broad Peak Central which included 70° ice and short vertical walls in the lower section and 65°–70° couloirs higher up. The summit climbers – Spaniards Oscar Cadiach, Enric Dalmau and Lluis Ráfols, and the Italian Alberto Soncini – left Camp III, at 7,350m (24,100ft) and climbed all day, bivouacing with little equipment

as later events showed) considered it unlikely that the Pakistani authorities would consider an ascent of Broad Peak to fall within that definition. The year after Messner and Kukuczka's ascents the trend for alpine-style ascents of Broad Peak continued. Two Polish women, Anna Czerwinska and Krystyna Palmowska, made the first female ascent – and a major contribution to the history of Himalayan climbing with the first wholly female ascent of an 8,000er. On 30 June, after a semi-alpine ascent with two camps, Czerwinska reached the col between the fore and main summits, Palmowska continuing to the main summit alone. Pure alpine-style ascents were also made by Andy Parkin and Al Rouse, Jean Afanassieff and Roger Baxter-Jones, Doug Scott and Steve Sustad, though the success of these teams was tempered by the death of Pete Thexton from oedema during an attempt with Greg Child.

1984 was a memorable year, Kurt Diemberger returning to the mountain. On 18 July, 27 years and 39 days after he had reached the summit with Hermann Buhl he stood there again, this time with Briton Julie Tullis. Despite being avalanched on their descent the pair made it safely off the peak. The day

at 8,000m (26,247ft), just a few metres from the top. At first light they summitted and returned safely to camp.

On his way to becoming the fourth climber to complete the set of all 14 8,000ers, in 1994 the Mexican Carlos Carsolio soloed a new route to the right of the original route, climbing over Pt6230. His third bivouac was below the headwall to the foresummit at the junction with the original route, where Camp III is usually placed. Bad weather then forced him to retreat. Later he climbed the original route to Camp III (the route had been prepared by other expeditions to the peak) and his earlier bivouac site. Here his stove exploded burning down his tent and removing his moustache. Undeterred by either loss he climbed the headwall directly to the foresummit, then followed the original route to the top. He reached the summit as night fell and returned to Camp III where he was helped by a Basque expedition. Also in 1994 Hans Kammerlander climbed the peak, his ninth 8,000er. As with Wielicki on Shisha Pangma, Kammerlander was fed up with climbers reaching the foresummit and claiming an ascent. He therefore left a piece of red and purple rope attached to a ski pole on the summit and asked climbers what they had seen there: in 1994 seven reached the real top, a further six the foresummit only. One of the true summiteers was the Swede Göran Kropp who soloed the peak in 18¼ hours.

The next year three Japanese climbers repeated the Polish route over the north, central and main summits, the only three of the 28 summiteers who did not follow the original route, taking seven days from base camp to base camp.

To date there are just four routes on the mountain (if the route to the Central summit from the Chinese side of the mountain is included), a small number for such a massive, in every sense, peak (attempts to add a fifth along the south-south-east spur to the south ridge, in 1997, firstly by the Basque Iñurrategi brothers and then by a two-man team, Briton Rick Allen and Australian Andrew

Lock, failed). It might be expected that, overshadowed by its near neighbour K2 and more difficult than the equally close Gasherbrum II expeditions to Broad Peak would be limited. Yet the aura of the peak being Hermann Buhl's last great climb has maintained a steady stream of climbers, almost exclusively following the original route and many deciding not to risk the long traverse from the foresummit to the main summit. Of the 14 peaks only Gasherbrum II has had more summit climbers.

Sunrise on the classic route

gasherbrun I 8,068m

'In the viewfinder of the camera I could hardly make out Peter at all. His dark figure merged with the black background of the sky. Only when he moved a few steps could I see his feet in the snow.'

REINHOLD MESSNER films Peter Habeler reaching the summit of Gasherbrum I

Gasherbrum I was K5 in the first Karakoram survey, but was named Hidden Peak by Conway during his 1892 expedition because it only came into view as he climbed the Upper Baltoro Glacier towards the west ridge of Golden Throne (Baltoro Kangri).

asherbrum I was K5 in the first Karakoram survey, but was named Hidden Peak by Conway during his 1892 expedition because it only came into view as he climbed the Upper Baltoro Glacier towards the west ridge of Golden Throne (Baltoro Kangri). However, before Conway named the peak it had already been referred to by its 'correct' name, the Alpine Journal of August 1888 noting the name Gusher-Brum which, it reported, Col Godwin-Austen had been told meant 'Sunset Peak'. As noted in the chapter on Gasherbrum II it is now widely believed that the origin of the name is the Balti rgasha brum, beautiful mountain, though it should be noted that Gasherbrum IV, the peak usually claimed to be the origin of the name, catches the evening light.

Hidden Peak was the accepted name for the peak until very recent times – the account of the first ascent uses the name, as does Messner in his book on the second ascent. But with the trend away from the use of western names for Himalayan peaks Gasherbrum I is now preferred.

Exploration

The early exploration of the Gasherbrum peaks is one shared with the other Baltoro peaks and is considered in more detail in the chapter on K2. Conway's expedition photographed the peak as well as naming it, and it was photographed again by Vittorio Sella during the Duke of the Abruzzi's reconnaissance trip of 1909. Further photographs, and mapping of the Abruzzi Glacier from which the South Gasherbrum Glacier heads north into the cirque of Gasherbrum peaks, were also obtained in 1929 by the Italian expedition of the Duke of Spoleto. Some of the Spoleto team also explored the Urdok Glacier, viewing Gasherbrum I from the east.

In 1934 Gunther Dyhrenfurth's International Himalayan Expedition (a curious venture which included actors and actresses as well as climbers, the former making a film which helped pay for the trip) carried out a more thorough exploration of the peak from the South Gasherbrum Glacier. Dyhrenfurth's team concluded that the only possibility of climbing it was from the south, either by the south spur which falls from a point on the south-east ridge (which links Gasherbrum I to Urdok I) or along another southerly spur to the east (a spur which later became known as the IHE Spur). Dyhrenfurth thought the latter the easiest, because although it offered a longer route to the top, the lower section of the IHE Spur was much less steep than the south spur and so easier for load carrying. Each of the spurs ends at a gentle snow plateau/basin below the south-east ridge. From the plateau the final summit (south-east) ridge appeared to offer little difficulty. Two of Dyhrenfurth's team, the German Hans Ertl and the Swiss André Roch, attempted the IHE Spur, fortunately reaching a height of only about 6,200m (20,350ft) when, on 6 July, they were caught in a violent storm. The two climbers were still 7 or 8 km (5

Gasherbrum I from the west near Advanced Base Camp on the South Gasherbrum Glacier. The icefall leads to the hidden Upper Gasherbrum Cwm and the Gasherbrum La

miles) from the summit, but were able to retreat safely: on Nanga Parbat, to the south, the same protracted storm was killing Merkl, Welzenbach and Wieland. When the storm eventually cleared Dyhrenfurth's team had neither the time nor the resources to make a further attempt on the mountain.

Two years later Gasherbrum I was attempted in earnest by a French team under Henri de Ségogne. The team included Pierre Allain, the greatest French climber of the time, and several other very experienced alpinists, as well as 35 Sherpas brought from Darjeeling. The French chose to attack the south spur rather than the IHE route and in poor weather established a series of camps, the final one (Camp V) at 6,800m (22,300ft). The intention now was to place one more camp near a subsidiary summit which the French called Hidden Sud (7,069m/23,192ft). Though still horizontally some distance from the summit the French believed that they would then have then been above the major difficulties and in a position to make a summit attempt. But at the crucial moment a storm broke. For 10 days it snowed unceasingly making not only further progress impossible, but an orderly retreat hazardous: at one point two Sherpas retreating from Camp III to Camp II were caught in a powder snow avalanche and carried 550m (1,800ft) down the mountain. The pair 'passed Camp II like meteors' and were lucky to escape uninjured. After the epic of the retreat the French were understandably reluctant to return to the peak and the attempt was abandoned.

First Ascent

In 1958, realising that they were running out of opportunities to climb an 8,000er, the American Alpine Club sponsored an expedition to Gasherbrum I. It was led by Nick Clinch and comprised Dick Irvin, Andy Kauffman, Tom McCormack, Dr Tom Nevison, the expedition doctor, Gil Roberts, Pete Schoening, the man who had held the fall on K2 during the retreat which ended in the tragic death of Art Gilkey, and Bob Swift. The team was completed by two Pakistani army officers, Mohammed Akram and Tash Rizvi who were in charge of the six Balti porters used for high altitude carries. The Americans used English, French and Swiss equipment almost exclusively – how things change, within a relatively short time many innovations in climbing equipment were being exported to Europe. The team also used English suppliers for much of their food: Bob Swift noted early on that there was a great deal of tinned oxtail and tinned ox tongue. As he was no lover of either he wondered often why it was that the English seemed capable of only breeding bovines with no middle sections. Swift's personal account of the walk-in is also refreshingly truthful. The Baltoro is often claimed to offer the world's finest trek, its sides

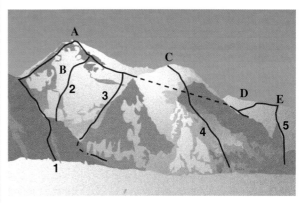

Above Looking North-east from Base Camp on the Abruzzi Glacier
A *Gasherbrum I* B *SW Face*
C *Hidden Sud* D *Urdok I*
E *Spur Peak*

1 *SW Ridge, Yugoslavians (1977); complete ridge Japanese (1990)*
2 *Kukuczka/Kurtyka (1983)*
3 *Spanish (1983)*
4 *Hidden Sud to first ascent, French (1980)*
5 *First ascent (1958), via Spur Peak*

Above North-west Face
1 *Germans (1982)*
2 *Swiss (1983)*
3 *Messner/Habeler (1975)*
4 *Italians (1985)*
5 *Japanese Couloir (1986)*
Main routes shown only; many variations, particularly of now-standard Japanese Couloir route

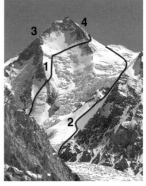

Above South-west Face
1 *Kukuczka/Kurtyka (1983)*
2 *Spanish (1983)*
3 *SW Ridge. Climbed in part by the Yugoslavians (1977) and fully by the Japanese (1990)*
4 *SE Ridge. Followed on the first ascent by the Americans (1958), and by the French (1980) and Spanish (1983) on their routes*

marked by an array of majestic peaks, but it can also be a nightmare. Swift notes 'June 3rd was misery' a sentence which sums up the effect of the sun on the ice, turning it into deep slush. He is also barely restrained about the difficulties with the Balti porters, though the best comment on this is from Schoening's account. He notes that one day's demand that the porters start walking at 10.30 in the morning was accepted, though the Americans did not know this until 10.29.

The Americans attacked the IHE spur (which they called the Roch Arête after André Roch) using fixed ropes to help load carrying to Camp IV at the edge of the snow plateau below the south-east ridge. On the plateau the climbers had to contend with waist-deep snow and wished they had skis. The snow slowed progress and when, on 4 July, Clinch, Kauffman, Nevison, Schoening and Swift climbed up to establish Camp V, despite using oxygen they could only reach a point at about 7,150m (23,500ft), over 150m (500ft) lower, but more importantly 800m horizontally, from the col below the south summit where they had hoped to place it. That night Kauffman

Nevison, Swift and Clinch leave Camp V during the first ascent

and Schoening remained in Camp V while the other three descended. The pair breathed oxygen not from masks, but from an open-pipe system which bled it into the space near their heads – a real incentive not to turn over during the night.

The next day the two set out at 5am using makeshift snowshoes formed by stamping their crampons through the plywood sides of food boxes and breathing oxygen, now through proper masks. The day was clear and sunny, but bitterly cold, slowing progress. When the slope steepened the box/snowshoes were abandoned, but they had been invaluable, allowing a relatively rapid rate of climb. In fact, when they changed to their second bottle of supplementary oxygen Kauffman and Schoening were able to increase the flow rate. On the final ridge the wind picked up, but the climbing was straightforward. At 3pm on 5 July they reached the summit, a broad snow dome. From it they announced their success to their team-mates at the lower camps using mirrors.

It had been planned that there would be one, perhaps two, further summit attempts, but none of the rest of the team felt fit enough to try, and the mountain was abandoned.

Later Ascents

It was 17 years before a climbing team returned to Gasherbrum I, a delay due to Pakistan government's refusal to open the area to foreigners rather than any lack of enthusiasm on the part of climbers. In the year the Karakoram was re-opened, 1975, two expeditions arrived at the mountain base, one a German team led by Hans Schell, the other the two-man team of Peter Habeler (from the Austrian Tyrol), and Reinhold Messner (an Italian Tyrolean). Since his involvement with big expeditions to Nanga Parbat, Manaslu and, more recently, Lhotse's south face, Messner had been wanting to try an 8,000er in alpine style, both as a reaction to the discipline of the big expeditions and to try to return to a purer style of climbing. His book on the Gasherbrum I expedition refers several times to the four-man team which climbed Broad Peak: Messner clearly saw such small expeditions as the way forward in Himalayan climbing, and saw Hermann Buhl as a father figure of the pure style.

Camp II during the first ascent. In the background are Chogolisa and Masherbrum

Schell had permission to climb Baltoro Kangri, but wrote to Habeler asking to be allowed on to their Gasherbrum I permit. At first Messner was pleased – Schell offered to pay for the permit and money was tight – but eventually was opposed to the idea. He was, in part, annoyed by Schell's assumption of agreement and lack of contact in Pakistan, but was also concerned that critics would seize on the fact that there was another party on the mountain to denigrate his and Habeler's climb. In the event, Schell's party climbed the IHE spur and so were an entire mountain away from Habeler and Messner.

The Tyroleans arrived in Pakistan with 200kg (440lb) of

Andy Kauffman on the summit after the first ascent

had given him 'an answer to the question of mankind's fundamental existence' and that he now saw himself 'in a new relationship with the world'. Though such cod philosophy gave his critics something else to chew on, there was no denying the magnitude of the achievement and that it really did open a new era in the history of Himalayan climbing.

Ironically, on the day after Habeler and Messner made the second ascent of Gasherbrum I, Schell's team climbing in the 'old-fashioned' style made the third, Robert Schauer, Schell himself and Herbert Zefferer following the original route to the top.

Over the next few years there were four further ascents of Gasherbrum I, three of them by new routes. In 1977 an eight-man Yugoslavian team climbed the south-west/west ridges): Andrej Stremfelj and Nejc Zaplotnik reached the summit, but Drago Bergar disappeared during a solo repetition of the climb. In 1980, the French pair Maurice Barrard and Georges Norbaud completed the French 1936 route over 'Hidden Sud'. To cross the snow plateau which had caused the Americans so much trouble the French used skis. Though purely alpine, the French ascent was also a feat of endurance: after climbing the south peak they were forced back to base by bad weather and in all spent over four weeks on the mountain. In 1981 a large Japanese expedition repeated the original route using oxygen on the summit climb, then in 1982 a German expedition led by Günther Stürm climbed a new route on the north-west face to the left (north) of the Habeler-Messner line. Stürm reached the top together with Michl Dacher and Sigi Hupfauer. At the same time a French team repeated the original route. The summit was reached by five climbers, one of them, Marie-Jose Valencot, making the first female ascent. Sylvain Saudan then skied from the summit to base camp, the first full ski descent of an 8,000er, though Manaslu had been substantially skied the previous year.

equipment compared to the 2 tonnes used by the Broad Peak team. On the first day of the climb proper Habeler and Messner carried rucsacs weighing 13kgs. On the second (summit) day they carried no sacs at all. Following the South Gasherbrum Glacier the pair bivouaced at 5,900m (19,350ft) below the mountain's north-west face. On 9 August they climbed the face, comparing it, in steepness and difficulty to the Matterhorn's north face. They bivouaced close to a distinct shoulder at 7,100m (23,300ft), then, on 10 August, starting at 8am, climbed the ridge between the north and north-west faces reaching the summit at 12.30pm, well before their self-imposed deadline of 3pm. Gasherbrum I was Messner's third 8,000er. The pair returned to their second bivouac site, but that night the weather, which had been near perfect, changed and violent winds almost destroyed their tent. Despite the storm they successfully downclimbed the north-west face on 11 August, being met by the Polish Gasherbrum II/III expedition who congratulated them on their step-change in the standard of Himalayan climbing. This was undoubtedly true. After the era of first ascents, and then the quest for hard routes – Annapurna's south face, Nanga Parbat's Rupal Face – the logical development was for smaller teams climbing in alpine style. Ultimately the two would be put together – two man teams on hard routes – and taken to its logical conclusion – solo ascents of hard routes. In his book on the climb Messner admits to the dangers in the approach – on a big expedition you have some chance of rescue by your team-mates – but claimed that the rewards justify the risk. Messner also claimed that the ascent

In 1983 the Polish Alex McIntyre Memorial Expedition comprising Jerzy Kukuczka and Wojciech Kurtyka, having already climbed a new route on Gasherbrum II climbed Gasherbrum I via the south-west face. The climb required three bivouacs, though two nights were spent at the second site as two attempts to climb the final headwall failed necessitating a traverse right on to a south-easterly spur. During the successful summit bid the Poles found one of Kurtyka's crampons dropped the day before on the abortive attempt on the headwall. While the Poles were completing their new routes on Gasherbrum I and II a Swiss team was attempting the two Gasherbrum peaks and Broad Peak, Erhard Loretan and Marcel Reudi completed a partially new route on the north-west face (joining the 1982 German line higher up), the climb being repeated by their colleagues Pierre Morand and Jean-Claude Sonnenwyl the following day. Also in 1983 all the members of a Spanish team under Javier Escartin reached the summit by a partially new route, following the south-west ridge of Hidden Sud, then continuing along the French line.

The following year Hans Kammerlander and Reinhold Messner traversed Gasherbrum I and II, the first traverse of two 8,000ers, and one accomplished with no route preparation or equipment caches. The pair climbed Gasherbrum II, then descended to Gasherbrum La and from there climbed the north-west face by a variant of the Habeler/Messner route before descending to the base of the north-west face which they climbed by a variant of the 1982 German route before descending to the South Gasherbrum Glacier.

Climbers on the now-standard route, the Japanese Couloir

1985 saw further new routes, the relatively easy-angled faces of the mountain allowing many variations. The Italian 'Quota 8,000' team, set up to climb all 14 8,000ers, completed two new routes on the north-west face, while the French pair of Eric Escoffier and Benôit Chamoux climbed a variant of the 1982 German line. The pair had previously climbed Gasherbrum II together, but Chamoux set off earlier than Escoffier on Gasherbrum I, bivouacing at nightfall. He was caught by Escoffier who started early the following day. Escoffier climbed the peak in 21 hours from the pair's base to the top and back. Their route was repeated

From a high camp a trail leads off to the base of the Japanese Couloir

a short while later by Gianpiero Di Federico the leader of an Italian team attempting the peak – the first solo ascent.

In 1986, during a period of renewed tension with India over Kashmir, Pakistan established a military camp on the Abruzzi Glacier on the southern side of the mountain and banned all expeditions from that area. The ban is still in place, the easy-angled south side of the peak remaining off limits. The original being unavailable, expeditions were now forced to find an alternative 'normal route' for ascents. This was rapidly provided by the Japanese Kiyoshi Wakutsu and Osamu Shimizu who, the same year, climbed a couloir which threaded its way up the north face above the Gasherbrum La. The Japanese Couloir is now the standard route on the peak. But the Japanese success was not shared by all the teams on the peak, a Swiss expedition attempting the north ridge direct from Gasherbrum La failing a heartbreaking 20m (65ft) from the top, stopped by winds which threatened to blow them off the mountain.

After the years of new route activity the peak received fewer ascents in the late 1980s, a combination of military activity between rival Indian and Pakistani forces, bad weather and avalanches keeping teams at bay. A notable attempt to climb the peak during this difficult period was that of a Japanese team who approached along the Sagan Glacier to the north. Bad weather and snow conditions halted the attempt at about 6,100m (20,000ft). In 1990 Wanda Rutkiewicz and Ewa Pankiewicz climbed yet another new line on the north-west face, and a Japanese team climbed the south-west ridge from its base, a new route as the 1977 Yugoslav route joined the ridge at a higher level. The climb involved a lot of fixed rope, a fact which allowed two teams to follow the line in the days after the Japanese had withdrawn. The 1990s saw many further ascents of the peak, chiefly by commercial expeditions. The closeness of Gasherbrum I to Gasherbrum II, a very popular peak with commercial expeditions, meant that many offered clients the choice of either (or even the chance of both) for a shared walk-in and consequent reduction in organisational requirements. There were still innovations though. In 1995 after ascents by a Slovenian team Marko Car, on a snowboard, and Iztok Tomazin, on conventional skis, skied down the Japanese Couloir, going from the summit to Camp II on the first day and on down to base camp the following day. The next year Frenchman Jean-Christophe Lafaille soloed Gasherbrum II and then Gasherbrum I in a four day climb. Lafaille was part of a large party attempting Gasherbrum II and left their Camp 1 at 5,900m (19,350ft) on the evening of 27 July. He reached the summit of Gasherbrum II at 9.10am on 28 July, then descended to a bivouac camp and was back in Camp 1 by the morning of 29 July. At 11pm he climbed Gasherbrum I by a route to the right

High on the Japanese Couloir route

of the Habeler/Messner line. He set up a bivouac at 7,450m (24,450ft) on 30 July, but bad weather forced him down to Camp 3 of other expeditions on the mountain. However, at 11pm he started up again and reached the summit on the morning of 31 July and was back in Camp 1 later the same day.

In 1997 Pakistan issued numerous permits for the Gasherbrum peaks, ostensibly to celebrate the country's Golden Jubilee of Pakistan. The effect was chaotic, with over 150 climbers crammed into the base camp area. Many believe that only perfect climbing weather prevented serious problems. Yet regardless of this number of summit aspirants only K2 of the Karakoram 8,000ers has had fewer summit climbers than Gasherbrum I. Despite the large number of routes on the peak, and the fact that there are still obvious lines – such as the north-east face – the (relative) ease of nearby Gasherbrum II is likely to ensure this remains the case for many years.

dhaulagiri 8,167m

> **' And then – there it was ... simply beyond words, mighty, unbelievably beautiful – Dhaulagiri. '**
>
> KURT DIEMBERGER

dhaulagiri

Peak XLII of the Indian survey is named from the Sanskrit dhavala giri, meaning white mountain. It is often, and correctly, said that travellers to the Himalaya, when asking the name of a prominent peak, were told it was dhaulagiri. It seems that when needing a name quickly, the local people chose an obvious one: most Himalayan peaks are, after all, substantially white.

Peak XLII of the Indian survey is named from the Sanskrit dhavala giri, white mountain. It is often, and rightly, said that foreign travellers to the Himalaya when asking the name of a prominent peak were told it was dhaulagiri, the locals not wanting to disappoint the man paying their wages and so, when needing a name quickly, choosing an obvious one: most Himalayan peaks are, after all, substantially white. But it is worth noting that to the east of Dhaulagiri are the Nilgiri peaks (nilgiri = blue mountain) and that the vast bulk of Dhaulagiri really is a mountain of purest white, a glowing, dazzling white when viewed from the south in the light of morning sun. This may have been even truer in the past as lately there has been a loss of ice from some Himalayan peaks (another product of global warming?). The surprise, perhaps, is that the imposing Dhaulagiri has as mundane a name as white mountain and has not been incorporated into a local legend or named for one of the pantheon of Hindu deities.

Exploration

Dhaulagiri was known from the early 1800s when Lt Webb made the measurements for which he was ridiculed, showing that the peak was 2,000m (6,600ft) higher than Chimborazo which was then considered the world's highest mountain. Though there were occasional sightings of the peak later – Lt James Herbert also surveyed it at the time of his advance into Nepal during the Nepalese War, confirming Webb's height – it was not until 1949 that the first photographs of the peak were brought back to Europe. They were obtained by Dr Arnold

The south face of Dhaulagiri is seen from the south east on the superb viewpoint of Poon Hill (3,194m/10,480ft) above the Ghorapani La

Heim, a Swiss scientist, who flew close to the peak, at an altitude of about 4,500m (14,800ft) during one of the earliest explorations of newly open Nepal.

The following year Dhaulagiri was one of the two potential targets for the French expedition under Maurice Herzog. The need to locate the mountain because of the poo quality of available maps meant that the French did not get very close to Dhaulagiri, but what they saw appalled them. Lionel Terray, one of the greatest French climbers of any era, claimed that the mountain would never be climbed and all those who saw it believed it was unclimbable from the northern or southern sides. Later, and hardly surprisingly, the history of climbing being full of those who have had to eat their words after seeing a team climb their 'unclimbable' route, Terray suggested to Max Eiselin (who led the first successful team) that the north-east ridge looked the most reasonable route. This assessment at least was prophetic, Eiselin's team following that ridge.

In 1952 a small British team carrying out botanical research on behalf of the British Museum made a more thorough exploration of the northern side of Dhaulagiri than time had allowed the French. They collected a good deal of information which was probably of value to a Swiss team which arrived in Nepal in 1953 with the intention of reconnoitring the north side and, if possible, climbing the peak. The Swiss, a seven-strong team led by Bernard Lauterburg, approached the peak along the Mayangdi Glacier which flows westwards from the northern side. The approach, particularly along the valley of Mayangdi Khola which required the team to hack their way through otherwise impenetrable jungle, was exhausting, but eventually a Base Camp was set up at the foot of the north face. Straightforward climbing on a rocky spur allowed progress to a height of about 5,900m (19,350ft), but the face above steepened sharply. A top camp (Camp V) was eventually placed at 6,500m (21,300ft) close to the base of a prominent feature of the face which the climbers called the Pear. Above this, it was hoped, they would be able to reach the west ridge, following it more easily to the summit. On 29 May Peter Braun and Ruedi Schatz, together with three load-carrying Sherpas, attacked the Pear. At the top of the feature the three Sherpas were sent down (one of them slipping on the way causing the three to fall 500m/1,600ft – a fall which they survived uninjured) while Braun and Schatz continued using oxygen. They reached about 7,600m (24,900ft), but guessed that it would take a further four hours to reach the ridge. With no way of assessing how long it might then take to reach the summit they retreated. The expedition then carried out valuable exploration work, reaching the north-east col and crossing the French and Dambush Passes to reach Tukuche.

DHAULAGIRI: ASCENT ROUTES

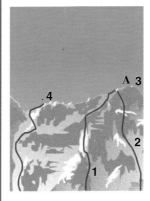

Above West Face
A *Summit*
1 *Kazakh (1991)*
2 *Czech (1985) but not to summit*
3 *SW Pillar (Czech/Italian/Russian 1988)*
4 *Czech route (1984)*

Above North Face
1 *First ascent (standard) route*
2 *UK/Russian (1993)*
3 *The Pear Japanese (1982)*

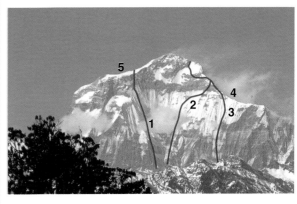

Above From Poon Hill
1 *Polish/Canadian (1986) but only to Japanese South Buttress route*
2 *Humar (1999) but not to summit*

3 *Slovenians (1981) but only to SE Ridge*
4 *SE Ridge Japanese (1978); approach was from the far side*
5 *South Buttress Japanese (1978)*

Above East Face
1 *SE Ridge, Japanese (1978)*
2 *East Face, Ghilini/Kurtyka/MacIntyre/ Wilczynski (1980)*

3 *East Face, Slovenians (1986) but not to summit*
4 *NE Ridge, first ascent/'classic' route*

In 1954 the first ever Argentinian team to one of the great peaks arrived below the north face. It was led by Francisco Ibañez, who had been the liaison officer on the French expedition to Fitzroy. The team of eleven established a base camp very early in the season and followed the Swiss 1953 route. High on the face where the Swiss had been unable to find level ground for a satisfactory camp the Argentinians used dynamite to blast a platform for their Camp VI – a dubious activity (though not the last debatable incident on an 8,000er)

Ernst Forrer at 8,000m during the first ascent

– a procedure which took three days. The Argentinians then climbed the Pear and set up Camp VII at about 7,500m (24,600ft). From it on 1 June four men, Alfredo Magnani, Austrian-born Gerhard Watzl and the Sherpas Pasang Dawa Lama and Ang Nyima, set out for the top. They reached the west ridge, but it turned out to be more difficult than they had hoped, unclimbable pinnacles

Diemberger, Schelbert, Nawang Dorje and Nima Dorje on the summit after the first ascent

forcing them to traverse on to the vast south face. Not until 5pm could they move back on to the ridge. They now bivouaced in a snow cave at over 7,900m (25,900ft) content that the way to the summit was straightforward, requiring no more than three hours climbing. But that night a violent storm broke and instead of the projected summit climb they were forced to battle down

to Camp VII where they found Ibañez waiting for them. Ibañez was severely frostbitten and could only make it down to Camp VI. The others, though also frostbitten and exhausted, continued down. It was five days before Ibañez could be rescued, his condition now so bad that he had to be placed in a makeshift stretcher and lowered down the mountain. On the march out, with echoes of the appalling journey of Herzog and Lachenal from Annapurna, Ibañez lost fingers and toes and then parts of his left foot. But there was to be no happy outcome: he died in hospital at Kathmandu.

In 1955 a German-Swiss team led by Martin Meier (who, with Rudolf Peters had first climbed the Croz Spur on the north face of the Grandes Jorasses) again attempted the north face route. The team was termed the 'Vegetarian (or Bircher-Müesli) Himalayan Expedition' as a requirement of their chief sponsor was that the climbers would have a meat-free diet. The team reached only 7,350m (24,100ft) on the Pear route, though this lack of success had less to do with diet than the lack of experience and expertise of the climbers (Toni Hiebeler had withdrawn from the expedition at an early stage concerned over just this) and the general disorganisation of the attempt.

The following year the Argentines returned, but they fared little better, the early arrival of the monsoon forcing them to abandon at a height only just above that achieved in 1955.

In 1958 the Swiss came back, this time led by Werner Stäuble. Again the Pear route was chosen, but after establishing a camp at 7,350m (24,100ft) an attempt to place a higher camp was thwarted by a violent storm. During this Max Eiselin and Sherpa Pasang Sona, marooned in the snow cave that formed Camp IV, were sealed into the cave by an avalanche. Their frantic attempt to dig themselves out were almost ended by their consuming the cave's remaining oxygen. Only on the point of black-out were they able to struggle free. Later Eiselin and his friend, the team doctor Georg Hajdukiewicz, observed the peak at length and became convinced that the best route to the summit was along the north-east ridge from the north-east col. Eiselin applied for permission to return in 1959, but this had already been given to the Austrian Fritz Moravec, the leader of the successful Gasherbrum II expedition. Eiselin therefore secured permission for 1960, but graciously told Moravec of his view that the expeditions to date had been going the wrong way.

The Austrian team did indeed make an attempt on the north-east ridge and initially made very good progress, Camp IV being established at 6,500m (21,300ft) as early as 24 April. Unfortunately the team was then struck a double blow. On 29 April Heinrich Roiss fell down a crevasse near Camp II. His disappearance was not noticed for a couple of hours and when he was eventually found it was too late: though he was still alive when he was dragged out he was in a very poor state and died during the night. At the same time bad weather destroyed the top camps, keeping the team low on the mountain. When the attempt could resume late in May a top camp was established at 7,400m (24,300ft) and from it Karl Prein and Sherpa Pasang Dawa Lama made several attempts to reach the top. They did not get beyond 7,800m (25,600ft), each time defeated by violent winds and bitter cold.

First Ascent

In 1960 Max Eiselin led an expedition which, though predominantly Swiss, was almost international in its make up.

Seen to the west from the pilgrim village of Muktinath, the sun sets behind Dhaulagiri

In addition to Eiselin, Ernst Forrer, Albin Schelbert, Michel Vaucher and Hugo Weber were Swiss, as was Jean-Jacques Roussi though he was then resident in Nepal. Kurt Diemberger was Austrian and Peter Diener German, while the team doctor Georg Hajdukiewicz and his assistant Adam Skoczylas were Poles. The final member was Norman Dyhrenfurth, the American (but Swiss-born) son of the Swiss-American Günter

On the north face during the Anglo-Russian ascent in 1993

Oskar Dyhrenfurth, who was to make a film of the expedition. The climbers were supported by a team of seven Sherpas under sirdar Ang Dawa (though he was demoted during the expedition for a combination of laziness and over-enthusiasm in eating the best of the expedition's food). The reason there were so few Sherpas was that the expedition was supported by a Pilatus-Porter glacier plane (painted red and yellow and christened 'Yeti') whose pilot and co-pilot/mechanic Ernst Saxer and Emil Wick became critical members of the team.

The plane was to be used to fly equipment and climbers to the north-east col, though an early acclimatisation camp was first set up on the Dambush Pass. The pass is at 5,200m (17,050ft), a world-record height for a plane landing. The north-east col is at 5,700m (18,700ft) and when landings were made there it (obviously) set a new world record. The use of the plane allowed the team to avoid a tedious walk-in and any possible disputes with porters, but the rapid height gain (from Pokhara to

5,200m in about an hour) caused all the climbers and Sherpas problems with altitude sickness. The plane was also not without its problems. Having successfully flown from Switzerland to Pokhara and made numerous flights to Dambush and the Col, it blew a cylinder forcing an emergency landing at Pokhara from which the pilots escaped unscathed. A replacement engine was obtained in a very fast time, but the plane later crashed on the Dambush Pass. Again the pilots escaped unharmed. This time the plane could not be salvaged, though by then all necessary supplies had been air-lifted to the Col. However, some expedition members and some supplies had to arrive the conventional way, on foot along the Mayangdi Glacier.

Max Eiselin's book of the expedition is a curious read. After a long chapter on the flight to Nepal (on which he was a passenger) there are longer ones on the early flights to Dambush and the Col, the engine failure and the crash. Only in the last few pages is the climbing of the mountain mentioned, by which time the team has already reached 7,800m (25,600ft). The first ascent of Dhaulagiri was, the reader gathers, merely a sideshow in the 'Yeti' story. When Yeti crashed Eiselin's concern was not how the mountain could be climbed without it, but how soon a replacement plane could arrive. To gain any real understanding of the difficulties of the north-east ridge it is necessary to read the accounts of the climbers, published elsewhere.

Early on it was discovered that the oxygen cylinders which had been supplied were useless, being virtually empty (for no apparent reason) and so if Dhaulagiri was to be climbed it must

Rob Hall and Veikka Gustafsson high on the classic north-east ridge route, the Annapurna Himal in the distance

The east and south-east ridge of Dhaulagiri and the notorious East Dhaulagiri Glacier are seen from above Larjung in the Kali Gandaki Valley

be without supplementary oxygen. The early arrivals on the Col – Diemberger, Diener, Forrer, Schelbert and several Sherpas – forced the route upwards, though one of their earliest tasks was to stamp out a runway for Yeti when its skis sank in soft snow. The take-off along this makeshift runway was a do-or-die effort by Ernst Saxer flying alone: fail to take-off and he and the plane would disappear into a crevasse; make insufficient height in time and he would crash into seracs. Take-off was successful and represented the most courageous act of the trip.

Using fixed ropes left by the Austrians in 1959, the 1960 team established a series of camps, the top one, Camp V, at 7,450m (25,450ft) being in place by early May, proving the usefulness of Yeti in moving supplies. From the camp a summit attempt was made on 4 May, but this failed at 7,800m (25,600ft) – at the point where the south-east and north-east ridges meet – because of the usual midday break in the weather. It was clear that another camp would be needed before an attempt with any hope of success could be made. But then a storm forced a temporary halt to progress.

When the second attempt was made the attitude of the climbers showed clearly that a new era in Himalayan climbing had begun. Gone was the altruism of the Annapurna and other early 1950s teams when success for the team was (usually) more important than that of the individual. Some summit fever had always been present, of course, better hidden or better controlled, but now it was rampant. On the north-east col Eiselin's plan for a steady push up the mountain was ignored, particularly by Kurt Diemberger (whose view of these events appears on pp.221–2 of *Summits and Secrets*). His view, according to the leader's account, was that on Broad Peak he had done all the hard work but been beaten to the summit and it was not going to happen again. Diemberger therefore climbed from the col to Camp IV in one day, together with Forrer, Schelbert and two Sherpas. The team doctor was appalled by the risks of this rapid climb, but Eiselin, faced with this minor mutiny, merely said 'oh well, it was all a question of tactics'

The next day, with Peter Diener having joined in as well, there were nine climbers at Camp V and, in essence, no one below them on the mountain in support. Roussi, Vaucher and Weber who had already spent a night of acclimatisation there, seemed to have been of the view that they deserved first go or, failing that, then the nine could survive one night huddled together. A row broke out and after that night the three descended. This was, with hindsight, a good decision as Vaucher became ill before the three had reached Camp IV and they were forced to take him down to the col. Back at Camp V the remaining six men now climbed on carrying one two-man tent. This was pitched at 7,800 (25,600ft) and occupied, the six, unable to lie down properly, taking up various, uncomfortable positions. In the middle of the night, Diemberger – who appears in some accounts to have been responsible for the row at Camp V – and Forrer asked Sherpa Nima Dorje, who was at the entrance of the tent, to make some tea. But Nima Dorje, who had already done that earlier, took his sleeping bag and mat and went outside, spending the night in the open. The next day, 13 May, was cold but clear and windless, a perfect summit day. The six men started on three ropes. Forrer and Sherpa Nima Dorje first, then Diemberger and Sherpa Nawang Dorje, and Diener and

Schelbert last. Later Diener and Schelbert unroped as Schelbert was moving much quicker. After starting out at 8am the top was reached at 12.30, 4½ hours for about 370m (1,200ft) of climbing including one passage of Grade IV. Although the climbing world might not differentiate between the six men, it is clear from the accounts that they did: Diemberger and Schelbert reached the rocky summit (big enough for all six to stand at the same height, but merely the highest bump on a long ridge whose undulations would confuse later climbers) first and were followed almost immediately by Nawang Dorje, then Forrer and Nima Dorje, and finally Diener. After an hour the six descended. Ten days later the climb was repeated by Vaucher and Weber starting from Camp V. Diemberger thus became, with Buhl (and, technically, Gyalzen Norbu who climbed Manaslu and was in the second team to climb Makalu on the successful French expedition), the only man to be first to the top of two 8,000ers.

Alpenglow on Dhaulagiri, seen from Poon Hill. In the foreground is the mist-filled Kali Gandaki Valley

The Swiss seemed to have had little difficulty in recognising the highest point though later summiteers seemed to have been less successful. Following several incidents in which climbers were accused of not reaching the true summit but a lower point on the long summit ridge a pole was placed on the top in 1998. Unfortunately this was placed on the very point (the lower one) which had caused the original confusion and merely added to the problems.

Later Ascents

Nine years after the first ascent an American team attempted to climb Dhaulagiri's south-east ridge, approaching from the East Dhaulagiri Glacier which is very broken and avalanche prone. On 28 April while a team of six Americans and two Sherpas were bridging a huge crevasse to allow further progress an avalanche engulfed them. Only Lou Reichardt survived.

In 1970 the mountain was climbed for the second time, a Japanese team following the original route and Tetsuji Kawada and Sherpa Lhakpa Tenzing reaching the summit on 20 October, achieving the first post-monsoon ascent. The Japanese used supplementary oxygen, a few full cylinders being left on the mountain and used in 1971 by the American Tom Bech and his wife who were looking for a safer way to reach the south-east ridge team than the 'suicidal' east glacier. Using Bech's photographs, an American team arrived in the spring of 1973 to attempt the south-east ridge by climbing to it from the north-east col. The ridge was successfully reached, but proved to be narrow and difficult. Realising they had neither the time nor resources to climb it the Americans transferred their attention to the original route. On 12 May, climbing without bottled oxygen, Lou Reichardt, the sole survivor of the 1970 tragedy, reached the top with John Roskelley and Sherpa Nawang Samden.

Dhaulagiri's reputation as one of the most difficult 8,000ers, and the number of obvious, but hard, lines now meant that expeditions were an annual event. In 1975 a Japanese team made a first attempt at the south buttress at the left end of the awesome south face but abandoned the attempt when an avalanche killed two team members, two Sherpas and a local porter. (This buttress is sometimes called the south-east pillar, a confusing name as it is on the west side of the south face and is actually a buttress on the south-west ridge. It is, however, to the east of the buttress on the west face, climbed in 1988, which is usually called the south-west pillar.) The following year an Italian team attempted the north-west ridge, but failed and repeated the original line instead, two men reaching the top. Then in spring 1977 Peter Habeler and Reinhold Messner led an international team in an attempt at a direct route on the south face. The extreme avalanche risk forced them to abandon the attempt. In the autumn of the same year the Japanese again failed on the south buttress, but were finally successful in the spring of 1978, Toshiaki Kobayashi and Tatsuji Shigeno reaching the summit on 10 May . Four more team members repeated the climb on the following day. Sadly one team member died of oedema after a bad fall. Post-monsoon the same year a Japanese team climbed the south-east ridge from the East Dhaulagiri Glacier, completing the American line. Six men reached the top, but three of the team were killed in an avalanche and another in a fall.

In 1980 the Poles Wojciech Kurtyka and Ludwick Wilczynski, Briton Alex McIntyre and Frenchman René Ghilini climbed the east face in an alpine-style ascent in atrocious weather. Having reached the north-east ridge they retreated down it (using the fixed ropes of a Swiss 20-year anniversary

Dhaulagiri and its south-east ridge rise steeply over the deep Kali Gandaki Valley in this view from east-north-east near Tukuche

spring 1982 Lutgaerde Vivijs, climbing with a Belgian team on the original route, made the first female ascent of Dhaulagiri. The expedition put seven people on the summit, one of whom, Sherpa Ang Rita, was making his fourth ascent. In the post-monsoon season of the same year a Japanese team finally climbed the Pear route, the summit team of Kozu Komatsu, Yasuhira Saito and Noburu Yamada using bottled oxygen for sleeping at the top camp and also for the climb along the west ridge. Later the same year a Japanese (Hokkaido University) expedition made the first winter ascent of the peak (and the first winter ascent of any 8,000er). The summit was reached on 13 December by Akio Koizumi and Sherpa Wangdu. Climbing with oxygen on the original route the pair began their summit climb from a snow hole bivouac at 7,930m (26,000ft). Their oxygen sets ran out before the top, making the last section and the descent a real trial. Under the strict rules of winter climbing the team's arrival in October and early work on the route in November meant that the climb was technically an autumn/winter ascent, but that seems to be splitting hairs unnecessarily.

Post-monsoon 1984 saw two significant climbs, a 20-man Czech team climbing the west face (rivalling Nanga Parbat's Rupal Face as the highest mountain wall in the world) after an epic, 60-day climb. Karel Jakes, Jan Simon and Jaromir Stejskal reached the top, but Simon, who had climbed ahead of the others, and descended first, was killed on the descent. He had retrieved a summit flag left by the French pair Pierre Beghin and Jean Noel-Roche who climbed the Japanese buttress on the south face alpine style. During the 1984/85 winter a Polish team made the first official winter ascent of the peak following the original route. The summit pair was Andrzej Czok and Jerzy Kukuczka (it was the latter's seventh 8,000er).

team), but then returned 10 days later to climb that route to their high point, continuing to the summit. The Swiss team was also successful, 14 climbers reaching the top including Fritz Luchsinger (then 59 years old) who had been in the first team to climb Lhotse, and Sherpa Ang Rita who reached the summit twice, on 13 May and again on 19 May. In 1981 the Japanese climber Hironobu Kamuro made a solo ascent of the original route, though he was supported as far as the north-east col and assisted on the route by ropes fixed, and a tent left, by an earlier, successful Anglo-Canadian expedition. Nevertheless, the climb, with four bivouacs on the ascent and two on the descent, was a considerable achievement.

In October 1981 the south face was climbed alpine style by a Yugoslav team of six following a route at the right side to the south-east ridge. The climb took 16 days, including nine bivouacs on the ascent and five days on the descent, involved hard climbing on rock and ice at never less than 50°. This magnificent achievement of endurance and climbing ability was unfortunately not capped by the team reaching the summit. The descent also had its moment of pure farce. Without food, fuel and tents the team stumbled on a Japanese south-east ridge camp, their joy being shortlived as a stove exploded when they attempted to light it leaving them fuel-less again. In

In the spring of 1985 Hans Kammerlander and Reinhold Messner also followed the original route. Dhaulagiri was Messner's twelfth 8,000er, climbed just three weeks after his ascent of Annapurna. Later the same year a Czech team climbed a very hard new route on the west face in alpine style. But having reached the south-west ridge (and, therefore, explored ground) they were stopped by violent winds. Later in the year, on 8 December the Swiss Erhard Loretan, Jean Troillet and Pierre-Alain Steiner climbed the Anglo-French-Polish route in 19 hours of night/day climbing, then sat out a second night, reaching the summit the following day, a remarkable achievement.

Post monsoon in 1986 a Polish team (which included two Canadians) had a similar experience to the 1985 Czech team, climbing a very hard new line on the south face as far as the 1978 Japanese route, but being unable to continue because of bad weather. The same year a Slovenian team climbed a new line on the east face, but were also unable to reach the summit. Two years later a Czech/Italian/Russian team completed an alpine style ascent of the south-west pillar (on the west face, to the right of the Czech 1985 line, a line that had been previously attempted by a French team in 1980) which involved pitches of grade VI+ and A2 on the huge (450m/1,500ft) headwall at 7,000m (23,000ft).

Winter sunset over Dhaulagiri from near Muktinath, on the Mustang border

Dhaulagiri's summit rises beyond outlying Jirbang (6,062m/19,888ft) in this view from the south west up the Myagdi Khola near Dharapani

The pace of exploration now, perhaps inevitably, slowed, but phenomenal climbs were still accomplished. In spring 1990, climbing as a member of an international team, Krzysztof Wielicki soloed the original route on 24 April, then on 9/10 May soloed a new route on the east face to the right of the Anglo/Polish/French 1981 route. Having reached the northeast ridge Wielicki did not bother to summit again, descending the line of his earlier ascent. The following year a Kazakh team pushed a new route up the west face, claiming that with long sections at 80° it was even harder than their line on Lhotse's south face. Ten of the eleven men team reached the top. Then, in 1993, a seven-man team (six Russians and the Briton Rick Allen) climbed a very hard direct route up the north face, all seven reaching the summit on 11 May.

In 1994 the Dutchman Bart Vos failed in a winter solo bid having spent a total of 36 days either in Base Camp or above. He returned to the peak in the spring of 1995, but finding too many people on the original route, soloed a line on the east face similar to the Anglo-French-Polish route, reaching the northeast ridge at about 7,400m (24,300ft). He was unfortunately forced to retreat from a point about 50m (160ft) from the top, but returned in the autumn of 1996 and soloed another new line on the east face (similar to that of 1994) claiming to have reached the summit on 17 October, thought this claim is doubted by many experts. Also in 1996 the French climber André Georges soloed Dhaulagiri, finding the body of Albrecht Hammann who had been a member of a 1995 multi-national team on the summit. Eleven days later Georges soloed Annapurna. Two years later the leading female climber Chantal Mauduit and her Sherpa Ang Tsering died in their camp at

6,500m (21,300ft) apparently of asphyxiation after snowfall had built up on the tent (though Mauduit had head injuries, possibly from falling ice hitting the tent). Mauduit had climbed 6 8,000ers, more than any other living female climber at the time. Ironically, post-monsoon in 1999 British climber Ginette Harrison, the new claimant to the title of most 8,000ers by a living female climber was killed in an avalanche on Dhaulagiri. The post-monsoon season had been notable for its snowfall and, therefore, avalanches – Alex Lowe was killed in another on Shisha Pangma – leading many to wonder whether global warming was affecting Himalayan weather and, if so, what the longer term consequences might be for high altitude climbing.

The tragedy slightly overshadowed a phenomenal climb by the Slovene Tomz Humar. In October he attacked the centre of the formidable south face solo, quickly reaching a height of 6,800m (22,300ft). There he was stopped by a rock wall which he had little chance of soloing at speed. He therefore traversed to the south-east ridge and climbed that to about 7,700m (25,250ft) where he traversed back onto the face. He continued up the face to reach the ridge again and followed it to the north-east ridge. At that point he abandoned any thoughts of a summit attempt ('I know I will die') and climbed down the standard route. During his descent, on 24 October, he found the body of Ginette Harrison. It is rumoured that when Humar returned to Europe he was met at the airport by Reinhold Messner. If true this would have been a fitting gesture; the man whose achievements had (arguably) dominated the first 50 years of 8,000m climbing, greeting and congratulating the man whose climb had set the seal on those years and laid down a marker for the next generation.

By the end of the century Dhaulagiri had had more ascents than any peak other then Everest and the 'easy' 8,000ers Cho Oyu and Gasherbrum II, a fact apparently at odds with its reputation as a difficult peak. It seems that the combination of challenging hard faces and ridges, which will continue to attract the top climbers, and a relatively straightforward normal route, together with the peak's imposing beauty make it irresistible.

The great pyramid of Dhaulagiri from Muktinath

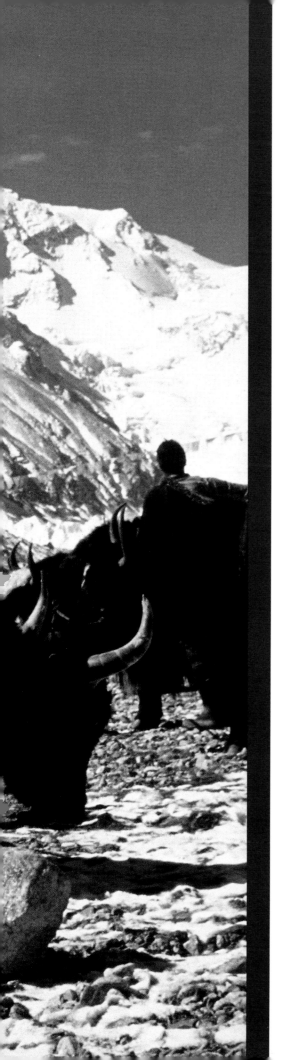

shisha pangma 8,046m

'The ridge grew increasingly narrow and sharp. The north side was powdery and steep, impractical and dangerous to traverse; the south side was steeper, vanishing immediately into a jumble of rock and sugary ice ...'

ALEX MACINTYRE on the summit ridge

Peak XXIII of the Indian Survey was for many years known by the Sanskrit name Gosainthan which translates as Place of the Saint. The existence of a Sanskrit name for a peak which rises from the Tibetan plateau was, and is, something of a mystery, but is assumed to originate from the mountain's proximity to Gosainkund, a holy lake of the Hindus which lies across the border in Nepal.

The existence of a Sanskrit name for a peak which rises from the Tibetan plateau was, and is, something of a mystery, but is assumed to originate from the mountain's proximity to Gosainkund, a holy lake of the Hindus which lies across the border in Nepal. Legend has it that Shiva rammed his trident into the ground near the pass between the Helambu and Langtang valleys, the holes filling to form the sacred lakes. Gosainkund is the scene of an annual pilgrimage by the Nepalese in August (at the height of the monsoon, a trying time for such a journey) when a ritual bath in its cold waters cleanses the body and soul. It is said that water from the lake is fed by an underground channel to the ponds of the Kumbeshwar Temple in Patan (across the Bagmati River from Kathmandu), some Nepalese choosing to take their ritual bath there rather than endure the long trek to Gosainkund.

The Tibetan name for the peak is Shisha Pangma, meaning the mountain crest above the grassy plain, a very descriptive, if somewhat mundane, name. After the Chinese occupation of Tibet (or liberation depending upon which version of history you favour) the new rulers tried to impose the apparently arbitrary name of Kaosengtsan Feng on the peak. When this failed they returned to the Tibetan name, but created a Sino-Tibetan version, Xixabangma which, they claimed, meant 'bad weather', presumably because of the weather systems attracted to the remote, solitary peak. In deference to the Chinese, who, after all, issue permits for the peak and for Everest's north side, this version is now frequently seen in the mountaineering literature.

Exploration

The exploration of Shisha Pangma has a relatively short history. In 1921 it was seen from a distance of about 45km (30 miles) by members of the British Everest reconnaissance, probably the first Europeans to view it. All subsequent visitors to this southern part of the Tibetan plateau, including later British Everest expeditions, would also have seen the peak.

In 1945 Shisha Pangma was sketched by Peter Aufschnaiter and Heinrich Harrer during their journey in Tibet after escaping from the Dehra Dun prisoner-of-war camp in which they had been interred in 1939. Then, in 1949, the British climber Bill Tilman led a small team (including Tenzing Norgay) into the Langtang Himal approaching to within 20km (12½ miles) of Shisha Pangma's west face. The following year the peak was photographed from the south-west by Dr Toni Hagen, a Swiss geologist, during an aerial survey of the Langtang and in 1951 was photographed from the east by Peter Aufschnaiter who approached to within about 10km (6 miles). In 1952 Hagen took more photographs of the peak when exploring the Langtang Himal on foot.

In 1961, with Shisha Pangma the only unclimbed 8,000er, the Chinese took an interest in the peak making a reconnaissance from the north. This first trip seems only to have concerned itself with approaches to the mountain, the first climbers to visit Shisha Pangma arriving in 1963. This party

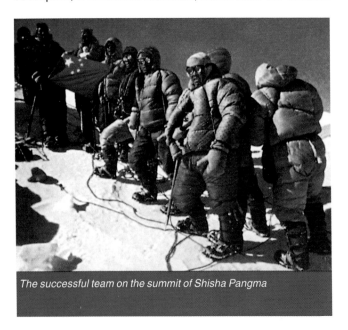
The successful team on the summit of Shisha Pangma

studied the north side in detail, watched the weather patterns closely and made some tentative climbs, reaching a height of 7,160m (23,500ft).

First Ascent

The Chinese returned in 1964 with an expedition numbering over 200 – climbers, scientists and porters – far too many to list by name even if all the names were known.

All the climbers had spent the previous winter in a fitness camp enjoying (or enduring) a regime which involved finger pull-ups and push-ups, forced marches, underwater swimming and much else besides, the camp's message being 'more sweat in training, less pain in climbing'.

The Chinese built a track for wheeled vehicles to a height of 5,900m (19,400ft) where, to keep the vast expedition happy, a small town was built, complete with cinema. The peak was approached along the Shisha Pangma Glacier, which flows from the north face. Three camps were established on it before the team climbed onto the north ridge. They traversed the western side of a peaked section of the ridge placing Camp IV near the col between this section and the main summit. Two more camps were placed on the ridge, from the last of which (Camp VI at 7,700m/25,250ft) ten climbers set out on 2 May climbing as three roped parties and apparently without using supplementary oxygen. There was one slight mishap, Wang Fu-chou (one of the three Chinese climbers to make the first ascent of Everest from the north in 1960: this is the usual western spelling of his name, the preferred Chinese version being Wang Fuzhou) slipping on bare ice and falling 20m (65ft) before being held by his colleagues. Finally, after 4½ hours of climbing the ten men – the Chinese Chen San, Cheng Tianliang, Wang Fuzhou, Wu Zongyue, Xu Jing (the team leader) and Zhang Junyan, and the Tibetans Doje, Mima Zaxi, Sodnam Doje and Yungden – reached the small pointed summit and took their turns in standing on it: Shisha Pangma's summit is a pyramidal snowy point on the mountain's long east-west ridge.

In the immediate aftermath of the climb many western climbers were sceptical of the Chinese claim. The 1960 Everest claim, with its night arrival at the summit and bust of Chairman Mao apparently installed there, and its lack of photographs invited such scepticism and the Shisha Pangma climb followed the same pattern. Again there was a claim that a bust of Mao had been carried to the summit and the summit photographs showed no background – just climbers against a blue sky: were they on top of Shisha Pangma or in a lay-by outside Beijing? But there were photographs taken from the top and later climbs showed that these had indeed been taken either on or very

SHISHA PANGMA: ASCENT ROUTES

Above From South
A *NW Face*
1 *Chinese, 1964, the 'classic' route*

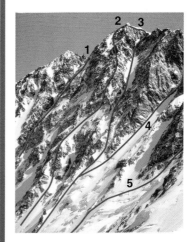

Left South-west Face
1 *Polish/Swiss (1990)*
2 *Slovenian, Kosjek/Stremfelj (1989)*
3 *British (1982)*
4 *Wielicki solo (1993)*
5 *Slovenian, Bence/Groselj (1989)*

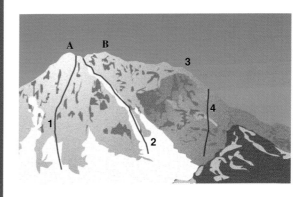

Above NW Face
A *Central Summit; the Main Summit lies behind and to the left of the Central Summit*
B *West Summit*

1 *'Esprit d'Equipe' (1990) but only to Central Summit*
2 *Hinkes/Untch (1987)*
3 *West Ridge, Polish (1987)*
4 *Lafaille (1994) but only to West Summit*

Shisha Pangma is seen from the north east above the usual Base Camp on the Tibetan plateau. Phola Gangchen (7,716m/25,315ft) rises left

close to the summit. Even then there were some who claimed, with little justification, that the Chinese had not reached the true summit but a lower point on the long ridge. Given later controversies over climbers claiming ascents of the peak when they have reached the central rather than the main summit this was understandable: those who stand on the central summit discover that a climb along a narrow, occasionally heavily corniced and dangerous, ridge is required to reach a summit just a couple of metres higher. This ridge can take several hours

to negotiate, though some have found it straightforward and climbed it quickly. However, today few doubt the veracity of the Chinese claim to have climbed to the main summit.

Later Ascents

After the Chinese climb the mountain was left alone for 16 years. Then, in 1980, the Chinese opened Tibet to foreign mountaineers. The Japanese went to Everest and a German team co-led by Manfred Abellin and Günther Sturm went to

making the first female ascent of Shisha Pangma in the company of two Chinese porters. Mrs Tabei did not use bottled oxygen. A month later Reinhold Messner and Friedl Mutschlechner also repeated the original climb, with a slight variation towards the summit. Shisha Pangma was Messner's fifth 8,000er. Messner and Mutschlechner had been members of a team which intended a direct route up the north face. When the early onset of the monsoon forced the team to abandon this attempt, the pair, climbing quickly to avoid being swamped by monsoon snow, reached the top in one long day from a bivouac at about 6,800m (22,300ft) during a brief break in the weather.

In 1982 a second route to the summit was climbed, a small British team climbing the 3,300m (10,000ft) south-west face. The ascent was made alpine style by Roger Baxter Jones, Alex McIntyre and Doug Scott with two bivouacs. The lower section of the route was over mixed ground at about 55°, the upper along a couloir of similar steepness reaching easier ground near the summit ridge. The descent was down the less steep south-east ridge and then the south-west face to the east of the ascent line. The following year saw more successes on the original line, but Fritz Luchsinger, a member of the first team to climb Lhotse and who had climbed Dhaulagiri at the age of 59, became Shisha Pangma's first victim at the age of 62, dying of pulmonary oedema.

In 1985, recognition of the relative ease of Shisha Pangma (as an 8,000er) encouraged the first commercial expedition to the peak, a successful Italian venture. At the same time all 12 members of an Austrian/German/Swiss team reached the summit. Post-monsoon in 1987 new routes were climbed on the peak. On 18 September Arthur Hajzer and Jerzy Kukuczka summitted after climbing the west ridge. Kukuczka made a partial ski descent from the top. With this ascent Kukuczka became the second man to complete the 14 8,000ers. His quest had taken nine years and on all but Lhotse he had climbed either a new line or made a first winter ascent. Also on the 18 September an international team of five (including Carlos Carsolio and Wanda Rutkiewicz) reached the top along the original route. As an aside, it is worth noting that the date of this ascent is disputed. Kukuczka claims the 18th in his book, but Wanda Rutkiewicz was adamant that it was on the 19th (though the difference is really only of academic interest). What is not in disputed is that Kukuczka, perhaps overcome by his situation, hung back from the rest as they approached the summit and was the last of the seven to reach it. A few days later the Briton Alan Hinkes and American Steve Untch climbed a new route on the north-west face, taking the central couloir. At the same time as these successes a large British team attempted the east face but decided it was too dangerous and

Shisha Pangma. On 7 May, after following the Chinese route on the north side of the peak, Michl Dachor, Wolfgang Schaffert, Sturm and Fritz Zintl reached the top, the climb being repeated by Sigi Hupfauer and Manfred Sturm five days later. In the post-monsoon period of the same year the peak was climbed again – the first post-monsoon ascent – by an Austrian team, also along the original route.

In 1981 a Japanese Women's expedition repeated the original route, Junko Tabei (the first woman to climb Everest)

instead attempted a climb along the connecting ridge between Pungpa Ri and the main summit. Luke Hughes and Steve Venables were forced to abandon the traverse at about 7,650m (25,100ft) after a miserable bivouac.

A Yugoslav (Slovene) expedition attacked the south-west face in 1989, producing two new routes. Between 17 and 19 October Pavle Kozjek and Andrej Stremfelj climbed the buttress to the left of the British route with two bivouacs,

On the first ascent of the British 1982 south-west face route

In the couloir, British 1982 south-west face route

while between 18 and 20 October Filip Bence and Viktor Groselj climbed a route that followed, for half the distance, the British descent route, reaching the south-east ridge which the pair then followed to the top. The following year, again in the post-monsoon period, the south face gained another new route. Just one week after climbing Cho Oyu, Erhard Loretan, Wojciech Kurtyka and Jean Troillet climbed the central couloir (which had been attempted by a Yugoslav pair in 1989, but not climbed after one of them contracted pneumonia). The couloir varied from 45°–50° and gave straightforward climbing. Starting during the evening of 2 October and carrying no bivouac gear the trio climbed to the summit ridge. Here Kurtyka rested, the Swiss reaching the central summit at 10am. They then descended, regaining base camp less than 24 hours after starting out. Kurtyka reached the central summit at 4pm, bivouaced during a 'pleasantly warm' night and descended next morning. Another new route was climbed in 1990 when an international team climbed the 'Esprit d'Equipe' Couloir on the north-west face (to the left of the Hinkes/Untsch route). The team – which included Hinkes, Benoît Chamoux and

After the miserable bivouac during the attempt on the Pungpa Ri to Shisha Pangma ridge

Pierre Royer reached the central summit but did not continue to the main summit.

In 1993 a Polish team, having succeeded on Cho Oyu's south-west buttress climbed the 1989 Slovene route alpine style. At the same time, one member of the team, Krzysztof Wielicki, soloed the 50° couloir to the right of the 1982 Scott route. After the climb Wielicki, who was climbing his tenth 8,000er, made an impassioned attack on people who climbed only the central summit, or those who climbed to the edge of the Cho Oyu plateau, and claimed the summit. These are not the tops he stated and should not be claimed. The problems of true summiteers were shown again in 1994 when only two climbers (one in spring, one post-monsoon) reached the main summit though many others reached the central summit. Frenchman Christophe Lafaille soloed the central summit but found it too windy to continue to the main top. Two days later he soloed a new route on the right side of the north face, reaching the west ridge and west summit. On this occasion he did not have sufficient time to continue to the main summit. The same year an attempted ski and snowboard descent failed when the skiers failed on the ascent at 7,990m (26,200ft) in the Hinkes/Untch north face route. Mark Newcomb skied down from this point.

In 1995 Erhard Loretan soloed the original route, starting at 5.30am from base camp (at 5,800m/19,000ft) and reaching the central summit at 11.30am the next day. He continued to the main summit, reaching it at about noon. Loretan was one of only three summiteers in 1995 to reach the main top. A new route was also added to the south-west face by a Spanish team. Reaching the top in thick fog they were dismayed to discover when it lifted that they were east of the main summit. There was deep snow on the ridge and they were too tired to contend with it and so descended. Then, having been somewhat shunted into the background as an easy 8,000er the mountain became headline news again in 1999 when the American Alex Lowe, widely believed to be the finest mountaineer of the time (a title he modestly eschewed) was killed on Shisha Pangma together with David Bridges. The pair were part of a team hoping to achieve the first American ski descent of an 8,000er.

With Shisha Pangma now firmly established as one of the easiest 8,000ers, and having the extra attraction of being in Tibet, the number of commercial expeditions has increased and the number of summit climbers – even allowing for the difficulty of deciding whether those who reach the central summit should be allowed to claim a 'real' ascent – is increasing. It is likely that it will soon lie fourth behind Everest, Cho Oyu and Gasherbrum II in total number. As with all the great peaks, the huge bulk of the mountain allows scope for many new routes and as the millennium closes Shisha Pangma still awaits a winter ascent.

List of Ascent Data For All 14 8,000ers

These data have been collected with the assistance of Elizabeth Hawley (the eight Nepalese peaks), Jan Kielkowski (the five Pakistani peaks and Shisha Pangma) and Xavier Eguskitza (the tables below). The early data on each peak is accurate, but the data for later years is more difficult to obtain. This is, in part, due to the climbing world as a whole being less interested in ascents of the standard routes on the peaks, so that the data is less assiduously collected at source, and the problems caused by disputed ascent claims. The latter are particularly problematic on peaks with more than one summit – the forepeak on Broad Peak, the central summit on Shisha Pangma – the lower being 'easier' to attain, or where reaching the true summit lies beyond some more easily attained point – for instance on Cho Oyu, where the true summit lies across a broad plateau. The advent of commercial expeditions to the 8000ers has added to the difficulty of collecting true ascent data as there are now many more climbers on the peaks, and there is an understandable enthusiasm for claiming a true ascent in order to justify the expenditure of time and money. Nor is this effect confined to the 'amateur' end of the market, the 'race' for the attainment of all 14 peaks and the 'hardest high-altitude climb in the world' leading to its own disputed claims because of the pressure to perform for sponsors and public opinion.

Total ascents of the 8000ers to 31/12/99

	Number of Climbers	Repetitions	Number of Ascents	Number of Ascents by Women
Cho Oyu	998	92	1,090	82 (79 women)
Everest	874	299	1,173	55 (52)
Gasherbrum II	456	12	468	43
Dhaulagiri	290	8	298	11
Broad Peak	212 (*1)	5	217	9
Manaslu	189	1	190	6
Nanga Parbat	184	2	186	9
Shisha Pangma	165 (*2)	2	167	7
K2	163	1	164	5
Gasherbrum I	161	3	164	6
Makalu	156	0	156	5
Kangchenjunga	146	7	153	1
Lhotse	128	1	129	3
Annapurna	106	3	109	5
Totals	(2,768*3)	436	4,664	247 (by a total of 170 women)

Note that apart from Cho Oyu and Everest there have been no repetitions by women.

*1 Main summit only, a further 107 climbers have reached the forepeak.
*2 Main summit only, a further 434 climbers have reached the Central summit.
*3 These data mean that 2,768 climbers have stood on the top of at least one 8000er.

Climbers with one or more 8000er ascents to 31/12/99

The number of peaks does not include personal repetitions of a particular mountain

Number of Peaks	Number of Climbers	Number of Peaks	Number of Climbers
14	6 (Messner, Kukuczka, Loretan, Carsolio, Wielicki, Oiarzabal)	7	4
		6	21
13	2 (De Stefani, Martini)	5	26
12	0	4	64
11	1 (Kammerlander)	3	150
10	13	2	408
9	7	1	2,060
8	6		

Deaths on 8000ers to 31/12/99

	Individual ascents	Deaths on descent	% of summiteers dying on descent	Total no. of deaths
K2	164	22 (*1)	13.4	49
Annapurna	109	8	7.3	55
Makalu	156	8	5.1	19
Kangchenjunga	153	7	4.6	38
Everest	1,173	40 (*2)	3.4	165
Broad Peak	218	4	1.8	18
Gasherbrum I	164	3	1.8	17
Dhaulagiri	298	5	1.7	53
Nanga Parbat	186	3	1.6	61
Manaslu	190	3	1.6	51
Lhotse	129	2	1.6	8
Shisha Pangma	167	2	1.2	19
Gasherbrum II	468	3	0.6	15
Cho Oyu	1,090	5	0.5	23
Totals	4,664	115		591

Note that deaths on Everest, K2, Kangchenjunga and Nanga Parbat include those which occurred on expeditions prior to 1950.

Deaths on descent are usually through exhaustion and falls, rarely as a result of avalanches: K2 is by far the most dangerous mountains in this regard. Deaths on ascents are often as a result of avalanches. Annapurna and Manaslu in modern times, as well as Nanga Parbat prior to 1950 are the most dangerous in this regard.

*1 Does not include the three Ukrainian climbers who died on 10 or 11/7/94. Two were found at a bivouac at 8,400m, the other had fallen, probably from around the same height. It is assumed they died while descending rather than ascending, but it is not known if they had reached the summit.
*2 Not including Mick Burke (26/9/75) and Pasang Temba (13/10/88) who probably reached the summit and died on the descent.

Annapurna ascent data

All climbs by first ascent route (North Face) except where stated.

3/6/50 M Herzog (France), L Lachenal (France); **20/5/70** H Day (Britain), G Owens (Britain); 27/5/70 D Whillans (Britain), D Haston (Britain) S Face; **13/10/77** M van Rijswick (Holland), Sonam Wolang Sherpa (Nepal); **15/10/78** I Miller (f) (US), V Komarkova (f) (US), Mingma Tshering Sherpa (Nepal), Chewang Rinzing Sherpa (Nepal); 30/4/78 Y Morin † (France), H Sigayret (France); **8/5/79** S Tanake (Japan), Pema Sherpa (Nepal); **1/5/80** G Harder (W Germany), K Staltmayr (W Germany), Ang Dorje Sherpa (Nepal); 3/5/80 K Schrag (W Germany), W Broeg (W Germany), Maila Pemba Shepa (Nepal), Ang Tsangi Shepa (Nepal); **19/10/81** K Aota (Japan), Y Yanagisawa (Japan) S Face; **4/5/82** W Bürkli † (Switzerland), T Hägler (Switzerland), Dawa Tenzing Sherpa (Nepal), W Wörgötter (Austria); **24/10/84** N Joos (Switerzland), E Loretan (Switzerland), E Ridge ascent, descent; **24/4/85** H Kammerlander (Italy), R Messner (Italy), NW Face; **21/9/86** A Giambisi (Italy), S Martini (Italy), F De Stefani (Italy); **3/2/87** A Hajzer (Poland), J Kukuczka (Poland); 8/10/87 R López (Spain), J M Maixe (Spain); 11/10/87 J C Gómez (Spain), F J Perez (Spain), Kaji Sherpa (Nepal); 20/12/87 T Kobyashi † (Japan), Y Saito † (Japan), T Saegusa (Japan), N Yamada (Japan) S Face, British (1970) route variant; **10/5/88** S Boyer (US), B Chamoux (France), N Campredon (France), S Dorotei (Italy), J Rakoncaj (Czech) S Face, British (1970) route variant; 2/10/88 J Martis (Czech), J Nezerka (Czech) NW Face; 3/10/88 P Aldai (Spain), J F Azcona (Spain); **28/10/89** L Ianakiev (Bulgaria), P Panayotov (Bulgaria), O Stoykov † (Bulgaria); **5/10/90** G Gazzola (Italy) (claim disputed); 20–1/10/90 G Denamur † (Belgium) S Face, British (1970) route; **21/10/91** B Stefko (Poland), K Wielicki (Poland) S Face, British (1970) route; 22/10/91 R Pawlowski (Poland), W Rutkiewicz (f) (Poland), R Schleypen (Germany), S Face, British (1970) route; 23/10/91 I Baeyens (f) (Belgium), M Sprutta (Poland), G Velez (Portugal) S Face, British (1970) route; 24/10/91 S Arsentiev (USSR), N Cherny (USSR); 26/10/91 V Bashkirov (USSR), S Isaev (USSR), V Obichok (USSR), N Petrov (USSR) S Face, British (1970) route; **26/4/93** Akbu (Tibet), Bianba Zaxi (Tibet), Rena (Tibet), Cering Doje (Tibet); **10/10/94** Park Jung-Hun (S Korea), Dawa Sherpa (Nepal), Ang Dawa Tamang (Nepal), Mingma Tamang (Nepal) S Face, British (1970) route variant; **29/4/95** C Carsolio (Mexico), D Karnicar (Slovenia), A Karnicar (Slovenia); 6/5/95 T Humar (Slovenia); **3/5/96** Kim Hun-Sang (S Korea), Park Young-Seok (S Korea), Kaji Sherpa (Nepal), Gyalzen Sherpa (Nepal); 15/5/96 A Georges (Switzerland); 20/10/96 A Marciniak (Poland), V Terzeoul (Ukraine) NW Ridge; 20/10/96 S Bershov (Ukraine), I Svergun (Ukraine), S Kovalev (Ukraine) S Face, British (1970) route variant; **3/5/98** Han Wang-Yong (S Korea), Ang Dawa Tamang (Nepal) (2nd), Phurba Tamang (Nepal), Arjun Tamang (Nepal), Kami Dorje (Dorchi) Sherpa (Nepal); **29/4/99** F Latorre (Spain), J Oiarzabal (Spain), J Vallejo (Spain), Um Hong-Gil (S Korea), Park Chang-Soo (S Korea), Ji Hyun-Ok † (f) (S Korea), Ang Dawa Tamang (Nepal) (3rd), Kami Dorje Sherpa † (Nepal) (2nd)

First ascents of subsidiary summits

East Summit: 29/4/74 JM Anglada (Spain), E Civis (Spain), J Pons (Spain) N Ridge. Middle Summit: 3/10/80 U Boening (Germany), L Greissl (Germany), H Oberrauch (Germany), to the E of the Dutch Rib

Everest ascent data

This list includes all climbers who have claimed they reached the summit, although there are doubts whether a few of them actually did. The questioned ascents are noted against the relevant ascent. The numbering is not necessarily the order in which climbers reached the summit, even amongst those within the same summit party. Some climbers have been to the top more than once, so the total number of mountaineers atop Everest is not indicated by the number assigned to the last person on the list. Although a person may have scaled Everest ten times, it is still counted as a single person.

All climbs by the first ascent route (Western Cwm, South Col, South-east Ridge) except where stated.

29/5/53 1 Edmund Hillary (NZ), 2 Tenzing Norgay (India); **23/5/56** 3 Jürg Marmet, 4 Ernst Schmied (Switzerland); 24/5/56 5 Adolf Reist, 6 Hansrudolf von Gunten (Switzerland); **25/5/60** 7 Wang Fu-chou (China), 8 Gonpa (China), 9 Chu Yin-hua (claim disputed) (China) N Col to N Ridge, 1st ascent from Tibetan side; **1/5/63** 10 Jim Whittaker (US), 11 Nawang Gombu Sherpa (India); 22/5/63 12 Lute Jerstad (US), 13 Barry Bishop (US); 22/5/63 14 Willi Unsoeld (US), 15 Tom Hornbein (US) W Ridge from Cwm up; SE Ridge to S Col down 1st ascent of W Ridge, 1st traverse of Everest; **20/5/65** 16 AS Cheema (India), 17 Nawang Gombu Sherpa (India) (2nd; first person to climb Everest twice); 22/5/65 18 Sonam Gyatso (India), 19 Sonam Wangyal (India); 24/5/65 20 CP Vohra (India), 21 Ang Kami Sherpa (India); 29/5/65 22 HPS Ahluwalia (India), 23 HCS Rawat, (India), 24 Phu Dorje Sherpa (Nepal); **11/5/70** 25 Teruo Matsuura (Japan), 26 Naomi Uemura (Japan); 12/5/70 27 Katsutoshi Hirabayashi (Japan), 28 Chotare Sherpa (Nepal); **5/5/73** 29 Rinaldo Carrel (Italy), 30 Mirko Minuzzo (Italy), 31 Lhakpa Tenzing Sherpa (Nepal), 32 Shambu Tamang (Nepal); 7/5/73 33 Fabrizio Innamorati (Italy), 34 Virginio Epis (Italy), 35 Claudio Benedetti (Italy), 36 Sonam Gyalgen Sherpa (Nepal); 26/10/73 37 Yasuo Kato (Japan), 38 Hisashi Ishiguro (Japan) First autumn ascent; **16/5/75** 39 Junko Tabei (f) (Japan) First woman to summit, 40 Ang Tshering Sherpa (Nepal); 27/5/75 41 Phantog (f) (China), 42 Sodnam Norbu (China), 43 Lotse (China), 44 Hou Sheng-fu (China), 45 Samdrub (China), 46 Darphuntso (China), 47 Kunga Pasang (China), 48 Tsering Tobgyal (China), 49 Ngapo Khyen (China) N Col to

(f) female climber

† died on descent

N Ridge; 24/9/75 50 Dougal Haston (UK), 51 Doug Scott (UK) SW Face First ascent of SW Face; 26/9/75 52 Peter Boardman (UK), 53 Pertemba Sherpa (Nepal) SW Face; **16/5/76** 54 John (Brummy) Stokes (UK), 55 Michael (Bronco) Lane (UK) Summit claim by Stokes and Lane is disputed; 8/10/76 56 Chris Chandler (US), 57 Bob Cormack (US); **15/9/77** 58 Ko Sang-Don (S Korea), 59 Pemba Nurbu Sherpa (Nepal); **3/5/78** 60 Wolfgang Nairz (Austria), 61 Robert Schauer (Austria), 62 Horst Bergmann (Austria), 63 Ang Phu Sherpa (Nepal); 8/5/78 64 Reinhold Messner (Italy), 65 Peter Habeler (Austria) Messner, Habeler first to summit without use of bottled oxygen; 11/5/78 66 Oswald Oelz (Austria), 67 Reinhard Karl (W Germany); 14/5/78 68 Franz Oppurg (Austria) 1st to top solo from last camp; 14/10/78 69 Hubert Hillmaier (W Germany), 70 Josef Mack (W Germany), 71 Hans Engl (W Germany) (used no oxygen); 16/10/78 72 Siegfried Hupfauer (W Germany), 73 Wilhelm Klimek (W Germany), 74 Robert Allenbach (Switzerland), 75 Wanda Rutkiewicz (f) (Poland), 76 Ang Kami Sherpa (Nepal) (not the same man as 21), 77 Ang Dorje Sherpa (Nepal) (used no oxygen), 78 Mingma Nuru Sherpa (Nepal) (used no oxygen); 17/10/78 79 Georg Ritter (W Germany), 80 Bernd Kullmann (W Germany); 15/10/78 81 Jean Afanassief (France), 82 Nicolas Jaeger (France), 83 Pierre Mazeaud (France), 84 Kurt Diemberger (Austria); **13/5/79** 85 Jernej Zaplotnik (Yugoslavia), 86 Andrej Stremfelj (Yugoslavia) W Ridge from S (from Lho La) First people to reach summit via entire length of W Ridge; 15/5/79 87 Stipe Bozic (Yugoslavia), 88 Stane Belak (Yugoslavia), 89 Ang Phu Sherpa † (Nepal) (2nd) First person to climb Everest via two routes. W Ridge; 1/10/79 90 Gerhard Schmatz (W Germany), 91 Hermann Warth (W Germany), 92 Hans Von Kaenel (Switzerland), 93 Pertemba Sherpa (Nepal) (2nd), 94 Lhakpa Gyalu (Gyalzen) Sherpa (Nepal); 2/10/79 95 Tilman Fischbach (W Germany), 96 Günther Kaempfe (W Germany), 97 Hannelore Schmatz † (f) (W Germany) (first woman to die on Everest), 98 Ray Genet † (US), 99 Nick Banks (NZ), 100 Sungdare Sherpa (Nepal), 101 Ang Phurba Sherpa (Nepal), 102 Ang Jambu Sherpa (Nepal); **17/2/80** 103 Leszek Cichy (Poland), 104 Krzysztof Wielicki (Poland) First winter ascent of any 8,000er; 3/5/80 105 Yasuo Kato (Japan) N Col to N Ridge (2nd) First person to climb north and south sides; 1st non-Sherpa to climb Everest twice; 10/5/80 106 Takashi Ozaki (Japan), 107 Tsuneo Shigehiro (Japan) N Face First ascent of N Face; 14/5/80 108 Martin Zabaleta (Spain), 109 Pasang Temba Sherpa (Nepal); 19/5/80 110 Andrzej Czok (Poland), 111 Jerzy Kukuczka (Poland) S Pillar to S Summit, SE Ridge First ascent of S Pillar; 1st time two new routes climbed in same season (and same month); 20/8/80 112 Reinhold Messner (Italy) (2nd) N Col to N Ridge to N Face. First completely solo ascent; used no oxygen; first person to climb twice with no oxygen; first summer ascent; **21/10/81** 113 Chris Kopczynski (US), 114 Sungdare Sherpa (Nepal) (2nd) S Pillar to SE Ridge; 24/10/81 115 Chris Pizzo (US), 116 Yung Tenzing Sherpa (Nepal), 117 Peter Hackett (US) S Pillar to SE Ridge; **4/5/82** 118 Vladimir Balyberdin (USSR), 119 Eduard Myslovsky (USSR), 120 Sergei Bershov (USSR), 121 Mikhail Turkevitch (USSR) Rib on SW Face to W Ridge; 5/5/82 122 Valentin Ivanov (USSR), 123 Sergei Efimov (USSR) Rib on SW Face to W Ridge; 8/5/82 124 Valeri Krichtchaty (USSR), 125 Kazbek Valiev (USSR) Rib on SW Face to W Ridge; 9/5/82 126 Valery Khomutov (USSR), 127 Vladimir Puchkov (USSR), 128 Yuri Golodov (USSR) Rib on SW Face to W Ridge; 5/10/82 129 Laurie Skreslet (Canada), 130 Sungdare Sherpa (Nepal) (3rd; first person to summit three times), 131 Lhakpa Dorje Sherpa (Nepal); 7/10/82 132 Pat Morrow (Canada), 133 Lhakpa Tshering Sherpa (Nepal), 134 Pema Dorje Sherpa (Nepal); 27/12/82 135 Yasuo Kato † (Japan) (3rd) first person to climb in three different seasons; **7/5/83** 136 Gerry Roach (US), 137 David Breashears (US), 138 Peter Jamieson (US), 139 Larry Nielson (US) (used no oxygen), 140 Ang Rita Sherpa (Nepal) (used no oxygen); 14/5/83 141 Gary Neptune (US), 142 Jim States (US), 143 Lhakpa Dorje Sherpa (Nepal) (not same man as no 131); 8/10/83 144 Louis Reichardt (US), 145 Carlos Buhler (US), 146 Kim Momb (US) E Face to SE Ridge, first ascent of E Face; 9/10/83 147 Dan Reid (US), 148 George Lowe (US), 149 Jay Cassell (US) E Face to SE Ridge; 8/10/83 150 Shomi Suzuki (Japan), 151 Haruichi Kawamura (Japan) S Pillar to SE Ridge, whole team used no oxygen; 8/10/83 152 Haruyuki Endo (Japan), 153 Hiroshi Yoshino † (Japan), 154 Hironobu Kamuro † (Japan), whole team used no oxygen; 16/12/83 155 Takashi Ozaki (Japan) (2nd), 156 Noboru Yamada (Japan), 157 Kazunari Murakami (Japan), 158 Nawang Yonden Sherpa (Nepal); **20/4/84** 159 Hristo Prodanov † (Bulgaria) (used no oxygen) W Ridge from S; 8/5/84 160 Ivan Valtchev (Bulgaria), 161 Metodi Savov (Bulgaria) W Ridge up, SE Ridge to S Col down, 1st traverse via completely different routes; 9/5/84 162 Kiril Doskov (Bulgaria), 163 Nikolay Petkov (Bulgaria) W Ridge up, SE Ridge to S Col down; 9/5/84 164 Phu Dorjee (India); 23/5/84 165 Bachendri Pal (f) (India), 166 Dorjee Lhatoo (India), 167 Sonam Palzor Sarapa (India) 168 Ang Dorje Sherpa (Nepal) (2nd, used no oxygen); 3/10/84 169 Tim Macartney-Snape (Australia) (used no oxygen), 170 Greg Mortimer (Australia) (used no oxygen) N Face; 8/10/84 171 Bart Vos (Holland) (claim disputed); 15/10/84 172 Zoltan Demjan (Czech) (used no oxygen), 173 Jozef Psotka † (Czech) (used no oxygen), 174 Ang Rita Sherpa (Nepal) (2nd, used no oxygen) S Pillar to SE Ridge up, SE Ridge to S Col down; 20/10/84 175 Phil Ershler (US) N Col to N Face to Gt Couloir; **21/4/85** 176 Chris Bonington (UK), 177 Odd Eliassen (Norway), 178 Bjorn Myrer-Lund (Norway), 179 Pertemba Sherpa (Nepal) (3rd), 180 Ang Lhakpa Sherpa (Nepal), 181 Dawa Norbu Sherpa (Nepal); 29/4/85 182 Arne Naess (Norway), 183 Stein Aasheim (Norway), 184 Ralph Hoibakk (Norway), 185 Havard Nesheim (Norway), 186 Sungdare Sherpa (Nepal) (4th; 1st person to climb 4 times), 187 Ang Rita Sherpa (Nepal) (3rd, used no oxygen), 188 Chowang Rinzing Sherpa (Nepal), 189 Pema Dorje Sherpa (Nepal) (2nd); 30/4/85 190 Richard Bass (US) (aged 55, oldest summiter so far), 191 David Breashears (US) (2nd), 192 Ang Phurba Sherpa (Nepal) (not the same man as no 101 or 337); 28/8/85 193 Oscar Cadiach (Spain), 194 Antoni Sors (Spain), 195 Carles Valles (Spain), 196 Shambu Tamang (Nepal) (2nd), 197 Ang Karma Sherpa (Nepal), 198 Narayan Shrestha (Nepal) N Col to N Ridge; 30/10/85 199 Noboru Yamada (Japan) (2nd, used no oxygen), 200 Kuniaki Yagihara (Japan), 201 Hideji Nazuka (Japan), 202 Etsuo Akutsu (Japan), 203 Satoshi Kimoto (Japan), 204 Mitsuyoshi Sato (Japan), 205 Teruo Saegusa (Japan); **20/5/86** 206 Dwayne Congdon (Canada), 207 Sharon Wood (f) (Canada) W Ridge from N; 30/8/86 208 Erhard Loretan (Switzerland), 209 Jean Troillet (Switzerland) N Face; neither man used oxygen in swift alpine-style climb; **22/12/87** 210 Heo Young-Ho (S

Korea), 211 Ang Rita Sherpa (Nepal) (4th, used no oxygen, first winter ascent without oxygen); **5/5/88** 212 Noboru Yamada (Japan) (3rd), 213 Lhakpa Nuru Sherpa (aka Ang Lhakpa) (Nepal), 214 Cerni Doji (China) N Col to N Ridge up, SE Ridge down; first N-S traverse; 5/5/88 215 Ang Phurba Sherpa (Thami) (Nepal) (2nd; not the same man as nos 101 and 337), 216 Da Cering (China), 217 Ringen Pungco (China) SE Ridge up, N Ridge-N Col down; first S-N traverse; 5/5/88 218 Susumu Nakamura (Japan), 219 Syoji Nakamura (Japan), 220 Teruo Saegusa (Japan) (2nd), 221 Munehiko Yamamoto (Japan), 222 Li Zhixin (China), 223 Lhakpa Sona Sherpa (Nepal) N Col to N Ridge; 10/5/88 224 Sungdare Sherpa (Nepal) (5th; first person to climb 5 times), 225 Padma Bahadur Tamang (Nepal); 12/5/88 226 Stephen Venables (UK) (used no oxygen), E Face to SE Ridge; 25/5/88 227 Paul Bayne (Australia), 228 Patrick Cullinan (Australia); 28/5/88 229 John Muir (Australia); 26/9/88 230 Jean Pierre Frachon (France), 231 Jean-Marc Boivin (France) (by parapente from summit to CII, 6,400m), 232 Gerard Vionnet-Fuasset (France), 233 Michel Metzger (France) (used no oxygen), 234 Andre Georges (France), 235 Pasang Tshering Sherpa (Nepal), 236 Sonam Tshering Sherpa (Nepal), 237 Ajiwa Sherpa (Nepal); 26/9/88 S 238 Kim Chang-Sun (S Korea), 239 Um Hong-Gil (S Korea), 240 Pema Dorje Sherpa (Nepal) (3rd) S Pillar to SE Ridge; 29/9/88 241 Jang Bong-Wan (S Korea), 242 Chang Byoung-Ho (S Korea), 243 Chung Seung-Kwon (S Korea) S Pillar to SE Ridge; 2/10/88 244 Nam Sun-Woo (S Korea) S Pillar to SE Ridge; 26/9/88 245 Marc Batard (France) (used no oxygen); fastest ascent to date; 29/9/88 246 Stacy Allison (f) (US), 247 Pasang Gyalzen Sherpa (Nepal); 2/10/88 248 Peggy Luce (f) (US), 249 Geoffrey Tabin (US), 250 Nima Tashi Sherpa (Nepal), 251 Phu Dorje Sherpa (Nepal), 252 Dawa Tshering Sherpa (Nepal); 13/10/88 253 Serge Koenig (France), 254 Lhakpa Sonam Sherpa † (Nepal); 14/10/88 255 Nil Bohigas (Spain), 256 Lluis Giner (Spain), 257 Jeronimo López (Spain), 258 Ang Rita Sherpa (Nepal) (5th, used no oxygen), 259 Nima Rita Sherpa (Nepal) (used no oxygen); 14/10/88 260 Lydia Bradey (f) (NZ) (used no oxygen, 1st woman to top without it) (claim disputed); 17/10/88 261 Jozef Just † (Czech) (used no oxygen) SW Face; **10/5/89** 262 Stipe Bozic (2nd) (Yugoslavia), 263 Viktor Groselj (Yugoslavia) , 264 Dimitar Ilievski † (Yugoslavia), 265 Ajiwa Sherpa (Nepal) (2nd), 266 Sonam Tshering Sherpa (Nepal) (2nd, used no oxygen); 16/5/89 267 Ricardo Torres (Mexico), 268 Phu Dorje Sherpa † (Nepal) (2nd), 269 Ang Dannu Sherpa (Nepal); 24/5/89 270 Adrian Burgess (UK), 271 Sona Dendu Sherpa (Nepal), 272 Lhakpa Nuru Sherpa (Nepal) (2nd), 273 Roddy Mackenzie (Australia); 24/5/89 274 Eugeniusz Chrobak † (Poland), 275 Andrej Marciniak (Poland) W Ridge from S via Khumbutse; 13/10/89 276 Toichiro Mitani (Japan), 277 Tchiring Thebe Lama (Nepal), 278 Chuldin Dorje Sherpa (Nepal) 279 Hiroshi Ohnishi (Japan),280 Atsushi Yamamoto (Japan); 13/10/89 281 Cho Kwang-Je (S Korea) S Pillar to SE Ridge; 13/10/89 282 Carlos Carsolio (Mexico) (used no oxygen); 23/10/89 283 Chung Sang-Yong (S Korea), 284 Nima Rita Sherpa (Nepal) (2nd), 285 Nuru Jangbu Sherpa (Nepal) W Ridge from S; **23/4/90** 286 Ang Rita Sherpa (Nepal) (6th; first person to climb 6 times, used no oxygen), 287 Pasang Norbu Sherpa (Nepal), 288 Ang Kami Sherpa (Nepal) (2nd), 289 Top Bahadur Khatri (Nepal); 7/5/90 290 Robert Link (US), 291 Steve Gall (US), 292 Sergei Arsentiev (USSR) (used no oxygen), 293 Grigory Lunjakov (USSR) (used no oxygen), 294 Daqimi (Tibet), 295 Jiabu (Tibet) N Col to N Ridge; 8/5/90 296 Edmund Viesturs (US) (used no oxygen), 297 Mistislav Gorbenko (USSR), 298 Andrei Tselinschev (USSR) (used no oxygen) N Col to N Ridge; 9/5/90 299 Ian Wade (US), 300 Daqiong (Tibet), 301 Luoze (Tibet), 302 Rena (Tibet), 303 Gui San (f) (China) N Col to N Ridge; 10/5/90 304 Ekaterina Ivanova (f) (USSR), 305 Anatoly Mochnikov (USSR) (used no oxygen), 306 Alexander Tokarev (USSR) (used no oxygen), 307 Ervand Illyinsky (USSR), 308 Mark Tucker (US), 309 Wangjia (Tibet) N Col to N Ridge; 10/5/90 310 Peter Athans (US), 311 Glenn Porzak (US), 312 Ang Jangbu Sherpa (Nepal), 313 Nima Tashi Sherpa (Nepal) (2nd), 314 Brent Manning (US), 315 Dana Coffield (US), 316 Michael Browning (US), 317 Dawa Nuru Sherpa (Nepal); 11/5/90 318 Andrew Lapkass (US); 10/5/90 319 Peter Hillary (NZ); 1st son of any summiteer to summit himself; 320 Rob Hall (NZ), 321 Gary Ball (NZ), 322 Apa Sherpa (Nepal), 323 Rudy Van Snick (Belgium); 11/5/90 324 Mikael Reutersward (Sweden), 325 Oskar Kihlborg (Sweden); 11/5/90 326 Tim Macartney-Snape (Australia) (2nd, used no oxygen); 1st person to go on foot from sea level to summit; 4/10/90 327 Alex Lowe (US), 328 Dan Culver (Canada); 5/10/90 329 Ang Temba Sherpa (Nepal), 330 Hooman Aprin (US); 331 Phinzo Sherpa (Nepal) 7/10/90; 332 Catherine Gibson (f) (US), 333 Aleksei Krasnokutsky (USSR) Gibson and Krasnokutsky 2nd married couple to top together; 4/10/90 334 Yves Salino (France); 7/10/90 335 Jean Noel Roche (France), 336 Bertrand Roche (France), 337 Nima Dorje Sherpa (Nepal), 338 Ang Phurba Sherpa (Nepal) (not same man as nos 101 and 192/215), 339 Denis Pivot (France), 340 Alain Desez (France), 341 Rene De Bos (Holland) Roches first father and son to top together; Bertrand Roche (age 17) youngest non-Nepalese to top; 5/10/90 342 Nawang Thile Sherpa (Nepal), 343 Sona Dendu Sherpa (Nepal) (2nd), 344 Erik Decamp (France), 345 Marc Batard (France) (2nd, used no oxygen), 346 Christine Janin (f) (France), 347 Pascal Tournaire (France); 6/10/90 348 Babu Tshering Sherpa (Nepal); 6/10/90 349 Pok Jin-Young (S Korea), 350 Kim Jae-Soo (S Korea), 351 Park Chang-Woo (S Korea), 352 Dawa Sange Sherpa (Nepal), 353 Pemba Dorje Sherpa (Nepal); 7/10/90 354 Lhakpa Rita Sherpa (Nepal), 355 Andrej Stremfelj (2nd), 356 Marija Stremfelj (f) (Yugoslavia) Stremfeljs first married couple to top together, 357 Janez Jeglic (Yugoslavia); **8/5/91** 358 Ang Temba Sherpa (Nepal), 359 Sona Dendu Sherpa (Nepal) (3rd), 360 Apa Sherpa (Nepal) (2nd); 8/5/91 361 Peter Athans (US) (2nd); 15/5/91 362 Mark Richey (US), 363 Yves LaForest (Canada), 364 Richard Wilcox (US), 365 Barry Rugo (US); 15/5/91 366 Eric Simonson (US), 367 Bob Sloezen (US), 368 Lhakpa Dorje Sherpa (Nepal) (2nd), 369 Ang Dawa Sherpa (Nepal), 370 George Dunn (US), 371 Andy Politz (US) N Col to N Ridge to N Face; 17/5/91 372 Mike Perry (NZ) N Col to N Ridge to N Face; 21/5/91 373 Mark Whetu (NZ), 374 Brent Okita (US) N Col to N Ridge to N Face; 24/5/91 375 Greg Wilson (US) N Col to N Ridge to N Face; 15/5/91 376 Edmund Viesturs (US) (2nd); 15/5/91 377 Mingma Norbu Sherpa (Nepal), 378 Gyalbu Sherpa (Nepal), 379 Lars Cronlund (Sweden) N Face (Hornbein and Japanese Couloirs); 17/5/91 380 Battista Bonali (Italy) (used no oxygen), 381 Leopold Sulovsky (Czech Rep) (used no oxygen) N Face (Great Couloir); 22/5/91 382 Babu Tshering (Ang Babu) Sherpa (Nepal) (2nd), 383 Chuldin Temba Sherpa (Nepal) N Col to N Ridge; 27/5/91

384 Muneo Nukita (Japan), 385 Nima Dorje Sherpa (Nepal) (2nd), 386 Phinzo Norbu Sherpa (Nepal) (not same man as 331), 387 Junichi Futagami † (Japan) N Col to N Ridge to N Face; 6/10/91 388 Jose Antonio Garces (Spain), 389 Francisco Jose Perez (Spain), 390 Antonio Ubieto (Spain), 391 Rafael Vidaurre (Spain); 7/10/91 392 Vladimir Balyberdin (USSR) (2nd, used no oxygen), 393 Anatoli Boukreev (Kazakhstan) (used no oxygen); 10/10/91 394 Roman Giutachvili (USSR), 395 Dan Mazur (US); **10/5/92** 396 Prem Singh (India), 397 Sunil Dutt Sharma (India), 398 Kanhayalal Pokhriyal (India); 12/5/92 399 Lobsang Sherpa (India), 400 Santosh Yadav (f) (India), 401 Sange Sherpa (India), 402 Wangchuk Sherpa (Nepal), 403 Mohan Singh Gunjal (India); 12/5/92 404 Ned Gillette (US), 405 Doron Erel (Israel), 406 Yick Kai Cham (Hong Kong), 407 Gary Ball (NZ) (2nd), 408 Douglas Mantle (US), 409 Rob Hall (NZ) (2nd), 410 Randall Danta (US), 411 Guy Cotter (NZ), 412 Sonam Tshering Sherpa (Nepal) (3rd), 413 Ang Dorje Sherpa (Nepal) (not same man as no 77 and 168), 414 Tashi Tshering Sherpa (Nepal), 415 Apa Sherpa (Nepal) (3rd), 416 Ang Dawa Sherpa (Nepal) (2nd), 417 Ingrid Baeyens (f) (Belgium); 12/5/92 418 Ronald Naar (Holland), 419 Edmond Oefner (Holland), 420 Nima Temba Sherpa (Nepal), 421 Dawa Tashi Sherpa (Nepal); 12/5/92 422 Alexander Gerasimov (Russia), 423 Andrei Volkov (Russia), 424 Ilia Sabelnikov (Russia), 425 Ivan Dusharin (Russia); 14/5/92 426 Sergei Penzov (Russia), 427 Vladimir Zakharov (Russia), 428 Evgueni Vinogradski (Russia), 429 Fedor Konyukhov (Russia); 12/5/92 430 Skip Horner (US), 431 Louis Bowen (US), 432 Vernon Tejas (US), 433 Dawa Temba Sherpa (Nepal), 434 Ang Gyalzen Sherpa (Nepal); 15/5/92 435 Lhakpa Rita Sherpa (Nepal) (2nd), 436 Peter Athans (US) (3rd), 437 Keith Kerr (UK), 438 Todd Burleson (US), 439 Hugh Morton (US), 440 Man Bahadur Tamang ('Gopal') (Nepal), 441 Dorje Sherpa (Nepal); 15/5/92 442 Christian Garcia-Huidobro (Chile), 443 Rodrigo Jordan (Chile), 444 Juan Sebastian Montes (Chile) E Face to; 15/5/92 445 Francisco Gan (Spain), 446 Alfonson Juez (Spain), 447 Ramon Portilla (Spain), 448 Lhakpa Nuru Sherpa (Nepal), 449 Pemba Norbu Sherpa (Nepal) S Pillar to SE Ridge; 15/5/92 450 Mauricio Purto (Chile), 451 Ang Rita Sherpa (Nepal) (7th, used no oxygen), 452 Ang Phuri Sherpa (Nepal); 15/5/92 453 Jonathan Pratt (UK); 25/9/92 454 Pitxi Eguillor (Spain), 455 Patxi Fernandez (Spain), 456 Alberto Iñurrategi (Spain), 457 Felix Iñurrategi (Spain); Iñurrategis first brothers to top together, they used no oxygen; 1/10/92 458 Josu Bereziartua (Spain); 3/10/92 459 Juan Tomas (Spain), 460 Mikel Reparaz (Spain), 461 Pedro Tous (Spain); 28/9/92 462 Giuseppe Petigaz (Italy), 463 Lorenzo Mazzoleni (Italy), 464 Mario Panzeri (Italy) (used no oxygen), 465 Pierre Royer (France), 466 Lhakpa Nuru Sherpa (Nepal) (2nd); 29/9/92 467 Benoit Chamoux (France), 468 Oswald Santin (Italy); 30/9/92 469 Abele Blanc (Italy), 470 Giampietro Verza (Italy); 1/10/92 471 Eugene Berger (Luxembourg); 4/10/92 472 Ralf Dujmovits (Germany), 473 Sonam Tshering Sherpa (Nepal) (4th); 7/10/92 474 Michel Vincent (France); 9/10/92 475 Scott Darsney (US); 9/10/92 476 'Poncho' de la Parra (Mexico), 477 Wally Berg (US), 478 Augusto Ortega Peru, 479 Kaji Sherpa (Nepal), 480 Apa Sherpa (Nepal) (4th); 9/10/92 481 Philippe Grenier (France), 482 Michel Pelle (France), 483 Thierry Defrance (France), 484 Alain Roussey (France), 485 Pierre Aubertin (France); **13/4/93** 486 Heo Young-Ho (S Korea) (2nd), 487 Ngati Sherpa (Nepal) N Col to N Ridge up, SE Ridge to S Col down; 22/4/93 488 Dawa Tashi Sherpa (Nepal) (2nd), 489 Pasang Lhamu Sherpa † (f) (Nepal), 490 Pemba Nuru Sherpa (Pemba Norbu) (Nepal) (2nd), 491 Sonam Tshering Sherpa † (Nepal) (5th), 492 Lhakpa Nuru Sherpa (Nepal) (3rd), 493 Nawang Thile Sherpa (Nepal) (2nd); 5/5/93 494 Ji Mi (China), 495 Jia Chuo (China), 496 Kai Zhong (China), 497 Pu Bu (China), 498 Wang Yong Feng (China), 499 Wu Chin Hsiung (Taiwan) N Col to N Ridge; 10/5/93 500 Alex Lowe (US) (2nd), 501 John Helenek (US), 502 John Dufficy (US), 503 Wally Berg (US) (2nd), 504 Michael Sutton (Canada), 505 Apa Sherpa (Nepal) (5th), 506 Dawa Nuru Sherpa (Nepal) (2nd), 507 Chuldin Temba Sherpa (Nepal) (2nd) S Col to SE Ridge; 10/5/93 508 Kim Soon-Joo (f) (S Korea), 509 Ji Hyun-Ok (f) (S Korea), 510 Choi Oh-Soon (f) (S Korea), 511 Ang Dawa Sherpa (Nepal) (3rd), 512 Ang Tshering Sherpa (Nepal), 513 Sona Dendu Sherpa (Nepal) (4th), 514 Rinzin Sherpa (Nepal); 10/5/93 515 Michael Groom (Australia) (used no oxygen), 516 Lobsang Tshering Bhutia † (India); 10/5/93 517 Harry Taylor (UK) (used no oxygen during ascent); 17/5/93 518 Rebecca Stephens (f) (UK), 519 Ang Pasang Sherpa (Nepal), 520 Kami Tshering Sherpa (Nepal); 10/5/93 521 Dicky Dolma (f) (India), 522 Santosh Yadav (f) (India) (2nd; first woman to climb twice), 523 Kunga Bhutia (f) (India), 524 Baldev Kunwer (India), 525 Ongda Chhiring Sherpa (Nepal), 526 Na Temba Sherpa (Nepal), 527 Kusang Dorjee Sherpa (India), 528 Dorje Sherpa (Nepal) (2nd); 16/5/93 529 Radha Devi Thakur (f) (India), 530 Rajiv Sharma (India), 531 Deepu Sharma (f) (India), 532 Savita Martolia (f) (India), 533 Nima Norbu Dolma (India), 534 Suman Kutiyal (f) (India), 535 Nima Dorje Sherpa (Nepal) (3rd), 536 Tenzing Sherpa (Nepal), 537 Lobsang Jangbu Sherpa (Nepal), 538 Nga Temba Sherpa (Nepal); 10/5/93 539 Mary (Dolly) Lefever (f) (US), 540 Mark Selland (US), 541 Charles Armatys (US), 542 Pemba Temba Sherpa (Nepal), 543 Moti Lal Gurung (Nepal), 544 Michael Sinclair (US) 16/5/93, 545 Mark Rabold (US), 546 Phinzo Sherpa (Nepal) (2nd), 547 Dorje Sherpa (Nepal), 548 Durga Tamang (Nepal); 10/5/93 549 Veikka Gustafsson (Finland), 550 Jan Arnold (f) (NZ), 551 Rob Hall (NZ) (3rd), 552 Jonathan Gluckman (NZ), 553 Ang Chumbi Sherpa (Nepal), 554 Ang Dorje Sherpa (Nepal) (2nd), 555 Norbu (Nuru) Sherpa (Nepal); 10/5/93 556 Vladas Vitkauskas (Lithuania); 10/5/93 557 Alexei Mouravlev (Russia); 15/5/93 558 Vladimir Janochkine (Russia); 16/5/93 559 Vladimir Bashkirov (Russia) (used no oxygen); 17/5/93 560 Vladimir Koroteev (Russia); 16/5/93 561 Josep Pujante (Spain), 562 Ang Phurba Sherpa (Nepal) (3rd); 17/5/93 563 Oscar Cadiach (Spain) (2nd, used no oxygen); 16/5/93 564 Joxe Maria Onate (Spain), 565 Alberto Cerain (Spain), 566 Jose Ramon Aguirre (Spain), 567 Jangbu Sherpa (Nepal), 568 Ang Rita Sherpa (Nepal) (8th, used no oxygen); 16/5/93 569 Jan Harris (US), 570 Keith Brown (US); 16/5/93 571 Park Young-Seok (S Korea), 572 An Jin-Seob † (S Korea), 573 Kim Tae-Kon (S Korea), 574 Kazi Sherpa (Nepal) (2nd); 27/5/93 575 Dawson Stelfox (Ireland/UK) N Col to N Ridge; 6/10/93 576 Park Hyun-Jae (S Korea), 577 Panuru Sherpa (Nepal) N Col to N Ridge; 6/10/93 578 Francois Bernard (France), 579 Antoine Cayrol (France), 580 Eric Gramond (France) (used no oxygen), 581 Gyalbu Sherpa (Nepal) (2nd), 582 Dawa Tashi Sherpa (Nepal) (3rd); 9/10/93 583 Alain Esteve (France), 584 Hubert Giot (France) (used no oxygen), 585 Norbu (Nuru) Sherpa (Nepal) (2nd), 586 Nima Gombu Sherpa (Nepal); 7/10/93

587 Juanito Oiarzabal (Spain), 588 Ongda Chhiring Sherpa (Nepal) (2nd) S Pillar; 7/10/93 589 Ginette Harrison (f) (UK), 590 Gary Pfisterer (US) (Spain), 591 Ramon Blanco (Spain) (age 60, oldest summiter so far), 592 Graham Hoyland (UK), 593 Stephen Bell (UK), 594 Scott McIvor (UK), 595 Na Temba Sherpa (Nepal) (2nd), 596 Pasang Kami Sherpa (Nepal), 597 Dorje Sherpa (Nepal) (3rd); 9/10/93 598 Martin Barnicott (UK), 599 David Hempleman-Adams (UK), 600 Lee Nobmann (US), 601 Tenzing Sherpa (Nepal) (2nd), 602 Nga Temba Sherpa (Nepal) (2nd), 603 Lhakpa Gelu Sherpa (Nepal), 604 Ang Pasang Sherpa (Nepal); 9/10/93 605 Maciej Berbeka (Poland), 606 Lhakpa Nuru Sherpa (Nepal) (4th; first person to climb by three different routes) N Col to N Face; 10/10/93 607 Jonathan Tinker (UK), 608 Babu Tshering Sherpa (Nepal) (3rd) N Col to N Face; 18/12/93 609 Hideji Nazuka (Japan) (2nd), 610 Fumiaki Goto (Japan) SW Face; first winter ascent of SW Face; 20/12/93 611 Osamu Tanabe (Japan), 612 Sinsuke Ezuka (Japan) SW Face; 22/12/93 613 Yoshio Ogata (Japan), 614 Ryushi Hoshino (Japan) SW Face; **8/5/94** 615 Kiyohiko Suzuki (Japan) S Pillar; 616 Wataru Atsuta (Japan), 617 Nima Dorje Sherpa (Nepal) (4th), 618 Dawa Tshering Sherpa (Nepal), 619 Na Temba Sherpa (Nepal) (3rd), 620 Lhakpa Nuru Sherpa (Nepal) (5th) S Pillar; 13/5/94 621 Tomiyasu Ishikawa (Japan), 622 Nima Temba Sherpa (Nepal), 623 Dawa Tashi Sherpa (Nepal) (4th), 624 Pasang Tshering Sherpa (Nepal) (2nd) S Pillar; 8/5/94 625 Shih Fang-Fang † (Taiwan) N Col to N Face; 9/5/94 626 Lobsang Jangbu Sherpa (Nepal) (2nd, used no oxygen), 627 Rob Hess (US) (used no oxygen), 628 Scott Fischer (US) (used no oxygen), 629 Brent Bishop (US); 630 Sona Dendu Sherpa (Nepal) (5th); 13/5/94 631 Steven Goryl (US); 9/5/94 632 Ang Dorje Sherpa (Nepal) (3rd), 633 Hall Wendel (US), 634 Helmut Seitzel (Germany), 635 David Keaton (US), 636 Ekke Gundelach (Germany), 637 Rob Hall (NZ) (4th), 638 Ed Viesturs (US) (3rd), 639 Nima Gombu Sherpa (Nepal) (2nd), 640 Norbu (Nuru) Sherpa (Nepal) (3rd), 641 David Taylor (US), 642 Erling Kagge (Norway); 13/5/94 643 Lhakpa Rita Sherpa (Nepal) (3rd), 644 Chuwang Nima Sherpa (Nepal), 645 Man Bahadur Tamang (Nepal) (2nd), 646 Kami Rita Sherpa (Nepal), 647 Dorje Sherpa (Nepal) (4th), 648 Ryszard Pawlowski (Poland), 649 Robert Cedergreen (US), 650 Paul Morrow (US), 651 Peter Athans (US) (4th), 652 Todd Burleson (US) (2nd); 19/5/94 653 David Hahn (US) N Col to N Ridge; 25/5/94 654 Steve Swenson (US) (used no oxygen) N Col to N Ridge; 26/5/94 655 Mark Whetu (NZ) (2nd), 656 Michael Rheinberger † (Australia) N Col to N Ridge; 31/5/94 657 Bob Sloezen (US) (2nd) N Col to N Ridge; 10/10/94 658 Muneo Nukita (Japan) (2nd), 659 Apa Sherpa (Nepal) (6th), 660 Chuwang Nima Sherpa (Nepal) (2nd), 661 Dawa Tshering Sherpa (Nepal); 11/10/94 662 Charlie Hornsby (UK), 663 Roddy Kirkwood (UK), 664 Dorje Sherpa (Nepal) (5th), 665 Dawa Temba Sherpa (Nepal) (2nd); **7/5/95** 666 Lobsang Jangbu Sherpa (Nepal) (3rd, used no oxygen); 11/5/95 667 Kiyoshi Furuno (Japan), 668 Shigeki Imoto (Japan), 669 Dawa Tshering Sherpa (Nepal) (2nd), 670 Pasang Kami Sherpa (Nepal) (2nd), 671 Lhakpa Nuru Sherpa (Karikhola) (Nepal) (6th; with Nima Dorje Sherpa (no672), first person to climb by 4 different routes), 672 Nima Dorje Sherpa (Nepal) (5th; see no 671) NE Ridge; first ascent of NE Ridge; 11/5/95 673 Vladimir Shataev (Russia), 674 Iria Projaev (Russia), 675 Fedor Shuljev (Russia) N Col to N Ridge; 13/5/95 676 Kazbek Khamitsatev (N Ossetia) (Russia), 677 Evgueni Vinogradski (Russia) (2nd), 678 Sergei Bogomolov (Russia), 679 Vladimir Korenkov (Russia), 680 Ang Rita Sherpa (Nepal) (9th, used no oxygen) N Col to N Ridge; 12/5/95 681 Piotr Pustelnik (Poland) N Col to N Ridge; 13/5/95 682 Marco Bianchi (Italy) (used no oxygen), 683 Christian Kuntner (Italy) (used no oxygen) N Col to N Ridge; 12/5/95 684 Ryszard Pawlowski (Poland) (2nd) N Col to N Ridge; 14/5/95 685 Mozart Catao (Brazil), 686 Waldemar Niclevicz (Brazil) N Col to N Ridge; 17/5/95 687 Graham Ratcliffe (UK), 688 Anatoli Boukreev (Kazakhstan) (2nd, used no oxygen), 689 Nikoli Sitnikov (Russia) N Col to N Ridge; 23/5/95 690 Michael Jorgensen (Denmark), 691 Crag Jones (UK) N Col to N Ridge; 12/5/95 692 Cheng Kuo-Chun (Taiwan), 693 Chiang Hsui-Chen (f) (Taiwan), 694 Mingma Tshering Sherpa (Nepal), 695 Lhakpa Dorje Sherpa (Nepal) (used no oxygen), 696 Tenzing Nuru Sherpa (Nepal) N Col to N Ridge; 13/5/95 697 Alison Hargreaves (f) (UK) (first woman to top in unsupported climb, used no oxygen) N Col to N Ridge; 17/5/95 698 Constantin Lacatusu (Romania) N Col to N Ridge; 26/5/95 699 Greg Child (Australia), 700 Karsang Sherpa (Nepal), 701 Lobsang Temba Sherpa (Nepal) N Col to N Ridge; 14/5/95 702 Reinhard Patscheider (Italy) (used no oxygen), 703 Teodors Kirsis (Latvia), 704 Imants Zauls (Latvia) N Col to N Ridge; 14/5/95 705 George Mallory (Australia), 706 Jeffrey Hall (US), 707 Jim Litch (US), 708 Dan Aguillar (US), 709 Kaji Sherpa (Nepal) (3rd), 710 Ongda Chhiring Sherpa (Nepal) (3rd), 711 Wangchu Sherpa (Nepal) N Col to N Ridge; 16/5/95 712 Colin Lynch (US), 713 Jay Budnik (US), 714 Steve Reneker (US), 715 Kurt Wedberg (US), 716 Phinzo Sherpa (Nepal) (3rd), 717 Jangbu Sherpa (Nepal) N Col to N Ridge; 14/5/95 718 Luc Jourjon (France), 719 Babu Tshering Sherpa (Nepal) (4th) N Col to N Ridge; 17/5/95 720 George Kotov (Russia), 721 Ali Nasuh Mahruki (Turkey) N Col to N Ridge; 24/5/95 722 Jeff Shea (US), 723 Lhakpa Gelu Sherpa (Nepal) (2nd), 724 Tshering Dorje Sherpa (Nepal) N Col to N Ridge; 26/5/95 725 Patrick Hache (France), 726 Robert Hempstead (US), 727 Lama Jangbu Sherpa (Nepal), 728 Babu Tshering Sherpa (Nepal) (5th, first person to make 2 ascents in same season) N Col to N Ridge; 27/5/95 729 Michael Smith (UK), 730 Patrick Falvey Ireland, 731 James Allen (Australia) N Col to N Ridge; 14/5/95 732 Josef Hinding (Austria) (used no oxygen) N Col to N Ridge; 15/5/95 733 Brad Bull (US), 734 Tommy Heinrich (Argentina), 735 Apa Sherpa (Nepal) (7th), 736 Arita Sherpa (Nepal), 737 Nima Rita Sherpa (Nepal) (3rd); 16/5/95 738 Tony TonsIng (US), 739 Musal Kazi Tamang (Nepal) N Col to N Ridge; 14/10/95 740 Jo Yong-Il (S Korea), 741 Zangbu Sherpa † (Nepal) N Col to N Ridge; 742 14/10/95 42 Han Wuang-Yong (S Korea), 743 Hong Sung-Taek (S Korea), 744 Tashi Tshering Sherpa (Nepal) (2nd) N Col to N Ridge; 14/10/95 745 Park Jung-Hun (S Korea), 746 Kim Young-Tae (S Korea), 747 Keepa (Kipa) Sherpa (Nepal), 748 Dawa Tamang (Nepal) SW Face; **10/5/96** 749 Anatoli Boukreev (Kazakhstan) (3rd); 750 Neil Beidleman (US), 751 Martin Adams (US), 752 Klev Schoening (US), 753 Charlotte Fox (f) (US), 754 Tim Madsen (US), 755 Sandy Hill Pittman (f) (US), 756 Scott Fischer † (US) (2nd), 757 Lena Nielsen-Gammelgaard (f) (Denmark), 758 Lobsang Jangbu Sherpa (Nepal) (4th, used no oxygen), 759 Nawang Dorje Sherpa (Nepal), 760 Tenzing Sherpa (Nepal) (3rd), 761 Tashi Tshering Sherpa (Nepal) (3rd); 10/5/96 762 Jon Krakauer (US), 763 Andrew Harris † (NZ) (Japan), 764 Michael Groom (Australia) (2nd), 765 Rob Hall † (NZ) (5th), 766 Yasuo

Namba † (f) (Japan), 767 Douglas Hansen † (US), 768 Ang Dorje (Chuldim) Sherpa (Nepal) (4th), 769 Norbu Sherpa (Nepal) (4th); 10/5/96 770 Gau Ming-Ho (Taiwan), 771 Nima Gombu Sherpa (Nepal) (3rd), 772 Mingma Tshering Sherpa (Nepal) (2nd); 10/5/96 773 Tsewang Smanla † (India), 774 Tsewang Paljor † (India), 775 Dorje Morup † (India) (claim disputed) N Col to N Face; 17/5/96 776 Sange Sherpa (India) (2nd), 777 Hira Ram (India), 778 Tashi Ram (India), 779 Nadra Ram (India), 780 Kusang Dorjee Sherpa (India) (2nd) N Col to N Face; 11/5/96 781 Hiroshi Hanada (Japan), 782 Eisuka Shigekawa (Japan), 783 Pasang Tshering Sherpa (Nepal) (3rd), 784 Pasang Kami Sherpa (Nepal) (3rd), 785 Ang Gyalzen Sherpa (Nepal) N Col to N Face; 13/5/96 786 Mamoru Kikuchi (Japan), 787 Hirotaka Sugiyama (Japan), 788 Nima Dorje Sherpa (Nepal) (6th), 789 Chuwang Nima Sherpa (Nepal) (3rd), 790 Dawa Tshering Sherpa (Thami) (Nepal) (2nd) N Col to N Face; 17/5/96 791 Hirotaka Takeyuchi (Japan), 792 Pemba Tshering Sherpa (Nepal), 793 Na Temba Sherpa (Nepal) (4th) N Col to N Face; 21/5/96 794 Koji Yamazaki (Japan) N Col to N Face; 17/5/96 795 Sven Gangdal (Norway), 796 Olav Ulvund (Norway), 797 Dawa Tashi Sherpa (Nepal) (5th), 798 Dawa Tshering Sherpa (Beding) (Nepal) (3rd) N Col to N Face; 18/5/96 799 Morten Rostrup (Norway), 800 Josef Nezerka (Czech Rep), 801 Fausto De Stefani (Italy), 802 Gyalbu Sherpa (Nepal) (3rd) N Col to N Face; 19/5/96 803 Alan Hinkes (UK), 804 Matthew Dickinson (UK), 805 Lhakpa Gelu Sherpa (Nepal) (3rd), 806 Mingma Dorje Sherpa (Nepal), 807 Phur Gyalzen Sherpa (Nepal) N Col to N Face; 20/5/96 808 Petr Kouznetsov (Russia), 809 Valeri Kohanov (Russia), 810 Grigori Semikolenkov (Russia) couloir between N and NE Ridges; 23/5/96 811 Thierry Renard (France), 812 Babu Tshering Sherpa (Nepal) (6th, used no oxygen), 813 Dawa Sherpa (Nepal); 23/5/96 814 Ed Viesturs (US) (4th, used no oxygen), 815 David Breashears (US) (3rd), 816 Robert Schauer (Austria) (2nd), 817 Jamling Tenzing Norgay Sherpa (India) (son of Tenzing Norgay), 818 Araceli Segarra (f) (Spain), 819 Lhkapa Dorje Sherpa (Nepal) (2nd, used no oxygen), 820 Dorje Sherpa (Nepal), 821 Jangbu Sherpa (Nepal) (2nd), 822 Muktu Lhakpa Sherpa (Nepal), 823 Thilen Sherpa (Nepal); 23/5/96 824 Goren Kropp (Sweden) (used no oxygen), 825 Ang Rita Sherpa (Nepal) (10th, used no oxygen) S Pillar to S Col; 23/5/96 826 Jesus Martinez (Spain) (used no oxygen) S Pillar to S Col; 24/5/96 827 Hans Kammaerlander (Italy) (used no oxygen) N Col to N Face; 235 hrs base-summit-base; descended most of route by ski; 24/5/96 828 Yuri Contreras (Mexico), 829 Hector Ponce de Leon (Mexico) N Col to N face; 25/5/96 830 Ian Woodall (S Africa), 831 Cathy O'Dowd (f) (S Africa), 832 Bruce Herrod † (UK), 833 Pemba Tenji Sherpa (Nepal), 834 Ang Dorje Sherpa (Nepal), 835 Lama Jangbu (Nepal) (2nd); 26/9/96 836 Clara Sumarwati (f) (Indonesia) (claim disputed), 837 Kaji Sherpa (Nepal) (4th), 838 Gyalzen Sherpa (Nepal), 839 Ang Gyalzen Sherpa (Nepal) (2nd), 840 Dawa Tshering Sherpa (Nepal) (3rd), 841 Chuwang Nima Sherpa (Nepal) (4th) N Col to N face; 11/10/96 842 Choi Jong-Tai (S Korea), 843 Shin Kwang-Chal (S Korea), 844 Panuru Sherpa (Nepal) (4th), 845 Keepa (Kipa) Sherpa (Nepal) (2nd), 846 Dawa Tamang (Nepal) (2nd); **26/4/97** 847 Apa Sherpa (Nepal) (8th), 848 Anatoli Boukreev (Kazakhstan) (4th), 849 Dawa Nuru Sherpa (Nepal), 850 Vladimir Bashkirov (Russia) (2nd), 851 Asmujiono (Indonesia); 2/5/97 852 Vladimir Frolov (Kazakhstan), 853 Andrej Molotov (Kazakhstan), 854 Sergei Ovsharenko (Kazakhstan), 855 Vladimir Souviga Kazakh (Kazakhstan) (used no oxygen) N Col to N Face; 7/5/97 856 Ivan Plotnikov † (Russia), 857 Nikolai Chevtchenko † (Russia) N Col to N Face; 20/5/97 858 Konstantin Farafonov (Kazakhstan), 859 Sergei Lavrov (Kazakhstan), 860 Dmitri Grekov (Kazakhstan), 861 Dmitri Sobolev (Kazakhstan), 862 Dmitri Mouravev (Kazakhstan), 863 Lyudmila Savina (f) (Kazakhstan) N Col to N Face; 22/5/97 864 Andy Evans (Canada) N Col to N Face; 7/5/97 865 Lee In (S Korea), 866 (Ang) Dawa Tamang (Nepal) (3rd) N Col to N Face; 8/5/97 867 Antoine de Choudens (France) (used no oxygen), 868 Stephane Cagnin (France) N Col to N Face; 20/5/97 869 Doytchin Vassilev (Bulgaria) N Col to N Face; 21/5/97 870 Nikola Kekus (UK), 871 Bjorn Olafsson (Iceland), 872 Hallgrimur Magnusson (Iceland), 873 Einar Stefansson (Iceland), 874 Babu Tshering Sherpa (Nepal) (7th), 875 Dawa Sherpa (Nepal) (2nd); 23/5/97 876 Mark Warham (UK, 877 Eric Blakeley (UK), 878 Hugo Rodriguez (Mexico), 879 Lhakpa Gelu Sherpa (Nepal) (4th), 880 Da Tenzi Sherpa (Nepal); 21/5/97 881 Danuri Sherpa (Nepal); 22/5/97 882 Franc Pepevnik (Slovenia) N Col to N Face; 23/5/97 883 Pavle Kozjek (Slovenia) (used no oxygen) N Col to N Face; 23/5/97 884 David Breashears (US) (4th), 885 Peter Athans (US) (5th), 886 Jangbu Sherpa (Nepal) (3rd), 887 Dorje Sherpa (Nepal) (2nd), 888 Kami Sherpa (Nepal); 23/5/97 889 Jamie Clarke (Canada), 890 Alan Hobson (Canada), 891 Lhakpa Tshering Sherpa (Nepal) (2nd), 892 Gyalbu Sherpa (Nepal) (4th), 893 Tashi Tshering Sherpa (Nepal) (4th), 894 Kami Tshering Sherpa (Nepal) (2nd); 23/5/97 895 Guy Cotter (NZ) (2nd), 896 Ed Viesturs (US) (5th), 897 Tashi Tenzing (Australia) (first grandson of any summiter), 898 Veikka Gustafsson (Finland) (2nd, used no oxygen), 899 David Carter (US), 900 Ang Dorje Sherpa (Nepal) (5th), 901 Mingma Tshering Sherpa (Nepal) (3rd); 23/5/97 902 Mohandas Nagapan (Malaysia), 903 Magendran Munisamy (Malaysia), 904 Na Temba Sherpa (Nepal) (5th), 905 Dawa Temba Sherpa (Nepal) (3rd), 906 Gyalzen Sherpa (Nepal) (2nd), 907 Ang Phuri Gyalzen Sherpa (Nepal), 908 Fura Dorje Sherpa (Nepal); 23/5/97 909 Andres Delgado Mexico (UK), 910 Tenzing Sherpa (Nepal) (4th); 27/5/97 911 Brigitte Muir (f) (Australia), 912 Kipa Sherpa (Nepal) (3rd), 913 Dorje Sherpa (Nepal) (6th); 24/5/97 914 Alexandre Zelinski (Russia), 915 Sergei Sokolov (Russia) N Col to N Face; 25/5/97 916 Wally Berg (US) (3rd), 917 Kami Rita Sherpa (Nepal) (2nd), 918 Ang Pasang Sherpa (Nepal) (2nd), 919 Pemba Tenji Sherpa (Nepal) (2nd), 920 Mingma Tshering Sherpa (Nepal), 921 Lhakpa Rita Sherpa (Nepal) (4th), 922 Nima Tashi Sherpa (Nepal) (3rd), 923 Tenzing Nuru Sherpa † (Nepal) (2nd); 27/5/97 924 Yuri Contreras (Mexico) (2nd), 925 Ilgvars Pauls (Latvia), 926 Dawa Sona Sherpa (Nepal); 29/5/97 927 Russell Brice (NZ), 928 Richard Price (NZ) N Col to N Face; 29/5/97 929 Daqimi (China) (Tibet), 930 Tenzing Dorje (China), 931 Kai Zhong (China) (2nd) N Col to N Face; **18/5/98** 932 Shoji Abe (Japan), 933 Toshiya Nakajima (Japan), 934 Pasang Kami Sherpa (Nepal) (4th), 935 Na Temba Sherpa (Nepal) (6th), 936 Ang Gyalzen Sherpa (Nepal) (3rd) N Col to N Face; 19/5/98 937 Hitoshi Onodera (Japan), 938 Hiromichi Kamimura (Japan), 939 Chuwang Nima Sherpa (Nepal) (5th), 940 Dawa Tshering Sherpa (Nepal) (4th) N Col to N Face; 18/5/98 941 Surendra Chavan (India), 942 Dawa Tashi Sherpa (Nepal) (6th), 943 Dawa Nuru Sherpa (Nepal) (2nd), 944 Thomting Sherpa (Nepal), 945 Nawang Tenzing Sherpa (Nepal) N Col to N Face; 19/5/98 946

Loveraj Dharmshaktu (India), 947 Phinzo Norbu Sherpa (Nepal) (2nd), 948 Nima Gyalzen Sherpa (Nepal) N Col to N Face; 18/5/98 949 Hidetoshi Kurahashi (Japan), 950 Masaru Sato (Japan), 951 Koichi Nagata (Japan), 952 Hisashi Hashimoto (Japan), 953 Shoji Sakamoto (Japan), 954 Ang Mingma Sherpa (Nepal) N Col to N Face; 20/5/98 955 Toshiaki Yano (Japan), 956 Yoshinori Kawahara (Japan), 957 Gyalzen Sherpa (Nepal) (3rd) N Col to N Face; 22/5/98 958 Kazuyoshi Kondo (Japan), 959 Dawa Sherpa (Nepal) N Col to N Face; 18/5/98 960 Alexei Bolotov (Russia), 961 Valeri Perchine (Russia), 962 Sergei Timofeev (Russia), 963 Yevgeni Vinogradski (Russia) (3rd) N Col to N Face; 21/5/98 964 Anatoly Mochnikov (Russia) (2nd, used no oxygen), 965 Gilles Roman (France); 22/5/98 966 Francys Arsentiev † (f) (US) (used no oxygen), 967 Sergei Arsentiev † (Russia) (2nd, used no oxygen) N Col to N Face; 18/5/98 968 Victor Koulbatchenko (Belorussia), N Col to N Face; 19/5/98 969 Peter Hamor (Slovakia), 970 Vladimir Zboja (Slovakia), 971 Vladimir Plulik Slovakia (used no oxygen) N Col to N Face; 24/5/98 972 Ci Luo (China) N Col to N Face; 19/5/98 973 Noriyuki Muraguchi (Japan), 974 Minoru Sawada (Japan), 975 Mingma Tshering Sherpa (Nepal) (4th), 976 Tshering Dorje Sherpa (Nepal), 977 Pasang Kitar Sherpa (Nepal) N Col to N Face; 19/5/98 978 Radek Jaros (Czech Rep) (used no oxygen), 979 Vladimir Nosek (Czech Rep) (used no oxygen) N Col to N Face; 20/5/98 980 Bob Hoffman (US), 981 Donald Beavon (US), 982 Pasquale Scaturro (US), 983 Charles Demarest (US), 984 Mark Cole (US), 985 Apa Sherpa (Nepal) (9th), 986 Pemba Norbu Sherpa (Nepal), 987 Nima Rita Sherpa (Nepal) (4th), 988 Gyalzen Sherpa (Nepal), 989 Chuldim Nuru Sherpa (Nepal), 990 Ang Pasang Sherpa (Nepal), 991 Arita Sherpa (Nepal) (2nd); 20/5/98 992 Jalal Cheshmeh Ghasabani (Iran); 993 Mohammad Hassan Najarian (Iran), 994 Hamid Reza Olanj (Iran), 995 Mohammad Oraz (Iran), 996 Dawa Tenzi Sherpa (Nepal) (2nd), 997 Chuldim Sherpa (Nepal), 998 Pemba Rinzi Sherpa (Nepal); 20/5/98 999 Jeffery Rhoads (US), 1000 Tashi Tshering Sherpa (Nepal) (5th); 27/5/98 1001 Jeffery Rhoads (US) (2nd; 2 ascents in one week), 1002 Tashi Tshering Sherpa (Nepal) (6th; 2 ascents in one week), 1003 Tom Whittaker (US) (first amputee to summit), 1004 Norbu Sherpa (Nepal) (5th), 1005 Lhkapa Tshering Sherpa (Nepal) (3rd), 1006 Dawa Sona Sherpa (Nepal) (2nd); 20/5/98 1007 Wally Berg (US) (4th) S Col to SE Ridge; 22/5/98 1008 Rustam Radjapov N Col to N Face; 23/5/98 1009 Svetlana Baskakova (f), 1010 Sergei Sokolov (Uzbekistan) (not same man as no 915), 1011 Marat Usaev (Uzbekistan), 1012 Oleg Grigoriev (Uzbekistan), 1013 Angrew Fedorov (Uzbekistan) N Col to N Face; 24/5/98 1014 Aleksei Dokukin (Uzbekistan), 1015 Ilyas Tukhvatullin (Uzbekistan), 1016 Andrew Zaikin (Uzbekistan) N Col to N Face; 25/5/98 1017 Khaniv Balmagambetov (Uzbekistan), 1018 Roman Mats (Uzbekistan) N Col to N Face; 24/5/98 1019 Lama Jangbu Sherpa (Nepal) (3rd), 1020 Lhakpa Gelu Sherpa (Nepal) (5th) N Col to N Face; 25/5/98 1021 Bernardo Guarachi (Bolivia); 25/5/98 1022 Khoo Swee-Chiow (Malaysia), 1023 Siew Cheok-Wai (Malaysia), 1024 Kami Rita Sherpa (Nepal) (3rd), 1025 Dorje Sherpa (Nepal) (3rd), 1026 Fura Dorje Sherpa (Nepal) (2nd), 1027 Nawang Phurba Sherpa (Nepal); 25/5/98 1028 Sundeep Dhillon (UK), 1029 David Walsh (UK) , 1030 Nima Gombu Sherpa (Nepal) (4th), 1031 Kusang Dorje Sherpa (India) (3rd), 1032 Nima Dorje Sherpa (Nepal); 25/5/98 1033 Russell Brice (NZ) (2nd) N Col to N Face; 1034 Sumio Tsuzuki (f) (Japan), 1035 Karsang Sherpa (Nepal) (2nd); 25/5/98 1036 Mark Jennings † (UK), 1037 Nima Wangchu Sherpa (Nepal) N Col to N Face; 25/5/98 1038 Craig John (US), 1039 Dawa Nuru Sherpa (Nepal), 1040 Lhakpa Rita Sherpa (Nepal) N Col to N Face; 27/5/981041 Richard Alpert (US), 1042 Robert Sloezen (US) (3rd), 1043 Panuru Sherpa (Nepal) (3rd) N Col to N Face; 26/5/98 1044 Alan Silva (Australia), 1045 Neil Laughton (UK), 1046 Edward Grylls (UK), 1047 Pasang Dawa Sherpa (Nepal), 1048 Pasang Tshering (Pangboche) (Nepal); 26/5/98 1049 Heinz Rockenbauer (Austria) N Col to N Face; 15/10/98 1050 Carlos Pitarch (Spain) (claim disputed); 17/10/98 1051 Kaji Sherpa (Nepal) (5th, used no oxygen in ascent) (claimed fastest ascent if summit claim is true), 1052 Tashi Tshering Sherpa (Nepal) (7th); **5/5/99** 1053 Peter Athans (US) (6th), 1054 William Crouse (US), 1055 Chuwang Nima Sherpa (Nepal) (6th), 1056 Phu Tashi Sherpa (Nepal), 1057 Dorje Sherpa (Nepal) (7th), 1058 Gyalzen Sherpa (Nepal) (4th), 1059 Na Temba Sherpa (Nepal) (7th); 18/5/991060 Charles Corfield (UK), 1061 Chuwang Nima Sherpa (Nepal) (7th, 2nd this season), 1062 Nima Tashi Sherpa (Nepal) (4th), 1063 Dawa Sona Sherpa (Nepal) (3rd); 5/5/99 1064 Graham Ratcliffe (UK) (2nd), 1065 Ray Brown (UK), 1066 Elsa Avila (f) (Mexico), 1067 Andrew Lapkass (US) Mexico (2nd, 1068 Pasang Tshering Sherpa (Nepal) (2nd); 13/5/99 1069 Michael Trueman (UK), 1070 Pasang Dawa Sherpa (Nepal) (2nd); 5/5/99 1071 Renata Chlumska (f) (Sweden), 1072 Goren Kropp (Sweden) (2nd), 1073 Mingma Tshering (Nepal) (5th), 1074 Kami Sherpa (Nepal) (2nd), 1075 Ang Chiri (Nepal); 5/5/99 1076 Bernard Voyer (Canada), 1077 Dorje Sherpa (Nepal) (4th) (not same man as no 1057), 1078 Chhongba Nuru Sherpa (Nepal); 6–7/5/991079 Babu Tshering Sherpa (Nepal) (8th, stayed at summit for 215 hours, used no oxygen), 1080 Dawa Sherpa (Nepal) 6/5/99 (3rd), 1081 Nima Dorje Sherpa (Nepal) 6/5/99 (2nd); 26/5/99 1082 Thomas Sjogren (Sweden), 1083 Tina Sjogren (f) (Sweden), 1084 Babu Tshering Sherpa (Nepal) (9th; 2nd this season, used no oxygen), 1085 Dawa Sherpa (Nepal) (4th, 2nd this season), 1086 Nima Dorje Sherpa (Nepal) (3rd, 2nd this season), 1087 Dawa Temba Sherpa (Nepal) (4th); 8/5/99 1088 Vasili Kopytko † (Ukraine) (used no oxygen), 1089 Vladislav Terzeoul (Ukraine) (used no oxygen), 1090 Valdimir Gorbach (Ukraine) (used no oxygen) N Col to N Face; 12/5/99 1091 Joby Ogwyn (US), 1092 Tenzing Sherpa (Nepal) (5th), 1093 Nima Gombu Sherpa (Nepal) (5th), 1094 Guillermo Benegas (US); 13/5/99 1095 Augusto Ortega (Peru) (2nd), 1096 Constantine Niarchos (Switzerland), 1097 David Rodney (Canada), 1098 Katja Staartjes (f) (Holland), 1099 Christopher Brown (UK), 1100 Martin Doyle (UK), 1101 Michael Smith (UK) (2nd), 1102 Michael Matthews † (UK), 1103 Lhakpa Gelu Sherpa (Nepal) (6th), 1104 Nima Gyalzen Sherpa (Nepal) (2nd, 1105 Kami Rita Sherpa (Nepal) (4th), 1106 Pasang Kitar Sherpa (Nepal) (2nd), 1107 Tshering Dorje Sherpa (Nepal) (2nd), 1108 Pemba Rinzi Sherpa (Nepal) (2nd), 1109 Dawa Nurbu Sherpa (Nepal); 12/5/99 1110 Lev Sarkisov (Georgia) (oldest summiter, 1 day more than Ramon Blanco, no 591), 1111 Afi Gigani (Georgia), 1112 Bidzina Gujabidze (Georgia), 1113 Benedict Kashakashvili (Georgia), 1114 Chewang Dorje Sherpa (Nepal), 1115 Nawang Tenzing Sherpa (Nepal); 13/5/99 1116 Ken Noguchi (Japan), 1117 Dawa Tshering Sherpa (Nepal) (5th), 1118 Nima Wangchu Sherpa (Nepal) (2nd), 1119 Nawang Wangchu Sherpa

(Nepal), 1120 Krishna Bahadur Tamang (Nepal); 17/5/99 1121 Conrad Anker (US), 1122 David Hahn (US) (2nd) N Col to N face; 18/5/99 1123 Jacek Maselko (Poland), 1124 Tadeusz Kudelski † (Poland), 1125 Ryszard Pawlowski (Poland) (3rd) N Col to N Face; 18/5/99 1126 Joao Garcia (Portugal) (used no oxygen), 1127 Pascal Debrouwer † (Belgium) N Col to N Face; 26/5/99 1128 Gheorghe Dijmarescu (US), 1129 Apa Sherpa (Nepal) (10th) N Col to N Face; 26/5/99 1130 Fred Barth (US), 1131 Nanda Dorje Sherpa (Nepal) N Col to N Face; 26/5/99 1132 Andrei Louchnikov (Russia) N Col to N Face; 26/5/99 1133 Hugo Rodriguez (Mexico) (2nd), 1134 Carlos Guevara Mexico, 1135 Lhakpa Nuru Sherpa (Nepal), 1136 Mingma Chhiri (Tshering) Sherpa (Nepal) (2nd, same man as no 920), 1137 Pemba Sherpa (Nepal); 26/5/99 1138 Merab Khabazi (Georgia), 1139 Irakli Ugulava (Georgia), 1140 Mamuka Tsikhiseli (Georgia), 1141 Man Bahadur Tamang (Nepal) (3rd) N Col to N Face; 26/5/99 1142 Sergio Martini (Italy), 1143 Maria Lago (f) (Spain) (used no oxygen in ascent), 1144 Samdu Sherpa (Nepal) N Col to N Face; 27/5/99 1145 Geoffrey Robb (Australia), 1146 Helge Hengge (f) (Germany), 1147 Kazuhiko Kozuka (Japan), 1148 Karsang Sherpa (Nepal) (3rd), 1149 Lobsang Temba Sherpa (Nepal) (2nd), 1150 Phurba Tashi Sherpa (Nepal) N Col to N face; 27/5/99 1151 Ivan Vallejo (Ecuador) (used no oxygen), 1152 Heber Orona (Argentina) (used no oxygen), 1153 Karla Wheelock (f) (Mexico), 1154 Fura Dorje Sherpa (Nepal) (3rd), 1155 Ari Piela (Finland), 1156 Antti Maniken (Finland) N Col to N Face; 28/5/99 1157 Akbu (Tibet), 1158 Luotze (Tibet) (2nd), 1159 Rena (Tibet) (2nd), 1160 Gui Sang (f) (China) (2nd), 1161 Jiabu (Tibet) (2nd), 1162 Bianba Zaxi (Tibet), 1163 Jiji (f) (China), 1164 Cering Doje (Tibet) (2nd), 1165 La Ba (China), 1166 Tashi Tshering (China) N Col to N Face; 28/5/99 1167 Amar Prakash (India), 1168 Kusang Dorjee Sherpa (India) (4th), 1169 Sange Sherpa (India) (3rd) E Face to SE Ridge, 1168 and 1169 are first from N, S and E; 29/5/99 1170 Cathy O'Dowd (f) (S Africa) (2nd), 1171 Ian Woodall (UK) (2nd), 1172 Lama Jangbu Sherpa (Nepal) (4th), 1173 Pemba Tenjee Sherpa (Nepal) (3rd) N Col to N Face

Nanga Parbat ascent data

All ascents via the 'Kinshofer' route on the Diamir Face at the left (north) end of the face: the first ascent climbed directly to the Bazhin Gap, then followed Buhl's route to the summit, but it is now more usual to traverse right and then to climb directly to the top) unless otherwise stated.

3/7/53 H Buhl (Austria) From Rakhiot Glacier via N Face of Rakhiot Peak, then E Ridge to Silver Saddle, across Silver Plateau and along SE Ridge; 22/6/62 T Kinshofer (Germany), S Löw † (Germany), A Mannhardt (Germany); 27/6/70 G Messner † (Italy), R Messner (Italy) Central Rib of SE (Rupal) Face; 28/6/70 F Kuen (Austria), P Scholz (Austria) Central Rib of SE (Rupal) Face; 11/7/71 I Fiala (Slovakia), M Orolin (Slovakia) Buhl Route; 11/8/76 S Gimpel (Austria), R Schauer (Austria), H Schell (Austria), H Sturm (Austria) S/SW Ridge at left (west) edge of Rupal Face, the 'Schell' route; 9/8/78 R Messner (Italy) (2nd) Right (west) edge of Diamir Face; 23/8/78 W Bauer (Austria), R Streif (Austria), R Wurzer (Austria); 28/8/78 A Imitzer (Austria), A Indrich (Austria); 5/8/81 R Naar (Holland) Schell route variant; 19/8/81 S Fassi (Italy), L Rota (Italy), B Scanabessi (Italy); 10/6/82 N Joos (Switzerland), E Loretan (Switzerland) Schell route; 14/7/82 H Engl (Germany); 17/7/83 E Koblmüller (Germany) Schell route; 31/7/83 N Nakanishi (Japan), M Taniguchi (Japan); 5/8/83 E de Pablo (Spain), JL Zuloaga (Spain); 3/6/84 M Ruedi (Switzerland); 27/6/84 L Barrard (f) (France), M Barrard (France); 7/8/84 O Cadiach (Spain), J Magrinyá (Spain) Schell route; 8/7/85 L de la Ferrière (f) (France), H Hanada (Japan), M Kikuchi (Japan), B Muller (France); 12/7/85 M Dacher (Germany), P Habeler (Austria); 13/7/85 C Carsolio (Mexico), AZ Heinrich (Poland), J Kukuczka (Poland), S Lobodzinski (US) SE Pillar of Rupal Face; 15/7/85 A Czerwinska (f) (Poland), F De Stefani (Italy), M García (Spain), M Gómez (Spain), S Martini (Italy), K Palmowska (f) (Poland), W Rutkiewicz (f) (Poland), R Vidaurre (Spain); 16/8/86 H Lanters (Holland), J Van Hees (Belgium), L Vivijs (f) (Belgium); 5/7/87 G Calcagno (Italy), B Chamoux (France), S Dorotei (Italy), T Vidoni (Italy); 9/8/87 F Alvarez (Spain), P Expósito (Spain), D Hernández (Spain), J Martínez (Spain); 19/8/87 K Matsui (Japan), R Okabayashi (Japan); 13/7/88 H Endo (Japan), Y Endo (f) (Japan); 29/7/88 S Hupfauer (Germany), T Mügge (Germany); 9/8/88 O Gassler (Austria); 13/7/89 E Gundelach (Germany), Atta-ul-Haq (Pakistan), Sher Khan (Pakistan), Mohammad Ullah (Pakistan), Rajab Shah (Pakistan); 1/7/90 H Kammerlander (Italy); 25/7/90 M Sato (Japan), R Portilla (Spain); 31/7/90 M Frantar (f) (Slovenia), J Rozman (Slovenia) Schell route; 11/8/90 P Nicolás (Spain), C Soria (Spain), A Fredborg (Norway); 12/8/90 R Joswig (Germany), P Mezger (Germany) Schell route; 18/8/90 M Todaka (Japan) Schell route; 21/7/91 R Mear (UK), D Walsh (UK); 29/6/92 Park Hee-Taek (S Korea), Song Jea-Deuk (S Korea), Kim Ju-Hyun (S Korea); 4/7/92 J Nezerka (Czech Rep), J Rakoncaj (Czech Rep); 8/7/92 C Häuter (Switzerland); 12/7/92 M Abrego (Spain), A Apellaniz (Spain), J Gozdzik (Poland), P Pustelnik (Poland) M Ruiz de Apodaka (Spain), J Oiarzabal (Spain); 7/7/93 P Barrenetxea (Spain), JL Clavel (Spain); 30/7/93 R Estiú (Spain), J Permanyé (Spain); 16/8/93 Y Mochizuki (Japan); 18/8/93 T Tonchev (Bulgaria); 24/8/93 R Pawlowski (Poland), B Stefko (Poland); 28/8/93 M Konewka (Poland), R Schleypen (Germany); 23/6/94 JR Agraz (Spain), J Castillón (Spain), L Ortiz (Spain); 23/7/95 T Akiyama (Japan), H Sakai (Japan), Y Yabe (Japan) NE Ridge of NE Peak to Silver Saddle then Buhl route; 1/9/96 K Wielicki (Poland); 15/6/97 Akbu (Tibet), Aziz Baig (Pakistan), Bianba Zaxi (Tibet), Cering Doje (Tibet), Jiabu (Tibet), Luoze (Tibet), Mohammad Ullah (Pakistan) (2nd), Rena (Tibet); 7/7/97 M Sawada (Japan); 7–14/7/97 A number of S Koreans from a team led by Yoon Kye-Joong (including Park Jun-Hun); 14/7/97 C Buhler (USA), I Dusharin (Russia); 18/7/97 V Kolisnichenko (Russia), A Volkov (Russia); 18/7/97 3 Japanese from a team led by M Kajiura; 19/7/97 3 Japanese from a team led by M Sawada; 27/7/97 J Bretcha (Spain), J Colet † (Spain), T Comerma (Spain), M Gioroianu (Romania), E Sallent (Spain); 31/7/97 S Bershov (Ukraine), V Terzeoul (Ukraine); 20/7/98 R Benet (Italy), N Meroi (f) (Italy); 21/7/98 A Hinkes (UK), A Lock (Australia), Kang Seong-Gyu (S Korea), Park Young-Seok (S Korea), Ra Kwang-Ju (S Korea), Han Wuang-Young (S

Korea), Rozi Ali (Pakistan); 6/8/98 T Kitamura (Japan); 10/8/98 L Fraga (Spain), JI Gordito (Spain), Y Tanahashi (Japan); **2/7/99** Asad Hassan (Pakistan), A Christensen (Denmark), N Cofman (USA), M Granlien (Denmark), P Guggemos (Germany), D Porsche (Germany), A Tremoulière (France), M Vincent (France); 12/7/99 Ang Dawa Tamang (Nepal), Um Hong-Gil (S Korea); 27/7/99 H Kurahashi (Japan), S Mori (Japan), Y Seino (Japan); 28/7/99 T Ikeda (Japan); 29/7/99 A Iñurrategi (Spain), F Iñurrategi (Spain), K Kondo (Japan), JC Tamayo (Spain)

K2 ascent data

All climbs by first ascent route (Abruzzi Spur) unless otherwise stated.

31/7/54 A Compagnoni (Italy), L Lacedelli (Italy); **8/8/77** S Nakamura (Japan), T Shigehiro (Japan), T Takatsuka (Japan); 9/8/77 Ashraf Aman (Pakistan), M Hiroshima (Japan), M Onodera (Japan), H Yamamoto (Japan); **6/9/78** L Reichardt (USA), J Wickwire (USA) NE Ridge/Abruzzi; 7/9/78 R Ridgeway (USA), J Roskelley (USA) NE Ridge/Abruzzi; **12/7/79** M Dacher (Germany), R Messner (Italy); **7/8/81** E Ohtani (Japan), Nazir Sabir (Pakistan) W Ridge/SW Face; **14/8/82** N Sakashita (Japan), Y Yanagisawa † (Japan), H Yoshino (Japan) N Ridge; 15/8/82 H Kamuro (Japan), H Kawamura (Japan), T Shigeno (Japan), K Takami (Japan) N Ridge; **31/7/83** A Da Polenza (Italy), J Rakoncaj (Czech Rep) N Ridge; 4/8/83 S Martini (Italy), F De Stefani (Italy) N Ridge; **19/6/85** N Joos (Switzerland), M Ruedi (Switzerland); 6/7/85 E Escoffier (France), E Loretan (Switzerland), P Morand (Switzerland), J Troillet (Switzerland); 7/7/85 D Lacroix † (France), S Schaffter (Switzerland); 24/7/85 K Murakami (Japan), N Yamada (Japan), K Yoshida (Japan); **23/6/86** M Abrego (Spain), L Barrard † (f) (France), M Barrard † (France), J Casimiro (Spain), M Parmentier (France), W Rutkiewicz (f) (Poland); 5/7/86 G Calcagno (Italy), B Chamoux (France), S Dorotei (Italy), B Fuster (Switzerland), M Moretti (Italy), J Rakoncaj (Czech Rep) (2nd), T Vidoni (Italy), R Zemp (Switzerland); 8/7/86 J Kukuczka (Poland), T Piotrowski † (Poland) S Face; 3/8/86 Chang Bong-Wan (S Korea), Chang Byong-Ho (S Korea), Kim Chang-Son (S Korea); 3/8/86 P Bozik (Slovakia), P Piasecki (Poland), W Wróz † (Poland) SSW Buttress; 4/8/86 W Bauer (Austria), A Imitzer † (Austria), K Diemberger (Austria), J Tullis † (f) (UK), A Rouse † (UK); **9/8/90** H Imamura (Japan), H Nazuka (Japan) NW Face; 20/8/90 G Child (Australia), G Mortimer (Australia), S Swenson (USA) N Ridge; **15/8/91** P Beghin (France), C Profit (France) W Face/NW Face/ N Ridge; **1/8/92** V Balyberdin (Russia), G Kopieka (Ukraine); 3/8/92 C Mauduit (f) (France), A Nikiforov (Russia); 16/8/92 S Fischer (USA), C Mace (USA), E Viesturs (USA); **13/6/93** S Bozic (Croatia), C Carsolio (Mexico), V Groselj (Slovenia), Z Pozgaj (Slovenia); 23/6/93 G Kropp (Sweden); 7/7/93 D Culver † (Canada), J Haberl (Canada), P Powers (USA); 30/7/93 D Bidner † (Sweden), A Bukreev (Kazakhstan), R Jansen (Denmark), R Joswig † (German), A Lock (Australian), P Mezger † (German); 2/9/93 D Mazur (USA), J Pratt (UK) W Ridge/SW Face; **24/6/94** A Iñurrategi (Spain), F Iñurrategi (Spain), J Oiarzabal (Spain), E de Pablo (Spain), J Tomás (Spain) SSE Spur; 9/7/94 R Hall (NZ); 10/7/94 D Ibragimzade † (Ukraine), A Kharaldin † (Ukraine), A Parkhomenko † (Ukraine) (see text); 23/7/94 R Dujmovits (Germany), M Gorbenko (Ukraine), M Groom (Australia), V Gustafsson (Finland), A Schlönvogt (Germany), V Terzeoul (Ukraine), M Wärthl (Germany); 30/7/94 S de la Cruz (Argentina), JC Tamayo (Spain) N Ridge; 4/8/94 A Apellaniz † (Spain), J San Sebastián (Spain) N Ridge; **17/7/95** A Hinkes (UK), R Naar (Holland), Mehrban Shah (Pakistan), Rajab Shah (Pakistan), H Van der Meulen (Holland); 13/8/95 J Escartin † (Spain), J Olivar † (Spain), L Ortiz † (Spain) SSE Spur; 13/8/95 A Hargreaves † (f) (UK), R Slater † (USA), B Grant † (NZ); **29/7/96** G Maggioni (Italy), L Mazzoleni † (Italy), M Panzeri (Italy), S Panzeri (Italy), M Todaka (Japan); 10/8/96 M Bianchi (Italy), C Kuntner (Italy), K Wielicki (Poland) N Ridge; 12/8/96 K Akasaka (Japan), M Matsubara (Japan), B Murata (Japan), A Shiina (Japan), T Tanigawa (Japan), Y Yoshida (Japan) SSE Spur; 13/8/96 M Alvial (Chile), W Farías (Chile), C Garcia-Huidobro (Chile), M Purcell (Chile) SSE Spur; 14/8/96 H Inaba (Japan), K Nagakubo (Japan), T Sano (Japan), K Takahashi (Japan), H Takeuchi (Japan), A Yamamoto (Japan) SSE Spur; 14/8/96 I Benkin † (Russia), C Buhler (USA), R Pawlowski (Poland), S Penzov (Russia), P Pustelnik (Poland) N Ridge; **19/7/97** K Nakagawa (Japan), M Suzuki (Japan), O Tanabe (Japan) W Ridge/SW Face variant; 28/8/97 Pemba Dorje (Nepal), Gyalbu (Nepal), M Kobayashi (Japan), A Nakajima (Japan), M Takine (Japan), Dawa Tashi (Nepal), Mingma Tshering (Nepal), R Yamada (Japan) W Ridge/SW Face variant

Cho Oyu ascent data

All climbs by first ascent route (West Ridge and West Face) except where stated. In the early years of ascents the route was generally approached from the South (Nepal), but is now more generally approached from the North (Tibet). Note: many Sherpas have the same names and have been identified by their home towns.

19/10/54 H Tichy (Austria), S Jochler, Pasang Dawa Lama (India); **15/5/58** Sonam Gyatso (India), Pasang Dawa Lama (India) (2nd); **25/4/64** F Stammberger (W Germany) (claim disputed); **29/10/78** A Furtner (Austria), E Koblmueller (Austria) SE Face; **10/10/79** M Saleki (Iran) (claim disputed); **?/10/82** H D Saucr (W Germany) (claim disputed); **5/5/83** M Dacher (W Germany), H Kammerlander (Italy), R Messner (Italy); 15/11/83 N Hertkorn (W Germany), R Klingl (W Germany); 17/11/83 R Klingl (W Germany) (2nd); ?/11/83 M Saleki (Iran) (claim disputed); **13/5/84** V Komarkova (f) (US), D Sterbova (f) (Czech.), Ang Rita Sherpa (Thami) (Nepal), Nuru Sherpa (Nepal); 20/9/84 A Llasera (Spain), C Vallès (Spain), Sambhu Tamang (Nepal), Ang Karma Sherpa (Nepal); 21/9/84 J Clemenson (France), J Pons (Spain); **12/2/85** M Berbeka (Poland), Z Heinrich (Poland), J Kukuczka (Poland), M Pawlikowski (Poland) South Ridge; 1/5/85

Renqing Pingcuo (Tibet), Danzeng Tobgyal (Tibet), Da Tobgyal (Tibet), Da Cering (Tibet), Xiao Tobgyal e (Tibet), Wanjia (Tibet), Gaisang (Tibet), Lawang (Tibet), Bianba (Tibet); 15/5/85 J Amezgarai (Spain), M Apodaca (Spain), J Oiarzabal (Spain), I Querejeta (Spain); 15/5/85 J Apellaniz (Spain), X Garaioa (Spain), F Uriarte (Spain); 28/5/85 M Gardzielewski (Poland), J Jezierski (Poland); 3/10/85 M Kitamura (Japan), T Mitani (Japan), N Nakanishi (Japan); 5/12/85 D Becik (Slovakia), J Stejskal (Slovakia); **29/4/86** R Gajewski (Poland), M Pawlikowski (Poland) (2nd) SW Ridge to W Face; 1/5/86 P Konopka (Poland), SW Ridge to W Face; 3/5/86 M Danielak (Poland), A Osika (Poland) SW Ridge to W Face; 5/5/86 P Habeler (Austria), M Reudi (Switzerland) SW Ridge to W Face; 9/5/86 R Schleypen (W Germany), J Smith (US) SW Ridge to W Face; 10/5/86 J Daum (W Germany) SW Ridge to W Face; 11/5/86 B Brakus (Croatia) SW Ridge to W Face; 11/5/86 J Frush (U.S.), D Hambly (UK); 12/5/86 H Vollmer (W Germany) (claim disputed); 16/5/86 M Lorenz (Austria) SW Ridge to W Face; 16/10/86 E Hino (Japan); **29/4/87** M Purto (Chile), Ang Phuri Sherpa (Beni) (Nepal), Ang Rita (Thami) (Nepal) (2nd), I Valle (Chile), F Graf (Switzerland), J Wangeler (Switzerland); 5/5/87 O Gassler (Austria), H Wagner (Austria), P Wörgötter (Austria); 6/5/87 K Wimmer (W Germany); 7/5/87 R Hofer (SWizerland); 8/5/87 R Strouhal (Austria); 9/5/87 P Ganner (Austria), K Hecher (Austria), H Pree (Austria), S Wörgötter (Austria); 12/5/87 B Vos (Holland); 20/9/87 A Hayakawa (Japan), K Kondo (Japan); 21/5/87 Y Okura (Japan), K Takahashi (Japan), T Kato (Japan), E Otani (Japan), Nima Dorje Sherpa (Beding) (Nepal), Ang Dawa Tamang (Nepal); 22/9/87 S Kobayashi (Japan), M Takahashi (f) (Japan), Lhakpa Tenzing Sherpa (Nepal), Ang Phurba Sherpa (Beding) (Nepal), Mingma Tenzing (Thami) (Nepal); 23/9/87 T Renard (France), Ang Rinzee Sherpa (Nepal); 30/9/87 T Karolczak (Poland), A Lwow (Poland); 2/10/87 W Berg (US); **6/2/88** F Garrido (Spain); 30/4/88 D Walsh (UK); 1/5/88 G De Marchi (Italy), F Spazzadeschi (Italy), L Zani (Italy); 2/5/88 O Forno (Italy); 10/5/88 H Engl (W Germany), G Schmatz (W Germany); 11/5/88 S Wörner † (Switzerland); 30/5/88 T Fischbach (W Germany), K Gürtler (Austria), P Konzert (Austria), H Bärnthaler (Austria), W Kuzendorf (W Germany), D Thomann (W Germany); 1/9/88 M Batard (France), Sungdare Sherpa (Nepal); 12/9/88 B Cormier (France), E Decamp (France), R Eynard-Machet (France), B Gouvy (France), V Perillat (f) (France), M Vincent (France), Ang Dorje Sherpa (Chaplung) (Nepal), Da Gombu Sherpa (Nepal); 13/9/88 A Busettini (Italy), E Fergio (Italy); 14/9/88 J Hoeffelman (Belgium), J Sesma (Spain), M Vincent (France) (2nd), Lhakpa Gyalu (Chaunrikarka) (Nepal), Da Gombu Sherpa (Nepal) (2nd); 17/9/88 S Martini (Italy), F De Stefani (Italy); 27/9/88 F Castenuovo (Italy), M Conti (Italy), L Mazzoleni (Italy), M Panzeri (Italy); 16/10/88 P Henschke (Poland); 2/11/88 I Tomazin (Slovenia) N Face ascent, W side descent; 5/11/88 V Groselj (Slovenia), J Rozman (Slovenia) N Face to W side; 6/11/88 T Saegusa (Japan), O Shimizu (Japan), N Yamada (Japan), A Yamamoto (Japan); 8/11/88 R Nadvesnik (Slovenia), M Prezelj (Slovenia) North Face; 9/11/88 B Jereb (Slovenia), R Robas (Slovenia) N Face to W side; **8/4/89** C Buhler (US), M Zabaleta (Spain) SW Ridge to W Face; 2/9/89 Hong Kyung-Pyo (South Korea), Lee Dong-Yeon (South Korea), Wangel Sherpa (Nepal); 17/9/89 A Brugger (Italy), R Zeyen (Luxembourg); 18/9/89 M Casella (Switzerland), P Giuliani (Switzerland), E Rosso (Italy); 19/9/89 M Capelli (Switzerland), C Margna (Switzerland), M Nos King (f) (Spain), M Verge (f) (Spain), Ang Phuri (Beni) (Nepal) (2nd); **27/4/90** H Kato (Japan), Y Tanahashi (Japan), Mingma Tenzing (Thami) (Nepal) (2nd), Pemba Tenjee Sherpa (Nepal); 30/4/90 B Chamoux (France), Y Detry (France), A Hinkes (UK), J Rakoncaj (Czech), M Rossi (Italy), P Royer (France), F Valet (France) (claim disputed); 11/5/90 M Groom (Australia); 19/5/90 G Haerter (Germany), G Lindebner (Austria), R Mueller (Germany), D Porsche (Germany), W Treibel (Germany) (claim disputed); 26/5/90 G Binder (W Germany), P Blank (W Germany), W Funkler (W Germany), B Hochstuhl (W Germany), G Hupfauer (f) (W Germany), S Hupfauer (W Germany), G Kurze (f) (W Germany), H Rössner (W Germany), U Schmitz (W Germany), F Stark (W Germany), J Tschoten (Austria), K Westphal (W Germany), U Zehetleitner (W Germany), K Zöll (W Germany), Nawang Thile Sherpa (Beding) (Nepal); 21/6/90 H Taylor (UK), R Brice (NZ), Dawa Nuru Sherpa (Phortse) (Nepal), Lhakpa Gyalu (Portse) (Nepal); 23/8/90 A Hubert (Belgium), L Lange (Belgium); 20/9/90 W Kurtyka (Poland), E Loretan (Switzerland), J Troillet (Switzerland) S-facing part of SW Face from N; 4/10/90 A Koncz (Hungary), J Straub (Hungary), R Wlasich (Austria); 6/10/90 K Aranguren (Spain), P Eguillor (Spain), P Fernandez (Spain), M Martinez (Spain), J Pujante (Spain), J Tapias (Spain), Ang Phurba Sherpa (Thami) (Nepal); 7/10/90 J Csíkos (Hungary), I Pajor (Hungary), C Tóth (Hungary), L Várkonyi (Hungary), L Vörös (Hungary); 8/10/90 S Nagy (Hungary), S Szendrö (Hungary), I Decsi (Hungary), P Tous (Spain), M Reparaz (Spain); 19/10/90 A Apellaniz (Spain) (2nd), R Portilla (Spain), J San Sebastian (Spain), A Trabado (Spain); **22/4/91** S Beck (Brazil), A Hantz (France), Man Bahadur Gurung (Gorkha) (Nepal), Iman Singh Gurung (Gorkha) (Nepal); 8/5/91 A Beetschen (Switzerland), P Kapsomenakis (Greece), I Konstantinou (Greece), M Rizzi (Switzerland), A Ruiz (Spain), Tirtha Tamang (Nepal), K Tsivelekas (Greece); 9/5/91, E Eder (Austria), W Maier (Germany), F Pantillon (Switzerland), T Pichler (Austria), M Respondek (Germany), N von Schumacher (Switzerland), E Wullschleger (f) (Switzerland), P Wullschleger (Switzerland); 27/5/91 A Albrecht (Germany), H Bauer (Germany), H Conrad (Germany), R Erardi (Italy), O Fangauer (Germany), R Gasser (Italy), G Hofer (f) (Italy), M Kumpf (f) (Germany), J Pallhuber (Italy), K Renzler (Italy), H Tauber (Italy), A Wiedemann (Germany) J Weissenberger (Germany), K Wolfsgruber (f) (Italy); 25/9/91 C Kuntner (Italy), S De Leo (Italy), J Reichen (Switzerland); 26/9/91 W Rutkiewicz (f) (Poland); 28/9/91 Tsindin Temba Sherpa (Nepal), T Ishikawa (Japan), Y Nezu (Japan), B Quetglas (Spain), T Watanbe (f) (Japan), Mingma Norbu Sherpa (Beding) (Nepal), Nima Temba Sherpa (Nepal); 29/9/91 C Armstrong (US), K Groninger (US), K Ikeda (Japan), C Richards (f) (US), Pemba Norbu Sherpa (Nepal), K Young (f) (US), M Mojaev (Russia), E Prilepa (Russia), V Skripko (Russia); 1/10/91 B Dimitrov (Bulgaria), I Dimitrova (f) (Bulgaria); 4/10/91 M Imbert (France), Dawa Dorje Sherpa (Makalu) (Nepal); 5/10/91 M Zalio (France), Kilu Temba Sherpa (Nepal); 20/10/91 S Bogomolov (Russia), V Pershin (Russia), I Plotnikov (Russia), Y Vinogradski (Russia), A Yakovenko (Russia) E Ridge from S; **7/5/92** P Debrouwer (Belgium), G Kropp (Sweden); 8/5/92 L LeBon (f) (Belgium), Danu Sherpa (Nepal), B Ongis (Italy), M Soregaroli (Italy), G Vigani (Italy), M Lutterjohann (Germany); 14/5/92 P Kowalzik (Germany), Musal Kazi Tamang (Nepal); 17/5/92 T Finkbeiner (Germany); 22/5/92 M Schneider (Germany);

4/6/92 P Guggemos (Germany), M Schumacher (Germany); 15/8/92 M Saleki (Iran), S Tsuzuki (f) (Japan); 17/9/92 A Aranzabal (f) (Spain), J Bereziartua (Spain), J Colet (Spain); 20/9/92 J Artetxe (Spain), P Ganuza (f) (Spain), Nam Sun-Woo (S Korea), Kim Young-Tae (S Korea), Mingma Norbu (Beding) (2nd) (Nepal), Nima Dorje (Beding) (2nd) (Nepal); 20/9/92 H Baba (Japan), A Hayasimoto (Japan), K Kondo (Japan), M Taniguchi (Japan), S Tsukamoto (Japan), T Suzuki (Japan), An Young-Jong (N Korea), Nima Sherpa (Taksindu) (Nepal), Mingma Tenzing (Thami) (3rd) (Nepal); 21/9/92 K Kanazawa (Japan), S Kimoto (Japan), Y Sato (f) (Japan), T Yanagihara (Japan), H Yatsuhashi (Japan), Ang Phurba (Thami) (2nd) (Nepal), Dawa Norbu Sherpa (Nepal); 20/9/92 F Airoldi (Italy), P Gugliermina (Italy); 21/9/92 A Cvahte (Slovenia), M Gregorèiè (Slovenia), S Lagoja (Slovenia), F Urh (Slovenia), M Urh (Slovenia); 29/9/92 A Ballano (Spain), J B Jimeno (Spain); **8/2/93** M González (Spain), F Guerra (Spain), M Morales (Spain), M Salazar (Spain); 10/2/93 L Arbués (Spain), M Chapuisat (f) (Switzerland), M A Sánchez (Argentina); 29/4/93 G Seifried (Germany); 2/5/93 Chiang Yung-ta (Taiwan), Tsai Shang-chih (Taiwan), Tenzing Sherpa (Nepal), Ang Kami Lama (Nepal); 4/5/93 Liang Chin-mei (f) (Taiwan), Liu Chi-man (Taiwan), Pasang Lama (Nepal), D Alessio (Argentina), R Mear (UK), E Tryti (Norway), C Giorgis (Italy), V Lauthier (f) (Italy), G Sacco (Italy); 4/5/93 M Fernandez (Argentina) E Ridge/Face (N); 5/5/93 P Stadler (Switzerland), A Würsch (Switzerland); 7/5/93 A Georges (Switzerland); 15/5/93 A Neuhuber (Austria); 16/5/93 P Y Guichard (Switzerland); 16/5/93 M Breuer (Germany), C Gabl (Austria), F Kühnhauser (Germany), R Ratteit (Germany), M Moreni (Switzerland), A Verzaroli (Switzerland); 10/9/93 Choi Byung-Soo (S Korea), Min Kyoung-Tee (S Korea), Um Hong-Gil (S Korea), J A Serrano (Spain); 18/9/93 M Bianchi (Italy), K Wielicki (Poland) W Ridge from N; 21/9/93 F Campos (Spain), B Sabadell (Spain); 24/9/93 J Garcia (Portugal), P Pustelnik (Poland) W Ridge from N; 30/9/93 D Caillat (France), J Cardona (Spain), F Faure (France), J Lafaille (France), J R Lasa (Spain); 8/10/93 T Akiyama (Japan), F Goto (Japan), R Hoshino (Japan), H Nazuka (Japan), Y Ogata (Japan), M Sato (Japan); 11/10/93 S Ezuka (Japan), O Tanabe (Japan), Pasang Tshering (Beding) (Nepal), Lobsang Jangbu Sherpa (Nepal); 12/10/93 T Miyazaki (Japan), T Terada (Japan), K Yagihara (Japan), F Yoshida (f) (Japan), Nawang Sakya (Beding) (Nepal), Dawa Tshering (Beding) (Nepal), Nima Dorje (Beding) (3rd) Mingma Norbu (Beding) (3rd); 8/10/93 J Garcia (Spain), C Pitarch (Spain); 10/10/93 J Elorrieta (Spain), J Gómez (Spain), Y Martin (f) (Spain); 31/10/93 M de la Matta (Spain), C Mauduit (f) (France); **26/1/94** J Garra (Spain), J Magrinyá (Spain); 26/4/94 C Carsolio (Mexico); 29/4/94 F Pedrina (Switzerland); 3/5/94 E Schwarzenlander (Austria); 4/5/94 H Katzenmaier (Germany), W Korber (Germany), H Spindler (Germany), L Protze (Germany), A Ratka (Germany), T Türpe (Germany); 8/5/94 J Delgado (Venezuela), M Duff (UK), C Jones (NZ), N Lindsey (UK), Pasang Gombu (Lokhim) (Nepal); 12/5/94 Z Hruby (Czech Rep), S Silhan (Czech Rep), A Giovanetti (Italy), O Piazza (Italy); 14/5/94 L Kamarad (Czech Rep), B Lodi (Italy); 16/5/94 A Oberbacher (Italy); 20/5/94 H Blatter (Switzerland), N Joos (Switzerland); 23/5/94 Y Yamanoi (Japan) SW Ridge ascent W Ridge/Face down; 25/9/94 Y Endo (f) (Japan), T Nagao (f) (Japan) SW Face; 26/9/94 G Frey (France), R Geoffrey (France), Y Salino (France), Ang Rita (Thami) (3rd) (Nepal), Pasang Jambu Sherpa (Nepal); 27/9/94 Park Young-Seok (S Korea), Ngati Sherpa (Nepal); 28/9/94 Cha Jin-Chol (S Korea), Han Sang-Kook (S Korea), Han Wuang-Yong (S Korea), Panuru Sherpa (Phortse) (Nepal); 29/9/94 T Harada (Japan), S Imoto (Japan), Kunga Sherpa (Rolwaling) (Nepal), Nawang Dorje (Rolwaling); 30/9/94 Akbu (Tibet), Daqimi (Tibet), Daqiong (Tibet), Jaibu (Tibet), Luoze (Tibet), Bianba Zaxi (Tibet), Rena (Tibet), Cering Doje (Tibet), Wangjia (2nd) (Tibet); 2/10/94 F Bibollet (France); 4/10/94 S Sasahara (Japan), H Tabata (Japan), Chhong Ringee (Beding) (Nepal), Lhakpa Gyalu † (2nd) (Chaunrikarka) (Nepal); 6/10/94 J Arnold (f) (NZ), R Hall (NZ), E Viesturs (US); **18/4/95** F Pepevnik (Slovenia); 6/5/95 H Eibl (Germany), B Zedrosser (Austria); 9/5/95 A Delgado (Mexico), H Ponce de Léon (Mexico), P Arvis (France), R Brand (Germany), P Brill (Germany), R Dujmovits (Germany), L Edel (Germany), A Haüsler (Germany), K Hub (Germany), P Hub (f) (Austria), F Prasicek (Austria), J Spescha (Germany), A Vedani (Switzerland), Nawang Thile (Beding) (2nd) (Nepal), H Konishi (Japan), Pembra Tshering (Thamo) (Nepal), M Yamamoto (Japan); 11/5/95 U Blasczyk (Germany), A Kraus (Germany), W Kuch (Germany), C Fox (f) (US), D Hahn (US), M Hutnak (US), Tenzing Phinzo (Phortse) (Nepal); 12/5/95 M Bazillian (US), J Findlay (US), H Macdonald (f) (US), R Sloezen (US); 16/5/95 B Hill (US), W Thompson (US), Dawa Nuru (Phortse) (2nd) (Nepal), A Van Steen (US); 17/5/95 C John (US), M O'Day (US), A Rausch (US); 29/5/95 I Peter (UK), P Walters (Australia), Nima Timba Sherpa (Nepal); 30/5/95 N Croucher (UK), Ang Temba Sherpa (Beding) (Nepal); 1/6/95 W Kleinknecht (Germany), E Resch (Austria); 13/9/95 F Iñurrategi (Spain), A Iñurrategi (Spain), Onchu Lama (Nepal); 25/9/95 H Hashiyada (Japan), J Miyakawa (Japan), T Yamamoto (Japan), Ang Phurba (Beding) (2nd) (Nepal), Dawa Tshering (Beding) (2nd) (Nepal), Nawang Tenzing Sherpa (Nepal), Dawa Tashi Sherpa (Nepal), B Separoviè (Croatia), B Puzak (Croatia), Nawang Dorje (Rolwalking) (2nd) (Nepal); 26/9/95 K Ikeda (Japan), Y Ogio (Japan), R Rosenbaum (Australia), Ang Temba Sherpa (2nd) (Nepal), Tendu Sherpa (Nepal), Nawang Sakya Sherpa (2nd) (Nepal); 26/9/95 J Arnold (f) (2nd) (NZ), R Hall (2nd) (NZ), L Harvey (Australia) D Mantle (US), Ang Dorje (Pangboche) (Nepal), Norbu Sherpa (Beding) (Nepal); 27/5/95 S Burnik (Slovenia), D Petrin (Croatia), F Seiler (Germany), J Stiller (Germany); 28/5/95 R Buccela (Italy), A Clavel (Italy), A Stremfelj (Slovenia), M Stremfelj (f) (Slovenia); 29/9/95 K Ito (Japan), J Sawataishi (Japan), Y Ueno (Japan), Pasang Kami Sherpa (Nepal), Ang Gyalzen Sherpa (Nepal), Man Bahadur Gurung (Sitalpati) (Nepal); 1/10/95 M Hatakeyama (Japan), T Tanaka (Japan), Na Temba Sherpa (Nepal), Ang Gyalzen Sherpa (2nd) (Nepal) Kunga (Rowaling) (2nd); 1/10/95 C Jager (France), A Thevenot (France), Kunga (Rowaling) (2nd) (Nepal) J Botella de Maglia (Spain) Gyalbu Sherpa (Nepal); 2/10/95 F Alvárez (Spain), A Gómez (Spain), A Pallarés (Spain), J L Sanz (Spain), Kami Tenzing Sherpa (Kumjung) (Nepal), L Drda (Czech Rep), R Hunter (US), H Magnusson (Iceland), V Mysik (Czech Rep), B Olafsson (Iceland), N Shustrov (Russia), E Stefansson (Iceland), J Tinker (UK) Babu Tshering (Taksindu) (Nepal), Lama Jangbu (Nepal); 3/10/95 O Louka (Czech Rep); 4/10/95 V Yanotchkin (Russia), P Sicouri (Italy), Lhakpa Rita Sherpa (Nepal); 6/10/95 J Kardhordo (Czech Rep), O Srovnal (Czech Rep); 7/10/95 P Athans (US), W Prittie (US), I Woods (S Africa), Lhakpa Rita Sherpa (2nd) (Nepal), Dawa Sherpa (Nepal); 8/10/95 T Hromadka (Czech

Rep); 10/10/95 A Cheze (France); 13/10/95 F Delrieu (f) (Spain), J Desplan (France), Ang Rita (Thami) (4th) (Nepal); **2/5/96** M Schmid (Switzerland), C Zinsli (Switzerland), C Bannwart (Switzerland), C Bitz (Switzerland), S Bonvin (Switzerland), R Laveikis (Latvia), J Osis (Latvia), A Rutkis (Latvia), Jangbu Sherpa (Nepal), Nawang Chokleg (Thami) (Nepal); 3/5/96 J Hermosillo (Mexico); 4/5/96 D Bieri (Switzerland), B Hasler (Switzerland), A Käslin (Switzerland), R Real (f) (Spain), M Boggelmann (Germany), A Heckele (Germany), K Schmidt (Germany), R Stihler (Germany), Nawang Thile (Beding) (3rd) (Nepal), Ongchu Sherpa (Karikhola) (Nepal), H Stockert (Germany), A Buhl (Germany), C J Schulte (Germany); 8/5/96 T Masuda (Japan), H Masunaga (Japan), N Miki (Japan), T Toda (f) (Japan), Tshering Dorje Sherpa (Nepal), Kunga (Rolwaling) (3rd) (Nepal); 9/5/96 T Saito (Japan), S Sato (Japan), M Yamaguchi (f) (Japan), S Yasukawa (Japan), Nima Sherpa (Taksindu) (2nd) (Nepal), Tshering Dorje Sherpa (Nepal) (2nd); 10/5/96 B Pederiva (Italy), (N) Kancha Nuru Sherpa (Khumjung) (Nepal) W Ridge/Face; 13/5/96 J Ellis (US), H Macdonald (f) (2nd) (US), T Richards (US) Dawa Nuru (Phortse) (3rd) (Nepal); 14/5/96 E Leas (US), J Race (US); 15/5/96 D Stefani (Italy), M Tosi (Italy), S Valentini (Italy); 16/5/96 A de Boer (f) (Holland), R Brice (2nd) (NZ), B Hasler (NZ), P Reynal-O'Connor (NZ), A Salek (NZ), M Whetu (NZ); 19/5/96 M Leuprecht (Austria), F Obermüller (Austria); 26/5/96 A Fink (Austria), C Haas (Germany), A Hinterplattner (Austria), P Perlia (Luxembourg); 27/5/96 E Gatt (Austria), S Gatt (Austria), S Greve (f) (Norway), I Gruber (Austria), E Huber (f) (Austria); 20/9/96 R Brice (3rd) (NZ), T Kurai (f) (Japan), J Tabei (f) (Japan), Karsang Sherpa (Nepal); 21/9/96 S Blackmore (UK), H Majima (f) (Japan), Lobsang Temba Sherpa (Nepal), Chuldin Temba Sherpa (Nepal); 23/9/96 Byun Mi-Jung (f) (S Korea), Kim Young-Ki (S Korea), Lee Sang-Bae (S Korea), Park Jung-Hun (S Korea), Nima Sherpa (Taksindu) (3rd) (Nepal), Ang Phurba (Thami No. 2) (Nepal), Chewang Dorje Sherpa (Nepal), V Bashkirov (Russia), A Klimin (Russia), A Kovalchuk (Estonia), B Mednik (Russia), A Paskin (Russia), V Pershin (2nd) (Russia), A Sedov (Russia), B Sedusov (Russia), Y Vinogradski (2nd) (Russia), G Tortladze (Georgia), N Zakharov (Russia), J Berbeka (Poland), A Boukreev (Kazakhstan), M McDermott (UK), Babu Tshering (Taksindu) (2nd) (Nepal); 25/9/96 K Noguchi (Japan), Pasang Tshering (Beding) (2nd) (Nepal); 27/9/96 K Boskoff (US), D Brown (Canada), R Dorr (US), C Feld-Boskoff (f) (US), D Robinson (Canada), L Hall (US), M Pfetzer (US), H Todd (UK), Pemba Dorje Sherpa (Pangboche) (Nepal), Jyamang Bhote (Nepal), P Mahenc (France), Kancha Nuru (Khumjung) (2nd) (Nepal), R Brice (4th) (NZ), S Tsuzuki (W, 2nd) (Japan); 28/9/96 P Morrow (US), Danuru Sherpa (Namche) (Nepal); 28/9/96 O Cadiach (Spain), S Ruckensteiner (Austria) North Ridge; 29/9/96 N Kekus (UK), I Loredo (Mexico), K Wheelock (f) (Mexico), Lhakpa Gelu Sherpa (Nepal), R Boice (US), M Buchan (UK), S French (f) (NZ), S Horner (US), E Viesturs (2nd) (US), Ang Dorje (Pangboche) (2nd) (Nepal), Chuldin Dorje (Khumjung) (Nepal); 1/10/96 A Arnold (Switzerland), B Huc-Dumas (France), M Kittleman (US), I Pauls (Latvia), Babu Tshering (Taksindu) (3rd) (Nepal, Pemba Tshering (Karikhola) (Nepal), Nima Sherpa (Karikhola) (Nepal), M Saul (f) (Canada), H Sovdat (f) (Canada), Nawang Phurba Sherpa (Nepal); 6/10/96 K Farafonov (Kazakhstan), S Gataoulin (Kazakhstan); 9/10/96 L Bečak † (Czech Rep), M Otta (Czech Rep); 10/10/96 M Penalva (Spain), O Ribas (Andorra); 14/10/96 S Gataoulin (2nd) (Kazakhstan), O Malikov (Kazakhstan), Y Moiseev (Kazakhstan); **27/4/97** D Beavon (US), S Bull (US), D Johnck (US), P Scaturro (US), K Tenzing (Khumjumg) (2nd) (Nepal); 28/4/97 C Demarest (US), B Hoffman (US), Pemba Norbu Sherpa (Nepal), Pasang Phutar Sherpa (Nepal); 30/4/97 H Rainer (Austria); 2/5/97 J Inhöger (Austria), H Nikol (Germany), S Allan (UK), J Sparks (US), Dorje Sherpa (Nepal), Lhakpa Gyalzen Sherpa (Nepal), H Rockenbauer (Austria), O Cadiach (2nd) (Spain), N Duró (f) (Andorra), J Tosas (Spain); 3/5/97 H Chlastak (Germany), H Goger (Austria), L Ioffe (Russia), E Lebedeva (f) (Russia), T Zoeva (f) (Russia), E Andueza (Spain), V Izquierdo (Spain), A Navas (Spain); 6/5/97 R Nicco (Italy), V Strba (Slovakia), J Leupold (Germany), M Walter (Germany), G Wiegand (Germany); 7/5/97 S Pasmeny (Canada) F Ziel (US); 8/5/97 T Slama (Czech Rep), W Turek (Austria); 12/5/97 M Mayerhofer (Austria), H Ortner (Austria); 13/5/97 K Braun (US); 14/5/97 H Dolenga (Germany); 15/5/97 F Alldredge (US), R Alpert (US), D Hahn (2nd) (US), T La France (US); 19/5/97 W Kugler (Germany), J Mayer (Germany), A Metzger (Germany), A Teuchert (Germany), Tenzing Phinzo (Phortse) (2nd) (Nepal); 20/5/97 C Arthur (UK), D Spencer (UK), S Stacey (UK), Mingma Dorje Sherpa (Nepal), Pemba Tshering (Karikhola) (Nepal); 19/9/97 Jang Hun-Moo (S Korea), Kim Hong-Sang (S Korea), Oh Jun-Young (S Korea), Park Young-Seok (2nd) (S Korea), Tashi Tshering Sherpa (Nepal); 20/9/97 Jang Kum-Duk (S Korea), P Schmidt (France), C Trommsdorff (France), Nawang Thile (Beding) (4th) (Nepal); 21/5/97 G Kotov (Russia), W Pierson (US) North Ridge; 21/9/97 Kim Seong-Seok (S Korea), Park Heon-Ju (S Korea), Panuru Sherpa (Phortse) (2nd) (Nepal), G Scaccabarozzi (Italy); 22/9/97 M Ellerby (US), Ang Pemba Sherpa (Nepal), M Jesús Lago (f) (Spain), Ongchu (Karikhola) (2nd) (Nepal); 26/9/97 I Beltrán de Lubiano (Spain), G Velez (Portugal), M Kadoya (Japan), K Maeda (Japan), K Tsubosa (f) (Japan), Dawa Dorje (Makalu) (2nd) (Nepal), Man Bahadur Gurung (Sitalpati) (2nd) (Nepal), P Garcés (Spain), J L Gómez (Spain), V Leontyev (Ukraine), V Kopytko (Ukraine), S Kovalev (Ukraine), G Cemmi (Italy), M Perego (Italy); 27/9/97 M Airoldo (Italy), G Harrison (f) (UK), G Pfisterer (US), Pasang Tshering (Pangboche) (Nepal); 28/9/97 D Jewell (NZ), R Koval (Ukraine), V Zboja (Slovakia), A Collins (NZ), G Cotter (NZ), D Hiddleston (NZ), Leung Yick-Nam (Hong Kong) Keith Kerr (UK), Ang Dorje (Pangboche) (3rd) (Nepal), Chuldin Dorje (Khumjung) (2nd) (Nepal), Khoo Swee Chiow (Malaysia), J Lean (Singapore), D Lim (Malaysia), M R Maarof (Malaysia), A Silva (Australia), Kunga (Rolwaling) (4th) (Nepal), Lila Bahadur Gurung (Nepal), M Dunnahoo (US), K Gattone (f) (US), S Greenholz (US), C Horley (US), L Lewis (US), R Link (US), A Mondry (US), J Norton (US), E Simonson (US), Tenzing Phinzo (Phortse) (3rd) (Nepal), Ang Pasang Sherpa (Nepal), A Nasuh Mahruki (Turkey); 30/9/97 A Akinina (f) (Russia), S Krylov (Russia); 3/10/97 V Saunders (UK), Y Contreras (Mexico), S Le Poole (Holland) W Ridge/Face; 13/10/97 E Escoffier (France), A Paret (France), I Singh Gurung (Gorkha) (2nd) (Nepal); 15/10/97 S Mondinelli (Italy), P Paglino (Italy); 6/11/97 J Martinéz (Spain); **21/4/98** Three Chinese led by Tang Yuan Xin; 28/4/98 N Pimkin (Russia), D Sergeev (Russia); 1/5/98 F Loubert (Canada), C-A Nadon (Canada); 6/5/98 J Hinding (Austria), R Hofer (Austria), G Kaltenbrunner (f) (Austria), T Prinz (Austria), F Scharmüller (Austria), H Wolf (Austria); 12/5/98 A Poppe (Germany), G Rösner † (Germany); 14/5/98 B Prax (US); 19/5/98 K-D Grohs (Germany),

R Rackl (Germany), Nawang Thile (Beding) (5th) (Nepal), M Della Santa (Italy), S Dotti (Italy), R Pizzagalli (Italy), C Romano (Italy), G Santi (Italy); 20/5/98 G Anders (US), G Bate (UK), P Falvey (Ireland), Nima Sherpa (Karikhola) (2nd) (Nepal), Phenden Sherpa (Nepal), A Wildsmith (UK), M Frankhauser (Austria), B Hirschbichler (f) (Germany), A Huber (Germany), G Simair (Austria), K Koomen-Staartjes (f) (Holland), Nanda Dorje (Khumjung) (Nepal); 21/5/98 M Pearson (UK); 22/5/98 B Friedrich (Germany), T Lämmil (Germany), R Lebek (Germany), R Roozen (Austria), M Staschull (Germany), G Weinberger (Austria), Y De Jong (Holland), S Terwee (Holland), H Van der Meulen (Holland), Chhong Ringee (Beding) (2nd) (Nepal); 23/5/98 K Schmid (Germany), A Blanc (Italy), M Camandona (Italy), W Niclevicz (Brazil), H Gogl (Austria), H Lechner (Austria), J Murg (Austria), P Perlia (2nd) (Luxembourg); 24/5/98 M Mlynarczyk (f) (Germany), Z Mlynarczyk (Germany); 29/5/98 A Smets (Holland); 31/5/98 A Dingemans (Holland), Nawang Chokleg (Thami) (2nd) (Nepal); 1/6/98 P Bergevoet (Holland); 24/9/98 R Tudor Hughes (UK), Sonam Tashi Sherpa (Nepal), Phurba Tashi Sherpa (Nepal), S Fear (f) (Australia), Nima Dorje Tamang (Kerung) (Nepal), M Blanchebarbe (Germany), Mingma Sherpa (Nepal), T Nousiainen (f) (Finland), Chhong Ringee (Beding) (3rd) (Nepal), Nanda Dorje (Khumjung) (2nd) (Nepal), C Lacatusu (Romania); 25/9/98 M Comes (Spain), Tarke Sherpa (Lokhim) (Nepal), K Morooka (Japan), A Jaggi † (Switzerland), Norbu (Beding) (2nd) (Nepal); 26/9/98 M Nukita (Japan), M Taniguchi (Japan), Nima Dorje (Beding) (4th) (Nepal), Mingma Tshering Sherpa (Nepal), Tashi Sherpa (Nepal), T Cowen (US), M Goddard (US) D Lambert (UK), A Lapkass (US), L Medina (f) (US), D Ryan (Ireland), Pasang Tshering (Pangboche) (2nd) (Nepal), R Benedetti (Italy), M Dibona (Italy); 27/9/98 G Ferlan (Yugoslavia), N Gubser (US), D Jacimović (Yugoslavia), A Mayer (Austria), D Mellor (UK), Pemba Dorje (Pangboche) (2nd) (Nepal), A Gil (Spain), J M Lete (Spain), J R Bacena (Spain), J L Bolado (Spain), A Cinca (Spain), J C Gómez (Spain), S Mingote (Spain); 28/9/98 S Woolums (US), J Robinson (US), B Ousland (Norway), E Urtaran (Spain), J Verdeguer (Spain); 9/10/98 T Riga (Estonia), A Sarapuu (Estonia); 11/10/98 R Plumer (Estonia), M Proos (Estonia), T Sarmet (Estonia), R Dujmovits (2nd) (Germany), R Eberhard (Germany), W Goering (Germany), S Mayr (Germany), H Steger (Germany), S Weiche (Germany), Chuldim Nuru Sherpa (Nepal), Ang Phurba (Beding No. 2) (Nepal), Nawang Thile (Beding) (6th) (Nepal); **13/4/99** J Gangdal (Norway), Tamtin Sherpa (Nepal), Dawa Tshering (Beding) (3rd) (Nepal); 23/4/99 A Delgado (2nd) (Mexico); 25/4/99 M Arbelaez (Colombia), M Barrios (Colombia), F González (Colombia); 26/4/99 A Boll (f) (Switzerland), M Borrmann (Germany); 30/4/99 C Soria (Spain), Sona Dendu Sherpa (Nepal); 1/5/99 M Küng (Switzerland); 3/5/99 A Delgado (3rd) (Mexico), A Ochoa (Mexico); 4/5/99 R Robinson (Canada), S Wyatt (Canada), A Bullard (f) (US), K Hess (f) (US), G Stanley (f) (US); 5/5/99 R Ariano (Colombia), N Cardona (Colombia), J P Ruiz (Colombia); 6/5/99 J Bach (US), J Gauthier (Canada), W Krause (Germany); 7/5/99 O Rieck (Germany), T Türpe (Germany) (2nd), M Abrego (Spain), A López (Spain), Tarke Sherpa (Lokhim) (2nd) (Nepal); 18/5/99 F Luchsinger (Chile), C Prieto (f) (Chile), Pemba Sherpa (Nepal); 19/5/99 T Fritsche (Austria), S Gatt (2nd) (Austria); 20/5/99 C Bäumler (f) (Germany), T Becherer (Germany), M Beuter (Germany), H Bielefeldt (Germany), M Bischoff (Switzerland), F Everts (Germany), M Farenzena (f) (Luxembourg), H Hackl (Germany), E Schmitt (Germany), T Zwahlen (Switzerland), Chuldim Sherpa (Nepal); 22/5/99 J Einwaller (Austria), J Koller (Austria), J Streif (Germany), R Benet (Italy), N Meroi (f) (Italy); 23/5/99 A Abramov (Russia), L Abramova (f) (Russia), N Cherny (Russia), V Elagin (Russia), J Khokhlov (Russia), S Larin (Russia); 25/5/99 T Klösch (Austria), R Knebel (Germany), W Scheidl (Austria), J Schoff (Austria); 26/9/99 Kang Seong-Gyu (S Korea), Kim Sang-Jo (S Korea), Moon Bong-Su (S Korea), Oh Hee-Joon (S Korea), Pemba Pasang Sherpa (Nepal), Pasang Gombu (Lokhim) (2nd) (Nepal), J McGuinness (NZ), I Okanda (f) (Japan), S Sakamoto (Japan), S Takahashi (f) (Japan), Man Bahadur Gurung (3rd) (Nepal); 27/9/99 B Johnson (US), P Kenny (US), C Warner (US), A de Choudens (France), S de Choudens (f) (France), S Juvet (Switzerland), C Mirmand (France), Nawang Thile (Beding) (7th) (Nepal); 28/9/99 J Marmet (France), B Muller (France), K Nagakubo (Japan), K Nakamura (Japan), M Okuda (Japan), T Tanigawa (Japan), A Collet (f) (France), Tarke Sherpa (Lokhim) (3rd) (Nepal), Ang Phurba Sherpa (Lukla) (Nepal), S Vetter (France); 30/9/99 F Oderlep (Slovenia), P Stular (Slovenia); 1/10/99 T Kitamura (Japan), A Lapkass (2nd) (US), J Litch (US), P Pappas (US) D Staples (NZ), K Tucker (US) T Aryama (Japan), Ang Dorje (Pangboche) (4th) (Nepal), Lhakpa Tshering Sherpa (Nepal)

Makalu ascent data
All climbs by first ascent route (NW Cirque, Makalu La and North Face) except where stated.

15/5/55 J Couzy (France), L Terray (France); 16/5/55 J Franco (France), G Magnone (France), Gyalzen Norbu Sherpa (India); 17/5/55 J Bouvier (France), S Coupe (France), P Leroux (France), A Vialatte (France); **23/5/70** H Tanaka (Japan), Y Ozaki (Japan) SE Ridge; **23/5/71** B Mellet (France), Y Seigneur (France) W Pillar; **6/10/75** S Belak (Yugoslavia), M Manfreda (Yugoslavia) S Face ; 8/10/75 J Azman (Yugoslavia), N Zaplotnik S Face; 10/10/75 V Groselj (Yugoslavia), I Kotnik S Face; 11/10/75 J Dovzan (Yugoslavia) S Face; **24/5/76** J Camprubi (Spain) SE Ridge; 24/5/76 K Schubert † (Czech), M Krissak (Czech) SE buttress to SE Ridge; **1/5/78** H Warth (W Germany), Ang Cheppal (Nepal); 10/5/78 H von Kaenel (Zwitzerland) K Landvogt (W Germany) Nga Temba Sherpa (Nepal); 21/5/78 K Diemberger (Austria), Nawang Tenzing Sherpa (Nepal); **15/5/80** J Roskelley (US) W Pillar; **25/4/81** R Schauer (Austria); 15/10/81 J Kukuczka (Poland) W Face to NW Ridge; **20/5/82** Heo Young-Ho (S Korea), Pasang Norbu Sherpa (Nepal) Ang Phurba Sherpa (Nepal) SE Ridge to E Face; 30/9/82 M Ishibashi (Japan), Y Michiwaki (Japan), K Yuda (Japan); 10/10/82 A Czok (Poland) N Face to NW Ridge, between Kukuczka route and W Pillar; **16/5/84** M Abrego (Spain), E de Pablo; 29/9/84 R Nottaris (Switzerland) Kukuczka route; **1/10/85** A Giambisi (Italy) S Martini (Italy), J C de San Sebastian (Spain), F Stedile (Italy), F De Stefani (Italy); **24/9/86** M Ruedi † (Switzerland), K Wielicki (Poland); 26/9/86 H Kammerlander (Italy), R Messner (Italy), F Mutschlenchner

(Italy); **12/5/87** C Pizzo (US), G Porzak (US), Lhakpa Nuru Sherpa (Nepal); 16/5/87 G Neptune (US), Dawa Nuru Sherpa (Nepal), Moti Lal Gurung (Nepal); **27/5/88** M Batard (France) W Pillar ascent NW side descent; 12/10/88 C Carsolio (Mexico); 14/10/88 T Kolakowski † (Poland), T Kopys (Poland); **6/10/89** P Beghin (France) S Face ascent NW side descent; **6/5/90** H Onishi (Japan) Nima Dorje Sherpa (Nepal); 18/5/90 K Calhoun (f) (US) J Schutt (US) W Pillar; 3/10/90 J Angles (Spain), A Bros (Spain), Lhakpa Sherpa (Nepal) Kukuczka route; **24/9/91** C Figueras (Spain), J Permane (Spain), X Robiro (Spain) Kukuczka route; 30/9/91 A Iñurrategi (Spain), F Iñurrategi (Spain), F Uriarte (Spain) Kukuczka route; 2/10/91 M Badiola † (Spain), E Loretan (Switzerland), F Troillet (Switzerland), C Valles (Spain) W Pillar; 5/10/91 Y Futamata (Japan), H Imamura (Japan), Y Okada (Japan), Ang Dorje Sherpa (Nepal); 7/10/91 T Ishizaka † (Japan), T Nagao (f) (Japan); **22/5/93** F Manoni (Italy), S Panzeri (Italy), D Spreafico (Italy), L Sulovsky (Czech Rep), Tirtha Tamang (Nepal), Mingmar Tamang (Nepal); **15/5/94** N Beidleman (US), A Bukreev (Kazakhstan); **5/5/95** B Chamoux (France) P Royer (France) NW side (claim disputed); 8/5/95 M Auricht (Australia), D Hume † (Australia), J Oiarzabal (Spain), B Ruiz de Infante (Spain), J Vallejo (Spain), Um Hong-Gil (S Korea); 9/5/95 A Zerain (Spain); 18/5/95 V Gustafsson (Finland), R Hall (New Zealand), E Viesturs (US); 21/5/95 T Arai (Japan), M Matsubara (Japan), O Tanabe (Japan), A Yamamoto (Japan) E Ridge to NW side; 22/5/95 T Ono (Japan), T Tanigawa (Japan), H Takeuchi (Japan), M Yamamoto (Japan), E Ridge to NW side; 9/10/95 A Collins (UK), D Mazur (US), A Nikiforov (Russia), J Pratt (UK) SE Ridge; **19/5/96** N Kogemiako (Russia), V Koroteev (Russia), I Plotnikov (Russia), G Sokolov (Russia); 23/5/96 V Bashkirov (Russia), S Bogomolov (Russia), V Foigt (Russia), Y Outechev (Russia), V Stalkovski (Russia), A Vegner (Russia); **21/5/97** A Bolotov (Russia), I Bougatshevski † (Russia), Y Ermatchek (Russia), N Jiline (Russia), D Pavlenko (Russia) W Face; **16/5/98** A Alexandrov (Russia), I Aristov (Russia), N Kadoshinikov (Russia); 19/5/98 O Cadiach (Spain), N Duro (f) (Andorra), A Horoaov (Bulgaria), Z Petkov (Bulgaria), J Simunek (Czech Rep), I Valtchev (Bulgaria) D Vassilev (Bulgaria), S Vomackova (f) (Czech Rep), Lahkpa Dorje Sherpa (Nepal); **30/4/99** M Jorgensen † (Denmark) M Stofer (Switzerland); 13/5/99 A Georges (Switzerland) NW side; 16/5/99 M Groom (Australia), D Bridges (US); 22/5/99 G Harrison (f) (UK), H Robertson (Australia); 23/5/99 A Hinkes (UK), Dawa Chiri Sherpa (Nepal); 25/5/99 W Pierson (US)

Kangchenjunga ascent data

All climbs by first ascent route (South-west Face) except where stated.

25/5/55 G Band (UK), J Brown (UK); 26/5/55 N Hardie (NZ), T Streather (UK); **31/5/77** P Chand (India), Nima Dorje Sherpa (Nepal) NE spur to N Ridge; **16/5/79** P Boardman (UK), D Scott (UK), J Tasker (UK) NW Face to N Ridge; **14/5/80** R Fukuda (Japan), S Kawamura, (Japan), N Sakashita (Japan), S Suzuki (Japan), Ang Phurba Sherpa (Nepal) NW Face; 15/5/80 G Ritter (W Germany), Nima Dorje Sherpa (Nepal), Lhakpa Gyalu Sherpa (Nepal); 17/5/80 M Ohmiya (Japan), T Sakano (Japan), Pemba Tshering Sherpa (Nepal), Dawa Norbu Sherpa (Nepal) NW Face; **9/5/81** K Fujikura (Japan), A Hosake (Japan), K Kataoka (Japan), S Suzuki (Japan), N Yamada (Japan), Nima Temba Sherpa (Nepal); 20/5/81 J Psotka (Czech), L Zahoransky (Czech) NW Face; 15/10/81 M Parmentier (France), J Ricouard † (France); **2/5/82** I Menbreaz (Italy), O Squinobal (Italy), Nga Temba Sherpa (Nepal); 6/5/82 R Messner (Italy), F Muschlechner (Italy), Ang Dorje Sherpa (Nepal) NW Face to N Ridge; **28/5/83** G Bachler (Austria); 17/10/83 P Beghin (France); 21/10/83 M Buchez (Switzerland), V May (Switzerland) NW Face; **19/5/84** T Ozake (Japan), Ang Tshering Sherpa (Nepal); 20/5/84 T Mitani (Japan), S Wada (Japan) SW Rib to S Ridge up, down in traverse of 3 summits; 18/10/84 R Marshall (Canada); **11/1/86** J Kukuczka (Poland), K Wielicki (Poland); 24/10/86 J Permane (Spain), Ang Rita Sherpa (Nepal); **25/5/87** F Bhutia † (India), P Dorjee † (India), C Tsering † (Nepal) NE spur to N Ridge; 31/5/87 S Limbu (India), C Singh † (India), B Singh (India), NE spur to N Ridge; 10/10/87 J Coulton (Australia), M Groom (Australia); **2/1/88** Lee Jeong-Chel (S Korea); 3/5/88 C Buhler (US), P Habeler (Austria), M Zabaleta (Spain) N Ridge; 17/10/88 M Unno (Japan), Nima Temba Sherpa (Nepal) (2nd); **9/4/89** V Elagin (USSR), E Kinezky (USSR), V Koroteev (USSR), A Sheinov (USSR); 16/4/89 Z Chalitov (USSR), V Dedy (USSR), A Glushkovsky (USSR), G Lunjakov (USSR), Y Moiseev (USSR), V Suviga (USSR), L Trotschinenko (USSR), K Valiev (USSR); 29/4/89 S Bogomolov (USSR), R Chaibullin (USSR), V Karataev (USSR), M Mozaev (USSR), V Pastuk (USSR); 1/5/89 S Bershov (USSR), A Bukreev (USSR), A Pogorelov (USSR), M Turkevitch (USSR), S Vinogradski (USSR), S Ridge to SW rib up and W Face down; grand traverse from Yalung Kang 30/4; 1/5/89 S Arentiev (USSR), E Kineszky (USSR) (2nd), V Khrichtchaty (USSR), V Suviga (USSR) (2nd); 1/5/89 V Babyberdin (USSR), Z Chalitov (USSR) (2nd), V Elagin (USSR) (2nd), V Karataev (USSR) (2nd), G Lunjakov (USSR) (2nd) SW rib and W Face to S Ridge up, SW down in grand traverse ending at Yalung Kang on 2/5; 3/5/89 N Cherny (USSR), S Efimov (USSR), Ang Babu Sherpa (Nepal); 18/5/89 P Ershler (US), C van Hoy (US), E Viesturs (US) NW Face to N Ridge; 21/5/89 R Link (US), L Nielson (US), G Wilson (US) NW Face to N Ridge; **15/5/90** M Udall (US); **1/5/91** S Bozic (Yugoslavia), V Groselj (Yugoslavia); 24/5/91 H Imamura (Japan), H Nazuka (Japan), R Oda (Japan) NE spur to N Ridge; 5/5/91 K Lal (India), S D Sharma (India), T Smanla (India) N E spur to N Ridge; **12/5/92** C Carsolio (Mexico) NW Face to N Ridge; **23/5/93** V Borko (Ukraine), A Kharaldine (Ukraine), A Serpak (Ukraine), M Sitnik (Ukraine), V Terzeoul (Ukraine) NE spur to N Ridge; 26/5/93 S Perkhomenko (Ukraine), I Zade (Ukraine) NE spur to N Ridge; **23/10/94** V Koulbatchenko (Belarussia); **5/10/95** E Loretan (Switzerland), J Troillet (Switzerland); 14/10/95 A Blanc (Italy), S Martini (Italy); **6/5/96** F Iñurrategi (Spain), A Iñurrategi (Spain), J Oiarzabal (Spain) NW Face; **24/5/97** S McKee (US) NW Face; **9/5/98** Akbu (Tibet), Daqiong (Tibet), Jaibu (Tibet), Luoze (Tibet), Baibo Zaxi (Tibet), Rena (Tibet), Cering Doje (Tibet); 15/5/98 F De Stefani (Italy), Gyalzen Sherpa (Nepal); 15/5/98 K Aksaka † (Japan), K Hirose (Japan), M Okuda (Japan), A Shiina † (Japan), T Tanigawa (Japan)

NW Face; 18/5/98 G Harrison W (UK), T Horvath (US), J Pratt (UK), C Shaw (US) NW Face; 18/5/98 K Auer (Italy), H Kammerlander (Italy); **12/5/99** Park Young-Seok (S Korea), Sherap Jangbu Sherpa (Nepal), Sange Sherpa (Nepal)

First ascents of subsidiary summits
South summit: 19/5/78 E Chrobak (Poland), W Wroz (Poland) W Face. Central Summit: 22/5/78 W Branski (Poland), Z Heinrich (Poland), K Olech (Poland) W Face. West Summit (Yalung Kang): 14/5/73 Y Ageta (Japan), T Matsuda † (Japan) SW Ridge

Manaslu ascent data
All climbs by first ascent route (North-east Face) except where stated.

9/5/56 T Imanishi (Japan), Gyalzen Norbu Sherpa (Nepal); 11/5/56 M Higeta (Japan), K Kato (Japan); **17/5/71** K Kohara (Japan), M Tanaka (Japan) NW Face; **25/4/72** R Messner (Italy) S Face; **22/4/73** S Hupfauer (W Germany), G Schmatz (W Germany), Urkien Tshering Sherpa (Nepal); **4/5/74** M Mori (f) (Japan), N Nakaseko (f) (Japan), Jangbu Sherpa (Nepal), M Uchida (f) (Japan); **26/4/75** G Blazquez (Spain), J López (Spain), Sonam Wolang Sherpa (Nepal); **12/10/76** M J Assadi (Iran), J Kageyama (Japan), Pasang Sherpa (Nepal); **28/4/80** Seo Dong-Hwan (S Korea), Ang Pasang Sherpa (Nepal), Ang Zawa Sherpa (Nepal); **7/5/81** H Von Kaenel (Switzerland), J Mecke (W Germany), Wangchu Sherpa (Nepal); 9/5/81 F Graf (Switzerland), K Horn (W Germany), A Loferer (W Germany), H Müller (Switzerland), H Zabrowski (W Germany); 19/5/81 W Heimbach (W Germany), J Millinger (Austria), R Schleypen (W Germany), Pasang Norbu Sherpa (Nepal), P Weber (Switzerland), P Wörgötter (Austria), S Wörner (Switzerland); 7/10/81 P Beghin (France), B Muller (France) W Face; 12/10/81 T Ozaki (Japan); 14/10/81 M Tomita (Japan), Y Kato (Japan); **10/10/82** L Audobert (France), Nawang Tenzing Sherpa (Nepal); **22/10/83** Heo Young-Ho (S Korea); 22/10/83 G Härter (W Germany), Ang Dorje Sherpa (Nepal), Nima Rita Sherpa (Nepal), H Streibel (W Germany), H Tauber (W Germany), H Wehrs (W Germany) S Face; **12/1/84** M Berbeka (Poland), R Gajewski (Poland) S Face; 30/4/84 E Loretan (Switzerland), M Ruedi (Switzerland); 4/5/84 S Bozic (Yugoslavia), V Groselj (Yugoslavia) S Face; 7/5/84 M Dacher (W Germany), F Zintl (W Germany); 11/5/84 N Joos (Switzerland), W Schaffert (W Germany), R Schaider (W Germany), Ang Cheppal Sherpa (Nepal), Wongel Sherpa (Nepal), G Sturm (W Germany); 20/10/84 A Lwow (Poland), K Wielicki (Poland) S Ridge to SE Face; **1/5/85** Ang Kami Sherpa (Nepal), W Studer (Austria) E Ridge to NE Face; 14/12/85 Y Saito (Japan), N Yamada (Japan); **10/11/86** A Hajzer (Poland), J Kukuczka (Poland) E Ridge; **7/10/87** J Etschmayer (Austria), W Hauser (Austria), Lhakpa Sonam Sherpa (Nepal); **1/5/88** B Fuster (Switzerland), U Huber (f) (Switzerland), R Ott (Switzerland) E Ridge to NE Face; 25/10/88 J Agullo (Spain), Ang Lhakpa Sherpa (Nepal); **9/5/89** B Chamoux (France), P Royer (France) S Face; 10/5/89 S Dorotei (Italy), J Rakoncaj (Czech) S Face; 11/5/89 Y Detry (France), F Valet (France) S Face; 12/5/89 A Hinkes (UK), M Rossi (Italy), Tirtha Tamang (Nepal) S Face; **26/4/90** F De Stefani (Italy); **6/5/91** A Makarov (Russia), V Pastuck (Ukraine), I Svergoun (Ukraine) S Ridge up, down; 25/10/91 H Brantschen (Switzerland), M Ferrari (Switzerland); **28/9/92** M Bianchi (Italy), C Kuntner (Italy), K Wielicki (2nd) (Poland); **2/5/93** J Brunner (Austria), G Flossmann (Austria), J Hinding (Austria), M Leuprecht (Austria); 13/10/93 S Mondinelli (Italy) S Face; 15/10/93 S Inhoeger (Austria); 19/10/93 V Lopatnikov (Russia); 21/10/93 E Ivanova (f) (Russia), I Khmiliar † (Russia); **19/10/94** A Georges (Switzerland), A Salamin (Switzerland); **7/5/95** J Bartock (Germany), S Thomas (Germany), M Zunk † (Germany); 8/12/95 A Baimakhanov (Kazakhstan), A Bukreev (Kazakhstan), S Gataoulin (Kazakhstan), O Malikov (Kazakhstan), J Moiseev (Kazakhstan), D Mouravev (Kazakhstan), D Sololev (Kazakhstan), V Sougiva (Kazakhstan); **3/5/96** Akbu (Tibet), Cering Doje (Tibet), Rena (Tibet), Bianba Zaxi (Tibet); 4/5/96 Daqiong (Tibet), Jaibu (Tibet), Luoze (Tibet), Wangjia (Tibet); 12/5/96 A Carsolio (Mexico), C Carsolio (Mexico); 24/5/96 C Mauduit (f) (France); 27/9/96 R Benedetti (Italy), L Campagna (Italy), T Ishikawa (Japan), S Martini (Italy), Nima Dorje Sherpa (Nepal), Tshering Dorje Sherpa (Nepal); 28/9/96 M Konishi (Japan), Pemba Tshering Sherpa (Nepal), T Sugiyama (Japan), Dhanjeet Tamang (Nepal); 30/9/96 M Mimura (Japan), H Arikawa (Japan); 13/10/96 A Blanc (Italy), A Favre (Italy), P Obert (Italy); 27/9/96 Um Hong-Gil (S Korea), Ngati Sherpa (Nepal); **19/9/97** Santa Bahadur Gurung (Nepal), K Kobler (Switzerland), Nima Tamang (Nepal), I Vallejo (Ecuador); 27/9/97 C Mace (US), A McPherson (UK); 8/10/97 Y Kato (Japan), T Mitani (Japan), Pertemba Sherpa (Nepal), K Takahashi (Japan), T Toyoshima (Japan), A Yamamoto (Japan); 8/10/97 J I Fernandez (Spain), J R Lasa (Spain), J Oiarzabal (Spain), I Querejeta (Spain); 8/10/97 M Rybansky † (Slovakia), P Sperka (Slovakia); 9/10/97 A Harada (Japan), M Hirose (Japan), Y Seki (Japan), Dawa Nuru Sherpa (Nepal), Phurba Tshering Sherpa (Nepal); **6/12/98** Park Young-Seok (S Korea), Kami Dorchi Sherpa (Nepal), Ang Dawa Tamang (Nepal); **22/4/99** V Gustafsson (Finland), A Montalban (Spain), J Noguera (Spain), E Vieslurs (US); 29/4/99 G Wiegand (Germany), G Stingl (Germany); 2/5/99 M Walter (Germany), V Tiller (Germany); 5/5/99 R Mittag (Germany), D Ruelker (Germany); 7/5/99 J Alzner (US), E Eriksson (US), M Manarik (Czech Rep) F Ziel (US)

Lhotse ascent data
All climbs by first ascent route (West Face) except where stated

18/5/56 F Luchsinger (Switzerland), E Reiss (Switzerland); **8/5/77** H Warth (W Germany), H Von Kaenel (Switzerland), Urkien Tshering Sherpa (Nepal); 9/5/77

G Sturm (W Germany), P Vogler (W Germany), F Zintl (W Germany); 11/5/77 M Dacher (W Germany), M Lutz † (W Germany), P Wörgötter (Austria), W Wörgötter (Austria); **5/5/79** W Axt (Austria), H Ladreiter (Austria); 10/5/79 I Exnar (Czech refugee in Switzerland), B Klausbruckner (Austria); 4/10/79 A Czok (Poland), Z Heinrich (Poland), J Kukuczka (Poland), J Skorek (Poland); 9/10/79 J Baranek (Poland), A Bilczewski (Poland), S Cholewa (Poland), R Niklas (W Germany); **30/4/81** H Prodanov (Bulgaria); **9/10/83** K Murakami (Japan), T Ozaki (Japan), N Yamada (Japan); 10/10/83 T Kagawa (Japan), T Miyazaki (Japan), Dawa Norbu Sherpa (Nepal); 14/10/83 Pemba Norbu (Nepal), S Suzuki (Japan), K Takahashi (Japan); **4/5/86** M Fukushima (Japan), T Haruki (Japan), Nima Temba Sherpa (Nepal), Nima Dorje Sherpa (Nepal); 14/5/86 A Lwow (Poland), T Karolczak (Poland); 16/10/86 H Kammerlander (Italy), R Messner (Italy); **28/9/88** D Becik (Czech), J Just (Czech); 2/10/88 Chung Ho-Jin (S Korea), Lim Hyung-Chil (S Korea), Park Hee-Dong (S Korea), Park Quay-Don (S Korea); 31/10/88 K Wielicki (Poland); **30/4/89** V Groselj (Yugoslavia); 14/10/89 Heo Young-Ho (S Korea); **24/4/90** T Cesen (summit claim doubted including claim to have soloed) (Yugoslavia) S Face; 13/5/90 W Berg (US), S Fischer (US); 16/10/90 S Bershov (USSR), V Karataev (USSR) S Face; **4/10/93** G Vionnet-Fuasset (France), Nuru Sherpa (Nepal); **9/5/94** O Kihlborg (Sweden), M Reutersward (Sweden); 13/5/94 C Carsolio (Mexico); 16/5/94 R Hall (NZ), E Viesturs (US); 1/10/94 E Loretan (Switzerland), J Troillet (Switzerland); 11/10/94 B Chamoux (France), R Pawlowski (Poland); **6/5/95** M Groom (Australia), V Gustafsson (Finland); 10/5/95 B Bishop (US), K Kerr (UK), Kipa Sherpa (Nepal), Danu (Danuri) Sherpa (Nepal); 27/9/95 A Iñurrategi (Spain), F Iñurrategi (Spain), Onchu Lama (Nepal); 2/10/95 J Oiarzabal (Spain), J Vallejo (Spain); **10/5/96** C Mauduit (f) (France); 22/5/96 S Darsney (US), J Pratt (UK); 23/5/96 D Mazur (US); 17/5/96 A Boukreev (Kazakhstan); **23/5/97** A Hinkes (UK), M K Jorgensen (Denmark); 24/5/97 I Outechev (Russia), N Tchernyi (Russia), S Zuev (Russia); 26/5/97 C Feld-Boskoff (f) (US); 26/5/97 V Babanov (Russia), V Bashkirov † (Russia), S Bogomolov (Russia), A Foigt (Russia), V Koroteev (Russia), V Pershin (Russia), G Sokolov (Russia), S Timofeev (Russia); 26/5/97 A Boukreev (2nd) (Kazakhstan), S Moro (Italy); 27/5/97 A Blanc (Italy); 28/5/97 J C Lafaille (France), M Panzeri (Italy), S Panzeri (Italy); 18/10/97 Han Wang-Yong (S Korea), Park Young-Seok (S Korea), Kaji Sherpa (Nepal); 21/10/97 K Nagaoka (Japan), S Sakamoto (Japan); **17/5/98** A Georges (Switzerland); 18/5/98 A N Mahruki (Turkey); 25/5/98 I Pauls (Latvia), Kami Sherpa (Nepal); 27/5/98 B Bull (US), T Heinrich (Argentina), A Lapkass (US); 13/10/98 Daqiong (Tibet), Bianba Zaxi (Tibet), Cering Doje (Tibet), Rena (Tibet), Luoze (Tibet); **21/4/99** I Ochoa (Spain); 12/5/99 J Simunek (Czech Rep), S Vomackova (f) (Czech Rep), Lhakpa Dorje Sherpa (Nepal); 13/5/99 J Moravek (Czech Rep), Z Hruby (Czech Rep); 22/5/99 M Doya (Japan), Man Bahadur Gurung (Nepal), Phurba Chhiri Sherpa (Nepal)

First ascents of subsidiary summits
East Summit (Lhotse Shar): 12/5/70 J Mayerl (Austria), R Walter (Austria) SE Ridge. Middle Summit: Unclimbed as of 31/12/99

Gasherbrum II ascent data
All climbs via first ascent route (SW Ridge, base of SE Face and E Ridge) except where stated.

7/7/56 S Larch (Austria), F Moravec (Austria), H Willenpart (Austria); **18/6/75** M Batard (France), Y Seigneur (France) S Ridge/E Ridge; 1/8/75 L Cichy (Poland), J Onyszkiewicz (Poland), K Zdzitowiecki (Poland) SW Ridge to col between GII and GII then NW Face; 9/8/75 M Janas (Poland), A Lapinski (Poland), WL Wozniak (Poland); 12/8/75 H Krüger-Syrokomska (f) (Poland), A Okopinska (f) (Poland); **9/8/78** G Brosig (Germany); 9/6/79 C Lucero (Chile), G Oyarzun (Chile); **31/7/79** K Hub (Germany), R Karl (Germany), H Sturm (Austria); 4/8/79 K Diemberger (Austria), Fayyaz Hussain (Pakistan), W Lösch (Austria), H Schell (Austria), A Schwab (Austria), W Weitzenböck (Austria); **2/8/80** P Aymerich (Spain), E Font (Spain), M Fukushima (Japan), K Imada (Japan), H Sato (Japan); **29/6/81** F Neumayer (Austria), G Neumayer (Austria); 3/8/81 R Nottaris (Switzerland), A Trabado (Spain), T Zünd (Switzerland); 6/8/81 E Beaud (France), P Grenier (France), C Janin (f) (France), Sher Khan (Pakistan); **9/6/82** G Markl (Austria), G Kaser (Austria); 10/6/82 M Grüner (Austria), R Renzler (Austria); 11/6/82 J Trattner (Austria); 12/6/82 L Barrard (f) (France), M Barrard (France), A Bontemps (France); 24/7/82 Sher Khan (Pakistan) (2nd), R Messner (Italy), Nazir Sabir (Pakistan); **15/6/83** F Graf (Switzerland), E Loretan (Switzerland), A Meyer (Switzerland), M Ruedi (Switzerland), JC Sonnenwyl (Switzerland), S Wörner (Switzerland); 1/7/83 J Kukuczka (Poland), W Kurtyka (Poland) SE Ridge over Pt 7200 and E Peak then E Ridge; **25/6/84** H Kammerlander (Italy), R Messner (Italy) (2nd); 31/7/84 J Demarolle (France), P Glaizes (France), P Guedu (France), F Maurel (France); 6/8/84 P Bournat (France), W Pasquier (Switzerland); **6/6/85** G Calcagno (Italy), G Scanabessi (Italy), T Vidoni (Italy) S Ridge/E Ridge; 15/6/85 B Chamoux (France), E Escoffier (France) S Ridge/E Ridge; 8/7/85 JM Boivin (France), L Chevallier (France), F Diaféria (France), Abdul 'Little' Karim (Pakistan), M Poincet (France), B Prudhomme (France), G Vionnet-Fuasset (France); 11/7/85 Mohammad Ali (Pakistan), G Casarotto (f) (Italy), R Casarotto (Italy), C Frémont (France), P Gévaux (France), G Hassan (Pakistan), Ibrahim (Pakistan), T Mayer (USA), A Molinaire (France), O Paulin (France), A Re (Italy), M Vincent (France), G Ubaldini (Italy), G Vionnet-Fuasset (France) (2nd); 14/7/85 JM Boivin (France) (2nd); 16/7/85 F Germain (Switzerland), T Kato (Japan); 28/7/85 M Matsumoto (Japan), T Takahashi (Japan); 31/7/85 PO Bergström (Sweden), N Campredon (France), G Flecher (France), L Le Pivain (France), M Metzger (France), P Mure-Ravaud (France), R Pillière (France), T Renard (France), T Sandberg (Sweden), P Weng (Sweden); 2/8/85 M Berquet (France), E Julliard (f) (France), H Sigayret (France); **6/6/86** R Carminati (France), G Chardiny (France), E Guillot (France); 9/7/86 JC del Olmo (Spain), R Vázquez (Spain); 3/8/86 Atta-ul-Haq (Pakistan), Fakhar-ul-Haq

(Pakistan), Abdul Jabbar Bhatti (Pakistan), Sher Khan (Pakistan) (3rd); 4/8/86 B Bisèak (Slovenia), V Groselj (Slovenia), P Kozjek (Slovenia), A Stremfelj (Slovenia); 16/8/86 J Altgelt (Germany), M Fischer (Switzerland), D Siegers (Germany), V Stallbohm (Germany), K Zöll (Germany); **28/6/87** D Heilig (USA), M Miller (USA), P Powers (USA), JP Hefti † (Switzerland), R Thorns (UK), G Hupfauer (f) (Germany), S Hupfauer (Germany); 10/7/87 M Dacher (Germany), G Halliburton (NZ), I Peter (UK), U Schmidt (Germany), D Stewart (UK); 8/8/87 E Berger (Luxembourg), F De Stefani (Italy), M Giordani (Italy), S Martini (Italy); 16/8/87 A Apellaniz (Spain), L Bradey (f) (NZ), J Little (Australia), C McDermott (NZ), J Oiarzabal (Spain); **22/6/88** G Lozat (France), B Muller (France), J Pons (Spain), JP Renaud (France), B Vallet (France); 23/6/88 N Joos (Switzerland), J Pêche (France), D Schaer (Switzerland), D Wellig (Switzerland), P Zehnder (Switzerland); 24/6/88 H Albet † (France), M Buscail (France), P Hittinger (France), Abdul 'Little' Karim (Pakistan) (2nd), Rozi Ali (Pakistan); 25/6/88 R de Bos (Holland), J Jacobse (Holland), H Van der Meulen (Holland), A van Waardenburg (Holland) S Ridge/SE Face to E Ridge; 25/6/88 H Hollwig (Germany), L Klembarova (f) (Slovakia), M Sterbova (f) (Czech Rep), H Wassmann (Germany); 5/7/88 R Borra (Switzerland), R Wellig (Switzerland); 7/8/88 H Sachetat (France); 8/8/88 I Baeyens (f) (Belgium), S Hashimoto (f) (Japan), J van Hees (Belgium), Ibrahim (Pakistan) (2nd), F Kimura (f) (Japan), M Kitagawa (f) (Japan), JM de Robert (France), L Vivijs (f) (Belgium), N Yanagizawa (f) (Japan), M Yasuhara (f) (Japan); 13/8/88 G Gadani (France), S Ravel (France); **30/5/89** C Forster (Switzerland), T Fullin (Switzerland), T Planzer (Switzerland), P Stadler (Switzerland); 12/7/89 R Lampard (f) (UK), W Rutkiewicz (f) (Poland); 13/7/89 X Erro (Spain), JM Goñi (Spain), A Ibarguren † (Spain); **18/7/90** R Lang (Germany); 19/7/90 P Pustelnik (Poland); 26/7/90 H Endo (Japan), Y Endo (f) (Japan), T Suzuki (Japan), O Tanabe (Japan); 30/7/90 L García (Chile), F Luchsinger (Chile), M Purto (Chile); 31/7/90 I Valle (Chile); 1/8/90 V Dewaele (Belgium), R Muys (Belgium); **28/6/91** C Haymoz (Switzerland), P Menu (Switzerland), Ali Mohammad (Pakistan), F Thurlir (Switzerland); 19/7/91 Han Sang-Kuk (S Korea), Kim Chang-Seon (S Korea), Kim Su-Hong (S Korea), You Seok-Jae (S Korea); 20/7/91 Cho Jae-Chul (S Korea), Han Young-Jun (S Korea), Jang Sang-Gi (S Korea), Lee Young-Soon (S Korea), Park Eul-Gyu (S Korea); **18/7/92** G Beggio (Italy), L Cárdenas (Mexico), G Figueroa (Mexico), R González (Mexico), V Lauthier (f) (Italy), J Pracker (Germany), G Schmieder (Germany), A Velázquez (Mexico), H Wittmann (Germany); 20/7/92 S Hasholzner (Germany), R Steffens (Germany); 23/7/92 M Benavent (Spain), G Dinev (Bulgaria), M Miranda (Spain), R Rachev (Bulgaria), JC Recio (Spain); **7/7/93** 3 Koreans from a team of 6 led by Yi Seok-Yang; 8/7/93 2 Koreans from a team of 6 led by Yi Seok-Yang; 21/7/93 R Gocking (USA), T Kieser (USA), C Landon (USA); 22/7/93 R Broshears (USA), C Mace (USA), SA McPherson (UK); 22/7/93 I Ogasawara (Japan), K Ohbayashi (Japan), M Sato (Japan), T Tanigawa (Japan), H Nagakubo (Japan), Y Yoshida (Japan) S Ridge/E Ridge; 28/7/93 L Hall (USA), A Lwow (Poland), P Snopczynski (Poland); 29/7/93 G Fuller jr (USA), C Haugh (USA); 31/7/93 L Bancells (Spain), J Barrachina (Spain), H Konishi (Japan), T Nagao (f) (Japan), A Serra (Spain), M Todaka (Japan), T Tonsing (USA), Y Yamanoi (Japan); 16/8/93 W Angermeier (Germany), P Kowalzik (Germany), M Putz (f) (Germany), H Wohlwent (Liechenstein); **1/8/94** O Banar (Ukraine), R Coffman (USA), BA Evensen (Norway), C Fox (f) (USA), J Giban (USA), T Hargis (USA), S Mordre (Norway), E Tryti (Norway); 2/8/94 J Garrido (Spain), JL Hurtado (Spain), JC Llamas (Spain), P Nicolás (Spain), C Soria (Spain), A Tapiador (Spain); **17/6/95** J Wangeler (Germany), D Porsche (Germany); 4/7/95 E Viesturs (USA); 4/7/95 C Carsolio (Mexico) SW Ridge and WSW Face to W Ridge; 7/7/95 Jawad Pirzada (Pakistan), Ali Raza (Pakistan), Nabi Raza (Pakistan), Mohammad Yousaf (Pakistan); 8/7/95 J Berbeka (Poland); 9/7/95 K Wielicki (Poland); 10/7/95 Akbu (Tibet), Bianba Zaxi (Tibet), Cering Doje (Tibet), Luoze (Tibet); 11/7/95 Daqiong (Tibet), Jiabu (Tibet), Rena (Tibet), Wangjia (Tibet); 16/7/95 M Sprutta (Poland); **24/7/96** V Terzeoul (Ukraine), Choi Byung-Soo (S Korea), Park Mu-Taek (S Korea), Ha Chang-Soo (S Korea); 28/7/96 JC Lafaille (France); 29/7/96 A Hinkes (UK), H Howkins (f) (USA), I Otxoa de Olza (Spain), R Portilla (Spain), JC Tamayo (Spain); **8/7/97** Danawang Dorje (Nepal), F Goto (Japan), Y Ogata (Japan); See Note 1; 10/7/97 R Naghavi (Iran), H Najarian (Iran), HR Owlanj (Iran); 13/7/97 P Egillor (Spain), A Gianotti (USA), E Havlick (USA), M Hernández (f) (Spain), K Knox (f) (USA), G Roach (USA); 14/7/97 Ang Chhiri (Nepal), Ang Gylazen (Nepal), Y Baba (Japan), A Bukreev (Kazakhstan), S Ezuka (Japan), S Iwazaki (Japan), T Miyazaki (Japan), H Nazuka (Japan), Norbu (Nepal), T Tajima (Japan), T Watanuki (Japan); See Note 1; 15/7/97 B Ader (USA), F Barth (USA), T Bradác (Czech Rep), K Gardyna (Poland), L Kamarád (Czech Rep), V Mysik (Czech Rep), G Neptune (USA), P Plsek (Czech Rep), M Reparaz (Spain), C Soles (USA), K Volz (USA), J Zurawski (Poland); 16/7/97 Ang Dorje (Nepal), G Cotter (NZ), D Mantle (USA), Um Hong-Gil (S Korea); 17/7/97 L Drda (Czech Rep), S Falcón (Spain), R Fernández (f) (Spain), Z Hruby (Czech Rep), J Kardhórdó (Czech Rep), C Mauduit (f) (France), J Natkinski (Poland), N Orviz (Spain), M Palacky (Czech Rep), Park Young-Seok (S Korea), together with two female S Koreans, L Pavlik (Czech Rep), Q Ruiz de la Peña (Spain), J Rybicka (Czech Rep), J Smid (Czech Rep), D Zulaski (Poland); 20/7/97 B Batko (f) (Poland), E Margueritte (France/Poland), R Pawlowski (Poland); 21/7/97 J Gozdzik (Poland), J Maselko (Poland), P Pustelnik (Poland) (2nd); **7/7/98** J Martínez (Spain), JA Martínez (Spain); 9/7/98 F Blanco (Spain), R Blanco (Spain), RF Brown (Australian), J Brunner (Austria), F Criado (Spain), J Davies (UK), D Hamilton (UK), A Hinterplattner (Austrian), M Leuprecht (Austria), S McIvor (UK), Ali Raza (Pakistan) (2nd), J Reynders (Belgium), S Stacey (UK), S Thorburn (USA), P Walters (Australia); 22/7/98 P Guggemos (Germany), Jin Hyun-Ok (f) (S Korea), H Rickert (f) (USA), B Zeugswetter (Austria) together with 6 Japanese from the 'Silver Tortoise' team of climbers aged 47–61 led by K Ikeda (including K Ikeda, T Ishikawa, Y Nezu and T Watanabe (f) and two younger Japanese who were filming the expedition) and Rajab Shah (Pakistan), Qurban Mohammad (Pakistan), Hashil Shah (Pakistan), Mehrban Shah (Pakistan) and two other porters; 25/7/98 E Bolda (f) (Austria), B Saxinger (Austria), H Weiss (f) (Austria); 26/7/98 M Gioroianu (Romania), A Gionvanetti (Italy); 29/7/98 F Facchinetti (Italy), J Hancock (USA), E Jensen (USA); 31/7/98 B Zacahry (USA); 5/8/98 Y Anciaux (France), A Delade (f) (France), CP Blondot (France), JF Janvier (France), C Mirmand (France), F Odine (f) (France), E Rambaud (France); 12/8/98 R Larrandaburu (France); **9/7/99** O Cadiach (Spain), S Corta (Spain), N Duró (f) (Andorra), P Garcés (Spain), P Goñi (Spain), D

Hamilton (UK) (2nd), C Jones (NZ), A Lock (Australia), I Ollé (Spain), LM Picabea (Spain), Ali Raza (Pakistan) (3rd), J Reketa (Spain), O Ribas (Andorra), Shakoor Ali (Pakistan), X Zubieta (Spain) 10/7/99 A Blanc (Italy), Cho Hyung-Gyu (S Korea), Choi Byoung-Woo (S Korea), Kim In-Kie (S Korea), C Kuntner (Italy), Lee Sang-Bae (S Korea), W Niclevicz (Brazil); 29/7/99 L Boucher (France), H Ponce de Leon (Mexico), R Real (f) (Spain), W Schmidt (Austria), C Tudela (Spain), F Wolf (Austria), W Zohrer (Austria); 31/7/99 JL Arnald (France), P Melani (France); 3/8/99 H D'Aubarede (France), M Guillemette (f) (France), Mehrban Shah (Pakistan) (2nd); 8/8/99 M Argeles (France), JC Stalla (France); 19/8/99 E Bladé (Spain), C Feld-Boskoff (f) (USA), X González (Spain), S García-Prades (Spain), J Rhoads (USA), G Ritchi (USA)

Note 1: In 1997 the large Japanese Gunma team attempted Broad Peak, Gasherbrum I and Gasherbrum II with supporting Sherpas. The whole team was divided into three groups each of which attempted two of the peaks. The Gasherbrum II groups were:

(and attempting Gasherbrum I = Team A)

H Nazuka (leader), Y Baba, S Ezuka, S Iwazaki and T Miyazaki together with Ang Gyalzen and Ang Chhiri

(and attempting Broad Peak = Team C)

F Goto (leader), R Hoshino, A Nozawai, Y Ogata, T Tajima, T Terada, T Watanuki together with Danawang Dorje and Norbu

On 8 and 14 July these groups are said to have put 11 Japanese and 4 Sherpas on the summit. This number is not consistent with the names quoted, which show 2 Japanese and 1 Sherpa summitting on 8 July, and 7 Japanese and 3 Sherpas on 14 July. It is likely that the names quoted are correct and that only 9 Japanese and 4 Sherpas summitted.

Broad Peak ascent data

All climbs via first ascent route (W Spur to Broad Col, then over forepeak to summit ridge) except where stated. NB Some of the ascents below may only have been to forepeak. Definitive details on summit reached are occasionally hard to obtain.

9/6/57 H Buhl (Austria), K Diemberger (Austria), M Schmuck (Austria), F Wintersteller (Austria); **8/8/77** K Noro (Japan), T Ozaki (Japan), Y Tsuji (Japan); **4/6/78** (Y Seigneur (France), G Bettembourg (France) – Bettembourg did not reach the main summit and claims that Siegneur also failed); **5/8/81** M Hernández (Spain), E Pujol † (Spain); **23/7/82** G Bachler (Austria), R Bärtle (Germany), P Gloggner (Germany), H Kirchberger (Germany), K Lewankowski (Germany), W Lösch (Austria), W Sucher (Austria); 30/7/82 J Kukuczka (Poland), W Kurtyka (Poland); 2/8/82 Sher Khan (Pakistan), R Messner (Italy), Nazir Sabir (Pakistan); **25/6/83** J Afanassieff (France), R Baxter-Jones (UK), A Parkin (UK), A Rouse (UK); 28/6/83 D Scott (UK), S Sustad (USA); 30/6/83 F Graf (Switzerland), E Loretan (Switzerland), K Palmowska (f) (Poland), M Ruedi (Switzerland), S Wörner (Switzerland); 2/7/83 P Morand (Switzerland), JC Sonnenwyl (Switzerland); **26/6/84** M Barrios (Colombia), T Hägler (Switzerland), A Reinhard (Switzerland), L Deuber (Switzerland), R Franzl (Austria); 27/6/84 G Calcagno (Italy), A Enzio (Italy), T Vidoni (Italy); 13/7/84 G Calcagno (Italy) (2nd), K Hub (Germany), R Schleypen (Germany), T Vidoni (Italy) (2nd); 14/7/84 W Fiut (Poland), J Majer (Poland), R Pawlowski (Poland), K Wielicki (Poland), H Zebrowski (Germany); 17/7/84 J Kukuczka (Poland) (2nd), W Kurtyka (Poland) (2nd) (W Ridge of N Peak, then along ridge to Central Peak, down to Broad Col and along first ascent route); 18/7/84 K Diemberger (Austria) (2nd), J Tullis (f) (UK); 8/8/84 R Joswig (Germany), R Schauer (Austria); **31/7/85** Fayyaz Hussain (Pakistan), Zahid Mahmood (Pakistan), Jawad Pirzada (Pakistan); 12/8/85 S Kashu (Japan), R Nishizutsumi (Japan), T Shigehiro (Japan), T Toyama (Japan), J Wada (Japan), M Yamamoto (Japan); **20/6/86** B Chamoux (France) (probably to forepeak only), S Dorotei (Italy), M Giacometti (Italy), M Moretti (Italy); 21/6/86 B Fuster (Switzerland), M Prechtl (Germany), D Wellig (Switzerland), P Wörgötter (Austria), R Zemp (Switzerland); 22/6/86 J Rakoncaj (Czech Rep); 23/6/86 H Koch (Germany), J Labisch (Germany); 7/7/86 S Hölzl (Austria), F Schreinmoser (Austria); 28/7/86 B Biščak (Slovenia), V Groselj (Slovenia); 29/7/86 T Cesen (Slovenia), R Fabjan (Slovenia), T Jamnik (Slovenia), A Stremfelj (Slovenia), M Stremfelj (f) (Slovenia); 30/7/86 P Kozjek (Slovenia); 4/8/86 D Jelinčič (Slovenia), S Karo (Slovenia), M Lenarcic (Slovenia), M Stangelj (Slovenia); 16/8/86 B Agnew (Australian), J Chester (Australian), P Cullinan (Australian), M Dacher (Germany), K Fassnacht (Germany), G Hupfauer (f) (Germany), S Hupfauer (Germany), P Lambert (Australian), T McCullagh (Australian), M Rheinberger (Australian), J Van Gelder (Australian), Z Zaharias (Australian); **29/5/87** N Joos (Switzerland); 7/6/87 B Honegger (Switzerland), E Müller (Switzerland); **27/6/88** S Matsumoto (f) (Japan), K Sakai (Japan), M Sasaki (Japan), K Shimakata (Japan); 1/8/88 C Schranz (Italy); 12/8/88 J Saito (Japan), M Taniguchi (Japan); 9/9/88 L Gómez (Spain), C Vallès (Spain); **12/7/91** K Hayasaka (Japan), I Ogasawara (Japan), M Sato (Japan), T Tanigawa (Japan), T Yawata (Japan); 16/7/91 R Beadle (UK), R Blanco (Spain), A Hinkes (UK); 30/7/91 M Abe (Japan), H Konishi (Japan), T Nagao (f) (Japan), Y Yamanoi (Japan), T Yoshimura (Japan); **2/8/92** D Hambly (UK), S McKee (USA), C Lacatusu (Romania), E Martínez (Spain), P Rodríguez (Spain), A Tapiador (Spain); **6/7/93** M Bianchi (Italy), C Kuntner (Italy); 7/7/93 A Brugger (Italy), S De Leo (Italy), T Heymann (Germany), F De Stefani (Italy); 21/7/93 Sarwar Khan (Pakistan), Rajab Shah (Pakistan), M Tamura (Japan), N Tsuji (Japan); 29/7/93 A Blanc (Italy), S Martini (Italy), Nima Temba (Nepal), Ali Raza (Pakistan); 24/8/93 S Ezuka (Japan), K Mino (Japan), T Nakamura (Japan), O Tanabe (Japan), K Uchida (Japan); **21/6/94** H Kammerlander (Italy); 2/7/94 G Kropp (Sweden); 3/7/94 A Busca (Italy); 9/7/94 C Carsolio (Mexico) (In two stages, going over Pt 6230 then WSW Spur to first ascent route then directly up headwall to forepeak); 10/7/94 E Morin (France); 23/7/94 B Christensen (Denmark), P Ibarbia

(Spain), J Mathorne (Denmark); **12/7/95** M Abrego (Spain), J Casimiro (Spain), Lee Jeong-Hyun (S Korea), J Oiarzabal (Spain), Park Hyun-Jae † (S Korea), Park Sin-Young (S Korea), Um Hong-Gil (S Korea); 20/7/95 T Hattori (Japan), T Kitamura (Japan), M Todaka (Japan) (W Ridge of N Peak, then along ridge to Central Peak, down to Broad Col and along first ascent route); 13/8/95 Ang Dorje II (Nepal), J Alzner (USA), S Ballard (f) (Canada), M Boyle (USA), Dawa Galjen (Nepal), J Ehrlich (Germany), C Feld-Boskoff (f) (USA), S Fischer (USA), P Goldman (USA), R Hess (USA), J Leupold (Germany), Lobsang Jangbu (Nepal), A Lish (USA), I Loredo (Mexico), A McKinlay (Canada), W Soroka (Poland), M Walter (German), F Ziel (USA); 23/7/96 Han Dong-Keun † (S Korea), Yang Jae-Mo † (S Korea); **13/7/97** A Iñurrategi (Spain), F Iñurrategi (Spain); 16/7/97 See Note 1; 19/7/97 J Coburn (USA), B Montoya (USA), M Schneider (Germany), T Tonsing (USA); 20/7/97 See Note 1; 7/8/97 A Lock (Australia); 9/8/97 JC Cirera (Spain); **5/7/98** R Bösch (Switzerland), K Kobler (Switzerland), I Vallejo (Ecuador); (29/7/98 E Escoffier (France), P Bessiéres (France) last seen on the summit ridge); **16/7/99** R Dujmovits (Germany), G Hafele (Austria), Qudrat Ali (Pakistan), J Rozas (Spain), S von Roth (Switzerland); 17/7/99 P Fessler (Austria), E Koblmüller (Austria)

Note 1: In 1997 a large team from the Japanese Gunma Mountaineering Association attempted Broad Peak, Gasherbrum I and Gasherbrum II with supporting Sherpas. The whole team was divided into three groups each of which attempted two of the peaks. The Broad Peak groups were:

(and attempting Gasherbrum I = Team B)

M Sato (leader), M Fukumoto, H Iwazaki, K Nakajima, S Yanase, H Yoshida and F Yoshida (f) together with Dawa Tsering and Arjun Tamang

(and attempting Gasherbrum II = Team C)

F Goto (leader), R Hoshino, A Nozawai, Y Ogata, T Tajima, T Terada and T Watanuki together with Danawang Dorje and Norbu

On 16 July 6 of the 7 Japanese from Team B, together with both Sherpas climbed Broad Peak. On 20 July F Goto and Y Ogata, together with Danawang Dorje, all from Team C, climbed Broad Peak. Other sources indicate that in total 3 Japanese and 2 Sherpas reached the main summit (probably including the three climbers of 20 July), the other 3 Japanese reaching the forepeak.

First ascent of subsidiary summit

Central Summit: 28/7/75 K Glazek (Poland), M Kesicki † (Poland), J Kulis (Poland), B Nowaczyk † (Poland), A Sikorski † (Poland) Main Summit first ascent route to Broad Col, then along the Central Summit's N Ridge

Gasherbrum I ascent data

5/7/58 A Kauffman (USA), P Schoening (USA) Roch Arête (IHE Spur) to SE Ridge; **10/8/75** P Habeler (Austria), R Messner (Italy) NW Face; 11/8/75 R Schauer (Austria), H Schell (Austria), H Zefferer (Germany) First ascent route; **8/7/77** A Stremfelj (Slovenia), N Zaplotnik (Slovenia) W Ridge; **15/7/80** M Barrard (France), G Narbaud (France) Over Hidden Sud to SE Ridge; **3/8/81** H Azuma (Japan), K Shimotori (Japan) First ascent route; **22/7/82** M Dacher (Germany), S Hupfauer (Germany), G Stürm (Germany) NW Face (German variant); 27/7/82 Mohammad Ali (Pakistan), JP Ollagnier (France), S Saudan (Switzerland), D Semblanet (France), MJ Valençot (f) (France) First ascent route; **23/6/83** E Loretan (Switzerland), M Ruedi (Switzerland) NW Face (Swiss variant); 24/6/83 P Morand (Switzerland), JC Sonnenwyl (Switzerland) NW Face (Swiss variant); 23/7/83 J Kukuczka (Poland), W Kurtyka (Poland) SW Face; 22/8/83 V Arnal (Spain), I Cinto (Spain), J Escartín (Spain), J López (Spain), L Ortas (Spain), A Ubieto (Spain) W Ridge of Hidden Sud, then French 1980 route; **28/6/84** H Kammerlander (Italy), R Messner (Italy) (2nd) NW Face (variant of German route); **9/6/85** P Camozzi (Italy), A Da Polenza (Italy) NW Face to the right (south) of Habeler-Messner line, then as Habeler-Messner; 19/6/85 G Calcagno (Italy), T Vidoni (Italy) NW Face (German variant); 22/6/85 B Chamoux (France), E Escoffier (France) NW Face (Swiss variant); 15/7/85 G De Federico (Italy) NW Face (Swiss variant); **2/8/86** O Shimizu (Japan), K Wakutsu (Japan) Japanese Couloir; 3/8/86 A Berthélemy (France), C Janin (f) (France), R Joswig (Germany) NW Face (Swiss variant); 17/8/86 R Lang (Germany) (but only to a point about NW Face 20m below the summit) (German variant); 18/8/86 A Bührer † (Switzerland), K Kölleman (Austria), M Lorenz (Austria), G Schmatz (Germany) NW Face (German variant); **20/6/88** R Gálfy (Slovakia), I Urbanovic (Slovakia) Japanese Couloir; 20/6/88 F Soltes (Slovakia) NW Face (Habeler-Messner); 12/7/89 Tsindi Dorje † (Nepal), H Endo (Japan), Y Endo (f) (Japan) Japanese Couloir; **16/7/90** T Katayama (Japan), E Pankiewicz (f) (Poland), Park Hyeok-Sang (S Korea), Ali Raza (Pakistan), W Rutkiewicz (f) (Poland), R Shah (Pakistan), T Yamane (Japan) Japanese Couloir; 26/7/90 G Derycke (France), A Estève (France), W Ridge; Y Tedeschi (France), Mohammad Ullah (Pakistan), M Yousaf (Pakistan); 29/8/90 P Bergeron (Canada), C Bernier (Canada) W Ridge; **25/8/92** Nazir Sabir (Pakistan), Rajab Shah (Pakistan) (2nd), Mehrban Shah (Pakistan) Japanese Couloir; **7/6/93** H Bumann (Switzerland), N Joos (Switzerland), M Stoller (Switzerland) Japanese Couloir; 3/8/94 S Martini (Italy), S De Leo (Italy), F De Stefani (Italy), G Vallc (Italy) Japanese Couloir; 4/8/94 F Lévy (France), JM Meunier (France), J Pratt (UK), M Staehelin (Switzerland) Japanese Couloir; 12/8/94 A Collins (UK), H Inaba (Japan), M Saeki (Japan), M Taniguchi (Japan), D Mazur (USA) Japanese Couloir; **5/7/95** M Car (Slovenia), I Tomazin (Slovenia) Japanese Couloir; 15/7/95 J Berbeka (Poland), C Carsolio (Mexico), E Viesturs (USA), K Wielicki (Poland) Japanese Couloir; 16/7/95 K Lasa (Spain), T Lete (Spain), LM López (Spain) Japanese Couloir; **10/7/96** D Carroll (UK), J Doyle (UK), A Hinkes (UK), A Hughes (UK), S Hunt (NZ), I Otxoa de Olza (Spain), J Tomás (Spain) Japanese Couloir; 11/7/96 M Alvarez † (Spain), A Juez (Spain) Japanese Couloir; 30/7/96 Y Karahashi (Japan), T Kawanabe (Japan), H Masaki (Japan) Japanese Couloir; 31/7/96 JC Lafaille (France) NW

Face (Swiss variant); **7/7/97** Ang Gyalzen (Nepal), Ang Chhiri (Nepal), Y Baba (Japan), S Ezuka (Japan), S Iwazaki (Japan), H Nazuka (Japan), T Miyazaki (Japan) Japanese Couloir See Note 1; 9/7/97 Ali Raza (Pakistan) (2nd), J Åkerstrom (Sweden), J Bermúdez (UK), R Foulquier (UK), D Hamilton (UK), Z Hruby (Czech Rep), Ji Hyun-Ok (f) (S Korea), J Kardhordo (Czech Rep), K Kimura (Japan), V Mysik (Czech Rep), J Oiarzabal (Spain), Park Young-Seok (S Korea), M Ryden (Sweden), S Silhan (Czech Rep), Um Hong-Gil (S Korea) Japanese Couloir; 13/7/97 Han Wuang-Yong (S Korea) Japanese Couloir; 15/7/97 A Giovannetti (Italy), J Gozdzik (Poland), J Maselko (Poland), R Pawlowski (Poland), O Piazza (Italy), P Pustelnik (Poland) Japanese Couloir; 16/7/97 T Kitamura (Japan), H Konishi (Japan), Rozi Ali (Pakistan) Japanese Couloir; **9/7/98** B Christensen (Denmark), J Mathorne (Denmark), M Granlien (Denmark) Japanese Couloir; 10/7/98 D Porsche (Germany) Japanese Couloir; 29/7/98 Y Iwasita (Japanese) Japanese Couloir; 31/7/98 J Martínez (Spain), JA Martínez (Spain) Japanese Couloir; **3/7/99** A Blanc (Italy), C Kuntner (Italy) Japanese Couloir; 17/7/99 P Garcés (Spain), A Lock (Australia) Japanese Couloir; 18/7/99 4 Koreans led by Lee Byong-Chui Japanese Couloir

Note 1: In 1997 a large team from the Japanese Gunma Mountaineering Association attempted Broad Peak, Gasherbrum I and Gasherbrum II with supporting Sherpas. The whole team was divided into three groups each of which attempted two of the peaks. The Gasherbrum I groups were:

(and attempting Broad Peak = Team B)

M Sato (leader), M Fukumoto, H Iwazaki, K Nakajima, S Yanase, H Yoshida and F Yoshida (f) together with Dawa Tsering and Arjun Tamang. No members of this ream summitted on Gasherbrum I.

(and attempting Gasherbrum II = Team A)

H Nazuka (leader), Y Baba, S Ezuka, S Iwazaki and T Miyazaki together with Ang Gyalzen and Ang Chhiri

These groups are said to have put 5 Japanese and 2 Sherpas on the summit. All of these were from Team A on 7 July.

Dhaulagiri ascent data
All climbs by first ascent route (North-east Ridge) except where stated.

13/5/60 K Diemberger (Austria), P Diener (W Germany), E Forrer (Switzerland), A Schelbert (Switzerland), Nawang Dorje Sherpa (Nepal), Nima Dorje Sherpa (Nepal); 23/5/60 M Vaucher (Switzerland), H Weber (Switzerland); **20/10/70** T Kawata (Japan), Lhakpa Tenzing Sherpa (Nepal); **12/5/73** L Reichardt (US), J Roskelley (US), Nawang Samden Sherpa (Nepal); **4/5/76** S Simoni (Italy), G Zortea (Italy); **10/5/78** T Kobayashi (Japan), T Shigeno (Japan) SW Ridge; 11/5/78 Y Kato (Japan), S Shimizu (Japan), Ang Kami Sherpa (Nepal), H Yoshino (Japan) SW Ridge; 19/10/78 A Abe (Japan), T Miyazaki (Japan), H Tani (Japan); 21/10/78 Nawang Yonden Sherpa (Japan), S Suzuki (Japan), N Yamada (Japan) SE Ridge; **12/5/79** I Aldaya (Spain), F J Garayoa (Spain), G Plaza (Spain), J Pons (Spain), Ang Rita Sherpa (Nepal); **13/5/80** H Von Kaenel (Switzerland), F Luchsinger (Switzerland), Ang Rita Sherpa (2nd) (Nepal); 14/5/80 J Buholzer (Switzerland), R Monnerat (Switzerland), H J Mueller (Switzerland), H Zimmermann (Switzerland); 17/5/80 H Bergstaller (Austria), H Eitel (W Germany), F Graf (Switzerland), M Ruedi (Switzerland); 18/5/80 M Ballmann (Switzerland), R Bleiker (Switzerland), Mingma Gyalzen Sherpa (Nepal), Lhakpa Gyalzen Sherpa (Nepal); 19/5/80 S Burkhardt (Switzerland), J Mueller (Switzerland), Ang Rita Sherpa (3rd) (Nepal); 18/5/80 W Kurtyka (Poland), A MacIntyre (UK), R Ghilini (Italy), L Wilczynski (Poland) E Face to NE Ridge; **17/5/81** A Burgess (UK), A Burgess (UK); 2/6/81 H Kamuro (Japan); **5/5/82** P Cornelissen (Belgium), R Van Snick (Belgium), Ang Rita Sherpa (4th) (Nepal); 6/5/82 M Lefever (Belgium), Ang Jangbo Sherpa (Nepal), J Van Hees (Belgium), L Vivijs (f) (Belgium); 17/10/82 T Mitani (Japan), J Tanaka (Japan); 18/10/82 K Komatsu (Japan), Y Saito (Japan), N Yamada (2nd) (Japan) N Face to NW Ridge; 13/12/82 A Koizumi (Japan), Wangchu Sherpa (Nepal); **18/5/83** M Gardzielewski (Poland), J Jezierski (Poland), T Laukajtys (Poland), W Otreba (Poland); 11/11/83 A de Blanchaud (France), M Metzger (France); **4/10/84** P Beghin (France), J N Roche (France) SW Ridge; 23/10/84 K Jakes (Czech), J Simon † (Czech), J Stejskal (Czech) W Face to NW Ridge; 21/1/85 A Czok (Poland), J Kukuczka (Poland); 15/5/85 H Kammerlander (Italy), R Messner (Italy); 8/12/85 E Loretan (Switzerland), P-A Steiner (Switzerland), J Troillet (Switzerland) E Face to NE Ridge; **3/5/86** G Härter (W Germany), J Hirtreiter (W Germany); 5/5/86 W Larcher (Austria), W Odenthal (W Germany), L Pfleging (W Germany); **16/10/87** 91 K Calhoun (f) (US), J Culberson (US), C Grissom (US); 2/12/87 M Batard (France), Sungdare Sherpa (Nepal); 4/12/87 M Kregar (Yugoslavia), I Tomazin (Yugoslavia) E Face to NE Ridge; **6/10/88** Z Demjan (Czech), Y Moiseev (USSR), K Valiev (USSR) SW Pillar; 14/11/88 Choi Tea-Sik (S Korea), Da Gombu Sherpa (Nepal), Wangel Sherpa (Nepal); **11/5/89** S Martini (Italy), F De Stefani (Italy); 18/5/89 J Inhoeger (Austria); **24/4/90** K Wielicki (Poland); 11/5/90 I Baeyens (f) (Belgium), R Dujmovits (W Germany); 30/9/90 K Kobler (Switzerland), H Roesti (Switzerland), P Rothlisberger (Switzerland), H Willi (Switzerland); 5/10/90 H Kindle (Liechtenstein), M Morales (Spain), C Pfistner (Switzerland), M Sanchez (Argentina); 6/10/90 S Silhan (Czech), L Sulovsky (Czech); 9/10/90 F Kimura (f) (Japan), Dawa Tshering Sherpa (Nepal), Changba Norbu Sherpa (Nepal), M Yasuhara (f) (Japan); 19/10/90 G Lowe (US); 31/10/90 C Buhler (US), D Makauskas † (USSR), Nuru Sherpa (Nepal); **10/5/91** A Bukreev (USSR), R Chaibullin (USSR), Y Moiseev (2nd) (USSR), V Suviga (USSR), A Tselishev (USSR) W Face; 13/5/91 V Khrichtchaty (USSR), Z Mizambekov (USSR), V Prisjashny (USSR), A Savin (USSR), A Shegai (USSR) W Face; 14/5/91 S Smidt (Denmark); 2/10/91 J Corominas (Spain); 11/10/91 T Nakajima (Japan), Keepa Sherpa (Nepal), K Yokoyama (Japan); **30/4/92** A Guliaev (Russia), V Kohanov (Russia), P Kouznesov (Russia), N Smetanin (Russia), N Zacharov (Russia); **11/5/93** R Allen (UK),

S Bogomolov (Russia), S Efimov (Russia), A Lebedikhim (Russia), Vi Pershin (Russia), I Plotnikov (Russia), B Sedusov (Russia) N Face; 30/5/93 Akbu (Tibet), Daqimi (Tibet), Daqiong (Tibet), Cering Doje (Tibet), Jiabu (Tibet), Luoze (Tibet), Rena (Tibet), Bianba Zaxi (Tibet), Wangjia (Tibet); 6/10/93 B Chamoux (France), M Koseki (Japan), A Nozawai (Japan); 9/10/93 V Gustafsson (Finland); 10/10/93 T Kirsis (Latvia), I Pauls (Latvia), I Zauls (Latvia); 11/10/93 S Sekiya (Japan), Mingma Tshering Sherpa (Nepal), J Vanmarsenille (Belgium), Dorje Sherpa (Nepal); **25/9/94** P-V Amaudruz (Switzerland), M Bianchi (Italy), C Kuntner (Italy); 26/9/94 S Albasini (Switzerland), R Caughron (US), J Garcia (Portugal), J Gozdzik (Poland), P Pustelnik (Poland); 27/9/94 P Boven (Switzerland), N Gex (Switzerland), O Roduit (Switzerland); 27/9/94 Y Ueno (Japan), Man Bahadur Tamang (Nepal), Pa Nima Sherpa (Nepal); 1/10/94 K Ikeda (Japan), T Ishikawa (Japan), M Konishi (Japan), K Netsu (Japan), Nima Dorje Sherpa (Nepal), Nima Temba Sherpa (Nepal), Wangchu Sherpa (Nepal), T Watanabe (f) (Japan); 3/10/94 R Henke (US), B Johnson (US), R Taylor (US); 4/10/94 R Green (US); 11/10/94 G Lebedev (Ukraine), I Svergun (Ukraine); 13/10/94 I Chaplinsky (Ukraine), T Ena (f) (Ukraine), V Gorbach (Ukraine), V Lanko (Ukraine), G Tchekanova † (f); **9/5/95** A Akinia (f) (Russia), D Botchkov (Russia), J Outeshev (Russia), V Solomatov (Russia); 14/5/95 V Bashkirov (Russia), V Khilko (Russia), S Krylov (Russia), E Popov (Russia); 15/5/95 C Carsolio (Mexico); 17/5/95 R Schmid (f) (Switzerland), M Kofler (Switzerland); 19/5/95 U Braschler (Switzerland), G Ennemoser (Austria), A Hammann † (Germany), N Joos (Switzerland); 4/10/95 M Sawada (Japan), Dawa Sherpa (Nepal) (2nd); 6/10/95 Hasta Bahadur Gurung (Nepal), H Tawaraya † (Japan); 6/10/95 K Narusaki (Japan), Pemba Rinzi Sherpa (Nepal), Arjun Tamang (Nepal), K Ueda (Japan); 6/10/95 T Hayashi (Japan), K Kondo (Japan), I Kuwabara (Japan), Pemba Tshering Sherpa (Nepal), Mingma Nuru Sherpa (Nepal), S Takeda (Japan); 8/10/95 A Bukreev (2nd) (Kazakhstan), R Rachev (Bulgaria); 9/10/95 T Tontchev (Bulgaria); 11/10/95 O Gigani (Georgia), B Gujabidze (Georgia); 12/10/95 B Dimitrov (Bulgaria), A Shinkarenko (Belarussia), I Vialenkova (f) (Belarussia); 14/10/95 Z Horozov (Bulgaria), D Vassilev (Bulgaria); 15/10/95 T Fritsche (Austria), R Mattle (Austria); **1/5/96** Um Hong-Gil (S Korea), Ngati Sherpa (Nepal); 5/5/96 A Georges (Switzerland); 17/10/96 B Vos (claim disputed) (Holland) E Face to NE Ridge; 21/10/96 A Mochnikov (Russia); 5/11/96 E Koblmueller (Austria), M Koblmueller (Austria), F Schmollngruber (Austria), H Schuetter (Austria); **27/4/97** Han Wuang-Yong (S Korea), Kim Hun-Sang (S Korea), Park Young-Seok (S Korea), Kaji Sherpa (Nepal); 25/5/97 A Lock (Australia), M Rogerson (Australia), Z Zaharias (Australia); 31/5/97 T Kitamura (Japan), H Konishi (Japan), Gyalzen Sherpa (Japan); 24/9/97 J Martinez (Spain), J A Martinez (Spain), J Rodriguez (Spain); 25/9/97 N Petkov (Bulgaria); **22/5/98** A Iñurrategi (Spain), F Iñurrategi (Spain), J Oiarzabal (Spain); 23/5/98 G Lacen (Slovenia), M Marence (Slovenia); 24/5/98 T Jakofcic (Slovenia), P Meznar (Slovenia); 26/5/98 T Bello (Italy), T Golob (Slovenia), J Meglic (Slovenia), D Polenik (Slovenia), M Vielmo (Italy); 30/9/98 H Kudo (Japan), T Saito (Japan), Y Shimoma (Japan), T Sugiyama (Japan), Pasang Gyalzen Sherpa (Nepal), Man Bahadur Tamang (2nd) (Nepal), Tul Bahadur Tamang (Nepal); **4/5/99** V Gustafsson (2nd) (Finland), E Viesturs (US); 16/10/99 T Strausz (Austria), P Walters (Australia)

Shisha Pangma ascent data

All ascents via the original Chinese line (Shisha Pangma Glacier/E Cwm/N Ridge/NE Face traverse) unless otherwise stated. NB Some of the ascents below may only have been to the Central summit. Definitive details on summit reached are occasionally hard to obtain.

2/5/64 Chen San (China), Cheng Tianliang (China), Doje (Tibet), Mima Zaxi (Tibet), Sodnam Doje (Tibet), Wang Fuzhou (China), Wu Zongyue (China), Xu Jing (China), Yungden (Tibet), Zhang Junyan (China); **7/5/80** M Dacher (Germany), W Schaffert (Germany), G Sturm (Germany), F Zintl (Germany); 12/5/80 S Hupfauer (Germany), M Sturm (Germany); 13/10/80 E Obojes (Austria), E Putz (Austria); **30/4/81** Jiabu (Tibet), Rhinzing Phinzo (Tibet), J Tabei (f) (Japan); 28/5/81 R Messner (Italy), F Mutschlechner (Italy) Chinese route variant; **28/5/82** R Baxter-Jones (UK), A MacIntyre (UK), Central Couloir; D Scott (UK) SW Face; 10/10/82 M Hara (Japan), H Komamiya (Japan), H Konishi (Japan); 12/10/82 T Chiba (Japan), M Ohmiya (Japan), M Tomita (Japan); **29/4/83** U Schum (Germany), J Walter (Germany), M Walter (f) (Germany); 30/9/83 M Browning (USA), C Pizzo (USA), G Porzak (USA); **6/5/84** D Howe (USA), M Jenkins (USA), D Kelley (USA), M Wingert (USA); 8/5/84 S Creer (USA), M Lehner (USA); **10/5/85** O Gassler (Austria), L Schausberger (Austria), P Wörgötter (Austria); 12/5/85 G Heinzel (Austria), B Kendler (Austria), A Vedani (Switzerland), T Schilcher (Austria), H Wagner (Austria), J Wangeler (Switzerland), M Wettstein (Switzerland); 16/5/85 G De Marchi (Italy); 19/5/85 L Karner (Austria), H Schell (Austria), T Schilcher (Austria) (2nd); 14/9/85 O Oelz (Austria), M Ruedi (Switzerland), D Wellig (Switzerland); **20/5/87** M Perry (NZ), M Whetu (NZ); 18/9/87 E Avila (f) (Mexico), C Carsolio (Mexico), R Navarrete (Ecuador), W Rutkiewicz (f) (Poland), R Warecki (Poland) Central Summit traverse (ie Central Summit to Main Summit); 18/9/87 A Hajzer (Poland), J Kukuczka (Poland) W Ridge to Central Summit to Main Summit; 19/9/87 A Hinkes (UK), S Untch (USA) Central Couloir N Face to Central Summit to Main Summit; 1/10/87 S Nagy (Hungary), A Ozsváth (Hungary); 8/10/87 Z Balaton (Hungary), J Csíkos (Hungary), L Várkonyi (Hungary), L Vörös (Hungary); **13/5/88** T Fischbach (Germany), K Gürtler (Austria), P Konzert (Austria) Central Summit traverse; 14/5/88 B Kullmann Germany), A Metzger (Germany), H Og (f) (Germany), K Schuhmann (Germany); 17/5/88 H Bärnthaler (Austria), T Hochholzer (Germany), W Kunzendorf (Germany), J Schütz (Germany), D Thomann (Germany); 5/9/88 P Berhault (France), F De Stefani (Italy), S Martini (Italy); 6/9/88 G Daidola (Italy), D Givois (France), P Negri (Italy); 24/10/88 T Saegusa (Japan), N Yamada (Japan), A Yamamoto (Japan); **16/4/89** K Suzuki (Japan), S Takamura (Japan), Y Tsuji (Japan); 19/10/89 P Kozjek (Slovenia), A Stremfelj (Slovenia) Central Buttress, SW Face; 20/10/89 F Bence (Slovenia), V Groselj (Slovenia) Right side of SW Face to S Ridge; **12/5/90** E Fries (Germany), J Neuhauser (Austria); 13/10/90 P Expósito (Spain), F

Gan (Spain), F Pérez (Spain), R Santaeufemia (Spain), J Martínez † (Spain), MA Vidal (Spain); **20/5/91** O Dörrich (f) (Germany), T Fritsche (Austria), G Härter (Germany), K Hecher (Austria), D Porsche (Germany), H Schnutt (Austria); 8/10/91 Kim Chang-Seon (S Korea), Central Couloir Kim Jae-Soo (S Korea) SW Face; **4/10/93** O Cadiach (Spain), M de la Matta (Spain), Central Couloir C Mauduit (f) (France) SW Face; 6/10/93 M Bianchi (Italy), P Pustelnik (Poland) Central Buttress, SW Face; 7/10/93 K Wielicki (Poland) SW Face between British route (1982) and Slovenia route (1989); **7/5/94** Akbu (Tibet), Bianba Zaxi (Tibet), Cering Doje (Tibet), Daqiong (Tibet), Daqimi (Tibet), Jiabu (Tibet) (2nd), Luoze (Tibet), Rena (Tibet), Wangjia (Tibet) Central Summit traverse; 28/5/94 J Kirschmer (Germany) Central Summit traverse; 4/10/94 N Kekus (UK) Central Summit traverse; **29/4/95** E Loretan (Switzerland) Central Summit traverse; 12/5/95 R Ratteit (Germany) Central Summit traverse; 13/5/95 P Kotronaros (Greece), Sonam (Nepal) Central Summit traverse; **1/5/96** N Joos (Switzerland) Central Summit traverse; 1/5/96 S Sluka † (Slovakia), P Sperka (Slovakia); 21/5/96 B Hasler (Switzerland), C Zinsli (Switzerland); 30/5/96 P Guggemos (Germany), M Schneider (Germany); 11/10/96 J Bereziartua (Spain), A Iñurrategi (Spain), F Iñurrategi (Spain) SW Face (British Route); **24/5/97** P Brill (Germany), R Dujmovits (Germany), K Hub (Germany), A Neuhuber (Austria), G Osterbauer (Austria), F Prasicek (Austria); **6/5/98** S Andres (Italy), C Kuntner (Italy); 14/5/98 A Blanc (Italy), M Comandona (Italy), V Niclevicz (Brazil) Central Summit traverse; 10/10/98 J Oiarzabal (Spain), C Stangl (Austria) Central Couloir SW Face; 11/10/98 I Querejeta (Spain) Central Couloir SW Face

In addition to the multiple ascents of the main summit given above, 14 climbers have made multiple ascents of the central summit. Mingma Norbu (Nepal) has made three ascents of the central summit. A Hinkes (UK), E Loretan (Switzerland) and Cering Doje (Tibet) have also climbed both the main and central summits on separate occasions.

First ascent of subsidiary summit
Central Summit: 29/4/83 G Schmatz (Germany) Main Summit's first ascent route with a final variant to the lower summit. Schmatz had become separated from his companions and was unaware that he was making the first ascent, believing he was climbing the main summit. Only on descent did he discover that he had climbed a different summit.

List of books of the first ascents of the 8,000ers

Annapurna
Annapurna by Maurice Herzog, Jonathan Cape, 1952.
There is also an account of the climb in *Conquistadors of the Useless* by Lionel Terray, Gollancz, 1963

Everest
The Ascent of Everest by John Hunt, Hodder and Stoughton 1953
There are accounts of the expedition and summit climb in Ed Hillarys autobiography *High Adventure* and Tenzings biography *Man of Everest*

Nanga Parbat
Nanga Parbat by Karl M Herrligkoffer, Elek Books, 1954
There is also an account of the expedition and summit climb in *Nanga Parbat Pigrimage* by Hermann Buhl

K2
Ascent of K2 by Ardito Desio Elek Books, 1955

Cho Oyu
Cho Oyu by Herbert Tichy, Methuen, 1957

Makalu
Makalu by Jean Franco, Jonathan Cape, 1957

Kangchenjunga
Kangchenjunga, The Untrodden Peak by Charles Evans

Manaslu
Manaslu 1954–6 by Japanese Alpine Club, The Mainichi Newspapers, 1956

Lhotse
The Everest-Lhotse Adventure by Albert Eggler, George Allen and Unwin, 1957

Gasherbrum II
Weisse Berge – Scwarze Menschen by Fritz Moravec, Österreichischer Bundesverlag, Wien, 1958. Not translated into English

Broad Peak
Broad Peak 8,047m: Meine Bergfahrten mit Hermann Buhl by Marcus Schmuck, Verlag Das Bergland Buch Salzburg/Stuttgart, 1958. Not translated into English. There is also an account of the climb in *Summits and Secrets* by Kurt Diemberger, George Allen and Unwin, 1971

Gasherbrum I
A Walk in the Sky by Nicholas Clinch, The Mountaineers, 1982

Dhaulagiri
The Ascent of Dhaulagiri by Max Eiselin, Oxford University Press, 1961

Shisha Pangma
Limited accounts of the climb can be found in *Mountaineering in China* by Guozi Shuddian, Foreign Language Press, Beijing 1965 and *Footprints on the Peaks: Mountaineering in China* by Zhou Zheng and Liu Zhenkai, Cloudcap, 1995

Picture Credits

All reasonable efforts have been made by the Publisher to trace the copyright holders of the photographs contained in this publication. In the event that a copyright holder of a photograph has not been traced, but comes forward after the publication of this edition, the Publishers will endeavour to rectify the position at the earliest opportunity.

All photographs researched and supplied via Mountain Camera Picture Library. Copyright in the photographs belongs to the following:
Front cover photograph: Doug Scott, Shisha Pangma. Back cover photographs: Doug Scott, Everest; Colin Monteath/Mountain Camera, K2; John Cleare/Mountain Camera, Kangchenjunga; Ian Evans/Mountain Images, Lhotse; John Cleare/Mountain Camera, Makalu; David D Keaton/Mountain Camera, Cho Oyu; John Cleare/Mountain Camera, Dhaulagiri; John Cleare/Mountain Camera, Manaslu; Doug Scott, Nanga Parbat; Darryn Pegram/Hedgehog House, Annapurna; Guy Cotter/Hedgehog House, Gasherbrum I; Doug Scott, Broad Peak; John Cleare/Mountain Camera, Shisha Pangma; Alan Hinkes, Gasherbrum II. Back flap photographs: l Tony Oliver, r Alastair Stevenson/Mountain Camera

The positions of the photographs on each page of the book are indicated as follows: t = top, l = left, c = centre, r = right, b = bottom
Duke of Abruzzi, National Mountain Museum, Turin 19 bc, 88 tl; Rick Allen 172, 188 tl; Peter Aschenbrenner 22 br; Bill Atkinson/Hedgehog House 161 br, 176; Pat Barrett/Hedgehog House 28, 184, 185 br; Fritz Bechtold 22 tl; Chris Bonington 36, 38, 39, 56 tl, 65 tl, 79, 90–91, 98 tl, tr; Brenner 21 br; Joe Brown/Mountain Camera 124, 126; Hermann Buhl 169 tl; John Cleare/Mountain Camera 20 tl, 37, 41, 48 br, 51 cr, 62, 65 tr, 72 tl, 82, 88 br, 89 t, 105 tr, 122, 128 tl, 142 tr, 149 b, 151 tl, tr, 174, 190, 195; Nick Clinch 178 tl, br, 179; Guy Cotter/Hedgehog House 3 br, 5 tl, 7, 50, 51 tl, 146, 160 bl, 163 bc; Henry Day/British Nepalese Army, Annapurna Expedition 26, 29, 30 cl, bl, 32 cr, 32–33, 33 tl, 34, 35 tr, c, 40; Kurt Diemberger Collection 78, 149 tr, 164 bl, 170 l, c, 171 (*K2 – The Endless Knot*), 186 br, cl (*The Kurt Diemberger Omnibus*); Grant Dixon/Hedgehog House 45 t, 46 bl, 85 cr, 151 tr; Ian Evans/Mountain Images 4 b, 42, 52, 89 br, 100, 102, 104 tr, 185 tr, 192, 194; John Fowler/Mountain Camera 199 tr, 200; German Himalaya Foundation, Munich 21 tc; Jon and Lindsay Griffin 115 c; Hall and Ball Archive/Hedgehog House 86 c, 90 tr, 103, 120 tl, 151 cl, 154 c, 188 br; David Hamilton 4–5, 9 br, 94 bl, 95, 156, 161 tl, bl, cr, 162 br, 163 t, 164 tl, 180 tc, 181; Bunshow Hattori 87, 91 cr; Karl Herligkoffer 66 bl, c; Alan Hinkes 2 l, br, 9 tl, 12–13, 65 cr, 67, 68 bl, c, 69, 76, 77, 80, 84, 85 tr, 86 tl, 92–93, 94 br, 97 tl, br, 99, 112, 121 tl, br, 139 tl, 143, 150 b, tr, 154 tr, 155, 159, 162 t, 165, 166, 173, 177 cl, cr, 180, 196; T. Imanishi (Mainichi Newspapers) 140 cl, 141 tl; Indian Air Force/Mountain Camera 148 bc; Tadashi Kajiyama/Mountain Camera 66 tl, 70, 71 tr, 72 cr, 73, 74 bl, 75 tl, 81; David D Keaton/Mountain Camera 3 bl, 54–55, 58, 60, 104 tl, 105 cl, 106 bl, tr, 107 bc, tr, 108 tc, b, 109 br, 110, 111; Col. Kumar 127 bl, tr; Louis Lachenal 31; Alex McIntyre 202 c; Helen Mason 14, 15, 18, 19 cl, 65 br; Colin Monteath/Mountain Camera 46 tl, 53, 56 cr, 59 bl, 185 cr, 189, 193; Fritz Moravec 158; Patrick Morrow 13br, 48 tl, 59 tr, 96, 119, 120 c, 132, 135 b, 152–153, 168, 182, 187; Mountain Camera Archive 19; Hugh Van Noorden/Hedgehog House 8, 44, 45 b; Steve Razzetti 11, 30 t, 30–31, 46 cl, 61 cl, 117 tr, 125, 128 cl, 133 tl, bc, 134, 136, 138, 144, 145l; Ernst Reiss 148 cr; RGS 20 br, 21 bl; RGS/The Times 49 tl; Marcus Schmuck 117 b; Doug Scott 25 tl, 61 tr, 64 bl, 71 bl, 75 b, 118 tc, 129 tr, b, 130 bl, 131 cl, tr, 169 tr, 199 cr, 202 bl; Eric Shipton 24 tl, bc; Will Siri 114; Dick Smith/Hedgehog House 118–119; Pip Smith/Hedgehog House 3 tr, 47; Frank Smythe 23; Geoff Spearpoint/Hedgehog House 135 tl; Lionel Terray 116; Herbert Tichy 104 bl; HW Tilman 25 tl; Jon Tinker 46 tr; Stephen Venables 6, 10 tc, b, 57, 203; Takayoshi Yoda (Mainichi Newspapers) 140 bc, 141 br, 142 bl; Zhou Zheng/Liu Zhenkai 198

Captions for the chapter openers are as follows: pp.26–27 This is the still rarely climbed northern flank of Annapurna. Finding a safe route through this jumble of ice and rock is no easy task; pp.42–43 The formidable northern flank of Everest from the Rongbuk Monastery as the first expedition would have seen it; pp.62–63 From this aerial viewpoint high over the Babusar Pass, Nanga Parbat –the westernmost peak of the Himalayan chain – dominates the skyline; pp.82–83 The spectacular first sight of K2 up the Godwin-Austen Glacier from the south near Concordia; pp.100–101 The southern – Nepalese – flank of Cho Oyu walls the head of the long Ngozumpa Glacier; pp.112–113 Among the old moraines near the snout of the Barun Glacier below the south-west face and south-east ridge of Makalu; p.122–123 A classic view of Kangchenjunga – 'the Five Treasures of the Great Snows' – from the south-west on the Milke Danda Ridge. The summits right to left are Kangchenjunga South, Kangchenjunga and Kangchenjunga West (Yalung Kang). On the far left is the formidable peak of Jannu; pp.136–137 Manaslu is seen westwards from Sama Gompa high in the Buri Gandaki valley; pp.146–147 Lhotse towers beyond the South Col where several tents and climbers can be picked out in this interesting view from Everest's south-east ridge; pp.156–157 The distinctive south-west and south-east spurs of Gasherbrum II fall towards the icefall of the South Gasherbrum Glacier; Gasherbrum III (7,952m//26,089ft) is on the left; p.166–167 Expedition porters rest near K2 Base camp below the formidable north eastern flanks of Broad Peak; pp.174–175 Gasherbrum I or 'Hidden Peak' seen from the south-west near Base Camp; pp.182–183 Wreathed in eerie morning mists, the southern flanks of Dhaulagiri are seen from the south-east on the famous viewpoint of Poon Hill; pp.196–197 Baggage yaks at Advanced Base Camp at about 5,640m (18,500ft) among the moraines of the Yabukangala Glacier